P9-ELG-830

ECHOES

The setting of Maeve Binchy's new novel is a small Irish seaside town in the 50s and 60s, where two very different children are growing up, shouting their hearts' desires into the echo cave, praying that their destiny will lead them far away from Castlebay.

Maeve Binchy brings to this story all the warmth and power of insight that characterised her bestselling first novel, LIGHT A PENNY CANDLE. The magic of her writing lies as much in the story as in her creation of a memorable supporting cast, including Angela O'Hara the schoolmistress whose priestly brother is not all he seems, and Garry Doyle, Castlebay's photographer and resident Romeo. Above all it resides in her uncanny ability to recreate the echoes of childhood or the memory of being a teenager in a very particular time and place.

**Also by the same author,
and available in Coronet Books:**

LIGHT A PENNY CANDLE
CENTRAL LINE
VICTORIA LINE

About the Author

Maeve Binchy was born in Dublin and went to school at the Holy Child Convent in Killiney. She took a history degree at UCD and taught in various girls' schools, writing travel articles in the vacations. In 1969 she joined the *Irish Times*. For the last eight years she has been based in London. She is the author of a number of stage plays and a television play, DEEPLY REGRETTED BY, which won two Jacobs Awards and the Best Script Award at the Prague Film Festival, as well as three volumes of short stories and the overnight bestseller, LIGHT A PENNY CANDLE.

Maeve Binchy is married to the writer and broadcaster Gordon Snell.

ECHOES

'Fully imagined, well-rounded, true to life characters . . . the pleasure lies in the accomplished, unpretentious story-telling and in Miss Binchy's clear recall of feeling and period'
Nina Bawden, Daily Telegraph

'The kind of a novel you can settle in with – long, leisurely and soothing . . . Ms Binchy has the true storyteller's knack of involving us in her characters . . . compulsive reading'
Observer

'An ideal novel for the deckchair'
Sunday Telegraph

'A thoroughly professional job full of tear-jerking moments . . . it left me feeling stunned'
Daily Express

'Vivid, evocative and skilfully-drawn pictures . . . A great, warm, gratifying read'
Irish Times

ECHOES

Maeve Binchy

CORONET BOOKS
Hodder and Stoughton

For dearest Gordon with all my love

Copyright © Maeve Binchy 1985.
First published in Great Britain in 1985
by Century Publishing Co. Ltd.

Coronet edition 1986.

British Library C.I.P.

Binchy, Maeve
   Echoes.
   I. Title
   823'.914[F]   PR6052.I7728

ISBN 0-7736-7114-5

Printed in Canada

*The characters and situations in this book are
entirely imaginary and bear no relation to any real
person or actual happening*

This book is sold subject to the condition that
it shall not, by way of trade or otherwise, be
lent, re-sold, hired out or otherwise circulated
without the publisher's prior consent in any
form of binding or cover other than that in
which this is published and without a similar
condition including this condition being
imposed on the subsequent purchaser.

Hodder and Stoughton Paperbacks, a
division of Hodder and Stoughton Ltd.,
Mill Road, Dunton Green, Sevenoaks,
Kent (Editorial Office: 47 Bedford
Square, London, WC1 3DP) by
Richard Clay (The Chaucer Press) Ltd.,
Bungay, Suffolk. Photoset by
Rowland Phototypesetting Ltd.,
Bury St Edmunds, Suffolk.

PROLOGUE

People seemed to know without being told. They came out of their houses and began to run down the main street. The murmur became louder, and almost without knowing they were doing it they started to check where their own families were. It was still just a figure, face down in the water. They didn't know for sure whether it was a man or a woman.

'Perhaps it's a sailor from a ship,' they said. But they knew it wasn't anyone who had gone overboard. No nice anonymous death of someone they didn't know. No informing the authorities and saying a few prayers for the deceased unknown sailor. This was someone from Castlebay.

They stood in silent groups on the cliff top and watched the first people getting to the water's edge: the boy who had first seen the waves leaving something frightening on the shore; other men too; people from the shops nearby and young men who were quick to run down the path. Then they saw the figures coming down the other path near the doctor's house, kneeling by the body in case, just in case there was something in a black bag that could bring it back to life.

By the time Father O'Dwyer arrived with his soutane flapping in the wind the murmur had turned into a unified sound. The people of Castlebay were saying a decade of the rosary for the repose of the soul which had left the body that lay face down on their beach.

PART ONE

1950–1952

It was sometimes called Brigid's Cave, the echo cave, and if you shouted your question loud enough in the right direction you got an answer instead of an echo. In the summer it was full of girls calling out questions, girls who had come for the summer to Castlebay. Girls who wanted to know would they get a fellow, or if Gerry Doyle would have eyes for them this summer. Clare thought they were mad to tell the cave their secrets. Specially since people like her sister Chrissie and that crowd would go and listen for private things being asked and then they'd scream with laughter about them and tell everyone. Clare said she'd never ask the echo anything no matter how desperate she was, because it wouldn't be a secret any more. But she did go in to ask about the history prize. That was different.

It was different because it was winter anyway, and there was hardly anyone except themselves in Castlebay in winter; and it was different because it had nothing to do with love. And it was a nice way to come home from school that way down the cliff road; you didn't have to talk to everyone in the town, you could look at the sea instead. And suppose she did go down that crooked path with all the Danger notices on it, then she could go into the cave for a quick word, walk along the beach and up the real steps and be home in the same time as if she had come down the street talking to this person and that. In winter there was hardly any business so people waved you into shops and gave you a biscuit or asked you to do a message for them. She'd be just as quick going by Brigid's cave and the beach.

It had been dry, so the Danger bits weren't so dangerous. Clare slid easily down the cliff on to the sand. It was firm and hard, the tide had not long gone out. The mouth of the cave looked black and a bit frightening. But she squared her shoulders; it looked just the same in summer yet people went in there in droves. She shifted her schoolbag to her back so that she could have both hands free to guide herself and once she got used to the light there was no difficulty seeing the little ridge where you were meant to stand.

Clare took a deep breath: 'Will I win the history prize?' she called.

'Ize ize ize ize,' called the echo.

'It's saying yes,' said a voice just beside her. Clare jumped with the fright. It was David Power.

'You shouldn't listen to anyone else, it's like listening in to confession,' Clare said crossly.

'I thought you saw me,' David said simply. 'I wasn't hiding.'

'How could I see you, didn't I come in out of the light, you were lurking in here.' She was full of indignation.

'It's not a private cave, you don't have to keep shouting Cave Occupied,' David retorted loudly.

'Pied pied pied pied,' said the cave.

They both laughed.

He was nice, really, David Power, he was the same age as her brother Ned – fifteen. They had been in Mixed Infants together, she remembered Ned telling someone proudly, wanting to share some experience with the doctor's son.

He wore a tie and suit when he came home from school, all the time, not just when he went to Mass on Sundays. He was tall and he had freckles on his nose. His hair was a bit spiky and used to stick up in funny directions, one big bit of it fell over his forehead. He had a nice smile and he always looked as if he were ready to talk except that something was dragging him away. Sometimes he wore a blazer with a badge on it, and he looked very smart in that. He used to wrinkle his nose and tell people that it only looked smart when you didn't see a hundred and eighty blazers like that every day at his school. He'd been at a boarding school for over a year but now it was closed because of scarlet fever. Only the Dillon girls from the hotel went to boarding school and of course the Wests and the Greens, but they were Protestants and they had to go to a boarding school because there wasn't one of their own.

'I didn't think it would answer really, I only tried it as a joke,' she said.

'I know, I tried it once as a joke too,' he confessed.

'What did you ask it as a joke?' she inquired.

'I forget now,' he said.

'That's not fair – you heard mine.'

'I didn't, I only heard eyes eyes eyes.' He shouted it and it called back the three words to him over and over.

Clare was satisfied. 'Well I'd best be off now, I have homework. I don't suppose you've had homework for weeks.' She was envious and inquiring.

'I do. Miss O'Hara comes every day to give me lessons. She's coming . . . oh soon now.' They walked out on to the wet hard sand.

'Lessons all by yourself with Miss O'Hara – isn't that great?'

'It is, she's great at explaining things, isn't she, for a woman teacher I mean.'

'Yes, well we only have women teachers and nuns,' Clare explained.

'I forgot,' David said sympathetically. 'Still she's terrific, and she's very easy to talk to, like a real person.'

Clare agreed. They walked companionably along to the main steps up from the beach. It would have been quicker for David to climb the path with Danger written on it, it led almost into his own garden, but he said he wanted to buy some sweets at Clare's shop anyway. They talked about things the other had never heard of. David told her about the sanitorium being fumigated after the two pupils got scarlet fever; but all the time she thought that he was talking about the big hospital on the hill where people went when they had TB. She didn't know it was a room in his school. She told him a long and complicated tale about Mother Immaculata asking one of the girls to leave

13

the exercise books in one place and she thought that it was somewhere else and the girl went by accident into the nuns' side of the convent. This was all lost on David, who didn't know that you never under pain of *terrible* things went to the nuns' side of the convent. It didn't really matter to either of them, they were no strain on each other, and life in Castlebay could be full of strains so this was a nice change. He came into the shop and, as there was nobody serving, she took off her coat, hung it up and found the jar of Clove Rock. She counted out the six for a penny that he was buying and before she put the lid on the jar she offered him one courteously and took one herself.

He looked at her enviously. It was great power to be able to stand up on a chair in a sweetshop, take down a jar and be free to offer one to a customer. David sighed as he went home. He'd have loved to live in a shop like Clare O'Brien, he'd have loved brothers and sisters, and to be allowed to go up to the yard and collect milk in a can when the cows were being milked, or gather seaweed to sell to the hot sea baths in bundles. It was very dull going back to his own house now to his mother saying he should really have some sense of what was what. It was the most irritating thing he had ever heard, especially since it seemed to mean anything and everything and never the same thing twice. Still, Miss O'Hara was coming tonight, and Miss O'Hara made lessons much more interesting than at school, he had once been unwise enough to explain to his mother. He thought she would be pleased but she said that Miss O'Hara was fine for a country primary school but did not compare with the Jesuits who were on a different level entirely.

Clare was sighing too, she thought it must be great altogether to go back to a house like David Power's where there were bookcases of books in the house, and a fire on in that front room whether there was anyone sitting in it or not. And there was no wireless on, and nobody making noise. You could do your homework there for hours without anyone coming in and telling you to move. She remembered the inside of the house from when she had been up to Dr Power for the stitches the time she had caught her leg on the rusty bit of machinery. To distract her Dr Power had asked her to count the volumes of the encyclopedia up on the shelf and Clare had been so startled to see all those books in one house for one family that she had forgotten about the stitches and Dr Power had told her mother she was as brave as a lion. They had walked home after the stitches with Clare leaning on her mother. They stopped at the church to thank St Anne that there hadn't been any infection in the leg and as Clare saw her mother bent in prayer and gratitude in front of the St Anne grotto she let her mind wander on how great it would be to have a big peaceful house full of books like that instead of being on top of each other and no room for anything – no time for anything either. She thought about it again tonight as David Power went up the street home to that house where the carpet went right into the window, not stopping in a square like ordinary carpets. There would be a fire and there'd be peace. His mother might be in the kitchen and Dr Power would be curing people and later Miss O'Hara would be coming to give him lessons all on his own without the rest of a class to distract her. What could be better than that? She wished for a moment that she had been his sister, but then she felt guilty. To wish that would be to want to lose Mammy and Daddy and Tommy and Ned and Ben and Jimmy. Oh and Chrissie. But she didn't care how wrong it was, she wouldn't mind losing Chrissie any day of the week.

The calm of the shop was only temporary. Daddy had been painting out in the back and he came in holding his hands up in front of him and asking someone to reach out a bottle of white spirit and open it up this minute. There was an awful lot of painting going on in the wintertime in Castlebay, the sea air just ripped the coats off again and the place looked very shabby unless it was touched up all the time. Mammy came in at the same moment; she had been up to the post office and she had discovered terrible

15

things. Chrissie and her two tinkers of friends had climbed on the roof of Miss O'Flaherty's shop and poked a long wet piece of seaweed through to frighten Miss O'Flaherty. They could have given the unfortunate woman a heart attack; she could, God save us all, have dropped stone dead on the floor of her own shop and then Chrissie O'Brien and her two fine friends would have the sin of murder on their souls until the Last Day and after. Chrissie had been dragged home by the shoulder, the plait and the ear. She was red-faced and annoyed. Clare thought that it was a good thing to have frightened Miss O'Flaherty who was horrible, and sold copy books and school supplies but hated schoolchildren. Clare thought it was real bad luck that Mammy happened to be passing. She smiled sympathetically at Chrissie but it was not well received.

'Stop looking so superior,' Chrissie cried out. 'Look at Clare gloating at it all. Goody-goody Clare, stupid boring Clare.'

She got a cuff on the side of her head for this performance and it made her madder still.

'Look, she's delighted,' Chrissie went on, 'delighted to see anyone in trouble. That's all that ever makes Clare happy, to see others brought down.'

'There'll be no tea for you, Chrissie O'Brien, and that's not the end of it either. Get up to your room this minute, do you hear. This *minute*.' Agnes O'Brien's thin voice was like a whistle with anger, as she banished the bold Chrissie, wiped the worst paint off her husband's hands with a rag that she had wet with white spirit, and managed at the same time to point to Clare's coat on the hook.

'This isn't a hand-me-down shop,' she said. 'Take that coat and put it where it's meant to be.'

The unfairness of this stung Clare deeply. 'We always leave our coats there. That *is* where it's meant to be.'

'Do you hear her?' Agnes looked in appeal to her husband, did not wait for an answer but headed for the stairs. Chrissie up there was for it.

'Can't you stop tormenting your mother and move your coat?' he asked. 'Is it too much to ask for a bit of peace?'

16

Clare took her coat down from the hook. She couldn't go up to the bedroom she shared with Chrissie because that would be like stepping straight into the battlefield. She stayed idling in the shop.

Her father's face was weary. It was so *wrong* of him to say she was tormenting Mammy, she wasn't, but you couldn't explain that to him. He was bent over in a kind of a stoop and he looked very old, like someone's grandfather, not a father. Daddy was all grey, his face and his hair and his cardigan. Only his hands were white from the paint. Daddy had grown more stooped since her First Communion three years ago, Clare thought; then he had seemed very tall. His face had grown hairy too – there were bits of hair in his nose and his ears. He always looked a bit harassed as if there wasn't enough time or space or money. And, indeed, there usually wasn't enough of any of these things. The O'Brien household lived on the profits of the summer season which was short and unpredictable. It could be killed by rain, by the popularity of some new resort, by people overcharging for houses along the cliff road. There was no steady living to be gained over the winter months, it was merely a matter of keeping afloat.

The shop was oddly-shaped when you came in: there were corners and nooks in it which should have been shelved or walled off but nobody had ever got round to it, the ceiling was low and even with three customers the place looked crowded. Nobody could see any order on the shelves but the O'Briens knew where everything was. They didn't change it for fear they wouldn't find things, even though there were many more logical ways of stocking the small grocery-confectioner's. It all looked cramped and awkward and though the customers couldn't see behind the door into the living quarters it was exactly the same in there. The kitchen had a range, with a clothes line over it, and the table took up most of the space in the room. A small scullery at the back was so poky and dark that it was almost impossible to see the dishes you washed. There was one light in the middle of the room with a yellow light

17

shade which had a crack in it. Recently Tom O'Brien had been holding his paper up nearer to the light in order to read it.

Agnes came downstairs with the air of someone who has just finished an unpleasant task satisfactorily. 'That girl will end on the gallows,' she said.

She was a thin small woman, who used to smile a lot once; but now she seemed set in the face of the cold Castlebay wind, and even when she was indoors she seemed to be grimacing against the icy blast, eyes narrow and mouth in a hard line. In the shop she wore a yellow overall to protect her clothes, she said, but in fact there were hardly any clothes to protect. She had four outfits for going to Mass, and otherwise it had been the same old cardigans and frocks and skirts for years. There were always medals and relics pinned inside the cardigan; they had to be taken off before it was washed. Once she had forgotten, and a relic of the Little Flower which had been in a red satin covering had become all pink and the pale blue cardigan was tinged pink too. Agnes O'Brien had her hair in a bun which was made by pulling it through a thing that looked like a doughnut, a squashy round device, and then the hair was clipped in. They never saw her doing this, but once they had seen the bun by itself and it had alarmed Clare greatly because she hadn't known what it was.

The dark and very angry eyes of her mother landed on her. 'Have you decided that you would like to belong to this family and do what's required of you? Would it be too much to ask you to take that coat out of my way before I open the range and burn it down to its buttons?'

She would never do that, Clare knew. She had hoped her mother might have forgotten it during the sojourn upstairs. But the coat was still going to be a cause of war.

'I told her, Agnes, my God I told her, but children nowadays . . .' Tom sounded defeated and apologetic.

Clare stuffed her school coat into a crowded cupboard under the stairs and took a few potatoes out of the big sack on the floor. Each evening she and Chrissie had to

18

get the potatoes ready for tea, and tonight, thanks to Chrissie's disgrace, it looked as if Clare was going to have to do it on her own. In the kitchen sat her younger brothers Ben and Jim; they were reading a comic. The older boys Tommy and Ned would be in from the Brothers shortly, but none of this would be any help. Boys didn't help with the food or the washing up. Everyone knew that.

Clare had a lot to do after tea. She wanted to iron her yellow ribbons for tomorrow. Just in case she won the history essay she'd better be looking smart. She would polish her indoor shoes, she had brought them home specially, and she would make another attempt to get the two stains off her tunic. Mother Immaculata might make a comment about smartening yourself up for the good name of the school. She must be sure not to let them down. Miss O'Hara had said that she had never been so pleased in all her years teaching as when she read Clare's essay, it gave her the strength to go on. Those were her very words. She would never have stopped Clare in the corridor and said that, if she hadn't won the prize. Imagine beating all the ones of fifteen. All those Bernie Conways and Anna Murphys. They'd look at Clare with new interest from now on. And indeed they'd have to think a bit differently at home too. She longed to tell them tonight, but decided it was better to wait. Tonight they were all like weasels and anyway it might look worse for Chrissie; after all she was two years and a half older. Chrissie would murder her too if she chose to reveal it tonight. She took upstairs a big thick sandwich of cheese, a bit of cold cooked bacon and a cup of cocoa.

Chrissie was sitting on her bed, examining her face in a mirror. She had two very thick plaits in her hair; the bits at the ends after the rubber bands were bushy and didn't just hang there like other people's, they looked as if they were trying to escape. She had a fringe which she cut herself so badly that she had to be taken to the hairdresser to get a proper job done on it, and at night she put pipe cleaners into the fringe so that it would curl properly.

She was fatter than Clare, much, and she had a real bust that you could see even in her school tunic.

Chrissie was very interested in her nose, Clare couldn't understand why but she was always examining it. Even now in all the disgrace and no meal and the sheer fury over what she had done to Miss O'Flaherty she was still peering at it looking for spots to squeeze. She had a round face and always looked surprised. Not happily surprised, not even when someone was delivering her an unexpected supper.

'I don't want it,' she said.

'Don't eat it then,' Clare returned with some spirit.

She went back downstairs and tried to find a corner where she could learn the poem for tomorrow; and she had to do four sums. She often asked herself how was it that with six people living in that house who were all going to school, why was she the only one who ever needed to do any homework?

Gerry Doyle came in as she was ironing her yellow ribbons.

'Where's Chrissie?' he asked Clare in a whisper.

'She's upstairs, there was murder here, she gave Miss O'Flaherty some desperate fright with seaweed. Don't ask for her, they'll all go mad if you even mention her name.'

'Listen, would you tell her . . .' He stopped, deciding against it. 'No, you're too young.'

'I'm not too young,' Clare said, stung by the unfairness of it. 'But young or old, I don't care, I'm not giving your soppy messages to Chrissie, she'll only be annoyed with me, and you'll be annoyed with me, and Mammy will beat the legs off me, so I'd much prefer you kept them to yourself.' She went back to the ribbons with vigour. They were flat gleaming bands now, they would fluff up gorgeously tomorrow. She couldn't get herself up to the neck in Chrissie's doings because there would be trouble at every turn. She must keep nice and quiet and get ready for tomorrow, for the look of surprise on Mother Immaculata's face, and the horror on Bernie Conway's and Anna Murphy's.

Gerry Doyle laughed good-naturedly. 'You're quite right, let people do their own dirty work,' he said.

The words 'dirty work' somehow cut through all the rest of the noise in the O'Brien kitchen and reached Agnes O'Brien as she pulled the entire contents of the dresser's bottom cupboard on to the floor. Tom had said that she must have thrown out the length of flex he was going to use to put up a light outside the back door. She was sure she had seen it somewhere and was determined that the project should not be postponed.

Tommy and Ned were going through the paper for jobs as they did every week, marking things with a stubby purple pencil; Ben and Jimmy were playing a game that began quietly every few minutes until it became a slapping match and one of them would start to cry. Tom was busy mending the wireless which crackled over all the activity.

'What dirty work?' Agnes called: a grand fellow, that Gerry Doyle, but you had to watch him like a hawk. Whatever devilment was planned he had a hand in it.

'I was saying to Clare that I'm no good at any housework, or anything that needs a lot of care. I'm only good at dirty work.' He smiled across, and the woman on her knees in front of a pile of tins, boxes, paper bags, knitting wool, toasting forks and rusted baking trays, smiled back.

Clare looked up at him with surprise. Imagine being able to tell a lie as quickly and as well as that. And over nothing.

Gerry had gone over to the job consultation, saying he heard there was going to be a man from a big employment agency in England coming round and holding interviews in the hotel.

'Wouldn't that be for big kind of jobs, for people with qualifications?' Ned asked, unwilling to think anyone would come to Castlebay to seek out him or his like.

'Have sense Ned, who is there in this place with any qualifications? Won't it save you shoe leather and the cost of writing off to these places if you wait till this fellow arrives and he'll tell all there's to be told?'

'It's easy on you to say that.' Tommy, the eldest, was

troubled. '*You* don't have to go away for a job. You've got your business.'

'So have you,' Gerry pointed to the shop.

But it wasn't the same. Gerry's father was the photographer; during the winter he survived on dances, and the odd function that was held. In summer, he walked the length of the beach three times a day taking family groups and then out again at night into the dance hall where the holiday business was brisk and where there would be a great demand to buy prints of the romantic twosomes that he would snap. Girls were his biggest customers, they loved to bring back holiday memories in the form of something that they could pass around the office and sigh over when the dance was long over. Gerry's mother and sister did the developing and printing, or they helped with it, which was the way it was described. Gerry's father expected the only son to take an active part, and since he had been a youngster, Gerry had tagged along learning the psychology as well as the mechanics of the camera.

You must never annoy people, his father had taught him, be polite and a little distant even, click the camera when they aren't at all posed or prepared and then if they show interest and start to pose take a proper snap. The first plate was only a blank to get their attention. Remind them gently that there's no need to buy, the proofs will be available for inspection in twenty-four hours. Move on and don't waste any time chatting when the picture is taken, have a pleasant smile but not a greasy sort of a one. Never plead with people to pose, and when gaggles of girls want six or seven shots taken of them remember they're only going to buy one at the most so pretend to take the snap more often than taking it.

Gerry's beautiful sister Fiona had long dark ringlets; when she wasn't working in the darkroom in their house during the summer she sat in the wooden shack up over the beach selling the snaps. Gerry's father had said that a town like Castlebay was so small you could never have a business if you tried to get big and expand and hire people. But keep it small and run it just with the family and there would be a great inheritance for Gerard Anthony Doyle.

But Gerry never had the air of a boy about to step into a secure future. He examined the paper with the O'Brien boys as eagerly as if he would be having to take the emigrant ship with them.

How did he know whether there'd be a living for him here? His father was always saying that all it needed was a smart-alec firm to come in for the summer and they'd be ruined. Who knew what the future would bring? Maybe people would want coloured photography, there could be newfangled cameras, it was living on a cliff edge his father always said. At least in O'Brien's they could be sure that people would always want bread and butter and milk. They'd want groceries until the end of the world and as long as the trippers kept coming wouldn't they be selling ice creams and sweets and oranges until the last day as well?

Gerry always made everything sound more exciting than it was. He saw a future for Tommy and Ned where they'd work in England and then, just when all the English would be wondering what to do and where to go for the summer holidays, Ned and Tommy would come back home to Castlebay, get behind the counter, help out with the shop and have a great holiday as well. And they'd be fine fellows at the dance because they'd be so well up in everything after being in England. Tommy complained that it wouldn't be much of a holiday coming home to work like dogs in the really tough part of the year when O'Brien's was open from eight o'clock in the morning until midnight. But Gerry just laughed and said that would be their investment, that was the only time of the year that there'd be work for all hands. The rest of the year they'd be falling over each other with no one to serve, but in the summer the whole family should be there to make sure that everyone got a bit of sleep anyway and to keep the thing going. It was like that in all seaside towns. Gerry was very convincing. Tommy and Ned saw it all very rosily, and really and truly Gerry was right, shouldn't they wait till the man came and had a list of jobs for them instead of scanning all the ads which told them nothing when all was said and done?

Clare had turned the iron on its end by the range; she was folding the blanket and the scorch sheet and wondering where to replace them since everything from the dresser seemed to be on the floor. Gerry Doyle was sitting on the table swinging his legs and she got a sudden feeling that he was giving her brothers wrong advice. They weren't capable and sure like he was, they were the kind of people who agreed with everyone else.

'Would this man who came offering jobs in the hotel, would he be offering the kind of jobs where you could get on or jobs you'd just have to work hard at?'

They were surprised that she spoke. Her father took his head out of the shell of the wireless.

'It's the same thing, Clare girl, if you work hard you get on. If you don't, you don't.'

'But trained like, that's what I mean,' Clare said. 'You remember when that Order came and the girls were all going to be taken off to do their Leaving Certificate and learn a skill if they became postulant nuns.'

Ned roared with scorn. 'A postulant nun! Is that what you'd like us to be, wouldn't we look fine in the habit and the veil?'

'No that's not what I meant . . .' she began.

'I don't think the Reverend Mother would take us,' Tommy said.

'Sister Thomas, I really think we're going to have to do something about your voice in the choir,' Ned said in mincing tones.

'Oh I'm doing my best, Sister Edward, but what about your hobnailed boots?'

'Sister Thomas, you can talk, what about your hairy legs?'

Benny and Jimmy were interested now.

'And you've got to give up kicking football round the convent,' said Ben.

'Nuns kicking football,' screamed Jimmy with enthusiasm. Even Mammy on her knees and having triumphantly found the bit of flex was laughing and Dad was smiling too. Clare was rescued unexpectedly.

'Very funny, ha ha,' Gerry Doyle said. 'Very funny Mother Edward and Mother Thomas, but Clare's right. What's the point of getting a job on a building site without any training as a brickie or a carpenter? No, the real thing to ask this fellow is nothing to do with how much, but what kind of a job.'

Clare flushed with pleasure. They were all nodding now.

'I nearly forgot why I came,' Gerry said. 'The father asked me to have a look at the view from different places, he's half thinking of making a postcard of Castlebay, and he wondered where's the best angle to take the picture from. He wondered would there be a good view from your upstairs. Do you mind if I run up and have a look?'

'At night?' Clare's father asked.

'You'd get a good idea of the outlines at night,' Gerry said, his foot on the stairs.

'Go on up lad.'

They were all back at their activities and nobody except Clare had the slightest idea that Gerry Doyle aged fifteen and a half had gone upstairs to see Chrissie O'Brien aged thirteen.

Nellie was on her knees with the bellows when David came in. 'I'm building up a nice fire for your lessons,' she told him.

Her face was red with the exertion and her hair was escaping from the cap she wore. She never seemed comfortable in the cap, it was always at the wrong angle somehow on her hair and her head seemed to be full of hairpins. Nellie was old, not as old as Mummy but about thirty, and she was fat and cheerful and she had been there always. She had a lot of married brothers and an old father. When David was a young fellow she used to tell him that she was better off than any of them, in a nice clean house and great comfort and all the food she could eat. David used to think it was lonely for her in the kitchen when they were all inside but Nellie's round face would crack into a smile and she assured him that she was as well off as if she'd married a Guard, or even better off. Her money was her own, she had the best of everything and every Thursday afternoon and every second Sunday afternoon off.

David started to help with the fire but Nellie stood up, creaking, and said it was going fine and wasn't that his teacher coming in the gate.

Angela O'Hara's red bicycle was indeed coming up the gravel path. She was tall and slim, and she always wore belts on her coats as if it were the only way they'd stay on. Other people had buttons, but of course other people didn't fly around on the bike so much. She had red-brown hair that was sort of tied back but with such a loose ribbon or piece of cord that it might as well not be tied back at all. She had big greenish eyes and she used to throw her head back when she laughed.

Miss O'Hara wasn't at all like other grown-ups. She wanted to know did they all get a refund of fees because the school had to close for the scarlet fever. David didn't know, he said he'd ask, but Miss O'Hara said it didn't matter, and not to ask because it might seem as if she was looking for more money, which she wasn't. David had forgotten that she was being paid to teach him, it wasn't the kind of thing you'd think about, he sort of believed that Miss O'Hara did it for interest. She had found that very funny. She said in many ways she would well do it for interest but the labourer was worthy of his hire as it said somewhere in the gospels, and if she were to do it for free what about the fancy order of priests he was with – they certainly didn't do it for free. David said he thought the main cost was the food and the beds in the dormitories, he couldn't imagine that the actual lessons would cost anything.

She came for an hour every evening, after she had finished up at the school and called in on her mother. Mrs O'Hara was all crooked from arthritis and David thought that she looked like an illustration of an old tree in one of the children's books he used to read. A book probably tidied away neatly by his mother for when it would be needed again. Miss O'Hara had two sisters married in England and a brother, a priest, in the Far East. She was the only one who had never travelled, she told him. He asked what would have happened if she had travelled and her mother had got all crippled living by herself.

'Then I'd have come back,' Miss O'Hara had said cheerfully. Since her sisters were married and her brother was a priest she would have been the one to look after her mother anyway.

The O'Hara house was out a bit on the road towards the golf course, and Miss O'Hara cycled everywhere on her big red bicycle with the basket of exercise books in the front. There were always copy books and when it rained she had them covered with a waterproof sheet. She wore a long scarf wound round her in winter and if there was a wind sometimes her long hair stood out behind her in a straight line. David's mother once said she looked like a witch heading for the cliff road and you'd expect her and the bicycle to take flight over the seas. But his father had refused to let a word of criticism be spoken of her. He said that nobody knew how much she did for that crippled mother of hers, morning noon and night, and wasn't it proof to note that when poor Angela O'Hara went on her two weeks holiday a year somewhere they had to have three people in and out of that house to mind the mother and it was never done satisfactorily even then. His mother didn't like Miss O'Hara, it had something to do with her not admiring things or not being excited enough about his mother going to Dublin for outings. It had never been said, it was just a feeling he had.

The table with his books on it was near the fire and Nellie would bring in a pot of tea and a slice of cake or apple tart.

Miss O'Hara always talked to Nellie more than she talked to his mother, she'd ask about Nellie's old father out in the country and the row with the brothers and had they heard from the sister in Canada. She'd giggle with Nellie about something new that Father O'Dwyer's housekeeper had said. The woman's name was Miss

McCormack, but everyone called her Sergeant McCormack because she tried to run not only Father O'Dwyer and the church but the whole of Castlebay too.

Miss O'Hara came in now, her hands cold from clenching the handlebars in the wind, and she held them out to the fire.

'God, Nellie, isn't it a sin having a great fire like this banked up just for David and myself. We could work in the kitchen, you know, beside the range.'

'Oh, that wouldn't do at all!' Nellie was horrified.

'You wouldn't mind, David?' she began . . . and then suddenly changed her mind. 'No, don't take any notice of me, I always want to change the world, that's my problem. Aren't we lucky to have this grand place in here, let's make the most of it. Nellie, tell me what are they building on the side of Dillon's? It looks like an aerodrome.'

'Oh, that's going to be a sun lounge, I hear,' Nellie said, full of importance. 'They're going to have chairs and card tables maybe in the summer, and tea served there too.'

'They'd need to have rugs and hot-water bottles if it turns out anything like last summer. Come on, college boy, get out your geography book, we're going to make you a world expert on trade winds, you're going to make them green and yellow striped with jealousy when you get back to that palace of a school of yours. We'll show them what a real scholar is, the way we breed them in Castlebay.'

Paddy Power was tall and thick-set, with a weather-beaten face. His face was beaten by weather of all kinds, but mainly the sharp wind that came in from the sea as he walked up lanes to people's houses, lanes where his big battered car wouldn't go. He had a shock of hair that grew in all directions as if he had three crowns on his head; it had been brown and then it was speckled but now it was mainly grey. Because of his bulk and his alarming hair he sometimes looked fierce, but that was before people got to know him. He had a great way of talking, a kind of good-natured bantering until he could see what was wrong;

his talk was merely to relax the patient until he could see where the piece of grit in the eyes was, or the splinter in the hand, the glass in the sole of the foot or feel for the pain in the base of the stomach without too much tensing and alarm.

He was a burly man who never found clothes to fit him and never cared about them either. Life was far too short, he said, to spend time in a tailor's talking rubbish about lines and cuts and lapels. But for all his bulk and his haphazard attitude to his appearance, he was a healthy man and he was able to go down the path from his own garden to the sea and swim for nearly six months of the year and to get a game of golf a week as well. But Paddy Power was tired today; it had been a very long day and he had driven seventeen miles out to see a young woman who would be dead by Christmas but who talked cheerfully of how she knew she'd be better when the fine weather came. Her five children had played noisily and unconcerned around the feet of the doctor and the pale young husband just sat looking emptily into the fire. He had also had to have an unpleasing chat with one of the Dillon brothers from the hotel and speak seriously about liver damage. No matter how carefully he tried to phrase it, he had ended up with a blank wall and a great deal of resentment. Today it had ended with Dick Dillon telling him to mind his own bloody business, and that Paddy Power was a fine one to talk, half the county could tell you that he was drunk as a lord three years ago at the races, so he was in a poor position to cast stones. There were two bad cases of flu in old people, where it was settling in on chests that were never strong, he could see both of them turning into pneumonia before long. People talked about the *good seaside air*, and the *bracing breezes*. They should be here in a doctor's surgery in winter, Paddy Power thought gloomily, there'd be less of the folksy chat then.

Molly said that David was getting on like a house on fire with his lessons, and that he did two hours on his own each morning.

'She's a fine scholar, Angela, isn't it a pity that she never got the recognition for it,' Paddy said, wearily taking off his boots and putting on his slippers.

'Never got any recognition? Isn't she a teacher above in the school with a big salary, hasn't she all her qualifications, that's not bad for Dinny O'Hara's daughter.' Molly sniffed.

'You miss the point, Moll. That's a bright girl and she's stuck here in Castlebay teaching children to be waitresses and to serve their time in shops. And what kind of a life does she have in that house? I mean the Little Sisters wouldn't do as much for their flock as Angela does for her mother.'

'Oh I know, I know.' Molly was anxious to leave it now.

'Still, a man on a white horse may ride into town one day for her yet.' He smiled at the thought.

'I'd say she's a bit past that now,' Molly said.

'She's only twenty-eight years of age, a year older than you were when we got married, that's what she is.'

Molly hated when he spoke about things like that in front of Nellie. Molly hadn't grown up here, she came from a big town and she had been at school in Dublin. She didn't like anyone knowing her business nor indeed her age.

She looked at herself in the mirror, no longer young but not too bad. She had made a friend of the buyer in that shop in Dublin and now there was no problem in getting clothes. Nice wool two-pieces, loose enough so that you could wear a warm vest and maybe even a thin jumper under them. You needed a lot of layers in Castlebay. And Paddy had given her nice brooches over the years so that she always looked smart. No matter who came to the house, Molly Power looked well-dressed and ready to receive them, her hair was always neat and well-groomed (she had a perm every three months in the town) and she always used a little make-up.

She examined her face. She had been afraid that the climate in this place might have made her lined or leathery like a lot of the women, but then they probably didn't use any face cream even.

She smiled at herself, turning her head slightly so that

30

she'd see the nice clip-on earrings she had got recently to match the green brooch on her green and grey wool two-piece. Paddy saw her smiling and came and stood behind her with his hands on her shoulders.

'You're right about yourself, you're gorgeous,' he said.

'I wasn't thinking that,' she said indignantly.

'Well, you should have been,' he said. 'A glamorous thing, not like a mother and wife.'

She thought about being a mother for a moment. She had believed it would be impossible. So many false alarms. The weeks of delight followed by the miscarriages at three months. Three times. Then two babies born dead. And then when she hardly dared to believe it, David. Exactly the child she wanted. Exactly.

Angela thought David was a grand little fellow. He looked like an illustration from those Just William books, with his hair sticking up, his shoelaces undone and his tie crooked. When he worked he sort of came apart.

Wouldn't it be lovely to teach bright children all the time without having to pause for ever for the others to catch up. She looked at him as he worked out a chart of the winds and gave it to her triumphantly.

'Why are you smiling?' he asked suspiciously.

'I don't know. I could be losing my mind. I've noticed myself smiling nowadays whenever any child gets anything right, it's such a shock you see.'

He laughed. 'Are they all hopeless at the school here?'

'No, not all, some are as smart as paint. But what's the point? Where will it get them?'

'Won't it get them their exams?'

'Yes, yes it will.' She stood up a bit like a grown-up who wasn't going to follow the conversation on with him. He was disappointed.

Angela cycled home from Dr Power's house into the wind. Her face was whipped by it and the salt of the sea stung her eyes. Any journey in winter seemed like a voyage to the South Pole, and she wondered for the millionth time would they be better if she moved her mother to a town. Surely this wet wind coming in through every crack in the cottage must be hard on her, surely it couldn't be healthy living in a place that was only right for seals and gulls for three quarters of the year. But then she mustn't fool herself: if they moved to a town it would be for herself, so that she could have some life. Let's not pretend it would be for her mother's poor old misshapen bones. And anyway what more life would there be for her in a town? She'd come in as a schoolmarm with an ailing mother, that's if she were to get a job at all. A schoolmarm who was freewheeling down to thirty. Not something that was going to light many fireworks. Stop dreaming, Angela, head down, foot down, pedal on, only a few more minutes now, the worst bit is over, you're past the blasts of wind from the gap in the cliff. You can see the light in the window.

People called it a cottage because it looked small from the front but in fact there was an upstairs. It was white-washed and had the formal little garden with its boxed hedge and tiny path up to the door.

She wondered how they had all fitted there when her father was alive, when they were children, they must have been crowded. But then her parents had slept in one room upstairs, the three girls in another and Sean, the only boy, in the third. And downstairs the room which she had now made into a bedroom for her mother had been a kind of sitting room she supposed. There had been no books in it in those days, there had been no shining brass ornaments, no little bunches of flowers or bowls of heather and gorse like she had nowadays. But of course in those times the small house had been home for a drunk, an overworked and weary mother and four youngsters all determined to get away from it as soon as possible. How could there have been time for the luxury of books and flowers?

Her mother was sitting on the commode where Angela had put her before going up to the Powers'. She had dropped her stick and the other chair was too far away so she had nothing to support her and couldn't get up. She was uncomplaining, and apologetic. Angela emptied the

32

chamberpot and put Dettol in it, she got a basin of soapy water and a cloth for her mother and helped her to wash herself and put on powder. Then she slipped the flannel nightdress that had been warming on the fireguard over her mother's small bent head and helped her to the bed in the room adjoining the kitchen. She handed her the rosary beads, her glass of water and put the clock where she could see it. She didn't kiss her mother, they weren't a kissing family. She patted her on the folded hands instead. Then Angela O'Hara went back into the kitchen and took out the essays which would be handed back next day. There was no doubt about the winner, that had been obvious all along, but she wanted to write a little paragraph on the end of all the others. They had done the essay in their free time to enter for the prize that she had provided. She wanted to give them some encouragement, some visible proof that she had read them, even the illiterate ones.

She wet a pot of tea and settled down with the wind howling outside and very shortly the sound of her mother's gentle snores about ten feet away.

Clare O'Brien had arrived early at school. The back of her neck was almost washed away, such a scrubbing had it got. The stain on her school tunic was almost impossible to see now, it had been attacked severely with a nail brush. Her indoor shoes were gleaming, she had even polished the soles, and the yellow ribbons were beautiful. She turned her head a few times to see them reflected in the school window, she looked as smart as any of the others, as good as the farmers' daughters who had plenty of money and got new uniforms when they grew too big for their old ones, instead of all the letting down and letting out and false hems that Clare and Chrissie had to put up with.

She thought the day would never start. It was going to be such an excitement going up there in front of the whole school. And there would be gasps because she was so young. Years and years younger than some of them who had entered.

Chrissie would be furious of course, but that didn't

matter, Chrissie was furious about everything, she'd get over it.

Clare walked to the end of the corridor to read the notice board. There was nothing new on it, maybe after this morning there might be a notice about the history prize. There was the timetable, the list of holidays of obligation during the year, the details of the educational tour to Dublin and also the price of it, which made it outside Clare's hopes. There was the letter from Father O'Hara, Miss O'Hara's brother who was a missionary. He was thanking the school for the silver paper and stamp collecting. He said he was very proud that the girls in his own home town had done so much to aid the great work of spreading Our Lord's word to all the poor people who had never heard of Him.

Clare couldn't remember Father O'Hara, but everyone said he was marvellous. He was very tall, taller than Miss O'Hara, and very handsome. Clare's mother had said that it would do your heart good to see him when he came back to say Mass in the church, and he was a wonderful son too, she said. He wrote to his mother from the missions, she often showed his letters to people – well, when she had been able to get out a bit she had.

Father O'Hara made the missions sound great fun altogether. Clare wished he would write a letter every week. She wondered what did Miss O'Hara write to him. Would she tell him about the history prize this week?

There was Miss O'Hara now, coming in the gate on her bicycle.

Mother Immaculata had a face like the nib of a pen.

'Could I have a word, Miss O'Hara, a little word please. That's if you can spare the time.'

One day, Angela promised herself, she would tell Mother Immaculata that she couldn't spare the time, she was too busy helping the seniors to run the potin still and preparing the third years for the white-slave traffic. But not yet. Not while she still had to work here. She put her bicycle in the shed and swept up the armful of essays wrapped in their sheet against the elements.

'Certainly Mother,' she said with a false smile.

Mother Immaculata didn't speak until they were in her office. She closed the door and sat down at her desk; the only other chair in the room was covered in books so Angela had to stand.

She decided she would fight back. If the nun was going to treat her as a disobedient child over some trivial thing as yet unknown, and let her stand there worrying, Angela was going to draw herself up so high that Mother Immaculata would get a crick in her neck looking up. Angela raised herself unobtrusively on to her toes, and stretched her neck upwards like a giraffe. It worked. Mother Immaculata had to stand up too.

'What is all this about a money prize for an essay competition, Miss O'Hara? Can you explain to me how it came up and when it was discussed with me?'

'Oh, I've given them an essay to do and I'm awarding a prize for the best one.' Angela smiled like a simpleton.

'But when was this discussed?' The thin pointed face quivered at the lack of respect, or anxiety at discovery.

'Sure, there'd be no need to discuss every single thing we did in class Mother, would there? I mean, would you ever get anything done if we came to you over what homework we were going to give them and all?'

'I do *not* mean that. I mean I need an explanation. Since when have we been paying the children to study?'

Angela felt a sudden weariness. It was going to be like this for ever. Any bit of enthusiasm and excitement sat on immediately. Fight for every single thing including the privilege of putting your hand into your own very meagre salary and giving some of it as a heady excitement which had even the dullards reading the history books.

It was like a slow and ponderous dance. A series of steps had to be gone through, a fake bewilderment. Angela would now say that she was terribly sorry, she had thought Mother Immaculata would be delighted, which was lies of course since she knew well that Immaculata would have stopped it had she got wind of it earlier. Then a fake display of helplessness, what should they do now, she had all the essays corrected, look here they were, and the children were expecting the results today. Then the fake supplication, could Mother Immaculata ever be kind enough to present the prize? Angela had it here in an envelope. It was twenty-one shillings, a whole guinea. Oh and there was a subsidiary prize for another child who had done well, a book all wrapped up. And finally the fake gratitude and the even more fake promise that it would *never* happen again.

Mother Immaculata was being gracious now, which was even more sickening than when she was being hostile.

'And who has won this ill-advised competition?' she asked.

'Bernie Conway,' said Angela. 'It was the best, there's no doubt about that. But you know young Clare O'Brien, she did a terrific one altogether, the poor child must have slaved over it. I would like to have given her the guinea but I thought the others would pick on her, she's too young. So that's why I got her a book, could you perhaps say something Mother about her being . . .'

Mother Immaculata would agree to nothing of the sort. Clare O'Brien from the little shop down by the steps, wasn't she only one of the youngest to enter for it? Not at all, it would be highly unsuitable. Imagine putting her in the same league as Bernie Conway from the post office, to think of singling out Chrissie O'Brien's younger sister. Not at all.

'But she's nothing like Chrissie, she's totally different,' wailed Angela. But she had lost. The children were filing into the school hall for their prayers and hymn. Mother Immaculata had put her hand out and taken the envelope containing the guinea and the card saying that Bernadette Mary Conway had been awarded the Prize for Best History Essay. Mother Immaculata left on her desk the neatly wrapped copy of Palgreave's *Golden Treasury* for Clare O'Brien for Excellence in History Essay Writing.

Angela picked it up and reminded herself that it was childish to believe that you could win everything.

Mother Immaculata made the announcements after prayers. Clare thought the words were never going to come out of the nun's thin mouth.

There were announcements about how the school was going to learn to answer Mass with Father O'Dwyer, not serve it of course, only boys could do that, but to answer it, and there must be great attention paid so that it would be done beautifully. And there was a complaint that those girls in charge of school altars were very lacking in diligence about putting clean water in the vases. What hope was there for a child who couldn't manage to prepare a clean vase for Our Lady? It was a very simple thing surely to do for the Mother of God. Then there was the business about outdoor shoes being worn in the classroom. Finally she came to it. Mother Immaculata's voice changed slightly. Clare couldn't quite understand – it was as if she didn't *want* to give the history prize.

'It has come to my notice, only this morning, that there is some kind of history competition. I am glad of course to see industry in the school. However, that being said, it gives me great pleasure to present the prize on behalf of the school.'

She paused and her eyes went up and down the rows of girls who stood in front of her. Clare smoothed the sides of her tunic nervously. She must remember to walk slowly and not to run, she could easily fall on the steps leading up to the stage where Mother Immaculata, the other nuns and lay teachers stood. She would be very calm and she would thank Miss O'Hara and remember to thank Mother Immaculata as well.

'So I won't keep you in any further suspense . . .' Mother Immaculata managed to draw another few seconds out of it.

'The prize is awarded to Bernadette Mary Conway. Congratulations Bernadette. Come up here, child, and receive your prize.'

Clare told herself she must keep smiling. She must not let her face change. Just think about that and nothing else

37

and she'd be all right. She concentrated fiercely on the smile; it sort of pushed her eyes up a bit and if there were any tears in them people wouldn't notice.

She kept the smile on as stupid Bernie Conway put her hand to her mouth over and over, and then put her hand on her chest. Her friends had to nudge her to get her to her feet. As she gasped and said it couldn't be true, Clare clenched her top teeth firmly on top of her lower teeth and smiled on. She saw Miss O'Hara looking round at the school and even looking hard at her. She smiled back hard. Very hard. She would never let Miss O'Hara know how much she hated her. She must be the meanest and most horrible teacher in the world – much meaner than Mother Immaculata – to tell Clare that she had won the prize, to say all those lies about it being the best thing she had read in all her years teaching. Clare kept the smile up until it was time to file out of the hall and into their class-rooms. Then she dropped it; it didn't matter now. She felt one of her ribbons falling off; that didn't matter now either.

The girls brought sandwiches to eat in the classroom at lunch, and they had to be very careful about crumbs for fear of mice. Clare had made big doorsteps for herself and Chrissie since her big sister was still in disgrace. But she hadn't the appetite for anything at all. She unwrapped the paper, looked at them and just wrapped them up again. Josie Dillon, who sat beside her, looked at them enviously.

'If you're sure?' she said as Clare passed them over wordlessly.

'I'm sure,' Clare said.

It was raining, so they couldn't go out in the yard. Lunchtimes indoors were awful, the windows were all steamed up and there was the smell of food everywhere. The nuns and teachers prowled from classroom to class-room seeing that the high jinks were not too high; the level of noise fell dramatically as soon as a figure of authority appeared and then rose slowly to a crescendo once more when the figure moved on.

Josie was the youngest of the Dillons, the others were away at a boarding school but it was said that they wouldn't bother sending Josie, she wasn't too bright. A big pasty girl with a discontented face – only when someone suggested food was there any animation at all.

'These are lovely,' she said with a full mouth to Clare. 'You're cracked not to want them yourself.'

Clare smiled a watery smile.

'Are you feeling all right?' Josie showed concern. 'You look a bit green.'

'No, I'm fine,' Clare said. 'I'm fine.' She was saying it to herself rather than to Josie Dillon who was busy opening up the second sandwich and looking into it with pleasure.

Miss O'Hara came into the classroom and the noise receded. She gave a few orders: pick up those crusts at once, open the window to let in some fresh air, no it didn't matter how cold and wet it was, open it. How many times did she have to say put the books away *before* you start to eat. And suddenly, 'Clare, can you come out here to me a minute.'

Clare didn't want to go, she didn't want to talk to her ever again. She hated Miss O'Hara for making such a fool of her, telling her that she'd won the prize and building up her hopes. But Miss O'Hara had said it again. 'Clare. Now, please.'

Unwillingly she went out into the corridor which was full of people going to and from the cloakrooms getting ready for afternoon classes. The bell would ring any moment now.

Miss O'Hara put her books on a window sill right on top of the Sacred Heart altar. There were altars on nearly every window sill and each class was responsible for one of them.

'I got you another prize, because yours was so good. It was really good and if you had been competing with people nearer your own age you'd have won hands down. So anyway I got this for you.' Miss O'Hara handed her a small parcel. She was smiling and eager for Clare to open it. But Clare would not be bought off with a secret prize.

'Thank you very much, Miss O'Hara,' she said and made no attempt to untie the string.

'Well, aren't you going to look at it?'

'I'll open it later,' she said. It was as near to being rude as she dared to go, and in case it had been just that bit too much she added, 'Thank you very much.'

'Stop sulking, Clare, and open it.' Miss O'Hara's voice was firm.

'I'm not sulking.'

'Of course you are, and it's a horrible habit. Stop it this minute and open up the present I bought you so generously out of my own money.' It was an order. It also made Clare feel mean. Whatever it was she would be very polite.

It was a book of poetry, a book with a soft leather cover that had fancy flowers painted on it with gold-leaf paint. It was called *The Golden Treasury of Verse*. It was beautiful.

Some of the sparkle had come back into the small face with the big eyes. 'Open the book now and see what I wrote.' Angela was still very teacherish.

Clare read the inscription aloud.

'That's the first book for your library. One day when you have a big library of books you'll remember this one, and you'll take it out and show it to someone, and you'll say it was your first book, and you won it when you were ten.'

'Will I have a library?' Clare asked excitedly.

'You will if you want to. You can have anything if you want to.'

'Is that true?' Clare felt Miss O'Hara was being a bit jokey, her voice had a tinny ring to it.

'No, not really. I wanted to give you this in front of the whole school, I wanted Immaculata to give it to you, but she wouldn't. Make you too uppity or something. No, there's a lot of things I want and don't get, but that's not the point, the point is you must go out and try for it, if you don't try you can't get anything.'

'It's beautiful.' Clare stroked the book.

'It's a grand collection, much nicer than your poetry book in class.'

Clare felt very grown up: Miss O'Hara saying 'Immaculata' without 'Mother' before it. Miss O'Hara saying their poetry textbook wasn't great! 'I'd have bought a book anyway if I'd won the guinea,' she said forgivingly.

'I know you would, and that eejit of a Bernie Conway will probably buy a handbag or a whole lot of hairbands. What happened to those nice yellow ribbons you were wearing this morning?'

'I took them off, and put them in my schoolbag. They seemed wrong.'

'Yes, well maybe they'll seem right later on, you know.'

'Oh they will, Miss O'Hara. Thank you for the beautiful book. Thank you, *really*.'

Miss O'Hara seemed to understand. Then she said suddenly, 'You *could* get anywhere you wanted, Clare, you know, if you didn't give up and say it's all hopeless. You don't have to turn out like the rest of them.'

'I'd love to . . . well, to get on you know,' Clare admitted. It was out, this thing that had been inside for so long and never said in case it would be laughed at. 'But it would be very hard, wouldn't it?'

'Of course it would, but that's what makes it worth doing, if it were easy then every divil and dirt could do it. It's because it's hard it's special.'

'Like being a saint,' Clare said, eyes shining.

'Yes, but that's a different road to go down. Let's see if you can get you an education first. Be a mature saint not a child saint, will you?'

The bell rang, deafening them for a moment.

'I'd prefer not to be a child saint all right, they're usually martyred for their faith, aren't they?'

'Almost invariably,' Miss O'Hara said, nearly sweeping the statue of the Sacred Heart with her as she gathered her books for class.

Chrissie and her two desperate friends Peggy and Kath had planned a visit to Miss O'Flaherty's to apologize. Gerry Doyle had apparently told Chrissie last night that this was the best thing to do by far. After all, she knew it

41

was them, they'd all been caught and punished by their parents, why not go in and say sorry, then Miss O'Flaherty would have to forgive them or else everyone would say she was a mean old bag who held a grudge. Chrissie hadn't gone along with this in the beginning but Gerry had been very persuasive. What could they lose, he argued? They didn't need to *mean* they were sorry, they only needed to say it, and then it would take the heat off them all so that they could get on with the plans for the party in the cave, otherwise they would all be under house arrest. Do it soon, and put your heart and soul into it, had been Gerry's advice. Grown-ups loved what they thought were reformed characters. Lay it on good and thick.

Clare was surprised to see the threesome stop outside Miss O'Flaherty's shop. She was sure they'd have scurried past but they were marching in bold as brass. She pretended to be looking at the flyblown window display that had never changed as long as she knew it, but she wanted to hear what was coming from inside the shop.

The bits that she heard were astonishing. Chrissie was saying something about not being able to sleep last night on account of it all, Peg was hanging her head and saying she thought it was a joke at the time but the more she thought of it, it wasn't a bit funny to frighten anyone. And Kath said that she'd be happy to do any messages for Miss O'Flaherty to make up for it.

Miss O'Flaherty was a big confused woman with hair like a bird's nest. She was flabbergasted by the apology and had no idea how to cope.

'So anyway, there it is,' Chrissie had said, trying to finish it up. 'We're all as sorry as can be.'

'And of course we're well punished at home,' added Kath. 'But that's no help to you, Miss O'Flaherty.'

'And maybe if our mothers come in you might say that we . . .'

Miss O'Flaherty had a jar of biscuits out. There would be no more said about it. They were harmless skitters of girls when all was said and done, and they had the good grace to come and admit their wrongdoing. They were totally forgiven. She would tell all their mothers. They skipped out of the shop free souls again. Clare was disgusted with them. Miss O'Flaherty was horrible and she deserved to be terrified with bits of seaweed. Why were they saying sorry now at this late stage? It was a mystery.

She didn't get much enlightenment from Chrissie, who was annoyed to see her.

'I'm sorry, Peg and Kath, but my boring sister seems to be following us around.'

'I'm not following you, I'm coming home from school,' Clare said. 'I have to come home this way, it's too windy to walk on the cliff road.'

'Huh,' said Kath.

'Listening,' said Peg.

'You're so *lucky* that you don't have any sisters younger than you,' Chrissie said. 'It's like having a knife stuck into you to have a younger sister.'

'I don't see why. We don't think Ben and Jimmy are like knives,' Clare argued.

'They're normal,' Chrissie said. 'Not following you round with whinges and whines day in day out.' The other two nodded sympathetically.

Clare dawdled and looked into the drapery. She knew everything off by heart in that window too. The green cardigan on the bust had been there for ever, and the boxes of hankies slightly faded from the summer sun were still on show. Clare waited there until the others had rounded the corner. Then she walked slowly on down the street towards the big gap in the cliffs where the steps went down to the beach, back home to O'Brien's shop which everyone said should be a little gold mine since it was perched on the road going down to the sea. It was the last shop you saw before you got to the beach so people bought their oranges and sweets there, it was the first shop you met on the way back with your tongue hanging out for an ice cream or a fizzy drink. It was the nearest place if you sent a child back up the cliff for reinforcements on a sunny day. Tom O'Brien should be making a small fortune there people said, nodding their heads. Clare wondered why people thought that. The summer was the same length for the O'Briens as for everyone else. Eleven weeks. And the winter was even longer and colder because they were so exposed to the wind and weren't as sheltered as people all along Church Street.

Molly Power said that it was lonely for David having no friends of his own and perhaps they should let him ask a friend to stay. The doctor thought that there were plenty of young lads in the town, boys he had played with before he went off to boarding school. But Molly said it wasn't the same at all, and shouldn't they let him ring his friend James Nolan in Dublin and invite him for a few days. His family could put him on the train and they could meet him. David was delighted, it would be great to have Nolan to stay, Nolan had sounded very pleased on the phone. He said it would be good to get away from home, he hadn't realized how mad his relations were. They must have got worse since he'd gone to boarding school and he hadn't noticed. David told him it would be very quiet after the bright lights of Dublin. Nolan said the lights of Dublin weren't as bright as that, and his mother wouldn't let him go to the pictures in case he got fleas. He couldn't wait to get to the seaside.

'And will my class increase by a hundred per cent?' Angela O'Hara asked him when she heard that Nolan was coming to stay.

David hadn't thought of that. He didn't know. It was something he hadn't given any thought to.

'Never mind.' Angela had been brisk. 'I'll sort it out with your parents. But we had a plan for twenty days' work to cover the time you were at home, if Mr Nolan arrives that will cut six days out of it. What are you going to do? Abandon it or try to do the work anyway?'

He was awkward and she rescued him.

'I think you'd rather not have Nolan seeing you taught lessons by a woman. It's a bit like a governess, a country schoolteacher coming to the house.'

'Oh no, heavens, nothing like that.' David's open face

was distressed. 'Honestly, if you knew how much I've learned since working with you, I'd be afraid to let on in case they'd never send me back to the school again, they'd put me into the convent here.'

He was a mixture of charm and awkwardness. It was very appealing. The image of his bluff kind father and yet with a bit of polish that must have come from his mother thrown in.

'Why don't I set out a bit of work for you and Mr Nolan to do each day. Say an hour and a half or two hours. I'll correct it, without coming in on top of you at all, and that way there's no embarrassment.'

The relief flooded his face.

'Is Mr Nolan as bad at Latin as you are?' she asked.

'A bit better, I think. He's going to need it too you see, he's going to do Law.'

'Is his father a barrister?'

'A solicitor,' David said.

'That makes it nice and easy,' she said with a bitter little laugh.

David was puzzled, but she changed the subject. It wasn't David Power's fault that the system was the way it was. A system that made it natural that David Power should be a doctor like his father, and James Nolan of Dublin a solicitor like *his* father, but made it very hard for Clare O'Brien to be anything at all. Angela squared her shoulders: hard, but not impossible. Hadn't Clare the best example in the land sitting teaching her? Angela, youngest daughter of Dinny O'Hara, the drunk, the ne'er-do-well, the man looking for every handout in Castlebay. And she had got the Call to Training, and higher marks in the college than any other student, and they had scrimped to send her brother to the missions, and she had nieces and nephews in comfortable homes in England. Nobody in the town could pity them when they walked behind her father's coffin five years ago. If Angela could do it with a drunken father and a crippled mother, then Clare could do it. If she cared enough, and today it looked as if she cared almost too much.

'So, College Boy,' she said to David, 'let's get on with the hedge school before the gentry come down from Dublin and catch us with our love for books!'

'You're great, Miss O'Hara,' David said admiringly. 'Wasn't it a pity you weren't a man, you could have been a priest and taught us properly.'

Molly Power was very anxious that things should be done right for David's young friend, and there were endless instructions to Nellie about breakfast on trays and getting out the best silverware until David begged that they just come downstairs as usual. Then they'd have to do their homework for Miss O'Hara before they felt free, but what a long day stretched ahead. Nolan loved the beach being so near, it was almost like having your own private swimming place, he said enviously, to be able to climb over a stile at the end of the garden and have a path going down to the sand and the caves. A path with *Danger* written all over it. Nolan tried out the Echo Cave and the other smaller caves. He wore wellington boots and slid and scrambled over the rock pools, he picked up unusual shells, he walked out to the end of the cliff road to see if the Puffing Hole was blowing. He walked the course on the golf links and planned that he and David should take lessons next summer. He couldn't believe they were allowed to go to the cinema at night. In Dublin he had only been to matinees and that was before his mother had heard of all the fleas.

Nolan was very popular in Castlebay. He was so handsome for one thing, small, with pointed features and hair that didn't stick out in angles like David's but fell in a sort of wave across the front of his forehead. He had very sharp eyes which seemed to see everything, and he wore his clothes with style, turning up his collars and striding round with his hands buried deep in his pockets. He used to joke about being short and said that he suffered from a small-man complex like Napoleon and Hitler.

He was polite to Mrs Power and insatiable for medical details from Dr Power. He praised Nellie's cooking and he said that he thought Castlebay was the most beautiful place in Ireland. In no time he was an honoured guest. Even Angela O'Hara liked him. He wrote out his preparation dutifully in small neat writing, and Angela had immediately sent him a note on the first batch of corrected work: 'Kindly make your writing much less fancy and much more clear. I have no idea whether or not you have written the correct ending on the cases of the nouns. I will not be mocked.'

'She must be quite a character, why don't we meet her?' he asked David.

David wasn't really sure, but he knew that it somehow reflected discredit on him. 'She's shy,' he lied, and felt worse.

Next day they saw a figure like a dervish flying past on a red bicycle. The machine did a dangerous turn and an envelope of papers was thrown from the basket to David.

'Here you are, College Boy, save me facing the winds over your way.'

David caught them neatly.

'This is the man who doesn't know the neuter plural from a hole in the ground,' she shouted cheerfully. 'You've got to make the adjectives plural too, my friend. No use just throwing them there and hoping they'll decline themselves.'

'Can't you come and teach us up at the house?' Nolan called out flirtatiously.

'Ah, too much to do, but aren't we doing fine by correspondence course?' Her hair stretched out behind her in the wind, blowing like someone in an open car in a film. She wore a grey coat and a grey and white scarf.

'She's gorgeous,' breathed Nolan.

'Miss O'Hara?' David said in disbelief. 'She's as old as the hills.'

They were still laughing over what age Miss O'Hara would be when Nolan was twenty-five, the age he thought he might take a bride, when they met Gerry Doyle. He had wellingtons and a fisherman's jersey and somehow he seemed much more suitable for the place than they were. Gerry was about the only one who would ever ask him what his boarding school was like, and what they had to eat and what kind of cars fellows' parents had.

'I was thinking they might burn that school of yours down if it has the plague,' Gerry said agreeably. He thought it was all more serious than they were being told, plague and pestilence and scarlet fever, otherwise why would they close down a big important school? He suggested too that they should look out for germs when they got back, in stagnant pools or in the curtains.

David made a mental note to talk to his father about it when he got home.

'Do you want to come to a midnight feast, isn't that the kind of thing you have in your place all the time, before the plague and all?'

'I was at one and we were caught,' David said sadly.

'I was at that and another, the other wasn't caught,' Nolan said as a matter of record.

'Yes well, tomorrow night in the Seal Cave starting at eleven-thirty. If you could bring a few sausages and your own bottle of orange or even beer.'

'Can we?' Nolan's eyes were shining.

'Why not? This is Castlebay, this isn't a backwater like Dublin,' David said bravely, and Gerry Doyle told them that there'd be girls and tins of beans and sausages . . .

Gerry Doyle had told Chrissie not to say a word to Tommy and Ned about the party in the cave. It wasn't that he had anything against them but they were the kind who could accidentally let something slip. He wasn't even telling his own sister, he said, because she was the same. Chrissie was pleased that Fiona wasn't coming and so were Peggy and Kath. Fiona looked a bit too attractive for their taste; she was fourteen of course, which would make her look a lot better, just automatically, than the rest of them but still they all felt a bit second best when Fiona was there. And of course Chrissie wouldn't think for a moment that Tommy and Ned should be invited, they were far too uncertain – they'd wonder aloud for days and in the end they'd all be found out and the picnic in the cave would be stopped. Gerry had said that there'd be about a dozen of them or so, no point in alerting the whole town. They were to meet there at eleven-thirty, and everyone was to try to make their own way in twos and threes at most. So as not to be noticed.

Clare stirred in her bed when she saw Chrissie's legs swing to the floor on the other side of the room. To her surprise, Chrissie was fully dressed. She was moving very quietly and feeling round for her shoes. The light of the Sacred Heart lamp fell on her as she was picking up what looked like a great lump of sausages and rashers from the shop! Chrissie was actually wrapping these stealthily in white paper and darting nervous glances at Clare's bed.

In a flash Clare understood she was running away. In a way this was great. She would have a bedroom to herself, she wouldn't be tortured by Chrissie morning noon and night any more. There would be less rows at home. But in another way it wasn't great. Mammy and Daddy were going to be very upset and the Guards would be here in the morning and Father O'Dwyer and people would walk along the cliffs when the tide came in looking for a body as they always did whenever anything happened in Castlebay. And there would be prayers for her and Mammy would cry and cry and wonder where she was and how she was faring. No, Clare sighed reluctantly, better not to let her run away, it was going to be more trouble than it was worth.

Chrissie looked at her suspiciously when she heard the sigh.

'Are you running away?' Clare asked casually.

'Oh God in heaven, what a sorrow it is to have such a stupid sister. I'm going to the toilet, you thick turnip you.' But there was fear in her voice.

'Why are you dressed up in your clothes and taking sausages and bacon if you're just going to the toilet?' Clare asked mildly.

Chrissie sat down on the bed, defeated. 'Oh, there's an awful lot of things I'd like to do to you, you're a spy, you were born a spy, it was written on you plainly, you'll never do anything else except follow people round and make their lives a misery. You hate me and so you destroy everything I do.'

'I don't hate you, not really hate,' Clare said. 'If I hated you properly wouldn't I let you run away.'

Chrissie was silent.

'But Mammy would be desperately upset and Dad too, I mean they're going to be crying and everything. It's not that I'm spying, I just thought I'd ask where you were going in case they think you're dead or something.'

'I'm not running away. I'm going out for a walk,' Chrissie said.

Clare sat up in her small iron bed. 'A *walk*?' she said.

'Shush. Yes, a walk, and we're going to have a bit of a meal on it.'

Clare raised herself up and looked out the window behind the Sacred Heart statue and the little red lamp. It was pitch dark outside. Not a thing stirred in Castlebay. 'Are Peggy and Kath going too?'

'Shush. Yes. And Clare . . .'

'Is it a picnic?'

'Yes, but you're not coming, you're not going to spoil every single thing I'm doing, you're not going to ruin it for me.'

'Oh, that's all right if it's only a picnic.' Clare had snuggled down under the blankets again. 'I just didn't want the fuss if you ran away. That's all.'

There was a small red travelling clock on the kitchen mantelpiece. David took it to bed with him. Nolan said that he'd wake all right in the spare room but David didn't want to take any chances. The clock was under David's pillow and its alarm was muted but it woke him from a deep sleep. For a while he couldn't think what was happening, and then he remembered. He had the bottle of cider and the sausages packed neatly in his school gym and games bag. Nolan had bought four bottles of stout and two packets of marshmallow biscuits which he said were great if you toasted them over a fire. Gerry Doyle had said there would be a bonfire in the back of the Seal Cave and that they knew it would work because they had tried it out already. There was a part of the cave which was perfect for it.

The only problem was Bones, the dog. David's father said that Bones would go up and lick the paws of any intruder or assassin but he'd bark the house down if you went in or out yourself. He was more of a liability than a watchdog. David and Nolan had decided to bring Bones with them to the midnight feast. It was either that or drug him and though Nolan preferred the notion of knocking him out for a few hours David had been too strictly brought up, in a house where even aspirins were locked away, to think that this was remotely possible.

He crept into the spare room and Nolan was indeed dead asleep but woke eagerly.

'I was only thinking with my eyes shut,' he said.

'Sure, and snoring with them shut too,' David said.

They shushed each other and crept down the stairs. Bones jumped up in delight and David closed his hand around the dog's jaw while stroking his ear at the same time. This usually reduced Bones to a state of foolish happiness and by the time Nolan had eased open the door they were safe. Bones trotted down the garden to the back wall ahead of them, finding nothing unusual in the hour. David and Nolan with their torches in their pockets stumbled. They couldn't shine a light until they were over the stile, it would surely be the one moment that David's mother was going to the bathroom and would look out the window and then waken the neighbourhood.

But down the path which said Danger they used their torches, and slipped and slid more than they walked. It was dry now but it had been raining earlier and the twisty path had a lot of mud.

'This is fantastic,' Nolan said, and David swelled with pride. When they got back to school Nolan would tell everyone of the terrific time he had in Power's place and the others would look at him with respect. He had always been slow to tell people about Castlebay, it sounded like such a backwater compared to the great places they all came from, but looking at it through Nolan's eyes he realized there was much more to it than he had thought.

Down on the beach Bones ran round like a mad thing, up to the edge of the sea and back again, barking excitedly, but he could bark for ever down here, the sound of the waves crashing and the wind whistling would carry it far away. Dr and Mrs Power wouldn't even hear it in their dreams.

The Seal Cave was dark and mysterious-looking. David was quite glad he wasn't on his own. There was a big fire at the back; Gerry was right, there *was* a part of it that was dry and not dripping with slime. They had begun the cooking and rashers dangled dangerously on long sticks and a couple of toasting forks. There were at least a dozen people around the fire. There were giggling girls nudging each other and breaking into loud laughter. That was Peg and Kath, he knew them to see; and Chrissie O'Brien from the shop. David looked around for Clare but she was too young probably. Chrissie couldn't be more different to Clare, he thought. Screeching with laughter and knocking the food off other people's forks. Clare was solemn and much gentler somehow.

David had never had stout before, but the others were drinking it. It almost made him throw up, it didn't taste like a drink should taste. Manfully he finished one bottle and began another. Nolan seemed to like it and he didn't want to look a sissy. Gerry Doyle seemed to notice though.

'You could have some champagne cider if you liked, it's a different taste, nice sort of drink,' he suggested.

David sipped some: now this was more like it. Sweet and fizzy, very nice indeed.

Gerry, small and eager, was hunched up over the fire. He looked very knowledgeable.

David held his glass up to the light. 'It's good stuff this,' he said appreciatively.

Later when he was getting nowhere after the groping had begun, Gerry marked his card again. No use trying anything with that one, she just laughed all the time. There was the one who would be more co-operative. A manly wink which David returned unsteadily. Gerry Doyle was a good friend to steer you in the right direction.

There were mystery ailments all over Castlebay next day, but against all the odds nobody broke ranks and the midnight feast was never discovered. Chrissie O'Brien had come back home covered in mud with cuts all down her legs where she had fallen coming up the steps from the strand, and she was sick twice into a chamberpot in the bedroom. Clare said grumpily she hoped that these midnight feasts weren't going to be going on all the time. Chrissie was too busy plotting the morrow and how she would explain her ripped and mud-covered coat, to answer Clare. In the end she decided she would go out early before anyone saw the state she was in and then she could fall again and be considered too sick to go to school. It worked too, nobody noticed that half the mud had dried and the scabs on her legs had started to heal. Chrissie's friend Peggy managed to get to school and stick the day but Kath had been sick in the classroom and had to be sent home.

Up in Power's house there seemed to be no explanation for the burn that had appeared as if by magic on James Nolan's mouth. In fact it had come from his eating a sausage directly from the long bit of skewer it was cooked on, but it was announced as being something that had come upon him unexpectedly during the night. Molly Power worried endlessly what his parents would say when he got back and fussed interminably about it when she wasn't fussing about David who was as white as a sheet and had to go to the bathroom every few minutes. The third peculiar thing in the house was Bones. He had apparently let himself out in the night and was found asleep in the garage with a cooked sausage in his paws. Dr Power told her that in the long run it was often better not to think too hard and try too earnestly to solve all problems. Sometimes it was better for the brain to let things pass.

Gerry Doyle's father told him at breakfast that there had been terrible caterwauling in the middle of the night and did he know anything about it? It sounded like a whole lot of women or girls crying on the doorstep. Gerry looked at him across the table and said that he thought he had heard that mad dog of the doctor's wailing and baying around the town during the night – could that have been it? It could, his father thought doubtfully and sniffed around him. 'This place smells like Craig's Bar,' he said to his wife and stamped off to what they all called his office, the front room beside the main bedroom. Gerry's mother got annoyed and started to slam out the breakfast dishes in a temper.

'Brush your teeth for heaven's sake, Gerry, and eat an orange or something before you go to school.' Fiona was not only kind she was practical.

Gerry looked at her gratefully. 'I had a feeling there might be a bit of a trace,' he grinned.

'Trace?' said Fiona. 'You nearly knocked us all out. Was it great fun?'

'It was in a way.'

'I wish you'd have let me . . .'

'No.' He was very firm.

'But I'm older even than some of them who were there.'

'That's not the point. You're not that type. No one must ever say that anyone was messing around with *you*. You are all I've got, I've to look after you.'

He was serious. Fiona looked taken aback.

'You've got all of us . . . like we all have . . .' she said uncertainly.

'What have we got? We've got Dad, who lives in his own world. When did Dad say anything that wasn't about the business?'

'He just mentioned Craig's Bar, didn't he?' Fiona laughed.

'Yes.' Absent-mindedly he took a peppermint out of his pocket and unwrapped it.

'What's wrong?' she asked, her big dark eyes troubled.

'I don't know. It's just he's so dull and unadventurous. How are we ever going to get on if we stay as timid as he is? And Mam . . . Well, honestly.'

'She's a bit better, I think,' Fiona said softly. They had not talked about this before.

'She's not. You say that because she went out to the garden and hung out the clothes. You think that's some kind of success. She hasn't been out of the house for six months. Six months. Tell me if that's normal or not normal.'

'I know. But what can we do? They don't want to tell Dr Power.'

'It's all his fault, he thinks that if we tell Dr Power there's going to be some kind of trouble.'

At that moment, Mr Doyle reappeared, small and dark like his son, with the same quick smile and almost elfin face. 'I'm only wondering does anyone in this house intend to go to school or have we all graduated without my knowing about it?'

'I'm just off. Dad, I may be going past David Power's house, will I ask his father to come and have a word with . . .?'

'If anyone needs a doctor they'll go and see Dr Power and if they're not able to go, Dr Power will be brought to them,' said his father sternly. That was that. Gerry went to brush his teeth as had been suggested, and met his mother creeping along by the wall, alarmed by the word 'doctor'.

'Don't worry, Mary, go back into the kitchen, there's no need for a doctor,' his father said.

He called at the surgery that evening.

'Well, Gerry?'

'I don't know, Dr Power.'

'It can't be too serious an ailment if you've forgotten it already.' The old doctor was cheerful.

'It wasn't an ailment at all.'

'Good, good. Was it something wrong with someone else?' The man's eyes were sharp.

Gerry seemed to hesitate. 'No, I suppose people have to look after their own illnesses, don't they?'

'It depends. If you saw a wounded man lying on the

road you wouldn't say he'd better look after his own illness.'

'No, it's not like that.'

'Would you like to tell me what it is like?'

Gerry made up his mind. 'No, no. Not now. I came to know if David and James Nolan would like to go out this evening? For a bit of a laugh like?'

Dr Power was thoughtful. 'I think there's been enough laughs for the moment. I think it's time the laughing died down for those two and they got a bit of work done.'

Gerry looked him in the eye. 'Does that mean they can't come out? Is that what you're saying?'

'You're as bright as the next man, Gerry, you know what I'm saying, and not saying.'

'Right. Tell them I called and was sorry they weren't allowed out.'

'No, I won't, because that's not the message. Tell them yourself if you want to.'

Gerry Doyle's great skill was knowing when not to push it any further. 'You're a hard man, Dr Power,' he said with a grin, and he was off.

Paddy Power wondered whether he had been going to ask about his anxiety-ridden father or his withdrawn, possibly phobic mother. Maybe the boy hadn't noticed anything wrong with either of them. He was a funny lad.

A parcel arrived for Angela, a small flat box. It was a beautiful headscarf from the parents of James Nolan. 'Thank you so very much for all the help with tuition, your pupils in Castlebay must be very lucky to have such a gifted teacher.' It was a square with a very rich-looking pattern on it, the kind of thing a much classier woman would wear. Angela was delighted with it. She showed it and the letter to her mother but it was a bad day and the old woman's joints were aching all over.

'Why shouldn't they be grateful to you, why shouldn't they send you something? It's money they should have sent. Doesn't the postman get paid for delivering letters?'

Angela sighed. She told David about it that evening. 'Wasn't it very thoughtful of them?' she said.

'They have great polite ways up in Dublin,' David said wistfully. 'We'd never have thought of giving you a thing like that, and we should have.'

'Don't be silly, College Boy. I was only telling you so that you'd know your friend appreciated the lessons and all that.'

'He thought you were very good-looking,' David said suddenly.

'I thought he wasn't bad himself, but a bit small for me. How old is he, about fifteen?'

'Yes, just.'

'Oh well, that's no difference at all, tell him I'll see him when he's about twenty-five, I'll be coming into my prime about then.'

'I think that would suit him fine,' David laughed.

It was shortly before the school re-opened that David met Gerry Doyle again.

'Have you had any good drinking nights since the cave?' Gerry asked.

'I think I'm going to be a Pioneer. I was never so sick. I was sick eleven times the next day,' David said truthfully.

'Well at least you held on to it until you got home,' Gerry said. 'Which was more than some people managed. Still, it was a bit of a laugh.'

'Great altogether. Nolan said he'd never had such a night.'

'He was telling me you've got a record player of your own, a radiogram in your own bedroom, is that right?'

'Not a radiogram with doors on it, but a record player yes, you plug it in.'

'How much would they be?' Gerry was envious.

'I'm afraid I don't know, it was a present, but I could ask.'

'I'd love to see it,' Gerry Doyle said.

David's hesitation was only for a second. His mother had never *said* he wasn't to have Gerry Doyle into the house but he knew she wouldn't approve. 'Come on, I'll show you,' he said.

Any other lad in Castlebay might have held back but not Gerry Doyle. He swung along the cliff road companionably with David as if he had been a lifetime calling on the doctor's house socially.

The summer houses looked dead, as they passed, like ghost houses and it was hard to imagine them full of families with children racing in and out carrying buckets and spades, and people putting deckchairs up in the front gardens.

'Wouldn't you need to be cracked to rent one of those for the summer?' Gerry nodded his head at the higgledy-piggledy line of homes.

'I don't know. Suppose you didn't live beside the sea?' David was being more tolerant.

'But if you had the money to rent one of those for a couple of months what would you spend it on that for, why wouldn't you go abroad to Spain or to far places like Greece even?' Gerry was beyond believing that anyone could pay good money for a place in his own Castlebay.

'But if you were married with children you wouldn't be able to take all of them abroad,' David argued reasonably.

'Ah well, I wouldn't be married, so I suppose that's the difference.'

'Not now, but later.'

'Not ever. Do you want to?'

'I thought I would,' David said.

'You're off your head, David Power,' said Gerry Doyle agreeably.

Mrs Power was in the hall arranging some winter branches in a vase.

'Hallo,' she said when the hall door opened. 'Oh hallo, Gerry, do you want to see the doctor?' She looked slightly quizzical. Her head had inclined towards the surgery entrance. Patients didn't come in the front door, they went in by the porch on the side.

'No thanks, Mrs Power, I'm coming to look at David's record player,' he said confidently.

'I beg your pardon?' She was polite, but frosty.

'Oh, I'm going to show Gerry the record player . . . how much was it, by the way?' David didn't feel as brave as he sounded.

'It was a present, David dear,' his mother said with a smile that wasn't in her eyes. 'We don't ask how much a present cost.'

'No, but maybe you could tell Gerry then, he was wondering if he might buy one.'

'I think it's a little beyond Gerry,' said David's mother in that tone he really hated. But Gerry didn't seem to notice in the slightest.

'You might well be right,' he said cheerfully. 'It wouldn't be until the end of the summer anyway, I work for pocket money but there's nothing really for me to do that's useful until the trippers come. Still it'll be nice to see it anyway.' He smiled straight into the disapproving face of David's mother and with his arm on the banisters and his foot on the first step he called to David. 'Is it up here?'

David followed him without looking back to see the grim expression that he knew had settled on his mother's face.

At lunch Mrs Power waited until Nellie had left the room. 'Paddy, could you ask David not to bring Gerry Doyle back here to the house.'

Dr Power looked up mildly from his newspaper. 'Well, he's sitting beside you, Molly, can't you ask him yourself?' he said.

'You know what I mean.'

'Is this some kind of row?' The doctor looked from his wife to his son.

'Not on my part,' David said.

'See what I mean,' said Molly Power.

'Well, it seems you are being off-hand with your mother. Don't be like that.' Dr Power went back into the paper.

'*Paddy*. Please. Explain to David that Gerry Doyle's

perfectly all right but he is not a guest in this house.'

Wearily he put down the paper. 'What's it about?' he said, looking from one to another.

There was no reply.

'Well, what did young Doyle do that caused the upset?' Again he looked from his wife's flushed face to his son's mutinous one.

'Nothing,' David shrugged. 'He came upstairs. I showed him my record player. He admired it. He went home.'

'Molly?'

'That's not the point, as you know very well. You're not an infant David, you know well what I'm talking about.'

David looked blank.

'Your mother is saying that she goes to a lot of trouble to keep this house nice and she doesn't want people tramping all over it. That's a reasonable request, isn't it?'

David paused, deciding whether or not to buy this explanation. Then he saw its flaws. 'Oh sure, sorry Mummy, I didn't know that was what it was about. I thought you had something against Gerry Doyle himself. You know, like Nolan's mother went through that bit of thinking everyone had fleas. No, that's fine, of course I won't ask people back without asking you first.'

Molly smiled uneasily. She wasn't at all sure that she had won.

'And I'll be going down to his house later on today, he said he'd show me the darkroom and let me help to develop some of the pictures his father took at a wedding.'

He smiled brightly from one parent to the other and helped himself to a glass of orange squash.

Gerry Doyle's sister was gorgeous-looking. She wore an overall, which was like an artist's smock, and she looked like an illustration in a book. She seemed a bit shy and answered yes and no when David asked her about anything. But she was very polite and helpful. She offered to go and make cocoa and said she'd run over to O'Brien's for a quarter of a pound of broken biscuits as well.

60

'Why didn't you ask her to the Seal Cave?' David wanted to know.

'Oh, you couldn't ask your *sister* to a thing like that. It's all right for Chrissie and Kath and Peggy and those, they're the kind of girls you'd expect to have at a thing like that, but not Fiona.'

David felt he had overstepped some limit he didn't know about. He felt awkward. He felt too that it was hard on the girls who had been there. They had all had great fun and played spin the bottle; and the boys had given them cider and beer and encouraged them like mad. Then the girls had got a bit silly and one or two of them were crying and Kath had been sick and they had fallen and everything. But it was all part of the night. It was a bit cruel somehow to think that Fiona was a different type of girl, one you wouldn't bring to a party like that, but it was true. When she came back with the tray of cocoa and biscuits David knew that he would not like Fiona to have been to a party like that either.

He would have liked to ask her to write to him at school. Nolan had a girl who wrote him long letters. But he thought it was too complicated to set it all up. Firstly if Fiona had said yes he would have had to explain the whole system where the letters were read by the priests and so the girl who was writing had to pretend to be another boy. Nolan's friend who was called Alice used to sign her name Anthony. She had to remember not to talk about hockey matches but say rugby instead, in fact the letter was in so heavy a code or disguise none of them could really work out what it meant. Still it was nice for Nolan to be able to get the letter and tell everyone how good-looking Alice was. It would be nice to do the same with Fiona. But if Gerry wouldn't let her come to a party in a cave down the road he would almost certainly be very much against her writing letters in code to a boy in a boarding school. That would be fast, and Fiona Doyle was not going to be thought of as fast. David noticed that he kept thinking of them as orphans even though they lived with their mother and father. That was odd.

'Your parents don't take much part in things, do they?' he said enviously.

'They work too hard,' Gerry said. 'It was always like that. It's a dog's life, and Mam hates the work but what else is there?'

'What would she prefer to be doing?'

'Arranging flowers on a hall table in a house like yours,' Gerry laughed. 'But isn't that what every woman would want?'

The roof didn't fall in and the skies didn't flash with lightning when David got back home that evening. He sensed that his parents had had a little chat. His mother was sewing the Cash's name tapes on some new socks and pyjamas for him. She seemed to have forgotten the row at lunchtime totally.

'I suppose in a way it will be hard to settle into all that studying again,' she said.

David was determined to be equally pleasant. 'Yes, but I'm very glad that I had Miss O'Hara, very glad. Nolan said we were dead lucky down here to be able to get someone like that, up in Dublin teachers are sharks, he said, they ask for a fortune for grinds and they smell of drink.'

David's father laughed from the other side of the fire. 'Your friend James is full of nonsense. You can't make generalizations about any job no more than you can about mine or his father's. Dear dear.'

'You know the way Nolan goes on,' David said.

'Of course I do, he's a very bright young fellow, we liked him, your mother and I did. Ask him down any time, or any of your other friends, the house is big and there's plenty of room. And it's nice to hear a bit of noise around the place.'

That's a different tune to the one they were playing at lunch, David thought to himself. Then I was invading the privacy of the house. He heard himself saying that he'd love to ask Nolan again, and he was very grateful to be allowed to invite people home. Nolan's mother was still fussing apparently and when she wasn't worrying about fleas she was worrying about ceilings falling down. Nolan said she was having a tonic for her nerves but it didn't seem to be doing much good.

On the last evening before he went back he said he'd like to go and say a proper thank you to Miss O'Hara, and maybe give her a small present. David's mother said that Angela O'Hara wouldn't like that at all, she had been paid adequately, but Dr Power said no, David was right, why not give her a book of some kind from the shelf, she always admired the books when she came to the house.

'You don't need to go up to Dinny O'Hara's cottage,' Molly Power said.

'Dinny O'Hara has been in the churchyard for five years, he's unlikely to come out and corrupt the boy now,' said Paddy Power, and David saw his mother's face get that tight-lipped look again.

Nellie helped him to wrap up a book about Irish place names. They took the torn paper cover off it and it was lovely underneath. Nellie looked at the small print in admiration.

'Imagine Angela O'Hara being able to read all this and understand it. Ah well, that's what comes of keeping to your books.' She had been at school up at the convent with Angela herself, and had been there the day the news came of Angela's scholarship to the big town. In those days the nuns had been so proud that one of their girls had won the scholarship they used to make the uniform themselves with their own hands. They had kitted out the young Angela for her secondary school because they knew that anything Dinny O'Hara would get into his hand went straight across a bar counter and he wouldn't do much to help his little girl get on.

'She deserved to do well,' Nellie said unexpectedly, as she was making a nice neat corner on the parcel and tying the string tightly. 'She never crowed about all her successes and her high marks and all. Nobody could say that it all went to her head.'

David didn't think that Miss O'Hara had all that much to crow about. To be teaching in that awful convent, to be here in Castlebay with her old mother – when she must have wanted to get far away. Why else did she go in for all those scholarships? He didn't think she had the huge success that Nellie seemed to think. But of course compared to Nellie it must be fine, she didn't have to clear out grates and ranges and scrub floors and make beds and cook meals and wash up and wash clothes and go out in the cold and see they weren't bashed down by the wind. Being a teacher must seem like a nice cushy job to Nellie.

He turned left outside the gate and went along the road towards the golf course. It was longer than he remembered, no wonder Miss O'Hara always flew round the place on her bicycle. There was a light downstairs in the O'Hara cottage: he hoped that her old mother wouldn't answer the door bent over the two sticks.

But the door was opened by Clare O'Brien. Clare was thin and alert, big brown eyes and fair hair tied in bunches. She always looked as if she was about to ask a question. He remembered meeting her in the Echo Cave and she had said that it would be like heaven on earth to have lessons from Miss O'Hara without the rest of the class. Maybe that's what she was doing now.

Clare seemed pleased to see him. 'She's putting her mother to bed, she's got awful pains altogether today, she can neither sit nor stand. Miss O'Hara said she'd be back in a few minutes. Will you come in and sit down?'

David was a bit put out that she was there; he had wanted to make a flowery speech to Miss O'Hara without an audience. But he could hardly order the O'Brien girl to go home or say that his conversation was private. He looked around the kitchen.

'Isn't it like Aladdin's Cave?' whispered Clare in awe.

It was a typical kitchen for a cottage in this area. The fire had been replaced by a small range. That must have come from Angela O'Hara's salary – it never came when Dinny O'Hara was alive nor from the widow's pension that the arthritic old woman got every week. Perhaps the brother and sisters abroad sent money, David wouldn't know. Miss O'Hara was very private, she never told you all about herself and her family like everyone else in Castlebay did all the time, that's why you were interested to know more. David looked up at the walls. Everywhere there were shelves. Each alcove had shelves from ceiling to floor, and there were ornaments and books and biscuit boxes and more books and sewing baskets and statues. Clare was right. Almost like a toyshop on a Christmas card. There was no inch of wall without a shelf, and no inch of shelf without an object. Most of the objects were books.

'She knows where every single thing is, would you credit that?' Clare's big brown eyes looked larger than ever in the semi dark of the room. There was a table with writing paper and a bottle of Quink ink and blotting paper. Miss O'Hara must have been writing letters with Clare when her mother took a turn.

'Are you getting lessons?' he asked. There was a touch of envy in his voice. He would have preferred to learn in this funny enclosed place where everything had a story and every item was known in its little place. It was a much better place to study than his mother's sitting room with the copies of *Tatler and Sketch*, and *Social and Personal* laid out beside *The Housewife* which came every month by post from England. When the copies were a couple of months old they went to the surgery, and of course there were all the encylopedias and big leather-bound books. But they weren't read and touched and loved like things were here.

'Oh no, I wish I could, no I'd like that more than anything. I'd be a genius if I had Miss O'Hara to teach me on her own.' She spoke with no intention of making him laugh. She was utterly serious.

He was sorry for her. It must be desperate not to have enough money for education. You always felt that came automatically.

'Maybe you could do things for her, you know, do the messages or cook or something in exchange.'

'I thought of that,' Clare said solemnly. 'But I think it's a bit unfair, she'd have to be looking round for things for me to do. It would be like asking for charity.'

'I see.' He did see.

'But I came up tonight because Miss O'Hara *is* going to help me, I'm to write to the convent in the town, a kind of letter that would make them think well of me, and inquiring about their scholarships in two years' time.' Her eyes were shining over the very thought of it.

'Miss O'Hara got a scholarship there herself, years and years ago. She says you have to be dead cunning, and look on it as a war.'

Angela O'Hara came into the room then. 'Don't give away all our secrets, Clare, maybe College Boy here might be disguising himself and trying to get into the convent ahead of you.'

Nolan would have made a witty remark. David couldn't think of one, he just laughed. 'I'm in your way, you're writing letters,' he said awkwardly.

'Don't worry about that, David, Clare's writing her own letter actually, and I am meant to be writing one to my brother. I find it so hard to know what will interest him about here. You know: got up, went to school, did not strangle Immaculata . . . every day it becomes a bit repetitive.'

'What does he write? I suppose his days are a bit samey too,' David said.

Angela took out an airmail envelope with the stamp neatly removed for the school collection. 'I was just thinking that very thing . . . My mother keeps all Sean's letters, every single one of them – look at the boxes of them – and he does seem to be saying the same thing over and over. But it's nice to hear.'

'When you get older I expect there's not much to write about,' Clare said helpfully.

'Or more when you don't really share the same kind of life,' David said. 'That's why I never had a penfriend in India or anything, once you'd described your life and he'd described his that would be it.'

'It is a bit like that,' Angela agreed. She picked up a thin piece of airmail paper and read to them:

Dear Mother and dear Angela,
Thank you so much for your letter which arrived here yesterday. We are in the middle of a rainy season which makes things very difficult but still it is thanks to all the great and good support that we get from home that God's work can be done.

I wish you could see the little Japanese children, they are really beautiful. I suppose I didn't have all that much to do with children before I came out here, on the missions. Perhaps little Irish children are even more beautiful . . .

Angela broke off and said it was easy known that he never had to pass one day of his lifetime teaching little Irish children in a convent or he would think otherwise.

'It's a bit like the letter he wrote to the school, isn't it?' Clare said.

'It's a bit like every letter he writes,' Angela said, putting it back in the envelope. 'There's nothing for him to say, I suppose, that we'd understand. I do ask him things myself sometimes, like do they ordain many Japanese priests out there, and what happened to all the Chinese they had converted before they left China, did they go back to their old religion or what. But he never answers those kind of things.'

She was silent in thought for a while. David coughed.

'I came to say goodbye and thank you,' he said. 'And to give you this book to tell you how grateful I am.'

Angela sat down and reached for her cigarettes without saying anything. When she spoke it was with a softer voice than either Clare or David had ever heard her use. 'That's very good of you,' she said and bent her head over the twine, fiddling with the knots.

'It's only old twine, you can cut it if you like,' David said helpfully and Clare found a knife. Miss O'Hara sawed through the string, and they all bent over the book. Time passed easily as they read why places they knew were called what they were called, and they were all enraged that Castlebay wasn't in it and said that the man who wrote the book hadn't travelled at all if he couldn't include a fine place like this. From the other room there were sounds of moaning but Miss O'Hara said not to take any notice, it was her mother trying to get into a comfortable position to settle for the night, it wasn't really sharp pain. They had a cup of tea and a bit of soda bread and eventually Miss O'Hara shooed them out into the night lest people think they had been kidnapped.

Angela told herself not to be so sentimental over David's present. It was very thoughtful of the boy certainly, but he came from a nice peaceful home where there was time to be thoughtful and there was ease and comfort. And his father was one of the most generous men that ever walked. It was in the boy's nature to be bright and generous. But it was so different to what she could expect from the children she taught up in the convent. Half of them would never do any kind of an exam, almost none of them would ever open a book again after they left her, except a novel or a magazine.

Not Clare of course. She was the one that would keep you going. Imagine teaching a class full of Clare O'Briens or of David Powers for that matter. She sighed. It was a pity as David had said that she hadn't been born a man. She could have become a priest and taught bright boys in a school where the principal would not go into shock if she asked for a globe.

She wondered did Sean ever regret his choice in teaching the children of Chinese and Japanese workers in pidgin English. Would he have liked the days spent in an ivy-covered college like the one that David and young Nolan went to? Would Sean have liked the evenings in study and chapel and walking reading a breviary in cloisters or discussing philosophy in a dining hall? It was a question that couldn't really make sense, since her brother Sean had never shown interest in any other life except the missions. He had followed the road that got him there without pausing to think or to wonder did people miss him. She missed him from time to time, his letters were no way of knowing him, and recently they had become very static.

You couldn't even hint at that to her mother. Every letter was kept in a box with the date it was received written laboriously on the envelope. As if someone was going to check them some time. The stamps were neatly cut off to add to the school stamp collection, they were never re-read but Mrs O'Hara knew almost by heart the names of the villages and the settlements and the places up country and down country. She knew them better than she knew the countryside around Castlebay, for it had been a long time since she could walk and see it. Angela wondered sometimes what her mother would think about all day if she hadn't a fine son who was a missionary priest to fill her mind.

Back at school Nolan told everyone that Power was a dark horse. They should see the great place he lived in, a big house on a cliff with its own private way down to the sea. They had a maid and a labrador and every single person in the place knew them by name and saluted them. David felt it was going a bit far to call Bones a labrador, but he agreed that the rest was mainly true. He also found himself the centre of attention because of having taken Nolan to a party where real sex games were played. This was the cause of a lot of questioning and David wished he knew how much Nolan had elaborated on the innocent kissing games they had played by the firelight before the drink had taken over and everyone had been too dizzy and confused to play any games at all. But it was good to be a hero, and he laughed knowingly about it all.

He was pleased too when Father Kelly said that he was an exemplary pupil and had kept up meticulously with the suggested course of study which had been handed out to all pupils on the day the school had closed because of the scarlet fever. The essays had been written, the poems had been learned, history questions had been written out and illustrated with neat maps and family trees, the maths and geography were completed, and the Irish and Latin exercises done in full.

'You got private tuition? Well, he was a good man whoever he was,' Father Kelly said in one of his rare moments of approval.

'It was a she actually, Father,' David said apologetically.

Father Kelly's brow darkened: he had been too swift with his praise. 'Ah, some of them are competent enough I suppose,' he said, struggling to be fair, but losing interest.

David told Nolan that Gerry Doyle had a smashing-looking sister, really beautiful, but that he wouldn't take her to the cave that night.

Nolan was very positive about this, as he was about everything. 'Of course he couldn't bring his *sister*,' he said as if it were obvious to a blind fool, 'I mean I wouldn't have let *my* sister go. We couldn't have taken Caroline to a party like *that*, where people would be . . . well you couldn't take Caroline there. Gerry Doyle was quite right. Is she going to write to you?'

'I didn't ask her.'

'Right, Power, you've got the technique, don't be too easy to get, don't be a pushover. Leave them wondering, that's what I always do.'

'Will Alice be writing again this term?'

'No, I think I've grown out of Alice,' said Nolan in a voice which revealed that Alice had grown out of him.

Nolan said his mother had got a bit better about things and that she had agreed to go away next summer for a holiday by the sea. Nolan's whole family had been wanting to do this for ages but his mother had always said the seaside was full of rats and beetles and sea snakes. St Patrick had only got rid of the land snakes according to Nolan's mother, but he had no power over the huge snakes calling themselves eels which came in on beaches all over the country. But now the tablets she was taking had made her forget, and they were going to inquire about renting one of those cliff houses in Castlebay. Because Nolan had come home with such glowing reports they were going to try there first. David was delighted: the summer would be full of adventure if Nolan and his family came to Castlebay.

Angela said that Clare must write the letter herself, it was no use putting grown-up words into a ten-year-old head. But she would monitor it for spelling, and style. She found Clare a writing pad that had no lines on it, but with a heavily-lined sheet you put under the page you were writing on. Clare should ask the convent whether there was any particular course of study she should concentrate on, since she was very anxious to prepare herself as diligently as possible for the open scholarship in 1952. Clare tried to remember the words diligent, concentrate, but Angela said no, she must use her own words, and she must sound like a real person, someone they would remember when the time came. She said to tell the nuns that her parents were business people. Clare wondered was that true; but Angela said, years ago she had told them her father was a substantial farmer who had fallen on hard times because of the Troubles, and since that was way back in 1932 it sounded reasonable. It would have done her no good to say she was the daughter of the town drunk and she was burning to get herself on in the world.

'Do you think there's any hope I might get it? You see I don't want to get myself all excited like I did . . . well . . .'

'Over the history essay.' Miss O'Hara nodded. 'No, I think you have a chance, a good chance if you work like the hammers of hell. Oh and don't tell anyone, it's easier somehow if you don't.'

'But David Power knows.'

That didn't matter, Miss O'Hara thought, he'd have it long forgotten. But Clare shouldn't mention it at school, or at home, it only got people into a state. Clare had thought there was too much going on at home without letting them get into another state over a scholarship in the distant future.

Tommy and Ned had been for interviews and they

couldn't wait to go to England. They had heard that there was massive reconstruction being done over there since the war, the place was full of bombed sites only waiting to be built up again, and roads from one place to another planned for, and housing for all those who lost their places during the raids.

The man who had come to Dillon's Hotel for two hours had taken their names and addresses. He had asked them very little but said they should report to him when they got there; they should wait till the fine weather until they came over. There'd be no trouble at all finding digs; the roads around Kilburn and Cricklewood were filled with Irish households only too delighted to have lads from home in to stay. They'd be like mothers to them, they wouldn't need to go near English strangers at all. The man said he was a businessman who could get a good deal for his own countrymen; he didn't like to see Irish lads being made fools of, he'd see them right when they came over.

Clare's father wondered could the man be a chancer. Why would he be doing all this for love? Why wasn't he an agency like any other agency that took fees? That way made sense, a person could understand that, but this way was hard to fathom. A man with an open shirt coming to Dillon's Hotel and giving them all a piece of paper with his name on it and saying he could be found any Friday night in one of two pubs in Kilburn – it sounded a bit suspicious.

But Tommy and Ned would have none of it. What had they to lose? If, after one week, he turned out not to be getting them their full wages, they could leave him and go on to one of these agencies that Da was talking about. They weren't bound to him. He had said he wanted nothing in writing, no complications of any sort. They should be delighted to have his name, and have him as a friendly contact over there instead of making such a fuss about everything.

Tommy had left school. He had no exams, no certificates and, after all his years in the Brothers, he could barely read and write. Clare thought wistfully of David Power

72

that night up in Miss O'Hara's kitchen and the book he had given to her as a present. Tommy would have thrown it aside. He couldn't even read what was written on a packet in the shop, if someone asked him. He didn't read the paper and he never opened a book of any sort now that he had been released from the classroom. He was meant to be helping his father get the shop to rights before he went off to London to seek his fortune. A lot of the time he spent just hanging around.

Clare's father was rearranging the shop, and that was hard to do while people were still being served. It meant that a lot of it was done in the evening when they were meant to be closed. Of course a place like O'Brien's could never close properly: if Mrs Conway came for a pound of sugar, or Miss O'Flaherty decided that she wanted some biscuits with her late night tea, there was no refusing them.

But there was less of a flow after six o'clock, less of the sound of the ping when the door opened and a figure stood letting in the cold sea winds until the door swung closed.

Last summer it had been so crowded trying to sell ice-cream in the middle of everything else, that this year he was going to move the ice-cream cabinet down to one side of the little shop. Chocolate and sweets would be high up over it, and fruit beside it, so the beach people could be served all in one area; while the people who had rented houses on the cliff road could ponder and deliberate and finally settle for cooked ham and tomatoes as they always did, on a less cluttered side of the shop. It was all fine in theory but it was hard to do and still keep track of where everything was. Each evening they scrubbed shelves and tacked on new oilcloth. The floor was a constant disappointment to them; the lino needed to be replaced but of course there wouldn't be funds for that, so instead new bits were nailed down near the door where the wear and tear was most obvious. Boxes that only contained a few things were emptied out and stored neatly in the storeroom. In the summer, visitors were mad for boxes and lots of the suppliers didn't leave any behind. It was best to have a pile of them ready.

It was worthy work but it ate into homework time. Miss O'Hara had drawn everyone in the class a map of Ireland, a blank map. They were to trace it or copy it and reproduce it every fourth page of their history exercise book. Then, when they learned of the battles and the treaties and the marches and the plantations, they could fill them in on their own maps and they would know what happened where. Clare was lost in the Battle of Kinsale, drawing little Spanish ships and Red Hugh's army on its way down from the north when she heard the voice calling. Perhaps if she pretended she didn't hear . . . This was the wrong thing to do. The door was thrown open and her mother stood quivering with annoyance.

'Aren't you a fine lady thrown on the bed when you're needed?'

'I'm not thrown, I'm filling in this map, look.'

'I've looked at enough of that childish nonsense, you're a grown girl, get downstairs and help your father at once. We've been calling and calling and not a word out of you.'

'It's my homework.'

'Don't be ridiculous, nobody has homework drawing ships and little men, stop that act and come down *at once*. Your father wants a hand to clean those top shelves before we put things up there.'

'But how will we reach them – what's the point of putting things up there?'

'Are you going to debate this from up here or come down like you're told!'

'Where are you off to, Chrissie? We'll be taking down all those old notices stuck to the windows this evening . . .'

'Oh, I can't stay, Mam, I'm going up to Peggy . . . she's going to teach me how to make a frock.'

'A frock?'

'Yes, she's got a pattern, she says it's easy to cut around it. Soon we'll be able to make all our own clothes.'

'Well, all right, but don't be late home.'

'No, I won't. Bye Mam.'

'Clare, what are you doing?'

'The trade winds. We've got to know all about where they come from and why they blew the fleets of . . .'

'Right, get a bowl of hot soapy water, will you, and come with me. These windows are a disgrace, you can't see through them in or out.'

'Clare, child, I know you work hard at your books but couldn't you give your mother a hand with the washing? She's got very thin on us altogether.'

'The washing, Dad?'

'Washing the clothes. I asked her to sit down and have a cup of tea and she said she couldn't, there was a pile of washing to do. You'll have to do washing when you have a home of your own, why don't you take a turn now and learn how to do it properly? There's a good girl.'

'What about Chrissie, Dad, could she do it tonight, and I'll do it the next time, I've this legend to learn. There's all kinds of desperate names in it.'

'Chrissie's gone to do her homework with Kath.'

'Uh,' Clare said.

'You could go on saying the names to yourself as you did the washing,' her father said.

'No, the book would get wet. Do I *have* to, Dad?'

'You don't *have* to. I thought you'd be glad to help your mother.'

'Tommy or Ned?' She asked without much hope.

'Well, if that's the kind of thing you're going to be saying . . .' he turned away in disgust. To suggest that *boys* would do the washing! Clare was being very difficult altogether.

'Oh, all *right*!' Clare slammed closed the story of Jason and the Golden Fleece. She only knew Jason, his father, his two wicked step-uncles and the name of the ship. There was a huge cast still to master, so it would mean waking up early . . . again.

'Clare, come here till I teach you to darn.'

'No, Mammy, I don't want to learn to darn.'

'You that wants to learn everything? Look, it's very

75

simple. Do you see this hole, what we have to do is to make a criss cross . . .'

'No, Mam, I'd like not to know how to do it. Ever.'

'Why, child? When you have a home of your own you'll want to know.'

'But if I know now, I'll be darning Tommy's socks, and Ned's, and Dad's, and Jim's, and Ben's, and maybe even Chrissie's.'

Agnes put her arm round the thin little figure, and smiled. 'Aren't you the funny little thing.'

'No, Mammy, I'm the sensible little thing. I'll never learn to darn, never.'

Agnes was annoyed to see her affection rejected. 'Have it your own way, and you can go and do the washing up if you're not going to take advantage of the lessons I was going to give you.'

'But . . .'

'Chrissie won't be in, their class have a special extra class today.'

'That's right,' Clare said glumly. 'Of course they do.'

'Have you a cold, Clare?'

'No, it's just a cough, Mam. Dust or something in my throat, I think.'

'Have a drink of water then.'

'Right.'

'Clare, don't spend all day in the kitchen, come back and help me with these boxes, and put a scarf or something round your mouth if you're breathing in all the dust.'

'Mam, when we've finished this lot, can I go and do . . .'

'Do your homework, do your homework. Why is it that you're the only one in this family who has to make the excuse of doing your homework? Look at the rest of them.'

'I know. Look at them, Mam.'

'What's that supposed to mean?'

'Nothing.'

Often Clare had to do her homework in bed, there was literally no other place and no other time. This made

Chrissie very cross. She grumbled loudly if Clare turned on the torch.

'You're spoiling my sleep and ruining your own eyes. You'll be blind soon and we'll have to take you round by the hand and you'll have a white stick,' Chrissie said with satisfaction.

'Shut up, Chrissie, I'm learning something. I can't get it into my head if you keep distracting me.'

Chrissie was surprised at the strength of the reply. 'I'll tell on you, if you don't stop that mumbling and learning and having a light on, I'll tell. *That* will put a stop to it.'

There was no reply. With her hands in her ears and eyes closed Clare was repeating under her breath the words, '*Do Ghealadh mo chroi nuair chinn Loch Greinne,*' over and over.

'You're as thick as the wall,' said Chrissie. 'You mean you don't even know one line after all that saying of it?'

'I don't know what *Ghealadh* means. It's hard to learn when you don't know what something means.'

'Ah will you come on out of that, you don't know what *any* of it means. How would people know what Irish poetry meant? It's just words.'

'It means something happened to my heart when I saw Loch Greinne, but I don't know what happened. *Ghealadh*, what would that mean?'

'It might mean Stop. My heart stopped dead when I saw Loch Greinne.' Chrissie laughed at her own wit.

'Didn't you learn it when you were in our class?'

Chrissie shrugged. 'We might have, I forget, I forget all of it. What's the point?'

Clare had gone back to her book.

'I mean it, I'll tell, and you'll be in right trouble then. I'll say you kept me awake with your caterwauling of poetry pretending you understand it. Wait and see. You'll suffer for it.'

'No I won't,' Clare said. 'I won't suffer from it at all, *you* are the one who'll suffer. It will be wondered why you do no homework, why you don't know anything. It might even be wondered what you and Kath and Peggy get up to. You're not going to say anything, and you know it so will you shut up and let me get this learned so that I can go to sleep.'

Angela waited in the surgery. There was only one other patient, old Mrs Dillon from the hotel. Angela would have thought that the doctor would have visited her privately, but Mrs Dillon whispered that she had come to see him secretly. She had pretended to her family that she was going to say the thirty days prayer in the church, but in fact she had come to explain that her daughter-in-law was poisoning her. Angela sighed. Poor Dr Power. He probably got as much of this as Father O'Dwyer did in the confessional. Angela settled down with an old copy of *Tatler and Sketch* and began to read about the happenings up in Dublin. She was in for a long wait. But in a few moments, Dr Power was ushering old Mrs Dillon out the door, and the woman was smiling ear to ear.

'You'll have time for the thirty days prayer after all, and say a few Hail Marys for me,' he called out after her.

'Sure you don't need them, Doctor, aren't you a walking saint,' called Mrs Dillon.

'She's only saying what's true.' Angela stood up and walked across the corridor with him.

'No. I'm a walking liar, that's all.'

'What did you tell her?'

'I told her I was in there during the week inspecting the place for hygiene and I have instruments that could detect poison a mile off. But there wasn't a trace of it in Dillon's Hotel. I said that the cold weather often made people think the taste of food had changed, that it was a common belief, then I gave her a bottle of rose-hip syrup and she's delighted with herself.'

Angela laughed: he looked like a bold boy who'd been found out telling a fib.

'And who's poisoning *you*, Angela, Mother Immaculata up at the convent, maybe?'

'Not a bad guess, I think she'd like to a lot of the time. No, it's not poison. It's sleep.'

'Too much of it or too little of it?'

'Hardly any of it.'

'Since when?'

'Three weeks, now.'

'Do you know what's causing it? A worry, a problem?'

'Yes, I do.'

'And is there anything that can be done about it?'

She shook her head wordlessly.

He waited, but nothing came. He reached for a prescription pad, shaking his head. 'I won't have you lying awake at night, of course you can have something. But Angela, child, it's no use just knocking yourself out with these.'

'I know. Thank you, Doctor.'

'And I'm not always such a blabbermouth, like I was there about old Mrs Dillon. If it would help to talk about it at all, I *could* keep it to myself. In fact I usually do.'

'You don't have to tell me that, Dr Power. Don't I remember always how good you were about my father.' But she was resolute. She thanked him and said she would go straight to the chemist now before they closed. She smiled a tired smile at him and he noticed she did indeed have the dark circles of sleeplessness under her eyes. As far as he knew it wasn't a man, he'd have heard in a small place like this. It was even more unlikely to be a casual sexual encounter resulting in a pregnancy – and anyway, Angela O'Hara wouldn't lie awake sleepless over something like that. She had been a Trojan in all that business of the child up in the convent who was pregnant: she had been so practical and down-to-earth when everyone else had been flying about in the air. It was Angela who thought of explaining to the girl how the infant would be born, and it was Angela who suggested that the girl's uncle should be shipped off to England with a warning delivered from enough tough people to make him believe that his life would not be safe if he were ever to return to Castlebay. That had been about four years ago; surely Angela herself couldn't have brought such a disaster on herself? He sighed and went in to the sitting room. Molly was reading by the fire.

'Nothing changes, nothing gets much better,' he sighed.

She looked up surprised. Usually he was an optimistic man, seeing hope where there was any kind of life. 'Is anybody dying?' she asked.

'No, nothing like that. Wasn't it a pity I wasn't a ship's doctor.'

'Paddy, don't be ridiculous, you can't dance well enough to be a ship's doctor. That's all they do. They don't have anything to do with sickness or curing people.'

She looked nice, he thought, when she was being enthusiastic and cheering him up, she looked young herself. It was when her face was discontented that she developed the pouting, double-chinned look of her mother – a woman who had been born disagreeable and lived to make life disagreeable for everyone round her until last year when she got a coronary right in the middle of complaining that she hadn't got enough presents for her seventieth birthday.

'I'm very ignorant all right,' he said and went over to the drinks cupboard. His hand hovered for a moment over the sherry but settled round the bottle of Irish. What could be so bad that Angela O'Hara couldn't tell him?

Angela got the sleeping tablets in the chemist and didn't correct Mr Murphy there who thought the pills were for her mother.

'It's a terrible curse, that arthritis, and you know there's no cure for it. Years ago people didn't know what it was; now they know what it is but they can't cure it. Not a great advance, when you come to think of it. These will give her a good night's sleep, anyway,' he said.

'Oh yes,' Angela said.

'You're not looking all that well yourself, Angela, you want to get a bit of rest too you know. Up in that school all day with the voices of those children, I don't know how you stick it. When we come up to see Anna and Nan in the concert we're nearly deaf from the shrieking of them all round the school, and then you have the poor mother . . .'

'I'm as strong as a horse, Mr Murphy,' said Angela and she dragged herself out of the chemist and into the post office. She had her foot on the doorstep when she realized she couldn't take Mrs Conway this evening – the bright artificial voice, the inquiries about how well Bernie was doing, the mention once more of the history prize. Angela would never get an answer to the question she wanted to ask, and today she wasn't strong enough to take Mrs Conway head on. Some days she'd be able to deal with ten Mrs Conways before breakfast. But that was all before she had got the letter.

The letter had arrived three weeks ago, with all the beautiful stamps which she usually cut off and put in the envelope on the mantelpiece at once. They saved stamps for the missions, foreign ones in one section and Irish ones in another. Once a year they got a letter at the school thanking them for their great Missionary Effort. Angela would always pin this up on the wall, knowing that somehow it annoyed Immaculata but there was no way she could fault it. She hadn't noticed that this letter was different to the others, that it had been addressed to her alone and not to her mother. She hadn't seen the word *Confidential* all over it. She could easily have opened it as she sat beside her mother.

The letter began: 'Angela, I beg you read this alone. I was going to send it to the school but I thought that would cause more fuss. You'll think of some reason why I put confidential on it. You'll think of something, Angela. Please.'

And it went on to tell her how Sean had left the religious house three years ago; how he was married to a Japanese girl; and how Father Sean had one child of fourteen months and another on the way.

Sean O'Hara had told the Brothers from an early age that he was going to be a missionary priest. They were pleased with this: it was far preferable to the other ambitions in the school, which seemed to be to drive the Dublin train or to own a sweetshop. Occasionally the Brothers tried to divert Sean to their own order; but firmly he said that what he wanted was not the job of teaching schoolboys who were already Catholics in Castlebay, he wanted to go out and meet savages and convert them to Christianity.

He was never a holy kind of boy, and none of his schoolmates thought that there was anything remotely pious in his vocation. They were slightly envious in fact to think that Sean would go off to all these exotic places. It was never firmly decided whether it would be Africa, or India or China. The Brother who taught geography was quite grateful to young Sean, as the boy was always sending off to Missionary Orders asking for details of their work; and in return for magazines and pamphlets Sean organized the silver-paper collection for them too.

He had even managed to get a missionary priest to come and give a talk at their school when he was around thirteen. The priest told him to slave hard at his books and maybe he would be taken into a seminary; but for everything in this life it was essential to be good at the books.

Sean was three years older than Angela but he found her a willing ally. She borrowed books for him from the convent; she shared the task of going round to look for their father each evening and finding a neighbour willing to help carry him home. It was she who insisted that a corner of their kitchen be made into a sort of study for them, and had the oil lamp fixed firmly to a shelf so that it couldn't be taken away from them. Their two sisters, Geraldine and Maire, were already planning to leave the nest. Geraldine had been in touch with a hospital in Wales where she could train as a nurse, and Maire had a friend who worked in a very nice store in London which was so smart that it wasn't like being a shop girl at all. Fifteen and sixteen, and their futures were certain. Within months they were gone. Holidays at home very rarely, letters from time to time, pictures of grandchildren never seen, never known, growing up with English accents and a promise to come home some day.

Geraldine and Maire had come home for their father's funeral. Grown-up, distant, wearing black coats and hats, startled that everyone else wore raincoats and headscarves. They had borrowed the black outfits specially. They had looked around with restless eyes at the wet cold church-yard, and at the entire population of Castlebay standing with bent heads against the wind. It was so unfamiliar to them after thirteen years in another country. They had looked pityingly at the small house that had been their home for over half their lives and shaken their heads sadly. Angela had been enraged. *They* didn't know how hard she had worked during her father's last illness to try to make the place look respectable, so that her mother would have some dignity at the end. So that she could give the neighbours tea and cake and whiskey without feeling ashamed of their home.

But of course the best consolation at the funeral had been Father Sean. He had been due back later in the spring but when Angela wrote to him and to the Superior of the Order – a measured letter explaining that her father would not be alive in spring, the liver damage was irreversible – the Order had acted swiftly and humanely. Of course young Father O'Hara could be spared from the mission fields a little earlier.

And home he came, stepping from the bus to a buzz of excitement; children ran ahead up to O'Hara's cottage to give the news that he had arrived. The long skirts of his habits he raised slightly to avoid the mud of Castlebay, the way they were used to avoiding the swamps of the Far East. Father O'Hara, home to give his father Extreme Unction and to say his Funeral Mass.

Father Sean had a word for everyone in Castlebay. His eyes didn't cloud with pity for the people, he didn't look sadly at his old home, his bent mother, nor did he close his ears from the life his father had lived. 'He was an unhappy man in this world, let us pray he finds that happiness he was always seeking in the next.' It was generous and forgiving and loving, people said. He had been away for most of his father's spectacular unhappiness, away in the seminary in the novitiate and eventually in the mission fields. But still, the principle was the same, and if he was able to forgive his father for all that neglect and trouble, people thought it was big-hearted of him in the extreme.

Angela's mother's bones ached less when Father Sean was around, and on the very last morning, before he went away again for five years, he said a little Mass at a side altar in the church just for the two of them. They didn't even have an altar boy; Angela answered the responses in Latin from her missal. Geraldine and Maire had gone back to their families in England with promises to return regularly.

When the Mass was over, Mrs O'Hara pressed eighty pounds into her son's hands for the missions; she had been saving it and hiding it for years waiting for his visit.

He had gone that day. The tears of goodbye were in the house, and the brave faces were at the bus stop opposite Conway's post office; there was a waving of handkerchiefs, and the pride of the widow that everyone in the town should see how her fine tall son had turned out.

And the letters never failed: thanks for the cuttings from the local paper, or for the news that their stamp collection had been the biggest in the county; sympathy to the Dillons when old Mr Dillon died, a holy picture to be given to the family with a few words of blessing written by Father O'Hara himself; less and less about what he did himself and more and more in response to their own tittle-tattle in the fortnightly letter which Angela now wrote for her mother since the arthritis had reached the old woman's hands.

Not long ago, Angela had written on her own behalf a little request: 'Sean, you're so good to be interested in all our petty goings-on here, but tell us more about you. In the beginning you used to tell us about the House and the various fathers who lived there, and the schools you all started. And I remember the day a bishop came to confirm everyone and there was a monsoon and they all ran off into their huts and no one got confirmed that year. It's *interesting* to us to know what it's like for you every day, and what you do all the time. If you were a priest here with Father O'Dwyer we'd know, but it's so different out there we find it hard to visualize . . .'

Why had she written that? If she had said nothing maybe she would never have had the letter that burned a hole through her handbag; the letter that told of the end of the vocation for father Sean but would spell the end of any kind of life at all for his mother.

Sean had written that he couldn't bear the deception any more, he said that Shuya and he found the letters from home unbearable now; they referred to a life long past. And when money arrived for Masses, it was spent on rent and food. Sean taught English in Tokyo. There had never been a religious house of his order there at all; the address on letters from Castlebay was in fact the house of Shuya's brother. Sean collected any mail from him.

The family spoke English, and were puzzled to know why he was still addressed as 'Father' on the envelope, and why their house was described as a religious foundation.

The other fellows had been terrific about it all, even his Superior. They had tried to change his mind at first and said that, even though Shuya was pregnant, surely Sean could come back to the House, and a provision be made for the child. They didn't understand that he loved her and wanted to have a family with her, and that long before he had met her, the conversion of the Far East had lost all sense for him. He could only see that they were fine with their own beliefs and he didn't think the Lord wanted them changed at all.

Eventually, when everything got more settled, he was going to send his plea to Rome to be laicized and released from his priestly vows. It happened much more than people thought. Then he would be free to remarry Shuya in a Catholic church, and their children could be baptized.

Shuya said she had no objection to the children being Catholics.

There was a finality about it that was chilling. The letter left no hope that Shuya was a dalliance, a shameful thing which you often heard whispered about when priests went abroad – something like that or two bottles of the local liquor a day. This woman was in his mind his wife. His fellow priests *knew* about her, they had been kind and supportive. His Superior knew. And Sean found the letters from home 'unbearable'. He couldn't 'bear' to read them now because they referred to a life that no longer existed. *To hell with him*, she thought in fury. He can bloody bear to read them for as long as we send them. I shall never tell that woman about the Japanese Shuya, I shall *never* tell her about the half-Jap grandson, called Denis after his grandfather. How could poor Mammy take it in and cope with it, if even Angela who was young and meant to be modern and intelligent couldn't take it in herself? And then there were other moods: poor, poor Sean, how desperate, with only one life to lead, and finding it empty. Led on and seduced by this Japanese woman with no religion and no morals. To her, a priest was the same as anyone else; she would have no idea what a sin it was, and what a terrible decision Sean had to make. At other times still she had moments of calm: it's not so bad, we'll say nothing, Mammy doesn't read my letters, I'll write him ordinary letters referring to his new life, and ask him to write the old-style letters referring to his old life. That way nobody will be hurt.

But in the night, when she had been asleep for about an hour and would wake with that start which she knew meant no more sleep for the rest of the dark hours, Angela knew that she was fooling herself. A lot of people had been hurt already. And in her moments of real self-pity she got up and lit a cigarette and looked out of the window: *she* had been hurt most of all. Struggling all that time, scrimping to send him money, even during her teacher-training when she was penniless from start to finish and wore away her legs walking because she had neither bicycle nor bus fares.

86

She had come back for a one-year appointment to the convent here, the year her father was dying. She had decided that she owed her mother that support and that the woman should have at least one of her children around for the bad months that lay ahead. She had been loath to leave the big, cheerful school in Dublin; but the Reverend Mother there had said she would certainly keep her job open for a year – Miss O'Hara was too good a prize to lose. She had walked the cliffs with her brother Sean when he was back for the death and the funeral. They had talked as naturally as they always had, the bond hadn't been shaken in the slightest. They had stopped at stiles and leaned on grassy banks looking out to sea where the gulls swooped and cried; and Sean had talked gently about ties, and duty, and doing what you felt you had to do. And she knew then that she wasn't going back to her job in Dublin, she was going to stay and look after her mother. She felt no resentment, then or later. She didn't hate Geraldine for not shipping her English husband and children over to Castlebay, nor Maire. How could they do anything of the sort? Sean was a missionary priest who had already given up his life to good, and anyway what use would a boy be around the house, even suppose he had been able to come home?

But somehow, now, in the dark sleepless hours where her heart was caught with a permanent sense of alarm and dread, she felt little love for him. How dare he talk to her about duty? How *dare* he? Where was his duty, she might ask. The first temptation and he leaves his priesthood, he closes his ears to what he had known since he was old enough to learn his catechism: that once a priest always a priest. He had slept with a Japanese woman, over and over, she was about to have his second child. Angela had never slept with anybody, and she was more entitled to try it than was a priest of God.

In his letter he said that he had told Shuya all about Angela, and Shuya had said it sounded as if she were strong enough to sort out the whole thing. Thank you very much Shuya, Angela thought in the night. Nice, helpful,

Japanese sister, thank you. Shovel it all on to Angela, as usual. Oh, you're becoming an O'Hara all right, Shuya, don't doubt it.

Clare received a letter from the nun in the secondary school enclosing the syllabus for the 1950 open scholarship. It arrived with the usual crop of bills, receipts and advertisements from suppliers which made up the O'Brien family post.

Agnes was sitting near the range so that she could supervise the lifting over of the big teapot and the spooning out of the porridge. The older boys and Chrissie sat on one side of the big kitchen table with its torn oilcloth; Clare and the two younger boys had their backs to the door. In winter, breakfast was one meal where they were unlikely to be disturbed. The ping of the shop bell never went before the family was off to school.

The kitchen was warm and not really uncomfortable, but it was so cluttered that it was almost impossible to move once any of them stood up from the table. There were clothes and schoolbooks scattered around on the dilapidated couch, there were bags that hadn't yet been sorted for the shop heaped up against the wall. The washing hung perilously from the ceiling and the dresser bulged with so many things that had been 'just put there for the moment' that it was impossible to see the plates and dishes.

Tom O'Brien groaned and sighed as usual over the brown envelopes, the ones with windows in them and the ones without. Then he gave a start. 'Well now, Clare, there's a letter here for *you*!'

Clare had never had a letter before, so it created a lot of interest in the O'Brien household.

'I suppose she's got some awful, ugly, scabby lover,' Chrissie said.

'Don't talk like that, don't be such a loud-mouth always,' said Agnes O'Brien crossly to her troublesome daughter.

'Well who is it from? Why don't you ask her? You always ask me everything, where I was, who I talked to. Why can't Saint Clare be asked anything?'

'Don't speak to your mother like that,' said Tom O'Brien, who was already in a bad humour. 'Come on, Clare. Tell us who the letter is from and stop all this mystery.'

'It's a list of books for exams,' Clare said simply, producing the roneoed sheet of paper that the nun had sent. She left the letter in the envelope.

'What do you want that for?' Chrissie scoffed.

'So there won't be any mistakes in what I have to study.'

Chrissie looked at the list. 'We did all those last year,' she said.

'Good.' Clare was calm. 'Then maybe you'd have the books for me to use later.' She knew that Chrissie's books were long torn up, or scribbled on, or lost. It was not a subject her sister would discuss for much longer.

Agnes O'Brien had more on her mind than book lists. She was preparing to send her two first-born sons to England, where they were going to live in a strange woman's house and go out to work with grown men of every nationality each day. It was a terrible worry. But what was there for them here in Castlebay? If they only had a few fields of land it would have been different, but a small shop like this one, there was hardly a living in it at all.

Clare decided to show the letter to Miss O'Hara after school, but she was careful not to be seen hobnobbing with the teacher in case anyone should suspect that she was favoured, getting extra help and advice all the way. She would go to the O'Hara cottage instead. Miss O'Hara never seemed to mind her dropping in, and surely she would be interested in the letter.

Mrs O'Hara answered the door slowly and painfully. Clare had been tempted to run off again when she heard the scraping of the chair that meant the old woman was beginning her long, aching journey to the door, but that would be worse.

'I'm sorry for getting you up.'

'That's nothing,' the old woman said. 'I may have to be

getting up to answer the door myself in a short time, that's the way things look.'

'Are you getting better?' Clare was pleased.

'No. But I may be on my own, that's the way the wind is blowing.'

'Miss O'Hara going to move out of the house?' It was incredible.

'And out of Castlebay, by the looks of things.'

'She can't!' Clare was stung with the unfairness of it. Miss O'Hara *had* to stay, until she got her scholarship. She *couldn't* leave now.

'Is she getting married or something?' she asked, full of hostility to the whole notion of it.

'Married? Who'd have that big long string of misery? Of course she's not getting married. Restless, that's what she's getting, restless. Her own words. She's up pacing the house all night long, you couldn't get a wink of sleep with her. What's wrong you ask her. Restless, she says. Ah well, nobody has any time for you when you're old. Remember that, Clare.'

Miss O'Hara returned just then. She looked very tired. She had been short-tempered at school too for some time, though not with Clare. So Clare didn't expect sharp words.

'*God Almighty,* am I to get no peace, at school, on the street and now at home?'

Clare was shocked.

'You give people an inch and they take a bloody mile. What is it tonight, Clare, is it the long division or is it the Long Cathechism? Tell me quickly and let's be done with it.'

Clare stood up and placed the letter from the distant convent on the O'Hara kitchen table. 'I thought you'd like to see the reply they sent me, since you helped me write the letter.' She was at the door now, her face red and furious. 'Goodnight, Mrs O'Hara,' she called, and was gone.

She marched down the long golf-course road, where more and more people were doing bed and breakfast in the season. Down towards the top of Church Street and straight into the town. She didn't even see Chrissie and Kath sitting on a wall swinging their legs and talking to Gerry Doyle and two of his friends. She didn't notice all the excitement in Dwyers' the butchers, when the mad dog belonging to Dr Power had run off down the street with a leg of mutton.

At home two suitcases were being packed even though the boys wouldn't leave for a few days yet. It was a rare thing to go on a journey; the packing was always taken very seriously.

Clare's father had found a good leather strap that would hold one case together – the locks had long rusted and wouldn't catch any more. They would probably use several layers of thick cord to hold the other.

Mam could hardly be seen in the kitchen behind the lines of washing. There were five bars – long wooden slats, and they went up and down over the range on a dangerous pulley system that only Mam could work, everyone else reached up by standing on a chair. But today there seemed to be a crisis of enormous proportions. The range was out. And Mam was standing on it at the back fixing what must have been a row of washing that had fallen, judging by the rage and the pile of ash-covered clothes in the corner of the kitchen.

Mam looked as if nothing would please her, and indeed nothing did.

'Can I do anything to help?' Clare asked after a moment, thinking that was a better approach that asking what had happened.

'It would be nice if *someone* did something to help,' Mam cried. 'It would be very nice if *anyone* in this house did something to help. That would be very nice. And very surprising.'

'Well, tell me what you want, and I'll do it, do you want me to make the tea?' Clare asked.

'How can you make the tea for eight people, don't be stupid, child.'

'Well, what do you want me to do?' Clare's voice was becoming querulous. What was the point of being nice to

91

Mam if she was going to be so bad-tempered? Clare wished she hadn't come into the kitchen at all but just gone upstairs to the bedroom.

'Why don't you go and stick your nose in a book, isn't that all you ever want to do?' Mam shouted and at that moment the rest of the clothes from the line, all of them damp and some of them almost dripping, fell on top of Clare's head.

There was a silence and then Mam was down ripping the shirts and sheets off Clare and flinging them regardless to the floor. 'Are you all right, child, are you hurt?' Mam was near to tears with the shock. Her hands tore at the clothes until she could see Clare's face. When she found it, it was laughing, from shock more than anything. Mam hugged her, with the damp clothes between them. Then she hugged her again. Normally any thought of pressing wet clothes would make Mam start talking fearfully about rheumatic fever. But not now.

'You poor little thing, are you all right, are you all right? That was God punishing me for being cross with you over nothing.'

Clare was bewildered and delighted. The accident seemed to have put Mam into a great temper for some reason.

'Now let me get you out of all this wet swaddling clothes . . . or we'll both have rheumatic fever. And I'll put on the kettle and you and I'll have a cup of tea, just the two of us with some biscuits, then we'll throw the whole bloody lot of this into the bath, it'll all have to be done again anyway. And we'll get one of those useless men of ours to mend the line.'

Mam looked happier than she had done for a long time.

David Power was in great trouble, and because of him so were the rest of the school. Father Kelly had read the letter out to Assembly not once but three times as a living example of how deceitful boys could be.

The letter was from a girl who was called Angela O'Hara and who apparently came from Power's home town. The letter was now almost known by heart throughout the school:

Dear David,
I have no objection to sending you the family tree of the Tudor monarchs with notes on how each one treated Ireland. I would have thought after all the money you pay in that great ugly castle up there, one of those priests who doesn't even have to make his own bed or cook his own breakfast could find time to do it for you, however. But I do not intend to join in your silly games of calling myself 'Andrew' when I write to you and filling the letter up with details of fictitious rugby matches. If that is the kind of hot-house nonsense that is encouraged in your school I am sorry for you, and for the men who are supposed to be in charge of you.
    I wish you continued success and also to your friend James Nolan.
Regards Angela O'Hara

The grossness of this letter had never been equalled in the memory of every single member of the Order. Imagine a boy writing to *anyone* else for a teaching aid, when it was known that this was the best school in Ireland and one of the best in the whole of Europe. Imagine describing it as, letting it be believed to be, 'a great ugly castle'.

To allow, nay encourage, such slurs on men who were the anointed priests of God, to make remarks about these priests not cooking their own breakfast – as if this is what they had been ordained to do! Worse still, to encourage deception, to ask this girl whoever she was to pretend to be a boy, to sign herself with a false name, to invent details of rugby matches to deceive the innocent guardians in whose care they had been placed. And more, to suggest that this was a common practice. That this had been going on undiscovered in the school before this sickening letter had been exposed. There would be thorough investigations and in the meantime those boys who knew anything were expected to come forward.

93

David apologized to everyone as best he could. He couldn't have known she would do a thing like this. She had been great altogether before, he appealed to Nolan, who in all honesty had to admit that this was so.

'She must have gone mad, that's the only explanation,' David said.

'Yes, that must be it,' said Nolan who was familiar with madness, if extremely annoyed to have been mentioned by name in the letter that shook the school.

The sleeping tablets were very odd. You could feel your legs getting heavy first, then your arms, and your head wouldn't lift from the pillow and suddenly it was eight o'clock in the morning. Angela felt that it took her until noon to wake up properly. Then she felt fine for the afternoon. So at least they bought her some good hours, hours when she could correct exercises, mark tests and try to undo some of the harm she appeared to have done during the first weeks after the letter from Sean, the weeks when she had hardly ever closed her eyes.

Mother Immaculata had said she was looking her old self again, which was irritating beyond words, and Sergeant McCormack, the priest's housekeeper, said she was glad that Angela seemed to have got over whatever it was that had made her so disagreeable. Mrs Conway asked was there anything in particular that Angela wanted – she kept coming into the post office and leaving again without making any purchase at all. And her mother said she was glad the pacing had stopped and added mysteriously that whenever Angela had any definite plans the fair thing to do was to tell them immediately.

But Clare O'Brien was not won back so easily, not in those alert hours of the afternoon. Angela looked at the small white face and the large dark eyes. It was only a few months ago that there had been those bright yellow ribbons and the big bright hope that she had won a history prize. Now there was nothing of that. There was the watchful look of a dog that has been struck once and won't let it happen again.

Angela had tried to put it right.

'Here's that letter back from Sister Consuelo. It's very encouraging really, isn't it?'

Clare took it with thanks.

'I was a bit hasty that day you came to the house, I had a lot on my mind.'

'Yes, Miss O'Hara.'

'So I'm sorry if I appeared a bit short-tempered, it had nothing to do with you, you know that.'

'Yes, yes indeed.'

'So why won't you come on back again, and we'll get a bit of work done, any evening you like.'

'No thank you, Miss O'Hara.'

'*God dammit*, Clare O'Brien, what do you want me to do, go down on my bended knees?' There was a silence. 'I'm going to tell you something now for your own good. You're a bright child. I would *love* to see you get the bloody scholarship. I don't mind working till midnight every night to help you get it. What better way could I spend my time? But you have a really *sickening* habit of sulking. Oh yes, you have. I remember you were just the same when you didn't win the history prize. *Nobody* likes a sulker, Clare, it's a form of blackmail. I didn't get what I wanted so I'm not going to speak to people. It's about the most objectionable vice anyone could have, so my advice is to get rid of it if you want to have any friends.'

'I haven't many friends,' Clare said.

'Think about it. That might be why.'

'Anyway, you're leaving, so why tell me you'll help me?' She was still mutinous.

'I'm leaving, am I? That's the first I heard of it. Where am I going?'

'Your mother said . . .'

'My mother doesn't know what time of day it is.'

'She said you paced round the house all night planning to leave.'

'Oh, Christ Almighty, is that what she's on about?'

'So you're not?' Clare had brightened a little.

'I'm not, but unless I see a marked change in your

95

attitude, I might as well have left as far as you're concerned. Come up to me this evening and we'll make a start. I need a bit of distraction to tell you the truth.'

'It'll soon be the bright weather and the long nights will be over.'

'Why do you say that?' Angela sounded startled.

'My mother always says it to cheer people up. I thought it was a nice thing to say.'

'I think it is.'

She decided not to send him a telegram, and it took her five weeks from the day she got the letter before she was able to reply. Only the thought of him waiting and watching for a Japanese postman to bring a letter made her put pen to paper at all. She began the letter a dozen times. The words didn't ring true. She couldn't say she was glad he had confided in her, she would prefer never to have known a thing about it. She couldn't say she sympathized with him because she didn't. She could find no words of welcome for her sister-in-law Shuya, her new nephew Denis, nor any enthusiasm about the arrival of the next child. Instead, her mind was full of snakes and worries slithering around. Would her mother have a stroke if she heard the news? Was there a possibility that the family might have to pay back some of the money spent educating Sean to be a priest, now that he had abandoned it all? Was it something that he might be excommunicated for, and the excommunication made public? Would all the priests in Ireland hear about it? Would Father O'Dwyer get to know through some clerical bulletin? She knew she should think kinder thoughts and treat him as a lonely frail human being; those were the words he used about himself, but then in the next sentence he said that he now knew perfect happiness, and understood for the first time why man and woman were put on this earth.

Several times she had her foot on the doorstep of Mrs Conway's post office prepared to send the wire telling him that his news had been received and urging him to communicate no further. But what would the town make

96

of *that* piece of intelligence. The houses and shops up and down Church Street and up the golf-course road and across on the far cliff road would buzz happily with speculation. If Angela wanted to send a telegram like that it would have to be sent from the next town. And it might provoke Sean into doing something really foolish. After all he had talked fondly, and insanely, in his letter of the day when he could come back to Castlebay and show it to his wife and children. *Father* Sean O'Hara show Castlebay to his wife and children! He must be raving mad! Not just *mad*, but sheer raving *lunatic* mad!

She tried to imagine what she would advise if it were somebody else. Her friend Emer back in Dublin, whom she had taught with and prowled the likely places with looking for husbands. Suppose it were Emer's brother. What would she say? She would probably urge a noncommittal kind of letter to tide things over. Fine. But once you started to write to your own brother about something like this you couldn't remain uncommitted. It was ridiculous to expect that you could behave like an outsider. So eventually she wrote from the heart.

She wrote that she was shocked that he had given up his vocation, and that he must realize everyone in Ireland would be shocked too, no matter how good and supportive his fellow priests in the mission field had been. She said that if he was absolutely certain that this was not a temporary loss of faith, then she was glad that he had found happiness in his relationship with his Japanese friend, and pleased that the birth of their son had given them both so much pleasure. She begged him to realize that Castlebay in 1950 was a place where understanding and casual attitudes towards married priests simply did not exist. She wrote that, as she sat in the dark room with the rain outside the window, and with her mother poking at the open door of the range with a rough old poker that she held in two hands, it became more and more obvious that their mother should never know. After her time, then they might all think again; but it would destroy the woman's life, and they had all agreed that when lives were being handed out

Mam had had a very poor one given to her. She said she knew it was hard; but could he as a higher kindness write letters that assumed he was still in the Order. And because Mrs Conway looked at every envelope that went through her post office, Angela had decided she was going to address hers in the way she always had done. Could he imagine the excitement if she were to drop the Father bit? She said she knew this was not the warm, all-embracing letter he had hoped for, but at least it was honest and it was practical and for the moment that was the best he could have.

It was on the dresser for two days before she could put it in the postbox. It was sealed and there was no fear that her mother would open it – the old woman thought that it contained the usual letter and the four folded pound notes for Masses. She half hoped it would blow away or fall down and be lost so it would never be sent.

Clare O'Brien, looking around her with wonder as she always did, spotted it. 'Can I post that to Father O'Hara?' she asked eagerly. 'It would make me feel very important posting a letter to Japan.'

'Yes, you post it,' Miss O'Hara said in a strange voice.

'Will we look at the globe to see how many countries it will go over before it gets to him?' Clare asked. She loved getting out the old globe which creaked when it spun round.

'Yes.' Miss O'Hara made no move to pass the globe which was near her.

'Will I get it?' Clare was hesitant.

'What? Oh yes. Let's see.' Angela lifted the globe on to the table. But she didn't start to move it yet.

'Well, it will leave Castlebay . . .' Clare prompted.

Angela O'Hara shook herself. 'That's the hardest part of its journey,' she said, like her old self again. 'If it gets out of Mrs Conway's sticky hands without being steamed open for Madam in there to read it, then the worst's over.'

Clare was delighted to be made party to such outrageous accusations about awful Mrs Conway, the awful mother of really awful Bernie Conway. She decided to take the letter to Japan by the westward route and brought it over the Atlantic to Nova Scotia where they said all Irish planes stopped first, and then she took it slowly across all the United States, going to Hawaii and then on to Japan. That's probably the way they'd take it, Clare thought, less land, less places to stop in. Could you choose whether it went one way or the other? Miss O'Hara shook her head. Clare supposed it depended on which way the planes were going first; she looked at Miss O'Hara for confirmation and to her surprise she thought she saw tears in her eyes.

'Will he be home soon at all?' she asked sympathetically. She realized that poor Miss O'Hara must miss her brother and maybe she shouldn't go on and on about how far away he was and how huge the world was. Maybe it wasn't tactful.

Chrissie said that Clare wasn't normal because her big toe was bigger than her second toe. This was discovered when Chrissie was painting her toenails and the bedroom smelled so much of lacquer that Clare had wanted to open the door.

'You can't do that,' Chrissie hissed. 'Everyone will smell it.'

'But nobody can *see* it under your socks. What's the point of it?' Clare had wanted to know.

'It's the difference between grown-up and being a stupid eejit like you are,' Chrissie had explained.

Clare had shrugged. There was no use in trying to talk to Chrissie about anything, it always ended up with an explanation that Clare was *boring* and that seemed to be the root cause of everything. Chrissie taunted her about every aspect of her life.

'Your hair is awful. It's like a paper bag, it's so flat.'

'I don't put pipe cleaners in mine like you do,' Clare said.

'Well, that's it. You're so stupid you can't even put curlers in.' And then on another tack: 'You've no friends at all at school. I see you in the playground on your own, you walk to and from school all by yourself – even your awful stupid class must have sense, they know not to be friends with you.'

'I *do* have friends,' Clare cried.

'Who? Name me one friend. Whose house do you go to in the evening, who comes here? Answer me that! Nobody!'

Clare wished devoutly that Kath and Peggy didn't come so often – it meant that she couldn't go to the bedroom, and downstairs she was always being asked to do something.

'I've lots of friends, different friends for different things you know, like I'm friendly with Marian in domestic science because we're at the same table and then I'm friendly with Josie Dillon because I sit beside her in class.'

'Ugh, Josie Dillon, she's so fat, she's disgusting.'

'That's not her fault.'

'It is too, she's never without something in her fat hand eating it.'

Clare didn't like Josie all that much: she was very dull, she couldn't seem to get enthusiastic about anything. But she was harmless and kind and she was lonely. Clare didn't like all the faces that Chrissie was making.

'Ugh, Josie Dillon, well if you had to have a friend I might have guessed that it would be someone like that big white slug.'

'She's not a slug, and anyway your friend Kath had nits in her hair, everyone in the school knows that.'

'Aren't you *horrible*!' screamed Chrissie. 'What a desperate thing to say about anyone. When I think how nice Kath always is about you.'

'She was never nice about me, all she said ever was shut up and go away, like *you* say.'

Chrissie was looking at Clare's feet. 'Put your foot out.'

'Why? I won't,' Clare said.

'Go on, just for a moment.'

'You'll put that awful red paint on it.'

'No I won't, I wouldn't waste it. Go on, let's see.'

Suspiciously Clare put her leg out of her bed and Chrissie examined her foot.

'Show me the other one,' she said after a while. Nervously it was produced. Then Chrissie pronounced that Clare was deformed. Her second toe should be longer than the big toe, Kath's was, Peggy's was, Chrissie's was, anyone you saw on the beach had feet like that. Clare fought back. Why was it called the big toe if it wasn't the biggest one?

Chrissie shook her head. 'Oh well,' she said.

Clare was frightened now. 'I think I'll go and ask Mam,' she said scrambling off the bed. A hand thrust her back.

'You'll do nothing of the sort, Mam will want to know why we were talking about toes, she'll want to see mine maybe, keep your awful complaints to yourself, and don't be seen in your bare feet.'

Clare crawled back on to her bed.

Chrissie looked at her and decided to be sympathetic. That was worse than anything else that Chrissie had ever done.

'Listen, nobody'll notice, and I tell you, I won't give you away.'

Clare looked miserable still.

'And Josie Dillon's not *too* bad. It's better than having no friend, isn't it?'

'Did you have a friend at school, Miss O'Hara?' Clare wanted to know.

'Yes, several. Why?'

'I just wondered, what happened to them?'

'Well, Nellie Burke is working up in Dr Power's house, she was a friend when I was about your age, and Margaret Rooney, she went to England and got married, she lives near my sister. And Cissy O'Connor became a nun God bless her, she's praying for all of us in a convent up in the North.'

'They weren't working like a demon like you were, like I am?'

'Oh no, they weren't working like demons at all, they thought I was mad.'

Clare was pleased with this, it made her path seem less odd.

'But when I got to the big convent, to the secondary school, it was different because there were lots of people there with the same interests, you didn't have to hide your work or anything. And when I went to the training college I had great friends altogether, still have in a way, but of course it's not the same now that I'm away, most of them teach in Dublin you see. But there'll be plenty of time for you to make friends, don't worry.'

Angela was being reassuring. Someone must have been getting at the child. Wouldn't you think they'd be delighted to see someone try to get on? Give some encouragement and support. But it had never been the way.

'I do worry a bit, I don't want to be abnormal.' Clare was solemn.

'Well, I hope you're not big-headed enough to think that you're something special. That would be a sin of Pride you know.'

'I suppose so.'

'You can *know* it, not suppose it. It's there in black and white in the catechism. The two great sins against Hope are Pride and Despair. You mustn't get drawn towards either of them.'

'Were you ever tempted a bit to either of them?' Clare was an odd mixture. She could be quite familiar and probing sometimes as if she were the equal of the teacher sitting opposite her, yet she could also be totally respectful, and up at the convent she never gave a glimmer of the intimacy they shared in the O'Hara cottage.

'If I was, I suppose it was a bit more towards Despair,' Angela said. 'Sometimes I used to think I'd never make it and what was it all for anyway. But I did and here I am, and I'm teaching the second great genius to come out of Castlebay, so will you open your books and not have us here all night talking about sins against Hope and friendships long gone.'

Clare giggled and got out the special copy books she had bought in Miss O'Flaherty's shop, a different colour to the school ones so that she would never get confused. They both knew that nobody at school would be pleased if they knew that Miss O'Hara was giving hours and hours of private tuition free to a ten-year-old. It was never mentioned. And at home Mam thought that Clare was getting help because she had fallen behind a bit. It was a devious business studying your books in Castlebay.

When the summer came David began to wish heartily that Nolan's family had never decided to rent the house on the cliff. First there had been the letters, they wanted the Very Best house, and could the Powers send them a list of accommodation. Castlebay wasn't like that, there were twenty houses on the Cliff Road that people let for the summer, usually a month at a time. And up towards the golf course there were other kinds of houses, smaller maybe but great for people who played golf all day. And then at the other side of the bay there was a jumble of houses, some owned by people who lived twenty miles away but who came out to stay there for the summer. People just knew the houses and knew what they wanted, it was very hard to explain all this to the Nolans. Molly Power was worn out from trying to explain.

She settled on Crest View and arranged the letting with Mrs Conway's sister who owned the house. She spoke of the professional people from Dublin, who would arrive with the three children and their maid and she insulted the Conways and all their relatives by suggesting that a coat of paint be put on the porch which was peeling somewhat under the constant wind and spray. But huffed though they were the Conways arranged that the porch be painted. They weren't going to have any professional family from Dublin casting aspersions on the house they were renting by the sea.

David was worn out inspecting Crest View with his mother and being forced to face unanswerable questions about where the Nolan parents would sleep, in this front room or that. And would Caroline Nolan share a room with the friend she was inviting? And did David think the room on the stairs was big enough for the maid? Dublin maids might have notions about themselves.

Nearer the time Mrs Power arranged to have a box of groceries delivered from the town to the kitchen of Crest View to welcome them. David had watched his mother while she dithered over the list.

'I don't think she'll notice really what you order,' he had said helpfully. 'Nolan says his mother is mad most of the time.'

'David will you *stop* that silly kind of talk!' his mother had cried out in rage. 'Here am I wearing my fingers to the bone trying to see that you have nice friends for the summer, and that they are comfortable when they get here and all the help I get from you is to say that some poor woman you've never met is mad. Honestly.'

'I did meet her when she came to see Nolan at half term,' David said.

'And . . .?'

'And it was one of her good days apparently.' He was unconcerned.

O'Brien's shop looked well, he thought, it had a new sign over it, and one of the ice-cream firms had put up a big tin sign as well so it looked much more modern than last year. He supposed they'd all be working in the shop: all the O'Brien family, cutting ice-creams, counting out sweets, putting oranges in white paper bags, giving change, getting greaseproof paper for the slices of cooked ham or the half-pounds of rashers. Wasn't it nice for Tommy and Ned to have that to do as a way of getting pocket money in the summer.

There was no sign of either of them. He asked Chrissie where they were and heard they had gone to England months ago. What for? To work on the buildings of course. It gave him a start.

Chrissie didn't know if they liked it or not. They only wrote very little on a Friday. They wrote every Friday? Well they sent something home of course. Of course. He'd forgotten. Mrs O'Brien was serving another family, young Clare was cutting ice-creams carefully and watched equally carefully by those who were buying them. It would be a disaster if a twopenny ice-cream were ever the teeniest bit smaller than the allotted ridge. Only Chrissie had time to talk.

'James Nolan and his family are coming to stay up in Crest View.'

'Oh, the fellow who burned his mouth.' Chrissie giggled.

'The very one.'

'Well he's in great time, Gerry's going to be organizing a picnic way down the sandhills of the golf links soon, he'll tell you all about it,' she hissed conspiratorially.

That was good news. David had been wondering whether this visit would live up to the last. A secret picnic in the sand dunes – that would be great.

'Does he have any sisters or anything? Gerry was saying there aren't enough girls. Though *I* think there are,' Chrissie said.

'He has a sister, Caroline, and she's bringing a friend but I don't think . . .' He stopped suddenly. It mightn't be polite to say that he didn't think *they* were the kind of girls you invited to somewhere that there was going to be messing.

Molly hadn't been so excited for a long time. To think that a Dublin family who were quite well known were coming to stay in Castlebay just on the word of a boy who had been a visitor in her house. She was very flattered. She hoped that young James Nolan hadn't exaggerated the style of their living.

The letters from Sheila Nolan had been courteous and warm, but alarmingly had given the impression that Castlebay was a little like Monte Carlo. She had said she so looked forward to going to the Spa each day with Molly. The Spa? She must mean the seaweed baths, but they were old and shabby and rusty, and only priests or cranky sorts of people went to bathe there. Molly could hardly have them transformed with a coat of paint as she had done with the house.

But wouldn't it be great to talk with Dublin people again, and laugh over Robert's at the top of Grafton Street, and wonder was that nice Miss so-and-so still in Switzer's and had Brown Thomas changed their displays. It was such a pity that there were so few people she could ask to meet the Nolans. The Dillons at the hotel were a very mixed bunch, and it was hard to think who else they could ask. The Nolans would think them very dull sticks.

Paddy had told her to relax, but men never understood anything. He said that he had seen the high and mighty of the land coming on holidays to Castlebay over the years and it was funny but they never seemed to want the comfort and style of home, there was something in the big bay, the cliffs and the sunshine that made up for everything else. He was certain it would be the same with the Nolans.

Yes maybe, but Molly wished they had the kind of life where friends dropped in for a sherry or they had a group of people to meet in the hotel. The danger of going out with Paddy was that every drunk and hopeless poor creature in the place would attach themselves with details of their symptoms. Molly also wished they had a conservatory. Wouldn't it be lovely to say to the Nolans, 'Do come into our conservatory with your coffee, we always sit here in the evenings.' Why hadn't she pushed Paddy more about it? Bumper Byrne who did most of the building in the town said that it wouldn't be hard to do but Molly had wanted someone with a little more style than Bumper. Now she had no conservatory at all.

Her heart fell when she remembered Sheila Nolan writing about where to shop. Shop? In Castlebay? Imagine a woman from Dublin who was used to going to places like Smith's on the Green having to stand in O'Brien's little shop and wait while those children laughed and skittered. That coarse Chrissie with the frizzy hair, and the thin worried-looking one, Clare, who often had a book in her hand if the shop was quiet. And they had nothing nice, nothing at all.

As she thought of O'Brien's with no pleasure she remembered that she hadn't put any flour or indeed any baking things at all on the list. The Nolans were bringing a maid after all, she might want to make scones or bread the first evening, they wouldn't know where to shop. Molly should have thought of a pack of brown flour, white flour, bread soda, it would show she understood that they didn't need to live off shop food all the time like people who knew no better.

Better do it now, she'd have so much on her mind tomorrow when they arrived and anyway she'd be getting her hair done and making the last-minute arrangements. A walk would do her good, it was a lovely day. She set off down the Cliff Road trying to look at Crest View quickly as if she were a stranger who hadn't seen it before. It certainly looked the smartest of the houses with its newly painted look. And Molly had seen to it that the grass was cut too, unlike some of the other places along the road. Down on the beach there was already great sign of activity, the season had begun, Paddy was surely right, the Nolans would love it.

She had hit a quiet time in O'Brien's, only Clare was serving, and she was deep in a book.

'Whenever you're ready,' Molly said.

Clare looked up, unaware that she should be paying attention to the customer. 'Did you do clouds at school, Mrs Power?' she asked.

'Clouds?'

'Clouds. Mam and Dad didn't and I was wondering about the cumulus. There seem to be lots of different kinds of them, I thought it was one name for one cloud.'

'I haven't time to talk about clouds now, I want to buy some flour, that's if you are serving. Perhaps I should wait for your mother . . .'

'No, no.' Clare put down the book guiltily. 'What did you want, Mrs Power?'

The child got the flour and the bread soda, she even suggested lard and then she added the items up carefully on the back of a white paper bag. She looked so intense that Molly felt a pang of guilt about having put her down so strongly. She was very young and after all it was good to see a child trying to study. But she looked so streelish in that faded dress which was much too short for her and too wide around the shoulders. Why couldn't Agnes O'Brien dress the child properly when she was on show for the summer, it gave such a bad impression of Castlebay. Molly's irritation returned.

'It's one pound four shillings altogether, Mrs Power.' Clare proffered the list but Molly waved it away and rooted for notes in her handbag.

At that moment a group of English visitors came in to be served and Tom O'Brien, hearing the ping of the door and the voices, came out to serve them. They were nicely spoken people staying at Dillon's Hotel and Molly looked at them with interest in case they might be possible company when the Nolans arrived.

Tom O'Brien stood like a landlord in an inn, pleased to see the civilized chat between Mrs Power and the visitors. It was only when the door pinged again to admit further customers that he thought he should speed up the process and serve someone.

'Well I hope I'll see you while you're here,' Molly said, pleased to discover that the two English couples had brought a car and a dog each on their vacation. This alone made them into people of standing.

She turned to Clare. 'I'll take my change now and rush along home,' she said.

'It's twenty-four shillings, Mrs Power.'

'I know, I gave you five pounds.' Molly was impatient.

'Hurry up, Clare, give Mrs Power her change. Come on now.'

Clare hesitated. 'You haven't . . . um given . . . me the money yet,' she said despairingly.

'*Clare!* Mrs Power said she gave you a five-pound note.' Tom O'Brien was horrified. 'Give her the change this minute. What did it come to? Twenty-four shillings. Give Mrs Power three pounds sixteen shillings and stop dreaming.'

'Mrs Power, you put the five pounds back in your handbag,' Clare said.

'I'm very sorry, Mrs Power.' Tom pushed his daughter

away from the drawer where they kept the money. He started rummaging for notes and coins.

'Look, Daddy, there isn't a five-pound note there. Mrs Power took it out but she put it back in her bag when she was talking to those people . . .'

Everyone in the shop was looking on with interest.

Two spots of red appeared on Molly's face. 'In all my life . . .' she began.

'Please forgive this, Mrs Power . . .' Tom O'Brien was mortified, he kicked the door into the back open so that Agnes could come out and help with the ever-growing group of spectators.

Molly had opened her bag and there on top of it for anyone to see was a five-pound note, hastily stuffed back there. She wouldn't have hidden it anyway, she told herself, but now there was no opportunity to do so. It was far too obvious to everyone. The flush deepened on her face.

'It's *perfectly* all right, Mr O'Brien, your daughter is totally correct, I did indeed put it back into my bag in error. How good that you have such a watchdog.' Graciously she handed over the note, waving Tom away and giving it deliberately to Clare.

Clare took it calmly and gave the change. She joined in none of the mumblings of her father, nor the assurances of how it could happen to anyone.

'Thank you, Mrs Power,' Clare said.

'Thank you, Clare,' said Molly Power.

The door pinged behind her.

'She'll never shop here again,' Tom O'Brien said to his wife.

It was a long day. Clare never got back to the chapter on clouds in her geography book. There was never a moment for her parents to speak alone with her or for her to explain the misunderstanding with Mrs Power. As the hours went by she became less repentant and more angry with Mrs Power. It was *her* fault after all, and she hadn't apologized, not in the smallest way. Clare hated her father for having humbled himself, she could have killed him for being all upset and sorry over something which was that woman's fault, not hers, not his.

The shop was empty for a couple of lovely minutes. Clare reached her hand out to her geography book and took it back. She looked across at her mother.

'It's all right, he'll forget it, it will all be forgiven and forgotten by tomorrow,' Agnes said soothingly.

'There's nothing to forgive! She didn't give me the money. Was I meant to give her three pounds sixteen shillings *and* her shopping? Was I?'

'Hush Clare, don't be difficult.'

'I'm not being difficult. I just want to know. If I am meant to do that, then tell me and I'll do it. I just didn't know.'

Agnes looked at her affectionately. 'I don't know where we got you, you're brighter than the lot of us put together.'

Clare still looked mutinous.

'There are some things that are neither right nor wrong, you can't have rules laid down for. Would you understand that?'

'Yes,' Clare said immediately, 'I would. Like the Holy Ghost.'

'Like what?'

'Like the Holy Ghost, we have to believe in Him without understanding Him, He's not a bird and He's not a great wind. He's something though, and that should be enough without understanding it.'

'I don't think that's the same at all,' said Agnes, troubled. 'But if it helps you to understand the problems of trade in a small town then for heaven's sake use it.'

It was eleven o'clock before they closed the door in O'Brien's. Tom O'Brien had a pain across his back from bending and stretching and lifting. He had forgotten the summer pain and the constant tiredness. This was just the first week: there would be another ten like it, please God, if they were to make a living at all. He was behind in paying one of the creameries and the bacon factory always allowed people a bit of credit until the summer pickings

110

were in. He sighed deeply, it was so hard to know about things. Last year everyone had wanted those shop cakes with the hard icing, this year he had only sold two of them and the rest were growing stale under his eyes.

Everything was so precarious nowadays, and a man with a wife and six children had nothing but worries morning noon and night.

He worried about the two lads gone to England; particularly Tommy, he was so easily led, so slow to work things out. How would he survive at all in England where people were so smart and knew everything? And Ned, though he was a brighter boy, he was still very young, not sixteen until the summer. Tom O'Brien wished that he had a big business, one where his boys could have come in to work with him, gone to other towns and served their time in big groceries and then come home to Castlebay. But it was only a dream. This was an outpost and it wouldn't be here at all, the community would have broken up and scattered long ago if it weren't for the yearly influx of visitors that began in the first week of June and ended sharply on September first. Eleven weeks to make sense of the other forty-one weeks in the year. He called out to Agnes, wanting to know if there was any hot water.

'What do you want with hot water at this time of night?'

'There's these bath salts we sell and there's a picture of a man with an aching back on the front and it says he gets great relief by putting these in his bath,' he said simply.

Agnes read the packet too. 'We'll boil up some. Clare child, before you go to bed will you fill a couple of saucepans, and Chrissie. Chrissie?'

'I think she was doing some holiday work with Kath and Peggy,' Clare said automatically. She knew that the amusements had started for the summer and the three were dolled up to the nines with their painted toenails freed from summer socks.

'That one should be running the country with all the homework and holiday work she does,' grumbled Tom O'Brien. 'Why is it that she gets these bad reports every term, I might ask.'

'They're fierce strict up in the convent now, it's not like the Brothers. They say awful things about everyone.' Clare was struggling with the saucepans. One way to buy an easy life was to keep Chrissie's cover, that way she got to stay out later and she tortured Clare a bit less.

Clare's mother was opening the packet of bath salts. 'It's hard to think that it would work,' she said doubtfully. 'Go on into the bathroom, Tom, and we'll see if it's any good.'

Clare was still there; the youngsters were asleep a long time; Chrissie would come home when the amusements had closed down, when she had won something on the roll a halfpenny table and maybe had a ride on the bumpers. Tommy and Ned were asleep in their digs in Kilburn.

'Go on up to bed, Clare child. You've been a great help today,' her mother said. 'I've got to fire a bit of energy into your father, we can't have him getting pains and aches in the first week of the summer season.'

Clare heard them laughing in the bathroom and it sounded comforting to Clare as she got ready for bed. She looked out the window and saw Gerry Doyle walking down towards the beach with a very pretty girl, a visitor. *That* would annoy Chrissie if she were to hear of it. She saw a crowd who had been in Craig's Bar carrying brown bags of bottles with them, they were heading off the Far Cliff Road on the other side of the bay; they had probably rented a house there. In the distance the music of the dance could be heard. That's where everyone was. Chrissie was dying to go, but not until she was sixteen; it was two years and five months away. The moon made a pointed path out over the sea, Castlebay was coming alive for the summer.

The Nolans arrived on the train from Dublin and the Powers had driven to the station in the town twenty miles from Castlebay to meet them. Dr Power called a porter immediately when he saw the amount of luggage that was assembling beside them. There would be two cars, the Powers' own Ford and a taxi. Sheila and Jim Nolan looked around them with interest and then spotted David running towards them. There were a lot of handshakes and much giggling from Caroline Nolan and her schoolfriend Hilary.

Mrs Nolan wore a very flowing sort of dress with huge red and green flowers on it as if she were going to a garden party of some type. She glanced around, sniffing the air as if suspecting it might be germ laden.

Dr Power took both of her hands in his and his face was wide with welcome, then he shook the hands of Jim and said what a pleasure it had been having their son to stay, and how everyone in Castlebay was waiting to welcome the whole family; he said his wife was organizing tea in the rented house for them, otherwise she would be here too.

Jim Nolan was a thin, fair-haired man of a slightly distracted appearance. He also had a role in watching out for the eccentricities of his wife. Sheila had a face which must have been that of a beauty when she was younger. Even now approaching her late forties she was handsome, with pale eyes and a disconcerting stare. She looked long and hard at Paddy Power.

'You are a good man, you are a man we could trust,' she said after a pause.

Dr Power was well used to intense stares like this. In his line of work he came across them regularly.

'I very much hope so, because you'll need to rely on me, on us for a bit until you get used to the ways of our strange country parts.'

With that he shooed them gently into his car with most of the luggage. David was to organize the taxi for the young people and Breeda, the Nolans' maid. There was a lot of waving and goodbyeing, until they would meet again in twenty miles' time in Castlebay.

It seemed to David that Caroline and Hilary seemed a bit scornful of everything they saw. They wanted to know where was the nearest big town to Castlebay, and giggled when they were told that they were in it. They asked when would they be on the main road and giggled even more when they learned they had been on it for three miles. They asked about tennis and were very disappointed to know that there wasn't a proper club, but they could play at the hotel. How did you meet people if there wasn't a club they wondered, and David found himself apologizing almost. Eventually, the taxi driver who also drove a hearse and had a half share in a pub, took over from him and explained Castlebay in much more attractive terms, talking about the quality who came every year and how the place was much sought after. English couples came too, often middle-aged people with a car and a dog and golf clubs. Fancy them coming all the way to Castlebay when they had the whole of their own country and Scotland and Wales to choose from. David realized that this was a much better way to go than his own style of excusing things. He brightened up and told them about the golf club and how this year he and Nolan were thinking of learning. You could hire clubs there.

Caroline and Hilary giggled and thought this was great, they might learn too.

You didn't really get a good view of the sea until you came over Bennett's Hill and David looked at them eagerly to see if it pleased them. Their faces seemed to say it all, so he sat back happily and exchanged conspiratorial winks with the taxi driver.

The girls were silenced for once as the whole coast spread before them . . . the tide was out so the beach spread out like a huge silver carpet, the headlands at each end looked a sharp purple and as they came to where the roads divided there was no need to explain any more, Castlebay explained itself. They drove down the main street – Church Street – with the big church on the right, past all the shops, well-painted and decorated for the summer, some of them with low whitewashed walls where holidaymakers sat and chatted in the sun. People were eating ice-creams and carrying beach balls and children had rubber rings and fishing nets. You could smell the sea. It was like paradise.

The taxi driver drove slowly down Church Street so that they could savour it all; the girls looked excitedly from the front of the big dance hall, to the entrance of Dillon's

114

Hotel. They saw Dwyer's the butchers with a big notice saying 'Get your holiday meat here'. Everyone seemed to be talking to each other or waving or calling, it was as if all the people on the street going down to the sea knew each other.

Majestically the taxi turned right at the Cliff Road so that they could have a good view of the beach.

'There's Gerry Doyle!' cried Nolan, delighted to recognize him. 'Who is that he's with?'

'That's his sister, I told you about her, Fiona,' David said.

The Doyles waved and James Nolan let out all his breath in a great rush. 'She's *gorgeous*,' he said.

The girls in the back were annoyed. They didn't have to say anything, you could just sense it in the way they rustled.

'How are we going to become great golfers if you're going to sigh like that over the first girl you see in Castlebay?' David said.

'Quite right.' Caroline was approving. 'We don't want the holiday spoiled by silliness and falling in love.'

'No indeed,' said Hilary very vehemently.

It was totally unconvincing but there wasn't time to debate it because everyone was getting out of the taxi and there was a joyous reunion on the lawn. David noticed that his mother had had her hair done, and was wearing her best dress. Bones was not there; he must be tied up at home on the very accurate assumption that he would not lend any tone to the gathering. The sun was shining down on the garden and Molly had brought Nellie with her in order to help serve a welcoming tea. There were canvas chairs and stools out in the garden, the cups were arranged on a tray in the porch and there were sandwiches and bridge rolls cut in half with egg on some and ham on others. There was apple tart too, on two large plates. Nellie had a small white hat on as well as her apron. James introduced her to Breeda who immediately took off her hat and coat and went into the kitchen to help.

Mrs Nolan was sitting back in her chair, eyes closed with

pleasure. 'What a *wonderful* welcome,' she said. 'What a beautiful place. James, we are lucky that you have marvellous friends like these to make it all possible.' Molly Power reddened with pleasure.

'Heavens it's very small and simple after Dublin,' she said in a tinkly voice that David didn't often hear.

'It's heavenly,' said Mrs Nolan. 'And the flies are going to be quite manageable I do believe.'

'The flies?' Molly was startled.

'Yes, but one has to expect them, I've been watching, you get about one bluebottle to eight flies, that's not too bad is it?'

'No, I suppose not.' Molly was puzzled.

'We brought quite a lot of muslin with us of course, but in the end we have to realize this is holidays, this is the great outdoors and . . . well they can't kill us?'

'Er . . . no?'

'The flies. They can't *kill* us. And I think this place is heavenly.'

And that put the seal on the summer. Dr Power had told her that it was one of the healthiest places in the world because of the sea and the ozone and the gulf stream, and goodness knows what else he had added for good measure; so now Nolan's mother need have no fear of fleas or damp or anyone catching anything. Mrs Conway's sister had come down to inspect the professional people from Dublin and had been slightly overawed to see eight people on the lawn of Crest View being served tea by two maids. But her curiosity got the better of her so she came in. She was given a chair, a cup of tea and fulsome thanks from Mrs Nolan as having provided the best house in Castlebay. Mrs Conway's sister took everything in, asked about eight searching questions and left to go to the post office and fill them in on the new arrivals. Dr Power had given his lecture about drowning. Every year he said for the past fourteen years there had been a death in the summer. All except one of them had been people who had just arrived; the accident had happened in the first few days, before they got used to the terrible undercurrent that pulled you out

116

and sideways after a big wave. There were notices all round the beach but people didn't believe them. There was a lifeguard – but there was only so much he could do and if a bather was swept out by huge waves, the call often didn't go up until it was too late. Dr Power was very grave. Caroline was enraged by the warning; she pointed out that she had had swimming lessons in the baths in Dunlaoghaire. Dr Power said that some of the people whose purple bodies he had seen had been swimming in other places for thirty years. Castlebay had a very very strong undertow and he would be a poor man to welcome them to the place if he didn't tell them that. He was solemn and they all fell quiet for a moment. It was enough to make it sink in. Dr Power turned his attention to the golf club then, and the chance of a game with Mr Nolan and whether they should make the boys junior members for the summer and get them lessons from Jimmy the Pro. Mrs Nolan wondered was there a nice hairdresser in the place, since Mrs Power looked so elegant there must be. Nellie and Breeda were in the kitchen having a chat about the dance, the amusements and the pictures.

Caroline stretched and said she felt filthy after the journey, would anyone mind if she changed? She and Hilary dragged cases upstairs and settled into their room. They came down not long after; Caroline had her hair loose now, not tied back behind her neck. It was curly a bit like Fiona Doyle's, but not as luxuriant. She wore a yellow shirt and white shorts. She looked really smashing.

'Will you show me the town of Castlebay?' she asked David.

It would be very nice to be seen with this lovely thing in white shorts and yellow shoes to match her shirt. He would love people to look as he took her for a tour. But it would have been bad manners.

'Sure I will,' he said, deliberately misunderstanding her. 'Let's all get our swimming things and meet here in ten minutes and I'll take the conducted tour to the beach.'

David thought that Caroline was a little put out. Great, he thought, she fancies me.

*　　*　　*

It *must* have rained some days. There had to be clouds and a wind would definitely have come up at high tide. But none of them remembered it. Hilary said it was the best holiday she ever had in her life and since she and Caroline had a fight the following term and were not best friends any more, it was her first and last time in Castlebay. Mrs Nolan grew stronger and got browner every day; she and Molly Power became firm friends and even took tennis lessons at the hotel in the early mornings when there weren't many people about. It was something they both wished they had done in their youth, but it didn't matter, they were catching up now. Nolan's father stayed for two weeks, then had to go back to work, but he came down every weekend.

They had their lunch outside almost every day and David usually ate with them. On Sundays they came to lunch at the Powers', a proper lunch with roast beef or two chickens, and soup first and pudding afterwards. And when the trippers had to eat oranges or try to boil cups of tea for themselves on the beach, the Powers and the Nolans could just walk up the cliff either to the doctor's house or to Crest View, and Nellie or Breeda would serve a real tea with sandwiches and biscuits and apple tart. It was heaven.

They went for picnics too, and because the Nolans had a primus stove they often cooked sausages which tasted much better in the open air. Mrs Nolan couldn't be told that they fried sausages on their own – she was afraid of conflagrations – but they kept the primus in the Powers' garage so that there was never any fuss.

It was the first summer for a long time that nobody drowned in Castlebay. One child did get into difficulties but Dr Power made him vomit up all the sea water and in an hour the incident was almost forgotten. A woman fell and broke her hip on the path going down to the beach and Dr Power went out in his shirtsleeves and hammered in a board nailed to a stick saying *Very very dangerous path*. The Committee didn't like it at all, and wanted it

118

removed. Dr Power said he was the one who had to pick up the pieces when people got injured and that if anyone removed his sign he would call the Guards. Eventually the Committee arranged a neater sign, properly painted and agreed to spend some money next year in making the path and steps less perilous.

Clare watched it all from the shop. It was like a different world to her, these carefree people with different clothes every day. Caroline Nolan, who had brown legs and white shorts, must have had seven different-coloured blouses. She was like a rainbow, and her friend Hilary was the same, and they were always laughing and the boys all stood round and laughed too when they were there. There were the Dillon boys from the hotel, and Bernie Conway's brother Frank, and David Power and James Nolan, and of course Gerry Doyle. Normally Gerry didn't join anyone's crowd, but he often seemed to be passing by, or perched on his bike leaning against the wall chatting to them.

They seemed to have endless money too, Clare noticed. Hilary bought ice-creams three or four times a day, and that Caroline thought nothing of buying a bottle of shampoo one day and Nivea Creme the next and three fancy hair slides the day after. Imagine having so much pocket money that you didn't even have to think before you bought things like that.

David Power was the nicest of them all, but then he always had been nice and he was from here. He didn't change because of his new crowd.

'Can you do me a favour?' he asked one day.

'Sure.'

'Nolan and I want to buy some things, but we . . . um don't . . . want to bring them home with us, can we pay for them and leave them here?'

'Do you want them delivered?' she said eagerly. Her father had been right – Mrs Power did not visit the shop any more. This might be the breakthrough.

'Oh heavens, no,' David said. 'You see we don't want them to know at home or at Nolan's, if you know what I mean.'

Clare made up the order for sausages, and bottles of orange and red lemonade, for bread and butter and biscuits. She even suggested tomato ketchup and when David wondered about a cake with hard icing on it, she said she'd put one of their own knives in the bag as well so that they could cut it.

'Is it a picnic in a cave again?' she whispered, eyes round with excitement.

'No, not a cave, down the sandhills,' David whispered.

'Oh great. When will you be collecting the food?'

'That's what I was wondering, could you sort of hide it outside somewhere, where nobody could find it except us? We'll be going about two o'clock in the morning.'

They debated putting it in the doorway behind the big potted palm. But suppose a dog got at it? Or if they put it anywhere too near the shop, Clare's father might think it was burglars coming to rob the place and raise an alarm.

'Is Chrissie going to the picnic?' Clare asked.

'Well yes, yes she is.'

'Then that's fine, I'll tell her it's in the press under the stairs and she can bring it with her.' Clare was satisfied she had sorted it out so well. She took David's money and gave him the change. Also a list of what he had bought so that he knew how the money had been spent.

'I'm sorry that you . . . I mean, I think it would be a bit . . .'

'I'm too young for picnics,' Clare said simply. 'Too young and too boring. In a few years I'll be old enough, I hope.'

David seemed relieved that she was being so philosophical.

'You will, definitely. Definitely,' he said, full of encouragement.

At that moment the floating, flowery prints of Mrs Nolan appeared at the door of O'Brien's.

'Do let's have an ice-cream Molly, in Dublin you couldn't be seen dead licking a fourpenny wafer. So full of *germs*, too. Isn't it marvellous to be here?'

There was no way that Molly could refuse to come in

now. Clare acted quickly. 'I'm sorry, we don't have any of those Scots Clan left,' she said to David in a clear voice. 'We'll be getting deliveries this afternoon.' She turned politely to the two ladies. 'Can I get you an ice-cream?' she asked.

'Is it all kept nice and *fresh*?' Mrs Nolan wanted to know.

'Oh yes, indeed. Look inside if you like, but why don't I open a fresh pack just in front of you?'

Mrs Nolan was pleased. David scurried out, unnoticed. Clare went to the kitchen and got a clean jug of hot water, and a clean sharp knife. She dipped the knife in the water and slit open the carton of ice-cream. She made the indentations on it firmly and cut two fourpenny wafers which she handed over gravely.

'This *is* a nice shop, Molly,' said Mrs Nolan.

'Oh yes, yes indeed,' said Mrs Power uneasily.

'I think it's a better place than where you told us to shop.'

'It's very good, all right,' Molly agreed, looking at the ceiling.

Clare prayed her father wouldn't come in and start fawning. She bade them farewell.

'Nice little girl,' she heard Mrs Nolan say. 'Very under-nourished looking, but a bright little thing.'

Chrissie said that Clare had a horrible gloating smirk on her that was terrible to look at, and that Clare would be unbearable now she knew about the picnic in the sandhills.

Clare sighed. She said that David's bag was in the press behind the coats, and there was one knife of theirs as well.

'Did he say whether Caroline and Hilary were coming or not?'

He hadn't, but Clare presumed they would be. Weren't they old enough?

'Oh they're old enough, but Gerry Doyle seemed to think they weren't.'

Chrissie was *hoping* they weren't. Gerry Doyle had too many eyes for Caroline Nolan altogether. She had seen

121

him laughing too much with her – over nothing. She didn't explain this to Clare but Clare seemed to understand somehow.

'They'll all be gone back at the end of the summer, and you'll still be here,' she said comfortingly.

'I know that, stupid,' Chrissie said, examining her face in the mirror. 'That's both good and bad.'

Nolan was very disappointed that Fiona Doyle wasn't in the number that giggled their way up the sandhills in the moonlight. He had decided that Caroline and Hilary could come – thereby making it respectable – and he was very annoyed with Gerry for putting it out of bounds to *his* sister.

'It's not as if there was going to be all that messing like we had in the cave,' he said to Gerry.

'I know, but she's just not going to come with us, not at night. Not in the sandhills.'

'You sound like as if you're talking about a nun, not about Fiona,' James Nolan grumbled.

Gerry gave him a smile that took all the harm out of it. 'Listen, I know what you mean, but Fiona *lives* here, you know. It's not just a holiday night out like it is for your sister, and for Hilary. If you live in a place, it's different. There's places in Dublin you wouldn't want Caroline to go, even though there might be nothing wrong with them in themselves.'

Nolan was impressed.

They had a wind-up gramophone and they had walked so far that nobody, not even the seagulls, could hear it.

They lit the primus and cooked the supper; and David had his arm round Caroline for a while, and Chrissie was snuggling up to Gerry Doyle – but he had to disengage himself a lot to open cans or to see to the stove and turn the sausages. Nolan found himself with Kath, who had improved a lot since last winter, he thought. Nobody paired off and disappeared, but as the light from the primus flickered and died and people didn't bother to wind up the

122

gramophone it became obvious that it had all worked out nice and neatly.

It was Gerry Doyle not Chrissie who decided when the party was over, and with a little laugh managed to get them all on their feet again, blouses being hastily rearranged and a few little giggles here and there. They walked back along the beach which was silvery and magic, stopped chattering when they reached the foot of the steps and then whispered and giggled their way home.

They weren't drunk this time, Kath and Chrissie giggled, but more experienced. Hilary and Caroline raced along the beach in the moonlight, putting their fingers to their lips and giggling. Hilary had been heavily romanced by one of the Dillon boys who had buck teeth but wasn't bad.

James and David walked at a more leisurely pace, James telling David he had put his tongue in Kath's mouth and it had been *horrible*. It was all full of spit. There *must* be some other way of doing it. David nodded with interest and said there must; he didn't reveal that Caroline Nolan's mouth had not been full of spit at all, but had been very nice indeed.

Caroline and Hilary were lying on the cliff top when Gerry passed by the next day.

'You didn't get caught?'

'Not a bit of it. Mummy takes so many sleeping pills she wouldn't know if we had had the picnic in the garden,' Caroline said.

'So does my mother, and pills to keep her awake and pills to calm her down.'

'Like Smarties,' Caroline giggled.

'It was a nice night,' Hilary said.

'Yeah, could have been better though.' Gerry seemed to be looking directly at Caroline.

'Yes. Well,' she said, flustered.

'I came to take your pictures for my wall,' he said,

'Oh we've lots of pictures already, nearly an album,' Caroline said.

'No, I don't mean the ones you bought, these are for

me, as souvenirs of the most gorgeous girls to come to Castlebay. Ever.'

They protested. They hadn't the right clothes, no make-up, nothing. He soothed them and they agreed. Hilary first, joking at first, making faces, then posing in silly ways then smiling, then looking straight at the camera. 'You must have a hundred there,' she said.

'At least. Now Caroline.'

There was less joking this time. Caroline seemed to relax immediately. 'I feel very foolish,' she said once. 'This isn't the kind of thing I do.'

'You're not doing anything,' Gerry said. 'You're just being yourself, you're fine. I think you look lovely through this, very nice indeed.'

She basked in his approval and smiled and leaned towards the camera. Without even realizing that she was doing it she ran her tongue across her lower lip and opened her eyes wider. It seemed quite natural to look at the camera as if hypnotized while Gerry clicked and clicked and talked on naturally too. He spoke about her skin and how it was very soft and tanned and he hoped that somehow by light and shade this would show up on a black and white film. She didn't feel embarrassed at these compliments in front of Hilary, and Hilary didn't giggle or feel embarrassed either. In fact she just wished she had put more into the whole thing the way Caroline was doing, then Gerry Doyle might have said something nice about her skin and her hair too.

He put his camera away.

'That's what I love, taking pictures of beautiful women. That's what I'd love to do all day, not sweating couples at the dance and hopeless family groups on the beach.' His voice sounded bitter. That was unusual for Gerry Doyle who was always so carefree.

'Why don't you do that then? You always seem to do what you want.' Caroline's eyes met his and she was saying more than the actual words.

'I do usually,' he grinned.

*   *   *

It seemed to Angela that more people than ever asked her about Sean that summer. People who had never asked about him before. Mother Immaculata wondered was he going to Rome for the Holy Year, so many fathers from all over the world were going to go to the Holy City. Angela thought he couldn't be spared from the mission fields. Young Mrs Dillon from the hotel told her excitedly that there were two guests who were actually going to Japan in September. Maybe they could take something to Father Sean for her, or go to see him. Angela said that by ill chance she thought September was the very month he had said he would be away touring the Philippines.

Sometimes she surprised herself with the way she could talk about vocations and missions, when she knew all that she did. What was the Lord thinking of all those years ago when he hovered over O'Hara's cottage and picked Sean? Didn't God *know* what was going to happen in the future? Why did He let Himself be mocked and bring such unhappiness on everyone? She was leaning the bicycle up against the wall of O'Brien's when she realized with a sudden shock that *everyone* had not been made unhappy, in fact very few people had. There was a possibility that only she was unhappy about it all. Her brother was totally content, learning as he said for the first time the meaning of true content. Her sisters Geraldine and Maire were quite content about it too. They sent him letters at Christmas and on his birthday and their children added bits in round unformed writing. And back up in the O'Hara house her mother who was sitting out in a chair watching the people walk up and down to the golf course, saluting and smiling and nodding at everyone who passed, she was happy too. Secure in the knowledge that she had a son a priest, interceding for her directly to God, making ready her place in heaven.

Angela didn't know whether to be pleased or outraged that she was the only one who suffered over Sean's predicament. She should be pleased, she supposed, that it meant that the sum of human misery was less. But the sheer *unfairness* of it all seemed huge when you began to think of it like that. Mouth set hard she marched in, and saw young Clare working away. Her face wasn't tanned golden like the girls who sat on the wall up in Cliff Road. She didn't wear a bright pink blouse that would have given her life and definition. Instead she looked shabby and wan, in a dress with faded yellow and pink flowers that must have been Chrissie's. She was furrowed with concentration, getting somebody change.

'I'm quite quick at change usually,' Angela heard her telling the woman. 'But when the shop is crowded and we are all at the drawer of money together it's easy to get flustered, that's why I'm being a bit slow.'

The woman smiled at the earnest child who didn't even have time to see Angela at the other side of the shop. Mrs O'Brien asked about Angela's mother, whether the weather was good for her bones, if there was any word of Geraldine or Maire coming home this summer, and how soon would his Reverence be back – wasn't it a pity he hadn't been able to come this year, he could have gone to Rome for the Holy Year. The Dillons were going to go there in October when the season was well over. Imagine going to Rome and being able to see the Holy Father. There had been talk of making a collection to send Father O'Dwyer, but nothing had come of it, the idea had come too late and everyone was working so hard now there'd be little time for meeting about it. Angela responded with a series of automatic grunts and replies. Often she felt that if you had been born dumb and never known the gift of speech you could converse quite happily with most of Castlebay. All you had to do was to listen and nod and smile and shake your head and make a sound. She knew she was right when she was packing her shopping in the basket of her bicycle and she overheard Mrs O'Brien saying to Miss O'Flaherty that Angela O'Hara was a very nice girl and it was no wonder the children were all mad about her. Angela smiled with pleasure at this and was only slightly taken down when Miss O'Flaherty's complaining tone which saw very little right with the world said that was all very fine but when was Angela O'Hara going to get a husband for herself.

That was indeed the question, Angela said to herself wryly. Suppose, just suppose she did herself up and went to the dance and found a nice fellow here for the summer holidays, he'd live in Dublin or Cork or Limerick, or Dagenham like the fellow she met three years ago did. What then? There was no point in thinking about it. If she had stayed with her mother this long she was going to have to stay the distance. There was a time five years ago when she might have left, but she couldn't leave now. She couldn't trust her brother not to blow the whole thing apart. Miss O'Flaherty, who was in a poor position to throw stones, would have to wait a long time before she saw Angela O'Hara getting a husband for herself.

Weeks later she met Dr Power. He slowed down his car to drive beside her along the golf-course road.

'I was thinking of dropping in to have a look at your mother.'

'Do that but for God's sake let me get in five minutes before you and put a clean blouse on her otherwise she'll be complaining all night that you saw her shabby.'

'I have to go up and see someone in the club first. I'll call on my way back.'

Wouldn't *he* be a lovely person to be married to, Angela thought. Old as the hills of course, but so calm and kind. That fusspot towny wife of his was very lucky; Angela wondered did she know how lucky she was or did she sit there restlessly examining her rings and her lightly painted nails and wish for a life of more sophistication. Was she grateful for that bright son of hers, did she love the big white house that looked straight out to sea on two sides and was she pleased every morning when she woke up to hear Nellie cleaning out the fires and making the breakfast? Nice laughing Nellie Burke who had wanted to be a film star when they were at school. Dr Power wasn't a saint exactly. Sometimes he was bad-tempered and impatient with people. But he was very kind and Mr Murphy in the chemist said that you'd travel far to find such a good doctor. If he was above in Dublin with a brass plate on the door of somewhere in Fitzwilliam Square he would be called a consultant physician and people would pay him a fortune. Angela hoped that Mrs Molly Power was never given this piece of information, for deep down Paddy Power was like herself, he wouldn't leave. He had been born on a big farm outside Castlebay and it had been his life since he could remember. He wasn't going to any square for any plaque on his door or any fees in his bank account.

She smartened her mother up, giving her a quick wash and a dusting of talcum powder. A clean slip in case Dr Power decided to feel her poor knee joints, and clean stockings of course.

She looked well when she was smartened up, Angela thought, the fine handsome face of Father Sean O'Hara got its good cheekbones from the mother's side, and her hair was curly and soft. Everyone looked a bit better when they were smartened up, Angela said to herself firmly, and changed her own dress and put on a little lipstick.

'Now we're like two tarts on a night out,' she said to her mother.

Mrs O'Hara looked round the room nervously in case anyone might have heard. 'You say terribly stupid things sometimes, I'm sure people get the wrong idea of you.'

'I bet they do, mother dear,' Angela said, as the doctor arrived.

It had been some visitor who played too much golf, no exercise at all, at home fifty weeks of the year, and then thirty-six holes of golf over a hilly course here, five days in succession. No wonder he had collapsed. There should be Danger notices on the golf course as well as on the beach.

'Will he be all right?' Angela asked.

'Oh, the worst he has to recover from is all the abuse from me. He'll be fine. I might have done him a good turn even, warned him about his way of life. He may live to a

128

hundred and thank me every day. Enough about him, how are you, Mrs O'Hara?'

Angela watched him as he felt the swollen joints of her mother's legs. And then he took the twisted lumpy hands in his own.

'It hasn't got much worse to the outside eye,' he said cheerfully, 'but I know that's not much help inside where it's all aches and pains.' He made it easy for them to complain a bit; Dr Power's patients didn't have to bite back their fears and their telling the tale of their illness. He had all the time in the world.

She walked him back to the car.

'Mind you, I think you put on a clean blouse and a clean face for me yourself,' he said, teasing her. 'Did you want to consult me too?'

'No, I'm fine,' she laughed.

'If you were fine you'd sleep at night,' he said.

'I nearly do now. I only take half one, not a whole tablet like I did in the beginning.'

'Is it any better whatever it is that's worrying you?' He was on one side of his car. She leaned over with her elbows on the roof of the car.

'It is a bit better, I suppose. It hasn't gone away but I've got used to it.'

'It's not any kind of sickness or health worry. You needn't tell me: I could tell you the name of a very nice doctor, someone strange to you?'

'No. It's not that, thank you all the same.'

'And if it's a man, we're not worth it. Not one of us is worth a woman staying awake one hour over us.'

'Stop fishing.' She laughed. 'You're fishing for information, *and* for compliments, half the town is sleepless over you Dr Power. I was only thinking that this evening in the house there, wasn't it an awful pity I wasn't around ten years earlier and I might have caught you.'

'Oh, you'd have had to be around long before that, I'm an old dog. A dull old dog.'

He got into the car and wound down the window. 'If you find a fellow you want to go off with, go now. Do you hear me, don't be thinking you have to grow old in that house there. I'll sort your mother out, I'll see she gets looked after. You live your life.'

'No, it's not that, honestly.' She smiled at him affectionately.

'Or a nun or anything,' he said suddenly.

'Oh it's *definitely* not that.' She pealed with laughter.

'No, well I suppose one in the family's enough,' he said and he was gone.

One was more than enough, Angela thought as she went back into the house.

Gerry Doyle had taken two smashing photographs during the summer. One was of David and Caroline playing with a beach ball and the big waves rolling in behind them. David thought it looked great, like an advertisement for Come to Sunny Somewhere, like you saw for English seaside resorts. The other picture was of Nolan sitting eating an ice-cream on the wall outside O'Brien's shop. He was surrounded by girls: Hilary was sitting on one side, and Gerry's own sister Fiona on the other, and at his feet sat Chrissie O'Brien and her two henchwomen Kath and Peggy. He looked like a sultan, tanned and powerful and surrounded by women, all he needed was the headgear. These pictures did Nolan and Power a great deal of good at school. In fact David began to wonder if half the pupils and their parents might turn up there next summer. The Seal Cave had become a legend for night adventures, the sand dunes for even more excitement, Brigid's Cave where you shouted a question and the echo answered. The tennis in the hotel and up on high stools at the bar afterwards for a lemonade, the lessons up at the golf club and the junior tournaments. Not only did they have the stories, they had the proof in these photographs. David kept the picture of Caroline under a piece of paper in the back of his atlas. It was awkward being in love with your friend's sister because you couldn't talk to him about it freely. You couldn't say that you had kissed her at the pictures and she hadn't asked you to stop. He couldn't tell Nolan that he had kissed Caroline in the sea and in the Echo Cave. He did tell Nolan that Caroline was going to write to him at school and call herself Charles, but Nolan was only mildly interested. Fiona Doyle, Gerry's sister, was going to write to Nolan calling herself Fred and Hilary was going to sign herself Henry. If Chrissie O'Brien could write she would probably have written too and signed herself Christopher, but it was deeply suspected however, that Chrissie was illiterate and so the question didn't arise. David Power and James Nolan decided that since she had Gerry Doyle right there in Castlebay she would be too occupied even to consider writing to people in boarding school. Gerry Doyle seemed to win all the girls without ever making the slightest effort.

They didn't know that Chrissie was growing more sure every day that Gerry Doyle didn't fancy her as much as he had at one time. She discussed it at length with Kath and Peggy, but they reached no conclusion. She had gone as far as she could go without going the whole way, or without even doing things that would embarrass them seriously in the broad daylight when they remembered it. What else were you supposed to do? Her spots had gone, her hair had got blonder, and, thanks to the pipe cleaners, was much curlier. She had a big bust and a tight red belt around her waist. She never plagued Gerry or bothered him or asked him to go steady. And still he seemed to have gone off her. It was a mystery. Kath and Peggy agreed, all fellows were a mystery.

'We must take up photography seriously, it seems to make you very popular,' Nolan suggested to David one day.

'I've a feeling it's more than that,' David said. He liked Gerry but he wished that Caroline didn't think he was so great. It was irritating to be in the middle of saying something to her and then to see her face light up and her hand go up waving. He knew that could only mean Gerry Doyle had been spotted again. And Gerry would just wave back with a friendly smile, he never came panting up eagerly like Bones did, shaking with enthusiasm and pleasure to

131

be noticed. Less like Bones, more like Gerry Doyle, that seemed to be the motto as far as success with women was concerned.

Success at school was easier. David came first in the class at the Christmas tests and Nolan came second. Nolan hated being second and the following Easter it was Nolan first and Power second. They made a pact not to work hard during the summer term and to spend all the time getting really good at tennis. Tennis was about the only game that Gerry Doyle didn't play and excel at. And that's because it was the only one he hadn't tried.

Chrissie said she wanted to leave school and learn something useful. Like what, they had asked her. She shrugged, anything, anything except boring school lessons. Nobody knew how time was wasted up in that convent she assured them, the nuns had no control and the children just sat there doing nothing all day. It was pointed out that Clare seemed to get on all right, but Chrissie said that proved nothing, Clare was distinctly odd, she had no friends, she was driven to study her books out of sheer despair that the rest of her life was so awful. This line of argument did not go down as well as Chrissie had hoped, there was no question of her leaving school at fourteen she was told, she would stay on another year and mind her manners too. Anyway it was wrong to say Clare hadn't a friend, hadn't she Josie Dillon?

Miss O'Hara had been very pleased with Clare's work over the months, she said that by any standards she would have to win the scholarship. She'd nearly get it this year while she was eleven, so next year she should have no problems at all.

'Sometimes I feel guilty teaching you, Clare,' Miss O'Hara had said one evening. 'You are able to read on your own now, and you actually enjoy it, all I'm really doing is sitting here praising you.'

'You won't stop?' Clare was terrified.

'No, of course not, I just meant that people like Josie

132

Dillon or the young Murphy girl might benefit more, at least they might leave school knowing how to read. That would be nice for them.'

'Josie *can* read,' Clare said. 'Of course she can.'

'But she doesn't, does she? I can't ask her to read aloud from the history book in class or the English book, she can't take any part in the plays we read aloud or we'd be all day and all night in the classroom. You know that.'

'She's not very interested, that's all.'

'What *is* she interested in? Her sisters were all right you know, not genius standard but reasonable. Josie'll never get a chance to go away to school like they did, it just won't be worth it.'

'Yes, she knows that.'

'Is it settled? I was only guessing. Does she mind?'

'No, I think she's quite glad, you know she doesn't really want to leave home, she's nervous, she doesn't want things to change.'

'You should give her a hand if you're a friend of hers, why don't you help her to get on a bit? And it would be good practice for you too.'

'Practice for what?'

'Practice for being a teacher. Hey, have you forgotten that's what all this is about? We're making a teacher out of you, Clare O'Brien.'

'Oh yes, yes of course.'

She hadn't realized that this is what Miss O'Hara saw as the end of the road. Being a teacher in a convent, either here in Castlebay and cycling home every afternoon, or somewhere else somewhere like this. She didn't know that Clare wanted to see the world, she wanted to be an ambassador or the head of a big company or an interpreter, not just a teacher. But of course it would be very tactless to say anything like that. It would be saying that Miss O'Hara hadn't done well enough for herself.

'So? Are you going to give her a bit of help? Not doing it *for* her, you know, explaining it a bit.'

'She'd wonder what was the point?'

'Well if she likes staying here, why not tell her that she

133

should work hard enough to get herself into some kind of commercial college, then she could learn book keeping and typing and shorthand and she could work in the office of the hotel when that old dragon of a grandmother of hers dies and lets any of them into the office.'

Clare was never so happy as when she was allowed in on grown-up viciousness like this. It made her feel very important. 'I'll see what I can do,' she said.

'It's better coming from you,' Miss O'Hara said. 'Most people think that any advice given by a teacher is bound to work out to their doom in the end.'

Josie had her twelfth birthday when all her sisters and brothers were away at school. Her mother, who was always called Young Mrs Dillon, said that they should put off the celebrations until the rest of the family came home on their holidays. Surprisingly Josie didn't agree, that's what had been said when she was ten and when she was eleven she said, it was not happening this year. This year she would like to invite Clare O'Brien to tea and then for them both to go to the pictures.

The pictures! At night, and during the week. It was unheard of.

Clare O'Brien said that her mother said it would be all right if Josie's mother said it was all right. Young Mrs Dillon looked at the large pasty face of her youngest daughter and was moved. It would be all right, she said. At least from what she could see the young Clare wasn't as much of a tinker as her sister Chrissie was, and perhaps it was good that poor Josie should have some friend even if it was a child from a huckster's shop.

While they were waiting for the picture to start Clare told Josie that she was so lucky to have a bedroom of her own and that was something Clare would like almost more than anything in the world.

'It's all right for you,' Josie said. 'You *like* studying.'

'I don't really *like* it, nobody could like learning things off by heart and nobody could like long division and

134

fractions and problems. I just do them so that I'll get what I want afterwards.'

'What do you want?' Josie looked at her with a dull face.

Clare wondered whether to risk it. 'Well, I sort of hoped that since we don't have any money or anything, not for secondary school, I wondered if I worked hard maybe they'd take me on free like, to encourage other people to work hard.'

'Who would?'

'Some secondary school.'

'I don't see why not, they should be glad to have hard-working people like you instead of lazy people who pay.'

Clare was heartened. 'So that's why I do it, you should too.'

'But we have money to send me to a school, there's no point. I don't want to go to one.'

'What *do* you want to do?'

'Stay here.'

'In the hotel?'

'Of course, where else would I go?'

'But you'd better learn to do something Josie, otherwise you'll be making beds and serving on tables there. The boys will all serve the time as hoteliers, won't they?'

'I suppose so.' Josie had never thought about it.

'And Rose and Emily, they'll do something I bet like a hotel management course or something.'

'Yes, well they might.'

'So to make sure they don't push you out of it, *you* should do something.'

'What could I do, Clare?' Josie looked at her pathetically.

Clare didn't want to come up with a solution too quickly. 'You could get trained for something they haven't done, so that you'd always be needed.'

'Like what?'

'Well suppose you did a commercial course, would you have anyone to stay with in the town so that you could live with them and come back home at weekends?' She knew that the Dillons had at least three sets of cousins in the town.

Josie remembered that slowly too. Yes, it was possible. 'But I'd be all on my own there.'

'Isn't it attached to the convent, the secondary school?'

It turned out that it was, and after all if Clare's plans went right she would be in the secondary school herself. They could barely concentrate on the film when it came on, real-life plans were more exciting.

'They'd only laugh at me. I'm no good at spelling and everything, I'd never learn all that stuff.'

'I could give you a hand if you like.'

'Why would you do that?' Josie was almost ungracious in her disbelief.

'Because you're my friend,' said Clare awkwardly, and Josie smiled from ear to ear.

It began then: the working in Dillon's Hotel rather than at home. It was much easier, and nobody seemed to mind. Clare wasn't one to be up to any devilment, not like Chrissie. If you passed the hotel you could even see the two of them working at an upper window with their books out. Clare helped her with the spellings first and Josie thought that it was a marvellous coincidence that Miss O'Hara announced a spelling bee at the very same time. The handwriting became neater, the exercise books were clean and orderly, and Josie even stooped less and seemed more alert. She once asked a question in class and Mother Brendan had nearly fainted. Clare frowned across at Josie, they had agreed the improvement must be gradual, and that she mustn't look so smart that they would decide to send her off to her boarding school and spoil everything.

The nuns had a rule that they never walked anywhere outside the convent alone, so it was common practice for a nun to ask a lay teacher or an older girl to accompany her to the post office, to Miss O'Flaherty's stationery shop or whatever errand it was. So Angela was not surprised when Mother Immaculata asked if she would accompany her down the town.

Together they walked out the convent gates and down the hill. It was never easy to find idle chat for Mother Immaculata at the best of times, and this was not the best of times for Angela. She had slept very badly despite the half pill taken with warm milk. She had a letter from Emer in Dublin with the great news for Emer that the engagement ring was being bought on the following Saturday. She wanted to know if Angela would come to Dublin and be her bridesmaid. Angela's mother had been very very stiff this morning and dressing her had been like bending painful wood to pull on stockings and to twist aching arms into garments. The children's voices had been shrill all morning, a child had been sick during religious instruction in First Year and despite open windows and Dettol the smell seemed to permeate the school. Now when she had been hoping for a cigarette and a look at the paper she had to waltz this ridiculous nun down town to buy a post card or whatever it was she wanted.

'Why don't they allow you out on your own, Mother? I'm delighted to accompany you of course, but I've often wondered.'

'It's part of our Rule,' Immaculata said smugly. Angela felt like punching her in the face.

'Are they afraid you'll make a run for it?' she asked.

'*Hardly*, Miss O'Hara.'

'Well there must be some reason but I suppose we'll never know.'

'We rarely question the Rule.'

'No, I suppose you don't, that's where you have my wholehearted admiration. I'd question it from morning to night.'

The nun gave a tinny little laugh. 'Oh, I'm sure you would, Miss O'Hara.'

Angela wondered again how old she was – possibly only ten years older than herself. This white-faced, superior woman was quite likely to be below forty. Wasn't it extraordinary. The children probably thought she was ninety, but on the other hand the children thought every teacher was ninety, so that was no guideline.

'I wanted to talk to you actually – that's why I seized this opportunity.'

'Oh yes?' Angela was wary. What was so urgent it couldn't be discussed within the confines of school? Could Immaculata possibly have heard Angela talking about the stink of the school being quite bad enough without having the children puking all over the place?

'It's about your brother, Father O'Hara.'

Hot bile in her throat and a feeling like a hen's wing of feathers in her chest.

'Oh yes?' She said it again, willing her face to look normal, reminding herself that this stupid, mannered nun paused for effect after every single phrase she uttered. There was nothing sinister in the way she waited.

'There's a sort of mystery, you see,' Mother Immaculata said.

'Mystery, Mother?' Angela played the game by the rules: the more quickly she spoke the quicker would be the response.

'Yes. I was wondering is he . . . well is he all right, you know? If everything is all right.'

'Well I sincerely hope so. It was when I last heard. How do you mean?' Angela could hear her own voice speaking briskly and marvelled at it. How great of it to come out with just the right responses when her brain had frozen solid and seemed to be unable to control it.

'You see there's this sister in our Community, she is not in this house but she was staying with us last year. You may not have met her – she was hardly ever in the school, she was mainly in the nuns' quarters. It was more or less a holiday that brought her to us.'

Angela kept a bright interested face in the monotone and swallowed the cry urging the nun to get on with it.

'And Sister has a brother who is in a seminary and he is about to go to their foundation house, and he hopes to go to the foreign missions, and you see this is why Sister came to me.'

She paused. The smile from Miss O'Hara was as polite

as that of any child who thought that favours were to be bought by courtesy.

'And Sister is in this predicament, because alas her family, far from being delighted that a second child had been called by God are standing in this boy's way. They say they want to know what kind of life it is out there and can they talk to any of the priests who have come back from the missions so that they can know what their son will be doing in his new life.' Mother Immaculata paused to tinkle an unsatisfactory little laugh. 'As if any of us could know what our lives in Religion were going to be like.'

Angela swallowed and nodded.

'So I told Sister about our Father O'Hara here from Castlebay, and I gave her the address. And Sister got this very strange letter back from him. Very strange.'

'She was writing so that he could tell her parents about the daily life out there, was that it?' Surprisingly strong and unfussed.

'Yes indeed, and Sister says that *her* letter was very clear, which I am sure it was, because she does express herself very well. Of course it's not easy to explain to an ordained priest that your family is not totally committed to the vocation of your brother, but I told Sister that she could write in freedom on that score. I told her that although I wasn't here at the time, I felt that Father O'Hara's own path to the ordination was not entirely spread with roses, that he had his own difficulties.' She smiled at Angela.

Bitch, Angela thought with a ferocity that frightened her, she told this blithering Sister all about drunken Dinny O'Hara and his outbursts.

'No indeed,' said the voice of Angela O'Hara, 'far from being spread with roses I can tell you.'

'Anyway, Sister had this very strange letter.'

'He couldn't help her?'

'Not that exactly, he *did* give a very detailed account of the daily life, and how they had to regroup after the expulsion from China, and he wrote about Christianity in

Formosa and in Macao and the Philippines, and of how they hope local people will train as priests and help in all this work.'

'So?'

'But it was strange, two things were strange, he said nothing at all about Japan, where he is himself, he said nothing of the work that the Foundation does there, and he also said . . . I think these were his very words, "I feel sure my sister will have told the community of some of my own problems here, so I am hardly the man to write to your parents on your brother's behalf". That was more or less it. I think those were his exact words.'

Oh, Angela thought, we can be sure those were his exact words. Immaculata, you must have them by heart now and the rest of the letter, but there's no mileage in quoting the bits that don't sound strange, that don't sound as if there might be the trace of scandal or trouble in them. No no, don't learn by heart and remember his words where he was helpful to this garrulous fool of a nun and her indecisive brother. Just the bit that might yield some gossip.

'Well well, what could he mean?'

'That's what we wondered, Miss O'Hara?'

'Oh, does Sister's family want him to explain himself more?' She was just within the bounds of manners but only just.

'Of course not, it's just that it's worrying.'

'What is?'

'The problems he has, his own problems, that he told you about that he expected you had told the community about. All that. And why he is hardly the man to help in this matter.'

'Because he's such a rotten letter writer.' Angela was amazed that Mother Immaculata didn't see it too.

'But the rest of his letter was very clear.'

'That's it, he can be marvellous describing the climate and the soil, I told him we should have him in the geography class. But he's useless about describing what he feels, and thinks. I think it's not just him, really. I believe that all men are hopeless at telling you what you want to know. My mother and I are always criticizing him for not giving us his feelings about it all . . .'

'But there must be more to it.'

'Exactly, Mother, that's what I always say, and what Mam says. There *must* be more to it. What's it like when he finishes a day in Tokyo, does he walk home through the crowded streets and look at the people's faces and think that he and the other fathers made progress today, that the Lord's word was spread among the people? Do the young Japanese children understand what it was like in Bethlehem, it's hard enough for us but what about them?' Angela was burning with indignation at this brother of hers who couldn't describe the everyday business of being a missionary to everyone's satisfaction.

In the end Immaculata gave up. They were at the top of Church Street.

'Where did you want to go?' Angela asked innocently.

'Nowhere.' Immaculata's mouth snapped like a mouse-trap. 'I just wanted to talk to you about all this.'

Angela was sunny-tempered about it. 'Well never mind Mother, I wanted to get some cigs anyway so you can accompany me into a shop for them. I'd go down to the end of the street to O'Brien's to give them the turn, but we might be late for class.'

She smiled like an angel, wrapped the scarf round her neck flamboyantly and went into a shop which was half a pub and stank of stout, so that Immaculata had to hover in a fury at the door.

She wrote to him that night as she had never been able to write before. She said that he had broken the agreement and broken it shabbily. How else might he have done this in ways that she didn't know? Must she live a tormented life wondering where would be the next weak link, the next confession of something wrong, something irregular? She said that she would prefer that he came home and asked Father O'Dwyer to allow him to announce it from the altar rails, rather than have any more of this. They had been through it a dozen times by letter and reluctantly he had agreed; now he was going behind their backs and allowing the worst, the most powerful thing that a place like Castlebay could ever know to run riot. Rumour, speculation, suspicion. She must have his word that this would happen no more. Why couldn't he have ended his letter to the mad nun where any normal person would have ended it? What was the need for this confused breast-beating, and to a community of nuns of all people on the face of the earth?

She added that she *knew* it must be hard, she did realize that. She knew he was trying to keep faith with people and she had managed to stop silver paper and sales of work for him, saying that the money was coming in different ways from the mother house. She really and truly *did* know that he was so transparently honest and generous that he hated hypocrisy, but surely he must know how everyone's hearts would crack in two if any of this were known. Since he must remember his home town it was only fair that he should keep faith with it and not hurt the people he claimed to love so much.

She put extra stamps on it, and for the first time she left out the word 'Father' on the envelope. She laughed at her silliness when she was buying the stamp from Mrs Conway.

'Heavens above, I forgot to put Father. Still I'll leave it rather than write it in a different ink. It's so hard to remember when it's your own brother.'

It was the right line to take. Mrs Conway laughed too, and said imagine what it must be like being the Pope's sister, you'd probably forget to call him your Holiness as well. Mrs Conway wondered when he'd be home and Angela said that she hoped soon.

She got a letter from him three weeks later. He had read what she said but none of it was important now. He had wonderful news. He had sent all the details of his situation to Rome, and he and Shuya were going to go to Rome themselves, together with Denis and little Laki, who was such a beautiful girl and so like her mother. They were all going to Rome.

He was going to plead his case; there was every belief

142

that he would be heard favourably, that he would be released from his vows, that he would be laicized. Then everything would be perfect. He could come home to Castlebay and bring his family.

The mills of Rome grind slowly. Another summer came and went and Angela learned to sleep at night without the tablets. Sometimes during that summer she took herself with a book out far to the rocks, but she rarely read. She stared at the sea.

At the beginning of term Fiona Doyle shyly presented her with an envelope: it was a picture of Angela, sitting on a rock looking at the sea. Taken completely unawares.

'Gerry's very pleased with it, he says it's a bit artistic,' Fiona said.

'Tell him it's very artistic and I'm very grateful, I'll put it on my wall at home,' Angela said. She looked at it again; it looked like a picture to illustrate The Lonely or The Mad or The Outcast.

That was the summer when Father O'Dwyer went out on a sick call one night and unfortunately passed a lot of parked cars on the Far Cliff Road over the other side of town. He was surprised to notice that there seemed to be people in all of them. Precisely two people, one male and one female. Father O'Dwyer was horrified by what he saw, and he wished he could think it had only been the trippers, the people from big towns whose morals might already have been in danger, but there was ample evidence to convince him that some of his own flock might have been involved.

At the beginning of September when the visitors had gone home he preached his horror and warnings and his threats about what would happen if any of this was noticed in winter time. Parents and guardians were urged to be for ever vigilant, young people were teetering on the edge of an abyss, and alas the world we lived in had lowered its standards and debased its values. Next year there might be a radical change in the leisure pursuits, the whole ethos of the Dance would have to be looked at again. Father O'Dwyer was purple in the face about it for three weeks and his housekeeper the Sergeant McCormack went round with her mouth in a thin line of disapproval that His Reverence should have been vexed so severely.

That was the summer when Josie Dillon and Clare O'Brien learned to play tennis at the hotel. They used to go to the courts early in the morning when Mrs Power and Mrs Nolan were having lessons; they would act as ball boys, and then afterwards because of their help and because Josie was a daughter of the house they got a short lesson as well. Chrissie was disgusted with this, especially since she and Kath and Peggy had been asked formally by Young Mrs Dillon not to come into the bar again. Barred from the hotel at the age of fourteen. It was so unfair, and there was goody goody Clare who was only eleven and the awful white slug Josie playing tennis as if they were somebodies. Clare had a pair of white shorts that Miss O'Hara had found at home, and she unearthed an old pair of Ned's games shoes which she whitened up with Blanco every night. Josie had got her an old racquet from the hotel, and with her white school blouse she was the equal of any of them. Angela saw her one morning as she ran earnestly up to the net to return a difficult shot and she paused, pleased that she had bought the child a pair of shorts in the Misses Duffy's shop. Angela had washed them once or twice and turned up the hem on the legs in order that Clare wouldn't think they were new. It was well worth it to see the child looking so confident, and was it her imagination or had Josie Dillon lost some weight? Certainly she was able to move around the court better than Angela would have expected.

That was the summer when David Power seemed very disconsolate. Angela had met him once or twice on his own, mooching around hands in pockets. Nolan was with Fiona Doyle morning noon and night, and Nolan's sister? Oh she seemed to have developed an interest in photography. Ha Ha. David laughed bitterly at the poor joke and the poorer situation. Maybe they could all have a double

144

wedding, you saw that sometimes, didn't you, brother and sister marrying sister and brother. Angela said you didn't see it all that much actually; and that the Doyles were like summer lightning; they were different to everyone else. They weren't *real* like everyone else, they didn't get involved in anything, they just floated around on the outside. David didn't understand, the Doyles had got pretty involved with the Nolans as far as he could see. No, Angela insisted, Fiona just goes her way and James follows along carrying the milk can, carrying the shopping, paying for the bumpers rides or whatever. Gerry goes around the beach with the camera, and Caroline trots behind him. Their father Johnny Doyle was the same years ago, everyone was fascinated with him, he was like a gypsy. David said he didn't think Angela understood, Angela said she was willing to have a bet with him, but it was unfair to take money off minors.

That was the summer Tommy and Ned O'Brien stopped sending home money from England. Mrs Conway noticed of course, almost before Agnes and Tom O'Brien did.

'Not helping out are they nowadays?' she asked with a show of great concern.

'Oh, we told them to keep that, they had to set themselves up a bit better over there, give themselves a bit of comfort, a start you know,' said Agnes O'Brien with a big smile that didn't manage to cover the hurt and worry.

It was also the summer when Angela got a letter from her friend Emer every week. Emer would just about forgive Angela for saying that she was too old to be a bridesmaid at the age of twenty-nine, she would overlook the insensitivity that was involved. After all didn't that make Emer a little bit old to be a bride at thirty? But what Emer would not forgive, or even countenance, was for Angela not to be at the wedding. They would be getting married next Easter; since Kevin and she were both teachers this was a very suitable time for them. The problem was that everyone seemed to be taking over the wedding on them. Emer's mother hadn't spoken to her for four weeks, her two married sisters were in and out of the house at all hours with advice that nobody wanted. Her father had said more than once in Kevin's hearing that he wasn't going to finance a great extravagant do for a third time. He had thought that all that was behind him now and since Emer wasn't exactly in the first flush of youth, he had thought it should be done quietly. Kevin's family were all religious maniacs; and there were old nuns who were getting permission to leave convents for the ceremony, and war to the knife among various priestly cousins as to who was going to do the marrying. Emer said it was like a three-ring circus with a Greek tragedy going on in the wings. Angela was to miss it at her peril.

The letters were light relief compared to everything else. Angela said that she would be there, of course. Nothing would stop her. She had to force herself to remember that these were indeed all real disasters and crises for Emer; the letters were so funny and full of ridicule they hid the hurt and the humiliation. Well so did Angela's own letters, perhaps. Wry accounts of life in a one-horse town with the demon Immaculata and the horrific Mrs Conway of the post office. Not a word about what it felt like to be trapped here for ever with the shadow of a mad brother – who had left the priesthood, taken up with a Japanese woman and produced two children – hovering on the horizon.

Dunne was to be Head Boy in their last year. David and James had agreed not to compete for the honour because they had been too busy keeping up their postal romances and working for their exams. They explained this to Dunne at the beginning of term so that he wouldn't get any notions about himself. Dunne however had become very authoritarian. He said they were talking nonsense and the Community wouldn't have dreamed of appointing either Nolan or Power to any position of trust since they were both unreliable and dishonest, and were known to carry on illicit relationships with the opposite sex. Nolan said that Dunne was showing all the signs of becoming a roaring homosexual. People who got all steamed up and purple in the face over other people's relationships, illicit or licit with the opposite sex, were queers, and that was widely known. David said that he heard Dunne had been called Daisy as a child and maybe they should revive the name. Dunne waged a war on them and saw to it that their every activity was monitored, their letters scrutinized, and even if they were going for a quick cigarette they were sure to be caught and reported.

In a way it was no harm, it gave them time to study, for what else was there to do? And for Nolan it was particularly helpful because it took his mind off the faithlessness of Fiona. David was mightily pleased to hear that Caroline was suffering the same kind of deprivation at her school. She had been expecting to hear from Gerry Doyle but a similar lack of communication seemed to be occurring there also. Nolan said that Caroline had been pretty annoyed when they had been home at half term. He had been in a very poor temper indeed on his return; he had telephoned the Doyles in Castlebay and spoken to Gerry. When he had asked to speak to Fiona, he was told that she was studying. Where? Upstairs. Well could she come downstairs? No, not during term time, she had to work. As cool as a cucumber. The rat, and not a word about Caroline either, Nolan had mentioned that she was home for half term, and Gerry Doyle had just said that was nice.

A few weeks later David got a letter signed Charles. The letter in its heavy code seemed to be saying that she was sorry the summer had been a bit complicated and she saw things more clearly now. He read it several times and the message definitely was one of reconciliation. He wrote back a short letter, saying he was too busy to get into correspondence at the moment, with the Leaving and Matric coming up, but he looked forward to seeing her next summer. A distant letter, and he signed himself David not Deirdre, just so that she'd get into trouble in her convent. She needed a little punishment for all she had done to him.

Gerry and Fiona Doyle's father was taken off to hospital in the town, and it became known that he would not come back. For a while there was a lot of talk that Mrs Doyle didn't go in to see him like you'd think she would have done. Then Dr Power let it be known that the poor woman had a kind of temporary condition, something to do with blood pressure, which meant that she found it very oppressive to go out of the house at all. Dr Power also suggested that poor Johnny Doyle was better not to be troubled with too many visitors since he found it hard to speak. Gerry drove his father's van everywhere now, and acted as an unofficial taxi service for anyone wanting to go into the town. The nurses said Gerry was an extraordinary visitor. He calmed not only his father but the three other men in the ward.

The screens were put around while Johnny Doyle hissed with what was left of his voice that Gerry mustn't expand, he must listen to nobody telling him that Castlebay was a boom town, there was a living, a small living, nothing more. It wasn't something like a dance hall or a hotel or even like an ice-cream shop that you could make bigger. There were just so many people and so many snaps of themselves they would buy. Gerry agreed, he nodded, he promised.

The old man died more peacefully because Gerry was there easing away his worries. Gerry told him that the business was doing fine, which it was, that Gerry would never expand it, which he would, and that Mam was getting much better, which she was not. Her agoraphobia was so bad now that she didn't even go to answer the door. Gerry had eased her guilt about not going to see her husband by saying that Dad was too tired to talk. He only took Fiona three times because it was too distressing.

Gerry was there when they closed his father's eyes. He didn't cry, he asked the nun was it always as peaceful as this, and the nun said no, Mr Doyle had been lucky, he had died with few worries, his son was reliable, his wife was cured and his business was in good hands. Not everyone had such peace at the end.

One of the old men in the ward asked Gerry Doyle to come and see them even though his father was gone. Gerry said he would come every week or so, but not regularly because he didn't want the men waiting on him. One of the young nurses who thought that Gerry Doyle was an extraordinarily attractive young fellow told him that he was quite right, and she congratulated him even more when another old man wanted to know if Gerry would take his picture. Gerry looked at the wasted face and the thin neck coming up out of the pyjamas and decided against it, but he explained that it was very hard to take pictures indoors with these white walls and he would wait till the weather was better. The weather became better but there were no old men left to take pictures of.

Gerry put all his efforts into his work, his mother got a bit better sometimes and at other times she got worse. He never let Fiona come home from the pictures in the dark by herself, and he helped her to do the housework, especially cleaning the windows and polishing the brass knocker on the door so that the place looked well on the outside. Since nobody much came in, the inside wasn't so important.

But if you saw Fiona Doyle with her shiny ringlets and her well ironed dresses, or Gerry Doyle with his elfin smile and easy ways, you would never know that there was a thing wrong in that house; or that their father had died from cancer, their mother was in the grip of her nerves and that the bank manager had offered to give them a big loan to expand the business. Gerry told his mother that Dad had told him to go ahead with any plans and his mother fretted and worried about that, but since she worried about everything it didn't make any difference to him.

Fiona must have understood that his father's wishes did not include any kind of expanding, but she said nothing. She was quiet and smiled gently but said very little. That's the way Gerry thought it was best to be for a girl. Otherwise you got your name up with people and you got talked about, and people misunderstood. He didn't want any of that for Fiona.

The letter from Sean had an Italian stamp. He had been five weeks in Rome, he said, and had wanted to get settled in before he wrote. Things were progressing but very slowly. He had no idea that there would be such an endless form-filling and waiting about and answering the same questions twenty times for some underling and trying forty times to see the person one step up but not being able to. Still the process was underway. He and Shuya had got here pretty exhausted after such a long journey and he was working now as a tutor to a very ancient family, real nobility. They had a house in Ostia which was at the mouth of the river Tiber and on the sea. It was a huge villa, and Sean taught the boys for three hours a day, which gave him time to go up to the Vatican to see how things were getting on. Shuya helped in the linen room because she was a wonderful seamstress. The children loved the place, they had a little lodge of their own to live in, they were well established there. It was torturing to be so near and yet so far. Last week he had seen a group of Irish pilgrims; they had all carried Aer Lingus bags with the name of the travel agency added to it. He had been dying to talk to them, but he was keeping his word. If Angela said it was so desperately important that nobody must know until after the laicization then she must have her reasons, he had held himself back from chatting to his compatriots. Sometimes when little Denis said the sea was beautiful Sean got an urge to carry him in his arms right back to the beach at Castlebay. He was longing to hear from her, and of course letters would travel much quicker to Italy than to Japan.

They would. Angela addressed the envelope to Mr and Mrs S. O'Hara and she changed her writing so that Mrs Conway wouldn't guess. Lord Almighty, was she becoming paranoid? There *must* be other O'Haras in the world, mustn't there?

Clare said that there was a typewriter in the hotel and Josie had got a book called *Teach Yourself Typewriting*. It didn't look too hard, but the bits with your little finger were crucifying, you had to keep typing Qs and As and Zs with your little finger so that you could do it without looking. Josie was full of confidence now. She had gone on a diet too, and she had her hair cut. She had also begun the process of convincing her parents that it would be a good idea to take this course. Angela had managed to manoeuvre Immaculata into a position where the nun had thought she had dreamed up the whole idea of Josie's future career herself, so they would be able to rely on her for support. Now the only real thing was Clare's scholarship. It would be held in the Easter holidays. Angela would be in Dublin at Emer's wedding, but that didn't matter. Clare could cope on her own now. In February she had asked Mother Immaculata if she thought she should enter, and once Immaculata began to think of it as her own project all was well. Nothing had changed, Angela had noticed, in nearly twenty years. The nuns were still enthusiastic that one of their pupils might win a place, they offered extra tuition here and there, all of which Clare accepted gratefully. She surprised them all with how much she knew already.

Funny little dark horse, they said in the Community room, you wouldn't believe she was Chrissie O'Brien's sister; remarkable little face with those big dark eyes and fair hair, you didn't usually get that mixture. The nuns were kind. They made her gifts – a lace handkerchief to bring with her, numerous holy pictures all mounted on bits of satin with sequins and decorations. One old nun gave her a fountain pen which had been sent for a feast day and another gave her a bright-coloured carved pencil box. Immaculata bathed in the glory of it and Angela O'Hara watched entertained from the sidelines.

'What have they said at home?' Angela asked her.

'I haven't said. You said not to say.'

'You'd better say now, otherwise they'll think you're holding out on them.'

'Right,' said Clare, 'I'll tell them this evening.'

Agnes O'Brien was looking into the big saucepan with no pleasure. 'This thing about getting cheap meat because

Chrissie works in Dwyers' is a mixed blessing,' she said. 'This is a pile of bones when all's said and done.'

'It'll make soup,' Tom O'Brien said, peering in at it.

'Yes. Again!' Agnes said. 'Still there's few enough mercies to be thankful for these days, I suppose I mustn't turn up my nose at meat got for half nothing.'

Clare took her books out of her schoolbag and covered them immediately with a paper bag. Any schoolbook left casually round that kitchen could well be covered in soup, spattered fat, dust from the range or a variety of stains.

'Something nice happened at school,' she said. She rarely spoke of school now. It had raised such scant interest. The very fact she announced it like that claimed their attention.

'What was that?' Agnes asked, transferring her glance from the big saucepan.

'Mother Immaculata and the other nuns think I should enter for the scholarship to the secondary school. In the Easter holidays.'

'Secondary school?' Tom O'Brien was astounded.

'I know Dad, I mightn't get it, there'll be people from all over going in for it. But isn't it great that the school think I should try?'

'A scholarship. That means they'd take you without paying, as a boarder and everything?' Agnes said.

'Yes, if I won it.'

'How do you win it, is it a competition?' Ben was interested.

'Sort of,' Clare said. 'Well yes, really. A lot of girls come and sit an exam, on one day, and the best one gets to go to the school.'

'For ever?' Jim wanted to know.

'Well for ever until school's finished, you know, sixteen or seventeen.'

'Would you stay at school *that* long?' Ben's eyes were round with interest.

'That's very good,' Agnes said slowly. 'Tom, what do you think of that, Clare going to the secondary school?'

'With the daughters of everybody,' Tom said happily.

'I haven't won it yet,' Clare said.

'Ah, but they wouldn't be putting you up for it if they didn't think you were in with a chance.' Tom O'Brien rubbed his hands delightedly. 'Mother Immaculata is a very intelligent woman, she knows what she's doing.'

Clare smiled to herself: it had all been kept from intelligent Mother Immaculata for nearly two years.

'I'll need to study very hard for the next few weeks. I'm not saying that to get out of things, you know that?' She looked from one to another.

'We know that, child, weren't we always anxious that you should be at your books?' Clare's mother really seemed to believe that she had been.

'Wait till everyone hears that,' Tom O'Brien said happily. 'There'll be very few who'll look at us crooked then.'

'Only if I get it.'

'You'll get it. Agnes, see to it that this child doesn't do one hand's turn of housework, do you hear me?'

'I was just going to tell you, don't have her out there lining shelves and running messages for you.'

They argued happily over the saucepan of mutton bones while Jim and Ben looked on.

The door opened and Chrissie arrived in her bloodspattered apron. 'God it's freezing out, and in the shop too with the door open. I nearly cut off my arm to give to Miss McCormack with the chops for the parish priest.'

'Clare's going to the secondary school,' shouted Jim.

'For years and years and it's all free,' said Ben.

'I'm *not* going,' Clare cried. 'I'm only entering a competition to go, you wouldn't say you'd won the crossword in the paper if you just did it, would you?'

But she was unheard.

'What do you think of that, your young sister has been chosen to go and enter for a scholarship in the school in the town,' Agnes said triumphantly.

'Look at that now,' said Tom O'Brien.

It was too much for Chrissie. A long hard day's work in

a cold shop, home for her tea and they're all praising Clare, horrible sneaky little Clare, going behind everyone's backs.

'Will you be a boarder?' Chrissie asked.

'*If* I win it, but I mightn't have a chance, I might never get there.'

'Oh, you'll get there, you get everything you want,' Chrissie said bitterly.

'I don't, I don't!' Clare cried. 'I hardly ever do.'

'Oh no, it's Saint Clare this and Saint Clare that. Well I hope you *do* get to your boarding school, then I'd have my room to myself for a bit without Saint Clare spying on me and making my life a misery.'

'Chrissie, stop that.' Her mother looked at the angry girl with the red face in the filthy butcher's coat. 'You should be delighted that Clare's doing so well.'

'They'll think all the more of you up in Dwyers' if your sister's in secondary school,' said Tom excitedly.

'Oh they wouldn't care there if she was in the county gaol,' Chrissie scoffed. 'But I'm glad all right, I really am, a bit of peace in this house at last.' She slammed out and upstairs, so Clare's hopes of taking her homework there vanished.

'Don't mind her,' said her mother, 'she's delighted really.'

Chrissie went upstairs and threw herself on the bed. It was too much, coming today of all days, today when Gerry had come in for a half-pound of minced meat. Chrissie had joked with him like she always did, how was it that he was doing the shopping, a man in a house with two women? He had said nothing, just smiled. Then she had asked, out of politeness, out of *niceness*, how was his mother, did she still feel she couldn't leave the house? Gerry had turned on her. In a low voice that the others couldn't hear he had called her a big-mouth. He had said the word several times. Big-mouth Chrissie, can never leave well alone, never knows when to say things and when not to. Big-mouth. She had stammered, what had she said wrong, wasn't she only inquiring after his mother? But Gerry hadn't smiled.

Chrissie should not use her big mouth to air other people's business in public, he had said.

Frightened, she had asked him would she see him at the pictures that night, a crowd of them usually went on a Friday evening.

'You may see me, you may not,' Gerry had said. His anger was over. He was distant now. She knew that just from a civil inquiry about his stupid old mother, whom she hadn't seen for months come to think of it, she was going to see no more of Gerry Doyle.

And now there was going to be a God Almighty fuss about Clare. Wasn't it desperate the way things never come singly. There was all that fuss about Tommy and Ned having left their digs in London, and when Mam wrote to the landlady to know why they weren't replying, the landlady wrote back this real snotty letter saying they had disappeared, owing her three weeks' rent. Dad had been very upset and nearly cried. They sent a postal order to the woman in England and their apologies.

The O'Brien boys had left their jobs: they were working with a different gang now. The landlady, who had become more friendly since the sudden and unexpected appearance of three weeks' rent, which she had said goodbye to a long time ago, told the O'Briens that the fellows their sons had joined were rough and not what they'd want. She said that everyone was paid on a Friday night in this pub so if they wrote a letter there it would reach them. And then of course there was a letter. Ned was sorry they hadn't written, but times were hard. They had changed jobs and changed where they lived; there wasn't much to spare at the moment and he hoped that Mam and Dad understood. Mam and Dad wanted no money – only please keep in touch. So the odd postcard arrived. Nobody in Castlebay liked getting postcards: it gave Mrs Conway a perfect right to comment on all your business. Agnes O'Brien sent Ned a pound note in an envelope addressed to the pub, asking him to buy proper envelopes and stamps: she didn't want the whole of Castlebay to know their business. And why was there never a word from Tommy?

155

Well, Tommy wasn't much for writing as they all knew but he was fine, getting on great.

Tom O'Brien wondered would the scholarship cover everything, supposing Clare did win it. Everything, Clare said firmly. She didn't know but she wasn't going to have it all debated now. Miss O'Hara had said that she should assume she was going to win and that when she won she was going to go, otherwise she would waste precious time worrying about things over which she had no control.

Dr Power said that he would drive her into the town on the day of the scholarship. He said he had to go once a month anyway so it might as well be that day. No, of course it wasn't too early. Angela had asked him this favour since the bus would have the child too late. He would pick her up in the evening, he said, and it would be a privilege. He hoped that he would have some part in bringing honours to Castlebay. When he said that Clare's parents were almost overcome, they hadn't realized that it would be an actual honour, they thought it might be just one more problem.

There were still six weeks to go. Clare came steadily to Miss O'Hara's house twice a week. Sometimes Miss O'Hara just gave her an essay title while she busied herself making her mother's meal or setting the place to rights. Then she would go over the essay, praising and correcting, discussing and debating. Clare never felt she wrote a bad essay, but she learned how to write one that would win her even more praise. She was to consider this day as an audition, her one chance. There would be no other.

She was writing an essay on the 'Rural Life versus the Urban Life' which had been one of the topics a few years ago on the scholarship paper, when Miss O'Hara gave a sudden start. Clare looked up and saw that the teacher was reading a letter. Old Mrs O'Hara looked up too, and they waited for some explanation.

'It's Emer,' Angela cried. 'She and Kevin are so sick of the whole fuss about the wedding, do you know what they're going to do? They're going to get married in Rome.

They have it all arranged, they're going to get married in a side chapel in St Peter's basilica in Rome on Easter Monday. A friend of Kevin's is a priest who's doing some postgraduate work . . .' Angela was reading from the letter now ' ". . . He has said there is no problem, we've sent all the documents and we will be married in the Holy City. Now nobody can object to that, can they? Even Kevin's awful cousins are struck dumb because they can't fault us, it would be like criticizing the Pope or something. And it's too dear for anyone to come, and it's too far. And I can wear what I like not what my sisters say, and we can have a honeymoon there as well. I can't think *why* we didn't think of it sooner." ' Angela hugged herself with pleasure. 'Isn't that magnificent?' she said to the old woman and the young girl who looked at her, dumbfounded.

'But that means you can't go,' her mother said.

'It does not. I was going to Dublin, now I'll go to Rome instead.' Angela threw herself into a chair and spoke to the ceiling. 'Now I do believe in miracles,' she said, smiling up at it.

Emer couldn't believe it. 'And you'll be my bridesmaid?'

'Why not? They've seen lions eating Christians in Rome, they must have seen ageing bridesmaids as well.' Angela was phoning from Dillon's Hotel – that way Mrs Conway would have had to tune in deliberately to hear her.

'We'll have a great time, and you can be round for the honeymoon bit too, can't you? You don't have to rush off home the next day.'

'No, I'll bring my best nighties and a frilly dressing gown and I'll get into the bed with yourself and Kevin. It'll be great.'

'Oh Angela, it's the very best news in the world that you're going to be there. Imagine you coming all the way to Rome. What a friend you are. I'll never be able to thank you.'

'When I get married I'll have the ceremony in Jerusalem, then we'll put you to the test.'

Emer laughed. 'I don't think there's much chance of a

romance between you and the best man, but you never know.'

'Oh you never know, Italian music and wine, it could be highly romantic.'

'Angela, isn't it *marvellous*. I feel like a young girl again.'

'So do I, truly,' Angela said.

Everyone seemed to know she was going to Rome. Dick Dillon – who had given up drink and was as bad-tempered as a weasel – called her into the hotel one day and showed her a lot of brochures. Apparently, because of the pilgrimages, the best way to go to Rome would be on an all-inclusive tour. That way she'd have a hotel booked already, and she'd be with people while she needed them. Angela was very grateful to him: she had feared the plane would be too expensive, but of course Dick Dillon was right. It turned out too that all Emer's party were going on a similar kind of arrangement.

Dick Dillon said he had been in Rome once and he had thrown coins into the fountain which meant you would come back again but he never had. He shook his head gloomily.

Angela said there was nothing stopping him going back any time he wanted to. He said that she didn't understand: now that he had given up the jar there was no point in going anywhere. Being in Italy and not being able to drink that wine? And the grappa, oh God, the grappa gave a fierce kick to the back of the throat, it was marvellous stuff. No, there would be neither rhyme nor reason going somewhere like Rome and drinking milk.

They got on to less heartbreaking subjects: Angela said she was glad that Josie was going to the commercial college next year, and hadn't she come on a lot lately? Dick Dillon agreed – she had been a terrible pudding of a poor thing but she seemed to have brightened up all right. Good for her anyway, *she* wouldn't be left on the side while the bright brothers and sisters got the pickings of the hotel; she wouldn't be left in a corner with no position, no status, just drinking her liver to bits like he was.

'But you're all right now, Dick,' said Angela a bit impatiently. 'Why can't you wrest your share back for yourself, or take control, or get in there and fight, or whatever you want to do?'

'I suppose I don't know *what* I want to do. That's the problem.' Dick Dillon was morose.

'Come to Rome with me as my escort,' she said.

'I could, I suppose, but I'd be no company and we wouldn't be able to go on anywhere they served drink,' he said, taking her seriously.

'You'd better stay where you are then, I'll send you a postcard of your fountain.'

David Power was furious that she was going to Rome.

'I was going to bribe you to go over my whole history course with me. You make it all sound so reasonable, as if they were normal people.'

'Then I must be getting it wrong, because most of them weren't.'

He was wrapped up in himself, his worries, his future.

'You'll be fine, David, you're very bright, you've worked hard, it's only nerves now after all the years. Anyway you've got weeks yet to cover the things you aren't sure of. Look at Clare O'Brien – she's really the one to pity, one shot, only one chance for a proper education. Your father's a very kind man, he's going out of his way to drive her to that scholarship next week. If she doesn't get it, that's it. And she's mad to learn.'

'I bet she's a bit fed up with you going off to Rome when she needs you.' He was still mutinous: it had never occurred to him that Miss O'Hara would be doing anything except waiting for chances to teach.

'No, oddly enough, she's very pleased for me, but then of course females are much more considerate than males, and generous, it's known.'

David smiled, his good humour restored.

'I hope she gets it.'

'I hope she gets it too. I remember this time seventeen years ago, it must have been the year you were born, I went over to the town to do the scholarship too, and I had no idea how many farmers' daughters there might be up against me. To be the brightest in Castlebay wasn't much, it was the rest of the county all around.'

'And when you got it, was it great?'

'No. Not really. My father was very drunk that day and very abusive. It had nothing to do with the scholarship. Well, not at first. Then he got upset about that and said that people were giving Dinny O'Hara's child their charity. No, the day wasn't great.' She brightened up. 'But it was great afterwards . . . How's James Nolan?'

'Languishing over Fiona Doyle – not over his revision I'm afraid.'

'And his sister? Languishing too?'

'She's got over her miseries. Much more fickle females are than males.'

'Has she transferred her attentions back to you?' Angela ignored his barb.

'There was a tentative move in that direction, but I discouraged it, until my exams were over.' He was as proud as punch. 'I'll play a bit hard to get.'

'Oh, I'm glad I'm not your age, you'd have my heart broken in bits.'

'Will you pray for me in Rome, Miss O'Hara?'

'Of course I will, Clare, in St Peter's itself on Easter Sunday, and again at the wedding on the Monday, and I'll go to Mass somewhere specially for you on the Tuesday, on the day.'

'That should work.' Clare was adding it up in her mind. 'Nobody will have that many prayers for them. I wish you were going to be here.'

'No, in a way it might be worse for you, might make you too anxious. You're probably better on your own.'

She was doubtful. 'There'll be no one to tell.'

'Yes there will, there'll be Dr Power in the car coming back; there'll be Josie, she'll be dying to know. And your mother and father. Now be sure to tell them all about it, they mightn't *sound* as interested as you hope, but in their own way they are.' Angela sought more people that Clare could talk to. It wasn't easy to find them, she would be wise to keep away from the convent: Mother Immaculata would depress her into the ground, with the Answers She Should Have Given and the Things She Ought To Have Said.

'You could always talk about it to David Power?'

'I wouldn't tell him about it, Miss O'Hara. He's a bit snobby.'

'No, he's not. His mother is, but he isn't, not at all. But suit yourself. Hold on till I get back. I'll be back on the Saturday night late, too late for you, but leave a note up in the house about how you got on, and come round after early Mass. We'll have breakfast together and you'll tell me step by step how you went in there, flags waving for Castlebay.'

Suddenly Clare threw her arms round Miss O'Hara, on the side of the road where it divided in three to go to the golf club, to the Cliff Road or down Church Street. There was nobody but a man on a bicycle and his dog passing by to see.

'You're so kind, you're the best help anyone in the world could have. I'll never be able to thank you.'

Angela was embarrassed but she hugged her back quickly and released her. 'That's all right, child, wait for the long weeks until we know, that's going to be the hard bit.'

Kevin was a lovely fellow, Angela thought. He was waiting with Emer at Kingsbridge station to meet her the night she arrived in Dublin. He ran up to take her suitcase and welcome her. He had freckles and reddish hair and he was as delighted with Emer as if she were a present that had been handed down to him from a Christmas tree.

Emer hadn't changed at all in the seven years since they had met. She had a brown corduroy pinafore dress and a white blouse; with her shoulderbag she could have been a student still. Angela touched her own face in some kind of reflex, she wondered had the years of living in wind, rain and sea spray with an invalid woman and teaching in a very narrow school taken their toll? She must look much, much older than Emer, when she was in fact over a year younger. And her clothes. They were drab and old. Though she had ironed them all and folded them with care in Castlebay now she wished she could lose the suitcase that Kevin was carrying as they swung along the platform to the bus. Emer had her arm linked and the years rolled away.

'I'll never be able to thank you for this, you know,' Emer said, looking at her with a shining face. 'It makes it all more normal, less odd if you know what I mean.'

Kevin was nodding too, eagerly: 'You're a very good friend, Angela, I can't tell you how pleased we both were, Emer danced round the room when you rang that day. It was terrific of you.'

'I couldn't wait for the post,' said Angela.

'My mother is pleased too, and Lord God nothing has pleased her since I don't know when. She remembers you coming to the house and she thinks you're much more reliable than any other friend I have.'

'Why on earth does she think I'm reliable, I'd hate to be reliable,' Angela said indignantly.

'Well you went and looked after your mother, didn't you? I mean how more reliable could another mother think one could be? You get all the points in the world for that.'

They laughed as if they had never been separated, and as if they had both known Kevin always. As they climbed on the bus and ran lightly upstairs so that they could smoke, Angela felt the first pang of envy for Emer. Wouldn't it be great to be on the verge of spending your life with this easygoing, happy man. They talked on the bus about the house they had bought, and how it needed a lot of doing up but it would be terrific in the end. They took her to the kind of a restaurant that hadn't existed when she was in Dublin. It had candles in wine bottles, and a foreign man serving them – it was like being abroad already.

Mrs Kelly was at the door waiting for them.

'Here you are at last, Angela,' she said crossly.

'What has she been up to, keeping you out till this hour? Why on earth were you not brought back here straight from the station, there were sandwiches made and all.'

'Isn't it wonderful news about the wedding! Imagine being married in Rome! Could you ever have believed it?' Angela was an expert at changing subjects and getting old women to talk about more cheerful things. And you didn't always do it in one step either.

'Well yes it is of course, but it's so far away, and the family . . . and I'm not altogether sure whether . . .'

Angela clapped her hands like a gleeful schoolgirl. 'I think you're all marvellous, Mrs Kelly, but I'd do the same if it were my daughter, if there were a chance of her seeing the Holy Father and having all the Easter ceremonies in Rome. *Anyone* can get married in Dublin but if it were my choice I'd much prefer to think a child of mine was able to have all this experience and there'll be the photos and everything.'

It was the right thing to say. An element that had not yet been introduced, that it was one up on everyone else. Mrs Kelly liked it. She liked it so much that she offered them both a sherry as a nightcap.

Emer was about to refuse and Angela hissed, 'Last night under this roof.'

So they all sat down and talked about how impressed people would be when they saw the pictures. Mrs Kelly asked Angela what kind of a hat she was going to wear. Angela had never worn a hat in her life and was momentarily stuck.

'We're going to choose it tomorrow morning,' Emer said.

On the way upstairs Emer said that it would be a great excuse to get out of the house for an hour or two, before the family came to wave goodbye and annoy them all.

There was a divan bed in Emer's room which was used as a settee when she was on her own but could be made into a spare bed. That was where Angela was to sleep, but they both sat on it and talked for two hours. In the end they remembered that they would still have days and days in Rome, and that from now on Angela was to come to Dublin every year and stay with Kevin and Emer in a house where nobody would interrogate you the moment you came in the door.

'I never spoke to you about money,' Emer said as she got into bed. 'Kevin asked me to say that the groom gives the bridesmaid a present, and he wanted me to find out tactfully if you'd like some of the money towards the fare instead of a gift. He said I wasn't to say it straight out but I can't think of how else to say it.'

'Isn't he very kind. You are so lucky, Emer.'

'I know.' She hugged her knees in bed, a schoolgirlish gesture. 'I can hardly believe how lucky I am. Well, what will I tell him?'

'Tell him I was touched to the heart but I'd prefer a present. I don't spend much in Castlebay you know, I live at home. I don't go anywhere much, I save a bit each week in the post office and I save that much again at home like a mad old lady in a box under my bed.'

'Why on earth do you not put it all in the post office?' Emer was amused.

'Because I wouldn't give it to that demon Mrs Conway to know how much I *have* managed to put by over the years. No honestly, Emer, I really do have the money, thank you and Kevin very much, and I don't spend much on clothes so I'm fine. I was always hoping that I'd have a great opportunity like this.'

Emer blinked away tears. Angela looked so sad lying on her elbow in the divan bed, her long brown hair brushed and tied loosely back with a rubber band, her face pale and worried looking. Emer felt guilty that her friend had such a sad life and was now spending her savings coming to Rome. Yet Angela seemed absolutely determined to be there, from the very first moment too. It was almost as if she had been looking for an excuse to go there and this was it. It was marvellous to have such enthusiasm as that, compared to everyone else moping and complaining. Emer drifted off to sleep happily, and didn't know that Angela smoked five cigarettes hoping that sleep would come, and when it didn't she took half a sleeping tablet with a sip of water.

They were meeting the best man in Rome, and so the party that set out on the plane were Kevin's cousin Marie who worked for Aer Lingus and could get a reduction, and Emer's Uncle David who was an artist of some kind and who went to the continent once a year to paint. It had all been balanced with great care. One relative from each side but no mothers or fathers, no clerics or nuns from either side and no sisters or brothers. Emer provided a bridesmaid and the best man who was working his way there by train was a friend of Kevin's and a teacher in the same school.

There had been a full day of discussion about whether the parents should come, but Kevin and Emer while pretending a certain enthusiasm had marshalled every possible argument against their making the journey. It worked. They were through the barrier at Colinstown airport in Dublin, with Angela, Uncle David and Kevin's cousin Marie. The wedding had begun.

He was waiting outside her hotel. She had *told* him not to come in person – it was a hotel where Irish pilgrims stayed, but he should leave a note for her saying where they should meet.

The taxi that Father Flynn had organized for Uncle David, Cousin Marie and Angela stopped outside the door. Sean jumped eagerly but Angela motioned him angrily away. Her first shock was that he was wearing a blue suit with a pale blue shirt open at the neck. It had never occurred to her that he didn't dress like a priest any more.

David and Marie spent ages being assured that she was fine, that she had her passport which she would need, that they knew of her at the desk, and then they all repeated to each other where they were going to meet for lunch the next day. At the foot of the Spanish Steps, on the bottom step, that way nobody could get lost.

Angela stiffened as she was aware of Sean listening eagerly to the arrangements. She wanted to keep him out of it, she wanted the two lives separate. She *hated* him for standing there mute and dying to join in. She hated herself too for keeping him at such a distance with a wave of her hand. Eventually, finally they went, back into the taxi and on to the hotel where Father Flynn and the happy couple had gone. Where the best man should be arriving tonight if all went well. Emer had been upset that Angela couldn't change her arrangements and stay at their hotel too, and that she wouldn't even try. But Angela had insisted that the booking remain the way it was. They would see plenty of each other, the hotels were only ten minutes' walk apart.

She was given the key to her room and pointed towards a very dangerous-looking lift. Sean came towards her.

'Are they gone?' he asked fearfully.

'Yes.'

'Oh Angela. *Angela*. Thank you, bless you for coming, bless you, and thank you from the bottom of my heart, Shuya says I must begin by giving you her thanks, she wants you to know that very specially.' He had his hands on her shoulders and his face was working uncontrollably.

'Don't . . .' she began.

'If you had any idea what this means to me.' He shook his head from side to side. There *were* tears in his eyes, she hadn't been mistaken.

'Please . . . I'll just go and . . .' She wanted to give him time to pull himself together, to stop this fawning tearful act, so unlike her confident brother the priest who was always so right and who knew what people should do and what they shouldn't do, and who knew about duty and staying with one's mother in Castlebay for all of one's life.

'I'll come with you.' He lifted the suitcase.

'No, you can't, what would they think?' She hissed this furiously at him.

In easy Italian he explained to the small fat man behind the desk. The man nodded, si si. Father Sean could still charm them, Angela thought bitterly.

There was barely room to breathe in the perilous lift.

166

Angela held her breath as it groaned up the flights. Sean opened the door of the small room. There was a single bed, a dressing table and a chair. On the wall were five hooks with hangers on them. Single rooms didn't have luxuries like wardrobes or washbasins. They had passed rooms called *Il Bagno* and *Il Gabinetto* on the corridor. Angela looked around her, this wasn't how she had wanted to meet her brother. She had wanted to come in and lie down and gather her thoughts. She had wanted to have a bath and change her clothes, hanging up her wedding finery and the new hat bought in Clery's this morning. Was it only *this* morning they had been in O'Connell Street with all those crowds? She had wanted Sean to leave her a letter suggesting a nearby café. She could have strolled there in the cool of the evening and they could have talked at a quiet table. Talked for hours if need be. She hated this hot, emotional, awkward meeting.

He had put her case on the floor and laid the big bag carrying her wedding hat carefully on the dressing table beside the big room key. And as she stood not knowing what was going to happen now, totally out of control on her first time staying in a hotel, her first time out of Ireland and her first time meeting her only brother since he had left the priesthood, Sean put his arms around her and with his head on her shoulder he cried like a baby. She stood there dry-eyed, wondering how could anything be as bad as this. He wasn't stammering how sorry he was that it had all happened, he wasn't saying that he had made a mess of everyone's lives. No, he was stumbling out words about the laicization and how long it was taking, and how glad he was to see Angela because he had been so afraid from her letters that she meant he was never to come back to Castlebay again.

They all found the Spanish Steps with no problem. Marie, the girl who worked in Aer Lingus, had been in Rome several times, and David the middle-aged artist had been there years ago. Emer and Kevin would have found the planet Mars if that had been the rendezvous point, so excited and full of energy did they seem. Father Flynn was excited too – this was *his* show, his town now, and he loved every minute of the role of organizer. Angela was the last to arrive but she was only minutes after the others. She had paused to buy dark glasses and had found herself always in the kind of shop where these glasses cost a fortune. In the end she paid a fortune, and the woman in the shop admired them and said that now she had a *bella figura*.

The others laughed when they saw the new Angela. They told her that it had not taken her long to go native and they joked about overindulgence in wine the night before. As they debated where to eat Emer asked Angela in some concern what she *had* done the night before.

'Wandered,' Angela said. 'You know me, wander and only half absorb where I am and what I'm doing. It's a beautiful place, isn't it?' Emer was satisfied. Years and years ago in Dublin Angela used to wander like that, for ages along the canal, or in the Dublin mountains, walking around for miles. It figured she would do the same in Rome. Emer went back to the argument about lunch, they dismissed the very notion of Babbington's Tea Rooms, an English-style place just beside them. They hadn't been in Rome for a full day yet, it wasn't long enough for them to start hankering over good old tea and scones.

They walked companionably to a place that Father Flynn knew. 'I haven't completely wasted my time here praying and studying,' he said happily. 'I've done some useful things like discovering where to eat and drink.'

A man in a cream-coloured jacket and a very showy handkerchief in his pocket made a play for Angela in the restaurant, jumping up from his table to ensure she had an ashtray and trying out his few lamentable words of English on her.

'I think these glasses suit me, I might wear them all the time,' Angela said when the man had backed out of the restaurant bowing and smiling and ogling. She hadn't seen that much attention in years.

Then they left her alone. Once she had made a little

joke they thought she was all right, she could opt out for a while and run the whole night over for herself as if it were a film. She had got Sean out of her room eventually, and he had written down the name of a café. She said she only needed an hour to calm herself and unpack; but as it turned out she did neither, her clothes remained in their suitcase and her anxiety grew ever more. She kept looking at the travelling clock and wondering why she had sent her brother, red-eyed, away. She was going to have to talk to him anyway, why hadn't she left the oppressive bedroom with him and gone to one of those picturesque squares?

They did walk to a square, the Piazza Navona. There were restaurants all around and the centre was full of people selling things and doing tricks as if it was a carnival. Not a person seemed to have a care except the O'Haras, she thought. They sat and ordered tiny coffees.

He had recovered himself fully. 'Let me tell you all about my family,' he began. She listened. She heard of Shuya and how he had met her almost immediately after they had gone to Japan to regroup after the expulsion from China; she heard of Denis who was three and the brightest child that had ever been known. And of Laki who was a baby of eighteen months, so beautiful it would make your eyes prickle when you saw her. And of the life they lived in Japan in Shuya's brother's house, and what they did here in the strange villa in Ostia, and how they would get married here in Rome as soon as the laicization came through. He talked like someone possessed: he had always been a great one to hold the floor, but that was because he was the only one who could, at home. He had been away to seminary and then on the missions, he was a priest of God who had more right to tell tales and get a hearing, who had better tales to tell. She listened. Nothing had changed much except the content. He was sure of his audience, sure that she was glad to know details of Laki's birth which had been a complicated one, sure that she was as absorbed as he was in the minutiae of the laicization process and his dealings with the Congregation for the Clergy.

Once or twice she tried to interject, but he raised his hand slightly in that clerical gesture which was only slightly a courteous request for permission to speak further – it was mainly a statement that he was *going* to speak further.

He wasn't going to go back tonight: it was too far, it would be too late. He would stay in Rome. Shuya had insisted, said it would be less tiring because surely he would want to talk to his sister again in the morning. As the monologue went on Angela became grateful that he was going to stay in Rome. Since she was obviously not going to get any innings at all, she would *need* the morning to try to explain to him some of the things that stood in the way of his sunny view of the future. But where would he stay? Much of his chat had included how short of money they were and how even fares were a big consideration. But he was fine for a bed. A friend of his, an English priest who was staying at the English College, said there would always be a bed there for Sean. It was nearby.

He talked of the priests he had met and the ex-priests, and of the spirit of change and questioning in the Church. He was prepared to talk for ever about such things. Angela nodded and made the necessary sounds as he spoke but all the time her mind was racing. It was just like getting his letters; he ignored every point she had made in her own letters, and had written as if Angela had addressed no thoughts, pleas or words to him at all. She had written to say that she was coming to meet him to explain to him face to face how impossible it would be – laicization or not – to return to Castlebay with a Japanese or any wife and two children. He seemed to have ignored the main part of her letter, and acknowledged only the first sentence, that she was coming to Rome to see him.

She hoped that a change of venue might change the tack of the conversation, so she suggested they have a meal. He hesitated. Angela said she would be glad to pay. He agreed. It was just that he felt so guilty spending anything on himself instead of on Shuya and the children. But nothing changed, he ordered for them in perfect Italian, bottles of mineral water as well as wine; told her he could make spaghetti thirty-four different ways now, and he made a salad every evening at home, often with leaves they plucked from the garden. You can actually eat *all* kinds of things like the leaves of flowers. Did Angela know that?

She didn't, but by the end of the evening she knew a lot of things like that. She could have gone into Radio Eireann at home and asked to be a panelist on *Information Please* after all she learned in the Piazza Navona, as the lights came on and the musicians played, and other people had beautiful Roman evenings. From her handbag she took a piece of paper and wrote down four words. Then she handed the list to him.

'What's this?' he asked, surprised and even a little amused.

'It's our agenda for tomorrow morning. When we meet in the daylight. I want to discuss the subjects written down there and nothing else.' She smiled pleasantly; she took a sheaf of huge Italian notes in almighty denominations and signalled for the bill.

Sean was reading aloud. 'Hypocrisy and Betrayal. Family and Community. What *is* this Angela? It looks very like the title of some sermon or a pamphlet in the Catholic Truth Society.'

She was still easy and relaxed. 'Let's leave it till tomorrow, will we? It's been a lovely evening and it's too late to start on these things now.'

He was genuinely bewildered; he wasn't acting. He sought to placate her. 'Right, sure, whatever you like. And we'll arrange for you to come to Ostia.'

She shuddered at that. She felt a slow sweat form on her shoulders and back at the thought of meeting this Japanese woman who shared a bed with her brother the priest, and a dread of meeting these two children.

'Not until after Emer's wedding, not until next Tuesday.'

She was firm: he was disappointed.

'But we were *sure* you'd come for Easter itself.'

'I'm going to go to the Holy Week Ceremonies tomorrow and all of the weekend with my friends. When that's all

171

over I'll come to Ostia.' If it's too awful to face, she thought, I can always pretend to be sick. To have a fever or something.

Sean was downcast. 'I had thought that . . .'

'It's all fixed.'

'No, I mean I thought that maybe you were going to ask us to the wedding. To Emer's wedding.'

She looked at him, stunned.

'I've met Emer, remember, I met her when you were in Dublin, and she came to Daddy's funeral.'

'Yes, she knows you as a priest.'

'But surely you've told her?' He was amazed.

A headache was beginning right across her eyes. 'Don't be ridiculous, Sean, of course I haven't told her, I haven't told *anyone*.'

'This is much more complicated than I thought,' Sean said, shaking his head. 'I thought it was only Mam you were keeping it from until the time was right. I didn't know that you had such old-fashioned views, and hard attitudes. I'm still a Catholic for God's sake, I haven't given up my Faith or anything. I still go to Mass and Communion.'

It was far too late to debate it now. The bill was paid and they walked amicably back to her hotel. All the time he pointed out places to her as if she were an ordinary tourist and he were her ordinary brother. He kissed her on each cheek and walked away into the night to his friend who was still a priest and who would not lie awake all night anguishing about what had happened to Father Sean O'Hara, and what course his life would take now.

She was businesslike in the morning. She said that she would prefer him to listen to her and only speak when she asked his view: otherwise her visit would have been wasted. He was startled but agreed. She examined the possibility of his coming back to Castlebay once more, once only and pretending to be still a priest. He was so horrified, he leaped up from the table. But she persisted. Examine it: technically, what would be the flaws, did he still have any clerical clothes, could he get away with it or would someone

172

from the Mother House hear of it? No, don't ask *why* was this necessary at the moment, just see could it be done? According to Sean, even if he wanted to do an insane thing like this he couldn't do it. He would be found out in days, and as he wouldn't say Mass in Father O'Dwyer's church, he would be an object of suspicion at once.

Could he say that since the Order had left China there had been a change in the Rule and priests had become workers and teachers and were working among the community more? Could he imply that *all* priests had been downgraded, not only Father Sean? No that was ludicrous too. You only had to read the papers to know that this was untrue, it wouldn't hold good for five minutes.

Could they pretend that he had died, been kidnapped? Sean looked at Angela as if she weren't all there. Why on earth should anyone begin such a tissue of hypocritical lies and bungling?

Angela's eyes flashed. She would tell him why, because if he told their mother the truth it would break her, literally *break* her. The only thing of value she had done was produce a priest for God, it was the only constant and hope in her soul and it was her only standing in the community. That's what Angela meant about Betrayal. To tell the old woman with the enlarged joints and crooked limbs that her priest wasn't a priest – that would be betrayal of a high order. Angela had come to Rome to beg her brother not to do this.

He was patient with her, he began to explain that once the process of making him a layman was completed, he had as much right before God to marry as anyone had, so he had anticipated it but it would then be regularized, post hoc. Angela silenced him with a word, this was *her* time: last night had been his. He was to decide between hypocrisy and betrayal. She would listen to no more speeches about breaths of fresh air blowing through the dusty corridors of the Vatican and new thinking and the Congregation of the Clergy. There was no fresh air blowing through Father O'Dwyer's church in Castlebay except what came in the windows on the day of the east wind. There was no radical rethinking in the O'Hara cottage, there was no spirit of brotherly love and understanding among people like Sergeant McCormack. Sean must decide between *hypocrisy* and *betrayal*. He must decide on the old principle of the greatest happiness of the greatest number. Which way would less people get hurt.

But, Sean protested, there could be no question of that, the truth was the truth, it was absolute. It couldn't be tinkered with and played with like plasticine, deciding who should believe what.

Their coffee cups were refilled over and over. Angela banged on the table to get him to stop talking and listen to her account of daily life in Castlebay. She didn't intend it to be humorous, but sometimes she said things that made him smile and she smiled herself to acknowledge that she did exaggerate in some areas. But not in the general picture.

She swore that it wouldn't matter all that much for her; to be frank she would prefer not to have the pitying and patronizing stance of Immaculata for the rest of her working life, and she would like not to have the knowledge that they had just stopped talking about it all every time she appeared. But she could live with it, she had lived with her father's reputation after all. She'd survive, but she was going to fight with every breath in her body for her mother not to have to try to survive it.

'When Mam dies, Sean, then I'll walk with you down Church Street in Castlebay. Don't come to her funeral, but six months later you can come back and I'll stand beside you.'

'That's the wrong way to do things,' Sean said. 'To wait till someone dies before you can bring your children home. How do you tell your son and daughter that you have to wait until their grandmother has been buried before they can come home, come home to where they belong?'

Angela's heart lurched again. He really and truly thought that these half-Japanese children and their mother *belonged* in Castlebay. She looked at her watch, and stood up to call for the bill again. It was time to go to lunch with the wedding party. He looked confused and unsettled.

'You will come, you will still come and see us?'

'Yes,' she promised.

'On Tuesday, and you'll stay a few days.'

'No, I won't stay the night, I might come again, but I'll just come for the day. Thank you all the same.'

'But why not? There's a bed there.'

'There's a bed in the hotel too, I'd prefer to come back.'

'Shuya will want to know do you send her a greeting.'

'Yes, yes of course.'

'What is it? What is the greeting?'

'Say I am happy to meet her.'

'It's not very warm,' he grumbled.

'It's all I've got. And you think about what I've said, because we have to sort it out. Will you discuss it with Shuya?'

'Yes, I suppose so, but it's hard, her family were so good, so welcoming, I don't want her to think mine are like a row of stones.'

'No. I understand.'

'Thanks anyway Angela. You're doing your best,' he said.

That's what did it, that's when the tears started, she threw some money on the table and stumbled away. *Doing her best!* God, wasn't she doing her bloody best! The ingratitude and lack of understanding were no longer possible to take. She ran almost blindly away. She heard him calling that he would collect her at the hotel on Tuesday and she nodded, not able to look back. She ran until she was well away, then she began asking directions and from the concerned looks people gave her she realized she needed dark glasses if not a full veil to cover her red-blotched face.

Father Flynn was a treasure, there was nothing he didn't know the answer to. He said it was going to be as dull as ditchwater when he got back to Dublin after all this, and the place was so gorgeous too. Dublin was so grey and gritty. Kevin's Uncle David, considered a little eccentric by the rest of Kevin's very straight-laced family, didn't usually go a bundle on priests: he said that normally they gave him a pain in the top of the stomach. But this little Druid was an exception. He wore a soutane which didn't at all suit his small round figure. Once when they were passing a lingerie shop which sold frilly waspie-waist corsets he asked Emer and Angela should he get something like that for himself to wear so that he would look good in wedding photographs. Father Flynn was full of stories about everyone and everything, all very ridiculous but not hurtful. And best of all, he could laugh at himself. He seemed to be well known everywhere they went. Italian shopkeepers setting out their cheeses on display would shout greetings to Fazzer Fleen.

But he had his serious side too and he told them that it was an honour to be married in St Peter's, and that obviously they would remember it all their lives. Nobody was so forgetful as not to recall where they got married, but this was something special. He took them down to the crypt chapel and they looked at it in awe on Holy Thursday afternoon just as the huge basilica was getting ready for its Holy Week ceremonies. Emer and Kevin were to be married here – it was almost too much to take in.

And the man seemed to know about clothes. He was fascinated by what they should wear at the wedding and thought that they would look absolutely great – apart from the shoes. There was something about Irish shoes that didn't look quite *right* in Rome. Late on Thursday evening the strange party wandered along the Via Condotti, and Angela and Emer tried on different footwear and paraded them for Father Flynn, Kevin, Marie and David. Marie became so excited that she started trying them on too, and Father Flynn said if his soutane didn't hide them he would be sorely tempted by those grey suede ones. Everyone in the shop was nearly hysterical, and when they settled on the fiercely elegant ones that all three had decided to buy, Father Flynn began to haggle like a fishwife about the price and brought the cost down enormously.

He stopped them at a flower stall where he was well

known too. He did great gesticulations and explanations about the colour of dresses, Emer's white with a blue trim, her hat blue with a white ribbon. Angela's dress was beige and her hat was white with beige and brown flowers. The family who ran the flower stall became highly excited over the wedding and fought amongst each other about what the bouquets should be. Soon they were all shouting at each other while the Irish group looked on amazed. Flowers were being held up to Emer first, then to Angela, heads were shaking, arms were waving and in the end a satisfactory combination of flowers and timings and delivery to the hotel and prices was arrived at. The family gave everyone a buttonhole there and then as a gift. There was hand-kissing and good wishes, and they seemed as pleased as if it were one of their own family.

'Could you imagine my mother being as pleased as that over anyone's wedding?' Emer said wistfully. 'Is it any wonder people would love to come here to get married, total strangers are delighted with us and at home there's been nothing but fuss.'

'My family would have half the geriatric priests and nuns on the move by now, all of them complaining,' Kevin said.

'Less of that attitude,' Father Flynn demanded. 'I'll be a geriatric priest some day, and when your children are getting married in about thirty or thirty-five years from now, I want someone to come for *me* in a wheelchair and take me to the party.'

He was *so* nice, Angela thought with a rush of affection. Despite all his joky going on he was one of the kindest people she had ever met. What a sensitive little man he was; wouldn't he be a great priest to have in a parish instead of dull old Father O'Dwyer; instead of people who couldn't even stay *in* the priesthood. *Stop.* She was not going to think about Sean until Tuesday: that was her little treat to herself. She hoped she would be able to keep to that promise and enjoy herself.

There had been a bit of a problem about the best man. He hadn't turned up. But Father Flynn had that sorted out too. If the best man wasn't there, couldn't David stand in? David was doubtful, he wasn't actually in the State of Grace, he said, he wasn't what you would call a conventional person to take part in the ceremony, as one of the performers, that was. Father Flynn seemed to regard a public announcement of being in a state of sin as the most normal thing in the world.

'There's no question of being a performer,' he said. 'You're only a witness, you could be alive with mortal sin, reserved sins and all, it wouldn't make a whit of difference to the ceremony. Of course, now that you're here in Rome, if you wanted someone to hammer a good confession job on you, I know plenty that would see you right.'

'Well, now I don't think . . .'

'No need at all, just letting you know it's there if you want it. I know a priest who's almost stone deaf, there's a queue a mile long outside his box but I could get you up to the top of the line by shameless pull and influence.'

It was hard to know if Father Flynn was joking or not. But in any event by the time they got back to the hotel after the wonderful warm afternoon wandering around Rome, the best man was there. His name was Martin Walsh. He was about six foot two tall and forty years old. He was painfully shy and he had got on the wrong train. He looked as if he was about to burst into tears. Father Flynn had it under control in minutes.

He couldn't have arrived at a better time the little priest said, because they were all going to split up now and meet again at nine o'clock. Martin would have *hours* to get over the shock of it all, and have a bath and a few cold beers and a chat with Kevin. Everyone else was perfectly capable of looking after himself or herself. He said this because Martin had kept babbling his apologies about not being there to organize the flowers and the bridesmaids. He had bought a handbook on the best man's duties and he seemed to have fallen down.

Father Flynn told him to throw away the book on the role of the best man. Everything was much simpler in

Rome. Martin's big sad face started to look human. Up to now he had looked like a thin wretched bloodhound.

The little wedding party walked with faltering steps into the huge basilica which they had visited every day since they came to Rome. Today it was different. There was a mixture of formality and casualness. People shouted good luck in different languages and a group of Germans took their picture. The walk seemed endless, but then they were in and down the marble stairs to the little chapels beneath. Father Flynn disappeared to robe himself, and the others knelt silently, heads down.

Angela prayed hard. She forced words to come into her head and she mouthed them to herself. She asked God to be kind to Emer and Kevin, and to make it a nice life. She explained to God that Emer had kept the rules and that it would be a good idea to reward her. Emer deserved to be happy. With her gloved hand she squeezed the white-gloved hand beside her and Emer grinned gratefully.

Father Flynn shone in his gold and white vestments. He was smiling at them all. The words began and Angela felt her eyes water when she heard Kevin's and Emer's uncertain voices. Then it was done. They were man and wife. They pecked at each other chastely and went to sign the huge register. The photographer was anxious to get them outside and grouped – on the steps first, then down to the centre of the square beside the big column, a great place to stand because you got a view of St Peter's in the background.

Sean was in the foyer when she came downstairs.
'Tell them you mightn't be coming back tonight, just in case, and in case they worry about you.'
'I'm coming back here tonight,' she said.
'It's so dear going up and down on the train,' he pleaded.
'Shall we go now?'
He shrugged; but soon he was in high good humour. Young Denis knew his Aunt Angela was coming. Angela shuddered and hoped he hadn't noticed the revulsion she

felt coursing through her. She asked what language he spoke. Apparently he spoke Japanese and English and now because they were in Italy they were using a lot of that. *Mia Zia*, Sean said dotingly.

'What?'

'*Zia*, the Italian for aunt. *Zio* is uncle. *Mia Zia*, my aunt.'

Angela wondered could this possibly be happening? Was she really having a language lesson as they walked? It had all the qualities of a dream where the wrong people are in the wrong places saying idiotic things. But this had been going on too long for it to be a dream. She wasn't going to wake up and find Father Sean still sending for stamps and silver paper from the Far East. That was long gone now.

She tried to tell him about the wedding – anything, rather than fall into the normality of his life with him. She didn't want to hear that this was the platform he normally sat on to wait for the cheaper train, she didn't want to become part of his ridiculous pattern of commuting from this new home and family to try to get audiences and hearings and advance his documents further with the Congregation of the Clergy. She wanted this *over*. She looked at the station, at the monument to Mussolini, who made the trains run on time for the first and only period in Italy's history. By the time she came back here tonight she would have met them. Sean's family. It wouldn't make her feel any different, she knew that.

'What would you like best to happen now?' he asked her suddenly as they sat on the train opposite each other.

'I don't know.'

'What would be the very best thing that could happen as far as you are concerned? Best for everybody.'

She looked out the window at the buildings with all the washing hanging from sticks and poles that jutted through windows.

'I don't know, Sean, I really don't. I suppose I'd like you to reconsider and to ask to go back to your Order, for

Shuya to see that this is your vocation, and for her to return to Japan with the children. I know it's not possible and it's not going to happen, but you did ask me what I would like.'

'Shuya must be a mind-reader,' he said happily. 'She said this is what you want.'

'I'm coming to see them, I'm doing that much – stop getting at me!'

'I know, and I'm so happy, soon you'll know them. A normal way of life is beginning for all of us.' He was like a child who thinks he's getting a bike for his birthday. Angela closed her eyes and kept them closed to discourage further conversation.

They waited in a hot noisy line of people for a bus and they didn't get a seat. Sean was smiling, blinking into the sunlight and bending down to look out, squinting for landmarks to point out to her.

After the bus ride, they walked for ten minutes. The gates of the villa were huge and wide, like the big gates of ruined Castlebay House at home. But the villa couldn't be more different: it was yellow-coloured with white shutters and there were flowers tumbling all over the walls. Sean looked through the gates with pride. Wasn't it beautiful? The Italians knew how to do things with style. The Signor and Signora didn't spend a great deal of time here of course, but they kept it up fairly well didn't they, when you considered everything. Angela wondered why they weren't going in. Maybe at this last moment he was getting some nerves, beginning to doubt the sense of the mad enterprise. It was only eleven o'clock in the morning and she felt she had put a whole day over her.

They moved away, to her surprise. It must have shown in her face.

'Our entrance is round here,' Sean explained easily. They went in a much narrower entrance a few hundred yards down the wall. It didn't need to say 'servants' entrance', that was so obviously what it was. Here the flower-beds were overgrown and the walls of the out-houses were peeling in the sun. But there were flowers too, and as Angela walked beside Sean, she saw some small, dark-eyed Italian children playing in and out of the open doors. It would be a good place for a child to grow up in some ways, a bit in the shadow of the Big House of course but it was safe and friendly and there would be plenty of other children to play with. She was walking warily now: she must keep her wits about her.

'There they are . . . we're home . . . Shuya! Shuya, she's here! Denis, come here . . .!'

The little boy had his hand up to his face, shy, not wanting to be the first to make the move, hanging back. Behind him came waddling a small fat baby with nappies hanging down underneath its knitted knickers. And leaning against the door was Shuya. Not in Japanese clothes as Angela had thought she would be, not wearing a bun with two sticks coming out of it, no big wide belt with a rose attached to it, no tiny pointed feet.

Shuya looked like an old, old woman. She had an Eastern face, like the face of a poor Chinese or Filipino woman holding out a begging bowl, the kind of face you saw in the missionary annals. Her skin was muddy grey, her hair was lank and tied back like Angela's own. She wore a shapeless dress and over it a long, faded cardigan. This could not be Shuya. Shuya must be inside waiting to come out, this was somebody else minding the children for her, an older friend. The thin tired figure smiled at them both. 'Welcome An-jay-la . . . wel-come. It is so good of you to come all this way to meet your family.'

Shuya's smile moved from brother to sister as she walked out of the shadow into the sunlight. Her smile was bright and it made her old thin face look less beaten, less resigned. Sean was staring at her with delight. In a flash Angela thought she understood it all. He was *lonely*. The poor stupid fool was *lonely* out there and she was kind to him, she was the first person to be kind and warm. That's what it's all about. It didn't make it any better, but it was some explanation.

'Hallo Shuya,' she said. Every word seemed leaden, but she forced them out. 'I'm very glad to meet you. Will you introduce me to the children?'

There was a pause. She must say something a bit warmer, Sean had probably built her up to the skies, described her as beautiful and generous and brilliant, just as he had built this sad creature up when he had spoken of her to Angela.

'This is Laki,' Shuya said. The toddler was whirling her two fat little arms round like a windmill in the effort to keep upright.

'Hallo Laki O'Hara.'

When the limelight was off Denis he realized it was safe to approach. 'I am Denis,' he said.

'I knew you were, I knew it the minute I saw you.'

There was no sending this lot back. Better banish the dream of Father Sean rediscovering his vocation, and his instant family being absorbed somewhere back in Japan. These were here to stay.

She went back on the train every day. Sean had been right, it would have been much easier to have stayed the night, but she had to stay true to her earlier words, and not let it appear that her first visit had been an inspection, and that she would stay if they passed the test. She brought them toys, she bought ridiculous over-decorated boxes of sweets. Laki sat on her lap and Denis wanted to know why she couldn't speak Japanese or even Italian. Shuya said little.

On Thursday, Sean had to see two priests who knew better routes than the ones he had been following. There was great hope they would steer him in the right direction. Angela said she would still come to Ostia, as usual. This was only her third visit but already it seemed natural. In fact she was glad that Sean would be away. Perhaps Shuya might talk more, might say the things that Sean reported her as saying. The woman was so quiet that Angela could hardly believe that she was the author of such philosophical announcements as Sean had always claimed. Shuya said

183

little or nothing in her presence, and served the simple salads and pasta as if she were a maid, sitting a little away from the others as they ate. But when Sean wasn't there she would have to speak.

At first she was content to let young Denis talk to his aunt, but Angela put a stop to that. She asked Denis to go and collect her ten different kinds of leaves, each one different, from the grounds, and lay them all out on a sheet of paper; then they would try to put names on them. Denis went off happily; Laki was playing with a fat Italian baby about her own age. The women were on their own. Shuya seemed to recognize it too: she sat with her hands folded, waiting for Angela to begin.

It was hard because Angela had to be in the role of questioner for such a long time. Shuya replied dutifully. She had three brothers, and two sisters. Her mother was dead and her father had married again. Yes, they did like his new wife, but now he lived with his new wife's people and they did not see much of him. Her family liked Sean. No, they didn't really think anything about his having been a priest. Or being a priest still, as Angela said. No, you see it was just a job to them – he had been teaching when he was a priest, he was still teaching. He had not been married before, now he was married to Shuya. It was so simple.

On close questioning Shuya proved to see some complications. She said that it was a very big thing, it was like being married to the Church and the Church would release you if you found a higher happiness. But there were a lot of formalities. That is why they were here, that is why Sean had gone to the Vatican again this day as he did so many days.

No, of course it didn't matter to her, not even a little bit, about whether this laicization happened or not. But since it mattered so much to Sean it had become important to her too. She wished it to happen to please him. Then they could get on with their lives.

This was a minefield. Angela had to tread carefully. Where did they see the rest of their lives? Shuya didn't really know. They did love Italy of course, and anyone with children would love to be here, the people adored all children. But after? Sean would want to teach in a school, possibly. He was so clever, and he could teach so well. He would want to teach and live in a school at the same time. Then Denis could go to the same school and there would be a school nearby for Laki.

And where would this school be? In Italy or Japan or where? Shuya didn't know exactly where, but it would be somewhere in Ireland. She wasn't sure if Sean knew himself, but of course it would be Ireland.

She began to explain to Shuya about Ireland, and about Castlebay. She was never interrupted as she had been by Sean. Shuya came out with no roaring denials and assurances that things had changed now. Shuya listened as if she were being told a tale from a far country. She listened as if Angela knew what it was like because that was her land. She was passive during the recounting of the struggle to get the money for Sean's ordination, and the moment of glory at his first Mass and then his first Mass in Castlebay, and even his return seven years ago for his father's funeral. So passive that Angela wondered if she understood any of it. Angela tried to explain that despite what all the clergy in Rome said to each other, it made not a bit of difference back home, whether a priest had been laicized or not. Even if his marriage was as white as the driven snow in the eyes of God and state, in the eyes of the community it could never be accepted.

She begged Shuya to ask her questions, to challenge what she said. Shuya said there was no reason to challenge anything. Obviously Angela must be telling the truth, but did this mean that Sean should never go back to Ireland? Was this what Angela was trying to explain?

Yes. That was it. That's what she had been trying to say to Sean in her letters, and again when she had met him in Rome. Had he not told her this? Oh he had told her, but then when Angela had agreed to come to see the family on Tuesday, and come back again Wednesday and today, he realized that he had been forgiven and that it would all be all right. He had hoped that this would happen and now it had.

Denis came back with his leaves. He was about to lay them out for discussion and identification. Angela passed a hand wearily over her forehead, she was in deeper than ever now. Her visit had been the positive green light that Sean had been waiting for. Was she ever going to get out of this mire of misunderstanding or was she walking everybody further into it?

For the first time Shuya seemed to take some action of her own. She suggested that Denis and Laki have their lunch and siesta in the house across the courtyard. Denis felt short-changed.

'Your Aunt Angela will be here when you come back,' Shuya soothed, marching them over the cobblestones, bringing some of Angela's sweets as a bribe. It was the house of a gardener and his wife, who also helped with the sewing in the linen room. When the gardener went to market his wife had a young lover in and on those occasions Shuya took her children: so it was a fair exchange. Angela was taken aback by the racy life in the servants' quarters and the casual way that Shuya had accepted it. But it worked in her favour and she was not going to criticize.

She seemed younger, stronger, when she came back and sat down. It was as if her listening had a different quality. She scented a problem where she had thought there was none, she wanted to hear, to learn and to see what could be done. This time she talked back, she asked questions, mainly unanswerable ones. Like why, if these people were very religious, would they not recognize and believe in a document signed by the Pope saying that Sean was released from his vows? Or why would people who say they follow a rule which is based on love for each other not give that love? Angela was helpless. But because she didn't bluster, because she didn't defend and make excuses, the conversation never became angry. In the end Angela asked about Japan: wasn't there some code of honour that they had too, some kind of thing that an outsider might think was odd? Shuya paused. They had *ko* which was a sort of filial piety, but it wasn't the same as what was being asked for here. With *ko* you had to be docile to your parents and for a woman in particular docile to your mother-in-law. But they didn't have anything which meant hiding the truth, and no notion that hiding the truth could ever be a good thing in itself.

The sun came in through the slats in the shutters and Angela felt a great sadness and tiredness. In Rome, Sean was bent over still more documents with still more clerics. In Castlebay the neighbours would have cleared away her mother's lunch things. It would still be cold and windy. Up at the convent Mother Immaculata would be getting the timetable ready for the summer term. In Amalfi, Kevin and Emer would possibly be holding hands after lunch in a restaurant by the harbour or be on a boat to Capri. In O'Brien's shop Clare would have told them about the scholarship exam and how she couldn't wait until Miss O'Hara got back to hear the details. And here she was with this woman discussing *honesty* and *truth* and *hypocrisy*. She felt as if she would like to curl up and go to sleep for a month, waking up only when everything else was sorted out. She was thinking about this so wistfully that she almost missed Shuya's words.

'I suppose then that the best thing is for us not to go to Ireland at this time. It is best for Sean to alter some parts of his dream?'

'What?'

'For him to change his hopes about going to Ireland at this time.'

'Do you think he will? He's so set in his belief that it will be all right. I wore myself out and he didn't change an inch, not an inch.'

'Well, I will explain to him.'

'Shuya, how can you explain, he will only think that I tried to browbeat you or go behind his back or something.'

'But that is not so.'

'I know it's not so. I'd have said every word in front of him, but he'd have interrupted me a thousand times, I

187

don't understand *this*, I haven't understood the *other*, Moral Law, Canon Law . . .'

'I know.'

She didn't dare to hope that this strange ugly woman with the lined face and the clothes of a beggar should be able to convince her big handsome brother of anything. 'Could you . . .? I think it would make everyone happier. Not just my mother, Sean's mother. But other people as well. They would be happier not to have to face it. I find that hard to say, especially since I know you and I know the children. I don't think it's fair or it's right, but I do think it's the way it is.'

Shuya nodded. 'I think it's the way it is,' she said.

There was a silence.

Could it be possible?

'What would you do if you didn't come to Ireland?' It was tentative.

'Stay here I suppose until the laicization, and after that . . .' she shrugged. 'I feel that may be a long time anyway, if it ever happens.'

'I suppose he'll keep trying.'

'He says it was like an official contract with his God. It was made formally, it must be ended formally. Like a business deal. His God wouldn't wriggle out of it, neither must he.'

'But in a way God *did* wriggle out of it, if He took Sean's vocation away.' Angela was trying desperately to be fair.

'The hardest bit is going to be the letters from your mother.'

'I know. I know. What should I do? Should I not post them, should I not write them? Will I just write a sort of account of her instead?'

'It's hard,' Shuya said. 'And on you it is most hard of all.'

Angela looked up, surprised and touched at this sympathy. Her brother had not sounded so soft and so understanding.

'I manage,' she said with a weak grin.

'Yes, but you manage alone, you manage without your

188

sisters in England. Nobody has mentioned them because obviously there is nothing they can or will do to help. You manage without the help of anyone in your town, your priest or your friends. And you do not complain, you spend your teacher's salary to come to see us even though you think that we should not be here, and that Sean should still be a priest.'

Angela couldn't find words, she stammered. 'It's not . . . it's not that easy on you, you have nothing either.'

Shuya's plain face smiled, a smile of disbelief. 'But I have everything, I have everything in the world,' she said. And on cue two figures started staggering across the yard, Denis weighed down under still more leaves and Laki, her face a red rim of pleasure from the tomato sauce she had eaten on her spaghetti lunch.

She came again on the Friday. Sean was still high with hope – the two priests he had met yesterday were really helpful. They had shown him how things could be simplified. Go for the direct route always, they had said. Don't be misled, don't go up side alleys. Angela's heart fell when she listened to him. She had been foolish to get buoyed up with hope that Shuya would change his mind. Then he said, 'Shuya and I were talking last night. She was saying something very interesting. She has the most extraordinary insights, you know.'

Shuya was up in the Signora's linen room at the time having insights about hemming frayed pillowcases and darning perfect small darns in white silk.

'What did she say?'

'It was about the difference between country and town. It's the same in Japan, it's the same here. In the country people are slower to see what's happening in the world, they resist change. It takes so much longer to persuade people in the country of anything. It's not their fault of course.'

She listened with a new patience. Perhaps she even looked like Shuya now, her hands folded, waiting for him to get to the point.

'Things will change of course, but in their own time. You can't rush people and expect them to go at your pace. In terms of absolutes you might be wise to hold off until the growth of acceptance is sufficient . . . until the ground swell of opinion has become so strong that there will be no doubt and no confusion. That way the hurt is lessened, the debate is less sharp and the lines of love rather than the letter of the law would mould people's attitudes . . .'

She closed her eyes with relief. In his convoluted way he was telling her that he wasn't going back to Castlebay.

They were all sad to be leaving Rome on the Saturday, and Father Flynn was at the airport to wave them off as he had welcomed them ten days before.

'It worked out all right, did it?' he said to Angela when there was no one else around – the others were all dealing with luggage.

'What?'

'What you had to do, sort out?'

She looked at him hard. Another Irish priest in Rome. Sean talking his head off everywhere he went about it all. It was only too possible that Father Flynn knew, and had known from the start. But she was going to admit nothing.

'Oh, I sorted myself out a great few days. I really love Italy. I'm heartbroken to leave, like they all are.'

'You might come back?'

'It would cost a fortune.'

'I'm sure it would be appreciated,' he said and let it drop. He was laughing and smiling and wondering what he would do next Tuesday when he had no big important wedding to officiate at.

The journey home was something she forgot. She must have talked to people, she must have said her goodbyes and gone to the station to get the train home. She caught the bus to Castlebay: Clare was waiting at the stop. At a hundred yards away Angela knew she had won the scholarship and she started to cry.

She was crying as she got off the bus, but Clare put a finger to her lips.

'Don't say anything, Miss O'Hara, don't say anything, only you and I know. Not Mother Immaculata yet, not Mam or Dad. I wanted to tell you first.'

'I can't tell you how happy I am, I can't tell you how glad.'

Clare picked up the teacher's bag. 'I'll walk you home. We can talk when there aren't people looking at us.'

She was right. It would only take half an hour for it to be known everywhere that the two of them were crying and embracing.

They walked up the golf-course road, Clare bubling about how the nun, the very nice nun in the town convent, had asked her to telephone the day before the official results, just in case there was any news. And Clare had telephoned this morning and yes, the nun had said it was definite, her Mother Superior was going to ring Mother Immaculata tomorrow. It was absolutely definite.

They had got to the O'Hara house and Angela let herself in.

'Do you want to be on your own . . . a bit?' Clare held back.

'Of course I don't. Mother! Mother, I'm back.'

The old woman was sitting in the chair and her face lit up. 'I was hoping you'd get the bus, was the plane very frightening? Did you have holy water with you?'

'I was laden down with it. Mother, I've got great news for you. The best, the best.' She had both her hands on her mother's shoulders as she spoke, and suddenly she remembered that for her mother the best news might be the imminent return of father Sean from the mission fields. Hastily she jumped in. 'Clare's done it, Mother, she's won it. Isn't that bloody marvellous!'

Angela threw herself down at the table and sobbed as if her heart would break. The tears that had never come in Rome came in a torrent. Her shoulders shook.

Clare and Mrs O'Hara looked at each other in alarm. Nothing could be heard but the heavy sobs from the table.

191

Mrs O'Hara reached out but was too far away to comfort Angela. Clare didn't know whether she should move towards the teacher or not. Tentatively she touched her on the arm and patted it awkwardly.

'Don't cry,' she said. 'Please.'

From the chair came support. 'Oh Angela, please stop that crying, we should be delighted for Clare, there was no crying in this house when *you* got the scholarship.'

Angela raised her head and saw the two stricken faces. Her own face was blotched and stained. But she found what they were both looking for, her good humour and her strength.

'It's the journey, and the shock and the pleasure, the sheer sheer pleasure of it. Well done, Clare, well done, may this be the first of many triumphs for you.' Her smile blazed out through the tears and suddenly Clare wanted to cry. But that would be ridiculous. Instead she did something much more ridiculous, she ran into Miss O'Hara's arms and together they swung around the room shouting with excitement. Mrs O'Hara clapped her hands in her chair and they laughed like people who had long forgotten what they were laughing at.

PART TWO

1957–1960

Clare hated sharing the room with Chrissie when she came home from school during the holidays. Chrissie's clothes smelled of sweat, she always had stockings rolled up and stuffed into shoes, the dressing table was covered with spilled powder and hair clips and combs with tufts of Chrissie's curly hair caught in the teeth. She used Clare's bed as a place to store her clothes and only very grudgingly removed them when the occupant returned from boarding school at the end of term.

Clare thought almost nostalgically of her small clean white bed in the dormitory, of the chair where her uniform lay neatly waiting for the morrow, with the stockings folded on top like a cross. It was always nice and airy in the dormitory, freezing sometimes, actually, but there was never that close smell of bodies that you had sharing a room with Chrissie. Worst of all were the blood-spattered white coats. It had never been defined who was to wash these coats and where the washing was to be done, but while it was in dispute two or more of them often festered on the floor. Clare would hide them under other garments so that she didn't have to speculate what part of what dead animal had bled over Chrissie's middle. She looked around her in disgust.

She *should* feel sorry for Chrissie, she knew this, but it didn't make it any easier. It was a desperate life standing up in Dwyers' butcher's shop and having to hack great bits of carcasses of dead sheep and cows. It wasn't a glamorous job, and it couldn't do her any good at the dance when fellows asked where she worked. Clare had suggested more than once that she try to work somewhere else. The chemist maybe? And be with that old bore Mr Murphy, Mr Murphy, a daily communicant who kept his own daughters under lock and key? No thank you very much. Or the hotel even? And be a skivvy passing round dinner plates or washing up for Young Mrs Dillon and her mad old mother-in-law, no thank you, not even if Clare was friendly with them. Thank you, Chrissie would prefer to earn her own wages and be done with the place as soon as she left it in the evening.

There had been a hope that she could have used the room they had called the Boys' Room, the downstairs room where Tommy and Ned used to sleep all those years ago when they lived at home. But Mam and Dad said that room had to be used as a storeroom now, and since the business was far better than ever before a storeroom was needed. The new caravan park up on the Far Cliff Road meant a great deal of trade. People in caravans had to buy everything; they didn't do much cooking so it was mainly cold ham and tins of things. When they trekked across from the caravan field O'Brien's was the first shop they met, perched as it was at the top of the steps going down to the sea. Very few of them went any further, and then the caravan people came back again to stock up for the day on the beach, and on the way home they would buy things for their tea. It was all great but it did mean that the Boys' Room was gone as a possible place to sleep, and Clare felt she must keep the rows to a minimum, only fight over things that were really important.

Miss O'Hara and Clare had another secret, another scholarship, another over-ambitious project. Clare O'Brien was going to go for the county scholarship. One student in the entire county would be offered a place in University College, Dublin, to study Arts, to do a B.A. degree. It was called the Murray Prize. A Mr Murray long dead had left his money for this, and the competition was fierce. Usually a bright boy from one of the seminaries won it, but three years ago it had been a girl, a very brainy girl whose father was professor already. Clare and Miss O'Hara had decided to take it on.

The prize was awarded on the strength of marks received in the leaving certificate together with a personal interview.

Those candidates with a sizeable number of Honours Papers and who had already announced their participation would be called to appear before a committee. Even to be called to interview by the Murray committee was an honour. But it was an honour that wouldn't happen until the end of August. The examination results had to come in first. Miss O'Hara had begged Clare to enjoy the summer, it might be her last summer of freedom. If she *did* get to university there would always be the need to study, and she would have to work for extra money – the Murray scholarship was not princely. If she did *not* get to university then she would be working during the rest of her summers, so there was even more reason to enjoy this last one. Have a bit of a fling, Miss O'Hara had advised her, and Miss O'Hara had said embarrassingly that Clare was turning into a fine-looking girl and she should make the most of it.

Clare looked at herself in the mirror. She wanted to lighten the colour of her hair: she used Sta-Blonde shampoo, which claimed to bring out the blonde highlights, but it didn't or else there were no highlights to bring out. She would have used some peroxide in the rinsing water like some of the girls at school did but, really, one look at Chrissie's peroxided fuzz would be enough to turn you against the stuff even if the smell of it didn't. Clare had grown tall, all of a sudden, when she was fourteen. Nobody had expected it, least of all Clare, and it was highly irritating. School uniforms had to have false hems and be let down to the last possible thread. She wore her hair in a pony tail with one of those nice plastic clips. Chrissie had said it made her look like a horse, but Clare had taken no notice. The great thing about going away to school was meeting so many other people and being able to compare Chrissie with them. Now she no longer believed her elder sister and didn't feel put down by the scathing insults heaped on her all the time.

Clare would like to have had blue eyes. Brown eyes were wrong in her face she thought, her complexion wasn't right for them. If she were like Ava Gardner, or had a dark smouldering face, then big brown eyes would be good; but she thought they looked out of place with her light hair and fair skin. Still. There was nothing she could do about them. Josie told her they were fine, and what's more they were unusual, so there. She should be delighted with them and stop complaining.

Josie was going from strength to strength these days. She was already in the office of the hotel, wearing a frilly white blouse and a cameo brooch. She had lost a great deal of weight in the two years she spent living in her aunt's house while she went to the commercial college. Her aunt was the meanest woman in Ireland and the meals that were served were extremely sparse. But it was all to the good and Josie's two sisters looked at her with shock each time they came home from their boarding school, and, eventually, the Hotel and Catering College. Slow, fat Josie could type letters like the wind, had understood book keeping and simple accountancy. She was helping Father and Uncle Dick and Mother with far more confidence than they seemed to be able to drum up. In fact Rose and Emily were quite jealous of the sister they used to call poor Josie. They even complained when they saw her change into whites and play tennis with that Clare O'Brien from the shop. But Josie was calm. She and Clare played tennis every morning from eight to nine; then they went to work, Josie in her family business, Clare in hers. They played again at seven in the evening. Rose and Emily had all day to play if they wanted to. It was unanswerable. Which was why Rose and Emily hated it; it was even further irritating to see that Josie and Clare played well and often played a mixed doubles with guests from the hotel.

Clare and Josie had more fun at the dance than Rose and Emily who thought, wrongly, that they would be exotic and a treat coming home as they had from Dublin. But the visitors didn't know where they had come from and the locals all knew the two girls who were around all the time; they were never without a partner.

Leaning over the balcony and watching Josie rocking enthusiastically to 'See You Later Alligator', Emily complained loudly one evening that the young ones had it very easy, didn't they? Nice cushy job ready made for them in the hotel, no studying hotel management, all plain sailing and life one long holiday. Chrissie O'Brien, another wallflower, watched her younger sister with equal rage and said that there was no justice in life. Rose and Emily had to disassociate themselves. Annoyed they might be, but they weren't going to ally themselves with terrible Chrissie O'Brien.

The Nolans still came to Castlebay, they were part and parcel of the place now. At least, Mr and Mrs Nolan did. Of James, there was no sign, Josie sighed.

'Maybe he'll come down this summer, and you'll dazzle him,' Clare said.

'No, I interrogated his mother, he's in France picking grapes with David Power. Can you imagine anything more stupid, those two picking grapes? They don't need the money, why aren't they here where they *are* needed?'

'It's a funny time of year to be picking grapes,' Clare said thoughtfully. 'I thought all that was much later on.'

'Maybe they're up to no good. They could have French mistresses.' Josie was deliberately making herself miserable.

'They should be working for their exams,' Clare said primly. David Power was about Fourth Med by now; and James Nolan had a B.A. in economics, but he still had to do his Bar Final. Josie was right; they were much too grown-up and sophisticated to pick grapes or whatever in France, but they were much too grown-up and sophisticated to come to Castlebay as well.

Molly Power was delighted with the letter. It said she was to let the Nolans know too. David and James would be arriving next Thursday week. Things hadn't worked out exactly as they had hoped in France, long explanations later, but meanwhile they thought they would come back to Castlebay. Waving the letter Molly ran out on to the drive as she heard her husband's car on the gravel.

'Great news, David's coming home next week.'

His face lit up with pleasure. 'David's coming back, Bones,' he said and the animal did three circuits of the car, barking delightedly.

Paddy Power took his wife's arm and they sat on the garden seat, looking straight out to sea. On a day like this it was paradise.

Nellie called from the kitchen window. 'You look very comfortable out there, stay as you are. I'll bring out your dinner.'

A polite protest.

'Sure why don't you act like the quality,' Nellie said and closed the window.

They smiled at each other, pleased greatly that their son was coming home.

'I arranged for old Mrs O'Hara to go into the County Hospital for a couple of weeks today. Observation, I call it.'

'And what is it? What has she got?'

'Nothing, as far as I can see. Nothing she hasn't had for years. But I want to give Angela a holiday, that's what it's really about. Angela hardly ever gets a break. I want her to enjoy a bit of this summer. Lord, she's living in a place that half of Ireland and indeed half of England as well seems to be descending on . . . but she never gets out to enjoy it.'

'You're very thoughtful.' Molly touched his knee affectionately.

'I've always liked her, always, she's got such pluck, I know it's a funny word, it's not a word for people like us, but that's it. Pluck. Do you know I often think young Clare O'Brien from the shop has it too. I always see her as sort of an echo of Angela O'Hara.'

'Do you?' Molly frowned.

'Same way of sticking their chins up and getting on with things, no matter what.' Dr Power smiled at the thought.

'I don't think so.' Molly was shaking her head. 'Angela had spirit certainly, and it's wonderful she got so far, considering . . .' She left unsaid the ripples of disapproval over Dinny O'Hara's behaviour, and her own remoteness towards the life looking after an old woman.

Dr Power hid his impatience. He hated Molly in that *grande dame* mood. 'Well the child Clare O'Brien has nobody to be apologizing for, just the fact that she was born poor and triumphed over it.'

'She was born sneaky, Paddy, you're too kind, you don't see these things. A woman would notice. She has deceitful eyes.'

'*Molly.*'

'Well, you say what you think, I say what I think.'

'But it's silly. Silly, to say such a thing about a child.'

'To me some of the things *you* do and say are silly. I don't pass remarks about them.'

'All right, Moll, all right. Life's short, let's leave it.' The day seemed less shiny somehow for him.

Gerry Doyle arrived at the O'Haras' cottage later in the afternoon. He was to give them a lift to the hospital. 'Take as much time as you like,' he told them. 'I'm in no hurry, so don't be rushing.'

But they were ready: Mrs O'Hara tremulous and afraid of a bumpy journey in that young tearaway's van, Angela pale and anxious. The little suitcase had been packed.

'Well will we head off then?' Gerry was a great person to drive them. He didn't care enough about Mrs O'Hara to be making inquiries about how she felt, and he had plenty of good casual chat to keep Angela distracted. Dr Power had said that since he went into the town every Tuesday to get equipment and supplies, he'd be the very man to give them a lift. Dr Power had even gone and called on Doyle's Photographics himself to save Angela the business of asking him for a lift.

He was kind and practical about getting the old woman into his van. 'Tell me first what movements hurt you most, and I won't drag you the wrong way,' he said.

Mrs O'Hara had to pause and think. The worst bit was having to bend her legs. Right, that was easily organized,

Gerry got a box for her to stand on then she sat into the front seat of his van and Angela eased her legs in as straight as it was possible to do. Mrs O'Hara settled in fairly cheerfully. Angela climbed into the back.

'You're very agile for a woman of your age,' Gerry said, smiling at her in the driver's mirror.

'Will you stop that nonsense, I could run rings round you. Your generation have no stamina.' She grinned back at him through the mirror. He was a handsome lad. She had always liked him. Much more than his sister, and she had often asked herself why she didn't take to Fiona Doyle, without ever coming to a satisfactory conclusion.

They were good youngsters both of them. Since their father's death, they had not only kept the business going, they had made it boom. The big increase in visitors had meant a huge demand for snaps. During the summer the Doyles hired another photographer to help out. They had smartened up their little booth on the cliff with bright paint, and they had been doing great business calling to the houses along the Cliff Road and the Far Cliff Road taking family pictures, which they enlarged and presented in a little cardboard frame. Nearly every family wanted to have a souvenir like that, something to show at home, the family in their own place. Messages used to be sent urgently to get young Jimmy back from the amusements, or call young Eddie up from the beach; Mother would change into her best dress and the milk bottle would be hidden away while the picture was being taken.

'I see your star pupil is home from school,' Gerry said.

'She is a star pupil,' Angela said proudly. 'I have great hopes for her, I really do.'

'So do I,' said Gerry, smiling roguishly. 'Great hopes altogether.'

'Stop sounding like the villain in a pantomime,' Angela said crossly. *Please*, she thought, don't let Gerry Doyle distract Clare before the interview. Don't let him get his hands on her until she's won the Murray Prize.

They were very nice to Mrs O'Hara in the hospital, and

202

the change suited her. Everything was new and interesting: the Little Flower ward with the big statue of St Theresa and the roses falling around the crucifix in her arms. Mrs O'Hara had always had a great devotion to the Little Flower. The woman in the next bed was some distant relative by marriage so they spent hours tracing people long dead and lowering their voices about people whose careers had not been too glorious. Angela felt nothing but relief that her mother was being well looked after. Dr Power had been right: the change would do Mam good. She spent the first few days after her mother left doing a kind of spring-clean. She never liked to paint the place while the housebound woman was there; the smell would be hard to bear. She pulled all the furniture into the middle of the floor, and began to take down the books and ornaments. It was a much longer job than she would have believed but it was a very peaceful one. She sat on a ladder dusting books and reading them at the same time, polishing ornaments and remembering who had given them or where they had come from. It was days before she actually began to paint. She had gone in twice and been reassured that her mother was happy and well looked after. This was a good break for her, housepainting in the morning, a stroll down to the hotel, a sandwich sometimes with Dick Dillon, still mourning the fact that he had been put off drink and pushed sideways in the chain of command in the hotel. Then she would go down to the beach, and swim. She would know at least twenty people that she passed, pupils present and past, people from Castlebay sunning themselves. But usually she took a book and sat on the grassy cliff base. Then when it got very hot she would run down into the sea and battle with the breakers. Once she came across a small child who was being constantly buffeted by the waves and knocked down every time she got to her feet. Angela swooped her up and carried her out of the water. She was just the kind of child who could be one of Dr Power's casualties. The kind of thing he was always worrying about, visitors who didn't know the pull of the current, the strength of the waves. She found herself telling the family tearfully that they must pay more attention to a child of that age or she would be swept out to sea. The child's parents were grateful and startled, and she overheard them saying as she left that possibly she had a child that was drowned herself and that's what had unsettled her so much. Angela didn't *feel* unsettled. She felt fine. But she realized that it was the first summer she had ever got a tan, been to the pictures regularly and gone to the dance.

She hadn't intended going to the dance. She thought women of thirty-five were pathetic in their summer dresses, their white cardigans and their newly lacquered hair queueing up at the ticket desk with the hope of a starry and glittery night ahead. Even when she heard that the Castlebay Committee were having a special dance to raise funds she didn't think of going. The Committee was going to charge a big price for the ticket, but there were going to be enormous spot prizes. Every business in the place was giving something. Gerry Doyle was going to take a family or group portrait free, Mrs Conway in the post office was offering a set of a dozen views of Castlebay on postcards with a small frame as well. Dwyers' were giving a leg of lamb. Miss O'Flaherty was offering a writing case with pad and envelopes. The O'Briens were giving two big tins of Afternoon Tea assortment, the best biscuits there were. The money they raised would go to make the place look more attractive, to build a proper car park possibly and prevent the road being cluttered with cars making it impossible to get in or out of Castlebay. Or maybe plant a big flowerbed on the way into town where the three roads met. Some people wanted to put up fairy lights down Church Street, and others wanted to have public lavatories built on the beach. It would all be debated long and excitedly during the winter, and the money raised would sit in Mrs Conway's post office for ages. Angela, as a teacher and respected member of the community, had been on the Castlebay Committee but it never occurred to her that she was expected to go to the dance. Dick Dillon said that this is what always happened when you had a bunch of old meddlers and busybodies running things, now they were all nicely stuck and had to go to the wretched dance or their lives wouldn't be worth living.

'Will you come as my partner?' he asked Angela in a voice filled with such doom he might as well have been asking her to leap off the cliff with him in a suicide mission.

'Certainly,' Angela said.

He looked at her suspiciously. 'You can collect me at the hotel then,' he said.

'No Dick, a gentleman collects a lady at *her* house,' Angela said in a parody of every Doris Day film she had seen. If Dick had seen the films he didn't recognize the parody.

'Very well,' he said. 'Seeing as how I don't drink any more I might as well get value out of the car by driving it.'

She hardly thought about the dance again, she was so busy painting the house. She decided that the only way to do it was to divide the big downstairs room into two halves, and when the first half was painted she would put back the books and knick-knacks before starting the other side. It did look much brighter and more awake. She was standing in a paint-spattered smock and her hair in an old scarf admiring it, when a car stopped at the door. James Nolan and David Power had come to call. Better than that, they had brought a bottle of champagne cider.

She was delighted to see them. She had followed their careers with delight and when nobody else remembered what exams they were doing, Miss O'Hara always did. She used to know the names of their professors too and she never asked embarrassing questions like did they have girlfriends, did they spend much money on drink, and what exactly were they doing in France?

They picked chairs and stools out of the heap of furniture and sat happily telling her about everything. David was tall and fair-haired with a peeling nose, and James small and dark-looking like a little Italian, so tanned was he after whatever they had been up to in France. They were full of plans for the summer. It was going to be two hours' work every morning and then free as the air all day and all night. They wanted to know was there any talent in town. Any gorgeous blondes or redheads with tiny waists and huge bosoms. Angela said she wouldn't have noticed if the town was full of them, but they'd have to look sharp before Gerry Doyle grabbed everything that was going.

'That fellow, is he still at it?' James Nolan said. 'I know I'm a small runt of a thing myself, but he's a dwarf. What *do* they see in him?'

'I can't believe he's *still* the Romeo,' David complained. 'He was always getting the girls without having to lift a finger. I'd have thought they'd have seen through him by now.'

'Different crop every year of course,' Angela said.

'But seriously, Miss O'Hara, seriously.' David looked lovely when he was trying to be serious. He pushed the long lick of hair on his forehead back so that it stood up like a fan. 'Now would you as a *woman* . . . well, as a *female* – would you tell us what's so attractive about him.'

'As a *female*, I would find it very hard to explain. He's good company, he has a nice smile, he smiles a lot. He doesn't try too hard to please, but he does seem to *like* women, without exactly flirting with them. Is that any help?'

She looked from one handsome student to the other as they sat in her upside-down house. They were both thoughtful.

'That's a great help, actually,' David said earnestly. 'Not trying too hard to please. I think that's where I fall down.'

'I don't think I *like* women like he does. I think I like the idea of women more than I like them as people,' said James Nolan.

'I'm sorry I don't have a couch free,' Angela laughed. 'You could lie down one by one and I could psychoanalyse you, maybe I could psychoanalyse half of Castlebay, and I'd make a fortune. Your father could send me a few patients, David, and maybe Father O'Dwyer could too. Oh and anyone left roaring and bawling after the dance could always come here for a midnight session, I'd straighten them out.'

She was great at knocking down their pomposity. David had been glad to hear from his father that the old woman was in hospital for the summer, he didn't like calling to see Miss O'Hara when her mother was there, you felt you should talk to both of them. He remembered why he had come.

'I really wanted to know if you'd like to come with us to the Castlebay Committee dance next week. Mummy and Daddy are going too and the Nolans and we were all going to have a drink in our house first and go together.'

Angela was flattered to have been asked; but she regretted that she had a date already.

They were excited when they learned it was Dick Dillon. A romance? A local love affair possibly? A slow-flowering friendship blossoming into a late romance? Would there be wedding bells pealing out from the church before long?

She said they shouldn't be so cruel and heartless and tease an old maid, a poor spinster of the parish. David said it was just because she wasn't an old maid they could tease her. It was the best compliment she had ever got, even though anyone else hearing it might have thought it inexplicable.

Clare came twice a week to rehearse the interview for the Murray Prize. They had found out who sat on the board: an uncle of Josie Dillon on her mother's side was one of them. He was a bank manager and the Murray money was in his bank so that gave him some kind of right to be there when it was being handed out. According to Josie he was mad and snobbish, and thought that Dillon's Hotel in Castlebay was rather beneath him. Angela and Clare were still working on their strategy for him. Clare arrived shortly after the boys had gone.

'The place stinks of drink,' she said accusingly.

'It's my age, at the change of life we women become all funny, we start shifting the furniture around and drinking on our own.'

Clare laughed. 'You're never at the change of life yet, Miss O'Hara?'

'*Of course I'm not!* God, remind me never to make jokes talking to children. Please Lord, let me never be ironic again. The drink was a gift from two young gentlemen callers. They came and brought champagne cider and invited me to the Castlebay Committee dance. How about that for a poor, old, decrepit, barren geriatric?'

'Who was it?'

'David Power and James Nolan.'

'And are you going?'

'No, I thought I'd leave the field free for younger, plainer women. I'm going with Josie's uncle. He did ask me first. Are you going?'

'I suppose I will, Josie and I'll go together. You don't need a partner. I think she'd rather like it if James Nolan was around, she fancies him a lot.'

'Tell her to pretend she doesn't even notice him, that will work. Come on now, do something to help me, lift one end of this contraption with me, I'm going to paint it out in the back. If I paint it here I'll stick to it every time I pass by. It's not going to rain they say on the wireless, so that should mean we'll have a nice fine evening . . .'

She broke off suddenly. Clare hadn't moved, she was sitting troubled and hadn't even been listening.

'What is it?' she said. 'You surely haven't got the results yet?'

The only thing that could make Clare's face so downcast must have to do with the Leaving Certificate results, but they weren't due for two more weeks.

'Tommy's in gaol,' Clare said simply.

'Tommy. Tommy?' It was so long since she had seen the O'Brien boys she had forgotten their names. It came to her a couple of seconds later. 'In gaol? In England? What did he do?'

'Housebreaking.'

Angela sat down. 'When did you hear? Who told you?'

'Just now. The afternoon post. I'm afraid I came up to you straight away. I couldn't bear to stand in the shop thinking about it. Mam will be furious. Still. I'll cope with that.'

'God Almighty, isn't that desperate. How do you know?'

'A letter from Ned. So as not to worry Mam and Dad immediately, but so as I could forewarn them in case it gets back to them. What *does* he want me to do? Tell them or not to tell them? It might appear in a paper he said, then again it might not. Thomas O'Brien is a very ordinary name he says, but Thomas O'Brien from Castlebay would place him pretty clearly. Here, you can read the letter . . . see if you know what he wants. See if you know what I'm meant to do.'

Angela didn't reach out to take the ill-written pages on their lined paper. She sat with her elbows on her knees and her head in her hands. There was a silence for a while. 'I don't need to read the letter, I know what he wants,' Angela said eventually. 'He wants *you* to make the decisions. He wants *you* to take on the responsibility.'

Clare was surprised. 'Why?'

'Because you're not Chrissie who wouldn't know what day it was, and you're not your mother who would cry her eyes out, and you're not your father who would get into a temper and you're not Ben and Jim who are too young to be taken into account. And because you're bright and got a scholarship, that's going to fit you and make you ready for any burden from now on.'

Clare was very startled at her tone. 'Miss O'Hara . . .' she began.

'What sentence did he get?' Angela asked crisply.

'Ned says two years.'

'That was more than ordinary housebreaking. He must have had a weapon. The great thick fool.'

'No wonder he never wrote home.'

'Tommy was hardly able to write if I remember rightly. What do you think you'll do?'

'I don't know. I've no information. If I thought it was going to get into the papers here I'd tell Ma and Da, but if not what's the point in hurting them?'

'I know, what we need is information as you say.'

'But I've no way of finding out . . .'

'I have. See can you find a writing pad under those

newspapers there, I'll write it now and you can get it into the six o'clock post.'

'Who? What will you say?'

'I have a friend in London. He's a priest – but not like Father O'Dwyer here or anything. He'd find out for us.'

'But could you ask him? Wouldn't he . . .?'

'No, he wouldn't be shocked, and he's one of the best men in the world to keep a secret. Have you the paper? I'll start straight away.'

Clare's eyes filled quickly with tears of gratitude as Miss O'Hara wrote her address across the top of the paper and then wrote: 'Dear Father Flynn, I wonder can you help me. Yet again . . .'

Father Flynn was magnificent. There was a reply in eight days. He had been to see Ned, who was working in a pub now, washing up. It was a rough sort of place, Father Flynn had got him a new job where he was better off – he could live in and the landlord would keep an eye on him. He had heard the details. Tommy had been in with a gang. They had done several jobs and six months ago, Tommy had got probation for his part in the theft of building supplies from a site. This time it had been a smash and grab raid on a small jeweller's shop. What they hadn't realized was that the jeweller was still in his shop when the windows were broken with crowbars and the goods seized. The jeweller's mistake had been to stand up. He had been hit on the side of the head by one of the gang – he could not identify it as being Tommy. But the rest of them escaped and were gone well to ground when the police came looking. Only Tommy was there still with some of the jewellery.

Tommy had said he didn't know who the others were, and couldn't give descriptions. He insisted that he had only met them that night and they didn't give their names. So, according to Ned, the gang were pleased with him and they would make sure he got his share when he came out. He would be out in eighteen months. Father Flynn had visited him in Wormwood Scrubs and reported that he was very pleased to have some contact with home. Since he had been asked to be totally frank, Father Flynn had to report Tommy O'Brien in poor shape, he was missing most of his teeth; he asked for nothing but comics to read from the prison library and he had all the appearance of a loser. Since it was hardly helpful to make such comments without offering anything more positive as well, Father Flynn wondered was there a way Tommy could be brought back to Castlebay when he was released. He did not seem a strong enough character to survive on either side of the tracks in the life he had found for himself in London. If Castlebay was not a realistic solution Father Flynn would try to keep an eye on him, but it would be hard. As soon as Tommy was released he would be given money to show approval that he hadn't squealed; and within three months he would be inside again, for he would loyally go along with the next job suggested to him, and be the patsy there as well. As regards publicity there would be none. The name T. O'Brien had appeared in a local evening paper in London; it would not be taken up by the Irish newspapers. Unfortunately, the arrest and imprisonment of people with Irish names was only too commonplace now. It didn't rate as news.

Angela and Clare read this glumly. He had certainly been as frank as they had asked him to be. But he had been exactly the right person to go and see what was happening. He made no judgements and expressed no shock or disapproval.

'I wonder how Tommy lost his teeth. A fight maybe?' Angela said.

'Maybe they just rotted away,' Clare said. 'He was very nervous of everything, Tommy. He wouldn't ever go to the dentist. I can't think how he was brave enough to get in with a gang of robbers, I'd have thought he would have run a hundred miles in the opposite direction.'

Her face was sad even though her voice was calm. She hadn't cried or shown any great shock when she read the priest's letter. She sat very still with her elbows on the table and her chin in her hands. Clare had the ability to be very still, Angela had noticed. When she was reading only the turning of the pages showed she was awake. When she listened it was the same. Now she heard of her brother's disgrace without expostulating, or making excuses.

'I don't suppose he had to be very brave to get in with a gang. Probably need to be brave *not* to get in with one. Will you write to him in gaol?'

Clare hadn't thought of this. 'Is there any point if he can't read the letters? Would we be better to pretend we didn't know he was there at all? I think that's what he'd like best,' she said without conviction.

'Too late for that. Ned wrote to you, remember? You can't pretend you don't know. You can keep it from your parents and the rest of them but you can't go back on what you know.'

'Yes.'

'So, will you write to him?'

'He never wrote to me, not in six years, nor to any of us, it would only be hypocritical, wouldn't it? And maybe even boasting. Look at me, how well I'm doing, I even have my sights on being a college girl, a graduate, and where are you? You're a gaol bird.'

'I don't suppose you'd write a letter like that.'

Her immobility had gone, her eyes flashed. 'You think I ought to, don't you? If it were you, you'd be sunny and forgiving and like a saint, the way you are about everything. But the world isn't full of saints, it's full of ordinary selfish people like Tommy who go stealing, and me who doesn't want to write him pious letters.'

Angela said nothing.

'I know I shouldn't say it's all right for you, I *know* you had your share of awful things years ago when your father was . . . but that's all long past you, people have forgotten that, you've no shames and no secrets now. You're where you want to be, and you're nice and safe as a teacher here, and your family are all respectable, and you've got a brother, a priest, for God's sake. I've got a brother with no teeth who can't read and who's in Wormwood Scrubs.'

'Clare,' Angela said sharply.

She looked up.

Angela paused. No, not now. It wasn't bad enough, it was only a fit of annoyance and self-pity. She wouldn't tell her.

'Nothing.'

Clare was surprised.

'If you don't get the Murray Prize remind me that I was going to tell you something this afternoon and I changed my mind.'

'Why won't you tell me?'

'I won't, that's all. Now are we going to waste any more time listening to how sorry you are for yourself? You asked me to find out about Tommy, I have. He's your brother, write to him if you want to, don't if you don't want to. I'm not spending one more minute discussing it. If you haven't the generosity to give some bit of hope and optimism to that poor eejit in there, then you haven't. I'm not involved in making you a nice person, nobody can do that for you. I'm only helping you to get on academically. Let's see, where were we?' She took out a notebook and checked the items they'd covered last time. 'Now we've been over a lot of current affairs and you're fine on Eisenhower and the Middle East and the end of Anthony Eden, and King Hussein of Jordan, but there's a good chance that none of the committee will have ever heard of them. Maybe we should concentrate on what they really know about, the Pope and de Valera. When was Pius XII consecrated as Pope . . .?'

'I'm sorry. Of course I'll write to him.'

'Write to who you like. Pius XII. And what was his name?'

'Pacelli, Eugenio Pacelli, he's eighty-one, he was elected in 1939, the year the war started, he was Papal representative in Germany.'

'*Nuncio, nuncio,* say it.'

'Nuncio.'

'And don't come out with it too cocky. Try not to sound as if you know everything. They won't like that.'

213

They laughed. Clare wanted to say more about Tommy, but she was headed off.

'De Valera . . . now this is a tricky one, they'll be bound to love him or hate him, but you're not expected to have any views . . . just facts. Born?'

'In New York in 1882, of a Spanish father and Irish mother, brought up in Bruree, County Limerick . . . but I do have views . . .'

'Of course you do, but when you are being tested for the Murray Prize is not the time to express them. If any of this lot are in their fifties or over they'll remember the Civil War. Not just remember hearing about it, they'll bloody remember it themselves, so will you go carefully and don't throw the whole thing away. We could concentrate on what Dev did in the last war, that shouldn't offend many of them, but if there's anyone with an Anglo-Irish accent there watch it, the English never forgave Dev over our staying neutral. No point in waving a red rag to a bull.'

'Thank you, Miss O'Hara.'

'Stop simpering and keep learning. Talking of simpering, did Gerry Doyle ask you to the Castlebay Committee dance?'

'Yes he did. I said no, Josie and I were going on our own, we'd see him in there.'

'It's you who should be teaching me,' sighed Angela.

Dick Dillon looked very cross when he came to collect Angela. She invited him in and offered him a cup of tea or a glass of orange. He looked around in surprise.

'You have it very nice, considering.'

'Considering *what*?'

'I don't know, just considering,' he said. Angela wondered why couldn't she have said to Dick Dillon that she'd see him inside? Why did she have to put up with this groaning and grousing?

'I painted it recently, while mother's in hospital. Dr Power said she should go in for observation. She'll be back soon.'

She heard her own voice, boring, talking trivia to this

old man. What did young Clare mean the other day when she said that Angela had got all she wanted? She did not want to be talking to a reformed alcoholic sitting there patronizing her little house. In as grouchy a manner as his own she flung his orange squash in front of him and very deliberately took a bottle of gin out of the press.

'Since I haven't been put off it yet, I am going to have a drink to get us through this night, Dick Dillon. So will almost everyone around you, so you might as well get used to it now.'

A slow smile of admiration came over his face. 'That's the first time anyone has treated me as a normal human being for seven years,' and he raised his own glass to her. 'Good luck,' he said beaming all over his face.

Molly Power had laid out little plates of biscuits with cheese on some and mashed-up eggs on others. The eggs ones had been a mistake. She had forgotten how quickly they would go soggy. She had nuts in little bowls and that afternoon she had gone and collected masses of gorse, which looked gorgeous in bowls and jugs all around the room. Their sitting room had yellow curtains and the chintz covers had a lot of yellow in them too. One day Nellie had brought in gorse and Molly had been about to throw it out – but Mrs Nolan had admired it. So now Molly had adopted it as her own idea.

David was rubbing Nivea Creme into his nose. 'I think all the peeling's gone now,' he said, looking at himself in the mirror over the mantelpiece.

'I told you to stop pulling at it and picking at it, it would have gone much sooner if you'd left it alone,' his mother said.

David sighed. There was never anything that Mother didn't know or wasn't right about.

'I know, I know,' he said wearily.

'Well it stands to reason. You're fair-skinned. You get burned. You must wait until the dead skin falls off. Don't pull at it.'

'I won't,' David said, exasperated.

'I don't know why you're getting into a mood.' Molly was annoyed. 'Here we are, having a party for all your friends before you go to the dance. You will have a marvellous evening and all you can do is snap at anyone who tries to help you.' She sounded aggrieved.

David said nothing.

'It's not as if your father and I ever interfere in your life or ask you what you get up to. When the dance is over, do we ever say you must come straight home? No we don't. We let you live your own life.'

'Ah, come on now,' David, trying to hide his anger without much success, laughed insincerely. 'Come on, Mother, I'm a grown-up man, not a little boy with a fishing net. I live my own life in Dublin – naturally I live my own life here too.'

'*Naturally*,' she said in her pouting voice.

He chose not to hear the sulk.

'Good, then we're both saying the same thing.' He squared his shoulders in his new jacket and gave himself one last look.

'Well, that will have to do. If I don't get the lovely Caroline away from Gerry Doyle tonight, I never will.'

'Gerry Doyle? Don't be ridiculous. He'll be there taking snaps.'

'Oh no he won't, he'll have a minion doing that. Gerry will be there on his own terms, making no effort and they'll all come crawling to him.'

'That's disgusting and all in your mind.'

'See for yourself tonight. Caroline's only one of a queue.'

'I never heard such nonsense . . . oh there you are Paddy, don't you look nice and clean?'

'Clean?' Dr Power roared. 'Is that all you have to say to me?'

'I meant dressed up and smart,' Molly laughed.

'Clean,' he snorted. 'What were you saying was nonsense, when I came in?'

'This belief that Gerry Doyle is some kind of ladykiller. Even Caroline Nolan. Caroline, with the whole of the university to choose from . . .'

'Caroline's here,' Dr Power said. 'There was a great tooting of cars and I saw her arriving up at the crossroads. She has a Morris Minor all of her own now. Anyway, she said she took it into her head to come to Castlebay, and I told her she picked a good night and that she was to come up here for a drink first. She got into a great fluster and said she'd have to wash her hair. I don't know why women go on so much about their hair. They're always washing it or having it done at the hairdresser's, and complaining if you don't know every rib of it that's been changed.'

'Well now we'll see if she's interested in that Gerry Doyle,' Molly said to David. 'And stop eating the cheese ones. If you want to eat anything, eat the ones with egg on them.'

Chrissie had given the dance a lot of thought. At one stage she was fully prepared to abandon it. A snobs' dance, an old people's dance. Catch Chrissie O'Brien dead at that? Then she saw that the feeling of the town was not the same as her own. In Dwyers' they discussed endlessly whether they should give mutton, beef or pork as a spot prize, and Kath and Peggy had even bought new dresses. Chrissie decided that she didn't want to be humbled watching Gerry Doyle ignore her. He only gave her the coolest of nods these days. She couldn't bear him to see her standing there as he whirled by with whatever new glamorous piece who had come to town. Even if he danced with her once or twice like he used to, that would be fine, but he had lost all interest. He didn't need Chrissie.

She sighed a lot when people asked her was she going to the Committee dance. 'Only if someone asks me,' she said. 'I'm too old to go to a dance without a partner.'

Kath and Peggy couldn't understand it. The *point* was to go without a partner and find a partner there. But Chrissie was adamant. Bumper Byrne the builder was buying meat and heard Chrissie O'Brien talking like this. He told his younger brother Maurice, or Mogsy as he had been called ever since anyone could remember. Mogsy came down to the shop.

'Will you be my partner for the Committee dance please?' he said across the counter. Mr Dwyer the butcher sighed with relief.

'What do you mean by being a partner exactly?'

'I mean I'll pay for you, I'll dance with you when you're not asked up by other people. I won't stand in your way if some fellow you want a spin around the floor with comes along, and I'll buy you minerals at the bar,' said Mogsy who wore his hat back to front and wasn't too bright.

Chrissie considered it. 'And what would *you* get out of it?' she asked ungraciously.

'I don't know.' Mogsy hadn't thought of it like that. 'I suppose I'd get the right to dance with you and put my arm around you and say you were my date for the night. Aren't you the best-looking girl in Castlebay?'

Chrissie smiled across the marble counter. 'Thank you very much, Mogsy, I'd be glad to come to the dance as your partner,' she said.

Best-looking girl in Castlebay. Well now. Not that anyone was saying Mogsy Byrne was bright or anything, but he wasn't *too* bad, and she would never be left standing, and she'd go in on his arm. That would show Gerry Doyle not everyone had to sit around and wait for him.

'Good, that's fixed then.' Mogsy was off.

'Have you a suit and everything?' she asked.

'I've a gorgeous suit,' he said.

'We'll show them, Mogsy,' she said.

Josie and Clare were putting on their make-up.

'It must be something to do with the colour of your lips to start with,' Josie said. 'Sari Peach looks quite a different colour on you than on me.'

They had bought one lipstick between them in Murphy's chemist. Mrs Murphy had said it was very unhygienic to share a lipstick, it could pass on germs. They had laughed the whole way home remembering how the whole school would share one lipstick at times and nobody had come out in a rash.

Clare wore a red corduroy skirt and a white frilly blouse: she had a red velvet ribbon on her hair. She dressed up in Josie's room because Chrissie had the bedroom at home commandeered. Josie had a lemon-coloured dress with a square neck back and front, trimmed with white broderie anglaise.

'Are you sure I don't look like a tank?' she asked for the tenth time.

'What am I going to do with you?' Clare wailed. 'You *don't* look like a tank, you haven't looked like a tank since you were twelve and you're nearly eighteen now. That's a third of your life you haven't looked like a tank and you still think you do!'

Josie laughed. 'I'm thinner than Emily and Rose. They hate it.'

'They hate everything. They're like posh versions of Chrissie. She says that I'm thin because of all the badness in me, it eats up the food from within, and you're thin because you've got worms.'

They fell about the room laughing. Which was worse, to have worms or inner badness?

'I don't think he has anyone else this summer, anyone serious that is,' Josie said, pouting at herself in the mirror.

'James?'

'Who else?'

'Not a sign of it. He and David have been playing golf a lot. Miss O'Hara told me. They call into her sometimes on the way there or back. No sign of women at all. His sister's arrived. Lady Caroline. I saw her rushing into reception downstairs asking for a loan of a hairdryer.'

'Did they give her one?' Josie wanted to befriend the beloved's sister.

'I think so, there was a great fuss – you know the way Lady Caroline talks, she expects things done.'

'I hope they got her one.'

'I don't, I'd like her to have rats' tails for once instead of looking like an advertisement.'

'I think she fancies Gerry Doyle.'

219

'Tell her to join the queue,' Clare said, applying more Vaseline to her eyelashes to get them to curl.

'I was just thinking,' Josie said. 'Suppose I won the spot prize we gave, you know the one the hotel gave.'

'Well, what would be so funny?'

'It's a weekend, all expenses paid, staying here. I could have a room with a sea view and have Emily bring me my breakfast in bed.'

Chrissie was just ahead of them at the ticket box. She was arm in arm with Mogsy Byrne who was in charge of the churns when the farmers brought the milk in. Tonight, he wore a suit. He looked a bit drunk already.

'I would have thought that the elegant Miss Clare O'Brien and her friend Miss Josie Dillon wouldn't be seen paying for their own tickets to the dance,' Chrissie said loudly.

She looked awful, Clare thought. After all that work and all that flinging of clothes and make-up around the bedroom. The pink satin dress was much too tight, the white cardigan was grubby and the glittery diamante jewellery looked flashy, like the bright red lipstick and heavy white powder. Still, other fellows were giving her admiring glances. Maybe she was more suitably dressed than Clare, perhaps the blouse and skirt were a bit dowdy, a bit schoolgirlish.

They were playing 'The Yellow Rose of Texas'; the ballroom was festive, with balloons and decorations all around, and a big banner saying that the Castlebay Committee welcomed everyone and thanked them for their support. There was a huge table, groaning with gifts, on the stage near the band, and a spotlight going around picking out lucky couples who would then be given a gift. The instructions were that not too many should be given early, and only the inferior ones. As Clare and Josie came in they saw a couple in the spotlight being presented with a small talcum powder and bath cubes in a presentation box. There were much greater things to come. They were heading across to a corner which they thought was a good vantage point when they were both asked to dance at once. This was a good omen, they thought, as they were whirled out on to the floor.

Dick Dillon said he was great at the waltz but he wasn't going to make a public display of himself over this jiving, and rock and roll.

Angela said the waltz was her forte too, just so long as they didn't twirl too fast. As luck would have it the band had announced 'Tales from the Vienna Woods' just as they came in.

'I suppose you'll want to go to the ladies' cloakroom,' Dick grumbled.

'Why would I?' Angela asked and they were off, round and round, bending and swooping, Dick looking over his left shoulder and Angela looking to her left. He held her firmly in the small of the back and didn't slip, even though the floor had been treated to make it shine. Angela's beige silk dress, the one she had bought for Emer's wedding, swirled round. If Emer could see this! It is *ridiculous*, she thought, I am a ludicrous figure. And she smiled to herself as she saw admiring glances, not laughter. She saw Dr Power pointing her out to Mr Nolan. That would have been her party if she hadn't agreed to come with this madman.

The madman in question spoke out of the side of his mouth. 'I think we're showing them a thing or two,' he hissed.

'I'd say they'll clear the floor any minute for the two of us to do a demonstration,' Angela said, and at that moment the spotlight landed on them and the band leader announced that they had won a leg of lamb kindly presented by Messrs Dwyer, the premier butcher in Castlebay.

Everybody was in good humour, and suntanned and cheerful. Simon, the handsome lifeguard, who wore a pullover tied casually round his shoulders, was talking to Frank Conway who was a guard, and very tall with a back like a ramrod. A lot of the girls were eyeing them with interest. Frank Conway kept glancing at the door. 'I was watching to see if I could see Fiona Doyle coming in,' he explained.

Simon smiled. 'I bet a lot of people are. But I wouldn't be surprised if the guard dog hasn't let her out.'

'The what?'

'Her brother. He is like a guard dog. He barks if anyone comes near. It's fine for him to do what he likes, but she can have no fun.'

Frank was disappointed but he wanted to stand up for Fiona. 'In a way, Gerry's right, you can't have *girls* doing what they like – it wouldn't be right.'

'You're not like that with your sister Bernie. She's a free agent.' Simon glanced at Bernie Conway, smooching with one of the visitors.

'Yes, well.' Frank was irritated now on every score. When the dance was over he went up to Bernie and invited her for the next waltz.

'This *is* a surprise,' she said, not altogether pleased.

'I think you should behave in a more ladylike way in public.'

'I think you should go and stick your fat head in a bucket,' said Bernie, and walked off the floor. Simon saw her free, and asked her back to dance.

'My brother is mad. Stark staring mad,' she said.

'Let's not talk about your brother,' said Simon, holding her very close to him and running his hand up and down her back.

Gerry Doyle never *asked* anyone to dance. He always seemed to be beside the girl that he wanted when the music started, and he would smile and hold out his hand. He asked Josie Dillon first, and she was glad to be seen out on the floor by James Nolan, who had just come in. Josie had noticed that Caroline's dark hair looked nicely set, so the hotel must have been able to find her a hair dryer all right. Gerry was a terrific dancer of course, and she was glad that she and Clare had spent some time learning the Twist at the beginning of the summer. The world was divided between those who could and couldn't do it. Gerry had probably been *born* knowing how to do it.

He admired her dress, he said it was a lovely sunny colour, that she and Clare O'Brien looked the classiest girls in the whole ballroom. She asked would Fiona be here, but he said she had a summer flu. They both agreed that Uncle Dick had turned out to be a demon dancer. He hadn't been off the floor since he came in and insisted on doing formal quicksteps to the rock and roll numbers.

James and Caroline Nolan had arrived, and Gerry had seen them. He escorted Josie back to where he had found her with a big smile. 'I wish they all danced like you, Josie Dillon, the Ginger Rogers of Castlebay.' Josie was pink with delight. She was about to tell Clare, but at that moment Clare was whisked off by Uncle Dick. Josie could have died of mortification. Why couldn't Uncle Dick just sit down like other old people, or venture gently into a foxtrot or something? Why did he have to make a fool of her by asking her friend to dance? The band announced a series of Latin American numbers beginning with the 'Blue Tango'.

'I'm not great at it, not a semi-professional like yourself,' Clare had confessed.

'Listen to me once, you're meant to be a bright girl. It's one step rock back, two steps rock back, three steps rock back. Repeat that.'

They hadn't started to dance yet. Clare repeated it.

'Right, hold on tight and follow me, none of this independent doing fandangos on your own.'

He stood beside her but facing in a different direction, he stretched their arms out as if they were pretending to be scarecrows in a field. He waited for the beat and they were off. The man was a wizard. She began to enjoy it and relaxed when it came to the turns. She noticed other people admiring them too, and saw from one part of the room Miss O'Hara, doing a very amateurish version of the same thing with Dr Power, smiling proudly towards her . . . Gerry Doyle – dancing with Bernie Conway – was looking at her in delight. David Power, dancing with Caroline Nolan, called her attention to the spectacular couple. Clare would have preferred it to have been a younger and more

223

dashing man but she forgot about that after a while. Especially when they went into the cha cha '. . . rock forward, rock backward, side close side . . .' he said and after a few bars she had all the confidence in the world. They won a spot prize too. A bottle of Jameson Ten Year Old.

'You can have that, my drinking days are over,' Dick Dillon said.

'Your dancing days sure aren't,' Clare said and went, flushed with success, to leave the bottle in the ladies' cloakroom and get a ticket for it.

The Committee were very pleased. They had charged a slightly higher price for admission, which was justified by the many gifts which would be given away, but it also kept out some of the riff-raff. Not *all* the riff-raff, they noticed, as they saw Mogsy Byrne throwing Chrissie O'Brien around in the way most calculated to show her knickers to the crowd. Still.

There was a brisk trade at the mineral bar. Oranges and lemons and ginger beers were passing with speed across the counter, and there was a percentage on all that for the Committee, too. No real drink could be served in the dance hall, on this night any more than any other. Dancers wanting a break to visit a pub applied for a pass-out card, and a good few had small bottles in hip pockets.

The band, which was there for the season, had dressed itself up to mark the special nature of the night. The men wore rosettes in their buttonholes, and Lovely Helena, the vocalist, wore a big rose at the waist of her tulle and net dress.

Out in the street, youngsters who were considered well below the age tried to peer in and every time the inner door swung open they caught a glimpse of the glitter inside. Through the ventilators the sound of the singing and the clapping of the announcement of yet another prize being delivered were heard, and then blasts from the band again. During the summer people became used to the sound of the dance hall. It was as familiar as the waves crashing on the shore, background music.

Sometimes people shook their heads with amazement and said wasn't it extraordinary that Lionel Donelly of all people would have had the foresight to build a dance hall, to borrow the money and build a big monstrosity that everyone said would be a white elephant. Now there were people driving to it from far and wide. Lionel, who never passed an exam in his life, had gone to England to learn the building trade and learned that people were building dance halls.

Clare went back to the dance floor. She thought she saw David Power coming towards her, but before he was near enough Gerry Doyle reached out his hand for her. It was a slow smoochy dance and he didn't bother holding her at arm's length for a few bars, he put his arms around her at once and she laid her cheek against his. They were the same height. She had worn her flat shoes.

The lights were dimmer for this number, the sparkles of the glittering globe cast a thousand little shines on people. 'Once I had a secret love,' sang the girl in the miles of net dress at the microphone. People sang the words softly to each other, oddly assorted people like David Power who sang them into Josie's ear because he hadn't got to Clare O'Brien before Romeo. James Nolan sang them into Bernie Conway's ear, because when he saw Gerry Doyle dancing with her, he thought she must be something special. Dick Dillon and Angela didn't sing them at all because they were concentrating on the curly bits and side chassis. Gerry didn't sing them because he didn't need to, and Clare had her eyes tightly closed.

At the last dance Josie was happy because finally James had seen her and flung her into a spirited version of 'California Here I Come'; and a great many other people were happy too. The Committee had made a great deal of money, the dance had been a social success, and all the people who had given spot prizes were pleased with the advertising.

'I have a caravan,' Gerry Doyle told Clare. They had

225

danced together three times, almost enough to be considered a lifetime commitment for Gerry.

'A what?'

'A caravan. All of my own. I'm looking after it for people. They only come at the weekend.'

'Really, that's nice,' Clare said innocently.

'So?'

'So what?'

'Will we go there? You and me?'

'Now?' she asked, her heart beginning to beat faster.

'Sure.'

There was a pause. He was looking straight at her. She must say yes or no. She was not going to make any blustering excuses.

'No,' she said. 'Thanks all the same.'

His eyes showed nothing, there wasn't a hint of persuading her to change her mind.

'Right,' he said. 'Goodnight sweetheart.'

Before her eyes, he went over to Caroline Nolan. She heard him sound surprised to see her, as if he hadn't known she was in the dance hall all night.

Clare watched Caroline smiling delightedly as Gerry suggested something. It was too far away to hear, but when he put his arm around Caroline's shoulder and they walked off together, she knew it had to do with his having a caravan.

Dr Power said he would give Angela a lift in to collect her mother. He never made that journey into the town without driving people in one direction or the other; he was the kindest man that ever lived.

'I saw you leaping about in great style with Dick Dillon,' he teased her.

'Well would you have believed it? The man could have medals for it. I never got such a surprise.'

'He's a very nice fellow, Dick. Never got a proper chance in that hotel. The old mother always preferred his brother. Still, he consoled himself fairly spectacularly during his day.'

Angela smiled, that was one way of describing a man who had been as heavy a drinker as her own father. Of course, Dick Dillon had been able to have the money to do it in comfort, and the trips to Dublin to be dried out, and now he had stopped. He had seen her home and come in after the dance; she had made tea and bacon sandwiches, and they had talked long into the night.

'What he needs is a steadying hand, Angela,' Dr Power said.

'Am I going to be hearing this for the rest of my life?'

'Probably. They'll say you could do worse. He's not a bad catch, sensible too nowadays, all the wild oats sown. Oh, they'll say that.'

'But it's not a question of catching, sure it's not? I always thought that if it happened it would be two people suddenly discovering they were more interested in each other than anything else. Not a *catch*.'

'It *should* be like that,' Dr Power said, negotiating a herd of cows and the boy who was halfheartedly moving them along the road.

'How about you?' She felt impertinent, but he could always laugh it off if he didn't want to answer.

'I met Molly at a dance in Dublin on my twenty-fifth birthday. She had a red dress on and she had her head back laughing and I thought to myself that I'd love her to be laughing like that at things I said. And that was it, I suppose. I went after her relentlessly. It was nothing to do with her being a catch, or me being one.'

'And she did go on laughing, didn't she?'

'Yes, mainly. Sometimes it's a bit quiet and dull here in the winter, and I wish she had more people to meet that would entertain her. Or that we had more children. If you have only one you concentrate on him too much. I'm always thinking about his medical studies and Molly's always wondering about his meals and damp clothes and what he does with himself in Dublin. If we had half a dozen it would be more spread out.'

'But David's sensible, isn't he, and he's as bright as paint.'

'He is, and we've managed to move very successfully from the notion of you and Dick Dillon.'

'He's an old man, with nothing on his mind except his long-lost days of drinking and sometimes the thought of an olde tyme waltz.'

'He's not ten years older than you. He's a fine man and he's lonely. Don't throw the idea aside too easily, Angela, girl.'

He was being serious. She decided not to make any more jokes.

'It was funny Fiona Doyle going off to London in the middle of the busy season to do that photography course.'

'It was bad timing, but I suppose she had to go when the opportunity came up.' Dr Power looked straight ahead of him at the road and the small white houses which broke the monotony of the hedges as they went along. Sometimes it was hard to be a country doctor and to hold the heartbeats and consciences of everyone in the parish. He knew only too well what bad timing it was for Fiona Doyle to have to go to London.

There had been a haze over the sea when Clare got up at six-thirty. It would be another hot day. A scorcher. Well, that's what they all wanted: eighty hot days with a little rain at night just to keep the farmers happy. Clare picked up all the litter from the corner of the shop which they had cleared for people to stand around having lemonades and fizzy orange, ham sandwiches and chocolate biscuits after the dance. It was good business: there was nowhere else to go except the chip van. But it was wearying clearing up in the morning. She put the returnable bottles all together in a crate, and stuffed the others into the rubbish bin. She opened the doors to let the fresh air in and glanced up the street with its white and coloured houses all still asleep. The winter painting done in Castlebay always looked at its best on an early summer morning; the town looked so clean, like sugared almonds. The pink of Conway's post office and the lime-green walls of Miss O'Flaherty's looked just right.

Clare went back to put on the kettle; her mother would be up soon, and not long after that her father would be down moving boxes, worrying over supplies and only just remembering to pause and shave before the early morning caravan people came in looking for their breakfast materials.

The kettle was boiling as Agnes came downstairs. Before she could reach for her shop coat which hung on the back of the kitchen door, Clare saw with a start how thin she had grown, and how tired.

'Why don't you have a bit of a rest today? I can cope with it.'

'*Rest*? On a day like today – it's going to be one of the busiest yet. Are you mad?' her mother wanted to know.

'You look very tired, that's all.'

'Of course I look tired, and Tommy Craig looks tired up in the bar and Young Mrs Dillon looks tired. Lord God, Clare, when would we not look tired if not in the middle of the season?'

'Shush shush, I'm not attacking you, Mam, I wanted to know if you could have a couple of hours more rest that's all.'

Agnes softened. 'No, I'll be all right when I've had a cup of tea, nobody looks anything until they've had a cup of tea.' Her thin face smiled a bit, but she wouldn't even sit down to drink it. She was hurrying into the shop and sure enough as soon as she was behind the counter the door pinged and the first customer arrived.

It was non-stop all day. A lot of people seemed to take advantage of the clear blue skies to plan picnics, and Clare was busy cutting sandwiches and wrapping up ice creams in several layers of newspapers.

Caroline Nolan was early. She ran in from her little Morris Minor, which spluttered and made noises outside.

'Picnic things,' she said to Clare, barely politely.

'For how many?' Clare asked.

'I don't know. Can I take things and if we don't need them bring them back?'

'No,' Clare said.

'What?'

'I said you can't. Suppose you brought back tomatoes or bananas that had been out in the sun all day – who else would want them?'

'I meant tins, or things that wouldn't spoil.'

'Why don't you just work out how many might be going?' Clare was impatient with this glowing girl, all fresh and summery in a white dress with big red spots; she looked so clean and awake and lively compared to Clare in her faded dress and her tired thin mother in the yellow shop coat.

'Maybe you can help me?' Caroline had decided to be charming. 'You see, a friend suggested we take a drive out to this place where you see seals, and I'm to provide a picnic. He, my friend, would bring a bottle of wine. And I'm not sure whether he meant us plural, like my brother and David, or whether he meant us singular, just me. You see my problem?'

'No,' said Clare. 'Ask him. Ask him did he mean you singular or you plural, then you'll know.'

Caroline left the shop.

Half an hour later she was back. 'He said he meant you plural,' she announced.

'Bad luck,' Clare said, and without being asked made a selection of the freshly made ham sandwiches and cheese sandwiches, apples, bananas, oranges, a packet of choc-olate biscuits and four bottles of fizzy orange.

Caroline took it in silence and packed it into the boot of her car.

Gerry came in for cigarettes a bit later.

'I thought you'd be off on your picnic,' Clare said.

'I'm going to join them later, I gave them directions to get to the seals. Why don't you come with us?'

'How can I? I have to work here. Anyway, I'm not asked.'

'You are, I'm asking you.'

Clare laughed. 'No thanks. How can any of us take a day like today off? How can *you* take today off, come to think of it?'

'Why do I pay someone to take pictures for me, if it's not to give me a day off. Come on, be a devil.'

'Stop it, you know I can't.' She was annoyed now, she wished he'd go. 'One day out of the summer? One sunny day?' He wasn't joking.

'Go away Gerry, go away.' Clare was laughing but her voice had a steely ring. 'We are going to take care of our business, even if others we wouldn't mention are letting theirs go down the plug-hole.' And anyway, Clare told herself, there was no point in going out with that gang without the proper ammunition. Clare had no crisp cotton dress with big red dots on it, Clare had no golden suntan, she had a faded mauve dress and long white legs in old-fashioned sandals. Hell, she wasn't going to compete with Caroline unless she had a chance of winning, and if she wanted the attentions of Gerry Doyle she wouldn't look for them now.

The good spell was set to last. In the days after the picnic, Clare decided that she hated sunshine. For other people it meant that the holiday dream was coming true, it meant a healthy out-of-doors life. For the young couples in their tents it was pure magic, for the Nolans and their friends just more long days lost in sandhills on seal beaches, on golf courses, and racing in and out of the waves. For children it meant rushing into the shop asking for a bottle of fizzy orange, open please and with three straws. But for Clare the sun just meant it was time to take the cakes and things that might melt from the window, and to make sure the stocks of ice cream were ready for Jim and Ben to cope with.

Gerry came in. 'I've a message for you, come on, up to the post office, now! Old Ma Conway said there was a phone message, they're going to ring again in fifteen minutes, well ten now, come on.'

Clare's heart was thumping as she ran up Church Street with Gerry. The hotel and the chemist and the dance-hall and the hardware shop passed in a blur. And then they were in Conway's.

'Oh you found her?' Mrs Conway looked disapprovingly over her glasses.

Please may it not be about Tommy. Oh Please God, I'll say the thirty days prayer, please Our Lady, I'll begin the thirty days prayer *today* if it's not some awful thing about Tommy.

'You must be very nervous,' Gerry said sympathetically.

Her heart gave another jump. 'How do you know, I mean what do you mean?'

'Your results,' he said simply. 'That's what it is, isn't it?'

It was. It was the convent, incoherent with delight – in all their years they had never been so proud. Clare had done nine subjects on her Leaving Certificate and she had got honours in *all* of them except mathematics; but of course she had passed that safely. And now wasn't there every chance that she would be called for the Murray Prize interview? Three of the sisters were starting a special novena today and Clare could be assured that the whole Community would remember her every day at Mass. She could hardly see Mrs Conway's pinched face, forcing itself to be congratulatory, having heard every word. Gerry lifted her off her feet and swung her round three times.

'Eight honours, eight honours, hell's bells and spiders' ankles!' he shouted.

'*Eight honours!*' Clare screamed. '*Eight!*'

'Well I must say I think congratulations are in order . . .' Mrs Conway said, her face pursed at the horseplay.

'I must tell Miss O'Hara, now,' Clare said. 'Now, this minute.'

'I'll drive you up in the van.'

She hesitated for a moment.

'I won't come in, I know you want to tell her on your own.'

Angela was out in front of the cottage, watering the scarlet geraniums. The sun shone in her eyes and she had to put up her hand to shield them as the van screeched to a halt. Clare tumbled out the door before it had properly stopped.

'Eight, Miss O'Hara, *eight!*' she shouted excitedly, and

Angela put down the water jug and ran towards her. She clutched the thin body – trembling with excitement – to her in a big awkward hug of delight.

They had both forgotten Gerry, who sat motionless in his van watching them with his dark handsome eyes.

The whole town knew by evening. Josie had been so excited when she heard that she put the lid on her typewriter and said she was taking some time off to celebrate. Agnes and Tom O'Brien were bewildered with pleasure and worn out shaking people's hands across the counter and taking praise on behalf of their bright, hard-working daughter. Dr Power was going past on his way to the caravan site and stopped to pay his respects. Sergeant McCormack had got wind of it, and it wasn't long before Father O'Dwyer's little car stopped outside O'Brien's as well. It was a miracle that anything was bought or sold, or money taken or change given in that shop all day with the comings and goings.

'Will you come to the dance to celebrate tonight?' Gerry said.

'Ah, there'd be too much of a crowd there, all the Caroline Nolans and all,' she said, smiling at him.

'We could go somewhere where there wouldn't be,' he grinned back.

'I don't think so, don't change any of your own plans.'

'There are eighty nights in the summer,' Gerry said. 'If you don't come tonight you'll come another night.'

She had a lovely night. She had a drink with Dick Dillon who taught her how to make a drink called a Pussyfoot which had no alcohol in it but sort of fooled you into thinking it had. Josie gave her a yellow blouse and a yellow ribbon to match it for her hair – she had been saving it as a surprise. Josie had a date with James Nolan and was in seventh heaven herself: they were going to the pictures and he had said he would meet her in the queue. She swore to tell Clare everything that happened and had worn a dress with a high collar in case he might start to fumble and she would have to decide whether to let him or not.

233

Clare walked down the Cliff Road. It was sunset and people could be seen indoors, finishing their supper or just sitting around with the dishes still on the table before heading off for the night's entertainment. It had been so long in arriving, this day. She was going to savour every minute of it.

It was getting dark now and she shivered a little in her new yellow blouse. Josie and James Nolan were well into the Main Feature and who knew what else at the cinema. Chrissie and Mogsy Byrne had gone down the sandhills, she knew that because she had seen Chrissie changing her slip and getting out her good knickers, the ones with lace on them. Gerry Doyle was in his caravan. No, she was *not* going to the caravan park. She would go up to the amusements and have two rides on the bumpers and then if she didn't meet anyone she would come home and pitch Chrissie's things to the other side of the room and go to bed. She would *not* go to the caravan park tonight.

There was never a greater demand for space than this summer. Somehow the word had spread that there was fun galore in Castlebay. Not all the visitors were desirable of course; this would be discussed by the Castlebay Committee during the winter. There had been a very noisy element with tents, and the dirt of the caravan people had to be seen to be believed. Dr Power said they weren't to be blamed until somebody put up lavatories and washbasins for them, and arranged proper bins and a rubbish collection.

There was hardly a day that Angela and her mother weren't approached by passing visitors asking for a night's lodging.

To her surprise her mother had said they should do it. Everyone else in the town made a profit out of the summer, why shouldn't they?

Angela washed sheets and tidied up the back room. Why not? It would be a few quid, and people were so grateful. She would point out that she had a mother who wasn't well and couldn't have anyone noisy. But it had been fine.

First a couple of girls who had crept in like mice after the dance, stayed four days and had both said that Gerry Doyle was the most gorgeous thing they had ever seen in real life. Up to now they had only seen his likes on the cinema screen. Then there had been a married couple, a quiet pair in their forties, dull, nothing to say to anyone or each other. Angela pitied them, and was puzzled when they said it had been a lovely visit and they would come back next year. Then two lads from Dublin, with accents you could cut, roaring laughing at nothing and saying it was the best fun they'd had in years. The night they had got very drunk they had the decency to sleep in the shed rather than trying to find their room. Angela told them they were marvellous and refused to charge them for the night's accommodation.

'You won't suffer for that, Missus,' one of them said. 'We'll send you our mates.'

And indeed there was a never-ending supply of Dubliners, lads from building sites, from factories, and then the two housepainters, Paddy and Con. God, they'd never seen the like of the place, they were going to have a swim immediately, they were sticking to themselves with the sweat after the train and the bus, and the sea looked a treat.

'Be careful,' Angela called automatically. 'There's a very high tide, it's treacherous at the end of August. They call it a spring tide.'

'Oh, you couldn't drown us,' called Paddy and Con.

She heard the cry about half an hour later. It was like a wail growing and fading, louder and softer. And she knew there was someone drowning down on the strand. She had been buying the bacon and eggs for their tea in O'Brien's. She had her bicycle with its carrier basket parked outside. Automatically she found her feet heading for the cliff top and there saw everyone clustered and pointing out beyond the caves and the fishing rocks. The waves were enormous.

On the edge of the water there was a commotion. Five or six men were trying to hold back the struggling figure

235

of Simon. Ropes and lifebelts had been thrown, to no avail. Angela's stomach lurched when she saw a hand raised desperately, far, far out, and beside it the head of someone else. There were two of them. She dropped the bacon out of her hands, and she knew that it was her lodgers, Paddy and Con.

They were shouting at Simon on the beach. 'You've been out twice, you've been battered, you can't do any more, it's suicide. You've done all you can. Simon, have sense.'

Simon's side was bleeding from where he had been scratched against the rocks.

'Let me go! Let me go!' His face was working and his eyes were full of tears. Gerry Doyle was gripping him, holding his arm behind him in a lock.

'What's the point in getting you killed? Look at your back, you've been thrown on the rocks twice. What are you trying to prove? You've done all you can, for Christ's sake, you warned them – you went out after them once and brought them back in.'

'They're new, they were all white,' Simon wailed, 'let me go.'

There was a great cry from the people who could see the figures.

'One's holding onto a rock, he'll be all right. Look! Look!'

But in seconds a huge wave pulled the small figure, its white arms flailing, down into the sea.

Helplessly the crowd watched. There was no boat, no swimmer, no throw of a lifebelt that would reach Paddy and Con. They would die in front of a thousand people.

Father O'Dwyer had been sent for, and as if by reflex, the people standing near him went down on their knees.

Father O'Dwyer called out the rosary and the swell of Holy Marys increased. Simon stopped struggling eventually and sat with his head in his hands, sobbing. Gerry Doyle sat beside him with an arm protectively around his shoulder.

There was no sign of the figures now, the waves kept

crashing as if they were unaware of what they had done. Men went for strong drinks, women gathered up their children and issued useless, angry warnings about the need to stay in shallow waters.

Clare had come out too. She felt a hand reaching for hers and to her surprise, it was David Power.

'Would it have been quick do you think?' she asked.

David shook his head.

'Oh,' she said in a small voice.

'I don't know. Not the first bit, not the being swept out, they'd have known what was going to happen.'

'I suppose so.'

'I have to go down there,' he said. 'With my father.'

'When?'

'When the tide comes in tonight, they'll be washed up.'

She was full of pity, and warmth, and she squeezed his hand.

'I don't *have* to, but I will. He just said that he'd like me to, and anyway I'll be a doctor soon myself. I'll have to then. It's just . . . it's just . . .'

'I know, it's just when its your own beach.'

He smiled at her gratefully. 'They might come in sooner.' He was full of dread.

'Would that mean they'd get battered up more?'

'I don't know.'

There was a great sound from the beach again and people were shouting and pointing. On the side of the beach near the caves, where it seemed calm, there was something that looked like a person. And near it was something similar. There was no movement, no waving or swimming. Then you could see they were face down. Bobbing on the water like the airbeds that they sold up at the top of Church Street. They didn't look like people: they looked like a bad joke.

Clare turned away, suddenly feeling a bit faint. This is what being dead looked like. She had almost forgotten she was still holding David Power's hand and when she turned it was towards him. She put her head on his chest. He put his arm round her shoulder. Then she pulled away a little.

'You've got to go down,' she said.

Gerry Doyle and two other fellows passed, helping Simon up the steps. The lifeguard's side had been examined on the beach by Dr Power, who had asked Gerry to get him away as soon as possible. Dr Power didn't want Simon there when the bodies came in. They would float in with the last minutes of the incoming tide.

Gerry Doyle looked at Clare evenly. 'If you've finished canoodling, you might go to your friend, Miss O'Hara – she's the one who's going to have to cope with it all and go through their things.'

'Why?' Clare cried, shocked. 'Why on earth will she have to do that?'

'Because they were staying with her, they're from her house, that's why.' Gerry put his arm under Simon's and continued to shove and push him along the street.

Clare saw Angela, standing by herself with her hands over her mouth in disbelief. Her hair blowing loose behind her, she was looking down on the beach while the crowds stepped into the shallow water and pulled the bodies of Paddy and Con on to the sand. Father O'Dwyer was there with his holy water, and his soutane, his long black skirt flapping in the breeze. Dr Power was urging people to keep the children well away and leaning on the chests of the dead men in the futile hope that there would be any life left in them. And in a minute beside him was his tall fair-haired son, helping too, looking calm and in control; not the trembling boy who had been standing moments earlier with his hand in Clare's.

Clare turned away from the scene on the beach. Gerry was quite right. If she was to do anything to help it should be for Miss O'Hara.

They talked about nothing else for days. The dance was cancelled that night as a mark of respect, and so was the cinema. They didn't know what to do at the amusements so they compromised by not playing the juke box. Clare and Angela had found an address amongst the few shabby belongings of Paddy and Con, and the Guards in Dublin were asked to go around and inform the families.

It had been strangely unreal for everyone and the greatest sympathy in the place was given to Simon. Nobody knew the families of Paddy and Con, any more than anyone had really met the lads in the short couple of hours they had spent in Castlebay between getting off the bus and being taken out of the sea. Simon's easy laughter had disappeared now. He was a very serious young man. He didn't go to the dance in the evenings and he had little time for high jinks on the beach. He sat nervously on a high stool that he had made himself from boxes, and he shouted angrily at children who played ball in his line of vision. One night in Craig's Bar he lost his temper and said that the Castlebay Committee were totally irresponsible encouraging people to come there with their plans for fairy lights and big car parks. They should build a pier and breakwater, they should enclose a swimming pool and only permit people who were known to be strong swimmers to venture beyond it. You wouldn't let people play with matches and jump through bonfires would you, he had said in a high nervous voice. They forgave him over and over, they told him of the children he had saved, of the cramp victim he had rescued, of the artificial respiration to the girl who swallowed so much water. They praised him for the countless others he had made safe by his daily parades up and down the beach edge. But his eyes got darker and they knew they would never see him again when the summer was over.

Angela and Clare didn't talk about it, not after the first night when they had found the address and folded all the clothes neatly into the two shabby grip bags. Talking about it only made things worse. Instead they rehearsed feverishly the kind of questions that Clare might face on the first Thursday in September when she had to meet the Murray Prize Committee.

They planned her appearance down to the last detail. She must look in need of their gift but not too needy. She must look quiet enough to be studious but not so quiet that she looked dull. Neat enough to be thought respectable but not so drab as to be thought dreary. Her good marks would impress them automatically, her grasp of current affairs was masterly, her simple direct explanation about coming from a family which was anxious for her success but not in itself academic was so patently honest it would have to convince them. She was not a fly-by-night either, she had always been ambitious, hadn't she got the scholarship to secondary school at the age of twelve?

In the end Angela said she was satisfied. There was literally no more they could do to prepare for this event. They would end up making her so nervous that she would not be able to speak at all.

Angela lent her a navy jumper and the good silk scarf that James Nolan's mother had given her all those years ago. It had lain idly in a drawer and this was an ideal opportunity to give it an outing. She wore her good blue skirt and a pair of Josie's shoes. Her hair was to be shining and in a pony tail, only the barest hint of make-up, like a trace of Sari Peach lipstick, rubbed on and rubbed off again.

If school hadn't started, Angela said, she would have gone into the town and waited nearby until Clare came out. It would have made it better for both of them.

But term would have started. Angela's twelfth year in the convent. For a woman who was going to stay twelve months, things had escalated. She felt no bitterness towards Sean about that now. It had been her own decision for a long, long time. She didn't even rebel at the thought of his unctuously clerical tones when he gave that advice. She had no more hate for Sean and the differences between what he preached and what he did. It had been a long time, teaching beside Mother Immaculata, certainly. But it had been a longer time for Sean in waiting for a laicization that never came.

Gerry Doyle called to the O'Brien house the night before.

'I have a job tomorrow, so I'll be going to town. I can give you a lift.'

'That's very nice, but I was getting the bus. The timing's all right for once and even if it's a bit late I'll be fine.'

'I'm going to the door,' he said. 'The Committee have asked me to photograph them and the shortlist of candidates. So go on the bus if you like but the lift is there.'

There were two girls and five boys. Gerry arranged them according to height and took several shots. He was able to relax them without having to clown around. It was a gift, Clare thought as she watched him. He never called her by her name. He was professional. It mightn't look good for her to know him, he was making sure she had nothing special about her one way or the other. He left her free to examine the competition. The girl was taller than Clare; she looked older and very studious. She had bushy, badly-combed hair and glasses. She could have been quite nice-looking but she had made no effort at all. There was a tear in her tunic – she wore a school uniform, for heaven's sake – and her shoes were down at heel. Anxiously Clare looked down at Josie's smart shoes and the neat cuffs of Miss O'Hara's good cardigan. Maybe she looked cheap and superficial?

'Makes us feel a bit like cattle,' said a small boy, who didn't look old enough to have done his Intermediate Certificate let alone his Leaving. But Clare was not deceived: this was the most dangerous one, she felt sure. Two of the others were clerical students: they wore black jerseys and were more reserved. There was a nervy boy who would irritate the committee and one who spoke after such a long pause each time, the interview would surely be over by the time he had answered anything.

The girl was nice. She had been at a convent about fifty miles away. She asked Clare how many honours she had got in her Leaving. Angela had prepared her for that and told her not to boast, and if at all possible to keep her great score to herself.

'I don't think they go on that any more,' she said. 'That's what I've heard, anyway. Nowadays it's not the number you have it's what they think of you.'

241

The boy who kept drumming his fingers looked up startled at this. 'Is that right? Then I'll be lost. I got six honours, I thought that was what was going to sail me through.' He laughed nervously, showing some broken teeth.

Clare thanked Miss O'Hara again and again in her mind. Miss O'Hara had beaten this nervous laugh out of her long ago.

They talked easily enough until the lady chairman came to address them. She was a self-important woman in a tweed suit; she had a huge chest and looked so like a pigeon, Clare was not afraid of her resounding voice. They were to be taken in alphabetical order. Clare was second last; the nervy boy was O'Sullivan, and he would be last.

She kept her mind calm. She refused to get up and go to the lavatory even when the others did suddenly. She knew she had eaten or drunk nothing that would make her need to go; she had eaten barley sugar sweets just as she had done when she was twelve and Miss O'Hara had been training her to get the scholarship to school. That had not been terrifying, neither would this. She had eight honours in her Leaving Certificate. She was the equal of any child in Ireland.

Gerry Doyle was told he would be needed in two hours. They would have come to their decision then. That surprised him. He'd thought they wouldn't decide there and then on the day. But it was better that she knew today. He didn't think she'd make it. Just from looking at them he thought the big untidy girl or the small boy who looked like a child prodigy were the most likely. Those were the kind of faces you saw in a newspaper with a paragraph underneath saying what they had won.

He came back in good time and sat in his van reading the local paper. There were three of his pictures in it this week: a wedding, a sand-castle competition and the foundation stone for the new wing of the Brothers' school in Castlebay.

The awful bossy woman with the big chest rapped on the window for him as if he were the gardener and called

242

him in to photograph the winner of the Murray Scholarship to University College, Dublin, Clare O'Brien.

Angela O'Hara asked Dr Power if she could have a word with him in his car. He was practically home and suggested she come into the surgery. She didn't want to. The house then, and have a sherry? No. It was something a bit unethical she wanted to ask, better to ask him on neutral ground. Unethical? His big bushy eyebrows rose. Angela? Nothing desperately unethical, she assured him, a fake doctor's cert, that was all.

'Get into the car,' he said. 'This is serious. If I'm going to be struck off we'd better make sure it's worth while.'

She laughed at his kind, worried face and told him what she wanted. She'd like to go to Dublin for a few days. Her best friend Emer had just had a baby, and now they wanted her to be godmother to the baby. Young Clare was going up to Dublin to start life at university, and it was a great opportunity to show her round a bit – not be a mother hen but just show her a few things so that she wasn't a total gobdaw when term started. It would be lovely to have a few days off school, but she couldn't ask for it. It was unheard of. Immaculata would have a blue fit. Was it possible that Dr Power could say she had something which meant going to Dublin?

He looked at her over his glasses, doubtfully.

'I never asked you before. I never in all my years up in that place asked for one day off.'

'You misunderstand me. Of course I'll do it. I think you should have a fortnight in Dublin . . . I'm only trying to think what you might have.'

She gave him a look full of gratitude. 'Would we say it was in my womb? That should embarrass Immaculata so much she'd shut up about it.'

'Yes, but there's no reason why you wouldn't go into the County Hospital if it were just a D and C,' he objected. 'It would have to be something that needed going to a specialist for or some kind of specialist hospital. A skin disease?' he suggested brightly.

243

Angela was doubtful. 'She might keep moving away from me and telling people not to use the same cups at our tea break.'

'Blood tests, you're a bit anaemic and I want it checked further.'

'You're a great sport,' she said. 'I was hoping I could rely on you.'

'I'm not doing it because I'm a sport. I'm doing it because you *do* need a break. I'd feel quite justified signing a certificate saying you are under great pressure and you need a change and a rest, but of course, if you wrote that to any of that lot of beauties up in the convent, they'd think you were naving a nervous breakdown and they wouldn't let you back again. Blood tests it will have to be.'

Emer and Kevin were delighted to see them.

They had to fight the nuns and nurses off to get baby Daniel home from the nursing home without having him baptized. They explained that the godmother had to come from the country but there had been terror that the baby's immortal soul would be lost during the delay. Anyway it was all settled now. Martin, the shy best man, was going to be the godfather, and best surprise of all, Father Flynn was going to perform the baptism. Wasn't that something! To gather the cast of the wedding in another city five years later!

They hadn't noticed the colour go from Clare's face when the priest's name was mentioned. She sat silently. She had been pleased to be invited to this warm, friendly house, to meet the laughing, undemanding friends of Miss O'Hara's. She had been delighted to be included in the christening party the next day, but she didn't want to meet this priest who knew all about her family and had been to see Tommy in prison. She would ask Miss O'Hara could she get out of it.

As they got the house ready on the evening before the christening Angela felt wistful as she often did in the presence of Emer and Kevin, they were so utterly complete as a pair, they hardly needed the rest of the world at all.

244

And their delight in this funny, creased, red-faced baby was so touching it would bring tears to your eyes. When they peered at him in his cot Angela thought she had never seen anything so happy.

She wished them so well that she didn't like the little feelings of envy that came to her unwillingly when she was with them. Nowhere else did she wish so strongly that *she* had found a Kevin of her own, someone she could share everything with. Someone she could laugh with about Dr Power and his kindness. Someone she could talk to at night about Sean and Shuya. She remembered, returning from her last visit to her brother's family: she had longed to take off her shoes and sit down by the fire and tell Emer and Kevin all about it. But it wasn't the same telling a story to a couple. When the evening was over they would go to bed, she in the neat guest bedroom with the gingham curtains and bedspread, they in their big double bed where they would lie in each other's arms and whisper low how terrible it was for Angela. She didn't want that sympathy, however loving and generous. She wanted a sharing. It was lonely holding Sean's secret for seven years.

She looked over at Clare, who was on a chair helping to put up the silver and white decorations they had organized for the sitting room. She had been rather short with the child there earlier on. She had no business being short with her; after all, she refused to talk to Father Flynn about Sean even though it was Father Flynn who had found the school in England for Sean to teach in.

She was just as much an ostrich as Clare, burying her head in the sand, and refusing to accept someone's help and thank them for it in a simple straightforward way. It was uncanny how alike their lives had been. Scholarships, first to the convent and then to college; neither of them came from scholarly families, and both of them had brothers in trouble. And Father Flynn was being a lifeline to both brothers – one despairing in an English school and waiting for a voice from Rome that would never come, the other reading comics in an English gaol.

*　　*　　*

The day was winding down, and Clare found herself near Father Flynn. 'Thank you very much for all you do for my brother, Tommy,' she said, forcing the words out. 'And for Ned too, getting him a job and seeing that he writes home. It's very good of you.'

Father Flynn looked at her. 'Oh, then you're Clare O'Brien, of course, that writes the letters to Tommy. He looks forward to them, and sometimes I read them to him – so don't say anything bad about me in the next one or I might find myself reading it aloud!'

Clare warmed to him. He hadn't shaken his head sadly and said it was a Dreadful Situation; Miss O'Hara was right.

'There's not really anything for him in Castlebay, you know, Father. I was thinking about it, he'd only be hanging around.'

'There's plenty of time to think yet, maybe he'd be better hanging round there than where he was hanging around.'

'Yes, that's probably true. Maybe I was just trying to keep him away, out of sight, out of mind.'

'But that's not true of you,' he smiled. 'He's not out of your mind. You're a generous girl. I hope you have a very successful career at university and that you meet a lot of people and read a great deal and have years that you'll always remember.'

Nobody had wished her well in such terms. Nobody had spoken aloud all her own hopes and dreams. She did want to read a great deal, and have time to read, and she wanted people to talk to, people who would talk about the things they read. This funny, fat little priest with the beady eyes knew just what she wanted.

She went to see Miss O'Hara off at the station. They had inspected the hostel where she was going to live, and Angela had said it wouldn't be bad at all because in a week it would be filled with girls from all over the country, united in their hatred of the nuns who ran the place and all as nervous as Clare, but none of them as clever. Miss

O'Hara had walked the legs off her round the city, and they now knew which side of Stephen's Green was which, and where the Physics Theatre was, which oddly was where a lot of the first Arts lectures would be held. She had registered and got her student's card.

Clare felt very experienced, catching a bus back from the station to O'Connell Bridge, she looked out eagerly at the city which was to be her home for three years. It was so bright – that was what she was going to find most hard to get used to. In Castlebay in winter there were hardly any lights on Church Street, none at all on Cliff Road or the golf-course road, but in Dublin even side streets, even lanes were lit up. And shops had their lights on in windows all night so that you could go and look at what they had for sale any hour at all. As the bus went up the Quays to the centre of Dublin the buildings were reflected in the river Liffey: the Four Courts, the big churches and the rows of tall buildings shimmered in the dark water. It was all so enormous, after home.

She had walked through the grand stores with Angela O'Hara, and looked at the rings and bracelets in the windows of jewellers'. She had been to the second-hand bookshops and bought all her texts for the first year. Angela had even climbed up on ladders in order to get better or cheaper editions for her. She had made herself known at the big red-brick hostel where she would stay. Angela had come with her and informed the nuns that this was no ordinary pupil, it was a Murray Prizewinner, and that her fees would be paid by the committee. The nuns were impressed. It reminded Clare a little of her secondary school, and she was disappointed that it had no garden or cloisters. It was part of a big terrace of Georgian houses, and the convent was in fact four of them all joined together. Angela had said she wouldn't have time for gardens. There was always Stephen's Green in the summer, and the fact that the hostel was so near the university meant it was worth its weight in gold. She could get out of bed literally minutes before lectures while other students had to cross the city.

Clare got off the bus at O'Connell Bridge and leaned across the parapet looking below to where two swans went by. They looked confident, even arrogant. They felt no unease about being swans in a place where everyone else seemed to be human beings. Clare smiled at the thought. She owed Miss O'Hara so much – or Angela as she must now call her. She owed her everything, including these last days, this great preparation.

She knew which bus would take her back to the hostel but she decided to walk. She would walk almost everywhere anyway, why not start now? She went up Grafton Street, pausing to look at fur coats, at household equipment, at pictures and frames, at a chemist's window full of perfumes and soaps and talcum powders. She saw books on display and furniture, big deep leather chairs in shops. She read the tariffs in hairdressers', she saw the sign to the little church in Clarendon Street. At the top of Grafton Street she wouldn't need to pause like so many new students, she knew to walk on along a side of Stephen's Green and on to her hostel. She had left her luggage there earlier, and they said that the young ladies would be arriving after six p.m. She had discovered that there wouldn't be supper, so she was that much ahead of all the rest who thought that there would. She looked up at its slightly forbidding outside, took a deep breath and walked into her new home.

There were going to be three in a room. She was the first so she could choose her bed. It was unlikely that there would be much study done here: it was too small, there wasn't much light, and anyway the libraries were meant for study. Clare took the bed by the window. It was the one where she would get most fresh air and she had checked, there didn't seem to be draughts. She thought of Chrissie alone in the bedroom at home, puzzling out her relationship with Mogsy Byrne.

The first room mate arrived. Mary Catherine was American, her father wanted her to have an Irish education, she had never been so cold in her whole life, she couldn't believe that they didn't have a bathroom attached to the room, she couldn't understand why there hadn't been a reception down there to welcome them, she was going to study English, she had majored in English Literature at her college, she was very confused, and where were the closets? Clare sat on the bed wondering how she was going to live with this voice for a year, when the door opened and in came a girl with short curly hair and tears streaming down her face.

'Isn't it *awful*,' she sobbed. 'It smells just like school, there's no supper or dinner or anything tonight, there's a list of rules as long as your arm, *how* are we going to survive it?'

She threw herself on the empty bed and sobbed into her pillow. Her luggage had the name Valerie painted on the end of each case.

Clare decided to take control. 'Of course it's awful Valerie – if that's your name – it smells even worse than school. I'm Clare and this is Mary Catherine and she's from America and she hates it because it's cold and it's not got a bath each and no closets, whatever they are. And of course there's no supper and no welcoming party because they don't know we're all expecting a bit of a fuss of it, but for God Almighty's sake let's not start moaning and groaning before we even start. Why don't we go out and have some chips and think what could make the place better?'

She could hardly believe that it was Clare O'Brien, the scholarship girl from Castlebay, speaking. She'd never really shouted at two totally strange girls, had she? But it had worked like magic.

The chips cheered them up so much they had apple pie and ice cream. Clare told them about the Murray scholarship. Mary Catherine said that her father was a mailman in the States, but he had told her to tell everyone in Ireland he was in government work – which in a sense was vaguely true. She was the only child. He had dreams of her marrying someone who owned a castle in Ireland. Valerie said her parents were separated. Her father lived in England with a fancy woman, and he had to pay for her education. Valerie didn't want to go to university but her mother said she must, and she must stay there for years in order to get as much out of that rat as possible.

They were immensely cheered by each other's life stories, and they learned what they would have expected: that none of them had any experience with men. Mary Catherine knew a girl in the States who went the whole way with four boys before she left school. No, amazingly, she didn't have a baby, but she didn't have a friend either. A girl in Valerie's school left hurriedly in the middle of Fifth Year but it had been a great mystery because she didn't have a boyfriend. There was a whisper round the school that it was someone in her family, her father or her brother. Clare offered some tales from Castlebay of things that had happened down the sandhills, but they were all second-hand and third-hand. She was going to say that she had her doubts about Chrissie and Mogsy at times; but Mogsy and Chrissie were such non-glamorous people she decided she wouldn't embark on it.

Full of food and confidences and friendship they stood up to go back to the room they were going to transform. They were going to buy a second-hand bookshelf on the Quays, they were going to buy coat hooks and screw them into the wall so that there would be more space for their clothes. They were going to price cheap reading lamps and buy one between them.

Just as they were leaving the restaurant, someone called from a crowded table. 'Hey it's Clare, Clare O'Brien!'

She was startled. All she could see was a sea of young men in duffle coats and scarves. One was waving. It was James Nolan. He stood up and came over to them.

'Well, well, well,' he said.

It seemed to be very little to say after coming all the way across the restaurant.

She introduced him to Mary Catherine and Valerie, smiling at him politely as if to assure him that she wasn't claiming any friendship.

'Well, well,' he said again. 'Is the rest of Castlebay up in Dublin too?' His eyes roamed over Mary Catherine and Valerie, assessing them.

'Josie Dillon might be coming up for a few days,' Clare said eagerly.

Josie had begged her to find out James Nolan's haunts, and said that she would love to come to Dublin if Clare could track him down. Imagine meeting him on the very first night!

'Josie?' He looked blank.

'Josie Dillon from the hotel.'

James Nolan shook his head absently.

'You must remember her, you were often with her in the summer,' Clare blurted out, and could have kicked herself.

'I don't think I do.' James was polite but bored by the subject. Clare would have liked to hit him hard.

'It's my mistake. I'm sure she doesn't remember you either.' Her eyes flashed a bit and he looked at her with surprise.

'No. Well. Listen, it's nice to see you girls. Oh, and there's a party on Saturday. All three of you of course. Here, I'll write it down.' He scribbled an address and time on a piece of paper.

'Ten o'clock! We have to be *back* at that place we're staying by eleven o'clock,' Valerie said, disappointed.

'Late pass, ask them for a late pass, cousin invited all three of you to twenty-first. The nuns love cousins, they think they're safe, sign of a big united family. They love twenty-firsts, it gives them a sense of continuity.'

They promised to be there and they linked arms, giggling as they went down the dark unfamiliar streets, and said that they'd all be lost if it had not been for Clare to guide them and tell them where they were and get them invited to a party on their very very first night in Dublin.

It was a great alliance. When other girls were lonely and self-conscious, they often looked with envy at the three girls; the tall fair one from the back of beyond with the dark brown eyes, the American with her outlandish clothes, and Valerie, the curly-headed terror. It was Valerie who made friends with a workman doing some building work on the

251

outside of the hostel wall. She pointed out that if he were to put three very sturdy bars jutting at intervals they could climb back into their room at night.

He was very nervous about it. 'You might get fellas climbing in to attack you,' he had protested. Nonsense; Valerie explained that there were three of them in the room, and any fellow climbing in uninvited would meet his match. She supervised the placing of the rungs carefully, and also their disguise. No passing nun could see them and realize what they were, a stairway to freedom. Valerie very cunningly asked that one or two extra rungs leading nowhere be hammered in as well. That way the purpose would never be discovered. And indeed it wasn't. They allowed very good friends to know the route, and regularly the light step of a girl was heard to fall into their room and someone, shoes in hand, would creep through, whispering a sorry or a thank you, but giving no explanations.

Clare and Mary Catherine didn't really use their escape route all that often but it kept them sane just knowing it was there. Only Valerie got real value from the contraption. She went dancing and to parties, and needed the footholds she had so cleverly organized at least three or four times a week. Valerie usually lay with her curls barely peeping from above the sheets when Clare and Mary Catherine were heading off to lectures. It was always kept as a polite fiction in front of nuns and other girls that Valerie was very lucky to have late lectures. Valerie rarely attended any of them anyway, no matter what time of the day they were held. As she told Clare and Mary Catherine, her mother had said nothing about passing any exams, only about using up the money for fees at university.

At Christmas, Valerie went home to her mother who was going to sit and curse her father all the time; Mary Catherine went to stay with American friends. Clare caught the train home. Her mother had asked Gerry Doyle to pick her up; he sent her a postcard, saying, 'Passion waggon will be parked in darkest side of yard outside station. See you then. Love, Gerry.' The other girls were intrigued. Even more when they heard that he was the heartbreaker of the country who had twice invited Clare to his caravan.

She felt cheerful going home. There was no guilt – she had written to her mother every single Friday, and to Tommy as well. She had written less to Angela. She had thought she would write more to her than anyone but it was very hard to describe it all: the National Library every afternoon, where it was peaceful and studious – you felt that everyone there was a real scholar, not just learning things with their hands in their ears for exams. She had read a great deal around the courses and everything on the course. She could meet every member of the Murray Committee, look each one in the eye and say truthfully that their money had not been wasted. Funny that she couldn't seem to write this to Angela.

She saw David Power on the train, and put her head back into her book so that he wouldn't notice her as he came along the corridor. It wasn't that she didn't want to talk to him, but it was silly, there she had been three months in the same city and never laid eyes on him, only to meet on the way home – it would be very forced.

He saw her only as they were getting out of the train and his face broke into a great smile. He thought she looked very nice, in her navy duffle coat, knitted navy and white scarf and her hair in a jaunty pony tail with a white bow on it. It was only the other day that she had been a kid. But then, his mother kept saying it was only the twinkling of an eye since he was in rompers.

He saw his father waving from the other side of the gate. 'Can we drive you home?' he said. 'I'm delighted I saw you in time.'

'I have a lift actually, but thank you very much,' and as they came to the barrier he saw Gerry Doyle leaning casually against the machine that wrote your name in metal.

Gerry wasn't bothering to move and wave and position himself as everyone else was doing, as David's own father

253

was doing. Gerry knew he would be seen when the time came. Clare raised her hand in salute.

'Second fiddle to Gerry Doyle, winter and summer, it's the story of our lives,' David said and went over to his father.

'Your mother's in the car, it's very cold. I didn't want her waiting in the draught.'

'Quite right,' David said. For some reason he couldn't explain to himself he was glad Clare hadn't accepted the lift. His mother didn't really get along with her. All right in her place of course, but David felt that his mother thought her place was behind the counter in O'Brien's, not as a university student and certainly not as a passenger in the doctor's car.

She had forgotten it would be so quiet, that it had always been so quiet at this time of year. There were no lights or Christmas trees in the windows, there was no traffic bustling up and down the street. She had forgotten how few people there were there, and how the wet spray stung your face when you went outside the door.

She had forgotten too how handsome Gerry Doyle was. He wore a leather jacket and his hair was long and shiny. In the station he had looked like a film star. He had brought a rug for her to wrap around her knees.

'Is there anything wrong?' Clare asked suddenly.

'Your mother had a fall. But she's fine. Fine,' he said.

'How fine?' Her voice was clipped.

'She nearly came to meet you with me, that's how fine.'

'Why didn't they tell me? Why did no one tell me? Where did she fall?'

'She fell on the cliff path. She broke her ankle. She wasn't even kept in hospital more than one night.'

Clare's eyes filled with tears.

'No, it's not bad, honestly, she hobbles a bit and that's all. Your dad's being very nice to her and he brings her tea in the morning.'

'She must be bad then. When did it happen?'

'About three weeks ago. Listen Clare, will you stop, I

254

was going to tell you just as we came into Castlebay so that you'd have no time to be going through all this useless kind of nonsense. So as you'd see her in five minutes and know she was all right.'

'She could have been killed.'

'She couldn't. Don't make it so dramatic. She's been through all that now, it will only make it worse if you start attacking them for not telling you and saying what could have happened.'

He was right. She admitted it grudgingly.

'Very well, tell me about other things. I'll see Mam soon enough.'

He told her that business was changing, as he had always suspected it would. More and more people were bringing their own cheap cameras to the beach, Murphy's chemist was demented with visitors wanting their holiday snaps developed. The demand for beach photographs was growing less.

But then he had always known it would, so the thing to do was to change direction, to expand. He was in portrait photography now, and doing special commissions for hotels and new buildings which wanted prestige pictures of their premises. It meant of course that he would have to improve his own premises. Big important places only came to you if they thought you looked big and important too.

Wasn't that risky, Clare had wondered. No, it was business, Gerry assured her.

He told her that Josie Dillon had managed to get a whole lot of people to come to the hotel for a bridge weekend, and it was such a success that bridge people from all over were going to come there regularly. Josie's Uncle Dick had learned to play bridge when he'd been ordered off the drink apparently, and he had been saying for years that they should do this but he'd done nothing about it. Now he and Josie were as pleased as punch. Josie's sisters were hopping mad and her grandmother claimed that it was all *her* idea in the first place.

She told Gerry about the size of the university and about the Annexe where they had coffee every morning and how there were hundreds and hundreds of nuns and priests studying too, which she had never expected.

Was Fiona back yet for Christmas, she wanted to know. It would be interesting to compare notes with her about what her polytechnic was like.

No, she wasn't coming home apparently, in fact Gerry thought he might go over and see her.

'Not coming home for *Christmas?*' It was unheard of.

Gerry kept looking at the road.

'But what's she doing that she's not coming home?'

He sighed, almost his whole body went into the sigh. 'Jesus, Clare, you're not an old biddy, why do you sound so amazed? She wants to stay there, that's all. Do I have to build up a story for you too, an explanation? Will everyone in Castlebay want a full account of what everyone else from Castlebay is doing for the rest of their lives?'

'I'm sorry, you're quite right,' she said contritely. 'I don't talk like this in Dublin, it must be coming home that makes me do it.'

'Yeah, well some of us never left home, don't forget that, but we grow up too in our own way.'

She wasn't sure what he meant but it sounded like a criticism. She nodded apologetically. They drove on in silence for a while.

'I'm going tomorrow in fact,' he said. 'I haven't told anyone else, I'll just go.'

'Sure,' she said, 'that's a good idea.'

'I might go to see Tommy and Ned while I'm in London,' he said unexpectedly. 'I haven't laid eyes on them in years.'

She jumped a little but he couldn't have noticed.

'Do you have their address to give me?'

'No,' she said. 'No, I don't.'

'Would your mother . . .'

'I think not.' Her mouth closed like a trap. She too stared ahead of her.

'Right,' he said eventually. 'As we were saying there's no reason why being brought up in Castlebay means you've got to be at everyone's beck and call the whole time.'

She smiled, biting her lip. She had as good as told him

256

now, hadn't she? She might as well have said the whole thing. It would have been easier in the long run.

Chrissie had got the ring for Christmas, she and Mogsy – whom she would now like to be referred to as Maurice – would be married next June. Mogsy – or Maurice – was building a house for them, a small place up near the creamery. Dwyers' had said Chrissie could go on working until there was a sign of a little Byrne coming along. They couldn't do fairer than that.

Clare's mother looked tired. 'Aren't you going to hare up and see your friend Miss O'Hara before you even sit down to talk to us?' she said the first night.

'Don't be giving out to me. I'm only just home.'

'Home! It's not much we'll see of you. Up there with the books, hardly a word to your own flesh and blood.'

'Mammy, why are you saying all this? I'm only in the door! I'm not going up to Miss O'Hara's, I'll go and see her tomorrow or the day after maybe, but you never minded that, you were always grateful to her too.'

'I know, don't mind me, I'm cranky these days.'

'What is it?' They were on their own.

'A bit of everything.'

'It's not Chrissie's wedding, you're not upset about that?'

'Not at all, for every shoe God made a stocking. I tell you those two were matched in heaven.'

'Well what then?'

'I suppose I get to thinking, I wonder about Tommy.' Clare's heart jumped. 'You'll know this yourself in years to come, there's something about the eldest one, I don't know what it is. But he never writes, he never comes back. Wouldn't it be great if he walked in this Christmas, that's what I was thinking I suppose.'

'Tommy never wrote more than his name in his life, you know that.'

'Yes, but I'm not settled about Ned's letters, he's hiding something. I'm going to ask Gerry Doyle when he comes in here will he go and see him, he's going to England tomorrow.'

'When did he tell you that? He said he was going to tell no one.'

'I asked him if he'd pick up some supplies for us before Christmas and he said he wouldn't be around, he just told me now, a few minutes ago when you were getting your stuff out of his van and being surprised at the sound of the sea all over again.'

'Gerry'd not have time to go finding Tommy and Ned.'

'Ah he will, he's a good boy for all that they give him a bad name around here. I'll have a word with him tomorrow.'

Clare left a note into Gerry Doyle's house that night. She said she wanted to stroll out to see the cliffs, her mother said she was stark raving mad but you might as well talk to a stone wall as to any of her children.

Gerry was sitting on the wall next morning as she had asked him. It was dark grey and threatening but it wasn't raining. They were both wrapped up well.

'There's a bit of a problem about Tommy,' she said.

'I thought there was from the sound of you.' He didn't sound triumphant or curious.

'Wormwood Scrubs to be exact,' she said.

'That's a bit of a problem all right.' He grinned at her comfortingly. 'And your ma doesn't know?'

'Nobody knows except Ned and me.'

'That's hard.'

'No, it's worse on him in the gaol, and the old man they beat up doing the robbery, those are the people it's hard on.'

'Sure, well what will I do, say I can't find him?'

'No, could you just ring Ned, I've his phone number here written out, and talk away to him and then tell Ma that Tommy's fine. Would that be all right?' She looked very young and very anxious in the cold morning air.

'That's fine, I'll look after it.'

'Thanks Gerry.'

She hadn't asked him to keep it to himself, she didn't need to.

'About Fiona,' he said.

'It's none of my business,' she said suddenly.

'No, but anyway, she's having a baby this week. A Christmas baby of all bloody things.'

Clare nearly fell off the wall with shock. But for Gerry's sake she hid it. 'She's lucky to have you,' she said.

'We're a great pair,' he said and leaped lightly off the wall. He helped her down.

'Happy Christmas anyway,' he said.

She looked at him gratefully. His small pointed face was cold in the chilly dawn. He had said as little as could possibly be said, offered little sympathy when there was nothing to say. He had told Fiona's secret just so that she would have something in return, so that the pain and shame of her telling could be written off in a balance on some kind of scales.

'Happy Christmas, Gerry,' she said. 'You're very very nice.'

'I've always been telling you that, you're the one that didn't realize it,' he joked.

'I don't mean *that* sort of nice,' Clare said, but she wondered as she said it was she being truthful. He was so handsome and kind, he had this great sense of being in charge, nothing could go really wrong if you told Gerry. Fiona had been very lucky to have a brother like that. Fine help poor Tommy or Ned would have been in such a predicament. She felt sorry that he wouldn't be around for the Christmas holidays. She felt this odd kind of wish to hold on to him. Not to let him go.

'I'd better head for foreign parts,' he said. He was still holding her hands since he had helped her down from the wall.

'Safe journey. I hope . . . I hope Fiona'll be all right.'

'I'm sure she will, she's going to give the baby for adoption, and then I suppose I'll have to teach her something about photography.'

'About *what?*'

'Photography.' He gave his familiar crooked grin. 'That's

what the whole place thinks she's been studying for the past six months.'

Angela was delighted to see her, no of course she wasn't too early, come on in and have breakfast like the old days.

'When I'm properly grown up and have my own place, I'll have exactly the same breakfast as you do,' Clare said, tucking in.

'What do I have that's special?'

'You have white shop bread and you have nice thin shop marmalade and you don't have thick homemade bread and awful homemade marmalade like people buy at sales of work.'

'Is this all your university education has done for you, made you whinge and whine about shop bread? Tell me about it all there, tell me about Emer and Kevin. Why don't you write to me, great long letters like you did when you were at school?'

'I don't know, I really don't know.'

'That's very honest of you.' Angela smiled, not at all put out. 'Anyway you're very busy up there.'

'It's not that.' Clare struggled to be honest. 'I write to my Mam, and to Josie and to Tommy. I *do* have time.'

'It might be easier in a while,' Angela seemed untroubled by it. 'Let me tell you about the place above. You won't credit this. Immaculata has gone totally and completely mad this term, the men with white coats will be stepping out of a van for her before Easter, mark my words.'

Mrs O'Hara frowned. 'You're very foolish and wrong, Angela, to say such things in front of a child. For all Clare's great marks she's only a child.'

'It's all right, Mrs O'Hara,' Clare said. 'I've heard it all, I say nothing, I keep my mouth closed.'

'You're the only one in this county who does then,' grumbled Angela's mother.

There was a long and insane story about Mother Immaculata having a Christmas pageant where everyone had to bring a toy for a poor child, they would all be gathered by the crib. Then one child had asked where they would go.

'To the *poor*,' Mother Immaculata had shrilled.

'But aren't we the poor?' the child had asked. 'There isn't anyone poorer than us.'

Clare laughed and while more tea was being poured she wrote Angela a note. 'I want to talk to you about Tommy, but not in front of your mother.'

Angela suggested that Clare come upstairs to see some new books that she had bought, and Clare sat for the first time in her teacher's bedroom. She was surprised at how sparse it was, with the very very white bedspread and the crucifix hanging over the bed head. There was a small press, Mary Catherine would have wept over the lack of closets. And a white chair. No carpet but a nice rug on the floor. Somehow it was a bit sad.

'I had to tell Gerry Doyle about Tommy,' she explained. She told everything except Gerry's secret.

'I had to tell him,' she said eventually when she saw Angela's troubled face. 'What else could I have done?'

'I suppose you could have let him find out and hoped he wouldn't tell your mother.'

'But it would have been so devious, such a long way round.'

'You might be right. I'm sure you are, it's just that now you've told him you're sort of in his power.'

'That's very dramatic.' Clare tried to laugh.

'He's a very dramatic young man. I've always thought that. Far too handsome and smart for Castlebay, he's dangerous almost.'

'I won't be in his power, honestly.' She looked straight into Angela's eyes. 'As much as I know anything, I know that. I'll never be in his control.'

David came into O'Brien's shop on Christmas Eve. Bones sat obediently outside the door.

'You can bring him in, everyone else brings their hounds in,' Clare's father said. 'In fact Mogsy Byrne brought in two cows a month ago.'

'I'd thank you to remember his name is Maurice, Dad, and he did *not* bring them in, they came in because the young fellow who was meant to be minding them wasn't.'

'Congratulations Chrissie, I heard you are engaged.' David was polite.

Chrissie simpered and showed him the ring. David said it looked terrific.

'No sign of you making a move in that direction yourself?' she said, arch woman of the world now, trying to encourage those who were hanging back.

'Oh, I think I'd better wait till I'm qualified. It's bad enough asking someone to take on a doctor but a medical student would be a fate worse than death, and we'd have nothing to live on.'

'Have you lost your heart up in Dublin?' Chrissie wondered.

'Chrissie, stop it, you're very forward,' Agnes said.

'No, I've been working too hard really to have any time for romance.' He smiled easily at them all. 'Is Clare here?'

'No, no sign of Clare – where would she be but up in Miss O'Hara's or in the hotel with Josie Dillon, there's no sign of her round here, I can assure you that.' Chrissie's voice was resentful. 'Sorry your visit was in vain,' she said spitefully.

'Not at all, I came for cigarettes,' he said easily. 'And for a tin of those nice biscuits as well for Nellie, and some black pudding.'

'Your mother got black pudding this morning,' Tom O'Brien said – it would be no use alienating a customer by selling the same thing twice.

'I'm sure she did but I bet she didn't get enough, I want six bits on my plate when we come back from Mass tomorrow morning. You've no idea how I miss black pudding in Dublin, they only have mean little slivers of it, and it doesn't taste the same at all.'

He wished them happy Christmas and they found a piece off the end of some cooked ham for Bones, and Bones gobbled it up and raised his paw in the air even though nobody had been offering to shake hands with him at all.

*　　*　　*

262

Clare was lying on Josie's bed telling her all about the hostel and the rungs up the wall and the laughs with Mary Catherine and Valerie. She told her about the lectures and the debating society on Saturday nights, and the hops, and how each Society had dances which were meant to make money.

Josie was disappointed that she had only met James Nolan on two occasions – in the café and at the very hot crowded party in somebody's flat. Clare revealed that he had danced with Mary Catherine twice, if you could call it dancing in those dark rooms; but he hadn't asked Mary Catherine out on a date or anything. Clare *didn't* tell her that James Nolan had forgotten her, she didn't think that was useful information; instead she said that she got the impression he was a bit fickle and faithless. But Josie said that was only when you didn't know him well.

Josie was thrilled about how she was building up the winter business in the hotel; and Uncle Dick had become really nice, not mad and grouchy like he used to be. Granny was totally gaga now; she had told Josie that Josie's mother had been putting arsenic in all their food for years now, and had even poisoned some of the guests, which was why they hadn't come back since. Her sisters Rose and Emily were home for Christmas and weren't a bit pleased about the bridge weekends; and they had almost told her to her face not to interfere. Clare didn't know how awfully quiet the place was in winter. When they were young they hadn't noticed it so much, but it was really so quiet you wouldn't believe it. She had learned to play bridge herself with Uncle Dick and sometimes the two of them went up to the Powers' and played a few rubbers with Mrs Power and Mr Harris, that auctioneer man who lived in a big house halfway between the town and Castlebay. He was *eligible*, Uncle Dick said, but he was also a hundred and ten. Well he was thirty-seven, eighteen and a half years older than Josie, twice their age. Uncle Dick must be mad. Clare agreed and told Josie not to dream of trapping the eligible Mr Harris.

They speculated about Chrissie and Mogsy and wondered what either of them could see in the other. Would their children be as awful as both of them, or twice as awful?

Father O'Dwyer went round to the houses of the sick on the night of Christmas Eve and brought them Holy Communion. He came to the O'Hara cottage as his last visit. Angela had prepared the place for his visit and had a little candle-lighting in front of the crib.

She had gone upstairs while the old woman's confession was heard and then when the Priest called her she came down to kneel while her mother received Communion. They were all silent for a few minutes, but after that Father O'Dwyer had a cup of tea and a tomato sandwich from which the crusts had been cut off.

'Isn't it a pity that Father Sean didn't make it over to see you this Christmas?' he said conversationally.

'Oh well, you know the way it is,' Angela said meaninglessly.

'You see he's in a part now where they don't even have proper postal services,' Mrs O'Hara said. 'That's why we have to write to their house in England in order that priests there can forward them or deliver them when they're going out.'

'Yes, yes,' Father O'Dwyer was soothing the way he listened to all old people, not taking in very deeply what they were saying.

'But maybe he'll come back next year,' he said.

'Please God, Father, please God. Still the way I look at it is that it's better that he's there doing the Lord's work with savages and people who never heard of God than here coming to see me.'

Her face was radiant in the firelight and the aftermath of receiving Communion.

Angela bit her lip hard.

Father O'Dwyer patted Mrs O'Hara on the hand and said, 'That's right, that's right, that's the spirit that sends the labourers into the vineyard.'

*   *   *

Dr Power had asked Nellie would she like to go home for Christmas.

'You ask me that every year and the answer's always no sir, thank you very much, I have a nicer time in this house, and a better meal and more peace. And I can go down to see them all in the evening.'

'If you're sure . . .' he said.

'Anyway sir, the mistress wouldn't like you playing fast and loose with the arrangements. I'd like to see her face, if I said I wouldn't be here for Christmas Day.'

'Stop trying to stir up a row, Nellie,' he said affectionately. 'This is a happy house now, do you hear me?'

'It is and all sir,' said Nellie goodnaturedly. 'I've been here since I was sixteen, that will be twenty years next year, and there's hardly a cross word ever said under this roof.'

'You've been here too long, Nellie. Why don't you go and marry someone?'

'And have a lout asking me to cook his dinner and polish his shoes for nothing for him, aren't I like a king here, with my own wireless that I can take upstairs and plug in in the bedroom if I want to, and a big chair beside the range. What would I want with marriage?'

'Will you sit with us and have your Christmas dinner at our table tomorrow?'

'God love you sir, you ask me that every year too, and I won't. The mistress would be annoyed for one thing, and for another I'd be dropping the food off my fork.'

'You're a very obstinate woman.'

'I've no brains but I'm not a fool, that's all.'

Clare had bought bright Christmas decorations while she was in Dublin. It had been marvellous going down Moore Street and Henry Street with Mary Catherine and Valerie listening to the women shouting their wares, and the last of this and the last of that in order to whip people up into a frenzy thinking things were running out. Clare had bought the last of the shiny chains, only to see dozens more coming from under the stall. She had also bought the last of the Christmas sparklers which were like low-key fireworks giving off little tinselly sparks. Jim and Ben had loved them and they were a treat in Castlebay so she felt it was a good buy. She had gone without lunches for three weeks in order to buy the gifts, and had stocked up on bread and butter from breakfast to keep her going through the day.

It was bright and cold on Christmas morning. The O'Briens went to early Mass from habit. There was no need to be back in case anyone would call to the shop. Nobody would admit that they had forgotten anything for Christmas, the family would be able to eat their meal undisturbed.

Clare had wrapped up all her presents and Chrissie eyed this pile of gifts with some suspicion.

'I hope you realize that being engaged and everything we have to put all our savings towards our future,' she said to Clare. 'We can't be wasting everything on silly gifts.'

'Sure,' Clare had said and resisted the temptation to pull out every hair of Chrissie's permed, frizzy head.

After their breakfast there was an endless amount of preparation for the main meal. Agnes, still frail and unable to move about, sat with her leg on a stool and gave instructions, lift the ham carefully from the water where it had been soaking. Carefully, don't drown the whole kitchen. Set the table properly. Properly, Chrissie, it *was* Christmas Day, take that dirty cloth off and find a cleaner one. And peel the potatoes Ben, not with your finger, with a knife, and move that holly Jim, before it sticks into people.

Tom O'Brien sat beside her, repeated her orders with increasing impatience, and added little asides of his own about how you'd think people would be glad to help when their unfortunate mother had been injured in a fall.

Clare did most of the work and when the meal was ready she was nearly exhausted. She couldn't understand why a lot of this work hadn't been divided up and done the night before, but a word of criticism would open the floodgates, and she kept her thoughts to herself.

After the plum pudding, she distributed her gifts. Mam

thought the scarf was very nice, a bit light for this kind of weather, but very nice for warmer weather, that is of course if you would wear a scarf at all in warmer weather. Her father looked with interest at the map of the county she had found with such trouble in a second-hand shop in Dublin, and then framed. It was very generous he thought; of course it would be a poor man who didn't know his own county, but maybe strangers might look at it. Jim and Ben genuinely *were* pleased with the puzzles and games she had got them. Chrissie looked at the manicure set with dulled eyes.

Clare had been so sure that Chrissie would love a manicure set, for as far back as she could remember Chrissie had been filing and painting her nails, her fingernails and her toenails, surely the set in the little red case would be exactly what she would like. But Clare must have been remembering a time too far back. Chrissie opened the parcel with her stubby fingers and Clare noticed that her hands were calloused and her nails were bitten short. Still, she thought hopefully, maybe.

Chrissie turned it over and said it was very nice, especially of course if you were a student and had time to be doing your nails. She put it aside and never looked at it again during the day.

Clare got a box of sweets taken from one of the shelves from her mother, and a tinsel card from Jim and Ben. Her father gave her £1 peeled from the notes in his pocket. She fought the stinging of the tears in her eyes. They were her family for heaven's sake, they didn't need to be going on with too much ritual. It was silly to get upset because of the lack of trappings.

Angela had warned her long ago that one of the dangers of going away to be educated was that you expected too much when you came back, and you built up a whole wall of disappointment that was unnecessary. It had been a bit like that when she came home from the scrupulously clean convent boarding school and had to share a room with Chrissie, it was the same now. After knowing people like Emer and Kevin with their politeness and consideration towards each other and everyone they came in contact with . . . this seemed a dull, leaden sort of day.

She remembered Mary Catherine reading somewhere that more people wanted to commit suicide on Christmas Day than any other day. She would not join them. Putting her elbows on the table full of dirty dishes and the wrappings of the presents that only she had given, Clare managed a big smile.

'Will we tell a ghost story?' she said.

'Who knows one?' asked her father.

'We could make one up as we went along, each person adding a bit. You start, Chrissie.'

'I don't know how to make up ghost stories.' Chrissie was not going to join in.

'Yes you do. Just start.'

The others looked eager.

'Once upon a time there was a ghost that had this desperate sister,' Chrissie began. 'It had four brothers who were all right but it had a really terrible sister . . .'

There was always a Christmas tree in the window of Dr Power's house. On the side where it could be seen from the road. There were presents which had arrived by post from the Nolans in Dublin and from cousins and friends all over the place. David placed his own gifts there on Christmas Eve night, wrapped in red crêpe paper and each one with a cut-out Santa Claus.

David looked at all the neatly labelled parcels. He glanced through at the dining room already set with gleaming glass and shining silver, decorated with holly and criss-crossed crackers. Why did it feel so empty and hollow? He hated Nellie being in the kitchen, although he knew she would never come and join them; he hated the games-playing, where he and his mother and father would pull crackers and read jokes and exclaim over gifts. If they only knew about some of the homes he visited in Dublin when he had been doing his practical work, then they'd find this kind of playing at Christmas very shabby. But his father must know.

They walked across in the cold Christmas air to Mass; everyone was good-humoured and cheerful despite the wind. Dr Power dealt with a young woman who had fainted, and reassured her it was just the result of a three-mile walk fasting on a cold morning. 'But I'd have to fast and go to Holy Communion on Christmas morning, wouldn't I?' the woman said, detecting some criticism in the doctor's voice as he bent her head down.

'Of course you would, that's just what the Lord likes on His birthday – people nearly killing themselves,' Dr Power muttered.

All through the day, David felt as if he were under some kind of spotlight. They were all anxious to know what David thought, what David wanted. Did David think they should eat now? Have a sherry? Would David like to open the presents? Was he sure he liked the sweater? If it wasn't big enough, if it wasn't the right colour it could be changed.

They had soup first, and little fingers of toast; and then the turkey was carved – was David sure he wanted the leg? There was plenty of breast.

They clapped when the flame lit on the plum pudding, and they raised their glasses to another good year and to the year that lay ahead. Molly Power wondered whether the Nolans were at this moment having their Christmas lunch in Dublin, and they drank a toast to them too.

'James' mother gets very odd at Christmas,' David said, to make conversation. 'Apparently last year she had a handkerchief on her head all through the meal.'

Dr Power burst out laughing. 'Did she say why?' he asked.

'Well, she did when Caroline asked her, she said you never knew with ceilings – then I don't think they asked any more.' David grinned back, thinking of the story.

'I don't like you telling stories like that about Sheila, she's different, she's unusual, that's all, you make her sound batty when you talk like that.'

'She is a *bit* batty, I think,' David said apologetically. 'You know, not dangerous or anything but definitely not firing on all cylinders.'

Dr Power frowned slightly and David understood.

'Sorry, I was just joking – unusual is more the word for it.'

Molly smiled, pleased. She didn't like her friend being defined as insane. She passed round the liqueur chocolates, exclaiming with delight as each centre was read out. Would she have kirsch or would she try cherry brandy? Which was more alcoholic? David fought down his wish to say that since there was less than half an eggspoonful of alcohol in each it was immaterial.

'*Do* you see a lot of Caroline?' Molly's voice was over-casual.

'A fair bit, but I'm working hard, very hard. People never believe this of students. We went to a party just before I came down here, she sent you both her love.'

'I think she likes it here, I think she's a Castlebay person at heart, she wrote a very nice note in her Christmas card saying it must be lovely in the winter.' Mrs Power was still fishing.

'Oh, I think just for holidays,' David said.

'You'd never know. A lot of people thought they'd come here for holidays and changed their minds, ended up staying here altogether.' Dr Power patted his wife's hand as he said this. David felt a sense of overpowering claustrophobia. Not only were they wrapping him in cotton wool while he was here; they were planning the day when he came back full time as a doctor to help his father; and they were now planning his wife for him.

'I think I'll go for a bit of a walk . . . all that food . . .' he stammered.

He stood up, anxious to be out of the warm room, the smell of mince pies and the beam of their attention.

But it was no use. They both thought that would be a great idea: Dr Power went to get his stick and Molly ran upstairs for her coat and gloves. David carried the tray of coffee cups out to the kitchen. Nellie was nodding off to sleep beside the big range with the wireless on, and Bones was fast asleep due to a surfeit of turkey.

He left the tray quietly on the kitchen table and wrapped his scarf round his neck.

He knew he was a selfish, selfish ungrateful so and so, but he wished that he had fourteen brothers and sisters to share the responsibility with him; or that he had no parents at all like one of the students in his year, who was going to spend the festive season with a lot of English people in Belgium. Everyone knew that English girls were outrageous and this fellow was going to have a really great time.

'Ready, David,' called Molly and everyone in the house woke up in confusion: David from his dream of permissive coach travellers, and Nellie and Bones from their kitchen sleeps.

The family walk was underway and soon it would be the family tea, and then tomorrow it would be the family Stephen's Day. David sighed heavily and hated himself for the sigh.

On New Year's Day Clare went for a walk on the beach to collect shells and make New Year's resolutions.

'I will not expect too much of my family.

'I will work out a better revision system, not just big pencil marks saying *must revise later*.

'I will get a job in a café one night a week in Dublin.

'I will have my hair cut in an interesting style.

'I will find a person to take me out on a date.

'I will write a proper letter to Angela O'Hara every single week.'

She found some nice cowries and put them in the box she had in her pocket. She heard a shout and there was David.

'I hoped I'd find you here. You and I are the only people who use the amenities out of season.'

'Or in season, they're all too busy to come down on the beach, my father can't even swim.'

'Anyway, here you are.' He looked pleased to see her, she felt suddenly a little embarrassed.

'Where's Bones, you don't look fully dressed without him.'

'Poor Bones, he has a cough. Believe it or not, he's coughing like an old man. My father has him dosed better than if he were the president but Bones is whooping and hacking away. Nellie has an old jumper tied round his neck, you never saw the cut of him.'

Clare laughed at the idea of it but said it was rotten to think of Bones not being well.

'Will you do me a favour?' he asked.

'Sure.'

'I want to go back the day after tomorrow . . .'

'But term doesn't start until . . .'

'Exactly. That's the point. I have to say it does, will you back me up?'

'Certainly, but I can't go back the day after tomorrow.'

His face fell. 'No, I suppose you can't.'

'No, I don't mean leaving here or anything, they wouldn't mind. It's just I've nowhere to stay. The hostel doesn't open for us till the first day of term.'

'Oh.'

'We could say medical school opens earlier, I could say that to anyone, but anyway what does it matter what I say? I don't meet your parents.'

'No, but if you'd gone back they'd know, everyone knows everything here, every single thing.' He sounded annoyed.

'I'm sorry,' Clare said. 'I know what you feel, and I wouldn't mind at all going back myself, but you do see . . .'

'You could always stay in our flat, my flat,' he said.

'No I could *not*.'

'I don't mean any funny business, you'd have your own room, one of the fellows won't be back until term starts.'

'We'd be killed if I was caught, and I'm damn well not going to risk getting caught for something I haven't done, or putting myself in danger unless I'm getting value out of it.' She was full of conviction and quite unaware how vehement she looked.

'All right, calm down. I see your point of view.'

'Did you have a nice Christmas?' she asked suddenly.

'Not very. Did you?'

'Not very.'

'Are you missing lover boy Gerry Doyle? I hear he went off to the bright lights of London.'

'No, I'm not missing him. I don't suppose I gave him a thought. I must be the only woman in the western hemisphere that isn't.'

'Aha then he'll go after you all the more,' David said.

'Have *you* a lover girl in Dublin that you want to be back to meet?' she asked.

'Yes and no. Yes there is a girl, but it's not only that. I feel a bit too *important* in the house. I'm all they've got. Do you know what I mean? I think they pay too much attention to me.'

'It's the reverse in my house. They don't pay enough attention to me. I'm not nearly important enough.'

He laughed. 'Nobody ever gets what they want, do they? Will I see you at all in Dublin? I could ring you in the hostel some evening.'

'Great,' she said.

He never rang, but that was no surprise.

Clare thought about it, and decided that David had never meant it, it was just the way the Powers had of saying goodbye. They couldn't actually say the word, it seemed too final, so they said something insincere instead, like promising to ring you at the hostel.

Perhaps it was just as well, she thought, making the best of it. There were thousands and thousands of men in UCD; she shouldn't try to get a date with someone from Castlebay who was on the other side of the cliffs so to speak.

Valerie had had a fairly uneventful Christmas, all things considered. She had nearly come to blows with her mother when they were playing Scrabble: her mother said Quorn was a word, and Valerie had claimed it was a proper noun and the name of a hunt somewhere. Her mother had flung things on the ground and said she wouldn't be patronized. They had an adventurous time with a cook book, each taking it in turns to make a dish, one more exotic than the other; apparently Valerie's father in England had refused to pay any actual money but would pay bills in the local grocery so they only chose dishes with very highly priced ingredients.

Mary Catherine had an adventurous Christmas too; James Nolan invited her to his house three times. She had thought Caroline was a *pain*. Caroline was finishing her thesis for her M.A. about Spencer and Ireland and thought almost everyone in the world was illiterate and that Americans were more illiterate than most. James Nolan showed a very unhealthy desire to go to the States in the summer: he said he would be sure to look up Mary Catherine and her family, and perhaps he could come to stay? She had agreed, and made sure not to give him her home address. Her mailman father told her when she married a man who owned a castle to keep her American side of things under wraps until the deal was done. James Nolan wasn't exactly a castle owner but he was an attorney almost, and that couldn't be bad. No, of course she didn't love him. But she wasn't going to pitch him overboard yet. Clare thought of Josie back home typing away in the hotel, organizing bridge conferences with Uncle Dick, fighting off her two jealous sisters Rosie and Emily. She sighed. It wouldn't be reasonable to tell Mary Catherine to hold her horses, because James Nolan couldn't remember Josie Dillon from a hole in the ground.

Mary Catherine came running up the stairs two at a time. 'There is a *dee-vine* young man downstairs asking for you, Clare. I said I would see if I could find you.'

'You mean thing! Why didn't you say I'd be down in two ticks?'

'Because I'm your friend. I wanted you to put on something good and to comb your hair and put on some make-up. I'm *too* good a friend, that's what I am.'

'Oh, it must be Gerry Doyle, he's the one who always gets that reaction.' Still, she did put on a little lipstick.

She picked up her duffle coat.

'Very confident he's going to ask you out,' Mary Catherine said.

'You should play hard to get,' Valerie suggested. 'He'll think it's too eager if you go down ready for the off.'

'That fellow only knows people who are too eager, that's the style he's used to. Anyway, we'll just go out for coffee, I imagine.'

'I think we should leave the window unlocked. You may need to climb the rungs tonight from the sound of it.' Valerie was pleased.

'He's not strictly good-looking. He's got an *aura*,' said Mary Catherine.

'You and your auras, you learned that word a week ago, everything has an *aura*.' Clare was gone before they could retaliate. She ran lightly down the stairs. Gerry was standing in the hall as relaxed as if he had been a regular visitor.

'This is a great surprise,' she said with genuine and unaffected pleasure. 'I didn't know you were in Dublin.'

'I'm not. I mean not in Dublin itself if you know what I mean, I'm passing through, on my way back from London. I got a longing to talk to you.'

She was going to say something joky—but his face looked tired.

'Great,' she said simply. 'Let me take you away from here before they devour you.' She tucked her arm companionably in his and they went out of the hostel and down the steps. 'Coffee or a drink?'

'A drink would be very nice. Do you know a pub?'

'There's two here, just round the corner. Shows you my virtuous life, though, I don't know what they're like. Have a look into the first one and tell me what you think.'

He came back in seconds, grinning. 'How many people are there in Dublin – half a million maybe?'

'More, much more, I think. Why?'

'In that pub, who do I see but David Power and Caroline Nolan looking into each other's eyes.'

'Go on. Well, we could have a Castlebay reunion, if you'd like that.'

'No. I wouldn't like that. I'd like to talk to you, that's why I came to find you.'

They went into the second pub. There was a mixed collection of drinkers: students in college scarves, workmen from a building site nearby, a few red-nosed old regulars.

'This is Paradise,' Gerry said. 'No one from home. Is it still bitter lemon or have you got more adventurous?'

'Still bitter lemon,' she said, pleased that he had remembered.

He told her about Fiona. The baby was a boy, born the day after Christmas. She called him Stephen. The old nuns had been very kind – disapproving of course, and thought Fiona was a great sinner – but kind in the end; and they had arranged the adoption when the baby was three weeks old. Fiona had a sort of depression apparently. That's why he had gone over again, to cheer her up, to reassure her that she had done the right thing. There was no other course open to her if she wanted to live her life in Castlebay. She had to pretend it had never happened. She *had* to keep it a secret.

Clare didn't want to hear about the baby's father, but Gerry wanted to tell her. He was a married man. Wouldn't you know? One of the crowd that came down golfing last year. He had told Fiona he was single; he had also told her when she wrote to him about the pregnancy that there was no question of his becoming involved; and that if she made any trouble all his friends had agreed to say that *they* had had her too. What options did she have? If this were known at home she would be a slut *and* a fool – what a combination . . .

He talked on about the business. Times were hard and getting harder. It hadn't been as easy as he had thought: there were all the expenses. If Clare could only see what he had to lash out on equipment – the new modern machines were so expensive, and of course they would eventually pay for themselves, but the trouble was *when*.

Even doing the place up had cost a lot of money. There had been some good commissions, but not enough.

'What are you going to do?' she asked sympathetically.

'Survive. Isn't that the only thing to do? What you and I have always been doing.'

He looked as if it might be quite an effort to survive. Shadows under his eyes, and his face pale. She felt very protective towards him suddenly, almost as if she would like to put her arm round his shoulder and draw him towards her soothingly. She had never felt like that about Gerry Doyle before, and had been rather relieved. It was as if she were the only girl in town who hadn't caught the measles. But this was different. This wasn't being keen on him like Chrissie and everyone else. This was wanting to look after him, he seemed defenceless and vulnerable sitting there in front of his pint glass.

She reached out and took his hand.

'So I thought I'd come and tell you about it. If there's anyone who'd understand, it's you.'

Pleased and surprised she asked, 'Why me?'

'Lord, it hasn't been easy for you to get where you've got. No one to help you on, just Clare do this do that, iron that shirt Clare, sort those potatoes Clare, when they should be so proud of you and helping you to study.'

He had noticed, all those years. He understood.

She was trying to lessen the intensity of his stare: he was looking at her as if his eyes were boring through her.

'You're different, Clare. I've always said that to you. You and I are the same type. We're the only two they produced in Castlebay. We belong together.'

She was startled now and not quite sure how to handle it.

'Look at that couple over there,' she said suddenly as a girl student, somewhat the worse for drink, started climbing on the lap of her companion. 'That's *belonging together* in a rather public way. How long before they're thrown out?'

She turned her bright smile back to him but his glance hadn't changed.

He grasped her hand. 'Stop talking about things that

don't matter. It's true. We *are* the same. And I know every thought you have, as you know mine.'

'I don't know yours, Gerry. Really I don't.'

'Well you will.'

'When will I? I have so much work to do here in this university I'll never have time to get round to reading people's thoughts?'

'Not *people's* thoughts. *Mine.* I'll wait for you.'

'It will be a long wait. I'm going to get a list of letters after my name, you know.'

'Stop trying to avoid it. I'll wait for you, no matter how long I have to wait. In your heart you know that.'

She looked at his troubled face, never so handsome as now, and wondered what he meant by all this. It had a very solemn air about it. Like a vow.

She met David Power not at all during the term, and got over her pique that he had promised to ring her. She went on one date to the Abbey Theatre. The serious history student who had asked her said he hoped she didn't mind being in the gods. By the time they got there they were nearly ready for a hospital bed. He told her that he didn't believe in spending money foolishly; and when they had a cup of coffee afterwards and he said, 'You *don't* want anything to eat, do you?' Clare agreed in her mind that indeed he was *not* someone to spend money foolishly. Or even at all. He asked her to go to the National Gallery with him on the following Saturday afternoon. But she didn't like him enough; and she preferred going there on her own anyway. And it was honestly *too* mean to ask someone on a date to a place that was free. She wrote about it to Josie, deliberately making it worse than it was. She didn't want Josie to know how much fun it was in Dublin. She didn't want Josie to know that she had met James Nolan either.

James always looked deliberately well-dressed, as if he were posing as a very elegant man at the races.

'Is your nice American friend Mary Catherine loaded?' James had asked her unexpectedly in the Annexe one morning when she was having coffee and reading an article in *History Today* at the same time.

'Loaded?' She pretended she hadn't understood.

'Loaded with money, weighed down with wealth.'

'I have no idea,' Clare said, looking at him with her big dark eyes opened wide in innocence. 'What a strange thing to ask.'

'Well I can hardly ask *her*,' he complained.

'But why not? If you want to know, isn't she the one you should ask?'

'It looks odd. And anyway women are so apt to take things the wrong way.'

'I know,' Clare said sympathetically. 'Isn't it sickening?'

'You're laughing at me.'

'I am not. I'm horrified by you if you must know.'

'It's just that I was half thinking of going to the States this summer – see how American I've become? I don't say "going to America" I say "going to the States" – and if I could stay with Mary Catherine's family for a bit it would cut down the cost.'

'Sure, but why would it matter if they were loaded or not? Couldn't you stay with them, if she asked you, even if they were just ordinary, and not wealthy? Wouldn't it be a bed wherever it was?'

James looked down into his coffee cup. 'Yes, but it is my last summer holiday before I settle down to work. I'd like to go somewhere where they have a bit of *style*. A swimming pool, a ranch or a big apartment on Fifth Avenue . . . She's very secretive about where she lives. That's why I asked you.'

'Why don't you just come back to Castlebay as usual? I think the complications about America are wearing you out.'

'You don't understand anything Clare, that's your problem.'

'I know,' Clare grinned at him. 'It's always been my problem. I'm as thick as the wall.'

They parted friends, and yet Clare felt guilty. This pompous man was being a real heel towards two of her friends. It was disloyal sitting in the Annexe and giggling with him.

Emer and Kevin said they would be delighted if Clare came to stay for Easter. She had offered them a deal: she would babysit, wash up every single thing that went into the sink and do two hours a day digging the garden. In return could she have a place to stay and a little food? She had written to Angela and said she couldn't bear to go back to Castlebay: this was just the period when she had to revise and prepare for her First Arts. She'd try to square David Power too. She left a note for him at the medical faculty. He rang her that night at the hostel.

'Why should I help you?' he asked in a mock temper. 'You never helped me at Christmas.'

'Your romance didn't suffer as a result of it,' she said sharply.

'Do you have a fleet of detectives?' he inquired.

'Please, David, it's just that I really do have to work, I'm the scholarship girl don't forget, I don't get chances to repeat things. And I don't get any time at home. It's not like your house.'

'OK. *I'll* go along with *your* lies.'

It annoyed her. 'Thanks very much, David. I'll see you in the summer, I'm sure,' she said curtly.

'Oh, I'm sure you'll have thought up something else by then,' he said.

She hung up immediately before she could lose her temper with him. *Spoiled, self-important pig.*

'They *don't* resent it.'

'They do, Clare. They mightn't even realize it, but you've grown in ways that they never will. You speak better than they do, than you used to. You look better. It's not just the book learning.'

Clare twisted her glass in her hand. She and Angela were having a drink in the corner of Dillon's Hotel lounge. There was a beautiful view of the beach. Shortly, Josie would be putting her cover on the typewriter and would come for the game of tennis. Some things hadn't changed over the years. But Clare realized that Angela was right. She did have much more confidence. Her own mother would never dream of coming into the hotel and sitting down in the cushioned chair looking out over Castlebay. That wasn't for the likes of them, she would say. Her father wouldn't stand at the bar and drink his pint in the hotel either, it would be Craig's or nowhere. Jim and Ben would be tongue-tied and shoving at each other. And as for Chrissie! She and Mogsy wouldn't be caught dead inside a stuffy place like that, she had said on more than one occasion. Clare sighed. Lord knew that Dillon's Hotel was hardly the sophisticated capital of the world, but wasn't it maddening to think that she was the only member of her family who would feel comfortable there having a glass of shandy.

'I'll be very nice at the wedding. All day,' she smiled at Angela.

'Good, I don't want to sound like a sermon on charity but you have had so much more than Chrissie and you always will have. Make it as nice a day for her as possible.'

'All I'll get for my pains is Chrissie giving out to me all day, and if I'm *nice,* that will be further cause for complaint.'

'You promised.'

'Yes. What about your brother, when he was being ordained? Was that a hard sort of day?'

'No.' Angela's voice seemed distant. She was looking out to sea. 'My father didn't have a drop to drink. Dr Power gave him some tablets and told him it was dangerous to drink with them. I don't know whether it was or not. And my poor mother had a hat with a veil. I'll never forget it – and gloves. No, that day was no trouble at all.'

'You don't talk about him much nowadays.'

'I'll tell you some time.'

'Sure. I'm sorry.'

'Here's Josie and Dick.' Angela looked up brightly. 'You're looking very well, Josie. Very pretty.'

'Thank you. I've been on another diet. The summer

visitors will be here at the end of the week. I'm trying to ensnare one of them.'

'One in particular, or just anyone?'

'Well, I have my eye on one. But he's a bit hard to get.'

Clare didn't catch Angela's eye. She had told her about Josie, and James Nolan going to the States for the summer; and debated whether or not she should tell Josie this.

Angela had said she should have let it fall casually ages ago, but Clare said it was very hard to let things *fall casually* when Josie sat up on her bed and hugged her knees and made plans for the summer.

'This is the last night we'll sleep together,' Clare said to Chrissie.

'I'm sure neither of us are sorry about that,' Chrissie sniffed. She was examining her face in the mirror with dissatisfaction. There was a definite spot on her chin.

'Well, it's the end of one part of your life. It must be exciting,' Clare soldiered on.

'Well, I'm twenty-one. It's time I was married.' Chrissie was defensive.

'It'll be a grand day.'

'Yes, it will. It'll be grand without any pats on the head from you, either.'

'I'm not patting you on the head. I'm just trying to say I'm pleased. That it's great. That it's the first wedding in the family. That's all.'

Her face was angry. Chrissie softened.

'Yes, well. All right. Sorry. I suppose I'm a bit jumpy and everything.'

'You're going to look terrific. The dress is fabulous.'

It was hanging on their wardrobe with an old sheet draped over it to keep it clean.

Chrissie looked at it mournfully.

'And your hair, it's super. I've never seen it so nice.'

'Yes, well. Peg's coming round in the morning to give it a comb out. You know, get it right for the veil.'

'Maurice will be delighted with you.'

'I don't know. Look at this spot. It's going to be desperate in the morning.'

'Listen. I tell you what to do. I'll dab a bit of Dettol on it. And don't touch it, do you hear? The Dettol won't work if you touch it, and then in the morning if it's not gone we can put some extra make-up on it. But it will have flattened a bit if you don't touch it.'

'Why were you never like this before?' Chrissie asked suspiciously.

'Like what?'

'Interested in spots, and ordinary things.'

'I always was, but you used to say I was mad, remember?'

Fiona Doyle said she'd be happy to look after the shop for them while they went to the wedding. She asked how thick she should cut the bacon and was there anyone she should or should not give credit to. Tom said she was a model shop girl and that if ever the photographic business folded, there'd be a job for her in O'Brien's ten minutes later. Agnes said that Fiona was a brick to come down so early because it gave them time to get ready themselves without rushing out into the shop every time the door opened.

There had been a pink card with 'All Good Wishes on Your Wedding Day' from Tommy, and a nicely wrapped tablecloth from Ned with a small greetings card wishing them every happiness, and regretting that he wasn't able to be there. Clare saw the fine hand of Father Flynn in both of these gestures.

Chrissie had been pleased. It hadn't struck her as remotely odd that neither of her brothers would return for her big day. Agnes was pleased too. She had somehow resigned herself to the thought that the boys weren't coming home again. Gerry Doyle had assured her they were well settled there, and wasn't it better in this day and age, when half the country were down taking the mailboat to England looking for jobs, that her two sons had got there first and got themselves established. In fact Agnes O'Brien was more cheerful than she had been for a long time. Her ankle had recovered now, everyone said that it was her accident which had finally been responsible for the Committee putting up the new steps and railings, so she was regarded as a bit of a heroine.

She dabbed unaccustomed powder on her nose and looked affectionately at Tom as he struggled into the new suit he had bought. He had needed one anyway, and this was the perfect opportunity. He struggled with the unfamiliar fabric which seemed hard and full of pointy bits and corners.

'I'm just so relieved,' said Agnes. 'Glad that she's settling down.'

'Mogsy Byrne isn't the worst, I suppose,' Tom O'Brien said reluctantly.

'No, when you think the way Chrissie *could* have gone.' They'd never spoken of it before, but they had been through their worries. Was Chrissie getting a name as being fast? Did she hang round with the girls who were known to be up to no good in the caravan park? They were lucky that poor Mogsy, not the brightest man in Castlebay, but the brother of Bumper Byrne who was certainly the sharpest, was going to take Chrissie on for life.

There had been a time when Chrissie had held out for Dillon's Hotel; but after a look at the menus, the rates and whole set-up she listened more carefully to her future brother-in-law's advice. Bumper and his wife Bid had advised Chrissie not to throw away her money just making the Dillons rich. Why pour out all that money so that Young Mrs Dillon could have a new fur coat? Chrissie had wanted the day to be very splendid, but she and Mogsy listened obediently and heard that it could still be splendid without paying out a fortune. And this way they could invite more people; which was always good for business, and it didn't insult people and cause grievances.

In fact Chrissie and her Mogsy had come round to the view that Dillon's Hotel would be a very stuffy place to have a wedding anyway.

So they were having it in the big room behind Father

O'Dwyer's house. It had been a storeroom once, but Dr Power and Miss O'Hara had somehow managed to persuade Miss McCormack that it should be used for the parish. Father O'Dwyer took very careful note of what she said. Now it was used for fêtes, and sales of work. They had the Irish dancing competitions there too, and recently it had been used for weddings or christening parties. There were long trestle tables covered with cloths, and there was a big tea urn. There would be plates of sandwiches, and bridge rolls, and sausage rolls. There would be jelly and cream as well as the wedding cake. Gerry Doyle was going to take the photographs, and cousins were coming from three separate towns for the occasion.

Chrissie and Mogsy had said they were keeping it small, but that still meant forty-five people. Just enough, Agnes thought, pleased for it to look respectable. There was no question of a rushed job. Nobody could say it was a hole-in-the-corner affair.

Clare was being very good over all the arrangements, Agnes noticed with surprise. And she was keeping Chrissie calm this morning; she had even bought some bath oil at Murphy's chemist and said that Chrissie should be allowed to have the bathroom to herself for half an hour so everyone else should wash quickly or else wash at the kitchen sink. Agnes hadn't expected Clare to be so helpful. Usually she and Chrissie had nothing but harsh words.

The young couple were going on a week's honeymoon to Bray: which was just another seaside resort, but still it would be miles away from Castlebay and that was the main thing. Then they would be back, a married couple living in the new house, and Mogsy would be organizing the churns and the milk collection; and Chrissie would be back in the butcher's shop, but with a new respect now. There would be two rings on her finger, she would be 'Mrs Byrne', and she could talk about 'my husband'. Agnes felt a great surge of sympathy for her large, brassy, argumentative daughter.

She could hear laughter coming from the bathroom. Clare was scrubbing the bride's back.

'You'll be next, Fiona,' she said to the beautiful dark-haired girl standing quietly in the shop.

'Oh, I don't know, Mrs O'Brien, who'd have me?'

'Tut tut child, aren't you the most beautiful girl in Castlebay?'

'I haven't got much life in me though. Fellows like someone with life in them. I'm like that advertisement up there on the wall: *Do you wake tired?* I seem to wake tired all the time.'

Agnes O'Brien had never heard the young Doyle girl utter a sentence as long as that in her whole life. She wasn't at all sure what to do. She wished Fiona had chosen a better time to confide in her.

'If I were you I'd go and have a chat with Dr Power, it might be tablets you need. Dr Power has great iron tonics in bottles too, they'd make you feel strong. Maybe it's a lack of iron.'

The thin, kind face of Agnes O'Brien under her unaccustomed hat and dotted with unfamiliar powder was concerned. Fiona shook herself.

'That's what I'll do, Mrs O'Brien. I'll go up to him the next chance I have. It could well be lack of iron.'

Agnes beamed; and then decided to hurry on the bride and her sister.

Peggy had now arrived dressed in her bridesmaid's gear and carrying a hairbrush and a can of lacquer. She pounded up the stairs.

'Your room looks different,' Peggy said, looking around. Clare said nothing. She didn't mention that she had put all Chrissie's clothes in the wash, everything that she wasn't taking on the honeymoon. Clare would personally transfer these to the new home. Chrissie had an alarming habit of saying that she'd 'leave this here' or 'leave that here for the moment'. She couldn't grasp the fact that she was actually moving residence. Clare had taken all the old shoes and put them in a box marked 'Chrissie's Shoes'. For the first time in years there was actually room to move.

Peggy began the back-combing and the teasing of the hair, expertly and with great intensity.

'Are you sure you're not in a huff because I asked Peggy to be the bridesmaid instead of you?' Chrissie asked for the twentieth time.

'No. I think you're quite right. I told you,' Clare said.

Chrissie examined her miraculously cured spot. 'It was just that we didn't know if you'd come or not. You see?'

Clare bit back her rage. There had never been any question of her not coming. 'I know,' she said sympathetically. 'I'll try not to be *too* jealous of Peg,' she added cheerfully, and Chrissie laughed.

Peggy shrugged her shoulders. Chrissie *hated* Clare! What on earth were they laughing like old friends for? Oh well. It was her wedding day. She was entitled to laugh if she wanted to. Not that marrying Mogsy Byrne was anything much to laugh about, Peggy thought sourly. She'd prefer to be a spinster of twenty-two than marry Mogsy.

Father O'Dwyer was waiting at the gate of the church when the wedding party arrived. The Byrne family were all installed. The O'Briens arrived together – it was only a five-minute walk from their shop up Church Street and this was the triumphal journey. Chrissie walked on her father's arm. She wore a white dress, which the dressmaker had said was far more suitable as a dance dress. Chrissie had giggled, and said why not, one day it would be a dance dress. Her veil was short and held in place by a headdress of wax flowers.

It was a sunny Saturday morning in June. The season hadn't really begun; the people would start arriving in the next few days. But the whole town saw Chrissie O'Brien go to her wedding. They waved and shouted from shops and houses. Josie Dillon waved out from the hotel. Miss O'Flaherty at her stationery shop; the Murphys were in the street in front of the chemist's shop. Dwyers' had a big sheet of paper with *Good Luck Chrissie* written on it. She was very excited when she saw it, and kept drawing people's attention to it.

Behind Tom O'Brien and his daughter walked Peggy in a very bright yellow which didn't suit her.

Clare and her mother walked next, with Jim and Ben. Clare wondered would she ever walk like this with her father, as she had seen so many other girls walk to the church. It was nice because everyone had a chance to see the wedding party without having to go up to the church uninvited and peer. But Clare couldn't imagine it. She could not see herself going through this kind of parade for anyone. It would have to be somebody quite extraordinary waiting up there in the church if she could endure this pantomime for him.

Just as she was wondering what kind of person it could be, Gerry Doyle appeared at her elbow.

'Stop dreaming about me and listen,' he said.

'You arrogant thing!' she laughed.

'I'll run on ahead. Make sure Chrissie stops yapping enough for me to get a proper picture of you all coming into the church. Do you hear me?'

'Just her and Daddy? Or all of us?'

'I'll want both, but she's so excited now she'll have half the town in the picture. I'm relying on you to calm her down.'

Clare smiled at him affectionately. Gerry Doyle understood how this album would be treasured for years, when Chrissie and Mogsy had few ceremonies to entertain them.

Yes, she'd calm Chrissie down for him. Even if it meant being bossy, superior Clare again.

Chrissie became very quiet in the church, and you could hardly hear her responses. Maurice Byrne resplendent in a blue suit, was almost as mute. Only the firm unchanging voice of Father O'Dwyer could be heard properly. Then it was over and it was into the room that was too small to call a hall.

There were photos cutting the cake; and then the going away photograph of Chrissie with one foot on the ground and one foot in the car, the big Cortina that her brother-in-law was letting them drive to the station. There was confetti too – the understanding being that the family would clear it up before nightfall. Then Mr and Mrs Maurice Byrne had gone.

Nobody worked hard in Second Arts. It was a year off in a way because there was no serious examination at the end of it.

Valerie had had an eventful summer; her father had gone to hospital in England and had written from his hospital bed a long apology for his life. What had her mother done? Instead of laughing hysterically and opening another bottle to give her further fluency to curse him, didn't she up and off to England? Her father had got better; and promised to abandon the fancy woman and come home. But not immediately. These things needed time, he had said. Valerie's mother, however, had become a different person. No more morning cocktails. In fact, no cocktails at all. There was now no question of wasting as much money as possible and making-that-bastard-pay-up. Now it was different. Valerie must work hard in UCD, and make full use of the generous fees her father paid for her; she must remember that money didn't grow on trees; and what's more, they had to spend the whole summer doing up their house and getting it in order for the return of the Prodigal Father. Since Valerie had only scraped First Arts this was going to be a hard year. She was full of gloom.

Mary Catherine had been very off-putting when James had asked if he could come and call. She had said that the family would be moving around a lot during the summer; and, really, it wouldn't be a good idea, because they were sure to be vacationing with friends whenever he arrived. James had tried to pin her down by giving her definite dates; but she had been adamant. James seemed much more interested in her this year; he had asked her to a dress dance. Mary Catherine had spent the entire summer working in a soda fountain making milkshakes. It was very wearying trying to explain Ireland to people – they thought it was full of cottages and leprechauns. Her mother worked in the garment district and her two younger brothers did paper deliveries all summer. She hardly saw any of them

289

until the big Labor Day picnic that the parish organized. Mary Catherine said it was nearly as difficult to explain America to the Irish as it was the other way round. She said she was hopeless at being an ambassador and that is exactly what her father thought that she was going to be when she graduated. Why else should she be so highly educated if it weren't to get herself a big job like that? Obviously he had decided that she wasn't going to marry an Irish nobleman with a castle if she hadn't nabbed one the first year and he was pinning his hopes on her becoming a career woman instead.

Clare said she hated anyone being secretive but she had very little to tell. It was a summer like any other in Castlebay. Chrissie's wedding had been exciting, and the weather had been good. Which was smashing, because that meant business was good and everyone was happy. Yes, she had met Gerry Doyle a bit. But he had been followed around by a very glamorous piece who had been meant to stay for three weeks. Her name was Sandra. And when the three weeks were up, Sandra decided that there was plenty to keep her in Castlebay, so she stayed the whole summer. Gerry Doyle had found her a caravan that wasn't being used. They were the talk of the town, but Gerry didn't take the blindest bit of notice. Apparently she was a student in Queen's University up in Belfast, and she had a red bathing suit which she wore all summer long, with open shirts of pink and purple and orange, all the colours that are meant to clash with red. She had a big mane of hair and she used to wash it in public with a shampoo, using the new shower that Dr Power had got the Committee to put up near the bottom of the steps to the beach. Valerie and Mary Catherine were rather sorry to think that the handsome Gerry had been so spoken for during the whole summer.

'Didn't you have any adventures and romances at the dance or anything?' Valerie asked interestedly.

'No. I hardly went to dances. I went to the Committee dance, because I had to, like everyone else, but I had no romances. I worked in the shop from morn to night, it was bloody exhausting. Do you know I find myself apologizing to Josie that I don't have romances in Dublin and to you that I don't have romances in Castlebay.'

It wasn't a light year for David. This was the year of his finals. He told James that he was going to put his head down and study, and he must be counted out of any socializing. James was affronted: it was his final year too, he insisted, and the Law was every bit as sacred as medicine. Wouldn't David come to this dance and make up a party? He had invited the American heiress who had played so hard to get during the summer.

David was resolute. He was going to work.

He found Caroline less than understanding these days. She had been very moody down in Castlebay, and had fought with her mother on every possible occasion. She had been obsessed with a rather trampish-looking girl called Sandra from Northern Ireland who seemed to be Gerry Doyle's choice for parading around the town. Caroline had even worn her own shirts loose over her bathing suit and had bitten the head off her mother when Mrs Nolan had complained mildly that Caroline seemed to have forgotten her skirt.

'Do you *still* find Gerry attractive?' David had asked her in exasperation. 'I thought you got over all that as a child.'

'Oh, don't be so patronizing,' she had snapped. '*Nobody* gets over Gerry Doyle. He's just there driving everyone mad all the time, isn't he?' She said it as if it were as obvious as night following day. He felt very irritated.

Or maybe he had just lost his way with girls. That could be it. He had taken Bones for long walks down the Far Cliff Road. Bones was nice and simple. He just wanted walks and for people to throw things which he would bring back. Bones imagined rabbits for himself and went happily in useless pursuit of them. It would be easier to have been a dog. Bones felt no guilt, no uncertainties. If he didn't get what he wanted he sat panting and smiling with his foolish face, and sooner or later, someone took him for a walk, threw him a stick or gave him a bone. Bones didn't sit smoking in his kennel at night and wondering what to do. Like David did. Well, his bedroom, but the principle was the same.

For the first time in his life he had not enjoyed the summer in Castlebay. He had grown away from Caroline so much that there was hardly any pleasure in being with her. She seemed to find him plodding, and yet she didn't really know what she wanted either. She was restless and impatient, she wouldn't talk about her career and her future. It was all too silly, she said, there she was with an M.A. degree and no chance of a job, she had to learn shorthand and typing like that patronizing halfwit Josie Dillon in the hotel who kept hanging on to her and giving her advice for some reason. *A nice commercial course* indeed! She had mocked Josie's accent. David had always liked Josie: she was far more pleasant than her two older sisters. And she had been such an ugly duckling when she was young – but Caroline wouldn't have known any of that. Anyway, David knew Josie was trying to cultivate Caroline from a deep interest in Caroline's brother. It was very transparent; and futile.

But that hadn't been the main problem of the summer: the main problem had been at home.

His mother had talked happily about his coming back to Castlebay to help his father in the practice. The way she put it reminded him of the times he used to help Nellie make shortbread, or help old Martin in the garden. She didn't understand that he was almost a fully qualified doctor. You didn't go round *helping* people if you were qualified, you practised medicine. He had his intern year to do first in a hospital before he was even allowed to practise; then he was going to do a year in paediatrics and a year of obstetrics and . . . but his mother had said in that really *irritating* voice, that it really wasn't necessary to do all that extra work. The best training was on the ground. His father needed all the help he could get. He even employed a young doctor to come and help in the surgery as a locum during the summer season – there was always something happening to the visitors. He had a heavy enough caseload with the people of Castlebay themselves . . .

David knew from Nellie all about the miscarriages and the two stillbirths that had gone before. He knew from unasked-for confidences from people like Mrs Conway or Miss McCormack, what a precious child he had been. 'To have come the full term, to have survived birth, to grow up strong and handsome.' To be nearly a doctor. It was a dream come true, people said. In his disgruntled moments, David had wondered how you got out of someone else's dream and started dreaming your own.

Clare had a very satisfactory second year. She set herself a very disciplined plan of work, and kept to it. Since nobody else seemed to be doing any work at all her efforts brought her to the attention of the tutors, and this is what she needed. Her plan was to do an M.A. thesis in history, and she would need the enthusiasm and support of the various members of the History faculty, she would also need their advice about how to get money to survive. The Murray Prize was for a primary degree. Once she got her B.A., that was it, she would be on her own.

But she was determined to have a social life as well. Every Friday was late pass night and Clare made the most of it.

Living in such cramped discomfort – three in a bedroom that should really only have housed one – Mary Catherine and Valerie were also involved by necessity in everything she did. They were all more or less the same size; which was both good and bad. Good, because it meant that in dire need one good blouse could be worn by any of them. And they had even bought a black polo-necked jumper between them and insisted that anyone who wore it had to use dress shields, and it had to be washed after the third wear.

But it was *bad* when they were looking for a favourite garment and realized that it must already be on the body of one of the other two. They learned to dress for their dances and their hops and their social outings of various sorts, each sitting on her own bed: if they all stood up it was like the bear cage in the zoo.

The dressing table was an area of war. Valerie didn't buy make-up. She claimed she didn't *use* make-up, but she wore a great deal of heavy black eyeliner. (Mary Catherine's); she made heavy inroads into the Sari Peach lipstick (Clare's); she was loud in complaint about spilled face powder but her own nose was suspiciously unshiny so she must have used it fairly regularly. Mary Catherine had a habit of leaving bits of cotton wool all over the room. Wool that had removed eye make-up, lipstick or the painted pancake which she sometimes spread on face, throat and shoulders.

Clare was accused of leaving combs filled with hair around the place. Just because she had long hair, they said, this was no reason why most of it should be distributed round the room.

But despite this, they never had a tiff that lasted longer than a few minutes – except the time that Mary Catherine discovered Clare had gone out wearing Mary Catherine's only smart shoes, and that Valerie had not only broken her mascara box but what was left of it was swimming in water and was a revolting grey puddle. *That* argument lasted a long time, and included three threats on Mary Catherine's part that she would go back to the United States where people were normal.

They would go to Bective, or Palmerston, or Belvedere or Landsdowne; they were the names of rugby clubs which held dances every weekend. It was funny to go to a rugby club; nobody in Castlebay knew anyone who played rugby. Possibly David Power's school had, but even the school the Dillon boys had gone to played proper football and hurling; and anyone from Castlebay who ever came to Dublin to see a match would come for the All-Ireland finals at Croke Park; they wouldn't dream of coming for rugby international at Landsdowne Road.

Clare went to a rugby match at Landsdowne Road, one cold afternoon, to cheer on UCD. It was called the Colours Match, played every year between Trinity College and

University College. The Trinity students were very upper class; and in order to pinpoint the difference even more all the UCD supporters would chant, 'Come on COLLIDGE, C-O-L-L-I-D-G-E, college.' It got a laugh no matter how often they did it.

Clare had a date for the match, a law student called Ian. She had met him at one of her Friday outings; and he had taken her to the pictures twice, and once out to a *bona fide*, which was a pub three miles outside the city. If you were a *bona fide* traveller you could go there and drink late. Clare didn't really like Ian – he seemed a bit pompous and superior. He didn't talk about normal things, it was all 'making an impression' and 'how things sounded', or 'how they looked'. But she had been having discussions with the girls; both Valerie and Mary Catherine united against her saying that Clare was becoming the devil to please, and you'd expect a law student to go on a bit and show off. That's what they were studying, for heaven's sake, that's what they'd be doing for the rest of their life in courtroom.

Ian had borrowed his parents' car and they went to a pub after the Colours Match. Then he took her for bacon and eggs in one of the big cinemas and to the film. They did a bit of necking during the film, but Clare kept lifting her head away from him, which annoyed him greatly.

'Later then?' he asked.

'Later,' she said staring at the screen.

They drove back to the hostel an odd way, through a lot of back streets. And then there was a bit of waste ground, where cars sometime parked during the day. Ian stopped the car.

It was all very embarrassing. Clare wept later, in the bedroom, while Valerie produced some vermouth to calm them all down. It wasn't a bit like the films, where people were able to say no without offending. It was *awful*. It was like the rugby tackles they'd been looking at during the match. And worse it was all *her* fault. She had *said* later, according to Ian. He called her all kinds of names. He had said she was a tease, and that it was physically bad for a male to be put into this state of excitement without being able to relieve it. That had worried her too. It was all her own silly fault. That's why everyone said you shouldn't go in for necking and groping and all. It just encouraged boys and made them sick if they couldn't go the whole way.

Valerie said it was ludicrous that you couldn't say yes or no, as you felt like it, like having sugar in your tea or not. But Mary Catherine said it was much more important than having sugar in your tea, and that it was so complicated because there were these limits. You were allowed to go so far, and it was all fine, you were a warm sweet responsive person; and then there was some line which, if you crossed it, meant you were going the whole way, and if you didn't boys got this awful thing about being in distress.

Though they discussed it in great technical detail, they couldn't agree from their limited experience where this line was, and how you crossed it. It had been different for all three of them. Maybe it was different for everyone, which was why there was always such an almighty fuss about the whole thing.

Clare said it had been a lesson to her. She was a scholarship girl, and the Murray committee had meant her to study, not to go round in people's parents' cars groping them and being groped and then being driven home in a black fury with accusations coming at her thick and fast. From now on, there was going to be no messing with men.

She had it all planned out. She would get her B.A. in Autumn 1960, then she would study for two years for her M.A. That would bring her up to 1962. Yes, fine. Then she would go to Oxford or Cambridge to do a doctorate, her Ph.D. She would tutor, of course, while she was there. That would get her to 1964. Then she would go to America, to Vassar or Bryn Mawr, for three years as a visiting fellow. In 1967, she would return and she would take a position as Professor of Modern History in either Trinity College or UCD – wherever the History professor died first. To make her mark on the place she should serve a seven-year term, writing, of course, all the time. Then, at the age of thirty-four, she would marry. It would be just in time for her to have two children, and no more. She would marry a don in some other field, and they would have a small unpretentious house covered with ivy, and lined with books. They would live near a café and they would eat out most evenings, all of them, including the babies as soon as they were old enough to get their hands around chips.

Valerie and Mary Catherine rocked with laughter at the long-term plan, it was so detailed – the names of the most prestigious universities in the world, the age at which everything would happen, and the need for chips nearby.

'It's not a joke,' Clare said, her brown eyes full of determination. 'I will *not* teach children in a school. I'm not going to have all this open to me and end up teaching rotten, stupid children who don't want to learn. I will not teach. And I will not get married until I'm good and ready. If I wanted to get married, I could have stayed at home in Castlebay and picked my nose like Chrissie.'

'She feels very strongly about it.' Valerie spoke as if Clare weren't in the room.

'I tell you, when she's settled down with a nice job, and a nice engagement to a nice young man, she'll remember this and laugh,' Mary Catherine said.

'You're nearly as stupid as boys, the pair of you,' Clare said, and drank some more vermouth.

Clare had a phone call from Dr Power next morning. She caught her throat in alarm, but he came quickly to the point.

'Mrs O'Hara died, Lord rest her, and since you and Angela were such friends, I thought you'd like to know.'

'When is the funeral, Doctor?'

'On Sunday, but don't you go spending all your money coming back now, it was just in case you wanted to send a Mass card.'

She rang Emer, who said she would send a telegram at once. Then Clare walked up to University Church.

The priest wrote Mrs O'Hara's name down in his notebook so that he would remember to include it in his prayers at Mass. Clare had two half-crowns in her hand. He shook his head.

'Isn't it five shillings, Father? I thought that's what it was for students?'

'It's nothing, child. I'll be glad to say a Mass for the repose of the woman's soul. Was she a friend of yours? A relation?'

'No, she wasn't really a friend. She was my teacher's mother, she used to sit there while this teacher used to give me extra lessons. She has a son a priest, and that used to give her a lot of happiness even though she was a sort of cripple.'

The priest was pleased to hear that. 'Well, she'll have a lot of Masses said for her soul by her own son, but don't you worry, I'll say a Mass for her as well. He wrote his name on a Mass card, on the dotted line beside the word 'celebrant', and Clare thanked him for his generosity. She wouldn't have minded paying five shillings for Angela's mother's Mass, but it did make things a lot easier now that she didn't have to. Guiltily she bought a stamp, and stood in the post office, writing a letter of sympathy. She wondered what would Angela do now.

It took a long time to answer all the letters of sympathy and to send notes of thanks for the Mass cards and the flowers. Angela did it methodically each night. She changed the position of the furniture in the cottage and put her mother's chair upstairs so that she wouldn't find herself looking over at it.

People had been so generous – even Immaculata had been human and offered her more days off than she was entitled to. Angela had said no, thank you, she would prefer to take a couple of days at the end of term. Immaculata hadn't liked that. Christmas, and the concert, and everything. That was it, Angela said. She would find it hard to put her soul into the Christmas concert this year. So Immaculata had to agree.

Geraldine and Maire had been more helpful than she

could have hoped during the whole time of the funeral. And they distracted people, in their black coats and their English accents, and their innocent and transparently honest concern that Father Sean hadn't been able to come home for his mother's funeral. Guiltily they admitted to each other that they hadn't written to him much and that they never got more than a Christmas card from him these times. Geraldine even went so far as to wonder was he happy in the priesthood; he had been so full of it all in the early days.

But Angela was never in the position where she had to answer a direct question about him, only mumble a regret that he wasn't there to say the Mass.

There was so much to organize: food for the people who would call, beds for Geraldine and Maire, dividing Mother's things so as to give the girls something to remember her by. They even had to talk about the cottage itself. It had been very hard to sit down with her two sisters who were almost foreign to her with their talk of shops and towns and seaside resorts she had never heard of in England. But it had to be done, they were entitled to a share of what small amount their mother left.

She showed them their mother's post office book: there was just over £100. She also had a burial policy so her funeral was paid for. Angela said they would divide the £100 into four. Maire wondered should they send it all to Sean for the missions: that was what their mother was most concerned about always.

For a short minute Angela was tempted to tell them. It was late: there would be no more callers to interrupt them. It would take it from her shoulders a little if she could lay it on theirs too. They lived in England, for God's sake, they could go to see him, decide for themselves about his plight and what their attitude should be. But something about Sean and Shuya seemed too vulnerable to let them be exposed to Maire and Geraldine and their strange, enclosed worlds. She wouldn't tell them yet.

Would her mother's soul think she was right to have told Sean nothing about the death? Was that the right

299

thing to have done in terms of real and genuine acting for the best? She was very much afraid that a lot of her protestations to Sean had been hypocritical. Why did she not let him come home now and declare himself? His mother was no longer there to feel the shame and the hurt. Was there a possibility that Angela was becoming a settled schoolteacher who didn't want things upset for herself?

Angela wondered why she had never told Clare about Sean. In ways she had been closer to Clare than to anyone. Clare had her own secret and disgrace with poor Tommy in gaol over in London. But there had never been the right time. And now it was almost too late.

Angela looked at Clare's letter of sympathy, and the Mass Card signed by a priest at University Church. The girl was very good to have written so soon and to have spent what little pocket money she had on having a Mass said. Angela knew what a sacrifice that would have been. Clare had written that Angela must have some consolation in knowing that she had always been there to provide a safe and happy background for her mother to live in; and that she had done it with no sense of grudging, but with humour and happiness; that it was a great gift to give a parent. And Clare said that she would never be able to do anything as positive herself. It was possibly the only letter that didn't say what a great consolation it must be to have Father Sean praying at this time and how sad it was that he hadn't been able to get back for the funeral.

Angela went to England during the last week of term. She told the children that she would like no Christmas cards this year and that she might stay away for Christmas with her sisters or with friends in Dublin. Everyone seemed to think this was a very sensible thing to do. No point in trying to celebrate Christmas in an empty house, although there were plenty of people who would ask her for the day.

It was cold and wet on the mailboat; and stuffy and uncomfortable on the train journey to London. She was puffy-eyed from lack of sleep as she got on yet another train to take her to Sean's school.

She walked a mile from the station, and remembered the day she had come with Sean to see the big house in Ostia where his wife and babies were tucked away in the courtyard. She recalled the sense of dread she had felt then at meeting them, and how it had been replaced by sadness.

She had been here to this school before, when Father Flynn had arranged the job, in the days when the cause at Rome had not been deemed lost. Sean had still been enthusiastic, and as busy in his letters to the Vatican as he had once been in his visits.

There had been little mention of it recently in his letters. He had written that Shuya had taken in a lot of work; and that Denis was doing very well in the Junior School; Laki was getting on famously at the nearby convent, and they both had lots of friends. It wasn't really permanent or anything, but it was a very good, expensive education for Denis that they wouldn't have been able to afford.

Angela wondered what kind of work Shuya was doing: surely in a school like this they wouldn't go along with her doing mending and sewing as she had been doing in Rome? But perhaps they were less hidebound in England: maybe a Latin master's wife might well take in sewing or even washing.

Angela arrived at the small gate lodge. The garden was much more cared for than when she was last here, even though it was midwinter. There were nice silver trees and golden bushes giving colour. The door was painted a bright, sunny yellow. It was a much more cheerful house than when she had seen it first.

She knew that Sean would be at school and she intended to meet him as he left his classes and came home for lunch. He had said that one of his greatest joys was to walk across the playing fields just for half an hour's peace in the cottage with Shuya, and then walk back. Angela understood only too well how welcome that break from the shrill little voices would be. She didn't have such luxury herself: Immaculata saw to that.

She tapped on the yellow door. Shuya. A smiling, delighted Shuya, arms outstretched.

'I saw you from upstairs. I ran down. Welcome, welcome. I can hardly believe it. I am so very happy. We are all so happy. And you have a suitcase, this time you will stay with us.'

'This time I'll stay with you, Shuya.'

They had tea, and Angela looked around. Shuya was *different* somehow. Younger-looking, smarter. She had her hair up in a chignon; she wore a light-green jumper and skirt, and a big white collar pinned with a brooch of Connemara marble.

Angela had brought it the last time she came to visit, and her heart was touched to think that this might be the only piece of jewellery that Shuya had. Shuya talked about the work she took in. It was far from washing and sewing. It was typing for theses; it was translations for Japanese businesses in London; it was roneoing and duplicating for anyone that needed it – one of her biggest customers was the school itself. They found it far better to pay Mrs O'Hara for neatly done examination papers, or notices, or leaflets, than to work a machine themselves and ruin reams of paper. She had quite a cottage industry going, she told Angela proudly; and she even employed a girl to come three afternoons a week to help her.

On the piano there were pictures of the children; grown now so much that Angela realized she would hardly know them. Denis, over ten years old and Laki eight. In another frame was a picture of her mother, the only nice one that had ever been taken. Young David Power and James Nolan had taken it years ago when they got a camera first and were busy snapping everyone in the town, to try to set up as some kind of rivals to Gerry Doyle. It had been a rare thing to catch her mother smiling, without the lines of pain on her face.

Her eyes rested on it. And Shuya noticed.

Very quietly she said, 'Have you come to tell Sean about his mother?'

'Yes,' Angela whispered.

'Is she very ill? Does she ask for him?'

'No. It's not that.'

'Because if it helps, he must go, go alone, dressed as a priest. If it is best. I will persuade him, if it is best.'

'No Shuya, no. She's dead. She died a month ago.'

'One month ago?'

'I know. I know. I had to make up my mind on my own. It seemed best.'

There was a silence.

'Please Shuya, wasn't it best? It took the decision away from him. Sean didn't have to decide.'

'Maybe he should have decided. Maybe he can't be protected all the time from having to make a decision.'

'I don't know anything any more,' Angela said sadly.

'Forgive me. Please, what am I thinking about? Your mother has died, and I give you no sympathy. I must be so cruel and thoughtless. Tell me about her death. Was it sudden?'

'Yes. Yes, she had a heart attack, you see. If it had been something slow then I would have let Sean know. But it would have been too late for him and I didn't want . . .'

'Please. Please. I think you did what was going to be the most painless for Sean. As always you acted for his good.'

Shuya stood up and put her arm around Angela's shoulders. 'You did what was best. I thank you for not having to go through all that with him. All the agonies. I thank you for giving us all this peace. He will become resigned to his mother's death. She has only been a dream to him, for thirteen years, since he last saw her. It is not a real person he will mourn. It is an idea.'

'You are wise, Shuya.'

'I think I shall be a teacher. I am doing examinations that will qualify me to teach typewriting and shorthand. I suppose they will recognize these examinations in Ireland.'

'Well, yes. But are you going to Ireland?'

'Sean talks of little else.'

* * *

Shuya pointed out the path she should walk to meet Sean. She said she would leave them alone in the house to talk. The lunch was all ready.

He wore a heavy overcoat with the collar turned up and his hands were in his pockets. He looked younger than a man of almost forty. His face split open into a big foolish smile . . . he started to run towards her and then stopped.

'Is it bad news?' he asked suddenly.

'Mam died very peacefully. She died without fear. It's all over.'

He blessed himself. 'The Lord have mercy on her soul.'

'I came when it was all over to tell you.'

'You're very very good to us.' He took her and hugged her to him.

'I hope I did right. It was all so quick and so sudden. I could have telephoned you. I rang people to tell Geraldine and Maire. But I just didn't, Sean. I thought that if Mam can see you she'll understand everything and it would have been too much on you, and, to be honest, on us.'

She felt better having admitted her own selfishness. He had his arm around her shoulder as she walked back to the gate lodge with him.

'Does Shuya know? Have you told her?'

'Yes.'

'What does she think? Does she think it was for the best that Mam is dead and buried without my being there?'

In a flash Angela understood what Shuya had meant. People *protected* Sean. They kept the world away from him. If she were to say now that Shuya gave her approval there would be the quick smile of relief and everything would be fine.

'Yes. Shuya said it was the right thing. She thanked me for giving you all a gift of peace, that was the way she put it.'

Sean smiled as she knew he would. 'I would like to have been there to hold my mother's hand. But if it all happened so suddenly, then thank you again for shouldering everything, Angela.' His arm was around her companionably still. 'Was it all very sad, very harrowing?'

'No. You know the way people say it was a blessing. It was, Sean. She was in *such* pain, all the time. Every movement was an ache or a stab to her. She couldn't dress herself, or move without help.'

His face was pained. He wouldn't want this to be part of his idea of his mother.

'Dr Power said that she had the worst arthritis he had ever known. And she was incontinent too, not because she really was, but because she couldn't get up in time.'

He closed his eyes with distress.

'It wasn't much of a life. She wasn't really happy from the time she woke up in the morning. It *is* peace for her. I look at the corner of the room where she used to sit and I think that all the time.'

'How long ago?'

'A month. I couldn't come any sooner, because of school. You know the way it is.' She smiled at him the resigned conspiratorial smile of one teacher to another.

They had reached the house. He looked anxious that Shuya wasn't there when they went in.

'She's gone into town. She said she'd leave us to talk, I told her there was no need.'

Angela found herself pouring the soup for her brother, even though this was not her house. She put on a kettle to make tea afterwards. She cut the bread. She had been in the door only a minute and already she was mothering him.

'I wish the children had seen their grandmother. They have no grandmother,' he said.

'Well neither did we, Sean, not to speak of. Dad's mother was dead before we were born, and Mam's mother died when I was a baby. You don't remember her, do you?'

'No. But Denis and Laki will have a better life than we did, things are different now. And they know that one day they'll go to Ireland. I have books, look, here . . . Lots of books about Ireland, so that they'll know. And we have books about Japan too. They're not going to grow up confused, and not knowing who they are like we did.'

'You want very much to come to Ireland, then?'

'But I've always said that.'

'I know. I know.'

Sean thought about his mother being dead and put his head in his hands. It didn't seem real to him, he said, he thought of her cheerful and full of chat and bursting with information about things and the centre of everything. She *had* been a bit like that perhaps in 1945, when Sean had last been home, when the glory of the priest-son in full regalia very largely compensated for the loss of the drunken troublesome husband who had been a heart scald to her for her whole married life. Yes, Mother was bright in her spirit then, even if she had pains in her joints. And Sean hadn't seen her since. He could be excused for thinking that she had been a woman with as clear a glance and a smile as she had in the photograph frame on the piano.

She played with her cheese salad while he talked about times gone by.

'We'll say the rosary for her tonight, all of us,' he said. 'That will make it important for the children.'

She wished she could get it out of her head that her brother was living in mortal sin and that it was quite incongruous for him to be organizing rosaries. And yet he seemed to see nothing out of character in it.

'Will the new Pope make any difference do you think?' she asked suddenly, reaching out and touching his hand. 'He looks kind.'

'It hasn't got anything to do with kindness. It's just as complicated and tedious as the civil service,' Sean said sadly. 'If I could *get* the papers to John XXIII then it would be a matter of days – but if I could have got them to Pius XII it would have been the same.'

'Does the fact that it's gone on so long mean there's more hope or less?'

'I don't honestly know. It means that there's more red tape, I suppose. If something has already been looked at by one person then other people are slow to take the file themselves.'

'Do they know here?' She nodded her head up to the school.

'At the very top yes. Otherwise no. I was very lucky to get in here.'

He was much less confident than he was before. There was a time when he would never admit that he was lucky to have got anywhere. It was all open to him, the whole world, whatever life he wanted. This whole business with Rome had changed his thinking.

But before they had the children with them, before they were all kneeling and saying a rosary for the dead grandmother the children didn't know and wouldn't have understood, she had to go back to his plans for Ireland.

'So you think you'd like to come back to Castlebay.'

'You wouldn't mind?'

'No. Of course not,' she lied.

'Well I know you said that, long ago in Rome. You did say that the only reason for me to stay away was because it would break Mam's heart.'

'That's what I said. I'm not going back on it.' She couldn't be any warmer. It just wouldn't come out as more welcoming. It would be lunacy. It would upset everyone, the enormity of the deception for all those years. Denis, a big boy of ten. How could he not see it?

'No, no, I know you're not going back on it. You've always been straight as a die, Angela. No one could have a better sister or friend.'

She made the tea, and poured a cup for herself. Her hand was shaking.

'It's been awful for you, all of it. What will you do now, will you live on in the house on your own?' His voice was full of concern.

'I don't know yet. I will for the moment.'

'Yes, yes.'

'Maybe you'll want the house? If you come back that is?'

Now she had said it, brought it right out in the open. This nonsensical idea of the priest going back to live in his native town with his Japanese wife and grown-up children.

To her relief he didn't seem to think that this was automatically the way things would go.

'Oh, I don't think we'd want to *live* in Castlebay. Where would I work? Where would they go to school?'

Angela fumed inside for a quick moment. What was so wrong with the convent where she taught? Or the Brothers, which had been good enough to educate Sean O'Hara. Still, this was all to the good.

'True, I suppose. But you do want to go back do you, and meet everyone – talk to Mrs Conway in the post office, Sergeant McCormack, the Murphys, the Dillons.' She had deliberately chosen awful ones to mix in with ordinary people. She had to tread carefully.

'Well, it's my home. It's where I came from.' He was defensive. She didn't want that at any cost.

'Don't I know it's your home – I'm offering you Mam's house to live in. Of course it's your home. I just asked what sort of way you'll be coming home. Will it be in the summer? Do you want me to let people know you're coming, or will you explain it all when you get there?'

'I thought that you'd . . . I don't know. That's something that can all be arranged later.'

'Of course it can.'

She went to see Father Flynn on her way back through London. He said they must go out and have dinner.

'I know now why people become priests. It's a licence to eat dinners out in restaurants for the rest of your life. I never ate in so many restaurants before or since as when we were in Rome.'

'Ah, those were the days all right. But this is half-work. Young Ned O'Brien asked me to the place he's working in. The landlord's just opened a dining room off the pub, and the bold Ned no less is running it. Wait till I turn up with his ex-school marm.'

'I don't think he'll be a bit delighted. Not that I ever taught him anything. I don't think we can lay his educational deficiencies at my door. And Tommy, he's out isn't he?'

'For the moment. That was something I was going to ask tonight.'

'I'll make myself scarce.'

'You don't need to. He knows you're in on it.'

'You're grand and easy about things, Father Flynn. Is it something that goes with the job, like deafness goes with teaching?'

They saw Ned, important and nervous at the same time. Father Flynn pretending ignorance of everything so that Ned could put him at ease. In the midst of doing this Ned lost a lot of his own nerves. He explained that there were three things you could have: steak, chicken or fish. And you got soup before and ice cream after, no matter what you chose. But the price depended on the main course. He could have Father Flynn as his guest but, to be honest, he wasn't sure about Miss O'Hara. Angela said that there was no question of her being a guest, she was going to have steak, the dearest, and was going to love it.

'I'm very sorry to hear about your mother, Miss O'Hara,' said the head waiter of the new dining area in which they were, as yet, the only guests.

'How did you know about it?'

'Clare writes to Tommy every week, regular as anything. She told him. I sort of . . . well, I read the letters to him. I'm very sorry.'

'Thanks Ned. She was old and in awful pain, it was for the best.'

'I don't think Tommy'll stay long with your friends, Father,' Ned hissed out of the side of his mouth.

'A pity. Why?'

'He keeps thinking these other lads will be looking for him. I don't think they want to see hair nor hide of him, but he has had a message that they're leaving him some money next week, his share like.'

'But if they don't want him in on whatever they're doing, then maybe he *might* stay with the Carrolls?' Father Flynn had got Tommy a live-in job with an Irish family who owned a small greengrocery. Tommy would be sweeping and helping at first, but they'd keep an eye on him; and if he was any way helpful at all, they'd give him a shop coat and let him serve the public.

'You know Tommy, Father. He's just a big baby.'

Angela sighed and wondered were all brothers big babies.

'What will I do, if Sean comes back to Castlebay?' she asked, later.

'You'll survive it, like you've survived everything else,' said Father Flynn.

She went back to Dublin in time to spend Christmas with Emer and Kevin. The boat was filled with returning emigrants, singing and happy to be on the way back to small villages or towns all over Ireland.

The house was full of holly and ivy and long paper chains across the hall. Emer hoped they weren't too cheerful. After all Angela had been recently bereaved. No, she assured her, they were exactly what she wanted to see. Clare would be dropping by that evening on her way to the station. She had a Christmas present for Daniel and Emer had invited her to supper.

Clare looked thin and tired, Angela thought, but was very cheerful. She told them she was hopeless with men and that once she felt her academic work was under control she was going to take lessons from someone who knew. It was apparently like bridge and driving a car: even stupid people could be good at it if they learned the technique.

Clare wished that she could stay here in this pleasant, easygoing household for Christmas, but shook the idea away. She was looking forward to seeing home again. There would be no Chrissie, and she had painted her bedroom before the summer ended. There was good news about Ned from London and no bad news about Tommy. Angela had been full of detail, and had even written a letter to Clare's mother to describe the elegance of Ned in his new job. Compared to everyone else's Christmas hers would be fine.

Valerie was going to have to face the return of the

long-lost father, and *Mary Catherine* had been invited to the Nolans and was wishing every minute of the day that she had refused. Clare thought about them both as she stood on the cold platform of Kingsbridge station waiting for the train.

On an impulse she went to the phone box and rang Val, who was still at the hostel.

'I'm in a great hurry. The train's nearly going. Tell him what you think, don't go along with all your mother's lovey-dovey bits. *You're* not in love with him. He's your father and he walked out on you. Tell him that you were greatly upset and that it might take a bit of time to be sure he's back for good.'

'What?' Val was stunned.

'There's no need to pretend that nothing happened. That's pretending that he's a madman. He left when you were thirteen and needed him. Don't just gloss over that, or he'll think it was a perfectly reasonable thing to do.'

'Then we'll spend the whole of Christmas fighting, and my mother'll come after me with a cleaver,' Val said.

'Nonsense, you can do it without a fight. Happy Christmas.'

She looked the Nolans up in the book and rang. James was surprised to hear her on the phone. 'Nothing wrong is there?' he asked.

'Heavens no, James. You're far too young to think a telephone call means bad news.'

He was annoyed – as she meant him to be – and went to find Mary Catherine.

'Tell them your father's a postman. Immediately,' Clare said.

'What?'

'The only reason you're not going to enjoy Christmas is because you're going to be up to your ears in pretence. Tell them, for heaven's sake, the moment they ask, or *before*. They're not going to throw you out in the street.'

Mary Catherine started to laugh.

311

'Well will you?' Clare said impatiently. 'I have to go for my train in a minute.'

'I guess I will,' Mary Catherine said. 'When you put it that way, there's no sense in not.'

The porters started shouting excitedly that the train was now backing into the platform and would be ready for boarding.

Clare wondered what would someone say to her if they were to give her good advice for Christmas just as she had been dispensing to others. She decided that Angela's age-old advice had always been the best. She must be *positive* and *cheerful,* and never let them think her education and her hopes were a threat to them.

She did all of that as if it were a Christmas homework she had been set to do. She helped her mother make a last-minute Christmas cake. She called to see her married sister's new house. She went with Jim and Ben on the back of a cart to a farm where they had a lot of holly and ivy and were glad to see people thinning it out. They decorated the shop and the house.

She went for long walks with her father down the Far Cliff Road, and discussed with him seriously the possibility of buying a soft ice-cream machine. There was little to discuss, really, except whether her father had the courage to borrow the money to buy one or not. It would obviously be a huge draw; sooner or later someone else in Castlebay would get one and a lot of trade would move to the place where the delicious whipped-cream cones were on offer. But Clare's father hunched his back and worried over and over about the wisdom of getting into debt for something that would only be used eleven weeks of the year. Clare said that people bought those soft ice-creams in Dublin even in the winter. You often saw people eating them in cinema queues. But her father puzzled and wondered . . .

Dad looked old and tired; and though he said he liked to get out in the fresh air to walk with her the wind seemed to hurt his eyes and make him seem frail. She debated telling him about Tommy; but the debate with herself did not take long. A man who couldn't decide whether or not

312

to get an ice-cream machine couldn't possibly cope with having a criminal son.

Josie was cheerful, but busy. She had decided all on her own to inquire whether there might be a demand for a Christmas programme, as it was called in hotels. And there was; they were going to have twenty-nine guests over Christmas and everyone was in a fever of excitement. There was bad blood between the family about it, and her sister Rose, who was meant to be coming into the hotel full time, said that since *Josie* seemed to make all the decisions nowadays, what was the point, and she was going to go to another hotel.

David Power came into the hotel that night for a drink and to wish them well in the Christmas programme. The guests were assembling and the Dillons were at their wits' end. They had never thought of finding someone who could play the piano. In the summer they always gave bed and breakfast free to any student who would play the piano in the lounge in the evenings.

Josie's mother looked at David appealingly. 'Just for about an hour, David? You would be helping us better than you could ever believe.'

'But I'm no good,' David protested. 'Clare, can't you play?' he beseeched.

'No. In my education, there was never time for it. But a renaissance man like yourself now. Every social skill . . .'

'I *hate* you, Clare O'Brien,' he said good-naturedly.

Josie thanked him profusely and led him to the piano. Haltingly, he got into a version of 'There Is a Tavern in the Town'. Dick Dillon, who was planted amongst the guests, began to sing and in no time they were all joining in. It was obvious after about three songs that he would be there all night. Dick got him a pint and left it on the piano. Bones, who had been sitting patiently in the hall, hoping that the music would stop soon, was taken into the kitchen and given a plate of soup. He fell asleep beside the Aga and dreamed of sandhills full of rabbits and big firm beaches when the tide was out, where people would throw sticks for him hour after hour.

In the summer of 1959 some people said that the world was going to end: it was the hottest weather ever known. Tom O'Brien cursed his cowardice as he saw people troop past his door to go to Fergus Murphy's soft ice-cream machine. Fergus built up a lot of business because people bought sweets and magazines and groceries while they waited for the ice cream queue to file by. The Castlebay Committee congratulated themselves on their foresight in organizing a booking register so that visitors could be directed to the available rooms in the resort rather than having to knock on doors. There were two full-time lifeguards and when the tides were high people had to bathe between two flags. Nobody drowned that summer in Castlebay, and nobody fell and hurt themselves on the paths up the cliffs because they were all finally built properly with rails to hold on to. People still went into the Echo Cave and asked it questions. The Dillons were very distressed to hear of plans for a new and huge hotel but were subsequently overjoyed to discover that two of the five businessmen who were going to start it were undisclosed bankrupts at the time, so that plan never got off the ground. Dr Power said he was getting old and slow and he was so proud that his big handsome son had passed Final Med with flying colours. He would do an intern year in Dublin and then who knew what would happen.

James Nolan was called to the Bar and did his first case in court. He said he thought he was never going to get another brief but he carried a great many papers tied with pink tape.

Fiona Doyle announced her engagement to Frank Conway, the pride and joy of Mrs Conway. Mrs Conway had never been anxious for her Frank to marry anyone, and she had her doubts about the Doyles in general. Gerry was as wild as anything and should be kept in a zoo if half of what you heard about him was true. And the mother was odd – some kind of phobia they said. She hardly ever went out. But you couldn't say a word against Fiona – a good-looking girl, great self-respect. She'd never let a man near her, even in the days when a girl was silly and could have her head turned. Mrs Conway sighed. Frank could have done a lot worse, she supposed. She gave them her blessing. And then that pup Gerry Doyle had the impudence to say he'd like a *talk* with Frank, since Fiona had no father. Mrs Conway never found out what the chat was about, but it had impressed Frank no end.

Chrissie Byrne discovered on her second visit to Dr Power that she was indeed pregnant, and bought a maternity smock on the way back from the surgery to the butcher's shop. Ned O'Hara came back for a flying visit to Castlebay with his fiancée, Dorothy. Dorothy thought everything in Castlebay was terrif. When she and her Neddy got old, like about thirty, they would come back here and start a restaurant. Dorothy thought the O'Briens' house was terrif. Dorothy's mother was Irish, and she wished that her mum had taken her to Ireland before – it was simply gorgeous.

That summer, a registered envelope arrived for Agnes O'Brien. There were twenty-five ten-pound notes in it and an ill-written note from Tommy saying he had been saving for years to get a present for his ma, and now he had.

Tom said immediately that they must tell nobody outside the house about it. They discussed long and secretly that summer what Mammy would do with the money. Chrissie was left out of the discussion because she was a Byrne now and if Bumper, Bid and Mogsy knew about it they'd be down like a flash.

In the end it was spent on a new coat for Agnes and the long and often discussed extension on the side of the shop. It was Tom O'Brien's one concession to the magnificent site of his business: he wanted a Perspex roof on an extra room where they could put a couple of tables and chairs. This way they could serve those who wanted to sit down for their Club Orange or their tub of ice-cream. And they were even going to add sandwiches and tea next summer. Tommy's gift made it possible.

In the summer of 1959, Mother Immaculata asked Angela O'Hara whether she intended to stay on in the school or, now that she was free to see the world, if she planned to travel. Angela, seeing that Immaculata would love Miss O'Hara to roam off around the world, said firmly that she was going to stay in Castlebay. It was also the summer that Dick Dillon asked Angela O'Hara to marry him and she said very gently that she thought they would drive each other mad within months, and the ambulance would be arriving from the town and they'd both be locked up in the asylum on the hill. Dick had smiled bravely and she had patted his knee and invited him to the Committee dance so that he would know she liked him greatly.

Clare's professors said she would get a First: they were all in agreement. *Clare O'Brien to get a First* – she said it to herself, not caring to believe it. Any student with a First was worth looking at. From then on she would never have to apologize again. Clare went off into one of her rare little daydreams in the National Library. Imagine it. Never would she have to tell people she was only a scholarship girl or she had to do this because of some Committee or other, she would be her own person. And a scholar. She tore a page from her ring file and decided to write to Angela O'Hara there and then. She wrote as she hadn't been able to write before, she said that somehow for the very first time she believed that it was actually happening. Only now did she feel it had worked, all that praying up in the church, and all the shouting in the Echo Cave and all the learning and learning, the disciplines that Angela had taught her.

Angela replied by return of post. She said that it was the most wonderful letter she had ever received in her life. It made everything – and everything included the seagull-faced Immaculata – all worth while. She said it was a letter written on the crest of happiness, and from that heady standpoint the world was there for the taking. She hoped that that would last for ever.

It was a warm and generous letter. Clare folded it in

four and put it in the little flap at the back of her big, black leather notebook. The book, which she carried everywhere, had been a gift from the nuns in the secondary school when she won the Murray Prize. Immaculata had sent her a picture of Maria Goretti, with a big padded frame of coral-pink velvet. Fortunately her mother had liked it and it hung in the back of the shop getting grimier and dirtier as the years went by. Gerry Doyle had given her a fountain pen. He had insisted. He had only been asked to do the pictures he said because there was a candidate from Castlebay. She knew this wasn't true but it was nice of him to say it. She still had the pen. She never lent it to anyone and she always put the cap on very carefully, clipped it to her notebook and then put a rubber band around the whole thing. She had so few possessions that she valued them all. She thought about Gerry. She could never write to him like she did to Angela but somehow she did want to talk to him. It would be nice if he came to Dublin again and they could walk by the canal maybe, or she could show him off to the girls. She sighed. She'd never get any kind of degree if she spent time daydreaming like this.

Still, she bought a postcard of O'Connell Street and sent it to him; a cheerful card saying it would be nice to see him if ever he passed through Dublin.

She heard nothing for ages.

She was annoyed.

Thank God she wasn't in love with him.

It was neither one thing nor another, being an intern; David discovered that very early on. Some people thought he was a fully-fledged doctor, who knew *everything*; others thought he was a schoolboy dressing up in a white coat and wouldn't ask him the time of day in case he got it wrong. And the hours! There was the solidarity of a prisoner-of-war camp in the Res, where bewildered young doctors coped with the unfamiliar and the frightening without any sustained sleep. They told each other that they would never sleep again. That their metabolisms would never recover from the strange hours and speeds at which they had to grab food. And even more immediate and urgent – their social lives were now finished for ever.

James Nolan, handsome, well-dressed young barrister, carrying his black bag that contained wig and gown casually slung over his shoulder, said he despaired ever of seeing David any more.

David was paged urgently, and rushed to the phone. 'Dr Power speaking.'

'Dr Power, this is Mr Nolan, barrister at law. I wondered if you would like to come and have a long boozy lunch with me. I got a cheque for seven guineas.'

'A lunch?' said David in disbelief.

'You *know*. You've heard of them. They're what people have in the middle of the day. Food and wine. You sit at tables.'

'You bloody don't do that here,' David said.

'Well, can you come? It's a gorgeous autumn day, walk a bit towards me and I'll walk a bit towards you.'

A wave of impatience came over David. How could James be so insensitive? He had no idea of what David's life was like. He had been up all through the night – but that made no difference to today's schedule. The ward round went ahead as usual. Blood tests here, a drip there, organizing an X-ray for another. The ward Sister – a poisonous woman – never gave him any information about the patients: she confided all that only to the consultants. The housemen were made to look fools as a result.

This morning a difficult patient had pulled the drip out three times, and so three times it had to be set up again. Then there was the teaching round with the consultant. And now he was in outpatients. He had been examining a man's swollen foot when James had rung.

As politely as he could, David told James that he would have to find someone else to celebrate the seven guineas and to lunch with. David's own lunch would be something very quick and not very nice. If he ate at all. Then it would be dealing with admissions, seeing the patients, getting the preliminaries sorted out before greater men came to deal

318

with them. And he was on call after that. Barristers? Lunches? Guineas? Bloody parasites.

He returned to the man with the swollen foot. 'I don't know,' he said honestly. 'I'd like to see the other foot. Can you take off your shoe and sock?'

The man was hesitant.

'So that I'll be able to compare,' David explained.

Reluctantly the man took off the other shoe and sock. The foot that he knew would be examined was nice and clean. The foot that he hadn't expected to be asked to bare was filthy. It was a foot that had not been washed in a long time. David stood slightly back from it to see if there was a similar swelling. His eyes met the eyes of the foot's owner.

'I didn't think, you see . . .' the man said.

'I know,' David said sadly. 'That's the trouble. We hardly ever do.'

He was on his own. He had never felt that Dublin was lonely when he was in the medical school, but now, isolated in hospital, it was different. That was your life. You didn't escape from it – or if you could you found nobody to escape with.

Full of self-pity in the darkening evening air, he walked up Kildare Street. People were going in and out of the National Library and the College of Art. The Dail had its guards at the gate, and that seemed to be bustling too. Everyone except David Power had something to do.

Suddenly he saw Clare leaving the library with her bunch of books. She looked lovely in the evening light.

'Clare! Clare, I was hoping to catch you,' he lied.

She was pleased to see him. He tucked his arm into hers. 'Will we go and have a coffee?'

'Sure. What were you hoping to see me for?'

'To ask you if you'd come out tonight. I know it's ridiculous short notice and everything but we never know in the hospital when we'll be on or off.'

She didn't seem put out by the shortness of notice. She'd love to. But first she had to go back to the hostel and see was there a message. Someone had said he was going to be in Dublin, possibly tonight, and if so she and her two friends were going to go out with him. If not then she'd go with David.

'I can't say fairer than that,' she said.

He grumbled as they walked towards the hostel: why three girls and one man? What kind of superman was this?

'It's Gerry Doyle,' she said simply, as if that explained everything.

A great and unexpected surge of annoyance swept over David. Gerry was so *cheap*. His line was so *obvious*. When he was a kid he had thought Gerry was good company, there was always a touch of the dangerous, the daredevil about him. But not now. Gerry was too slick. And too *much*.

'I thought you'd have outgrown him,' he said in a very superior voice.

Clare was surprised. David Power didn't usually talk like this. 'Nobody outgrows Gerry,' she said. It was an echo of what Caroline Nolan had said to him. A flash of anger came over him.

'What's so great about him? Has he some new technique as a lover or something?'

'I wouldn't know.' Clare was cool.

'Well, what *is* it then? It's not his intellectual conversation is it? Surely Gerry Doyle isn't a rough diamond concealing a poetic soul?' His face was twisted in a way she had never seen before.

'Why are you so cross?'

'I'm not cross. I'm just disappointed with you for making yourself so cheap. You've always been different. Why be so bloody predictable? Following as soon as Gerry Doyle raises his little finger. Gerry's a nobody, Clare. He's just *trashy*, you deserve better.'

She was unaware of the crowds moving up and down the street and even the people who had to move off the footpath because they couldn't get past the angry young couple.

'You keep your disappointment to yourself, David

320

Power. Don't come bleating it out to me. You can take yourself off with your insults and your jeers. *You're* the one that's cheap, not me. I've been working here all day, and now I've finished. I'm going back to my friends and if Gerry's around he'll cheer us all up and make us laugh. He'll make no comments about whether we're predictable or not. He'll be nice to us. That's what you'll never understand in a million years. Gerry is *nice* to people. He's *glad* to see them. He smiles and he asks them questions and he listens. He *likes* people. And I'm *glad* he's coming to Dublin tonight, and Val will be glad, and Mary Catherine will be glad.'

'I didn't mean . . .'

'Oh, go away and leave me alone. I'm tired.'

'I'm tired too. I've been on duty since I don't know how long. I'm cross-eyed with tiredness.'

'Yes,' she said briefly. 'I see that.'

'Can I still come along with you, if he's there, or . . .'

'No. You cannot. I'm not going on an outing with you both knowing that you've said he's cheap and flashy and what was it . . . trashy. I'm not going to sit in a pub with you and know that you mocked at him and his lack of education, and made fun of his intellectual conversation. You can find your own company tonight. And whoever it is, she has my sympathy.'

Clare turned away. David watched her as she walked in a rage along Stephen's Green.

Clare had a letter from David a week later.

People often make jokes about medics being illiterate and now I see why. It's so long since I wrote anything that wasn't an examination answer, a report on a case, or notes at a lecture, I'm not sure how to begin. But I want to say I was in an extremely bad mood the other day when we met and I am very sorry indeed for taking it out on you. I really do apologize. You were minding your own business, you were loyal to a friend. I just behaved like a boor. I don't know why I said all those things about Gerry Doyle. Reluctantly, I have to put it down to simple, unattractive jealousy. I've always envied him his easy charm. I envied his reputation as a ladies' man. And that night in particular I envied him because he was going to go out with you when I wanted to. It's hard to say all this, and I'm sure I'm saying it very badly but I want you to know I regret it all very much. There's a Halloween dance in the hospital. I'd love you to come as my partner . . .

Clare sent him a postcard. David turned up at the hostel, in James Nolan's car, to collect her. She wore the same yellow and red dress that Mary Catherine had worn to the dance with James.

'Same dress, same car, only the cast has changed,' Mary Catherine said as she looked out the window.

'Don't they breed them handsome in Castlebay,' said Valerie watching David in his dark overcoat and white silk scarf, tucking Clare into the car.

They had decorated the Res up with funny faces cut into turnips and little nightlights burning inside. There were pictures of witches on the wall, and the lights were covered in red or black paper. They had apples hanging from a string and you had to bob for apples too. Everywhere there were basins and baths and the fronts of shirts were wet as heads were pushed far into the water. The hilarity was more important than the actual trapping of the apple. They had a big selection of records; and a lively nurse with her leg in a plaster cast was responsible for playing them three at a time, saying after the third, 'Thank you very much, end of dance, thank you.'

David was very popular, and much in demand for the Ladies' Choice. Clare was nearly knocked down in the rush of nurses towards Dr Power. It was funny to hear him called that. She kept expecting to see his father.

He introduced her to other doctors, interns and even registrars.

'Who's looking after the sick tonight?' she asked.

There was a system of call, and about a third of the

people there couldn't drink in case they were needed.

'Those are the ones to watch out for,' a bearded doctor told Clare. 'If they can't drink, their minds are very definitely set in other directions.'

'I'd better stay with the winos then, if I want to keep my virtue,' she laughed. David seemed proud of her, and she saw him with new eyes. In this world he was relaxed and funny. She never thought of David Power as someone you laughed with. In fact, when his face came to her mind, she used to think of him as being a bit solemn. Either with his parents when he was young, or walking with Bones along the beach in winter.

Of course when the Nolans had come to Castlebay he had been fairly excited and laughing during those summers when she had been stuck behind the counter in the shop . . .

'What are you thinking about?' He was dancing close to her.

'About you,' she said truthfully.

'Good. Were they happy positive thoughts?'

'Yes, I suppose they were. I was thinking how well you fit in here, how happy you seem.'

'I think that about you too. You always disapproved of me in Castlebay.' He was half teasing.

'Jealous, I suppose. You had more freedom. You could have such a good time.'

David smiled. 'I used to envy all of you. A sweetshop, you could come and go as you liked, they weren't sitting waiting for you to come in, hanging on your every word . . .'

'No one's ever satisfied with what they have. I told you that. Do you remember?'

'I remember. I didn't think you would,' he said. 'I remember it because I thought it was a sad sort of thing to say and to mean.' His smile said he wanted her to cheer up.

She laughed at him, and at that point the music changed to a faster beat, and Mary Catherine's red and yellow dress was swung into a very energetic version of 'Down by the

Riverside'. It was actually a Ladies' Choice but David and Clare hadn't noticed. Several nurses retreated in defeat.

The supper was magnificent. Real Halloween food: colcannon, mounds of mashed potatoes with chopped-up onion and kale in it as well as threepences and rings. There were plates of sausages, and afterwards huge amounts of toasted barm brack, with extra rings pushed in so that there could be a lot of happy screaming at the thought of a marriage within a year.

Clare got a ring, which she nearly swallowed. 'Lord above, how frightening,' she said.

'Did you nearly choke?' David asked.

'No, the thought that I'd be married in a year.'

They were sitting in an alcove of the big room, a window seat away from the crowd. They had brought their glasses of red wine, and the noise was away in the background.

'Would that be the end of the world?' he asked.

'Yes. It would. The end of *my* world.' She explained her plans, the M.A. the Ph.D. the terms in the United States, in Oxford or Cambridge and finally the history professorship. She felt he was smiling inside.

'I will, you know. I really will. If I got this far I can get to the moon.'

'I know.' He was gentle.

'You don't know, David. You really don't. For all that you were brought up beside me, you don't know how hard it was to get here. I don't want to go on and on about it. But, you see, it's not just like saying I want to be a film star, or I want to be the Pope, for me to say I want to be a professor of history. When I was ten I wanted to be an Honours university student. And who would have believed then that I could?'

'You give me very little credit. I do know. Of course I do. It's you knows nothing about me. What do you think I want for my career? Tell me. Go on.'

She paused. 'I suppose you'll go home and be a doctor with your father,' she said.

'See, you don't know a thing. I'm not going back to Castlebay for ages. If at all. Being a doctor like that in a

324

small place . . . You choose it. You can't have it chosen for you.'

'But everyone thinks . . .'

'Everyone thought when you were a small girl in the convent that you'd leave school and marry someone from up the road. Like Chrissie. But you didn't.'

'It's not the same. If you didn't want to be a doctor why did you become one?'

'I do want to be a doctor. But I haven't become one yet. I have years more to do, at least four or five in different hospitals learning under specialists, seeing the new developments . . . There's much more to being a doctor than saying tut-tut-poor-thing and knowing when to call the ambulance.'

'So will you be a specialist?'

'I don't know. I think I would like to be a GP, like my father. But not yet. And not in Castlebay. Can you see anything so stupid as sitting down with my mummy and daddy, like I did when I was a young boy, coming home from school, and describing How I Spent My Day?'

She giggled. 'I know, it does sound silly. But perhaps you'll marry someone and then it won't be like that. It will be more normal.'

'Not yet. And if I'm going to wait for you to be thirty-four, I'll be nearly forty.'

'Oh, I wouldn't go back to Castlebay even when I'm thirty-four. You'd better not marry me,' Clare said, anxious that there should be no misunderstandings. 'I just said I'd be ready to marry then, not give anything up like my Chair of History.'

'I think you'd be too complicated for me. I think I'd better marry someone else all right.'

'Caroline Nolan? Would she be suitable?'

'Not really.'

'Why not?'

'I don't know. My mother thinks she'd be suitable. Her mother thinks she'd be suitable. Her brother thinks it too. That's probably why.'

'Does *she* think she'd be suitable?'

'I don't know,' David laughed. 'Let's dance.'

A red-haired doctor with a Cork accent asked David if he would lend him the lovely lady in the red and yellow dress for one dance. He was called Bar. He said most people in Cork were called some form of the name Finbarr, with his being the patron saint. Bar said that he was a registrar and very important in the hospital and that David's whole career would depend on Clare being nice and willing and co-operative and giving herself in every way to Bar. Clare pealed with laughter at this and asked whether this line of chat ever worked.

'Sometimes,' Bar said gloomily. 'But less often than you'd hope. Women seem to be brighter these days. They have minds and things.' Was she David's girlfriend? No. Good. Just a girl next door from Castlebay, that was nice. Clare said it wasn't exactly next door, but this was never a concept you could explain to anyone in Dublin; they all thought that you were rewriting Cinderella if you explained the gulf of difference between the O'Brien and Power families.

Bar was holding her very tight and saying that he was on call so he couldn't have a drink, which made the party a bit of a bore – but on the other hand it did sharpen his awareness of who were the best-looking girls.

Diplomatically, Clare released herself in order to help him choose the best-looking girls. Bar found this irritating but he couldn't fault her. They were discussing the attributes of a group of girls in the corner when David rescued her.

'Thank God,' she said as she danced with David again. 'That fellow's like an octopus.'

'I'm disappointed that groping is out,' he said.

'David! You'd never grope. You'd make sophisticated gestures when you knew the feelings were returned. Aren't I right?'

'You are. God you are,' David said, holding her close to him but not allowing his hands to roam like those of Registrar Bar, the octopus as he would be known for evermore.

On the way home he parked the car. Clare looked up in alarm.

'It's all right. I haven't turned into an octopus. I just wanted to talk for a bit. It's one of the few nights I'm not crashing to the ground with sleep. James says I'm the most boring friend to have. I have no time off, and I can't stay awake when I do.'

They talked on easily, happily, like old friends.

'We should go out together, sometimes . . . you know, the pictures or a coffee. What do you think?' He looked enthusiastic and casual at the same time. He didn't sound as if he were asking her for a date, or a commitment, just friendship.

'I'd like that, certainly. Of course I would,' she said.

'There'd be nobody to bother us here,' David said. He didn't need to mention that there would be plenty of people to bother them in Castlebay. He gave her a kiss on the cheek to settle it and drove her back to the hostel. He watched in alarm as she climbed up the iron rungs and disappeared through a window.

'Was he nice?' Mary Catherine asked sleepily as Clare climbed in the window.

'Very.'

'Did he jump on you?'

'No, no. Nothing like that.'

'But it's desperately late, what else were you doing?'

'Talking. Just talking.'

'God, that's serious,' Mary Catherine said, waking up.

'Don't be silly, go back to sleep, I've hung up your dress, it's not too sweaty.'

'What is it?' Valerie was awake now.

'Clare's back. She *talked* to him all night. They're in love.'

'Great,' Valerie snorted and settled down again.

'I'm *not* in love. Even if I wanted to be in love with David Power I couldn't. So there.'

'Why? Is he in fact your long-lost brother? Why not?'

'Because his mother would throw a cordon of Guards around the big house on the cliff if she thought that any of the O'Briens from the huckster's shop had notions about her son. That's why.'

Clare had snuggled down in her bed and pulled the sheets to her chin. Mary Catherine was wide awake and concerned. 'You can't let that kind of crap stand in your way! You're not going to tell me that . . .'

'I'm not going to tell you anything till tomorrow. *Goodnight* Mary Catherine.'

Ned's letter was short. Tommy had left Mr Carroll's greengrocery shop on a Friday. He had said that he wouldn't take his week's wages. He had got another job and it wasn't fair to ask to be paid for the last week. The Carrolls had telephoned Father Flynn, but no one could find Tommy. Until the following Wednesday, when the police found him. In a stolen car which had crashed during a police chase. The car was being chased because it was seen leaving the scene of a robbery with violence. Tommy had ended up with a dislocated shoulder, a broken jaw and a nine-year sentence. Ned just wanted to ask Clare whether someone should tell Mam and Dad now or was the pretence to go on for ever.

Poor, stupid, *stupid* Tommy. She couldn't think of him as bad Tommy, dangerous Tommy, in with a gang of thugs and joining in their violence. She could hardly remember him, but he had seemed nice like Ned was last summer when he came home.

She would tell them. But not by letter. And not making a special visit.

She would tell them when she went home for Christmas.

It was hard to choose the moment to begin. There never seemed to be any time when they were all together. Mam was thin and tired, but she was always on the move, from range to table, from kitchen out to shop, from shop to storeroom. Dad was always fiddling with things, and Jim and Ben were coming in one door and out another.

After tea, the first night home, she thought she had them all in one room, at least.

'I have some bad news about Tommy,' she said loudly, to get their attention. 'He's not injured, or sick, or anything. But it *is* bad news.'

They all stopped what they were doing. She certainly had their attention.

'So will you sit down, and I'll tell you,' she said.

'Stop acting like a judge and jury. What is it? If you've something to say, say it.' Her father was annoyed.

'I wanted to tell it to you from the start. Jim, why don't you put the sign up on the door?'

'How long is this going to take, for God's sake?' Tom O'Brien was now worried.

'Tommy . . . Tommy . . .' The tears were already starting to form in Mam's eyes.

One by one, they sat down round the table and she could hedge no more.

'I had a letter from Ned. Tommy's in gaol. He's going to be there for . . . for a long time.'

'How long?' Mam's voice was almost steady. She didn't ask what he had done, or why he was there. Just how long.

'This is hard, Mam. Very long. Nine years.'

She looked at the table. She couldn't bear to see the shock round her. They had all thought that Tommy was living an ordinary life until twenty seconds ago. Now they had to try to understand all this at one go. She *should* have told them ages ago.

'You can't mean nine *years*,' Agnes said. 'You can't mean *years*.'

Clare told them what Tommy had done. She told them what he had done before. It seemed like a story about somebody else's brother as she was telling it. She looked at her mother's face, and realized that it certainly sounded like the story of someone else's son.

Gerry Doyle came in while she was telling them.

Mam was crying. Dad was throwing back his head and saying what would you expect. Jim and Ben were round-eyed, and teetering between a grudging admiration of their

329

brother for doing something as brave as running with a gang and a sense of horror about the disgrace that was going to fall on the family.

'I didn't think *Closed* meant me,' Gerry smiled around the kitchen door.

'It does tonight.' Clare gave him a smile that wasn't a smile, and to her relief he understood.

'Sure. It was only a packet of fags. I'll take one and run. Pay you tomorrow. All right?'

He was gone. Clare settled down again for the abuse. How dare she play God and decide to hold the first bit of news back from them? What did she and Ned think they were playing at, telling packs of lies? How could anyone know now if *this* was the whole truth? And who was this priest that none of them knew, fiddling in their affairs? And did Ned's fiancée know all about it too? Was she in on the whole deception?

Clare soldiered on. Already it was getting easier. The more they knew, the less frightening it became. She wished that she had told them ages ago, she admitted this to them, but she said truthfully that since she had hoped that Tommy might have just had that one phase, it would be a pity to damn him in their eyes for ever.

Mam wondered did anyone else in Castlebay know. And Clare looked her straight in the eye and said that nobody knew. She decided that she could trust Angela and Gerry. They had kept it to themselves so far; there was no reason for them to speak now.

The news made them look older. All of them. Clare wondered had it done that to her too when she got the first letter from Ned. Mam's thin shoulders stooped more under the navy cardigan she wore, and Dad's face looked grey and set while he painted the new extension that would never bring him a day's happiness now that he knew it was built with stolen money. Jim and Ben lost a bit of their good spirits. Clare saw that they stayed in the house more than usual, rather than roaming the town looking for divilment with their friends from school.

Chrissie arrived on visits, the size of a mountain now,

and said that it was like going to visit a graveyard instead of your own family at Christmas time. If this was the cheer that Clare brought home with her she might as well have stayed in Dublin.

Clare said she was going to spend a day with Angela. They were going to go over a lot of work Clare had to do for her finals.

'Don't be telling her our business now,' Agnes warned.

'Why would I tell her anything of the sort?' asked Clare. She had planned to spend hours discussing it, if Angela had the time.

She lost the sense of time there. They must have had tea, or a meal. There was certainly drink, a bottle of port wine was on the table.

At one stage Dick called, and Angela asked him to go away.

It wasn't all Clare's tale.

The story of Father Sean O'Hara was told too. Not only had he left the priesthood years and years ago, but he had a grown-up family nearly. And they were all coming to Castlebay for the summer. They had booked a caravan. Father Sean O'Hara was coming back to show his home to his Japanese lady friend, and to show his children their roots.

In Dublin Clare could meet David anywhere she liked. He could come to the hostel to collect her, she could take a bus up to his hospital and they could have coffee in the canteen. They could go to the pictures or to have a drink. Nobody took any notice. In Castlebay it was almost impossible to do any such thing. Without even saying it they knew they were going to be further apart for the two weeks they spent in Castlebay than if they were on different sides of the Atlantic. They didn't have to tell each other that it would be awkward to invite the other home. They knew. Like they knew about spring tides, and about Father O'Dwyer's sermons. Clare would not be invited to the Powers' for supper. David could chat easily with the O'Briens across the counter, but they wouldn't let him in to see their kitchen with its old rusty range, its torn lino and its boxes of supplies all round the place, an inelegant overflowing storeroom for the shop which had never been properly organized.

They couldn't go and sit in Dillon's Hotel for hours on end, or the whole town would know about it. Clare didn't play golf, and Castlebay would have mocked her if she had learned. It wasn't for the likes of Clare O'Brien. That meant the golf course and its rolling dunes were out. If they went to the pictures together there would be talk.

And they didn't want talk. It wasn't worth it. They weren't in love with each other. They were friends. They were great friends. But such a concept didn't exist in Castlebay, and if it were going to exist it was very unlikely it would develop between the handsome, eligible son of the doctor and the bright perky little girl from the store.

They went for a long walk with Bones. David had had a bad row with his mother that morning and was not going to apologize in order to keep the peace. He had said he was going to the pictures that night and he was thinking of asking Clare. Molly had said very sweetly that it wouldn't *do* at all. It would be unfair on the girl. It would give her ideas. Raise her hopes. Furious, he had said this was rubbish, that he often met Clare in Dublin and neither of them had any hopes, just a good friendship. Molly had raised her eyebrows very high and said she thought David could have done better for himself, a professional man, than to be going out with the sister of Mogsy Byrne and Chrissie O'Brien. He had laughed in his mother's face and said that since she couldn't find anything to blame Tom and Agnes for, she had to draw in the least respectable member of the family and her eejit of a husband to complain about. Molly Power, with two bright spots of red on her face, had stormed out of the room and upstairs. His father had already gone out on his rounds but the whole thing would be aired again this evening. He almost told Clare but stopped. She might take it as a slight, even though she was always making jokes herself about confusing the rank and file of Castlebay.

Clare nearly told David about Tommy. He was so nice and understanding, so solid and unshockable, he might well reveal that both his mother's and father's parents had been in gaol for years. But she didn't want him to have more things to apologize for when he met her. Nellie had told Chrissie that there had been an almighty row this morning already about David meeting Clare at all. Better not let him know she was the sister of a criminal in an English prison as well as being one of the poor O'Briens, God help us.

There were New Year's Eve celebrations in Dillon's Hotel but Clare didn't feel any heart for going. She suggested to her mother that they ask Angela O'Hara for supper.

'We're not the kind of people that have people to supper,' her mother said.

'Maybe we should be,' Clare said. Her father said he didn't mind, it was no concern of his what the women did or didn't do.

The evening was a surprising success. Angela taught them to play rummy and even Agnes began to enjoy it. She had been hesitant at the start and wanted to stay out of it. Angela said more than once that it was very nice to spend New Year's Eve with a family.

'Oh, you wouldn't call this much of a family,' Tom said disparagingly.

'Why ever not? One daughter married and going to give a grandchild this spring. Another, the town genius. Two lads in England making their own way, two here, and please God there'll be work for them when they leave school. A good business . . . what more of a family could you want than that?'

Agnes said when you looked at it like that it was true, they had a lot to be thankful for. But she sighed a sigh that went down to her feet almost as she said it.

'Everything isn't as it seems,' Tom O'Brien said darkly, shaking his head.

Angela nodded enthusiastically at him. He was absolutely right, nothing *was* as it seemed, there wasn't a family in Castlebay without its own sadnesses and worries and confusions. She often thought that at Mass on a Sunday, people kneeling there so calm-looking and only the Lord knew what was in their hearts. Every one of them had a worry. She had hit it just right. This gloomy-sounding old soothsaying cheered up the O'Brien family greatly. They weren't alone in their cross. In fact Clare's father was so cheered that he thought it was time for everyone to have a glass of something to see the sixties in. They wished each other Happy New Year and shortly afterwards Angela left: she had promised Dick Dillon to look in on him in the hotel and wish him the compliments of the season.

Clare walked her up the road. She felt very wide awake and restless. She went to the seat that the Committee had put up last summer, the big green seat just at the top of the steps. A perfect vantage point for surveying the beach on a crowded summer day. Tonight you could just sit and look at the stars and the bright clear night. The sea looked navy somehow, and the cliffs like cardboard cut-outs.

Gerry arrived, silently, and sat beside her.

'You pad around like a leopard or a cat,' she said. 'You frightened the life out of me.'

'Happy New Year,' he said taking a half bottle of brandy and two little metal cups out of the pocket of his leather jacket.

Clare clapped her hands in delight.

'Aren't you one of the wonders of the world. Do you go round with mobile picnics and parties in your pocket all the time, or is it only on festivals?'

'It's only when I see you on your own. I was coming out of the hotel. I saw you coming down here, and raced home for the supplies.'

They toasted each other and looked out to sea.

'This is *the* year, isn't it? The finals, the big degree?'

'Yes, Lord I'll have to work when I get back, I'm doing nothing here. I thought I was going to get lots of reading done, but I haven't opened a book.'

'I'm sorry for intruding the other night. Was it a family conference?'

'It was about Tommy.'

'Don't tell me. It's not my business.'

'Oh no, it's all right. You know anyway. But he did it again, and this time they wounded a man so badly he'll be in a wheelchair and Tommy's gone to gaol for nine years.'

Gerry let out his breath like a whistle. 'Nine years. Lord.'

'So this time I decided I would tell them at home. They have a right to know. They were very low as you can imagine. Angela cheered them up a lot tonight. But they think nobody knows, so I swore that nobody did.'

'Sure.'

He was easy and her restless feeling was fading fast. Or maybe it was the brandy. He had put his jacket around both of them. It kept out the wind, and it was companionable. He kissed her, a long gentle kiss. She didn't pull away. He put his arms inside her duffle coat and held her to him as he kissed her again.

She felt something touch her leg and jumped.

It was Bones looking at her eagerly, waiting for her to disentangle herself from Gerry. Behind Bones, a dozen yards away, was David.

'I was just going to say Happy New Year,' he said. 'I'm sorry. I didn't mean to disturb you.'

He turned very quickly and walked along the Cliff Road home.

Bones looked hopefully at Gerry and Clare, in case there was going to be any fun and games for him. But deciding there wasn't, he cantered off after David who was walking unnaturally quickly through the bright starry night.

His parents were still at the hotel. Nellie had gone to her family. The house was empty. David nearly took the door from its hinges with the bang he gave it.

He was going to sit down in the sitting room where the fire was still warm and have a drink to calm him down but the fear that his parents would come back and that he would have to talk to them civilly was too great. He poured himself a large whiskey and went up to his bedroom. He pulled back the curtains and looked out at the sea. Years ago, when Gerry Doyle had first seen this room, he had said in admiration that it was like a ship. You could see no land unless you turned your head or leaned out to see the garden beneath.

There were two big rooms with bay windows upstairs, and his parents slept in the one next door. David had a window seat running round the three windows of the bay. His toys had been kept inside it when he was young. He looked to see were they still there and indeed, there was a small cricket set, a blackboard and easel, there were boxes of soldiers and boxes of playing bricks. His Meccano set was still there and there was a box which said David's Colouring Things.

It annoyed him to see them still there. And yet what should his mother have done with them? Given them away? They were his after all, and one day he might want them for his children . . .

But anything would annoy him tonight.

It had been a very boring evening. He had made a very tactless mistake with Josie Dillon. Apparently Clare had never mentioned that Mary Catherine had been an off-and-on girlfriend of James Nolan since the Lord knew when. Josie had been distressed by the news but even more by the fact that Clare hadn't told her. She had become quite weepy and had gone off to bed before the singing of 'Auld Lang Syne', so that would have to be sorted out.

But nothing had prepared him for the strength of his feelings when he saw Clare in Gerry Doyle's arms like that. He felt sick all over until he was nearly shaking to think of it again. Him, with his arms around her, inside her coat, fondling her, and kissing her, there on the bench in the dark, with a cheap half-bottle of brandy at their feet. David had walked up to them because he recognized Clare's duffle coat, and the moonlight was shining on her fair hair. It was quite obvious who she was. He hadn't really seen Gerry; it was dark that side of the bench, and they weren't kissing when he started to walk over. If only Bones hadn't rushed across he might have been able to escape without speaking to them.

But even so it was churning his stomach to think of Gerry Doyle's mean, small, dark face pressed on Clare's. To think of *him* giving her brandy and forcing himself on her. And to imagine that bright Clare, lovely, bright, sunny Clare, could be so stupid as to fall for it. Why was she letting him crawl all over her?

David felt so sick he couldn't finish his whiskey. He poured it down the wash basin, and lay back on his bed.

He was pale at breakfast and his mother asked him whether he might be getting flu.

'There are two doctors in this house, Mother. Leave the diagnosis to us,' he snapped.

Dr Power looked up in alarm. 'I heard a kind courteous inquiry after your health from your mother who is concerned about you,' he said quietly.

'Yes. I'm very sorry. That's what I heard too. I apologize, Mother.'

'That's all right.' Molly was gracious. At least he was able to say sorry now, a few days ago when she had said something perfectly harmless about the young O'Brien girl he had leaped down her throat and he had *not* apologized on that occasion.

'I'm in surgery all day, David. Do you want to take the car and drive off somewhere? It might be a nice break for you.'

'That's very nice, Dad.' He paused. He'd better make the offer. 'Would you like to go for a drive, Mother?'

Fortunately it was a bridge afternoon and she had to get ready for it. But it was nice of him to ask her. Honour had been satisfied.

New Year's Day or not, people would have their ailments and Dr Power shuffled off into the other side of the house. Nellie made David a big turkey sandwich with lots of stuffing in it and a flask of tea. He didn't even notice where he was driving until he came to a wild rocky place

337

he had only seen from the road before. He parked the car and got out.

It must have been the same for centuries, he thought. Bleak and unwelcoming, the sea washing on it endlessly, as remote in the summer as in winter. Who would walk for forty minutes as he had through thickets and briars and down stony crumbling paths to get to a place that didn't even have a sandy beach? He threw stones into the water mechanically, one after another in a kind of rhythm. He couldn't be so obsessed with Clare that he shivered at the thought of Gerry touching her. He was only awake last night because he had drunk too much, because he had a stupid quarrel with Josie Dillon, because he was worried, as he was always worried, about this business of coming home to live like a child again in the house with a mummy and a daddy and a doctor's coat.

But her face was there, and her shoulders, and her hair. And her bright smile, and the way she was always so interested in everything and had so many views on any subject. He remembered the day he had felt so annoyed with her outside the National Library in Dublin when she was running back to her hostel to know if Gerry had rung. He remembered the relief that she didn't seem to be at all interested in the amorous Mr Doyle. Her work plans were daunting and over-ambitious, but she was certainly destined for a first-class B.A. and acceptance as an M.A. student. So why was she behaving like a cheap tramp last night? That's what it was. The cheapest way to go on, with a bottle of spirits and right in public. And with Gerry, who had felt up and touched every girl who was any way attractive and quite a few who were not.

His hand throwing the stones into the sea paused and he dropped the stone and clenched his fists. Gerry Doyle would never touch her again. Never. He would keep his hands to himself. He would not go near Clare O'Brien, he wouldn't dare. Last night had just been silly, a New Year silliness, to be excused but never to be repeated.

He would explain this to Clare, and she would understand. They would even laugh about it.

But what would he explain?

He wished he had taken Bones with him. Just looking into the dog's foolish face helped; but he hadn't known where he was going to go and the dog could have been a liability.

What would he say to Clare?

The wise man would say nothing. The wise man would make a little joke and forget the scene on the cliff top.

But David began to think he was not a wise man. He could not forget the tableau and he couldn't stop a feeling of light sweat forming on the back of his neck at the memory.

He couldn't want Clare that badly for himself. He couldn't. It must be pure bloody jealousy that Gerry struck lucky on New Year's Eve in the cold, while he, David, had a boring evening listening to old-timers singing 'Darling, You Are Growing Old' – which was too painfully true – having a totally ludicrous conversation with a tearful Josie Dillon, and then coming across Love's Young Dream on the bench.

No. It was more. He wanted to see Clare. Now.

He wanted to tell her that she was special. And to ask her to give him a chance to prove himself her lover as well as her friend.

It was highly awkward, but as sure as he knew anything he knew he loved her.

Clare didn't know why she felt so furious all next day. There was no way she could fault David. He hadn't been rude. Under the circumstances he had been polite. His voice hadn't dripped with sarcasm, as it had that time he had unleashed a tirade about Gerry in Dublin when he called him trashy.

But she wished he hadn't come along. It had been nothing, it had only been a couple of kisses, and she didn't think it would have gone any further. It was too public a place for one thing; and she *wouldn't,* for another.

But she had this feeling that David was always on the verge of going on to another level in their friendship. She had never admitted this to the girls. She kept telling them how unsuitable the liaison would be, and they made jokes about the security forces Mrs Power would need to employ and where she should station them around Castlebay. But Clare knew it wasn't just a joke.

She felt they talked as she never could with anyone. They didn't just talk gossip or plans. She was always interested to know what he thought about things. He never bored her. And she had the feeling that he was delighted with her. But he had never touched her or kissed her. So she was a bit in the dark about what he really felt. She would like to have been close to him, closer than she was, but she didn't want to push it because she had no idea at all how he felt.

Anyway it might be just hero worship. When she'd been the poor little girl in the shabby cotton dress in the shop, David and James Nolan had been swaggering round Castlebay like gods. Now she was their equal in a way. He sought her out and didn't meet other people at all.

It was all such bad timing. If only she had stayed at home. Or gone straight home. Or said no to Gerry Doyle. Or if only that big idiot of a dog hadn't spotted them and come like a detective to find them out.

She'd never know now what David Power had felt about her, if anything. It would have vanished on that cliff top last night. *Damn* Gerry Doyle, to the pit of hell.

Very few people came in on New Year's Day. It was a holiday of obligation and they had all been to early Mass. Clare hadn't looked round to see if David was in the church. She thought she saw his father, but she didn't want to meet any of them. She hurried home afterwards, down the quiet cold street.

Clare decided that she would invite Josie to supper, too. If only her mother would get out of this servile approach things would be much better. There was no reason why Josie Dillon shouldn't have sausages and beans, and brown bread-and-butter in their kitchen. She would enjoy it.

Clare had tried to catch Josie's eye in the church, but

Josie looked away every time. Possibly she hadn't seen her.

The shop doorbell went. Her father was cleaning the paintbrush out in the back. Ben and Jim were reading the funnies in a paper. Chrissie had arrived for a woman-to-woman chat with Mam and was sitting on a hardbacked chair while Mam ironed. Clare had been half reading a very dense account of the differences between common law, equity and statute law, for what she had been hoping would give her a better understanding of the history of the English courts.

'I'll go.' Chrissie quite enjoyed meeting the public and serving them now that she was such an important person in the town. Mrs Maurice Byrne, and seven months pregnant too.

'It's young Dr Power, for Miss O'Brien,' she said scathingly on her return.

Clare went out and pulled the kitchen door a little closed behind her.

'Please come out with me now. Please,' he said as if preparing for a long debate about it.

'Right,' she said and took down her duffle coat from the hook.

She was surprised to see the car outside the door.

He held open the car door for her, and then ran round the other side. 'I wanted us to go for a drive,' he said. His eyes looked very bright but he didn't look upset.

'Yes, of course.'

They drove to that strange rocky place, bleak and dangerous. They got out of the car and looked down at it. Apart from the seagulls, there wasn't a soul around.

'I was down there this morning,' he said.

Clare said nothing.

'I was down there for a long time. Throwing stones in the sea. And I realized something.'

She looked at him.

'I realized I love you,' he said.

'I love you too.'

She didn't know why she was crying, it was ridiculous

341

to cry when this happened. This was the best thing in the whole world that could happen. Why did the tears come down out of the corners of her eyes? She could taste them mixed with the spray, the salty spray which came up and whirled lightly around them as they kissed each other and held on to each other on the cold New Year's Day of 1960.

PART THREE

1960–

David's father and mother drove him to the train; Dick Dillon and Angela drove Clare.

'There's David,' Angela said, pleased, as they stood on the platform.

Clare was casual. She had a book in her hand already. Everyone knew she was going to study all the way to Dublin. David waved cheerily, and his mother nodded, a kind of bow as if she had hurt her neck. Dr Power had gone to the newsagent's stall to buy David a magazine for his long journey.

When the train was half a mile from the town they were in each other's arms in the corridor, each whispering the other's name over and over. They were going back to Dublin. City of freedom. So Clare was in a hostel run by nuns and David was a resident doctor in a big city hospital. Compared to where they came from this was licence and freedom.

The book on the history of law and the magazine just bought at the news stand lay beside each other on the seat of the train unread. The train was not crowded. They had a compartment to themselves for most of the journey, and when they were joined it was by an elderly American who said it was the coldest country he had ever visited in his life and he had visited a few. David encouraged him to wrap something round his feet – it was the extremities that often felt most cold. The American had a huge muffler and they tied it loosely around his ankles. He was asleep in no time and they kissed and held hands and snuggled up to each other happily in the corner without interruption.

They had two whole days in Dublin before anyone knew they were back. Clare's hostel didn't open till Sunday; and

David wasn't expected in the hospital until eight a.m. on the Monday morning. It was only Friday night. They had made no plans, almost as if they both felt it might be unlucky.

Now in the winter evening outside Kingsbridge they walked past the line of taxis and to the bus. Clare had one small case, David two huge ones. She accused him of having brought all his washing home for Nellie to do and he opened his eyes wide. Didn't everyone do that?

She wanted to ask him what they were to do now. Or better, she wanted to tell him all her options: she could stay with Kevin and Emer, if he wanted to go and stay with James for example. She could go to the hostel and throw herself on the mercy of the nuns. They thought she was one of the most reliable girls they ever had, so they would grumble only a bit and let her into her room – even though it hadn't been aired for her and no hot-water bottles had been put in the small iron beds.

She had £18 in her wallet. They could stay in a guest house: there were lots of them in Glasnevin, she knew lots of students who had cheap digs out that way.

But she thought she should wait and see what David had in mind. Her throat closed over once or twice in case he suggested that they sleep together. She hoped and prayed he wouldn't ask her to. Not yet. She had to think. It was all too sudden.

As they got on the bus to O'Connell Bridge, David said easily, 'You know the flat I used to stay in before they locked me up in the hospital?'

'Yes.'

'I still have the key. And I can go there always. There'll be nobody back until Monday. And there's lots of rooms. You could go in the one I used to have, it's one of the nicest. And I could go . . . well anywhere. Far away from you, I think, so that I won't come and break down the door and get at you.'

She smiled at him, relieved that she hadn't spoken, pleased that he felt the need to break down the door,

346

and very grateful that he wasn't going to. He had said absolutely the right thing.

They had a honeymoon without sex. They held hands and she took him on tours of her Dublin. He had never been inside the Bank of Ireland to look from within at what had once been the Irish Parliament. He said he must have known that but somehow he had forgotten. She promised to take him on a weekday.

She crossed the road with him and showed him the book of Kells in Trinity College. He said he had known it was there and he had been going to see it one day.

They climbed Nelson's Pillar to look out over the city. It had a long, dark, windy staircase. There was a lot of pausing to catch breath and to kiss. David embarked on a long tale of a doctor who was married but having an illicit romance with another married lady. They couldn't go anywhere to make love because they were too well known, so they used to meet twice a week inside Nelson's Pillar and make love on the stairway. If any tourist climbing up or down was troublesome enough to interrupt them they just flattened themselves against the wall.

'That's why I brought you here of course.' She laughed and jumped lightly ahead of him so that he'd know she wasn't contemplating it for a moment. She took him down the Quays to St Michan's, an old Protestant Church where they had a totally preserved mummy in the vaults.

In the evenings they made themselves meals. David was rather better at preparing them than Clare.

'I thought you'd be very domesticated, big family, all those brothers to cook for,' he teased.

'I'd be fine throwing a big dinner for eight on the table, lump of bacon, half a ton of spuds. But I've never cooked just for one or two. We get the food handed to us up in the hostel.' She sounded apologetic.

'It's not the end of the world, Clare. Stop looking so mournful!'

'What will we have tonight? Will we go out and get something or what?' She hoped he'd say that they'd get chips from the place down the road.

'Oh, there's lots of eggs there – why don't you just make an omelette?' He was talking absently, concentrating on clearing out the grate.

Clare looked stricken.

'There's a bit of cheese there, isn't there? We could have a cheese omelette,' he called.

'I'll do the fire, *you* do the omelette.'

'Don't tell me you can't make an . . .' David stopped when he saw her face.

'We never had them at home. If you show me, I'll know then.'

'Listen, it doesn't matter, scrambled eggs, anything . . .'

'Show me how to make an omelette. I want to know.' Her face was set and determined.

'All right then.' David was good-natured. 'It doesn't matter a damn, you know, you *do* know that, don't you?'

They kissed over the frying pan. It didn't matter a damn.

On Sunday night, he asked her. 'What are we going to do?'

'I don't know.'

They sat for a long time on the floor with a bottle of wine between them.

'It's too soon isn't it? We met too soon.'

'We met when we were babies, David.'

'You know what I mean. Now. It's too early.'

'I love you. The other seems unimportant. I wouldn't want to be a history don somewhere without you.'

'I don't want to be anywhere without you.'

'Maybe we can go round the world only taking universities that will have research facilities for both of us.' She smiled nervously.

'But in real life . . .' he said.

'Yes. Real life. Which begins tomorrow.' She looked stricken.

He kissed her and rocked her in his arms. 'Nothing bad can happen now, I was never more sure in my life. I'll love you for ever. I half loved you always and didn't know it.'

'No, nothing bad can happen now,' said Clare.

*   *   *

They knew immediately of course. Mary Catherine and Val. There was no point in denying it.

'Do you mind if I don't talk about it,' she said.

'Yes we bloody do,' Valerie said indignantly. 'What kind of nonsense is that? We've told you everything, every pant and groan.'

'It's very unfair to hold out on us now. It's secretive and it's not like you at all. I can't understand it.' Mary Catherine was upset.

'But there's nothing to tell. I beg you, there's no new panting and groaning in it, in fact there's a lot less than there was with Ian that night in the car. So now, will that satisfy you?'

'It will not. How did it happen? Did he say he loved you, did a thousand violins start to play? I *must* know.' Valerie was sitting on her bed, legs crossed like an old-fashioned tailor. She looked very young, Clare thought. They were all young, nobody was twenty, she was too young to feel the way she did. The realization swept over her.

'You see I'm too young,' she said stupidly.

'For what? God Clare, you're very irritating when you put on this dramatic bit. Does he think you're too young for him or what?'

'No, but it's all right for him. He's old, he's twenty-five. His life's nearly over. In terms of studying I mean.'

'This is very tedious,' complained Valerie.

'I *told* you it was tedious,' Clare said defensively.

'It may pass over. Seriously, if you've known the guy all your life and never thought about him in that way until ten days ago, it's bound to blow over.'

'It won't. That's what really is going to be tedious for you. I can't think of any better way to put it than this and it's going to make you vomit.'

'Say it,' said Valerie grimly.

'I feel as if I'd been looking and looking for something I'd lost and now I've found it. It's like going home, except much nicer than going home, it's like you think going home should be.'

'It's a bit soppy,' Val said objectively.

'I'm afraid it is.'

'Will you be any fun do you think, ever again?' Mary Catherine asked.

'Oh I hope so, but do you see what I mean, it's no good my talking about it, I can only use these awful, sickening words.' She looked from one to another.

'It's going to be very hard,' said Val. 'In the middle of a perfectly normal conversation about sex or about who we're going to set our sights on at a party we'll remember that you've had this coming home feeling about the boy next door.'

'Will you do me one favour, will you get it into your heads that he is not the boy next door. Whatever he is, he's not that.'

He was hungry for every detail of her, he told her that he used to envy the O'Briens as children going off with their jam jars picking blackberries, or with the same jam jars on strings trying to catch pinkeens. There were always children running in and out of the shop and calling to each other winter and summer while his own house was very big and you could hear the clock ticking in the hall.

She told him about how terrible Chrissie had been and somehow they made her into a comic character. All her cruelty, and pulling Clare's hair, and trying to persuade her she was abnormal didn't matter any more.

He told her about his father and how he tried hard not to drag David back to the practice but he really wanted him there. Tomorrow. David admitted that his mother sometimes drove him mad. She was full of childish nonsenses; but years ago in a man-to-man talk his father had urged him not to be impatient, and said that Molly had given up a lot of bright lights and fun to come to a backwater as a country doctor's wife. It irritated David greatly that his father should be somehow grateful to his mother for this. It was her choice after all. And there was the history of miscarriages and stillbirths so she had to be forgiven her little silliness from time to time.

He told her that his mother came to Dublin every year to spend a few days with the Nolans; and he used to be ashamed of her carry-on, sitting in the lounge of the Shelbourne, or the Ibernian or the Gresham having afternoon tea. Far too dressed up, and asking at the top of her voice who all the other people were, then trilling with affected laughter when David hissed that he didn't know and saying that really he was quite a recluse. Clare was sympathetic. It was probably because Mrs Power wanted to feel important just for a couple of days; she could go home and remember that so and so had saluted her and so and so had made a fuss of her. It was like a child really. David's father indulged her just like a child. Some people always got that kind of treatment.

After a while she told him about Tommy. She wasn't going to. He didn't need to know and it seemed disloyal to them all at home with this sad secret they hugged to themselves. It seemed somehow indulgent to confess it in the great heat of love. Maybe David shouldn't have to hear it either. But she told him suddenly, when he had been talking so honestly about his own life and hiding nothing. She told him quickly and unemotionally. He reached across the table and held both her hands tight. He was upset but not shocked. If Tommy were such an eejit as to get in with this kind of a crowd, maybe the safest place for him was in gaol. And since he'd always been such a nice fellow he wouldn't get beaten up by the other prisoners or the warders or anything.

'When you and I go to London some time . . . we'll go to see him,' David said expansively. 'And that'll show him that he's not cut off or anything.'

Go to see Tommy? In a *prison*, on *visiting day?* She nodded at him, unable to speak.

He reached out and stroked her face. 'I don't think you have any idea of how much I love you, you are part of my soul. I would do anything for you. Going to see Tommy would make me happy if it were to give you some ease and pleasure. I'd go tonight on the mail boat.'

She closed her eyes and held his hand to her face.

'I don't deserve you. I'm so narrow and one-track and self-obsessed. Why do you love me so much?'

'I've no idea. It's just there. Filling all those empty spaces I used to have. There's no more doubt now. I just want you and what's good for you.'

He sat opposite her in the little café, his face tired from lack of sleep, his shirt collar open at the neck, his smile enormous and all over his face, lighting it up.

'You look like a man that's won the Sweep,' she said admiringly.

'Now you're just feeding me lines so I'll say that I *have* won the Sweep when I've won you,' he said.

As they left the café he asked whether anyone else knew where Tommy was.

'Angela. She was the one who insisted I write to him every week. Oh, and Gerry Doyle,' she said.

He frowned. Why had she told Gerry? He tried to keep his voice casual but she knew he hated Gerry knowing the family secret before he did.

'It was a long time ago. Gerry was going to London and my Mam asked him to go and find Tommy. I had to tell him what was happening. I couldn't have him going around investigating it and turning it up for himself, and then not knowing what to say. It was easier to tell him straight out. He never said a word, naturally.'

'Naturally.'

'Why are you studying in bed?' Valerie complained.

'Because I did nothing today. I met David for two hours, I went back to the library and I wrote him a letter. That was another hour. Then I spent an hour thinking about how nice it would be to go to London with him. Then I spent about half an hour working out how he should tell his father he can't possibly go back to Castlebay until he's done three years at least in Dublin hospitals. Then I went to this place where they do your hair cheaply in the afternoons, then I went out to the hospital with my new hairdo and had a cup of tea in the canteen with him, and gave him the letter. Then I came home. That's the work I did today, that's the amount of work the Murray scholar has put in towards getting her first-class honours degree.'

'All right, all right.' Valerie hadn't intended to bring on such an onslaught.

'No. It's not all right. I didn't know this would happen.' Clare looked mournful.

'Christ, you're only having a bit of fun. One day, one day, Clare O'Brien, with this fellow – it's not as if it were something stupid, like me making eyes like a sheep at that fellow who doesn't even know that I am alive, or Mary Catherine going out with James. You've got the real thing, what we all want. Stop *bellyaching*.'

'I know it must *sound* like bellyaching . . .'

'It does.' Valerie was grumpy.

'But if you knew how annoyed I am for doing nothing today. If you knew.'

'I'm *beginning* to know. For God's sake will you get out of bed, put on your coat, sit at the dressing table and work properly. Stop hanging out of the bed and trying to read with the light on the floor. Do it properly. I'll get to sleep. Don't mind me.'

'Valerie, stop making yourself into a tragedy queen,' Clare said.

Val laughed at the scorn; but she said that it was no harm to take Professor Clare O'Brien down a bit. She talked about her studies as if they were a sacred ritual. Clare had to smile as she climbed out of bed and put on clothes so that she wouldn't freeze.

A girl they didn't know tapped on the window, having climbed up the rungs. Clare let her in and she thanked them profusely.

'You three are a legend in this place,' she said breathlessly. 'I mean you're so old, and so settled, and make all your own rules.'

'We're also mad,' Val said from the bed. 'We take it in turns to get up and get fully dressed in the night to keep guard over the others.'

The girl was startled and said she should be off.

'You have to make a cup of tea for us as your payment for going through the room,' Clare said, as a joke – but ten minutes later the girl crept back with two cups of tea.

'I presume your friend is still out,' she said, nervously looking at Mary Catherine's bed.

'Of course she is,' said Val. 'It's only three o'clock in the morning.'

Clare said that Valerie was giving them all a reputation for being stone mad. Val said that she wondered what on earth Mary Catherine and James Nolan could be doing until after three in the morning if they weren't in bed together.

About ten minutes later, Mary Catherine came through the window. She and James Nolan *had* been in bed together, and it had been all right. Not *great*, but *all right*, and she would like them to start a novena this minute because her period was due in exactly nine days' time, so if ever a novena was called for it was now.

Dick Dillon told Angela that he hadn't changed his mind. That he wasn't much of a catch for her, and he wasn't as well read, but at least she knew that he'd never turn into a drunk on her. Then he remembered that a drunk is exactly what Angela's father had been and he apologized so much for the remark that she had to tell him to shut up or she would beat him to death with her bicycle.

But *seriously*, he said. Wouldn't it be a good idea? Angela was lonely in that cottage, he was lonely in a little corner of the hotel, his bedroom and sitting room. He would be agreeable to whatever she wanted – live in her cottage, build a new place, he could get a site easily. Angela could go on teaching if she liked. The ban on married teachers had been lifted now. Or she could take a rest from it. He so enjoyed her company. He was never one for the flowery words, but genuinely he had flowery thoughts in his heart.

Angela was thoughtful. She said that in her heart she still felt it would be the single most foolish act since the partition of the country but she wouldn't think of it now.

There was something else to the forefront of her mind. But the thing that was in her mind would be out of it one way or another at the end of the summer.

Then she would sit down with him seriously and discuss his suggestion, without any jokes or smart-alec remarks.

'It's not so much a *suggestion*, it's more a *proposal*,' he said, affronted. 'This . . . thing, this worry in the summer. Is there anything I could do to make it easier for you?' he asked.

She looked at him. He had a very kind face. 'No, Dick. Thank you all the same.'

'It isn't another man?' he asked anxiously. 'You're not making up your mind about another person or anything like that?'

'No. There's no other man in that sense at all.'

'You're not thinking of entering the convent?' He was fearful of all the rival possibilities.

'Immaculata would have the place closed down rather than let me into the community,' she said.

'Well, sure one religious in any family is enough,' said Dick Dillon, unerringly putting his finger on the one thing that was guaranteed to set every nerve end jangling. Father Sean O'Hara. Who still wrote excited letters about how much they were all looking forward to the summer.

Paddy Power said it was a very clear day altogether, you could see cliffs and headlands miles and miles away. Nellie had told him he was back early: it would be half an hour before the lunch was ready, the potatoes were still like bullets. Molly said she'd walk a bit along the cliff with him since it was so bright and fresh out.

'Will you go up to see Sheila? You like going there in January.'

'Yes. I was thinking of it. David was a bit offhand on the phone when I suggested it.'

'Offhand?'

'He said he might find it very hard to get any time off to meet me, he just said that he'd like to warn me in advance.'

'Well that's fair enough. I remember it was like that in my time as well, you don't have a minute of your own.'

'Oh, he has minutes of his own all right.'

'What do you mean?'

'He said to me that he heard the Guards had to be called to Dillon's Hotel, I asked how he heard that – we hadn't told him – and he said that he had met Clare O'Brien and she'd told him. Josie Dillon had written to her all about it, apparently.'

'Well?' Dr Power couldn't see where all this was leading.

'Well it shows he gets enough minutes off to meet that Clare O'Brien.'

'Molly, don't be giving out about that child. You've always had a down on her.'

'I've had nothing of the sort. I just mentioned to you in passing that it's odd our son has time to meet her when he's not going to be able to have any time to meet his own mother.'

'Now, now, now. He ran into her – what more natural than they talk about Castlebay?'

'No, he didn't say he ran into her, he said when he met her, as if they met all the time. And stop sounding exasperated with me like that. I *know*, I tell you.'

'If he *is* meeting her, would that be the end of the world?'

Molly looked triumphant. 'A minute ago I was drawing conclusions, I was imagining things. Now all of a sudden I'm right.'

'Yes, Molly . . .'

Valerie said you couldn't do a novena for something like that. God just wouldn't listen. Clare said that if anything had happened it had happened now and no amount of prayers could change it. Mary Catherine said that neither of them had understood the nature of prayer. In her parish back in the States it had been very clearly explained. God knew in advance that you were going to pray later. It was foreknowledge, not predestination. They had endless debates about it, but fortunately events overtook them and on the appointed day the news was good, so there was a great sigh of relief from the bedroom of the three ageing eccentrics.

Mary Catherine said she wouldn't run the risk again, although James had said that he would Look After Things. She said she didn't really want to either. She couldn't think why she had in the first place except that she was so sick of him pestering her about it, and saying no, and finding excuses, and thinking up reasons why not. She said he had nearly dropped dead when she said she would go back with him to this flat. The same one that David had lived in . . . They all brought their girls there, it seemed.

But Mary Catherine said they probably talked much more than they actually seduced. James said he was fairly experienced, but without being too technical Mary Catherine thought he wasn't. No honestly it would be too detailed, she couldn't say any more. And she had asked him very casually if he thought that David Power was a ladies' man, and he had said that David was being terribly secretive and the belief was that he was having it off with a fast nurse up in the hospital otherwise why wouldn't he come out to play with the rest of them?

Mary Catherine said she couldn't see the need for secrecy but if it was so desperately important to Clare and David, she'd go along with it. She didn't care much one way or the other she said, she had a far bigger worry of her own. How to brush off James politely. Far from casting her aside once he had his way with her, he was on the phone morning noon and night, presumably hoping to have his way with her over and over again. She didn't want to turn him down too brusquely and she certainly didn't want him to tell everyone that she was a good thing.

In the safety of daylight and public places Clare and David talked about sex. David told her that he never had it with anyone, he had implied to the lads that he was at it all the time, but he actually never had. There was a sort of a near miss on one occasion but he needn't detain her with that.

Anyway that had all to do with drink and nothing to do with love.

They discussed almost abstractly what they would do if they had the opportunity presented to them. Suppose now for example that Clare had her own flat where nobody would bother them. Suppose David had his own place. Would their resolution be so strong?

Clare said that she could never go through the anxiety. She didn't like to tell tales on Mary Catherine, but it turned out that David knew anyway. This was a bit alarming, but they couldn't fault James really since Valerie and Clare knew all about it as well.

David said that there were probably ways round the anxiety bit, and what with being a doctor and everything he'd have more access to the ways round it than anyone else. Anyway people went to the North of Ireland where you could get contraceptives legally, so there should be no problem there.

'That's *if* we were thinking of it seriously,' Clare said.

'Yes, that's if we were,' David agreed.

Emer rang Clare at the hostel and asked her would she do her a great favour. Kevin had been asked to go and find out about new educational aids in London. For three whole days. And would you believe it, she was going too. Her mother was looking after Daniel. And what she'd really like is if someone were to stay in the house, to keep an eye on it. Would Clare like to? Clare said she'd like to very much.

She contemplated not telling him. For two whole hours.

Then she told him. He asked for his three days' leave at that time.

'I hope we won't have to be doing any more novenas,' Valerie grumbled.

'Suppose I never want to see you again afterwards?' she said as they went to the bedroom.

'Why wouldn't you want to see me again afterwards?'

'Mary Catherine didn't with James.'

'They don't love each other. They're only just pretending to.'

'So being in love would make all the difference?'

'That's what I've always heard.'

David stroked her long fair hair on the pillow afterwards. He kept moving his hand from the top of her head to the end of the hair. He was afraid to speak in case she was hurt or unhappy.

Her eyes were open as she lay there beside him but he couldn't read her face. Was she frightened? Or disappointed? Had she felt anything like the pleasure that he had, or the peace he felt now?

'David,' she said. Her voice was very small.

He gave a great cry of delight and gathered her up in his arms and held her to him. He couldn't believe that it was possible to be so happy.

James Nolan tracked David down eventually.

'I thought you'd been murdered and the body buried,' he said. 'Nobody knew where you were.'

'Is anything wrong?' David asked quickly.

'Depends how you view it. Your mother's coming to stay with mine tomorrow. Both maternals are a bit shirty that you couldn't be found. I think you'd better ring your own to pat down ruffled feathers. Where were you anyway?'

'Wouldn't it *have* to be this weekend she was looking for me? Wouldn't you bloody know.'

James shrugged. 'I did my best. I thought maybe you'd gone off with a bird. I said there was a match on and that you might have gone to that.'

'A match for three days!'

'I said it was in Northern Ireland.'

'OK, that'll do. Thanks, James.'

'Don't hang up, where *were* you?'

'As you said. At a match.'

'I'll deal with you. You're meant to be coming to lunch with us on Sunday.'

Molly Power was martyred, on the phone.

'Please don't think I'm checking up on you. I don't mind where you go on your time off. Your father's always saying you're a grown man. I agree entirely.'

'I'm glad to know you're coming up to Dublin,' he said, gritting his teeth.

'It's just that the Nolans thought it was so *odd* that you couldn't be found. I mean, David, nobody wants to keep checking up on you, I've told you that, it's just that if anything happened to your father — God forbid that it should — and we were looking for you . . .'

He held the receiver at arm's length. He would like to have smashed it against the wall.

' . . . do you think you'll be able to *tear* yourself away from *whatever* is occupying you so much to come and meet us when I'm in Dublin?'

'I'm really looking forward to Sunday lunch,' he said, willing an eagerness into his voice.

'Am I not going to see you *until* Sunday?'

'No . . . I meant that, in particular . . . of course I'll see you before then.'

He leaned his head against the wall when the three minutes were up. 'Clare,' he whispered to himself. 'Clare, Clare.'

'Are you all right Doctor?' A young nurse with freckles was looking at him. A lot of the young housemen went a bit loopy, she had been told, and she thought it could well be true.

Angela read the letter with great surprise. If Clare had got into a political group, or become very active in a cause, she would not have been so surprised, but David, lovely big nice David Power who was coming back to Castlebay next year to share the work with his father? How had it happened? And what would Clare do if she married him? She would marry him, it seemed, reading between the lines. Clare had said how they both felt as strongly as each other and they couldn't bear to be apart. She said he had it as badly as she did. Angela was bewildered, reading the outpourings. Bewildered because there seemed only one thing to say. So she said it:

I suppose you must work as hard as you possibly can, get your First as you know you can, then relax, and do your Higher Diploma. And then, who knows? I might be put out to grass here and you'd be over-qualified, but I'm sure they'd take you in the school. But as Mrs Power, young Mrs Power, would you *want* to work? Would you want to teach all day . . . ?

Clare read the letter in dismay. She had been *stupid, stupid, stupid,* to tell Angela. The woman understood *nothing.* There was *no* question of going back to Castlebay. That was what all the *agonizing* was about. David didn't want to, she didn't want to. The *root* of the problem was how to explain this to David's father without breaking his heart. In a million *years* Angela wouldn't understand. She had been too long in Castlebay, that was her trouble.

'I'm going to meet your mother-in-law and your intended on Sunday,' Mary Catherine said.
   'How on earth . . . ?'
   'James has asked me to lunch. He said Mrs Power was coming and that David would be there too. Didn't he tell you?'
   'Yes. It slipped my mind.' David hadn't told her. She was furious.

'I didn't want to talk about anything bad, that's all.'
   'Your mother coming to Dublin isn't bad.'
   'Yes it is. It makes it all more real, it brings that side of things into our life here.'
   'She comes every year. You don't have to announce to her at lunch in the Nolans' house that your plans for the future have changed.'
   'No. But I'd prefer to be with you on Sunday. Not there.'
   'Mary Catherine's going. They must be having a big do.'

'*That's* an idea. Why don't I get James to ask you too?'

'Are you stark staring mad?' she asked.

The ideal thing would have been to find somewhere near the hospital, but the roads were too posh and the prices of flats were too high. If they went far out of the city they could afford somewhere nice but then it would be pointless, David would hardly ever be able to escape to somewhere so far away. They read the small ads in the evening papers and couldn't believe how quickly any reasonable-sounding bed-sitter was snapped up. Sometimes they found long queues on the doorstep of a place that had only been advertised that very day. They got to know other young people and exchanged information. Rathmines wasn't too bad, people said. It was about twenty minutes' walk from UCD. Lots of people had bed-sitters there. They went on an expedition, just knocking on every door: that was meant to be as good a way as any. Clare looked around at the area. There was a big main street and a lot of tall houses which had once been family homes but now housed several families. Some were very well kept with well-painted halls, nice half-moon tables where the post for each flat dweller was laid out in neat rows. Others had torn lino, walls badly in need of papering and a faintly unpleasant smell about them. These were the ones they were going to be able to afford.

It was a nice area, they decided. A bit like a village or a place all on its own rather than part of the Dublin they knew. But there were buses constantly back and forth, it was near the canal for walks and, because this was where a lot of young people had flats, the shops stayed open later. There was also a chip shop nearby. Clare looked at it gratefully. This might be very useful indeed.

They looked at the small grimy room up three flights of stairs, in the big house with the uncared-for garden and the peeling paintwork. They looked at each other and said yes. They handed over the first month's rent and moved in on Saturday. The landlord said he hated students usually

362

but seeing that this was a young married couple, that was quite different. He did hope that there was no question of a child yet because they would understand he had to run a quiet house. They shook their heads. No, there would be no question of that and they quite understood.

David had given her a plain ring which cost fifteen shillings; one day it would be a proper one. Like one day it would be a proper place to live. They had an oil stove, and the place smelled of paraffin; the bed was a bit lumpy and the little cooking ring was very dirty after the last tenants. The bathroom was down two floors. But it was their own. And apart from Valerie and Mary Catherine who had to know everything, nobody else in the world knew where they were.

They went out to buy bacon and sausages and a bottle of red vermouth for their first supper. They bought a bookcase at a second-hand shop because the landlord said he didn't like his walls being mutilated. The walls were so rough and uneven, and had such shaky plaster, they would have been hard put to take a nail let alone a shelf. Clare felt settled when the books were in place.

He kissed her hands and looked up at her face. 'Look, it's all going to be all right. You'll study and I'll come to you every minute I can. You'll get your First and I'll finish my year and start somewhere else, just as if it were the most natural thing in the world. I won't be an intern, we can live together like this, only better. I'll be getting real money.'

'So will I,' Clare said excitedly, 'if I'm tutoring.'

'We haven't a worry in the world. If we can do this . . .' he waved his hand expansively around the small shabby room '. . . if we can do this in a few days, can't we do anything?'

It was a lonely Sunday, but all Sundays could be a bit down in Dublin.

Clare scraped at the cooking ring for a while, then she went out to buy a Sunday paper. A bell was ringing and great crowds were going into the big church in the main street of Rathmines. She hurried past. There had been five Sundays since she was in mortal sin. She had gone to Mass as usual the first Sunday, but it was ridiculous, she couldn't say any prayers, it was hypocritical to kneel there knowing that she was going to commit further mortal sin. For all her brave words to David, it *was* a sin, and that was that. There was no point in acting the part of a person who was praying. If Clare were the Lord she'd prefer those kind of people not to come to church at all.

Val had gone to a lunch where six people were going to make a curry. It sounded awful, yet Clare would like to have been there. She didn't feel she could ask Emer and Kevin if she could call, it seemed like using them, and anyway she did feel slightly embarrassed going back to their place even though they had no idea why she should be. Mary Catherine was at this Nolan lunch and so was David. Perhaps she should have said yes, and agreed when, in his innocence, he had suggested she should be invited too. It would have been hard to take: Mrs Power's rage and scorn would have communicated itself to everyone there and Clare didn't really like James or Caroline Nolan enough to think they might have supported her. But still this was very hard too, this hanging around and waiting.

It was like being in love with a married man, like that girl who was so depressed in the hostel last year. She had been having a romance with one of the lecturers; she was suicidal at weekends.

'Don't be so silly,' Clare told herself aloud. 'There is no comparison. We have a flat together of our own. He'll be coming back here. It's his *mother* he's seeing, for God's sake, not a wife. Why feel so chilly? Why this awful sense of doom?'

There were five cars parked in the drive in front of the Nolans' house: Mr Nolan's, his wife's, Caroline's and James's. David didn't know who the last one belonged to. He ran lightly up the steps. Breeda opened the door. She took his coat, and put it in the breakfast room, where a lot of other coats were already hanging and draped.

He went up the stairs to the first-floor drawing room. His mother was standing by the fireplace, leaning on the mantelpiece. She looked very made-up and a bit fussy, David thought. Too many frills at her neck and her cuffs. He didn't have time to see who else was there, since Molly gave a scream of welcome.

'The *prodigal*! He's torn himself away!'

He wished she hadn't. It made such a commotion. He should have gone in quietly and greeted James's mother and father. But now because she had called such attention to him, he had to go straight to her.

'You're looking marvellous, Mother,' he said, kissing her on the cheek.

'Oh, you're a worse flatterer than your father,' she said, still in this high silly voice that he hated.

He looked around. Mrs Nolan looked vague and sort of fluttery as usual. David wondered yet again why his mother didn't see how strange Sheila Nolan was, how dotty, for want of a more technical word.

'Lovely to be here, Mrs Nolan,' he said dutifully.

'Oh, David.' She looked at him as if she had never seen him before but as if she had learned his name to make him feel welcome. 'How good of you to come to see us. Your mother is here too you know.' Sheila Nolan looked around vaguely.

'Yes, yes. I've just seen her.' David was beginning to feel trapped, to experience the hunted sensation that Mrs Nolan managed to create all around her.

'David – they tell me you love sherry. Sweet or dry?' The woman stared into his eyes as if waiting for the Meaning of Life in his answer.

'Dry would be very nice, Mrs Nolan.' He *hated* sherry of any kind.

He saw James had managed to get a gin and tonic, but it was too late, the sherry glass was in his hand. Caroline was talking to Mary Catherine by the window. Two priests were talking to Mr Nolan. One of them looked familiar, yet David hadn't met him before. Breeda came in and passed round cheese straws and little bits of celery filled with cheese.

The voices of his mother and Mrs Nolan talking archly at him receded, and David wanted Clare and their little room and a tin of tomato soup. He wanted to be miles from this overheated room and babble of chat. He answered the questions automatically: yes, it was pretty hard work, no, he didn't know that specialist, but of course he knew him by name, and how nice of the Nolans to say they'd have a word. He asked his mother about home, and about his father, and had Bones recovered from the terrible paint incident. Molly Power said that Bones had never looked beautiful but nowadays he would actually frighten you to look at him. They had cut off so much of his coat where the spilled paint had all hardened and matted. He looked very odd but had no idea that his appearance had changed. Old as he was, he still ran round in circles barking happily. Molly said you couldn't take him for a walk anywhere because the explanations were so lengthy when you met anyone, and the memory of finding him lying on his back on the kitchen floor in a pool of red paint was not one you wanted to relive.

'Will you be down before Easter to see him? And us indeed,' she asked.

'Not a chance . . . oh and about Easter . . .' he began, but Sheila Nolan had clapped her hands. Lunch was ready.

They moved to another very overheated room with nine places set around a table, two bottles of wine already open and a huge joint of beef on the carving table.

'Isn't this the life,' said Molly Power wistfully as they went into the room with its heavy dark furniture and thick curtains. Her voice was envious for a life which could assemble people around a table like this, far from Castlebay.

David took his mind from the dingy bed-sitter not two miles away, and forced himself to feel some sympathy for his mother. Dad had always said that she needed very little to make her happy. And it was true, there she was, revelling in the showy lunch that Sheila Nolan had organized in her honour. He was not going to be rude to her. He wasn't going to spoil her visit. He'd tell her about Easter later.

David was sitting between Caroline and one of the priests. Caroline was in high form and full of confidences and whispered questions.

'Do you think James is serious about the Yankee lady? Oh go on, he must tell you. I don't believe this strong silent act. Men do tell. I know they do.'

'But you are so wrong, Caroline, men are much too gentle and sensitive to discuss their emotions, would that we had the strength of women, able to bring anything out in the open, air it, examine it and dust it down.'

She laughed. 'Do you think they're *involved*, if you know what I mean? Once upon a time he used to be only interested whether she had money, now he's a bit lovesick, I think.'

They both looked at Mary Catherine, who was battling with interrogation from Mrs Power and glances of fluttery hostility from Mrs Nolan.

'Why don't you ask her? She'd tell all, the way women do.'

'No, she's like a tin of sardines that one, I wouldn't get to first base, to use her own kind of language.'

'And how about your own romances. Are you the toast of the Incorporated Law Society?'

'You only ask me that to break my heart. You know I think of no other man.' Caroline waved her eyelashes up and down at him jokily.

'What chance would a humble country hick like myself have with a sophisticated girl like you?' David smiled. He had always liked Caroline. He had fancied her of course when he was very young, and in phases ever since, she was so easy to talk to, so joky, and she took nothing too seriously. He remembered with a start that his mother had always regarded them as a likely match, and with some alarm noticed that Mrs Power and Mrs Nolan were looking at them fondly.

Caroline was unaware of it. 'I never tried seriously to

capture you, David, I hate failure, I feel that with you I have to bide my time, wait till you're ready for me, and fall into my arms like a ripe plum. Maybe on the rebound from some other female.'

She threw back her head of dark hair and laughed. Clare had once said that Caroline Nolan had too many good, white, even teeth, it was a sign of great money and breeding, rich people didn't rot their children's teeth with sticky things, and rich people took their children to the dentist regularly.

Caroline did look very healthy.

She looked very attractive too: she had a lemon-coloured jumper and a green and gold sort of tartan-type skirt. She wore a big amber necklace. She said that she must have been mad to listen to the nuns who said that a degree was the answer. It wasn't the answer, it was the question. You had to ask yourself what to do then. Fortunately now that she had done the boring secretarial bit she was nicely installed in her father's office as a solicitor's apprentice where she should have been years ago. Before she became old and grey.

She turned to pass the vegetables in their heavy tureens and David found himself talking to the priest with the small buttons of eyes.

'I know your face from somewhere, Father. Would there have been a picture of you in the paper or anything?'

'I hope not. I'm in bad enough books with the archbishop already. No, I don't think I've come across you – I know you're from Castlebay. Your mother was telling me before you arrived.'

'I'm not such a genius as she makes out,' he said.

'She didn't make you out to be a genius at all,' the priest said.

'I don't know if that's good or bad.'

'We do have a mutual friend though. Angela O'Hara. She and I met at a wedding in Rome, oh it must be eight years ago now. A long time. But somehow we all remained great friends. A couple called Quinn got married . . .'

David remembered why the priest was familiar. He

was the Father Flynn whose round face shone out of the wedding photos in Kevin and Emer Quinn's bedroom.

The photo that he had looked at for a long time as Clare slept in his arms in the big bed that belonged to Kevin and Emer.

Mary Catherine didn't like David's mother one bit. She thought that Clare was going to have a hard time of it with this one.

'Tell me about Castlebay,' she said brightly, smiling her perfect smile and pretending an interest she didn't feel. 'I hear it's one lively town.'

'You hear wrong,' Mrs Power said definitely. 'It's a small community, very, very small, swollen to about twenty times its size in the summer. A lot of *riff-raff* have been coming recently, and *loud* people. It used to be a wonderful family resort. Remember, Sheila, when you all came down . . . ?'

Molly caught David's eye and realized that she mustn't run down the place she was trying to get him to come home to. ' . . . But I think that's just my age, really. For young people, for young *professional* people, *working* there, for the *doctor* or the young *solicitor*, or the people in the hotel, it's a wonderful life. And a lot of very nice people a few miles back from the coast. Very nice indeed. Wonderful big estates and everything.' She nodded owlishly.

David raged within. She had never been invited to any of the big estates nor did she even know anyone who had. Why did she try to impress people with a line of chat which was just making her pathetic?

'I was thinking of spending a few days there this summer. When I do my degree I'll have to go back to the States, so best see a bit of Ireland while I can.'

Molly was a little nonplussed. On the one hand the girl had been talking about her father being a postman and her mother working in a clothes factory of some sort, hanging garments on rails. On the other hand, the Nolans seemed to think that James was serious about her. Who knew what way to jump?

'Well, that would be very nice, dear,' she said noncommittally. 'Be sure to let us know when you arrive, and come to see us.'

'Thank you, Mrs Power.'

'Will you stay in Dillon's Hotel?'

Mary Catherine spoke without thinking. 'I guess Clare will find me a bed . . .'

'Clare?'

It was too late. Clare had asked her not to bring up her name at all, but it was done now.

'Clare O'Brien, I share a room, I've been sharing a room with her.'

Molly Power sniffed. 'I doubt if there's going to be any room for you with the poor O'Briens – but maybe Clare didn't describe it to you properly. It's not a place that anyone could *stay* in.'

David's face flushed a dark red.

Mary Catherine spoke quickly. 'I explained it badly, I meant to say that Clare said she would book me in somewhere. But heavens, who knows if I'll ever get there, there's so much work to do . . . Was your last year full of frights and horrors, Caroline?'

'Dreadful. I didn't know you shared a room with Clare O'Brien.'

'You never asked,' Mary Catherine said with spirit.

'I know Clare O'Brien,' said the small priest. 'A very bright girl. She won that scholarship for three years from your county, didn't she? I always think it must be the most terrible pressure on young people when they get that kind of bursary . . .' He chattered on lightly, knowing there was some tension in the air but not knowing where it came from.

'So you know Clare O'Brien too, Father? My goodness, doesn't she get about?' She turned to Sheila Nolan. 'Remember them, Sheila? Big, straggling family, not a penny to bless themselves with?'

'I don't think so.' Sheila Nolan's vacant blue eyes were vaguer than ever.

'Oh you *must* remember them, we used to go in to buy

370

ice creams there. Though I never particularly liked dealing there. Not terribly *clean*.'

'Why did we buy ice creams there, then?' Mrs Nolan was bewildered.

'It was near the beach, that's why, I think.'

'I would never have bought ice creams there had I known it wasn't clean.' Mrs Nolan's thin hand went to her throat as if regretting the possible germs that might still lurk there.

'No, no. That's not the point. I was just telling you who the family were. One of them put her mind to her books and she's come a long way. Everyone here is on calling terms with her except you and me . . .' Molly Power looked fussed and annoyed. Sheila Nolan looked confused and worried about possibly unhygienic ice creams eaten in the past.

Father Flynn thought he saw the lie of the land. He asked his colleague, Father Kennedy who was the new curate in the Nolans' parish, to tell them all the story of the archbishop's garden. It was a harmless little tale but it distracted them.

Father Flynn looked at David levelly. 'People often sound much more cruel than they are. In their hearts they're probably very kind.'

'Yes,' David mumbled.

'Eat up. That's lovely beef. I bet you don't get food like that in the hospital.'

David didn't respond.

'And there's nothing for concentrating the mind like eating.'

David had to smile. 'I knew the clergy were dangerous,' he laughed.

'That's better. Give Clare my love.'

'Were you the priest who was so helpful about her brother?'

'You must be a *good* friend if she told you all that. Yes. Not that I was all that much help as it turned out.'

'Clare said you were great.'

'Is she going to get a First? She was very eager about that.'

371

'I think so. I'll keep her at it.'

They spoke low and stopped when Caroline turned to join the conversation.

At the other end of the table Molly whispered behind her hand to Sheila. 'I can't explain it, but I *never* liked that girl. She didn't ever do anything against me, but I don't *trust* her. Do you know the feeling?'

'I do.' Sheila was equally conspiratorial. Her glance rested on Mary Catherine. 'That American girl is going back where she belongs,' she said.

'The pity of it is, that it's hard to say where Clare O'Brien belongs now and where she should go back to,' Molly whispered.

She was lying on the bed reading the verses in the In Memoriam column. 'Listen David, listen to this one: "Now every year upon this day/We ask just why you went away."'

Clare pealed with laughter. 'They couldn't could they? Each year on her anniversary, they sit down and say, "What *could* have happened to her?"'

He sat beside her. 'Why aren't you studying? You said you'd have a full day without me, what are you doing reading this rubbish? Where are your books?' He looked around, there was no sign of study.

'Don't give out to me. What was it like?'

'Oh, very Nolanish, you know.'

'I don't know.'

'Men are hopeless at describing things, you're always saying that. There was too much to eat.'

'I know. You smell of food.' She nuzzled him.

'Oh, and your friend Father Flynn was there. He's over for a few days' holiday.'

Her face was bright at the thought of him; then it looked puzzled. 'How did he know you knew me?'

'Castlebay and everything.'

'Yes.' She looked at him. 'David. Was there any more?'

'I nearly lost my temper with my mother and walked out . . .'

'Tell me the whole thing.'

It wasn't *so* bad. Nothing they hadn't known already: that David's mother did not think the sun and moon and stars shone from Clare. That was all. Why was David so upset?

'I didn't want to be there. I wanted to be here.'

'You're here now.'

Much later they did the boldest thing they had ever done. They ate a tin of pears, with spoons, straight from the tin, and bits of the juice kept falling on their bodies and they had to lick it off their shoulders – or wherever it fell. Towards the end of the tin they were covered in the sweet pear syrup and so was the bed. They laughed until they both ached. They dropped the pear tin down on the floor, and put their sticky arms around each other again.

'Is this squalor? Is this what we live in?' Clare asked.

'It's lovely, whatever it is,' David said.

Father Flynn decided to go to Castlebay to see it for himself. He booked himself into Dillon's Hotel, made a courtesy call on Father O'Dwyer, and told Sergeant McCormack that he had heard her highly spoken of, which inspired her to make scones for his tea. Choosing his time well, he went to O'Brien's shop and told them that Tommy was getting on well, with a prison visitor who was bringing him picture books of wild flowers and he sometimes drew them. They marvelled at some English woman who would take the time to go to visit an Irish boy with no teeth in gaol for robbery with violence. Father Flynn said he knew it was hard, but the odd letter, with no criticism or abuse but just descriptions of what life at home was like, would work wonders. Clare had been unfailing in her letters. Agnes was proud to hear that. Clare had never got uppity despite her great success and advances, she told Father Flynn.

'You must be hoping she'll find a good man and marry him and settle down,' the little priest said.

'That one? Marry and settle down? She's going to be a professor, no less. She never had much of an interest in boys when she was young, and I used to think that was a mercy. Chrissie had far too great an interest in them. But not Clare. I suppose in a few years she might meet a professor somewhere, but she'll be gone from us in Castlebay, I knew that the day she got into the secondary school.'

'Suppose she were to marry and come back here?'

'But who would she marry here, father? Hasn't she more book-learning than anyone in the parish?'

He called on the Powers too, because deep in his heart he was a man filled with curiosity. A big, square house, built to withstand the gales and spray from the sea. Father Flynn noted that it must have to be painted every year. There was a large garden, part of it obviously leading to a cliff path down to the sea. It wasn't an elegant house; but it was sturdy and substantial.

Inside too it was comfortable. No antiques, nothing very old, but nice furniture and good carpets, big arrangements of flowers and greenery on window sills and surfaces. A pleasant maid with wispy hair and a broad smile showed him into the drawing room while she went to get the mistress. Molly was delighted to meet him again, and flattered that he should have come to call.

Father Flynn liked David's father enormously: a bluff, kind man who was an old-style adviser to his patients. Probably does a lot of the work that dry stick Father O'Dwyer should be doing, Father Flynn thought ruefully. Over a drink, a lot of admiration for their magnificent view of the sea and some words of sympathy to an elderly mad dog, half-shaved, half-particles of red paint, he talked to the big warm man. He told him about the work with the emigrants in Britain, some of its lighter side as well as its gloomy overtones; that it was often the weakest and the least prepared who were the ones who had to emigrate.

Dr Power told him of the good and bad things in Castlebay. People would never die of loneliness, as they

374

might in a big English city; but attitudes could be cruel, and tolerance was low. In nearly forty years of practice here he had seen a lot of intolerance: families couldn't cope with what they called 'shame and disgrace'. He was sure Father Flynn knew well what he meant. You didn't stamp out young love and young desire by refusing to face up to the consequences.

Dr Power said it was great to have lived through the years that saw TB being wiped out. When he started off, people still hid the fact that they had tuberculosis in the family. It was denied, and if anyone had a spot on the lung it was considered a disgrace and something that would prevent other members of the family being able to marry well.

Father Flynn said he had had the pleasure of meeting Dr Power's son, a fine boy, in Dublin. What were his plans?

Dr Power didn't know, precisely. If the boy were going to work back home then the sooner he came back the better. He would want to find a wife for himself; and it would be wiser for him to be installed here, and choose from here, rather than starting off a life with some girl in a big place with lots of life in it and then asking the poor woman to come back here with him. There was a slight sadness which Father Flynn thought must be hearking back to his own situation.

'And do you think he's met anyone that suits him yet?' he asked.

'Divil a fear of it. He's having too good a time with all those nurses up in the hospital,' said Dr Power with a laugh.

Father Flynn talked about it with Angela too.

'Aren't you a terrible old woman?' she teased him.

'Terrible. That's why I'm so good in confession. I'm never bored and I like to meddle in other people's lives.'

'Are you meddling with David Power and Clare O'Brien?' she asked.

'It worries me a bit, and I only know the fringes of it,' he said. 'I don't know why I feel that it's so doomed. But that's the word that keeps coming to me.'

'It could just be First Love.'

'It could.' He was doubtful. 'But I must get over this tendency to play God. Are you going to let this brother of yours come here and upset everyone?'

'I promised him in Rome. Those were my words. That's how I bought him off from doing it years ago. I can't go back on that now. He's like a child, you can't go back on a promise to a child.'

'Children can do dangerous things. Sometimes promises needn't be kept.'

'Is it dangerous for him to come home? He's had his heart set on it. I don't have children, you don't. We don't know all this about showing them their roots. I mean, I don't think it matters, and you don't. But suppose it's everything? Then he should do it. I'll survive it if I have to.'

There was a silence. He drank his tea, and looked admiringly around the book-lined room. When he spoke, it was with the voice of one introducing an entirely new subject.

'That's a very civilized fellow in the hotel, Dick Dillon, brother of the man running it, I think. Very pleasant sort of a man altogether. Someone you could always rely on, I'd imagine, if there was a crisis.'

'I'm sure you imagine right, Father Flynn. Such a pity that you got over this tendency to play God, isn't it? You could have had a field day there.'

Before he left Castlebay Father Flynn decided to buy a few postcards of the place: not the garish ones which looked like everywhere else, but those nice black and white ones full of outlines which Angela often used to send him.

He asked Josie Dillon where they were on sale.

'We haven't had them for ages. I used to put them up just to please Gerry Doyle – that's the photographer – he took them, you see. But visitors mainly preferred the coloured ones. But now you mention it, he never brought any replacements. You could ask in Doyle's, it's the place with the big bright sign, Doyle's Photographics. You can't miss it.'

You couldn't miss it. Josie Dillon was right.

There was a small, dark-haired man inside.

'Father? What can I do for you?'

He was a likeable fellow, with an easy smile.

'This is a very grand place.' Father Flynn looked round in admiration. 'I'd not have thought Castlebay would have something so fine as this.'

'Don't let my mother hear you, or my sister, or, Lord rest him, my father. They would all agree with you.'

'Well I'm not a businessman – what would I know? Is it too small an order to ask do you have those nice pictures of the place, the black and white ones. They were very good. I kept the ones people sent me.'

Gerry flushed with pleasure. 'Go on, is that a fact?'

'I can't find them in the shops.'

'I didn't bother. Hold on till I see where they are.' He pulled out drawers here and there, and called to an assistant. There was difficulty in finding them.

'It doesn't look as though I'm much of a businessman either,' Gerry grinned.

'If it's too much trouble . . .' Father Flynn began.

'No. It's a matter of honour now.' He found them. 'Here they are.'

'Could I have . . . er a dozen, please, assorted views.' Father Flynn had been going to buy three cards, but after all this trouble on his behalf he felt it would seem piffling.

Gerry had made a bundle and thrust them at him.

'There's more than twelve there.'

'Nobody else ever praised them before. I'd like you to have them. As a present.'

'That's extraordinarily kind of you . . . Mr Doyle,' Father Flynn said in some embarrassment.

'Not at all. You keep sending them to bishops and priests

and tell them to get their ordinations and enthronements recorded by me.'

'You're a very fine photographer. I'd be delighted to put any work in your way. But I'm sure you hardly need it.'

Father Flynn looked around again at the big counter, the carpeted floor, the large framed photographs on the wall. It had all the appearances of a studio in a large city. He recognized a picture of Clare on the wall – taken a few years ago, but very recognizable as the same face.

'Is that Clare?' he asked.

'Do you know Clare?' Gerry was pleased. 'That was when she got the Murray Prize, a scholarship to UCD. They sent me to take the winner. I never believed it was going to be Clare. I hadn't enough faith. Fortunately she did.'

'She works very hard, certainly. I met her with friends in Dublin.' Something made him uneasy about the way Gerry was looking at the picture.

'She's very unusual. For Castlebay that is. I don't think she's from here at all. I think she's a changeling. I've always thought that. Like myself.' He laughed to take the oddness away from the statement. 'That's why I'll marry her. When she's ready. When she's got all this studying out of her system.'

'And bring her back here?' Father Flynn sounded politely doubtful: inside he felt a slight tremor of anxiety.

'Oh, no. Clare's grown well beyond Castlebay. And as soon as I get this business organized, so will I.'

'Tell me about Gerry Doyle. The photographer,' Father Flynn asked Dick Dillon.

'Trouble from way back,' said Dick. 'But the women won't hear a word against him. Even a sensible woman like Angela O'Hara says he's got a nice way with him.' Dick Dillon snorted, and Father Flynn shivered a little in the sunshine.

Sometimes they finished at about ten o'clock, and everyone else in the Res went for a few drinks before closing time.

But David never joined them. These days, he would hare out of the hospital down to the bus stop.

'I don't know why you even call it the Residence,' one of the other doctors said to him. 'You barely reside here at all.'

David grinned. 'I had no idea we were going to be on call so much, I thought we'd have far more freedom.'

'No, you didn't. You knew you'd be cooped up here, you just didn't think you'd meet such an available girl.' The red-headed registrar laughed at his own perception.

David Power's face was cold and hard. 'I beg your pardon?' he said.

'It was only a joke . . .'

'I didn't think it was a bit funny.'

'No . . . Well, I'm sorry. I mean I don't know anything about it, I know nothing.'

'That's right, you know nothing, which gives you licence to say everything. That about sums you up.'

He marched, white with anger, out of the Res sitting room, having thrown his white coat over the back of a chair.

'What did I say?' Bar pleaded to the empty room.

It was cold and wet. The bus took for ever to arrive and even longer to get to Rathmines. He burned with rage still. A nice, *available* girl. *Available. Clare.* How dare he?

David was tired and very much on edge when he climbed the stairs. Clare was at the makeshift desk they had rigged up for her with planks of wood and builder's bricks. She was wearing mittens on her hands which made her look so endearing he stopped and stared at her with pleasure.

Her eyes were tired and had circles under them. 'Lord, are you home already? Is that the time?'

He was pleased she called it home, but a little disappointed that she hadn't been waiting for him, looking out for him.

'Did you get a lot done today?'

'I'm back into it again, thank heavens. I didn't notice

379

the time or anything. I heard a man selling oil so I rushed downstairs with the can and got some.' She looked proudly at the glowing little oil heater.

'It's lovely and cosy. What are we having to eat?'

She looked stricken. 'There's nothing. I meant to get something.'

'There must be something. Toast even?'

'No. There's nothing.' She opened the little press. 'Look, real Mother Hubbard stuff. Bare. We'll go out and get chips,' she added when she saw how disappointed he was.

'I only just got in,' he said. 'I'm dog tired.'

Clare got up and reached for her coat. 'Stay here, I'll go out for chips and bring them home.'

'Then I'll be here all on my own,' he grumbled.

She looked at him startled. This wasn't his way of talking.

'Darling Clare, I'm sorry. I'm just desperately overtired, I hardly know what I'm saying.'

She was full of concern. 'What are you apologizing for? Sit there. Rest for ten minutes. I'll be back and we'll have a feast.' She wouldn't hear of him moving.

She took his shoes off and pulled the two pillows into a bundle behind him. She said no to money, she had some. Dinner would be her treat. She was gone down the stairs, and he felt guilty.

What a way to come home. Like a typical husband shouting, 'Where's my tea?' This was a hopeless way to go on. Both of them so tired they could hardly talk. No money, no comfort. If they had more money Clare could have lived in a flat near the hospital: they wouldn't have this smelly stove, and this filthy house with bicycles, and the smell of urine downstairs in the hall.

He felt restless, got up and walked over to her desk. In her big, firm writing with the funny old-fashioned fountain pen and ink, not a ballpoint like everyone else, she had pages of notes.

She had been concentrating on economic history lately. The works of John Maynard Keynes were this week's project . . . she had taken notes in the library, now she had been sorting them out and fitting them into her scheme. She was so bright and hungry to know. He wondered had he lost some of that himself, he used to feel a bit that way at school, and so did James Nolan then. Nowadays James was so languid it was hard to know what he felt, and David was so tired and so used to sleeping with an ear ready to be called to a ward that he would have thought that hunger for information was a luxury.

There was a letter to Clare on the desk in a brown business envelope. The odd thing was that it was addressed here, to this flat. Nobody knew they lived there, *nobody*. And even worse, it was addressed to her as Clare O'Brien. They had told the landlord they were married. It had a Castlebay postmark.

David had never read anyone else's letter in his life. This time he justified it. He wanted to know. If he asked her she would tell him, and there would be an explanation; but he had already been so testy and crotchety tonight he didn't trust himself. He would just have a quick look and then nothing need be said. He pulled the short letter out of the envelope. It was on headed paper which said 'Doyle's Photographics' and it was signed Love Gerry.

Clare had bought them a choc-ice each as a treat. The man in the shop said they must be supermen to eat ice cream in weather like this. She unwrapped the chips and found plates. There was an awful plastic flower in a pot which they always put on their table for meals and made jokes about Doing the Flowers. They had tomato sauce and salt as well as the vinegar that the shop had provided. Clare chattered happily about the advantages of living in bed-sitter land where you could go out any hour of the day and night and get food.

David said nothing.

'Lord, you really are tired. Maybe you should just go to bed a couple of the really bad nights there, so you don't have to drag yourself up here.'

'Maybe,' he said.

381

'Did anything happen?'

'No.'

'Is anything worrying you, then?'

'That letter.' He pointed to the desk.

'What letter?' She stood up. There were two letters: one was from her mother addressed to The Ladies' Reading Room at UCD. She had said that this was a quicker way of getting your post and her mother hadn't questioned it.

'This one?' she held up the brown envelope.

'Yes.'

'If you read it, why are you worried?' Her voice was cold now.

'I didn't read it. I swear to you. But I know who it's from. And I was wondering why you gave him our address and told him you lived here. This is our secret. And we're meant to be man and wife. Why the hell is Gerry-bloody-Doyle allowed into anything and everything? And don't tell me what everyone says when his name is mentioned, that *it doesn't count telling Gerry*, or *Gerry knows everything*, or *everyone loves Gerry*, because I find that sickening.'

She had taken the letter out of the envelope and was reading:

Dear Clare,

I did what you asked me, I hope to hell it doesn't get lost in the post or I'll look a nice criminal.

The place is full of activity here, your Chrissie getting ready to produce your nephew or niece, our Fiona getting ready to marry Frank Conway, Josie walking out with a very suitable older man. I suppose you know all the details. Only you and I left around from the old guard.

Send a card or something so that I know it arrived OK.

Love Gerry.

She read this, brushing aside his protestations that he didn't want to hear it. She threw the letter on the bed at him, she reached into a drawer and took out a post office book and threw that too.

'I asked him to get my post office book for me from my room at home in Castlebay. I didn't want Mam asking what I needed my savings for. I need my savings, you bloody, suspicious, mean-minded pig, because now that I live here I have to buy things that I didn't have to buy when I lived in the hostel. Like milk, and bread, and tea, and sugar, and packets of soup and Vim. And I pay a share of the rent here. And it all costs money. And I don't have a penny left. In fact I owe Valerie three pounds. So in order not to appear a kept woman or a hanger-on, or to define even *more* the fact that I am poor Clare O'Brien and you are rich David Power, I sent for my savings account.'

Her eyes blazed with rage. 'I asked him to send it here because I didn't want a valuable thing like a post office book with sixty-three pounds in it, money I've been saving for three years, to get lost in college or get mislaid at the hostel. And Gerry Doyle doesn't give a tuppenny damn if I live here or on the top of the Dublin mountains, so I gave him this address. *And* I was not going to tell him that I am pretending to be your wife, so I gave him my name. *And* the landlord no more thinks we're married than he thinks that he's charging us a fair rent.'

Her hair had fallen over her face as she spoke. She lifted her plate of chips and poured them roughly onto David's plate.

'I have no appetite now, I'd do anything rather than share a meal with such a mean-minded human being.'

'Come back . . . come back!' he called.

'I'll *not* come back. Not tonight. I'll come back tomorrow when you've gone.'

She had grabbed up a few papers and put them into her duffle bag, she had pulled the nighty from under the pillow.

'Clare, you can't go out in that rain . . .'

'I went out once, to get *your* supper, didn't I? To give *you* time to poke around and make accusations. Go to *hell*!'

383

She ran faster than he did and jumped on the last bus going towards the city. She got off and slipped round behind the hostel looking left and right. She climbed the rungs, praying that Valerie and Mary Catherine might be out. But it was not a night for prayers to be answered.

They were reading magazines and listening to Chris Barber on their small portable record player. When she came through the window, furious and dripping, they were convulsed with laughter. They laughed as they got one of the younger and more frightened occupants of the hostel to go for tea, and they laughed as they gave her a big bath towel and ran a bath for her in the big old bathroom at the end of the corridor.

They felt that it called for even more than tea, so the brandy was taken out from the drawer. And eventually she laughed too. She laughed as she dried her hair and sipped the tea with brandy in it and told them the outline of the story. And then eventually she went to bed in the third bed.

Valerie and Mary Catherine had fought like tigers not to have a third girl. They said that since Clare had paid until Easter anyway it would be double letting, and the nuns couldn't do anything as dishonest as that, could they? Secretly Mary Catherine had been certain that Clare would be back: she felt that the romance with David was not going to get beyond first base. But she said none of this as Clare sighed happily and settled back into her old familiar place. Neither did Valerie.

'I'm really sorry. It makes me such an eejit,' Clare said.

'Nonsense, it makes you much nicer,' said Valerie. 'Now we know you're still normal, and not all this awful sickening peace and calm of true love. That was the distressing bit.'

Bar apologized to him formally as they were having coffee the next morning.

'I'm afraid I spoke out of order last night. I meant no disrespect.'

'That's fine. Sure. Thanks,' David mumbled.

'You look a bit rough. I don't want to say anything that you'll take amiss, but are you all right?'

'Sure, I'm fine.' David swallowed his coffee and went back on the wards. He had spent about three hours tidying the flat. He had removed all the rubbish, including the uneaten chips. This morning he had gone out and bought supplies of tea, coffee, milk, sugar, cornflakes, sardines and oranges. He had arranged them as well as he could, and he had bought a vase too. He left the vase on the desk with a note:

This is for the flowers I would like to bring you tonight. I'll understand if you don't want me. But I will be heartbroken. You are all I ever dreamed of and hoped for. You are much, much more. Please know that I didn't think I was mean-minded. But I realize I am. I don't want you to put your arms around me and say it's all right, that you forgive me. I want you to be *sure* that you do, and to know that my love for you will last as long as I live. I can see no lightness, no humour, no joke to make. I just hope that we will be able to go back to when we had laughter, and the world was coloured, not black and white and grey. I am so sorry for hurting you. I could inflict all kinds of pain on myself, but it would not take back any I gave to you.

He had written it over and over to try to take out the phrases that sounded tired. He tried to make it just himself. But he was in such unaccustomed low form, it didn't end up sounding like him. Perhaps he should have just left a card with a heart on it, or should he have gone round to the hostel after her last night? He had telephoned from a phone box and asked to speak to Mary Catherine. The nun on duty had asked did he know the time, all the young ladies were in bed, he could leave a message in an emergency. He had hung up. Perhaps he should have feigned illness at the hospital and taken a day off. He could have waited at the bottom of those rungs, Clare would have had to come down that way, she wasn't meant to be a resident. Perhaps he should have stood in the hall up at UCD and waited till she came in for lectures.

Most of the morning was spent speculating between beds.

The secretary at the front desk handed him a note as he passed. 'This just came for you, Dr Power.'

In her big firm handwriting she had written:

> It was just our First Row. That's *all* it was. Of course I love you. I'm hot-headed and impatient and I'm very sorry for that too. I am ashamed I ran out and left you there, tired and depressed. I love you and I'm greatly looking forward to those flowers and whatever else you might think of as a way to spend the evening.

They were often too tired to talk, too tired to make love when they went to their bed, but not irritably tired. They looked forward to David's proper leave days with excitement and planned them down to the last detail. They went to the zoo, which was lovely in the winter because it wasn't crowded, and they went out to Bray on the train one day and climbed Bray Head to look all over County Wicklow and County Dublin.

Sometimes they ate out, and they had gone to the pictures with Mary Catherine and Valerie one night. But they didn't mix much with David's hospital set, and they didn't look up old friends. James had given up on Mary Catherine and he seemed to be in a very social set. David and Clare didn't need James Nolan, they didn't need anyone but each other.

They had decided not to think about the future yet. David was going round doing interviews for hospitals where he would do his Post Intern year once he finished his present post in July. Clare had her mind fixed firmly on her degree.

By next September they would both be earning money, they would afford a better place, they would not get married yet, they just skated over that bit, but neither of them wanted to bring on the storm. Up here in Dublin in their own little world, nothing mattered, nobody bothered them.

They would be all right unless something happened.

Coming up to Easter two things happened.

Dr Power had a mild stroke.

And Clare discovered she was pregnant.

It was Angela who found him when he passed out. He was just getting into his car, which he had parked a quarter of a mile from the golf club in order to give himself a little walk. He had bandaged the finger of the barman, delivered a strong lecture on the danger of sharp knives, and explained that it didn't matter whether a lemon was finely sliced for drinks but it did matter if dangerous knives were left where people could cut their hands on them.

He walked cheerfully down to the car and then felt everything go dark. He realized that he must be about to faint and lowered himself to the ground beside his car. He tried to call out but he could hear a rushing sound and knew that he was losing consciousness.

Angela was hanging up some clothes on the washing line. She saw the car, and just as she was about to turn back into her house, she saw his black bag thrown on the ground. She ran quickly and was at his side when he was recovering consciousness.

'Did you have a fall?' she said.

'No, Jhangelgha,' he said. 'Shmore a vainting . . .' His voice sounded very odd. As if he were drunk. She was practical as he would have expected.

'Tell me what to do in yeses or nos. Can you stand up if I help you?'

'Yesh.'

'Will I open the door and put you sitting in the car?'

'Yesh.'

He started to speak again, she had the door open and the big man seated in the passenger seat.

'Now, do you want me to get your wife, or to go to a phone and call the hospital in the town? Sorry you have to answer yes or no. Will I get Mrs Power?'

'No.'

'Will I phone the hospital?'

'No. Drive.'

'No, Dr Power. I could curse myself to the pit of hell but I can't drive. Let me get someone to drive you . . . is it safe to leave you here?'

'Yesh. Shafe.'

'Very well, I'll get my bike, I'll be back in five minutes . . .'

'Anjheala.' He seemed agitated.

'Trust me, trust me. I'll get the right person. Are you better here or would you like me to help you back to my house?'

'Alrigth.'

She was a blur of bicycle wheels and then he heard a car coming. Dick Dillon and Gerry Doyle stepped out. The two men he would have picked himself in the whole of Castlebay.

They had been marvellous to him in the hospital, masking their shock that it was the man himself who needed a bed, not one of his patients.

One of his oldest friends Tim Daly was with him in no time. 'That's a light one, Paddy, take more than that to put you in a wheelchair,' he said.

That was what Paddy Power wanted, no fancy chat, no pretending nothing had happened. He knew a stroke when he saw one, and even more so when he had just been through one.

He pointed at his mouth. 'Shpeesh,' he said.

'Sure, that can go on for a day or two even in the slightest of strokes, you know that.'

'Shide,' he said indicating the side of his body.

'Same thing, it's not paralysed in any strict sense, it's just a bit numb.'

'Yesh.' Power's face was sad.

'Will I drive out to Molly myself, and tell her we're keeping you here for a few days, bring her in with me maybe?'

'Itsh far.'

388

'No it's not. It's no trouble. And would you like me to tell David? There's no need, as you well know. You could stay here and come out and he need never be any the wiser. Is that what you'd like?'

'Yesh.'

'Sleep a bit, Paddy. It's hard I know, but it's what will do you good . . .'

'Tim . . . Tim . . . locum.' He was straining.

'I have it in hand. I've told him three weeks, you're not to get frightened. I said that, so that you can have a real rest, maybe a week away somewhere with Molly.'

Dr Power closed his eyes, secure at last that everything was under control.

Tim Daly was right. It was a very light one. So light that it was never even referred to as a stroke. Dr Power said that it wouldn't give a young mother confidence if she thought that the doctor attending the birth of her first baby might keel over paralysed. It was described as a little turn and it caused hardly any comment in Castlebay. The locum doctor was a nice man too and not a bit put out by people saying that if he didn't mind they'd wait until Dr Power was ready before they'd have their stitches out or go for those blood tests.

Dr Mackey had lived for a long time in the North of England in industrial towns. He thought the peace of Castlebay was something that should be bottled and put on prescription for those who were tense or anxious all over the world.

'Faith and there's a fair few very tense and anxious here all the same,' Paddy Power said to him. He, Dr Mackey, and Dr Tim Daly were all having a progress discussion. Paddy had been out of hospital for a week: Dr Mackey was still booked for another ten days. The speech had fully returned to normal and there was no more trace of numbness. But Paddy agreed that it was a warning, and agreed further that his own advice to anyone in similar circumstances would be cut down drastically. He knew there should be no more night calls. He would in fact have to cut out a lot of his long drives over bad roads on home calls. He needed someone else to help him. Since there would not be a living for two doctors, he would need a younger man as an assistant. That man should be the one who intended to follow him. David.

'I have written to him. It was easier to write than to say.'

'You're not asking him much,' sniffed Dr Mackey. 'To come back to a ready-made practice. You can teach him all he doesn't know already. You won't be a dog in the manger trying to keep the good will – an *ideal* set-up for any young doctor.'

Dr Power sighed. 'Ah yes, but this young doctor was all set to do his paediatrics and then obstetrics and then the Lord knows what . . . he hadn't it in his mind to come back now. That's what I said to him, I said I knew it was bad timing. He's coming home tomorrow. The hospital gave him compassionate leave. He had to tell them I was at death's doors but he'll be here tomorrow.'

Molly came in with Nellie and a tea tray. Molly had surprised them all by being so calm. They had expected hysterics and they had got a very practical woman. She had even agreed that David should not be alerted until they knew the extent of the trouble.

Tim Daly thought that he must have misjudged her. He had often said to his own wife that Paddy Power had deserved someone less feathery and citified than Molly; but maybe he had been wrong. Anyway there was never any doubt about that son of his, a big, square, handsome, bright lad. Tim Daly sighed again thinking of the strange hand of fate that had dealt him five daughters in succession and no boy anywhere along the line.

David knew about his father before he got the letter. He had heard from Angela almost immediately after it happened. She wrote that she was becoming increasingly unable to mind her own business as she grew older and unable to avoid meddling in other people's affairs, but just in case he would need more time to think about it than he would get, his father planned to write to him in a few days and tell him of a mild stroke which was genuinely believed to have been slight and no threat to his life, but which would mean that he might need David much sooner than expected. Angela said that he mustn't acknowledge the letter or anything, it was just sometimes nicer to be forewarned.

She had written to him at his hospital, and without her having to put it in writing he knew she hadn't written to Clare. It was to give him time to think. It was all bad news but he thanked her deep in his heart.

He thought. Three times he was pulled up for not paying attention, and on one occasion a patient said to him that he looked as if he was on another planet.

He went into a cubicle in casualty and sat on the bed. Suppose he did go home? In July, when he finished this intern year? Suppose Clare studied on, back and forth from Castlebay to Dublin? Suppose she took her degree and was accepted for M.A.? It was by thesis. You could write a thesis anywhere, couldn't you? He was desperately vague. Could you do it from Castlebay?

He rang the admissions office of the university, and the voice kept saying he would have to come in and discuss it.

'*God damn it!*' David cried. 'There must be a *rule*. Can people do their M.A. without being in the university or not? *Yes* or *No*? Is that too much to ask?'

It was, or the tone in which he asked was too much to reply to.

He couldn't go back to hide in the cubicle, it was time to go back to work.

He had hidden nothing from Clare up to now and there was no point in pussyfooting around and trying to get non-existent information about her degree. Anyway, their futures were together. She deserved to know anything that he knew.

He would do no special pleading.

He wouldn't try to sell her on the idea of going home. He wouldn't apologize for his father's ill health.

He would tell her no flowery tales about how much she would love his mother once David and Clare were married.

391

He would gloss over nothing.

But he must tell her.

There was no bus coming so he decided to walk. He saw her coming up the road towards him, hands in pockets, thoughtful.

'You came to meet me,' he cried.

'Yes, I wondered if we could go somewhere just to have a drink maybe?'

'That's great.' He tucked her arm into his. It would be easier to tell her in a pub that their life in Dublin, their freedom, their study, was going to be cut short.

He carried the drinks to the corner table. He would tell her at once.

'David. You're not going to like this. But it's no use putting it off. I'm pregnant.'

There was a long silence.

'I'm very sorry. But it's confirmed. I sent a sample to Holles Street. It's positive, and I . . . well, I know . . .'

'But you *can't* be . . . we took such care.'

'Not enough, it seems.' She looked very small and young and frightened.

'Oh Clare, Clare,' he said. 'What will we do?'

'I don't know. I've had two weeks to wonder and worry. And I still don't know.'

'You should have told me.'

'What was the point? Silly, frightening both of us to death unless it was definite.'

'And it's *definitely* definite?'

'It is David. It is.'

He put his head in his hands. 'Oh *Christ*,' he said. '*Christ, God*, isn't that so unfair. Isn't that *all* we need.'

His drink was untouched and so was hers. Nobody was near enough to hear them or have any idea what they were talking about.

She sat icy and withdrawn. She had hoped he would touch her, put his arms around her. Now she felt she would kill him if he tried.

He took his head out of his hands, hair tousled, face flushed. 'I'm sorry,' he said.

392

'What for?'

'For it happening. I'm meant to be a doctor. Some medical knowledge I have.'

'Don't worry about *that*. It's not an exam. Nobody's going to give you marks or take them away for it.'

'Clare!'

'Well? What else is there to say?'

'I don't know. I suppose we should think what we'll do . . .'

She was silent.

'Make plans . . . It's just, just such a shock, and such a bloody shame. Now of all times.'

'Yes,' she said.

Her face looked small, white and hurt. He remembered suddenly that he hadn't told her about his father. She didn't even know that side of it. He remembered too that she was in the most feared condition of any girl from any small town and maybe any big town in Ireland. She was In Trouble.

He reached out for her hand. 'We'll sort it out,' he said.

She pulled her hand away.

'You haven't touched your drink,' he said awkwardly.

'Neither have you.' The pint looked too big and too sour.

'I think I'll have a brandy,' David said. 'Would you like that, for the shock? Doctor's orders.' He tried a watery smile.

'No. Thank you,' Clare said.

When he came back, she leaned across the table. 'I'm terribly, terribly sorry. I can't say any more. I know how frightening this must be for you, David. I'm trying to keep calm and think what on earth we're going to do. But you probably don't know what you feel yet. It's probably still unreal to you.'

'Yes. That's right,' he said, grateful that she understood that much.

There was another silence.

He drained his brandy. 'Will we go home?' he said.

They stood up and left, each afraid to touch the other and walking several paces apart.

Out in the street the yellow light shone down and made their faces look even more strained. They walked in silence towards the bus stop where David had been heading less than an hour before. They sat silent on the bus, too. Once or twice they looked at each other as if to say something but the words didn't come.

About two stops before their own David stood up. 'Will we get out here?' he asked her diffidently.

'Yes. Of course.' She was very polite. Under normal circumstances she would have questioned him and joked and argued.

They were beside the canal. 'Let's walk a little here,' he said.

They walked in silence and both stopped when two swans glided up to them.

'I only have a bit of chewing gum,' Clare said in almost her ordinary voice. 'Do you think they'd like it, or would it stick their beaks together?'

'Will you marry me?' David said.

'What?'

'Will you marry me. Please.'

'David?' her voice was low and unsure.

'*Please,*' he said again.

'David, you don't have to say anything yet. Don't say anything now. I don't expect you to . . . you don't have to. Honestly. We'll talk, we'll make plans, it's not the end of the world.'

'I know. I love you,' he said.

'And I love you. That's never changed, that never will.'

'So,' he said, eyes shining. 'We'll get married. Now rather than later. Won't we? Say yes. Say, "Yes David."'

'You know I'd love to, but there are other things, other possibilities which we should discuss. You know that.'

'Not with *our* baby, our own child. No other possibilities.'

She stared at him, her eyes filling with tears.

'You haven't given me your answer, like they do in stories.' He was eager and still not sure what she would say.

She paused and took his face in her hands. 'If you mean it . . .' she began.

'That's not an answer, that's a conditional clause,' he said.

'I would love to marry you. Yes. Yes, *please*.'

They walked home and bought chips, and wine, and a chocolate cake. They sat down by their oil stove to make plans and to think about the future.

'Can we get married here? In Dublin? I couldn't bear it at home.'

'That's not the way my wife is going to talk about our big day!'

'You know what I mean.'

'Yes. Of course we'll get married here. Wherever you like. London. Paris. Rome.'

'And then we'll come back and get ourselves a bigger flat, and wait till the exam and the baby. There's a month between them. The finals are over at the end of September and the baby arrives in October, the third week.'

He held her hand between his. 'Isn't it marvellous,' he said again.

'I'm so glad you're pleased. I was afraid that when you get your job in the hospital, you wouldn't like coming home at night to a baby.' She smiled at him. He said nothing.

'I mean it's not what a young doctor, a junior hospital doctor wants to come back to, a flat of nappies and a wife at her studies . . .' She was worried by his sudden silence. 'But the great thing is that I *will* be able to do a lot of work at home, I was discussing it with one of the postgrad students. She said that as long as they know your circumstances and can see that you're in there and doing the work and consulting every week or so, you don't have to present yourself every day or anything.'

'Oh.'

'What is it?'

Then he told her about his father's stroke, and that they would have to go back to Castlebay.

*   *   *

Because of Angela's letter, they had five days. Five terrible days. Sometimes they raged at each other, sometimes they just clung together. There were times when they were calm and worked out the alternatives. There were no alternatives. Sometimes Clare taunted him and said he was a Mummy's Boy. No other man would throw his whole career away. Sometimes he wounded her and said that her love was meaningless and shallow if it could change because of place. True love survived wherever it lived. They knew of a doctor that Clare could go to – he had been struck off the medical register, but he did a steady practice in terminations. Because he was a doctor, it wouldn't be dangerous. Then they could think again. But they never talked of that seriously. The miracle of a child of their own seemed about the only cheerful thing in the middle of all the tears and confusion. They would solve none of the dilemma if the baby were taken out of the picture. The pregnancy, and having to tell both families, was not the biggest thing.

The biggest thing was going back.

Neither of them wanted to.

David was going to.

That's where it stood when David got the letter from his father.

Clare cried and cried when she read the letter. It was so generous, so understanding. The old man had put down on paper all the things they had been talking about during the week. He said he regretted so much asking this of David that he barely had the strength to write it. He set out clearly the impossibility of asking another doctor to hold the fort for three or four years until David might feel ready to return. He sympathized almost dispassionately with David.

What is very hard, for both of us, is this emotional blackmail. I hate to ask you back: you hate to give up your plans. But I have to ask and you have to say yes or no. If I had died, then your decision would be much more clear cut. If you had not wanted to take over this practice then it would have been far easier for you not to have done so. Your mother might have moved to Dublin and nobody would have been greatly hurt or let down. This, I am afraid, is the hardest way and I am well aware of it.

All I can do is try to make it as attractive for you as I can. This house is yours, as you know, but you might feel more independent if you had a place of your own. We could do up the Lodge for you so that you could have a private life of your own and not feel like a little boy again. But the other thing of course, David, is that a doctor in a small community like this can't have much excitement in his private life, if you know what I mean. It's all very hard on you, boy, it's a letter I hate having to write to you . . .

The Lodge. It was a small house just within the half-acre garden of the Powers' residence. It needed a new roof. It had about four rooms, David thought. No kitchen, and only an outside lavatory. They had always been intending to get it done up. At the moment it just housed extra furniture.

It would be their new home.

They travelled back on the train together.

This time they were quiet. They looked out as the fields and telephone wires flashed by. At one place where the train slowed down there were children at a gate waving excitedly at the passengers. A six-year-old held up a fat baby who waved like mad with his two fat arms and his face split into a grin showing one tooth. David and Clare automatically reached for each other's hand. By Christmas they would have something like that. Not as big, not with a tooth, but a bit like that. They gave each other encouraging smiles. They weren't silent out of pique, or despair. It was just that they had been over the plans so often they didn't even want to mention them again.

* * *

The plans were complicated. Clare was going to stay on the train while David left as one of the first passengers. His mother would meet him and he would hasten her out of the car park as quickly as possible. Clare had asked Angela to arrange for someone to meet her. She had telephoned Angela at school, and could almost see the disapproving face of Immaculata.

Clare had said that for reasons she would explain later she didn't want to be met by Gerry Doyle, but anyone else, and for reasons which she would also explain she would be the last person to leave the train, well after Mrs Power had cleared the car park. Angela said she understood perfectly.

She felt sick when he went through the ticket barrier without a backward glance, as they had arranged.

She waited till a porter walked through the train picking up newspapers before she got out.

The ticket checker was surprised. 'Well, now! I was off to my tea. Fall asleep on the train, did you?'

Clare smiled at him. Lucky man. Just his tea to worry about.

In the car park Dick stood, waving enthusiastically and coming forward to carry her bag.

Molly Power wore driving gloves. She had been told that they gave you a better grip on the wheel. She looked very well, David thought, her hair freshly done, a nice wool two-piece in a soft green – not the fussy, insecure, over made-up woman he had met a few short months ago at the Nolans' house.

She was calm and practical about his father too. She understood the nature of his attack and the need not to exert himself. There was no evidence of panic or anxiety. She spoke pleasantly of Dr Mackey the locum, of the great delight that David had returned home so quickly to discuss things, of the conversation she had held with Bumper Byrne about getting the Lodge fixed up.

David raked her face for clues of how she would react

in a couple of hours when she knew she was going to have Clare O'Brien as a daughter-in-law.

Dick Dillon was easy to talk to. He talked about things, not people. She asked was it easy to learn to drive, and he said it was very easy. He showed her the pedals at his feet and said he'd have the theory of it taught to her by the time they got back to Castlebay. And indeed he had. A was accelerator, B was brakes and C was clutch.

She studied his big feet in their neatly-laced, shiny brown shoes as he told her what he was doing each time. 'I see, you have your foot heavy on C and lightly on A and as you release C you press A. I have it,' she said excitedly. 'And now you're pressing B because you want to slow down at the crossroads,' she said.

'I want to *Stop* at this crossroads, Madam. Because I see a big sign saying *Stop*.'

'That's great. I have the hang of it. I'll get a licence as soon as I can.' She would need to know how to drive, and to drive far, if she were going to be living in Molly Power's garden.

His father listened attentively. David said they had hoped to marry in a couple of years' time and he had hoped to get further experience in Dublin hospitals. But now, since circumstances said otherwise, they were happy to come back and start both married life and practice all at the same time.

His father looked thoughtful. Weren't they very, very young to settle down? Clare wasn't twenty yet, well, only barely twenty. Still very young.

No. David was firm. Circumstances had changed so they would marry now. In a few weeks' time in Dublin.

'So Clare is pregnant.'

'We're very very pleased,' David said defiantly.

'You may well be. But is it the best start for a marriage, for a young girl like Clare, for the baby?'

'Dad, whether it is or not, it *has* started. We never thought for a moment of trying to unstart it.'

'No. No. I'm glad of that.'

'So, I suppose what I'm trying to say is, that once we've told Mum and once Clare has told her family, we'll just get on with it.'

'Is Clare home?'

'Yes.'

'You didn't say . . . Molly didn't say she was with you.'

'We thought it best to come separately from the station.'

Dr Power gave a very deep sigh.

'I'm sorry to have to break it to you like this, Dad.'

'You're very irresponsible, really, you know.'

'Well we didn't mean it to happen, obviously. But then, as you know, I'm sure only too well from all your years here, it just does happen.'

'I didn't expect it to happen to my own *son*. You shouldn't have taken advantage of her. It's not *fair*. Just because you knew her from home, because you knew she was going to be timid.'

'There was no taking advantage of her. You don't understand. In Dublin nobody thinks of Clare as poor little Clare O'Brien from the shop. That's only here. And not everyone here. It's mother, and a few people. I didn't think *you'd* be like that.'

'I'm not being like anything, boy. I realize you're upset. I'm just saying it was a pity that this had to happen to you. You, with your whole life ahead of you.'

'Ahead of us now, Dad. That's what I'm trying to tell you.'

'She's only a child, a child herself. She doesn't know what she wants.'

'Oh she does, she very much does. She's going to finish her degree, you know. Her finals are a month before the baby is born. So we want to get married as soon as possible.'

'It won't be soon enough for Castlebay.'

'Well to hell with what they think.'

Dr Power poured himself a very small brandy.

'It's medicinal. I prescribe it for myself now and then.'

400

'Are you going to drink my health? *Our* health?' David asked.

'Not immediately.'

'You're not shocked, Dad.'

'Not in that sense. I don't know. You're very young, David. You've only got one life. You don't have to marry Clare if you don't want to. You can be very honourable and just without marrying her. You can acknowledge the child and give her maintenance. But there's no shotgun at your head. Not today, not in 1960.'

'You've got it all out of proportion. The fact that Clare is pregnant is only part of a much bigger thing, which is that I love her. I love her desperately, Dad. I'll never want anyone else in the world. I couldn't contemplate anyone else marrying Clare. I didn't explain that properly.'

'I think I'll let you explain that to your mother. You'll have to do a fair bit of explaining there, so there's no point in doing it twice.'

'Do you think I could have a medicinal brandy?'

'No. I don't. I think you can make your explanations without any stimulant.'

'If I'm to be your partner in this practice, then I can prescribe too. I prescribe myself a brandy twice the size of yours.'

Dr Power laughed and poured it for him. 'Go to it, son,' he said.

'Aren't you coming with me?'

'No, I'm a man who mustn't have too much excitement. I'm going into my study.'

Agnes O'Brien had noticed that the tourist trade was beginning to have a bit of a surge at Easter. More and more people who owned their own caravans up in the site thought they should get value from them by coming more than once a year. She wasn't surprised to hear a ping on the door. She was very surprised to see Clare.

'What brings you back? You never said you were coming?'

'I got a chance, suddenly. So I came,' Clare said.

'You never wrote or anything.' Her mother was full of wonder. In her world people wrote letters announcing what they were going to do; *then* they did it.

'No. As I said, I just got the chance.' She must hide her impatience with her mother. 'Will we have a cup of tea or anything?'

'What am I thinking of, I didn't expect you, you see, come on in, give me your bag.'

'You look much better, Mam, how's your leg?'

'Oh, that's long forgotten, now haven't I enough to be worrying about without thinking of old ailments? No, thank God, I walk fine now, not even a bit of a limp.'

'That's great, Mam.'

'Well come on in, and don't stand there staring around as if you'd never seen the place before.'

'Where's everybody?'

'Your father's gone with Ben to get him a job, or we hope he will. There's a new garage opening out at the crossroads. They want two young fellows to work there. They'll have them trained by the summer, when the business will be great. Your father's gone up there with Ben. Ben's not great to give an account of himself.'

'When did they go?'

'They were to meet the man up there at six. Why?'

'I want to talk to you.'

Clare had put the Closed sign on the shop door. Agnes laid down the kettle without filling it.

'Mother of God, you're pregnant,' she said.

It took time for her mother to stop crying. Clare had time to fill the kettle, boil it, make the tea, cut them two slices of fruit cake and find two paper table napkins for her mother to use as a handkerchief.

'How you can sit there, as bold as brass, and tell me this? How you can do it? It's beyond belief!' her mother wept.

'Mam, I've told you nothing. I just nodded when you asked me was I pregnant. Then you started to cry. Now let me tell you what I really came home to tell you . . .'

'Oh! You weren't going to *bother* with this then, were you? This isn't *news* at all. This is something we were meant to expect, along with your high and mighty ways.'

'*Please*, Mam. Let me tell you. I'm getting married.'

'A bit late in the day for that isn't it?'

'No. Listen. I was going to get married anyway, and this just means we get married a bit sooner, that's all. Honestly, that's all. But it was the getting married bit I wanted to tell you about.'

'I'm not stopping you, tell me about it.' Agnes's eyes were red, she hadn't touched her tea and cake.

'It's David, David Power. We're getting married in a few weeks' time in Dublin, and then he's coming back here – I mean we're both coming back here. His father hasn't been well and . . .'

Agnes stood up. 'David Power! You let *David Power*, the doctor's son, make little of you, and get you into trouble? I don't believe it. I can't believe my own ears.'

She knew this was her mother's vocabulary. In advance she had warned herself of words like *disgrace* and *get into trouble*. But it still didn't make them easy to hear.

'I wish you wouldn't put it that way. At this moment he's up in his house telling his parents too. And whether this had happened or not we were going to get married anyway. So don't talk about people *making little* of other people, or of him *disgracing* me. I was just as eager, all the time, as he was.'

'Don't boast of it, you little tramp. Don't stand there like a slut in my kitchen and tell me what you were eager for and what you weren't. You've ruined us all in this family. We'll be the laughing stock of the place – marrying into the Powers no less. Do you think that Mrs Power is going to let the likes of *you* cross her doorstep? Do you think that woman is going to let her son, with the fine education he has, marry a girl from a shop in Castlebay? A girl who is no better than she should be?' Agnes was laughing now, a twisted, ugly laugh. 'Now, *I* never did even my Primary Certificate. *I'm* not college educated like you. And yet *I* can see with the two eyes in my head that there'll be no marriage. There'll be an *explanation*. David almighty Power will have to go abroad to finish his education – or some such excuse. Don't be fooling yourself, girl. There's going to be no wedding for you. Only *disgrace* and a child to bring up. And there's going to be nothing for us but jeers.' Agnes started to cry again.

Clare found herself pitying the thin woman with the rolled-up table napkins crying at her kitchen table.

She spoke very gently. 'Mam, listen to me. I know this is hard to believe. But it's true. David is twenty-five years of age. He's a grown man. He doesn't have to ask their permission for anything. We've arranged the marriage, and the priest. It *will* happen. If his mother turns against him, let her turn. She'll turn back eventually. You know the Lodge up in their garden near the cliff edge, well, Bumper Byrne is going to get it done up and that's where we're going to live. *Mam*. And when Chrissie's baby is born, she'll wheel hers down to see you, Mam, and I'll wheel mine along the Cliff Road. And there's no disgrace. No jeers. It's all *grand*. Don't you understand?'

Her mother looked up with tear-stained face. 'It's all very simple for you, Clare. But life isn't like that.'

'It is, Mam. I'm as good as David. In every way. He knows that. And so do I.'

'If you think that you'll be the only two in Castlebay who do,' her mother sniffed.

'Mam, drink your tea. Please, Mam.'

'When is it going to be born?' She looked at Clare's stomach.

'End of October. Just after my exams.'

'You're never going to go on with your exams.'

'But I have to. That's what it was all about, the three years. I've got weeks in hand. They may have to cut a hole in the desk for me to fit into it, but still I'll manage.'

'Don't say things like that.' Her mother had sipped the tea; she was getting back to normal.

'So what I was going to suggest was this: that we say David and I are getting married in Dublin, not having a big fussy wedding because we're both still studying, and then as soon as the house is done we'll be back. No need to mention anything else at all, is there?'

'But people aren't fools, Clare. They can count to nine like the rest of us. If someone gets married in April and has a baby in October, they'll know.'

'But what will they know that matters?' Clare's impatience was beginning to show.

Her mother sighed deeply. 'You'll never understand. And, Clare, child, if you believe they'll let you be happy here you'll believe anything.'

David decided to say it quickly.

'Mother, I've just had a long chat with Dad and it's all sorted out. I finish my internship, and come back here at the beginning of July.'

Her face brightened. 'I knew there'd be no problems. Paddy kept saying it was a pity to call you home before your time, but I said you'd be happy to come.'

'You were right. And I love the idea of the Lodge. I'll talk to Bumper Byrne myself tomorrow.'

'There's no real hurry with the Lodge, is there? Your room is there . . .'

'Well . . . you see . . . I've other plans too, Mother. This is my big news. I'm getting married.'

'*David!* You can't be *serious*. You've never told us a word . . . we didn't even know you were courting. Paddy, Paddy . . .'

'He's gone to the study. I wanted to tell you myself.'

'But haven't you told him . . .?'

'Yes. He knows.'

She suspected trouble.

'I just thought I'd tell you myself, in my own way. I'm going to marry Clare O'Brien. Very soon. In four weeks' time. In Dublin. And as soon as she has finished her degree she will come back here and we will live in the Lodge.'

The colour had gone from Molly's face. She was standing, she had jumped up in her first excitement. Now she swayed slightly, and held on to the back of the chair.

'We intended to get married later on, and live in Dublin. But, of course, now, with Dad needing me back at home that's all changed.'

'*Clare O'Brien.*'

'So we're not having any big wedding, or any fuss. But Father Flynn, do you remember him, he's going to be over again, he's going to be based in Dublin now and he's going to marry us . . .'

'I don't believe it.'

He deliberately misunderstood her. 'Oh, but he is. And he's been very helpful about it all.'

'You know what I mean. I cannot believe that you are being forced to marry that girl. No matter what you may have done.'

'Not forced. We want to. I've explained that. We've planned this for a long time.'

'When you discovered she was up the pole.'

David swallowed. He had rehearsed with Clare how they would behave when their parents said the unforgivable things, when the accusations started. Somehow he hadn't thought his mother would use such a coarse expression. 'That's a vulgar way of describing it.'

'She's a *vulgar* girl.'

He was very calm. 'No, that's not true. Clare isn't in the least vulgar. She is gentle and sensitive, she is bright and well educated and considerate. I would never think of her as vulgar. Never. But she is poor. And her family are poor and uneducated. And her sister Chrissie is most definitely vulgar.' He spoke without any anger.

'David. You *mustn't* do this.'

'I'm going to say this very carefully. So please listen to me. Just listen, and then talk later. It's very important. Nothing you say, *nothing*, will make me change my mind. I love Clare. I *will* marry her. And we *will* be happy. And we will have a child in October. And any harsh words you say now will only make things difficult between us, always, so I'm going to beg you not to say anything until you've had some time to think . . .'

She was without words. Looking at him.

He moved towards her. She stiffened as if forbidding him to touch her.

'I don't know what to do, Mummy,' he said, using the form of address he hadn't used for years. 'I really don't. You see I want to talk to you about it all now, and tell you about how happy I am and how much Clare means to me. But I'm afraid . . . I'm afraid you'll say something so hurtful that I'd find it hard to forgive.'

She nodded mutely.

'So I'm going to go out with Bones for a bit. I'll come back in at half-past eight. And then I'm going to meet Clare at nine in the hotel. She will have told her family then too.'

'*David* . . .' It was a sad cry.

He left the room and, pretending he didn't see his father hovering at the study door, called for Bones. He looked back at the end of the drive, and he saw the two silhouettes in the window. He saw his father put his arms around his mother, who was obviously crying on his shoulder.

Ben had been taken on at the garage, so Tom O'Brien returned in a fine good humour.

'What's all this? The Closed sign on the door?' he asked. 'Ben's not going to be able to keep the lot of us with the job he's got. Why are we closed, will you tell me?'

'Clare's home. She came unexpectedly. We were having a chat.'

'Clare's back?'

'She's engaged, Tom. Engaged to be married.'

'Clare? Never! To some college fellow, is it?'

'To David Power.'

'Our David Power? But I thought she hardly knew him in Dublin?'

'That's not the way it would appear.'

'Well that would beat the divil.' He scratched his head, not sure what to make of it, looking at his wife's face for guidance. Agnes's eyes looked a bit too bright, but she showed no signs of crying.

'Isn't that a bit odd?' he searched her expression, but got nothing. 'Isn't the whole thing odd?'

Clare came down the stairs. 'Have you heard my news?'

'You have me stunned,' he said.

'Is that all I get? Where's the congratulations? And the delight? Where's the looking at my ring . . .' She held out a small diamond for admiration. It had been bought with the remains of her savings and the money the pawnbroker gave David for his good sheepskin coat.

She approached her father to give him an unaccustomed hug. He looked at Agnes and, seeing what he considered approval, gave her the hug. Then she hugged her mother.

'Mam says it won't be easy. But nothing's easy, is it?'

'I suppose it isn't, child. But I'd say you've taken on the World Champion when you're taking on Molly Power.'

She didn't mention the baby to her father, and though his eyes seemed to ask many a time, neither she nor her mother took him up on the unspoken questions.

Clare looked at the clock. There was still half an hour before she met David in the hotel.

She had a sudden feeling of fear. Suppose they had talked him out of it? Suppose she had come all this way to meet him, and to agree to going back cheerfully to Castlebay, suppose she had made all those concessions and somehow that mother of his had talked him out of it? Suppose he was at the hotel gate, and said with fallen face that he had agreed to wait until the baby was born before they married? Then she really would feel *cheap*, and *betrayed*.

They were both in the hotel lounge by five to nine. They entered by two different doors. Bones was with David, refusing the polite request to sit in the corridor outside.

They nodded at each other.

The worst was over.

'What will I get you to drink, Mrs Power?' he asked gently.

She smiled at him.

Rose Dillon was behind the counter. She had always tried to include David in her parties and picnics without success. She smiled at him coquettishly still. 'To what do we owe this honour? We don't see nearly enough of you in Castlebay.'

Clare watched fascinated: Rose Dillon didn't even acknowledge that she existed, sitting in the chair by the window. She only had eyes for David.

'I'll be coming home for good soon.'

'Oh, that will cause a flurry – they'll be dying to marry you off,' she twinkled.

'I'll be married off sooner than you think,' David said.

Rose frowned. She looked over at Clare O'Brien and shook her head. *No*. That would be *ridiculous*.

They walked up to Angela's cottage to tell her. She was the one person they hoped would be totally delighted. She could see that from their faces. She was touched.

'Will you come to the wedding? Please? It's going to be a bit tense.'

'I'm great at tense weddings,' Angela said.

'Father Flynn will be marrying us.'

'He and I could nearly set up a company, awkward weddings catered for. A speciality in fact.'

'Will you though?'

'If Immaculata lets me. I don't want to anger her too much – after all, the big guns will be out in the summer when the prodigal returns.'

'What's that?' David asked.

'You didn't tell him about Sean? That was good of you, Clare, but in love and marriage you can tell all. It's allowed.'

David looked bewildered.

'Listen, David. Your marriage, which is going to raise a few eyebrows and the imminent birth of your child – which has not been announced to me but I am sure is a likelihood – will raise a few more. But let me assure you that those eyebrows will have you long forgotten when the other excitement hits the streets of Castlebay. When

Father Sean O'Hara, much respected missionary priest, returns to stay in a caravan with his Japanese wife and his two children.' She laughed when she saw David's face. 'I hate to take the limelight away from the pair of you, but prepare to live in obscurity . . .'

Dr Mackey delivered a nine-pound baby to Chrissie Byrne. It was a boy, and Chrissie and Mogsy said he was going to be called John Fitzgerald after the President of America. Clare went to see her. And got little thanks for her visit.

'You were always one to steal someone else's thunder, Clare. You must have announced your engagement just to spite me as soon as you heard that John Fitzgerald had arrived.'

'Don't be a goon.'

'Always the same,' grumbled Chrissie.

'Here, let's see him.' Clare was eager.

'Don't touch him. You'd drop him.'

'I just want to look at him.' Clare peered in at the little bundle in her sister's arms – a red face and lots of black hair.

'He's beautiful,' she breathed, with such admiration that Chrissie was slightly mollified.

Clare decided she had better ask her. Life would be intolerable if she didn't.

'David and I are having a very small wedding, as you know. Just his family and ours, and a couple of friends. Will you and . . . er Maurice . . . be able to come?'

Chrissie looked doubtful. 'It's very soon, altogether. I'd have John Fitzgerald with me. Maurice and I have been discussing it. I think with regret we will have to refuse.'

Clare looked just disappointed enough, but not too upset. Nothing that would make Chrissie go back on her decision. 'I'll keep you some of the wedding cake,' she said.

'Imagine you marrying the gentry,' Chrissie said. 'What I can't understand is why you're going back to college.

Haven't you done it now? Haven't you got what you were out to get? A rich husband?'

It wasn't at all as she would have expected. Mrs Conway had been pleased. She made a point of crossing the road to tell Clare that she wished them well. 'I always thought my Frank could have done worse than marry you,' she said – which was a high accolade.

Josie, oddly, did not seem as pleased as Clare would have thought. She was very formal about the news and only offered the most distant of congratulations.

Josie had been walking out with Mr Martin Harris, the auctioneer. Martin was *mature*, which meant old; and *responsible* which meant dull. Josie, who had never been jealous of anything Clare had done, was now very envious of Clare coming back to Castlebay and snatching the only attractive man, and the only *catch*, from under their noses.

Father O'Dwyer wrote out her letter of freedom. It was an odd thing not to get married in your own parish, but this Father Flynn had been a very decent person and he was sure he would do it right.

Angela had begged her to call on Immaculata. There was great false excitement in the convent over the ring, which was admired by the whole community. There was genuine excitement about how Molly Power would take the new daughter-in-law.

They kept the meetings with the families as brief as possible.

David shook Tom's hand and thanked him for letting him marry Clare.

'Divil much a say I had in it one way or the other,' Clare's father said.

'I know you'll be pleased to have her back in Castlebay,' he said manfully to Clare's mother.

'I suppose it *may* turn out all right,' Agnes O'Brien said.

Up in the big house, Molly waited nervously at her fireplace; she had rearranged everything in the room a dozen times, and shouted at Nellie who was sulking in the kitchen. She had changed her dress twice.

She saw them walking up the drive. Laughing. The girl was *laughing*, instead of shaking in her shoes.

David had his own key.

'Mother, we're here,' he called.

Clare was tall. Molly had forgotten that. She was tall and thin, and her face seemed pale.

'Well.' Molly looked her up and down. It was just on the right side of being a calculated insult. But only just.

'Hallo, Mrs Power,' Clare said. Her voice was steady.

'So,' Mrs Power said.

I won't let her annoy me. I will not rise to her bait, Clare told herself, fists clenched by her sides.

David wasn't saying anything, which was what they agreed.

'David has told you our news, and our plans, Mrs Power.'

'Oh yes.'

'So I just wanted to add that I hope very much that I will make him happy, and that eventually I will make you and Dr Power pleased that we married.' Not too confident. It angered Molly more than anything had ever done in her life.

'I doubt if that will ever be the case,' she said holding back the temper that was threatening to spill out. 'I am here to greet you. Would you like me to ring for tea?'

'Thank you, but no, Mrs Power. If I may, I'll just go and pay my respects to your husband. I have a lot of things to do before going back tomorrow. Thank you for welcoming me to the house, and I'll look forward to seeing you at the wedding.'

I could kill her, Molly thought. *I wish she were dead.* The feeling swept over her and was gone. She felt shock and guilt. It confused her and she didn't make her farewells as she intended to.

'What . . . oh . . . yes. Yes, the wedding day. Yes.'

Clare had smiled and was out of the door.

'Thank you, Mother,' David said. His face was in a pleasant smile but his eyes were cold.

It was much later when she saw him. Sitting on the wall, by the hotel.

'You were going to run out of town without telling me.' He was cold and unsmiling.

'Don't be ridiculous.' She forced a light laugh that she didn't mean. 'Of course I was going to tell you. If I hadn't seen you tonight I'd have left a note for you.'

'You're a liar.'

'Now stop that,' she said, her anger rising. He was not going to upset her, she would not let him, but *hell*, he wasn't going to call her a liar. Especially since he was right.

'You had no intention of telling me,' Gerry said.

'Why wouldn't I tell you? Don't *dramatize* everything so much. I've been telling all my friends that I'm getting married. Why wouldn't I tell you?'

'Because you knew what I'd say.' There was no answering smile on his lips.

'And what would you say? What will you say?'

'That you're mad. You musn't do it.'

One more attempt, thought Clare. Just one more, to get this on to some kind of normal plane and then I abandon it.

'Well, listen to me, just because you and I were the only people left, everyone else getting hitched, that's no reason why I'm going to stay single just to keep you company. I'm delighted with it all. And I won't put up with any nonsense from you.'

'Don't do it. *Clare*.'

'Stop it. Can't you wish me well? Like ordinary people?'

'I do wish you well. But not married to David Power. And you're not ordinary people, I've always told you that. Neither am I.'

'You're certainly not like generous people or mannerly people,' she said.

'You can't marry him. You have to marry me. You always knew that.'

413

She looked anxiously at his pointed face for the lopsided smile, the grin that made anybody else grin too. There was none of it there. She stared at him, shocked.

'Well, I don't suppose there's anything more to say.' Clare moved towards the entrance gate.

Lithe as a cat, Gerry leapt to the ground. 'Don't go yet.'

'Of course I'm going. I'm not talking to you for one more minute. How dare you upset me and say all these things? How *dare* you? If it were you that had got engaged, I'd be so pleased and wish you well.'

'Got engaged? Got engaged? You and David haven't *got engaged*. You're getting *married* in three weeks. What does that mean? Well? What does it mean?'

'Go to hell.' She turned and ran past him.

He ran beside her, half jumping, half running. 'It's the wrong thing to do. Girls like you, like Fiona, you shouldn't be just forced to make fools of yourselves. *You're* not tramps. You're too trusting. If something goes wrong then you should work it out properly . . .'

She stopped and looked at him levelly. 'In my case, *nothing* went wrong. *Nothing*. Do you hear me? Everything is fine, as right as can be. Our marriage is a bit sooner than we intended but it's exactly what we wanted. It's going to be perfect.'

Gerry had stopped opposite her. He looked straight into her eyes. 'Your marriage to David Power is not going to be perfect. You foolish, *foolish* girl. Your marriage is doomed.'

The girls had been magnificent. They had been through the entire hostel in search of clothes, and since everyone was so much in awe of Valerie and Mary Catherine, clothes were forthcoming. They had a huge selection for Clare to choose from.

There was a nice pink suit which fitted Clare very well. They took a wine-coloured hat from another girl, and a very expensive black bag. Now all she needed were wine-coloured gloves and good black shoes.

They bought her the gloves between them, and she bought the shoes herself. She was kitted out.

Mary Catherine was to be bridesmaid, and James Nolan the best man. David seemed a little cool with James. Clare didn't know why. Anyway they were all in such a frenzy with study and getting clothes ready and dismantling their flat in Rathmines and finding a better one, that there was little time to speculate.

Clare had received a note from Caroline Nolan wishing her well, expressing surprise at the suddenness of it all, and regret that the Nolan family offer of hosting the wedding hadn't been taken up.

Clare had been adamant about that. It was not going to be on Nolan territory. It was to be on neutral ground, the hotel near the church. Father Flynn had discussed the menu and suggested one that seemed not too ambitious. David and Clare had opened a bank account: the manager loved young doctors and David, without actually saying it, implied that he was well on the way to being a consultant in Fitzwilliam Square. They had a small overdraft. It would pay for the wedding. There was no way the Nolans could get their hands on Clare's day.

They went through the list. There were the *relaxed* and the *tense*. The relaxed seem to outweigh the tense. David's father, Angela, Father Flynn, Emer and Kevin, Mary Catherine and Valerie. And James and Caroline would be all right, wouldn't they. Snobby, Clare thought, but all right. And what about Ben and Jim? *Tense*, Clare said, and if by any unlucky chance they did become relaxed it would mean that they had become hooligans.

Well, that was a fair number of easy people. On the other side of the scales would be David's mother, who would look like an avenging angel all day long; both Clare's parents, who would be so timid and fearful of doing the wrong thing they would have everyone's teeth on edge; and there would be the Nolan parents, who seemed to regard this marriage as in the same class as the loss of the *Titanic*.

'It's great that we're able to laugh about it,' Clare said.

415

'That's the only thing that makes me feel it's not doomed,' David agreed.

Clare didn't like the use of that word. It made her shiver.

The O'Briens came up by train the night before. Jim had never been in Dublin before; Ben had been once on a school trip. Clare met them at the station. She was taking them by taxi to the hotel where they would all stay the night. Mr Ryan, the owner, had arranged a very good rate. There were three rooms booked: one for Clare's parents, one for her brothers; and one for herself, where the girls would come tomorrow to help her dress.

Her heart filled with pity for them, for all she was putting them through, as she saw them getting out of the train. Blinking after the long journey, tired and nervous about what lay ahead . . . Their suitcase was enormous and very shabby – surely there were a couple of *small* bags at home? But then, they rarely went anywhere.

Ben and Jim were chastened by the hugeness of Kingsbridge station. The boys were squeezed into the front of the taxi. Clare's parents looked nervously out of the car on each side. She chattered: there would be tea and sandwiches in the hotel, Mr Ryan was going to have it ready. There wasn't a bar as such, but he said that he could get a few bottles of stout for them. Clare's father brightened; and so did Ben, but Ben was told that there was no question of a bottle of stout for him. There wasn't much need for conversation. They were all so tired that the tea and stout were enough to close their eyes.

Ten times Clare's mother asked what time they had to leave. Ten times, without complaining, Clare told her that they would walk across to the church – a distance of fifty yards – at eleven o'clock.

It was a beautiful sunny day. Mary Catherine and Valerie arrived giggling in their finery. They had the hat and the good black bag with them. Those were only borrowed for the day: the owners were so terrified to let them out of their sight, they had promised to return them before nightfall.

'I brought some brandy. In case,' Val said.

'Not now,' Mary Catherine said, 'We have to dress the bride.'

Clare looked pale so they rouged her up. She also looked extremely smart. The outfit was a work of genius and Clare blessed the anonymous donors. She felt that it was taking the Something Borrowed superstition a little too seriously, and they were all laughing at that, when Clare's father arrived beating on the door nervously and saying they had only twenty minutes – should they be on their way?

Clare didn't know there would be music. She was surprised to hear the burbling sounds of a church organ. Her father's arm stiffened in fright.

The altar did seem a mile away, but soon she was near enough to see them turning round. She saw the admiration in Angela's face first, and it was warming. She saw Angela clutch Emer, and they were both nodding with delight at her. Her unnaturally clean brothers seemed surprised too at how well she looked and this made her hold her head high. She saw Caroline's eyebrows go up, and that was pleasing too, as was the big smile from Dr Power. But best of all was the way Mrs Power's face changed just a fraction. The superior look which seemed to be built into it as she was whispering to Mrs Nolan left it for a moment. And because Clare felt so exhilarated, her smile was sparkling.

By the time David turned round she was glowing with confidence and happiness; transformed, almost, from when she had started to walk up the aisle. He had never known she could look so beautiful. He looked at James standing beside him and smiled. James smiled back encouragingly. The coldness, the tactless words James had spoken, were forgotten. David was stepping out of the pew to take his beautiful, beautiful bride to the altar.

The Powers were not taking any photographs. If the Nolans had brought a camera it was not produced. Kevin Quinn had a camera though; and when Father Flynn saw the sparsity of picture-taking he gave Jim O'Brien some money and sent him off to a nearby chemist to get three more films.

'Keep snapping,' Father Flynn hissed to Kevin. 'You're the official photographer.'

They walked cheerfully enough across to the hotel. Mrs Power looked at it as though it were some kind of museum piece. She was annoyed to hear the Nolans saying they hadn't known it was there, and what nice antiques in the hall. Mr Ryan had taken the decision to serve the drinks out in the conservatory, which opened on to a garden. There were flowers and plants and rays of sun coming through coloured glass.

'It's not bad at all,' hissed Valerie through clenched teeth. 'The way Clare was going on, I thought we were in for a place smelling of cabbage, with sauce bottles on the table.'

'There's nothing wrong with the place,' Mary Catherine said. 'But isn't the mother-in-law a *bitch*.'

'She'll soon see she's outnumbered,' Angela said. They jumped. They had not intended anyone else to hear. 'I agree, she's behaving like a bitch, but she's got no confidence, herself. When she sees the rest of us thinking it's marvellous, she'll come round.'

'I'll go and talk at her for a while,' Val said. 'Blind her with tales of my background.'

Mr Ryan called them in to lunch. There was cream in everyone's tomato soup, and a little chopped parsley on top.

Mrs O'Brien wondered whether it was just a decoration; Father Flynn solved that by spooning his own down noisily the moment grace had been said. Agnes saw what to do, and her family followed her. The rolls were slightly warm; and there were little clusters of bottles on the table: red wine, white wine, orange squash, and stout bottles artistically arranged at intervals.

The seating plan was a miracle of diplomacy. No O'Brien was left without a friendly neighbour. Clare and David felt the breath they had been holding all day begin to slip out naturally. It was too big a number for general conversation, but there was a nice buzz; and by the time Mr Ryan and his two waitresses had cleared the chicken à la crème away and dusted the table for the bringing on of the ice cream and cake, it was far more friendly than anyone could have believed possible.

Molly Power was flanked by Kevin Quinn on one side and Father Flynn on the other. Without being deliberately rude, there was nothing she could do but respond.

Agnes O'Brien was on the other side of Father Flynn, and then there was Valerie. They had dispensed with the traditional order of seating since that would have been a *certain* recipe for disaster.

Father Flynn had instructed James in some of his duties: he asked him to call upon Miss O'Hara to speak, and to ask David's father to say a few words too.

'It's not *traditional*, Father,' James complained.

'Whose side are you on, boy?' Father Flynn had replied sharply.

It worked. Tom O'Brien's bumbling words, the studying of his piece of paper, went almost unnoticed. If it had just been Tom, and the fluent young barrister James Nolan, the difference would have been very marked.

Dr Power was warm and cheerful. Doctors were often apt to say at weddings that they brought the bride or the groom into the world, as if that gave them special standing in the community. In this case he had brought both of them into the world, and had considerable responsibility for the existence of the groom. He wished them long, happy years in Castlebay – which as everyone knew was the centre of the Universe, and would those people who had not yet been to Castlebay please hurry up and go there.

Angela, more hesitant than she ever had been at school, spoke about how sentimental teachers always became once the pupils were out of their hands.

James was flowery. It was very nearly over. David stood up to speak last.

Clare had to fix her eyes firmly on the heap of telegrams

419

so that she would not cry at his words. He was speaking simply and directly about his happiness and his hopes for both of them. He was thanking everyone there by name for all they had done. Nobody could be more happy than he was at this moment.

They all clapped. Molly's gloved hands; Agnes's thin bony hands; Jim's and Ben's scrubbed clean hands – examined before they were allowed out; Father Flynn's plump little white hands and Angela's long artistic hands.

Clare went up to change, to remove the pink suit – on which not a crumb or drop had been spilled – to place the hat and the handbag back in tissue paper. She wore Valerie's good grey dress and a set of cheap wine-coloured glass beads, which matched her gloves. She grabbed up her own shabby bag. She was ready for Going Away. James had said he would give them a proper present later when they were settled into their new home. In the meantime perhaps the car might be useful. David thanked him again warmly as he took the car keys in his hand.

'It's good of you, James. And thanks for all the marvellous support. At the meal. You know.'

They stood awkwardly waiting for Clare to come downstairs. 'It was all great,' James said.

'Yes. Yes, of course.'

'And it will all turn out marvellously well.'

'Yes,' David said.

They were both thinking of the days when they could say anything to each other. A long time ago.

For the three-day honeymoon they had said they were going to a quiet hotel in Wicklow and everyone had nodded sagely. They were in fact going back to their new flat, which was in total chaos. They wanted nobody else. They wanted no gaiety or candlelit dinners, they just wanted each other and the knowledge that the day they had dreaded was over.

James Nolan had left champagne cooling, and when they got back to the Nolan house, Breeda was ready with a tray of glasses.

'This is more like it,' Caroline said.

'It was very nicely done, very nice,' her father said.

Dr Power took his glass of champagne and walked out into the well-kept garden. A man was mowing the lawn. For other people it was an ordinary working day.

Molly saw him standing by himself and went out to him. She stood beside him wordlessly.

'You were very good, Moll,' he said.

'Good?'

'You didn't want it, but you didn't let that spoil their day. Even though your heart wasn't in it.'

'Clare . . .' she paused.

He said nothing.

'She looked very well, I thought. The outfit was smart.'

Inside, the champagne was flowing. Caroline wanted to know why Clare hadn't carried that super handbag away with her when she was leaving. 'There was a fearful coldness between James and David, did you hear? James was nearly not going to be the best man?' She was giggly and conspiratorial.

'I *didn't* know,' Valerie said, giving her the cue to go on.

'*Apparently*, when David told James about the marriage, and the *hurry* and the *dramas* and all, James said, very reasonably I think, but anyway he said *bad luck* or something, and David said what do you mean, and James said that *really* David didn't *have* to marry a *scrubber*, and David poured his glass over James – it was in a hotel bar all this – and walked out, and James had to run after him. Gosh, it was *awful*.'

'Wasn't it?' Valerie said fervently. 'Wasn't it about as *awful* a thing to say as anyone could think of.'

'No, what I mean is . . .' Caroline saw she had put her foot in it.

'Isn't it *quite* extraordinary how James ever managed to make it to being an attorney with a mind like that,' Mary Catherine said in amazement.

June had always been a stifling month, waiting for the end of term.

Angela had written to Sean and Shuya in reply to their excited letter. Yes, indeed, she would be here, she would be in the cottage as always, and once they had decided what they were going to do, they could come and tell her, she would be happy to see them all, as she was always happy to see them.

Sean had said no, he hadn't written to anyone in Castlebay about his changed life, who would he write to? But Angela had been very firm on that one: it was Sean's story to tell, not hers. He must be the one to decide who to talk to and what to say.

No letter with any change of plans came. There was no reprieve.

They would be here on Saturday.

On Saturday morning, panic came over her as she was buying meat in Dwyers'. Chrissie, back at work, wanted to know if Miss O'Hara was going to have a party.

'No. Why?' Angela said, alarmed.

'Well you're just after buying enough meat to feed an army.'

Angela looked in horror at the huge lumps of meat. Without thinking she had bought dinner for Sean and his family. She felt dizzy and leaned against the wall.

'Are you all right?' Chrissie asked, frightened. 'Jimmy! Give Miss O'Hara a hand.'

She had steadied herself again.

'I'm very sorry. I've got a bit of summer 'flu, I think.' She paid for the meat, put it in her bicycle basket, and wheeled it home. She didn't dare to get on the bike for fear she might faint. Though in a way it wouldn't be a bad time, if she had to die, to die now. She sat at home glumly all day. Why had she not had the courage to tell people after her mother died? Why had she lied to them, and gone along with their messages of sympathy, their requests for prayers? She had never taken a penny of their money: she had said that it should all be sent to the missionary headquarters. But they wouldn't remember that.

She thought of the nice, honest people who always asked after him, the people she had fooled, rather than the awful people who would crow with horror. She didn't care all that much about the Sergeant McCormacks and the Mother Immaculatas. She thought about Dick Dillon, and her heart went down to her feet.

It was a beautiful day, the kind that they would sigh over, the trippers in for the day, the visitors down for the month, the shopkeepers who had been hoping for weather like this all year.

Shuya and Sean would sigh with pleasure too, and Denis and Laki would be as delighted with the long golden beach and the bright blue sea. She never remembered feeling so sad.

She had shown herself she was a person of no courage. She hadn't the courage to beg them not to come, nor the courage to go to the station and welcome them with open arms. What a useless, spineless friend and sister she had turned out to be.

They would have been here three hours at least now. They had taken the overnight boat from England, the morning train to the town, and since there was no one to meet them to take them to Castlebay, they would wait for the bus. They would have been in their caravan for an hour.

Had they taken the children for a swim? Had they gone to O'Brien's shop to buy provisions? Had Sean leaned eagerly across the counter and shaken Tom O'Brien's hand?

'Don't you remember me, Mr O'Brien? I'm Dinny O'Hara's son Sean. And this is my wife, and these are my children. Say hallo to Mr O'Brien, Denis . . .'

Were they on their way up the street now? Had they reached the corner? Were they turning down the golf-course road?

She had said she would be in her cottage. She wanted to run away.

She never remembered the clock ticking so loudly or her heart moving so oddly in her chest.

She sat and waited.

And waited.

By the time the children should be well in bed, there was a knock on the door. She steeled herself and went to it slowly. There was no sound of voices on the step. Perhaps they were upset that she hadn't come to meet them.

She opened the door.

It was Dick Dillon.

'Hallo,' she said faintly. She stood leaning against the door. She made no move to ask him in.

'I was wondering if I might come in at all? Or would that be out of the question? I do come to call here occasionally, you know.'

'Dick, I'm sorry. Come in.'

'I know you said you didn't want to come up this week, and that you'd explain it all later.'

'Well it didn't do much good my telling you that, did it?'

'I knew it was all right to come.'

'That was very arrogant of you.' Her voice was weary.

'No. It wasn't arrogant. I knew I could come. I knew they weren't here.'

'What?'

'I knew I wouldn't be blundering in on top of them. They're sitting down on the seat at the end of the town looking at the sea.'

He had discovered them by complete accident. He had seen them getting off the bus, he had looked because of the foreign woman, and the children being half foreign-looking.

'He didn't recognize me. I was in my drinking mode when he was here last. I'd only have been a blur to him or indeed he to me.'

'So how did you know?'

'The boy said when were they going to see Aunt Angela, and the woman said they were going to their caravan first, and Aunt Angela would be waiting up in her cottage for them later when they got settled in, today or tomorrow.'

'I'm sorry, Dick. I'm very, very sorry.' Angela wept. 'I'm such a coward, I'm so bloody weak, I couldn't tell you.' She put her head on his shoulder and sobbed like a child. His arms went around her, and he patted her comfortingly.

'It's going to be all right,' he said, as if to a very small, very upset toddler. 'Dick is here, he'll look after things.'

They sat in the sunset and watched the red ball disappear down behind a big navy line of horizon. Behind them, the music of the amusements and the cries of laughter, and around them the chitter-chatter of holidaymakers.

Denis and Laki were both fast asleep, exhausted. Already he had pointed out the Brothers' School where he had gone every day, he had shown them the big rock pools where he used to play, and he had taken them into the Echo Cave to shout their questions.

Sean had remembered O'Brien's shop. But it had been much smaller then; he didn't know the boy serving there – it must be one of the young sons. He saw Mrs O'Brien in the background; but he was shy suddenly. It wasn't the place to catch her eye and begin the great comeback. He had bought a colouring book and pencils in Miss O'Flaherty's shop, but she was busy serving someone else and he didn't know the young woman who served them.

On the street, a child of about eight looked at Laki with interest. 'What land do you come from?' she asked.

'I was born in Japan, I am half-Irish, half-Japanese,' Laki said proudly.

'I had a Japanese doll when I was young. It didn't look a bit like you,' the girl said curiously.

They had eaten their meal and made plans for the next day; there would be swimming and a picnic lunch on the beach. But first they would call on Aunt Angela. The children had thought this perfectly satisfactory.

'This is a good place to have as another home,' Laki said. Sean had been talking about Castlebay as their 'other home' for as long as the children could remember. But this time he said nothing.

'I'll show you the town,' he had suggested to Shuya. But when they came to the bottom of the street, he hung back; he didn't want to go to the dance, he was too old to take her to the amusements. A middle-aged couple on the bumpers? It would be idiotic. Then, in the hotel, sitting drinking, and seeing other groups: would he go up to them? If so, would he give his name? He remembered the Dillons vaguely, but he hadn't known any of them well.

He had hesitated as they approached Church Street. It was Shuya who pointed out the nice bench.

'That wasn't here, years ago,' Sean said. 'Probably afraid that people might sit here and cuddle or do something outrageous like that.'

She put her arm around him. She sensed his unease, the flatness about everything.

'It's changed a lot, of course. Everything,' he said.

'It must have. Was that big amusement centre always there?'

'Much smaller, much shabbier. And I don't think the dance hall was like that. Of course, in those days I wasn't likely to be going into it, so I hardly noticed it.'

'It's funny,' Shuya said. 'Most people, when they go back, find that things have grown smaller. Here you find they have all grown much bigger.'

'You wouldn't know the place in ways,' he said. 'It's very painted and bright and the shops have all got things hanging outside them, buckets, and water wings and sun-hats. There was none of that in my day.'

There was a silence.

'Would you like us to walk up to your home, to see it, even if you don't want to go in?'

She was trying hard. It worked.

'Yes, that would be an idea. I don't think we'll go up Church Street, we can go up the Cliff Road, it's longer but it's very nice.'

'Let's go by the Cliff Road,' said Shuya.

They walked on to the golf-course road. Late golfers were coming back from their drinks after the last hole.

It was a warm, balmy evening. They walked on till they

426

saw the house. The curtains were drawn and there was a light in the main room. Angela must be waiting there for them.

'Is it cheating to walk past it, and not go in?' he asked.

'Angela said come any time we were ready. I don't think you're ready now,' Shuya said gently.

'No. I'm not, somehow.'

'Well then, it's not cheating.'

He pointed out where his room had been, and which had been the window he used to climb out of if he wanted to race out and have an early-morning swim. They marvelled at the energy of a boy who could have raced down a half mile to the sea and a half mile back . . . he would run on the road, and there would be cows going for milking . . . he would be back in his room and studying again before anyone in the family got up.

He showed her the little geraniums that his mother had planted in the window boxes and said that it was wonderful they had survived so well. He pointed out the chimney where the birds had made a nest, and the porch where they had to scrape off the snow in winter in case it became too heavy and broke the glass.

Shuya whispered that now she had a very perfect picture of the way he used to live.

They walked together back down the road, arm in arm, to the caravan park; again by the quiet cliff road, not the bustling Church Street with all its lights and the fun of the season getting underway.

Dick Dillon came downstairs; he had been peeping through the dark bedroom window.

'They've gone,' he said.

They had heard whispering outside and he had crept upstairs to have a look. Angela had remained at her post. If they knocked she was to let them in and Dick was to leave the back way. He would not stay and greet them – otherwise they would get the impression that the whole of Castlebay would accept him as willingly. They had to make their decisions according to the facts, not just from meeting Dick.

'What do you think they were at?' she asked.

'We'll probably never know that,' he said.

'Would you stay the night, Dick?' she asked suddenly.

'What?'

'I don't mean in the bed with me, I'm not inflicting that on you. Just in the house.'

'I'd love to stay with you, and since you're on the subject, it would be no infliction at all if you weren't to bother to go to all the trouble of making up another bed.'

'Ah, it's no trouble, Dick,' she laughed.

'I was hoping maybe you might have no bedclothes aired.'

'They're aired, and it's the middle of summer. Will there be a hue and cry for you if you don't go back to the hotel?'

'Angela, my girl, they don't know whether I'm there or gone, whether I live or die in that place.'

'Stop playing on my sympathies, you'll have your own bed here, I'll go and make it for you now.'

'I'd be no trouble to you, that's a grand big bed you have up there. I was just looking at it and speculating.'

'Speculate away. Dick?'

'Yes.'

'Thank you *very* much.'

She thought they would go to late Mass, so she was surprised to see the four of them at First.

When she saw Sean and the two children go to the altar to receive Communion she closed her eyes. Castlebay would forgive a lot but it would never forgive that.

She left before the Last Gospel. She was buying her Sunday paper from Mickey Mack outside the gates when she heard a farmer say to his wife, 'Did you see the Chinese woman at Mass, and the two half-caste children, going to the rails and all?'

'Isn't China full of Catholics?' said Mickey Mack: he

wasn't an ignoramus just because he couldn't read the papers he sold.

She had plenty of soda bread, and cornflakes for the children. Dick had gone back to the hotel and he wouldn't come to the house until she sent for him. She could always phone from the golf club if there was an emergency.

She sat down to read the paper, calmer now. Nobody had recognized them.

They must have been having some kind of second thoughts if they had come to look last night but had not come in.

She waited for them with a dread that was much less sharp around the edges. And she didn't feel too bad about herself either. Last night Dick had assured her that she had behaved most honourably. She felt less of a coward today.

Today she could take them.

They arrived excitedly, chattering like starlings. There were hugs and a present for Aunt Angela and delight at the breakfast.

Shuya wandered round the room entranced by the books and objects. 'You never told me it was like this, Sean.'

'It wasn't, when I was here.' He seemed sad. Shuya was praising the one thing that didn't date from his time.

Casually, very casually, Angela asked him had he met any friends to introduce to Shuya.

'No.' He seemed troubled. 'Not yet.'

'Of course, a lot of Sean's friends would have been made through his mother, and through you, Angela. When he came home, she would gather people round and because of his status as priest, people would call.'

Shuya understood.

'I don't seem to know anyone from school.'

Angela clenched her fists. *Know anyone from school?* The man was mad! Thirty years ago, little fellows running in and out of the Brothers? Who in the name of God would he know?

'No, I suppose you've grown away, and they have,' she said cautiously.

'You know, it's very changed, Angela. Do you not find that?' he said.

This was it. If she moved carefully, this might be the lifeline that was being thrown. There would be no point in coming back to a *changed* Castlebay.

'Oh I do,' she sighed. 'I think what it used to be like in the old days, room to walk on the footpaths, only a few families on the beach . . . You knew everyone to say hallo to.'

Shuya was playing the game too. 'Sean told me last night that it has changed too much, become big and what was the word you used . . .?'

'A bit *brash*. Hasn't it? To be honest, Angela, it's getting a bit like those places in England, that used to be so nice, but very noisy and full of trippers.'

'What can you do?' Angela cried. 'I often think of leaving it myself, getting a better job in a bigger school. I don't know why I hang on, but like you, I suppose it's roots.'

Shuya said levelly, 'If *you* left, Angela, you could always come back. To see people. After all, you do have friends here. Sean doesn't have many.'

'I wouldn't say that . . .' He didn't want to appear friendless.

'No, you'd know a lot of people, of course, Sean. But Shuya's right. They're Mam's friends, not our own. Really, the best of ours went away. It's the same in a lot of small places.'

He repeated it. 'The best of ours went away. It's true for you, Angela. True.'

The children came in from the garden: it was scorching, could they go for a swim? Of course they could. Would Angela join them on the beach? No. If they didn't mind. But she'd be here tonight. She had bought a lot of meat, would they come and have a big supper?

'Which is a nice, quiet part of the beach . . . um . . . for the picnic?' Shuya called.

Angela told her the part where there was least chance of Sean O'Hara being unmasked.

'We were thinking, Angela, that it would be a pity not to see a bit of the rest of the countryside around here, now that we're this far.'

Her breathing was short – it was going to happen. 'I think that's a good idea. Take day trips, is it?'

'No. Go on and see a few other places, places they can remember, write about in their projects and scrapbooks.'

Shuya said, 'And I want to see Dublin. I was promised Dublin.'

'Well, of course, that would be nice. But the caravan?'

'There's people queuing up to get into caravans, they'll even let us have the balance back, which is very fair.'

'But you'll come back again? To Castlebay? Before you leave Ireland?'

'No. It wouldn't make sense. We'd be retracing our steps.'

'I see. Yes. You're right, of course.'

Shuya said, 'So we thought we might start out tomorrow. They can let the caravan from lunchtime.'

Angela said nothing. Her heart was too full.

Sean mistook the silence for disappointment. 'I don't want you to think we're running out on you. I'll never be able to thank you for the welcome. It's just . . . it's just . . .'

'I think I understand. Some things have changed a lot.'

'And some things haven't changed at all.'

'The bus leaves early. We must rise very early . . .' Shuya said.

'I have a friend – you won't remember him – Dick Dillon. He could give you a lift to the town, and you could start out from there . . .'

'Would he mind?'

'Not at all. I'll tell him tonight.'

431

'Angela . . . there's just one thing . . . about this Dillon man.'

'What's that?'

'You won't tell him who I am? You see I'd prefer in a way if people thought . . .'

'I won't tell him who you are – didn't I say I'd leave it to you to tell who you want.'

She came down the Cliff Road with them all and kissed them goodbye at the corner by the seat that looked out to sea. They walked on up to the caravan park. She told them Dick Dillon would pick them up at the caravan site at a nice civilized time, like ten o'clock.

When she went home she prayed on her knees, long sobbing prayers of thanks to a Lord that she had thought recently had been hard-hearted.

The days fell into a hypnotic routine. They got up early. There was no one on their part of the beach so they went down the steps beside the Lodge to the beach for an early swim. Bones knew about this, and even though he was so old he had to be helped back up the steps again, he always came with them. There was no one to see the swelling of Clare's stomach except David, who patted it lovingly as they went out into the early-morning waves.

Then they ate bacon and tomato, which they loved. David joined his father, and Clare walked down the Cliff Road to her old home. She had a cup of tea in the kitchen, did any shopping that was needed. Then, while it was still early, she would walk back the Cliff Road watching the families getting ready for the day on the beach, and she would let herself into the Lodge. The day would pass in studying. David usually found time to come in at least twice before he was home for the evening. They rarely went out to the hotel, and apart from the Committee dance they had no social outing. It was peaceful in the evenings, the sunset looking like an exaggerated picture from their own window. And sometimes they did a little desultory painting of the upstairs rooms. Bumper Byrne's contract had only gone so far as to get the place habitable and have the downstairs part decorated. 'After all, who'll be looking at the upstairs except the pair of you?' he had said cheerfully. David and Clare were so happy to be into the place they didn't argue.

There were three rooms upstairs: their bedroom, the room they would make into a nursery and the storeroom. Clare had thought of having that made into a study. Wouldn't it be great to have a place you could spread your books and papers and never have to take them up when a meal was needed or when you had to tidy the place up? But, David had said, what was the point of having a study upstairs? Wouldn't it be a bit antisocial, locking herself away there, and when the baby arrived . . .

Clare agreed. She would leave it till later.

They painted the nursery a sunny yellow colour, and as soon as they started murmuring quietly about hoping to start a family around Christmas, Nellie became very excited and made curtains for them with all kinds of nursery-rhyme figures on the fabric.

David took his toys from the window seat of his old bedroom, slowly bit by bit, and always when his mother was out. He wasn't stealing them, he just did not want to have to mention the child. Her face froze over in a mask when the subject was hinted at. David dreaded thinking about how she would react when the baby was born.

'I think she'll come round. Not to me, but to the baby.'

'We should make sure she has some time with him herself. Or her, of course.'

They were convinced that it would be a boy. He was to be christened Patrick Thomas.

As the days went on it seemed impossible they had lived any other kind of life. The hectic, rushed meetings in Dublin, the dirty flat with the smelly hall and the unpainted, uncarpeted stairway in Rathmines seemed from a different life lived by different people. David said he could hardly remember the name of the registrar with the carroty head who was always fighting with everyone in the Res. Clare said that if she were on a torture rack she wouldn't be able to remember anything at all that she and

Mary Catherine and Valerie talked about for two and a half years.

Now they talked about David's patients. He delivered three babies that summer. But, actually, Mrs Brennan had done most of the work, she was a marvellous midwife he said, reassuring and practical. The women loved her. That interested Clare, she had always thought Mrs Brennan was an almighty bossy boots but this cast a new light on her. David told Clare the secrets of the town, knowing that she wasn't going to speak of them to anyone. Josie Dillon's grandmother had senile dementia and was in the county home; very quietly, the whole thing was done, but that was where she was. Mrs Conway was going to the town shortly to have a hysterectomy. Father O'Dwyer had such a bad chest David's father had told him that it was an act of suicide to continue smoking and the Lord would look on it very poorly indeed. Father O'Dwyer had told Dr Power to keep his religious pronouncements to himself and concentrate on medicine. 'I am concentrating on medicine, you stupid man,' Dr Power had roared at him, and there had been a slow process of reconciliation in which David had to be the middle man.

She learned that her own brother, Jim, was very hard of hearing – not just slow, and stupid, as they had all thought. He was going to have a hearing aid, and David said that there could well be total hearing loss.

'Maybe you could teach him lip-reading, after finals.'

'Teach him what?' Clare laughed. 'I don't know how to lip-read.'

'But you could learn, couldn't you? It could make all the difference. Otherwise he'll just end up like Mickey Mack or someone.'

Clare was shocked. Yes, of course she could learn. There must be books on the subject, and diagrams. Yes, of course, she would.

David was becoming like his father already, concerned and involved in everything that happened. In a few weeks people had stopped thinking of him as a boy helping his father and holding the fort until the real doctor arrived.

434

The day came when a woman said to David's father that she had begun with young Dr Power and she thought she would continue with him if that was all right, he had been so helpful.

David's father took out a bottle of sherry at lunch that day, and Molly had laughed with pride and told Nellie about it as the meal was being put on the table. And as they smiled about how well David was settling into the practice, no mention was made of his wife sitting fifty yards away, bent over her studies with a cup of soup.

There was no phone in the Lodge yet but there was a buzzer from the house, so that David could be woken for night calls. It was awkward, because it meant he had to go up to his parents' to hear the details before setting out. Still, they had been promised a phone soon, and were at the top of the priority list.

Clare heard the buzzer with surprise one morning; David had long gone on house calls, they must have known she was on her own. Resignedly she walked to the house. Molly was in the hall.

'There's a call from Dublin for you,' she said and held the receiver out as if it might contaminate her.

'I'm sorry for disturbing you,' Clare said.

It was Mary Catherine. She and Val had the most marvellous flat, they were installed now and they would keep it for a year. Val was going to do a Higher Diploma in education and Mary Catherine was going to do a Diploma to be a librarian. Any time Clare wanted to come and stay, there was plenty of room.

A longing so great came over Clare, it almost made her faint.

Miles and miles away from Dracula, who was sighing as if the phone were needed urgently. Molly was just in earshot, fiddling with some flowers that didn't need adjustment.

Clare sighed too.

'Well? Can you come up? Will you?'

'I'll write to you about it.'

'Can't you talk?'

'That's right.'

'Do your best. We'd love you to come. David, too, of course, if he can get away. We've got a big double bed in the spare room.'

'Sounds great.'

'So you'll try?'

'As I said, I'll write.'

She told Mrs Power pleasantly that her friends were inviting David and herself to visit.

Mrs Power gave a tinkling laugh. 'That's *very* nice of them, Clare dear. But David's never been short of a place to stay in Dublin. Heavens *no*. We've *lots* of friends there, and the Nolans' house has always been a second home to him.'

Clare smiled. And before her face cracked with the effort, she returned to the Lodge and started to bang things, hard, with a ruler. She was so angry she was shaking. She tried to concentrate on her work but *that woman*'s superior voice rang in her ears. She was going out.

She left a note on the table in case David called in, and marched out nearly taking the door from its hinges. She walked first to Bumper Byrne's lean-to shed that he called his office, and spoke to him sharply about their gate. It was meant to be a proper entrance, with a gate, and tarmacadamed path. What was it but a hole in the hedge? No. It was *not* perfectly adequate for the moment. She would like it done. This week. Could he tell her which day? No? Well then, she'd wait here till he *could* tell her which day. No. She didn't mind waiting at all. In desperation Bumper said he'd have someone up there on Thursday, and she thanked him warmly.

Then she went to Peter O'Connor who had a saw and used to cut down trees. He'd be about the only person in Castlebay who could advise her on how to build a hedge.

'I want to plant a hedge that looks small and harmless now but will grow up like a flash and make a big forest,' she said to him.

He knew why she wanted the hedge.

'I'm not great on the pronunciation but I think it's called Cupressors that you want.'

'That's the Latin for a cypress tree, is that what you mean?'

'The very thing. I could get you a set of nice young plants . . .'

'Not *too* young, Mr O'Connor.'

'When do you want them in?'

'This afternoon. And I'd like them to grow twenty feet tall by next week.'

'Come on, now. She's not as bad as all that?'

Clare laughed. 'Of course not. Just as long as it's grown fairly soon.'

She called to see her mother. The shop was full.

'Do you want me to get behind the counter and give you a hand?'

'Are you out of your mind? The doctor's wife? Serving? Have some sense.'

She went into the hotel.

'Will you have lunch with me Josie? A real lunch in the dining room? I'll pay . . .'

'I can't, Clare, not in the middle of the season. Mummy'd go mad and Rose would make another scene. We're meant to leave those tables for the paying customers.'

'I would be a paying customer,' Clare said crossly.

'No, real people. Not us. It's ages since I've seen you. How are you, anyway?'

'Like a weasel,' said Clare and left with a wave.

She thought she would go up to Angela's cottage. She bought a bottle of sherry in Costello's, and snapped the head off Teddy Costello who called her Mrs Power.

'God Almighty, Teddy, we were in mixed infants together – you called me Clare until a few months ago. Am I to start calling you Mr Costello?'

He stammered, he thought it was what she'd like, what Mrs Power senior would like. He was sorry.

'You know what they say in the films: "You're beautiful when you're angry, Miss Jones."' It was Gerry. He had been behind her, and she hadn't noticed.

She laughed, in spite of herself. 'No, *really*, Gerry, this Mrs bit is the last straw.'

'Fiona likes it. She says it makes her feel grown-up.'

'It doesn't do that for me. It makes me feel we're all in some school play or other.'

'You see, I told you,' he sighed. 'You should never have married him. Go off and abuse the rest of the town. You've demolished Teddy fairly successfully,' he added good-naturedly, and disappeared.

Just as she was leaving the shop she saw Angela carrying fruit and a big bottle of orange over to the back of Dick Dillon's car.

'Are you going on a picnic?' she asked enviously.

'Just a few miles down the coast. Dick has a day off, we thought we'd explore a bit.'

'Great.'

'Why aren't *you* at your work by the way?'

'I came out for a bit of air.'

'And a something to keep you going?' Angela eyed the bottle-shaped parcel.

'Yes. Well.'

'I hope it helps the studying,' Angela said cheerfully and waved goodbye.

Disconsolately Clare walked back to the Lodge. Her anger with her mother-in-law was gone. But so was a lot of her good spirits. She hoped that David had been in and out while she was on her travels. She didn't feel like talking to him now, she wouldn't be able to get the despondent note out of her voice. There was a note on the table beside her books.

Glad you went out, it's the best day of summer. Why don't we take a day off together and go down the coast a bit? I was in seeing Peter O'Connor's child who got burned and he told me you'd ordered little saplings for the garden. That's a great idea, he's going to look them

438

out for us and bring them tomorrow which is very speedy for Castlebay!

I love you my darling, and I'll see you this evening.

He wrote his name with a heart round it.

She sat down at her table and cried till the tears showered down on her big handwriting in all the files of notes.

He was the most generous and loving man in the whole world and here she was marching around the town trying to build a drawbridge and moat between him and his family. She felt wretched and shabby: maybe some of the things that Dracula believed about her were right? She just wasn't good enough for David.

They had their picnic down the coast. There were gulls and two small seals, and a school of porpoises too. They lay in the sun, happy and rested; they ran in and out of the sea; they drank their bottle of wine and their flask of coffee and ate their hard-boiled eggs and brown bread and butter. And the ice cream, which hadn't melted, wrapped up in six newspapers.

They kissed and laughed, and David accused her of having given Peter O'Connor unmentionable favours in order to make him do the hedge so quickly, and even more favours to Bumper Byrne and his gang, who had suddenly produced a very presentable entrance, having promised it since last April.

Clare said all his female patients were in love with him and that Rose Dillon at the hotel was definitely out to get him, married man or not. They wished they had taken old Bones with them; he would have loved this beach but he was getting a bit creaky now and he might have found the walk down and back too much for him.

They were as happy as they ever had been.

On September first she went to Dublin on the train. She had fourteen days before her exams began. David was going to come up for two weekends, and then to collect her and take her home when the exams were finished.

439

She said it would be a waste for him to come with her now.

'I wish you all the luck in the world, my girl,' Dr Power had said, 'but you've never done anything except come in the top league in every examination you ever did. Do you remember my driving you into the town all those years ago, to do your scholarship? I remember it as if it were yesterday . . .' Dr Power beamed at her, and sighed at the way the years had flashed by.

Molly had decided to be charming. 'I hope you get all the questions you're looking for,' she said. 'Maybe that's not a very intellectual way of putting it but you know what I mean . . .'

They drove round by O'Brien's and she went in to kiss her mother goodbye.

'Lord, child, it's not the ends of the earth you're going to,' Agnes said.

'I know, Mam, but this is *it*, this is the B.A., the degree.'

'Well I know, Clare, and we all hope you'll do very well, but that's all behind you now, isn't it?'

Her mother came to the door and waved, puzzled at the exasperation that had come into Clare's face. After all, she had only said what was true. A lot of people didn't think that Clare should have bothered to go back to college to do that exam after getting married.

It was somehow like showing off.

'Will we have to learn first aid?' Val asked fearfully as Clare took off her shoes and eased her back with a cushion.

'What do you mean?'

'In case your man gets born here, what do we do? I know you need a watch to time things.'

'Not a chance. Week beginning October fifteenth. David's father hopes it's going to be the eighteenth, that's the feast of St Luke apparently, and Luke was a doctor in his time. What is it?' she asked suddenly as she saw Mary Catherine looking at a diary.

'Oh dear. You'll miss Conferring,' she said.

'I will *not* miss Conferring. I will bloody not. If Patrick Thomas is three days old, I'd be well enough to travel, wouldn't I? I *can't* miss Conferring. Maybe he'll come early . . .' Clare addressed her stomach. 'Be a good boy now and please your Mammy . . . arrive around the end of September, maybe the twenty-ninth, so that Mammy will be ready to come back up to Dublin and get Conferred.'

Mary Catherine was still looking at her diary. 'That would be quite a good day, actually. Feast of St Michael and all the angels.'

Clare clapped her hands. 'Right! Did you hear that? Be here on September twenty-ninth and we'll add Michael to your names.'

'I thought this yucky mumsy stuff only started *after* they were born,' said Valerie.

It was just as she had dreamed it would be. Plenty of room, books all around the place, cups of coffee being made all day and all night, friends dropping in. Down to the National Library where people noticed her condition and smiled congratulations. In to UCD where people noticed her condition and were surprised. She had been a quiet student, and only the people in her own group knew her well.

She paid her examination fee, and got her number. It made it seem very close when she had the card with her own number.

She went to see Emer and Kevin and she noticed from their faces they were surprised to see how pregnant she now looked. Perhaps she had been holding herself in at home: everyone here seemed more aware of it.

Clare discussed the work she had done with her tutor.

'I didn't think we'd ever hear from you again,' he said.

'Why on *earth* did you think that?' Clare asked furiously.

'Well, married bliss, and a summer in Castlebay, a *summer* there, mind, not a week. I thought you wouldn't open a book again.'

'*My* only worry is the B.A.' Clare smiled at him. 'I suppose I sound a bit intense, and off my rocker to a lot of people. But when it's so hard, you get a kind of Holy Grail thing about it.'

'I know, I wish they all found it as important as you do.'

'Wish me luck then.'

'You don't need luck, Clare O'Brien . . . or whatever your name is now. You're the grade, everyone in the department knows it.'

They knew. Now all she had to do was prove it to them. She smiled as she went to sleep that night.

She had phoned David. He had just returned home after his second visit to Dublin. The Lodge was lonely without her, but in under ten days she would be back and they would wait. Together.

He wished her courage and energy and confidence. He couldn't say he loved her because he was standing in the hall, but he did say, 'And everything,' which was their code word.

She turned over and went to sleep happily.

Mary Catherine woke up in alarm.

'Come quickly! She's groaning, and shouting!'

'What? Who?'

'Clare. She's doubled over. Jesus, Mary and Joseph, I think she's having the baby. After all our joking about it.'

'Don't be ridiculous. It couldn't be. It's not for weeks yet.'

'Shut up. It could be a miscarriage. No, it couldn't, it's much too late . . . I don't know. Get an ambulance.'

'She keeps saying no.'

Clare was white-faced, with sweat coming down her forehead. 'It's all right,' she gasped. 'I couldn't be having it. I couldn't. These aren't those pains you have. No downward pull or whatever they said.'

'We don't know any doctors here, we're not on anyone's list, we're calling an ambulance, Valerie's phoning it this minute.' Mary Catherine was trying to be calm.

'Please don't. I can't go to hospital. The exam . . . There's nothing wrong.'

'Please, Clare. Just go in and be a false alarm, will you? Just for us? Please. Then you can come out twenty minutes later, and we'll all laugh at it. Please.'

She kicked the door closed with her foot so that Clare couldn't hear Valerie explaining down the phone how bad the patient was. 'Then we'll all go in and do the exams calmly.'

'I don't want you to be up half the night,' Clare cried.

Valerie came in, looking pale. 'We'll get dressed. We'll go with her.'

'*No!*' screamed Clare.

The ambulance was there in ten minutes. The girls had packed Clare's things quietly, and out of her line of vision.

The ambulance men were reassurance itself.

'It's all a false alarm,' Clare said with a tear-stained face. 'I'm so sorry and you see we're all starting our exams tomorrow. Our finals.'

She bent over with pain.

The ambulance men exchanged glances, and the driver leaped smartly into the driving seat and switched on the siren.

The pain was beyond anything she could possibly have imagined; nothing helped; not panting like a dog as they had taught her, nor reciting poetry very fast in an undertone, nor writhing and wriggling into different positions. A lugubrious student midwife kept telling her to relax. Clare wanted to kill her.

She was in labour for two hours before they told her that something was wrong. The midwife, listening for the third time to the foetal heartbeat, straightened up with more than usual gloom.

'The baby's in some distress.'

'Oh my God,' cried Clare wildly. 'What's wrong? Can you tell what's wrong?'

'The heart's not standing up to the contractions.'

'But will it be all right? The baby, I mean?'

'I can't say,' said the midwife, 'I shall have to report it.'

It seemed like hours. Clare felt pure terror; and the most intense longing for David. It had never occurred to her that the birth would be anything but straightforward; now it appeared that the baby was being killed by something uncontrollable inside her own body. Before she had held it, kissed it or even looked upon its face, her baby would die; and there was nothing she could do about it.

She was holding her breath as though that might ease the baby's distress when the door swung open to admit Bar, the red-headed doctor whom David disliked so much. The examination took seconds.

'Cord's dropped,' he said. 'I'm very sorry. I know how disappointed you will be. We shall have to do a Caesarean. We'll also have to ask you to sign a piece of paper giving your consent.'

'A Caesarean,' said Clare, high-voiced with joy. 'Oh thank God. Thank God. I'd forgotten all about Caesareans.'

Later she knew that a dropped cord was the worst emergency after a haemorrhage. Then she was only aware of Bar, now in a white mask and a green overall, giving clipped instructions. His face, which before had seemed rather heartless, now looked blessedly confident and know-it-all. Sister McClusky, summoned because she was an 'expert at cords', was an enormous, jovial woman who stuck her hand inside and gave Clare a running commentary on how well the baby was coping, all the way to the operating theatre.

'I love you,' she said, then they put her under. She felt the first violent pain of the knife, heard someone say it was a beautiful baby girl, before the anaesthetic took effect and she knew no more.

She woke up in the recovery room where the first person she saw was David holding their baby in his arms.

'She grinned,' he said. 'I've been holding her for an

hour, waiting for you to come round, and she gave me the biggest grin you've ever seen.'

'She's not normal, is she?' said Clare.

'Darling, she's *perfect*.'

'You're lying to me, she's a mongol.'

'Here, see for yourself, she's beautiful.'

'Babies don't grin until they're six weeks old.'

At this point the baby began to cry, steadily angrily; and Clare, taking her in her arms for the first time, made two extraordinary discoveries. The first was that on contact with her mother the baby instantly stopped crying; and the second was that she was indeed utterly, perfectly, beautiful. True, the nose was a bit squashed, but her eyes were big and clear, and she had masses of hair. Her fingers looked as if they'd been soaked too long in washing-up liquid, but they were slender and graceful with long, pointed nails – almost as if they'd been specially manicured for her debut. Round one minute wrist and one ankle were plastic bands stating that she was Girl Power, and the date and time of birth.

With a flash of insight, Clare suddenly wished that they could all stay here forever, the baby safely cradled in her arms, protected by the hospital staff. For with this new love came also a new and terrible vulnerability, from which there would never be an escape. How shall I endure chicken pox, and tree climbing, and reading about children dying in fires? she thought. Life stretched away in an infinity of dangers and she felt afraid.

PART FOUR

1960–1962

There were all the explanations: nobody got their arithmetic wrong, but it was the strain and the stress of the exam that brought the baby on; or she was genuinely a baby that was kicking and screaming to be born and would not wait the time; or Clare had been eating all the wrong food and not taking enough rest.

She had a very small face, but it wasn't nearly as red as the faces of other babies in the hospital; and her eyelashes were longer than any they had ever seen. She was so delicate and fine, that suddenly John Fitzgerald Byrne became a huge, hulking monster in comparison, and any other baby was crabbed and ugly.

Clare and David looked at each other and back at this magnificent person they had created. They kept saying over and over that they couldn't believe it. They said it so often in front of Father Flynn that he said he thought that's what they wanted her christened.

They decided they would give her a name that nobody else had, nobody else they knew. She wouldn't be Molly or Agnes; nor would she be Chrissie or Caroline or Angela or Emer or Valerie or Mary Catherine. She would not be a Fiona or a Josie or a Bernie. She would be a name that nobody had used before and put a shape into like wearing a jumper.

They didn't know any Victorias, and neither of them knew anyone called Martha; so those two were considered. Then David thought of Olivia, and the more he said it the more the tiny baby seemed to suit it; and the more they liked it. Olivia Power. It was a name that sounded made for her.

'You'll have to have a saint's name as well,' said the nurse who knew everything.

'I don't mind, any saint,' Clare said cheerfully.

'Mary's always nice,' said the nurse.

'What's your mother's name?' Clare asked David suddenly.

'It's Molly, you know that.'

'Yes, but what's it short for?'

'Margaret.'

'Right. We'll call her Olivia Mary. I just didn't want to let poor Saint Agnes feel left out. Da was put out enough about John Fitzgerald Byrne, I'll tell you that . . .'

Olivia Mary Power was ten days old when she left the hospital. Her mother was still pale, and rather shaken-looking. Olivia would need more bottles than a baby which had gone the full nine months, but she was perfectly well and healthy. She had a small christening, with champagne, in the private room which had been found for Clare when they realized she was a doctor's wife and not the hysterical student they had taken her for when she was admitted. There were flowers and cards, and a great deal of admiration.

At no time did anyone say that it was a pity that this of all babies had to be premature since they were going to pretend in Castlebay anyway that it was a premature birth even if it were six weeks late.

And at no time did anyone mention to anyone in the room that it was a pity that Olivia Mary Power could not have delayed her arrival for ten days so that her mother could have sat the examination for the degree she had so much wanted.

There was so much delight about the new baby, it would sound unwelcoming to say anything about bad timing.

'Do you think she minds desperately and isn't saying?' Valerie asked Mary Catherine.

'I have no idea. I know I was about to show her the examination papers and something stopped me. And I never mentioned them again.'

'It's funny, I've never been afraid to ask her anything,

450

and even when I was on my own with her and the baby the other day, I couldn't ask.'

'Neither could I. That plausible attorney called me to ask me out, and in the midst of my saying no, he suddenly cut in and asked was she going funny in the head about the exams. He said that since he met her as a kid she's been talking about getting a degree, and now she doesn't mention it.'

'I don't *think* she minds. I think she's so goddamned pleased about the baby.'

'There's a bit in the New Testament about a woman getting all pleased about a man being born into the world.'

'Spare me your interpretations of the Bible, Val. Nobody in Ireland has ever read the book as far as I can see.'

'Wasn't that the worst luck ever? Poor Clare.'

Dick and Angela were learning to cook from a book, and each week they made something new in Angela's kitchen.

Angela agreed. 'I thought it would be the end of the world, and that we'd hear the tears of her the whole way from Dublin. But it seems she's not taking it badly at all.'

'I suppose, now she has the baby . . .' Dick broke off and frowned into the bowl. 'Is this the pale and light in texture that I should beat it until?'

'The people who write these books should be hanged. It looks pale and light in texture to me, but how would you know? This one says cook till ready. If we knew when "ready" was, we wouldn't need their stupid books.' She banged round the kitchen a bit.

'I suppose she could always sit it again next year.'

'She could. But people don't. It's like that. And with a small child she won't keep up her studies. How could she?'

'You're worried about her.'

'I am, but don't mind me. I worry about everything.'

Agnes read the letter out to Tom: the way the child's hair came forward and sideways from the crown like a little star. How the tiny toes each had a perfect little pink nail on them. How David had to bring all the things for the baby when he came up in such a rush, and he couldn't find half of them so he had packed table cloths and sheets and teatowels instead of the little matinee coats and vests.

'She seems to be delighted with the child,' Agnes said, pleased.

'Didn't it arrive a bit early? Isn't that what people will think?' Tom O'Brien looked at her over his glasses, waiting to see what reaction he would get.

'Wasn't it *miles* too early? Isn't that why she missed her exam?' Agnes said.

'But even if . . .'

'Tom, will you stop that, doesn't everyone know that the child wasn't expected for an age. Clare thought she was going to be doing her B.A., and everything.'

'Yes. Yes.' He saw there was going to be no scolding and complaining on the home side, which was a great blessing. 'Queer sort of name they gave it,' he grumbled.

'Oh you can be sure that's the Powers' doing. Some fancy choice of Molly's. That's what it will turn out to be. But saying nothing, that's always the best.'

Nellie wanted to know when they'd be home. She had been down to the Lodge on her day off in order to have it right for them. She hadn't liked Clare coming in there at first, she was sure there would be airs and graces. But as the months went on Nellie had felt sorry for the girl, stuck in there at her books all day. If ever you passed the window she wouldn't even look up, reading and studying and learning.

Nellie had known from the word go that there was a child on the way, and she knew better than anyone how enraged it had made the Mistress. The trouble was that the Mistress had no real friends she could talk to, and was sore to the bottom of her heart about it. She woke bad-tempered and she went to bed bad-tempered.

Nellie pitied her. She wasn't a bad woman – full of nonsense, of course, but everyone had something a bit wrong with them. Of course she'd have liked David to have got a finer girl than one of the O'Briens from the shop. David Power was the equal of anyone, but if he *had* got the little O'Brien girl into trouble and if he *did* seem happy to marry her, then Nellie thought that the best should be made of it all. There was no point in conducting a war across fifty yards of garden. Maybe it would be better when the baby came back, but you didn't need to be a genius to see that the Mistress was even more livid that the child had arrived so early. Now there was *no* way of covering up.

Molly said that they'd be arriving on Saturday.

'Will I set the tea for all of you in the dining room?' she asked.

Molly was about to say no, then she thought again. 'Yes, that's right, set it for all of us.'

Nellie smiled to herself, at least she had done that much for the young couple, they wouldn't have to be banished to their own little place and wait till the Mistress buzzed for them.

Dr Power was waiting on the platform, eager as a child.

They were in the front of the train, so they passed him, blinking happily into the carriages. Clare felt the tears come to her eyes, and David leaped up to wave out the window. 'Father, father.'

They didn't like Dr Power to drive on his own now, so he had brought Mrs Brennan with him. She had wanted to do a few things in town. She was waiting now in the car. Molly had said she'd prefer to meet them at home and because she had arranged a welcome-home supper, Paddy hadn't argued with her.

He hurried until his steps were a run down the platform and he peered into the white bundle. He took off his glasses and wiped them and put them on again.

'Isn't she perfect, God bless her, perfect little girl,' he said.

Clare was very nervous of anyone else touching the baby; but there she was thrusting it into her father-in-law's arms. He joggled her around expertly. He was so sweet that other people started to look at them.

'We're making a circus of ourselves,' he said. 'Come on, Clare, girl, let's go home.'

They walked to the ticket gate and Dr Power showed off his grandchild. Mrs Brennan in the car admired the baby with all the right words.

'Am I holding her right, do you think, Mrs Brennan?' Clare asked.

It was very much the thing to have asked. Mrs Brennan's face softened to the girl she had thought of as a bit of a madam up to now. All the way back to Castlebay they had lessons on supporting the head, and keeping the spine firm and the way to tilt the bottle. Dr Power hid his smile of pleasure when he saw how genuinely interested Clare and David were in what the woman was saying.

Six months ago they would both have crossed the road to avoid talking to Mrs Brennan. Now they hung on her every word.

Dr Power drove to the door of the big house.

'Molly has supper for you all here. Will we go straight in and show her the baby or would you like to go to your own house first?'

There was no doubting which he wanted.

David looked at Clare quickly.

'We'd love to come in and show off the baby,' she said.

Molly had been to the hairdresser, and she was wearing her best knitted two-piece. She was standing in the sitting room as if the gentry were coming.

David ran in and kissed her, and then stood back.

Clare put the baby straight into Molly's arms, which startled her. She had expected to bend over Clare and admire the child that way. Now she was holding her grandchild all on her own.

They couldn't stop admiring the baby. Clare looked at Molly occasionally, when she wasn't looking; Dracula was absorbed in the baby.

Nobody was going to be forgiven for anything, like

blighting David's young life, forcing him to marry a girl from the lower classes, a shotgun wedding and an early baby. But given all that, at least Molly liked her granddaughter. At least she wasn't going to reject the child. Things were looking up.

At Mass next morning they met Gerry. He was full of congratulations.

'Olivia, that's a fine posh name for Castlebay,' he said approvingly.

'Ah, they're sick of these Davids and Clares and Gerrys, the dull old names,' Clare laughed.

'I hope they won't call her Olly,' David said.

'Make your own nickname then,' Gerry said.

'Livy?' Clare suggested.

'Liffey even?' Gerry said. David was buying the papers from Mickey Mack.

'I'm sorry about the exam,' Gerry said in a low voice.

'It doesn't matter,' she said brightly.

'Of course it does.'

'No, really. It sort of faded away. I didn't think it would.'

'You can't fool me. I know that's what you wanted so much, so don't throw my sympathy back at me as if it was worth nothing.' He stamped off.

They insisted that Angela come back to the Lodge where Nellie was minding Olivia.

They had coffee and toast, and Angela said she was going to give the baby a book, not a matinee coat, because she couldn't knit for one thing and everyone else gave matinee coats.

'You gave me my first book, remember,' Clare said. 'To console me for not getting the Prize.'

'*A Golden Treasury*. And it turned out better in the end.'

Clare cradled the new infant to her, and her thin white face looked misty remembering all that struggle ten years ago.

Angela wondered, as she saw Clare plant a kiss on the baby's forehead, did she regard this child as a consolation prize for not having got a history degree? And did she think it had all turned out better in the end?

Chrissie was the only one who mentioned that they had only been married five months when the baby was born. 'I'm disgraced in front of the Byrne family,' she said.

Clare sighed. 'Weren't you able to tell them the baby came early?' she asked.

'No baby comes *that* early.'

'Is there a chance that you'd like to look at her at all? I brought her to see her cousin. John Fitzgerald seems in great form.' Clare struggled as she felt she had been struggling for years just to get some kind of normal reaction from her sister.

'Oh I have nothing against the child, poor creature, it's none of her doing.'

'Good, then here she is to have a look at.' Clare handed her over. She had found that this was a sure-fire way of making people enthusiastic about the baby, once it was in their arms they felt different.

'She's grand, isn't she?' Chrissie said. 'A bit small of course.'

'That's to do with being born prematurely, I told you,' Clare said.

Chrissie had to laugh then.

'Come here to your Auntie Clare.' Clare picked up John Fitzgerald and gave him a cuddle.

'Well now, you're a big fellow. Six months old. You're a fine big fellow.'

'If you knew all the trouble I had with him being born,' Chrissie said.

'Well I do a bit. It's not a bundle of laughs, is it?'

'What are you talking about? You didn't have to give birth to this little thing at all! Wasn't she lifted out of you?'

'It's a way of describing it, I suppose.' Clare gritted her teeth.

'Sure there'd be no problem, we'd all have a half dozen if that's all there was to it. You wait, Clare, you wait for the next one, and see what it's like. I was in labour

456

for fourteen hours. *Fourteen hours!* But of course that wouldn't be right for the wife of a doctor. They wouldn't leave her pushing and shoving for a whole day and into the night.'

'It must have been desperate all right.' She would have been happy to push Olivia into the world too. But useless to say that to Chrissie.

'Well it was, it wasn't something you forget in a hurry. Still it's more natural, in a way more normal. Imagine, you're only the same as me now, after all the grand plans, all the studying.'

'I know, isn't it strange?' Clare said without rancour.

Chrissie felt guilty. 'Well, you'd done enough anyway, hadn't you?'

'Oh definitely.'

All the patients seemed pleased that David was a father. It was nice to have a family man, they said. They sent soft toys for the new baby, they embroidered little dresses. Often the people who had little or no money to pay a doctor were able to give gifts, and they loved an excuse.

A man gave him a pair of hares that had been shot that day. 'Tell your wife to make a nice jugged hare, very good for a baby that is.' Another gave him potin to wet the baby's head and a woman whose house was always thought to be of the illest fame sent a miraculous medal to the little girl and said that this medal would protect her all her life.

Clare became more deft at giving the bottle but it still took a long time. In fact everything about Olivia took a long time. Clare looked with awe at the women trailing six or seven youngsters around with them. How had they managed? Maybe it was only the first that was such a problem, after that you had a team to help you. Now that she came to think of it she remembered giving a bottle to Jim and to Ben, while Mam was in the shop.

Olivia was so sweet you could play with her for hours. Just poking her gently in the tummy made her wave her arms and legs a bit. And she smiled, long before babies smile Olivia was smiling.

'I'm sure everyone must feel a bit like that, but they don't have the time to say it and think about it,' Clare said, looking at the small white bundle in the cradle.

'I don't have all that much more time to say it and think about it, I'm off again.' David finished his cup of tea as he pulled on his coat. 'I don't know how Dad looked after a quarter of this, I really don't, and yet he must have, you don't hear any complaints about him.'

He kissed his wife and daughter and ran through the rain to the car. He was becoming more and more involved in the work and all the patients; he said you'd learn as much in a month in Castlebay as in a year up in the hospital.

In the first few weeks there was no question of doing any studying, and Clare had no intention of beginning it until after Christmas. Everyone said a baby needed your full attention for the first three months. What nobody had said was that a baby took every ounce of your energy for the first three months too. But maybe you were meant to know that.

Olivia was a good baby they said, people who knew, people who had had babies like Mam, and Molly Power and Chrissie and Young Mrs Dillon and Anna Murphy and a dozen more. And the amount she slept was good. But sometimes she cried for long long times. Clare was despairing one morning and just before she took her child up to its grandfather in the surgery she discovered that a nappy pin was open and sticking into the tiny leg.

'How could I have done that to you? How?' Clare wept and held the small baby so close that the howls started again as the child began to feel suffocated.

The bath took a long time. You had to be very careful to hold her properly, she was so slippy, and you had to keep the soap from her eyes and yet make sure she didn't get cold.

And then the bottle. This was a slow day, she kept pushing it away. Finally it was almost finished and she was laid down. But she wouldn't settle. Over and over Clare took her up. It seemed an age before she agreed to sleep, even though her eyes were fighting to stay open.

Then there was the washing. Nellie had offered to help, but unfortunately she had offered when Molly Power was there, raising her eyebrows. So Clare thanked Nellie profusely, and said not at all. It was quite impossible to imagine that a tiny baby like that could provide such a mound of washing. Not to mention David's shirts. At home nobody changed their shirt every day. Dad would wear his shirt for four days maybe. And the boys . . . Lord knew when they changed theirs. But David had a fresh shirt every single day. It took seventeen minutes to iron each bloody shirt in the beginning. Now it took eleven. It was still far too long. Eleven minutes. That was a whole hour on five shirts one morning, and it was easier to do five at a time because otherwise he used to seem disappointed that he hadn't a choice.

'If you hate it so much I'll do it, it might be quite restful,' he had said once when she protested.

'No you damn well won't, the very first day you do one your mother will call and see you, and I might as well throw my hat at it after that.'

Today she had decided to iron three. But in the middle of the first one Olivia woke up again, and since it was nearly time for her bottle that was the end of the shirts. Then David was home for lunch. Then she had to tidy herself up. This was the day she had been invited for a cup of tea in the big house. Molly talked almost entirely to Olivia, in baby talk, and twice asked the baby, who was not yet three months old, whether she thought that matinee coat was a little bit too tight.

Clare answered, as the baby didn't. It was a fine fit.

'Why then, Olivia, do you have these little red marks on your arm, little sore marks? *Poor* Olivia.'

Clare wanted to hit Molly with one of the big hard

uncomfortable cushions on the sofa. Instead she sat back and swallowed her thin tomato sandwich.

David rang her later in the afternoon.

'What's wrong,' she asked, alarmed.

'Nothing's wrong, I'm just celebrating that we have the phone that's all.'

'Yes, it's marvellous. No more buzzing from the Great House.'

'Now, Clare!' he laughed.

'Sorry. Sorry. Will you bring home some chops from Dwyers'?'

'It might be closed when I'm coming back. Why don't you ring them and ask them to deliver?'

'And have Chrissie calling me Lady Muck for a month.'

'Oh well, do what you can. I have to go. I thought I'd just ring.'

'There was nothing you wanted to say?'

'Only that I loved you.'

She hung up, and realized she should have said she loved him too.

She asked Nellie to look after the baby in the kitchen and walked down to Church Street and a confrontation with Chrissie.

Her mother-in-law moved the curtain in the sitting room and watched her go.

She wrote to Valerie that evening but tore up the letter. It was a list of complaints and moans and grouses. It was the kind of letter you would hate to read. Then she put the pieces in the range in case anyone ever found them torn up in the bin and pieced them together. She wondered was she going mad to imagine anyone piecing together one of her letters to Valerie.

David was called out twice in the night.

When the phone went the second time Olivia woke too. Clare went to pick her up. David was putting on his socks and shoes as he talked to the woman on the phone.

'It's no life this, is it?' she said jiggling the crying baby up and down in her arms.

'It's not for that woman.' David nodded at the phone which he had just put down. 'Those bloody dogs they have out there have just eaten the face off her baby.'

'*No!*'

David had his clothes on by now.

'What will you do?' Clare asked, stricken.

'Hope the baby's dead, properly dead. Hope we can get its mother to agree to go into the hospital. For a couple of days, anyway. She'll need more than just a sedative after that lot.'

He was down the stairs and into the car. It was three hours, and dawn, before he came back. Olivia was asleep again. Clare was in the kitchen, she had a kettle ready and made some tea. He took the mug gratefully.

'Was the baby dead?' she asked.

'Not quite,' he said.

She waited. He said nothing.

'And Mrs Walsh? Is she all right?'

David still said nothing. His shoulders were shaking. He was crying, but he didn't want her near, he went to the window and looked out at the dark sea and the shapes of the cliff heads only becoming visible now. He stood there for a long time and she found no words or gesture to help him.

She went over to the big house to take the paper back. She had read it from cover to cover. There was a voice in the kitchen, talking to Olivia. She thought David must be back, but she didn't see his car. It was Gerry. He was dangling a little woollen ball, a brightly coloured pompom, in front of the baby who was looking at him eagerly.

'Gerry?' She was not pleased. He had given her a fright, and anyway, how dare he come in uninvited?

'I don't remember asking you in,' she said.

'I don't remember a time when friends in Castlebay had to wait to be invited in. Maybe it's different here in the . . . um . . . in the Lodge.' He made the name of the house sound laughable.

461

'What do you want?'

'I came to see your daughter and ask her would she like her photograph taken. That's all.'

'Don't be childish, Gerry. What do you want?'

'What I said. Would you like a picture of the baby . . . as a wedding present?'

'No,' she said quickly.

'What nice manners they teach up at the Lodge.'

'No thank you. I'm sorry. No thank you very much.'

'Why not? I take nice pictures of babies. They like me.'

Olivia was indeed gurgling up at him and the red, black and yellow ball of wool.

'I'd prefer not, if you don't mind. Thanks, though. Sorry about my manners.' She smiled, hoping he'd go.

He stood up. 'She's beautiful,' he said. 'I sometimes think *I'd* like one.'

'Well, nothing's stopping you.' She tried to be light. 'You know how to set about it.'

'Ah, but it would be no use if it weren't yours too.'

She flinched.

He put up both his hands in peace. 'I'm off, I'm off. Take that look off your face.'

He did have his camera with him, in its shabby black bag that he had always used. 'Whenever you think she's old enough, I'd love to.'

'Sure. I'll talk about it with David,' she said.

'Do that.' He smiled and was gone.

She felt very uneasy and didn't know why. He only wanted to take a photograph. He had only made those sort of flattering remarks that he made to everyone. Why did she feel so bothered?

She invited her mother-in-law to see the baby being bathed. She spent the whole day tidying the place up first.

Molly came to watch the ritual.

Clare tested the heat of the water with her elbow, feeling very experienced.

'Do you do that? How strange,' Molly said. 'How very strange, with all the thermometers and everything. Ah well.' She sighed as if her granddaughter was being brought up by a thick, ignorant peasant who knew nothing.

One grey morning she heard a timid tapping on the door. It was her mother.

'You haven't been down for a bit. I called to see you.'

'That's great. Come on in.'

Agnes O'Brien looked around as if fearful someone might ask her what she was doing there. 'Have you done up the parlour yet?' she asked.

'You're always asking me that. What would we need a parlour for or a sitting room or drawing room or whatever we'd call it? This is where we live.'

Agnes jerked her head up towards the big house. 'But wouldn't they expect . . .?'

'Let them expect what they like. David and I want to make this a nice bright room that we can live in. Armchairs and bookshelves and the advantage of it being the kitchen as well.'

'And when are you going to start?' her mother asked innocently.

'Will we have a cup of tea?' Wearily she emptied the tealeaves from the pot and put it on the range.

'Are you not using a kettle?'

'There's just the two of us, Mam.'

She was wrong.

Molly Power was at the door.

'I thought you might want something from town, I'm going in with Mrs Dillon this afternoon. Hallo, Mrs O'Brien.'

'Good morning, Mrs Power. Good morning.' Agnes stammered a little.

'Come to admire the baby?'

'Yes, well, Clare hasn't shown her to me yet.'

'Clare dear, do show the baby to your mother.'

Clare fumed. Her mother had made it seem that she had never seen her granddaughter at all. Mrs Power made Clare feel like a very unsatisfactory hired help.

She went upstairs for Liffey. She was not only wet, her nappy was filthy. The clean nappies were downstairs.

She went down to get them.

'Oh, don't bother dressing her up specially.'

'I'm not,' Clare hissed.

She did a rapid change job and Liffey, alarmed by the speed and lack of gentleness, cried in fright. Clare handed her first to her mother.

'I don't know whether I should . . .'

Why did Mam have to be so humble?

'You had six of your own, I'm sure you won't drop her.' Her voice was sharp. The teapot was hissing. Trying to shield her actions from her mother-in-law, Clare put four spoons of tea into the boiling water and pulled it aside.

'What a funny way to make tea,' Mrs Power said clearly.

'I've told Clare a dozen times not to do that,' Agnes said. Awkwardly she passed the baby over to Mrs Power. For a few minutes Molly Power cooed at her grandchild, and by magic the child stopped crying.

'There you are,' said Molly triumphantly, as if she alone knew the secret.

She refused a cup of tea without actually shuddering, and left.

Clare and her mother were full of gloom.

'You shouldn't let her see the house like this, Clare, really.' Agnes looked at the heap of dirty clothes in a corner, the unwashed saucepans on the draining board.

'It's my house. I'll have it look exactly the way I want to.'

'Oh all right.' Her mother was about to take offence and leave.

'Not you, Mam, sit down. I mean her. Why should we bow down before her? I'm damned if I'll do everything the way Lady Molly wants.'

'No, but you could do a bit of cleaning and cooking, that's not bowing down before her,' Agnes said coldly.

Clare knew that she wouldn't drop in again casually; she would have to go and invite her from now on.

She had been very entertained by Angela's attempts to learn to cook; and decided it wasn't a bad idea. She might well do the same herself. She made shortbread biscuits one morning and took a plate of them up to the house for Molly.

'Won't you come in and have coffee with me?' Molly said.

'I left her there on her own,' Clare said.

'Oh well. Another time then.'

The woman could have said, go back for her, couldn't she?

She lay on her bed resting one morning, and her mind just drifted off. She wasn't asleep for more than a moment. David came in.

'Hey, you worried me. I thought you weren't here.'

'What is it? What's wrong?'

'Clare, what *are* you doing? Olivia's crying her head off downstairs, Bones is sitting looking at her, and there's no lunch.'

'It's not lunchtime.'

'It's half past one, I thought I'd be late.'

'Christ, I'm sorry, David. I must have fallen asleep.' She leaped from the bed and raced down the stairs. With Olivia in one arm she grabbed a saucepan and broke three eggs into it, she reached for some butter.

'What are you doing?'

'David my love, I'm making you a scrambled egg. I'm sorry, I'll make a proper dinner this evening, I tell you I must have drifted off to sleep. I feel so tired sometimes.'

'I know. I know. It's all right.'

'It's not all right, I'm dreadfully sorry.'

'Look, will I make toast or something?'

'No, hold your daughter, I'm quicker.'

She swept the breakfast things away and into the sink.

'I don't want you to feel you have to cook a lunch for me every day, don't think that . . .'

'Darling David – will you stop it. One day, just *one* day I fell asleep. Every other day I love to have lunch with you. I love it. I used to be very lonely when you were up with your mother and father and I was there at the window working.'

They both looked over at the window as she spoke. No books there now, just a big arrangement of dried flowers.

'Aren't you going to start studying again?'

'What for?'

'Clare, please. Don't be like that. For your degree of course.'

'I studied for it once, why should I do it again?'

'Because you didn't take it, you clown. You were happy studying.'

'Not all the time I wasn't. A lot of the time I was worried and anxious.'

'Will we go to the pictures tonight?'

'Are you trying to entertain me by any chance?'

'A bit I suppose.' He looked troubled.

Clare asked Angela was there any kind of Christmas present you could make for people, by cooking, something that would look as if you'd gone to a lot of trouble over it.

'I suppose you could make fudge,' Angela said doubtfully, 'and put it in nice coloured boxes. But why do you want to make things? You're worse than me. And I think they'd expect a bit more than fudge from you.'

'Who'd expect? I don't care what they expect, I'm so tired, I tell you Angela I can't stay awake these days. It's such an effort to go into town, and there's nothing here . . .'

'Well stay awake long enough to go into town just one day. Make a list of what you want. Come in with Dick and me on Saturday afternoon.'

'Yes, I could do that. I'll ask her Ladyship would she mind Liffey.'

'Liffey. Isn't *that* a name, now. How did you think of it?'

'I just made it up,' Clare said. She didn't want to tell anyone that it was Gerry Doyle's idea.

'Am I going to teach you to drive, Clare? Remember we set it all up. You learned the theory all at once.'

There was a silence at the back of the car.

466

'I think she's asleep, Dick,' Angela said.

'No, sorry, what was it?'

'Will I give you driving lessons after Christmas?'

'I don't know if I'd have the time. It's very kind of you. If I have the time . . .'

Molly and David were sitting by the fire in the big house when she came back.

'You look exhausted,' David said.

'David, you must get Clare some nice clothes, it's terrible to have her dragging round in all that studenty-type thing. No wonder the girl looks so dawney.'

Clare let them talk about her.

'Why don't we all have a sherry, you've provided the excuse.' David leaped up.

'A really nice coat in a good bright colour, something that would put some colour in her face.' Molly was thoughtful. 'A cherry red maybe.'

David handed them both a sherry.

'Thank you, my dear,' Molly said.

Clare said nothing.

'Was it exhausting?'

'It was very tiring all right,' Clare said.

'Did you leave your parcels in at the Lodge?'

'No. This is all I got.' She had a small shopping bag with a few little things in it.

She sat on a stool looking into the fire and eventually David and his mother went back to talking as they had been before she came in. They didn't even try to bring her into the conversation.

David bought all the Christmas presents in the end. He even wrapped them and wrote the cards. He put the Christmas cards she was to send to Mary Catherine and Valerie in front of her and she wrote Love from Clare on each of them.

When David opened his Christmas present from Clare he said he was delighted with the shirt. It was just what he wanted. You couldn't have enough shirts. He said this one was particularly nice, and he put it away hastily before his mother could see it had been bought in the shop in Castlebay and was exactly the same as half a dozen which he had already.

David had bought Christmas tree decorations when he was in town: he couldn't bear anyone in Castlebay to see him buying them locally. He brought a tree home from one of his country calls, the man whose child had been sick was delighted to give the young doctor a fine green tree.

'Your wife will enjoy decorating that, Doctor,' the man beamed as they fitted the tree into the back of the car.

'Oh, she's going to love it,' David said with a smile he didn't feel.

He looked carefully at his mother's tree that evening and did something a bit similar to their own; Clare looked up at him gratefully as he stood on a chair.

'That's terrific, David, it looks really lovely. I'd do it myself but I'm just worn out.'

It was cold clear weather, from the window David saw his parents warmly dressed and in their comfortable walking shoes setting out with the dog. He knew they would head far along the cliff away from Castlebay and they would point things out to each other, and see the birds swooping low and hares running through the fields. They would come back to a hot lunch. They would sit on either side of a big well made-up fire and read. He looked over at Clare to know if she too would like a walk. She was sitting at the kitchen table. She had been reading, but in fact she had dropped off over her book.

There was a call for the doctor to come quickly. A child. Come quickly. They rang off. A five-year-old had fallen over rusty farm machinery and opened his eye.

David remembered Clare saying that she had cut her leg years ago on the rusty spikes of half-hidden machinery.

He felt a surge of anger about people raising children so casually among all these dangers.

Soothing, reassuring, and speaking confident words he didn't mean, David wiped the drying blood from the child's face. It wasn't too bad. Calming and chatting to distract their attention he said it wasn't bad at all, it would all be fine, now now, could someone start to make some tea. Then he took out his bag and put five quick stitches into the small face. He examined it critically. It wasn't bad. The child looked at him trustingly.

'Isn't that fine,' David said.

'I'm Matthew.'

'Of course you are, and you're better now.' David gave him a hug just as the tea tray was being brought in.

'Aren't you the cut of your father, and the same grand ways with you.' Matthew's mother was holding one of his hands between both her own.

'Thank you.'

'We were all delighted when you married a local girl, not getting yourself a fancy wife from Dublin.'

'I'm glad.'

'And how's your own little girl, Doctor?'

'Oh she's beautiful, thank you. Simply beautiful.'

'I'm glad to hear that, you give so much to other people's children, it would be very sad if you didn't find happiness in your own.'

Liffey was crying when he got in. She was wet. Her little legs were red and chapped, and the napkin soaked. As it was cold, she had obviously been lying like that for some time.

Clare was lying in bed reading a recipe book.

'I thought I'd make drop scones, they don't look too hard,' she smiled at him.

'Sure, that would be fine, Liffey's very wet.'

'I'll see to her in a minute.'

'She's been wet for ages, Clare.'

'Oh all right.'

David spoke sharply. 'No, I'll do it, it'll be quicker.'

'Oh good.' She went back to studying the recipe book.

Clare went back to bed early, so she should have had a fair bank of sleep when Liffey woke. But the child cried and cried and Clare never turned over in bed.

David got up. He fed and changed her again, but she still wouldn't settle. He walked her up and down. Eventually, she slept.

About ten minutes before he intended to get up Liffey began again. He poked Clare gently.

'You get her this time, love, will you, I want to grab a few minutes' sleep.'

Clare swung her legs out of bed and put her woolly dressing gown on over her long nighty. She picked up Liffey with a few words of comfort and carried her downstairs.

When David had washed and shaved and come down for his breakfast, Clare was sitting at the table, asleep. The kettle was on the range, hissing and spitting; Liffey was screaming from her cradle.

That was the morning David told his father in halting, broken sentences that he thought Clare was suffering from post-natal depression.

His father said that these things were too easily defined and put into categories. Clare was a bit low. Life was very different and less demanding than it had been last year, and it should never be forgotten that the child had missed her degree. That would be hard enough on any girl but on a little girl who had fought like a tiger to get there it must have been harder still.

David said it was more than that. If it was only that they could talk about it and sort it out, but she was so physically tired, she was drowsy all the time, and without losing any love for Liffey she seemed to have lost interest in her.

David's face was white and his eyes were dark and sleepless-looking. His father was full of pity for him.

'I think you should still try other ways before you say that we should treat it, or send her to someone.'

470

'I don't want to send her to anyone, but couldn't she be put on Tofranil? Wouldn't that sort her out in a month or two? Dad, that's what we'd say for anyone else. Why can't we say it for Clare?'

'Because it could be a lot of other things, she could be lonely, she could be unsure of herself, Molly might be making her feel inadequate. Talk to her. Talk, and tell her things and maybe you'll see. It's not a question of her being some unfortunate woman who has no one to understand her. She's got a fine husband, a great husband.'

'I can't be all that great if she's changed so much.'

'Do you still love me?' he asked her.

'David, what can you mean? I love you more than ever.'

'That's the third time you've been too tired to make love.'

'I'm sorry, I just felt a bit weary. OK. I don't mind, now I'm awake.'

'It's too late now.'

'Oh David, stop sulking.'

He swung his legs out of bed and plugged in the electric fire. He wanted to talk and he didn't want them to freeze.

'I promise you on my oath I'm not sulking. But when I think the way we were jumping on each other this time last year, it seems as if we were two different people.'

'This time last year we were in Dublin and we hadn't all the responsibilities we have now,' she said.

'This time last year, you were working fourteen hours a day for your exams, I was working fourteen hours a day in that hospital, we had to get round the city on buses, we were up to here in anxiety. Now we have our own house, our own child, our freedom to jump on each other morning, noon and night if we wish to do so, I have a gentle and satisfying amount of work to do rather than the mayhem as an intern, you have no official things to do and we're still too tired.'

'You're not, I am,' she said, correcting the facts.

'But why, Clare, *why*? I'm not just being a raging beast

471

like all men trying to demand my rights, or more rights, or anything. Why are you so tired?'

'There's so much to do,' she said.

'Are you sure you love me, and you know I'm not picking a fight?'

'Yes, of course.'

'Then let me tell you what you did today. You got up and *I* got breakfast. And *I* changed Liffey. And I said I'd get a leg of lamb in Dwyers' on the way home and you said no, *you* would. Before I went out I brought in some potatoes from the bag outside. *I* peeled a few, *you* said leave them. I came home for lunch. You had been asleep all morning. Liffey was wet and bawling . . . you were upset because there was no lunch. Clare . . . this is terrible. This isn't meant to be a row, do you understand, I'm just trying to find out why you could be tired? I made us a tin of soup and we had some of Nellie's bread while you got the bottle for Liffey. This time I insisted on getting the meat. I left it back in the house at three o'clock. You were asleep in the chair. Clare, *I* put the bloody meat into the oven, and that's how we had dinner. I thought we'd go to the pictures but *you* said *you* were too tired. You've been asleep all morning, all afternoon and now you're weary, you say, when you come to bed. I'm your doctor as well as your husband. Of course I'm worried about you.'

'I'm very sorry. When you put it like that, it's indefensible.'

'Darling heart, I'm not blaming you, I'm only asking you as my best and dearest friend, can you tell me what's wrong?'

'I don't know. I didn't think anything was.'

'But we can't live like this. I mean, you can't go on like this – if I weren't a doctor I'd bring you to a doctor.' He smiled and put both his hands on her face.

'What do you think?' she looked like a worried child.

'I think it's a depression.'

'I'm not sad.'

'No, a clinical depression.'

'But I swear I'm not depressed.'

'And your exams?'

'Yes, but I've got over that. Honestly I have. I had harder things to fight against ten years ago. Now I'm a nice middle-class married lady, no worry about the fees. If I haven't the guts to do it again it's my own fault, not anybody else's. Not Liffey's fault, not yours, only mine.'

'And will you have the guts to do it again?'

'I think I'm too tired. There, I've said it again.'

'I'd like to give you an anti-depressant.'

'More energy, like?'

'No, I'm not going to talk to you as if you were an ignoramus, they've got nothing to do with iron or energy, they work on the chemicals, on amino acid in the brain, and on the nerve endings. It would take about three weeks to make any difference.'

'What does your dad think?'

'I'll ask him.'

'I'm sure you have asked him, it doesn't matter, you have to ask him things.'

'He thinks you're just lonely and unsure of yourself here.'

'And you think it's a post-natal depression, and I think it's just tiredness.'

'It could be a bit of all of them,' David said.

'Well feed me the medicine, Doctor, and let's hope we see a miracle cure.' She smiled at him, a smile from the old days, and he went to sleep feeling a little better than he had felt for some weeks.

Next day he suggested that they take Liffey to see Mr Kenny, and Clare said that was a great idea: the nice old solicitor had sent them a lovely silver spoon for the baby. But when David got home expecting Liffey and Clare to be ready, the baby hadn't been changed or dressed, and Clare said she felt very tired today.

David said fine, they'd go another day and without making any big drama out of it he started her on a course of Tofranil.

'I was up this way and I wondered if there was a cup of tea going.'

'Nobody's up this way, but you can have a cup of tea,' she said.

'You never come down town any more,' Gerry said.

'And how would you know whether I do or not?'

'Your mother mentioned it to me, as it happens.'

'Oh Lord. I meant to go to see her this week.'

'This week? Clare, she's only ten *minutes* away. She thinks you've joined the gentry.'

Clare felt very guilty. The days ran into each other, yes, it was a whole week since she had brought the baby over to her mother, it must be three days at least since she had seen her mother-in-law.

'Do you feel all right, Clare?' Gerry asked gently. He was sitting at the kitchen table.

She was pouring the kettle of water into a teapot.

'Thank you very much for all this interest, Dr Doyle. Have you become a medical consultant now as well as a home counsellor, bearing me advice from my family?'

'I'm serious, Clare.'

She brought the tea to the table.

'I'm tired, that's all. It's very exhausting looking after a baby.'

'That one doesn't seem to need much looking after. She's fast asleep.'

'Ah, but they wake up, Gerry, that's a little trick they have.'

They drank their tea.

'And is the handsome young doctor giving you anything for your tiredness?'

'Yes of course he is . . . a course of tablets.'

'Good. I'm glad he noticed.'

'Please don't speak badly of David, Gerry, it makes me very upset.'

'I'm not speaking badly of him. I'm just saying he's wrong for you.'

'Now you really must go.' She stood up, coldly. 'Friend or no friend, Gerry, you are not coming into my house when David is not here and saying that. No you bloody can't.'

'You're only getting upset because it's true.'

'Oh don't be ridiculous. You can win any argument if you say things like that. The truth is I am upset to hear any bad reference made to David at all, and if you ever knew what it was like to love someone rather than just . . . well . . . use them . . . then you'd understand.'

'I love you,' he said.

There was a silence.

Then she threw her head back. 'Don't be idiotic. You only say that because you once or twice made a pass at me and I didn't give in. You feel it's broken the track record for you, it's not one hundred per cent. Bingo! Isn't that it? That's what it's all about. I pity any girl you really say that you love because you don't know what the word means.'

He sipped his tea. 'In this case I suppose it means that I'd do anything to have you, anything.'

She felt frightened.

'Please . . .' she began.

'I saw David one day last week kneeling in the middle of the road. I thought of putting my foot on the accelerator. Nobody would have blamed me. He was in the middle of the street, any court would have let me off. Then I saw he was looking after a puppy someone had run over. I couldn't do it.'

Clare stood up. 'You aren't serious, you're just saying these things to make yourself sound like a villain.'

'No, it's quite true. Quite true.' His voice was calm.

'But *why*?'

'Who knows? Who knows anything about why people love other people? Anyway I decided that it could never be done that way, and even if David had an accident, a genuine accident, and you were a grieving widow, that mightn't work. It might take years for you to get over him. So it has to be a different way entirely.'

'This is a game, is it?'

There was another silence.

Clare didn't like him sitting there looking at her. 'I'll tell you something, maybe it's foolish but I'll tell you anyway.

I don't feel all that well, I think I have a sort of depression, and honestly I can't take any more upset. I would be sitting here day and night in a panic if I thought that anything you were saying, *any* of it, were true. Can you reassure me that it's not? Please?'

'I thought you had a depression,' he said sympathetically. 'Remember Fiona did too, in England that time. But she got over it, and so will you. Is he giving you proper tablets for it?'

'Yes.'

'You'll be fine, and you'll be back at your books, and madam there will grow up to be a pride and joy to you.'

It was as if he hadn't said any of the other terrible things. Clare felt dizzy.

'So put everything out of your head. I'll just love you quietly from a distance. For ever. You know?'

'Or until summer,' she said.

'No, for ever. But you're right, there's no point in getting you upset, you're to get yourself better now.'

He got up to leave.

'Yes. Yes I will, I'll be fine.'

'And go to see your Mam, eh? And Josie, right?'

'Right. Goodbye, Gerry.'

The baby woke just then and began a little cry.

'Aren't you going to pick her up?'

'Yes, in a minute. I was just seeing you off. Hush, Liffey, I'm just coming.'

'Liffey?' he smiled from the door. 'You call her the name I gave her.'

'I think we're going to have to come to terms with pastry,' Angela said.

'I came to terms with it years ago, I love it.'

'No, I think we should make it. We've been avoiding all these recipes that begin telling you to roll out the crust. Let's make the damn thing tonight.'

'Right,' he said. 'Will I get the ingredients?'

'No, I'll call into O'Brien's on the way back from school,

I think it's only flour and lard or something, but I might be wrong.'

'I can't think of any other woman of your age who doesn't know how to make pastry,' he said, teasing her.

'Less of that, you got yourself an intellectual as a girl-friend, you should be delighted with yourself and counting your blessings all the time.'

'Are you my girlfriend?' he said, pleased.

'Of course I am. I didn't mean to be but I am,' she said.

The following night they made the pastry. It was night-marish. The book had said you could use lard *or* butter *or* margarine.

'Why doesn't it tell us what ordinary people use?' Angela fumed.

It had told them to Rub The Fat Into The Flour.

'That actually is not English, you rub something out, or you rub something, you don't *rub in*. God, these people.' They made it look like breadcrumbs which is what it said, but it also said use a Light Hand.

'That's the most stupid thing I ever heard. How can you be light with all this rubbing?' Dick had an apron on over his good suit. Angela had insisted.

'I don't know what you wore a good suit like this for, just to do cooking,' she scolded. But she knew well . . .

It was the same reason that she had worn a smart blouse and washed her hair.

The question had to wait until they worked out what Bake Blind meant. By process of elimination they dis-covered it meant that you put the pastry into the oven and you cooked it by itself first. Angela wrote a short note to the book's publishers saying that it should be withdrawn for its general misinformation.

Then they sat down and poured themselves a drink. Dick stood up again and said he would like Angela to marry him.

'Dick, are you sure? You've been asking me a long time you know.'

He put his glass of orange squash down on the table and took her hands. 'I thought that maybe when you let slip that you were my girlfriend that we had made a bit of progress,' he said.

'I'm very difficult,' she said.

'I know,' he said.

'And you're set in your ways of course,' she added.

'I am *not* set in my ways. When I got to know you, which is not today or yesterday, I was set in my ways. Now I do all kinds of things I'd never have done before. I read long books, I cook great meals. I'm cheerful instead of miserable. What do you mean, set in my ways?'

'Yes, please.'

'What?'

'I said yes please, I'd love to marry you.'

Angela tried the beautiful ruby ring on, the ring that Dick Dillon had bought long ago hoping for the day it would be needed. It was perfect.

'I'll make you a good wife – not a peaceable one mind, but I'll be good to you, and love you and look after you.'

'The love bit is the most important one,' he said shyly.

'It is for me too, I just felt awkward saying it.'

'We don't need to feel awkward any more,' he said, and they sat in the firelight, as the pastry burned black in the oven and the red ruby glittered and shone.

'Do you have this funny feeling that it's all over? It's all happened? Like everything went into the past tense instead of the future tense?' asked Clare.

David looked at her. He had no feeling like that at all. 'I know, I know,' he said, his heart heavy.

'Oh good. I was afraid it was just me. I suppose we'll get used to it, and adapt.'

'I think that's what happens to people,' he said.

'It's not regrets or anything. You know that?'

'Of course.'

'But you must find that too. I mean you don't regret coming back here, but the kind of work you do, the life we lead, it sort of happened a bit soon, didn't it?'

He patted her hand. She *was* much brighter than before, she was far more aware of Liffey and spent hours playing with her. She had taken driving lessons from Dick Dillon. David had even seen some of her history textbooks out by the window again.

Perhaps Clare was just too young and unprepared to settle down so quickly. Perhaps she would never settle down. It made it all the harder to tell her that he *loved* this life. He liked caring for sick, frightened people, and curing them with medicines from his black bag; or sewing up their wounds; delivering their children sometimes or closing the eyes of their dead. A couple of years ago he might have been mildly tolerant of his father's brand of medicine, preferring instead to think of a more scientific approach. Now he couldn't see anything that would be better for the patients than to see a face they trusted, an old face and his son a newer face. This gave them some confidence and very often that was three-quarters of the battle.

It all made him feel unsettled. He didn't worry about Clare's health any more but he felt that the great closeness they had grown used to, and accepted as if it was their natural right, had disappeared. The words were the same, the interest was there, she was eager to hear about his cases and discuss them. But it was as if she believed that somehow they had been shunted into a siding and forgotten about, and they were trapped in this middle-aged world, so they had better play the role of old people as cheerfully as possible.

Dick and Angela were married in Dublin. There had never been the slightest discussion about it. They knew they wanted nobody from Castlebay, not one of Dick's hotel relations, and Angela said that she certainly didn't want to draw sisters and brothers and the whole of Japan on her either. It was arranged with no fuss, Father Flynn again, of course, and Emer and Kevin.

Just the five of them at a small side altar early one morning.

'It's not festive enough for you,' Father Flynn complained.

'Our life is festive enough, Father, we don't need it on a wedding day. Honest.'

He gave in grudgingly.

They went back to Emer's and Kevin's house and they had scrambled eggs and bacon and a cake that Angela and Dick had made themselves from the section called 'Simple Cake Making' which they said was another example of lies in cookery books. Reluctantly they allowed Father Flynn to take one photograph of the occasion which, when it came out, was so ludicrous that Angela said it could illustrate an article called Christmas Day in the Asylum.

They took the picture out occasionally if they wanted a good laugh, but they didn't need anything to remind them of the best day of their lives. That's just what it was, Dick said, pure and simple. The best day ever. And for once even Father Flynn found himself without a word to say.

It came as a great surprise to hear that the Nolans were going to take a house on the Cliff Road again. Mr Nolan hadn't been well: he had been told to take things easy and get a bit of sea air. Caroline had finished her apprenticeship and was in the throes of looking for a job. She thought she would have a break. James said that he could prepare his few briefs just as well in Castlebay as anywhere else.

That was the way the news was broken to David by letter. He read it to them all with suitable James gestures and Clare was surprised to see how pleased they all were.

Even Nellie was delighted. 'It puts the Mistress into great good humour when that lot comes down, and their Breeda's a very nice girl, I'll be glad to see her again myself.'

Mrs Power started in a mad rush to get the garden done up. There was a nice corner with lupins and she wanted to be able to have afternoon tea served there. She had all the deckchairs of course but they looked a bit shabby.

'I'll paint the deckchairs blue for you, and we'll look

like an ocean-going liner. What do you think?' Clare looked at her mother-in-law.

'I don't think so . . .'

'Oh go on, you've got blue and white china, you could get blue paper serviettes. It would be terrific.'

Mrs Power seemed to regret having shown how flustered she was to Clare, she wished she hadn't admitted her wishes to impress the Nolans, she began to take it all back.

'Well, thank you, dear, for the idea anyway,' she said dismissively.

'Are we going to do it?' Clare cried, 'because if we are I'll ring Bumper and ask him to get some cans of paint round here right away.'

'I think not, Clare. Thank you, no.'

Two red spots burned in Clare's cheeks. 'A bit flashy, might it be?'

'Since you say the word, that's just what it might look like, you know, a little . . . well, a little overdone.'

'Common?' Clare asked.

'No, no, heavens what a thing to say about your idea, but you know . . .'

'I know,' Clare said grimly and walked back to the Lodge.

'You've got a common flashy mother,' she said to Liffey, 'a mother who is a little . . . what's the word again . . . overdone.'

Liffey seemed pleased with the attention and the tone of Clare's voice.

'And Liffey, you also have an almighty bitch of a grand-mother, I never want you to forget that. She is in the major league of bitchiness as your godmother Mary Catherine would say, she is a Class A bitch.'

Clare felt better when she had defined everything. Liffey was a good listener.

Caroline looked very elegant. Clare remembered when she had come to Castlebay first, and she had been so jealous of all the fun Caroline and her friend Hilary had been having with David, James and Gerry Doyle.

How strangely it had all turned out. She felt uneasy when she thought of Gerry and his strangeness.

She was surprised when Caroline, languidly reclining in a deckchair with Liffey on her lap, said, 'Is Gerry Doyle still the Main Attraction?'

'I think so,' Clare said carefully. 'I'm not as in touch as I used to be. Possibly the younger ones have other heroes, but I think he does very well.'

'Well, I think I'll stroll down later and have a look at him,' Caroline said. 'Now that you've taken the most gorgeous man in Castlebay, I'll have to start looking round at the second bests.'

She laughed, and they all laughed. David too.

Clare was furious. The *bitch* – why did she say that in front of Molly? Clare had seen the look of regret come over Molly's face. Suppose David and Caroline had married, now wouldn't that have been something special? Suppose she and Sheila Nolan had been cooing over Liffey. Molly would have much preferred that than have Liffey also the granddaughter of O'Brien's shop.

Valerie came to stay in the Lodge for a week.

'I can't stand Caroline Nolan,' she said. 'Stop being so nice to her, Clare.'

'I'm only being civil. Not nice. She'll be gone in a couple of weeks.'

'I wouldn't bet on that, she's asking that old man the solicitor friend of David's father . . .'

'Mr Kenny.'

'Yes, she's asking him are there any openings for a solicitor round here, a country practice would be so much more interesting than a city one, you'd see all sides of the law.'

'But she couldn't be a solicitor in Castlebay, there isn't any need for anyone apart from poor old Mr Kenny and most people go to the town.'

'Aha, that's what he told her, she's going into the town today to investigate possibilities. Gerry Doyle's giving her a lift.'

'That's all baloney, as Mary Catherine would say, she's just gone to get a quick feel from Gerry Doyle, she fancies him rotten, she always has. She pretends it was David, but I remember all those years. It was Gerry this and Gerry that.'

'I hope you're right,' Val said.

'I wish you didn't have to go, you make me feel safe,' Clare said.

'You are safe, stupid.'

'Well, normal, then.'

'Come to the dance tonight,' Valerie said suddenly.

'No, I'm too old, too dull. David's going to be out all night, nearly, he rang. Mrs Brennan says there are complications in a confinement.'

'You come anyway, David would like that, I know he would.'

'I don't want to, I feel wrong, somehow.'

'I won't go either and I was so looking forward to it.'

'Damn you, Valerie, now I have to go. I have to wash my hair and go.'

'Yes you do,' said Valerie, pleased.

They all had a drink at the hotel first, Caroline, James, Josie and Martin, Valerie and Clare, then they crossed the road and headed for the dance hall. The sound of the band hit them as soon as the swing doors opened.

'I feel that old excitement, just like when we were young,' Caroline said.

'So do I,' James Nolan said, eyeing Josie Dillon speculatively.

Martin said nothing.

Inside, the familiar smell of sweat and perfume and suntan oil came to them, and the band struck up a Paul Jones.

Clare remembered the excitement of the Paul Jones years ago when you could stop opposite literally anyone, and half the girls in the ballroom wanted to stop in front of Gerry Doyle. She forced herself to relive that sense of excitement.

Come on girls, get into the ring,' she called.

'Good to see the grass widow enjoying herself for a change,' Caroline said.

Clare refused to wonder what that meant. It probably meant nothing. It was a clever-clever thing that Caroline *would* say.

She stopped opposite a boy of about sixteen, red faced and sweating with nerves. It might even be his first dance.

'Hallo,' she smiled. 'I'm yours, I think, for the dance.'

'Um, thank you, I'm not a great dancer,' he said.

'You couldn't be any worse than I am,' Clare said cheerfully and she made him feel so confident in their gallop around the room that she knew he would come back and claim her over and over, unless she told him.

'That was lovely,' she said. 'I'm married to the local doctor here. We have a little girl. It makes me feel nice and young again to dance like that.'

He was gone like a bow from an arrow. A married woman! Heavens!

Valerie seemed to be happy, Clare thought later as she looked down on it all from the balcony, a freckled man in a check suit had asked her to dance several times over, he looked nice and they were chatting away too. James Nolan, the smooth, two-faced rat, was dancing cheek to cheek with Josie Dillon who was admittedly very foolish indeed to allow and encourage such a thing. Clare didn't approve, but she could have foretold it. She could also have foretold that Caroline and Gerry Doyle would have found each other out too.

She leaned with her elbows on the balcony looking at them. Caroline was taller than Gerry, but who wasn't? Saying not much but smiling a lot, not groping but dancing very close. Very sure of each other. Clare wished that Valerie would leave the check-suited man and come up here for a moment. Then she would get over this silly idea that Caroline Nolan was a troublemaker with eyes for David. Anyone could see that Caroline had eyes only for Gerry Doyle.

Clare remembered the days when she and Josie would

484

come to the dance and be rushed off their feet. Not so for Josie tonight, she never left James Nolan's side. Not so for Mrs Clare Power, the doctor's wife, and mother of the doctor's daughter. None of the boys who used to ask her to dance would approach her now, and it wasn't the Castlebay Committee dance where she would have found older people to dance with. She didn't mind being a wallflower, she didn't really wish David was here, she felt she had grown away from the dance. Not too old for it, just away from it.

Three little things happened before they played the national anthem and the night was over. Martin told Josie in a shaking voice that he was leaving now and would she like to come with him or not. He put a lot into the question, and Josie answered head on. No, she would not, she would like to stay. Thank you.

Then Bernie Conway came up to Clare and said it was marvellous to see her again, she had been such a recluse in the beginning.

'I suppose it was the shock of the baby coming so early.'

'It must have been,' Clare agreed.

'And who's looking after her tonight? David?'

'No, no, if he were free he'd be here, Nellie Burke loves to have her from time to time.'

'Oh, the resident domestic. Nice,' Bernie said.

There was a pause.

'I'd never have expected to see you here on your own . . . after . . . after everything,' Bernie said.

Clare wanted to push her out the window on to Church Street but decided against it. 'I'm not really on my own, I came with about five or six other people, I'm just not being danced with at the moment,' she smiled sweetly. 'Like you.'

And the third thing was that Gerry Doyle and Caroline waved casually and went off into the night towards the caravan park.

Caroline's father said she was very sensible to get experience in a country town, there was nothing as useful as learning the business on the ground at every level. They were all congratulating her on having got a position in the town twenty miles from Castlebay.

James said he hoped she would get the firm to send all the cases to advise to him, he needed a good country contact. Sheila Nolan said she would come down and help to settle Caroline in, and then she could come across to Castlebay and see Molly for a winter weekend. Dr Power said that she'd find it a real change from the summer, in fact some of the Castlebay Committee didn't agree with Josie Dillon that visitors should be allowed in the place in winter at all, let them think it was the land of eternal summer.

Clare was silent. She remembered how she had laughed when Valerie said that Caroline was a schemer and that she was plotting to be down in this part of the country. Was Caroline really a bit keen on David as Valerie had all but said? It couldn't be. Hadn't she taken up her romance with Gerry Doyle exactly as she was planning? Perhaps she was scheming to be near Gerry Doyle. Surely not. Caroline had too much intelligence for that.

They often had tea in the garden at Crest View, Caroline seemed to be able to summon it up with a wave of the hand, while Molly Power would fuss for three days about any entertaining, Sheila Nolan never seemed to think of it, and Clare never suggested it in the Lodge since she thought none of them would want to come there.

But Caroline just knew automatically that what people loved around five o'clock was a huge pot of tea, and plates of nice thin tomato sandwiches. Even Dr Power loved dropping in, for half an hour or so. Caroline had painted all the deckchairs bright red.

'Do they belong to us, strictly?' James asked.

'Of course not, but they were so tatty. The old bat who owns the place will be delighted with us.'

Molly said it was a *very* clever idea. And very *tasteful*.

She took Liffey sometimes but not always. A ten-month-old baby was lively and needed attention, Caroline had limited time for babies. And this summer it seemed as if Caroline was calling the shots. After all she was planning to become a native. Almost.

David did seem to find her good company, but then he always had. They had been friends, and now he seemed to laugh and relax more with Caroline than he did even with James.

She sat with her hand on the pram, rocking the sleeping Liffey. Mrs Nolan was describing some dream in elaborate detail; Molly Power listened enthralled. Dr Power and James Nolan were discussing the business of calling doctors as expert witnesses in court cases. Breeda was refilling the teapot and setting out further plates of sandwiches. David and Caroline were sitting on the whitewashed wall of Crest View watching the beach below.

What am I doing here? Clare thought. This isn't *my* place. I'm not meant to *be* here with these people.

It was like an echo of what Gerry Doyle had said.

'I always hated saying goodbye to this place,' Caroline said. 'Now it's not goodbye at all. I *am* glad about the job.'

'So are we,' David said eagerly. 'But won't it be very dull? Honestly, Caroline, you've no idea how quiet it can be in this area. I know the town is bigger but it's still small after Dublin.'

'How could a town with Gerry Doyle be dull? Answer me that.' Caroline was being light and joky but she saw immediately she had said the wrong thing.

'Oh, him,' David said.

'I was only teasing you, I don't think he'll form part of my winter social life, hardly the suitable escort for the legal profession.'

'You must choose your own friends, I'm only a stick in the mud.'

That *wasn't* so, and anyway she'd find it hard to make friends at first. 'I'll be relying on you and Clare to introduce me round.'

'We hardly know anyone.' He wasn't apologetic, he was stating a fact.

'We'll have to take up golf again, will we do that, have a game every now and then?'

'I'd *love* that,' David said. 'Yes, that's something I really would like. I'm meant to have an afternoon off in the middle of the week, I hardly ever take it.'

'Well now.' Caroline smiled at the marvellous notion. 'There we'll be, old country doctor, old country solicitor, out for an afternoon's golf.' Her laugh pealed out like a bell. 'Who would have thought it, David, that we'd come to this?'

Clare listened to them from her red-painted deckchair. Old country doctor, old country solicitor, and there was Clare – old country nothing.

The wasps were dying, the seaweed was coming in on the tide, the visitors were packing up. Angela was getting her books and charts ready for school.

Clare came to the door, wheeling Liffey in a push chair.

'She must be nearly a year.'

'Next week. Is Dick here, Angela?'

'No . . . oh hell he is, he said to say he was out if anyone came. But for you. Come on in.'

Dick was at the table with plans spread out all over it. He jumped guiltily.

'It's only Clare, love,' Angela said.

'We were going to tell her anyway.'

They were going to make their cottage into a small hotel. Dick was getting his share out of Dillon's, which would suit everyone there, and they were going to open a small twelve-bedroom hotel of their own. Angela owned the field behind the cottage: they would build a hotel just for golfers, with places to leave their clubs, with early breakfasts if they wanted it, with late suppers. They might not get a licence to serve alcohol; but people could order a bottle of whiskey or whatever and it would be supplied in their room. Their plan was to open it next June, Angela was going to leave the school.

'Is that why you've been doing the cooking?' Clare asked eagerly.

'The one thing we *proved* is that we have to hire a cook

before anything else, we'll make the beds and wash up but *not* cook!'

They had tea and looked at the plans. 'That should cost a fair bit of money,' Clare said.

'I'll be owed a fair bit of money out of Dillon's,' Dick said.

'Will your brother be pleased or furious?'

'He'll be delighted I'm out of his hair, but he'll be furious about this, that's why it's a secret you see, the money bit goes through this week. A firm in the town are handling it, in fact that girl – what's her name? – was here.'

'Caroline Nolan?'

'The very one. Nice girl for a Dubliner, very straightforward.'

'Um,' said Angela.

'Um indeed,' said Clare.

'What did you want Dick for, by the way?' Angela remembered why Clare had called.

'I was wondering would you give me a few secret golf lessons when Angela went back to school, I thought you'd have some time on your hands, but now I see you won't.'

'I'm not the one to give you lessons, I'm very bad.'

'I don't mind only learning a little.'

'No Clare, you don't understand, I'd teach you the wrong grip, the wrong stance, you'd have to unlearn it all over again.'

'Why don't you go up to Jimmy the Pro?' Angela wanted to know.

'I wanted to learn secretly, without anyone else knowing.'

'That's why you can't ask David,' Angela said.

'Right.'

'What about Gerry Doyle, he's a good golfer?' Dick suggested.

'No, I'd probably spend most of the lesson on the flat of my back in the sand dunes,' Clare laughed.

'I'll tell you – that girl Caroline, *she* loves golf, she says she's going to come over here and play as much as she can. *She* might be the one.'

Dick Dillon's face shone with pleasure at having solved a problem.

'I'm sorry, Clare,' Angela said, 'some men are as thick as the wall. But you mustn't worry.'

'I don't know what you're complaining about, you've come up with no suggestions. I've given two, and they've been laughed out of court,' Dick grumbled.

'I'll solve it for you,' Angela said, 'why don't I book lessons with Jimmy and you could so-called come along and watch, and join in, it wouldn't look like you learning.'

'It would really, and anyway you don't want to learn.'

'If I'm to be the genial co-proprietor of a golfing hotel I'd better know how to play the damn game,' Angela said. 'I'll talk to Jimmy, and you come up casually like around Lesson Two or Three.'

'You're always helping me,' Clare said. 'It's probably very silly.'

'No, I think you're quite right,' Angela said seriously, in a way that let a shiver of cold go through Clare.

Josie was in tears at the Lodge that evening. Martin never wanted to see her again. He said she had made a fool of him over James Nolan. Oh how stupid she had been, Josie could kick herself from here to Dublin and back, she was so annoyed. What should she do? Clare was so good with men.

'I am not good with men, what makes you think that?'

Well hadn't Clare got David Power as her husband, and the town Romeo Gerry Doyle was saying only the other night in the hotel that he wished he had moved in before the young doctor.

'Gerry was saying that. In front of people?'

'Yes, yes.' Josie was much more interested in her own disasters. Should she write to Martin? Did James have any *real* interest in her? What did Clare think . . .

'I can't tell you what I think until I know what you want,' Clare said, exasperated. 'If you tell me straight out what you want, I'll tell you what I think you should do.'

'I want James Nolan, but I don't think he wants me, so

if I'm sure of that and that there's no hope there, I want Martin. Now is that honest and truthful enough for you?'

'You wouldn't just like to be on your own for a bit and let life go by, and eventually meet someone else?'

'No thank you.' Josie was firm.

'That's what I think you should do.'

'I told you what I wanted, it's easy for you to say that, and all this bit about being independent, you have a husband, a child, and Gerry Doyle ogling you as well.'

'Right. I'll drive you out to his house, you can put a letter under his door: "Dear Martin, I behaved stupidly, I suppose I wanted to see did you really care about me . . ." that sort of thing. Not too cringeing, not too apologetic, but don't be defensive either, we'll write it now if you like . . .'

'I don't think James Nolan will ever . . .'

'I agree. I don't think James Nolan ever will either . . .'

Two weeks later Josie and Martin bought the ring. Three diamonds in a cluster.

'You're a genius, Clare,' Josie breathed to her a few days after the announcement.

'That's what I am,' Clare agreed.

But Clare couldn't be a genius for herself.

She despised women who were coquettish to men, and during those heady days when she and David had been so in love that Dublin just seemed like the backdrop on a stage for them, he and she used to laugh at the posturings of women who thought flirtatiousness was attractive, and the men who were fools enough to be taken in. They had sworn then that they would always be able to tell each other how they felt and say it straight out, the other was allowed ten minutes to be upset but after that he or she was to remember that this was the Love of the Century and that any plain speaking was a part of the very special relationship they had.

Clare wondered would it work if they went back to Dublin and raced round in duffel coats in the rain. In the winter and spring of 1960 it had been easy to talk, in the winter and spring of 1962 they had lost it.

491

She wrote him a letter one day. A long letter trying to recapture how it had been. But she re-read it and it sounded like a list of complaints so she tore it up.

She even tried to talk to his father about it. Very obliquely. But she realized soon that the old man thought that everything was fine between them. He acknowledged that Clare had been a little low after the birth of the baby, perfectly normal under all the circumstances, he saw no yawning gaps or wide distances now. It would have been cruel as well as pointless to try to tell him about them.

She found it very hard to study again. Almost impossible.

She wrote to the cheerful tutor who had said he never expected to hear from her again. She said that he might have heard what had happened on the day she was ready to sit her finals, but that the baby was now almost a year and a half, and that Clare would like to get back to work again. He wrote back saying that she had to apply formally of course, but he knew there would be no trouble once people knew the facts, the very dramatic facts. He admired her courage for starting again, because in eighteen months she must have got out of practice. He said to be sure to contact him if she were in Dublin.

And that was it. No other way of getting back into the frame of mind she had been in once. She looked at her notes. How had she been so intelligent? How could she have written those paragraphs on the left-hand side of each double page, paragraphs headed 'essentials' and then on the other side quotes, references, details. Was there a possibility that she once knew all this? Did other people up in Dublin know this kind of thing now?

Should she go to Dublin for a few days? Would that make it more real?

She discussed it with David. He said he thought she should go.

She planned to stay with Emer and Kevin and the now monstrous Daniel. They were dying to see Liffey, having met her only at the christening. Would David come too? Just for a couple of days?

No, he said. It was the worst time to leave. Old people got pneumonia at this time of year. But he'd love her to go, really and truly.

'Have you gone off me, David?' she asked him that night without rancour.

'Well really, what nonsense,' he said. 'Are you sulking because I can't get away?'

'Of course not, I meant it much more generally.'

'I haven't gone off you, sweetheart, why should I?'

'I don't know, who knows why people love and they don't?' She was standing in the same spot of the kitchen as she had been when she had heard Gerry Doyle say those words from the kitchen table. She had echoed them unconsciously.

She shivered a little.

'Well I know. I know I love you and I haven't gone off you. So there.'

'Are you happy, David?'

'What's happy?' he asked, shrugging his shoulders.

'This room is beginning to be like the Echo Cave,' Clare said. 'You asked me a year ago was I happy, when you were telling me that I wasn't loopy. You asked me then was I happy.'

'This is very intense. What did you say?'

'Don't you remember?'

'No, and love, don't pick a fight because I can't remember every word of every conversation we have had in two years. If I were to quiz you, there must be many things you've forgotten.'

'That's fair. I'll tell you what I said. I said I was happy. And you said "But . . ." asking a question and I said, well, "But . . . we'd sort of got a bit settled down hadn't we" and you said yes you felt that too.'

'Well, what's the production?'

'The production is that we've changed a lot, you were the one who was beseeching *me* and wanting to know how *I* was, now I'm the one.'

'I've had a hard day, a really hard day. A woman of forty-four died today. Down the coast. She'd been fine,

493

not a thing wrong with her. Cancer all over her in two months. She had six children and a big stupid husband and I had to stand there and talk about the good side of it. Clare, there was no good side to it, believe you me there was no good side.

'I came back and sewed up the eye of a child of five whose father hit her with a chair, the father is in a worse state than the child. I have to write a report of it all for Frank Conway. Frank Conway asked me how his mother was and I had to tell him she won't come out of hospital.

'Then Dad asked me if I'd mind looking after everything on my own for a week in about a month's time, he's feeling very tired he says, he wakes at night with his heart racing, he'd like a little rest.

'Rest? He's hardly doing a quarter of the load, so if he wants a rest at this level of work the man is really bad. Then I come back here and I'm met with pleas and beggings to come to Dublin which I can *not* do much as I might like to. And now the whole fabric of life has to be analysed.'

There was a silence.

'I'm sorry,' she said.

'There's no reason why you should be. These are the joys and horrors of my day, not yours.'

'What *would* you like from me? What would have been best tonight? Tell me.'

'I suppose a bit of peace, chat about other things, not about us and where we were going and who loved whom more.'

He stood up and put his arm around her. 'It's all right, Clare, it's not magic all the time, but people in jobs like ours, well like mine and when you were studying feverishly you were the same, you understood . . . in the time off you need just to relax, not to have to think of what love is and what it isn't.'

'I see. I do,' she said.

The telephone rang. David answered it.

'Oh hallo.' His face broke into a smile. She knew it was Caroline Nolan, who understood what people wanted in their time off. They didn't want *concepts*, they wanted a nice effortless exchange of words and an arrangement to play golf.

She wrote to Emer and said she wouldn't come just yet, she wanted to stay at home to sort out a few things. Emer said there was no bother, the bed was always there. Mention of the beds in Emer's house always caused Clare to feel a little guilty.

Angela was a very good golfer, Jimmy the Pro said. She had a swing like a man. Angela did not regard this as the high praise which Jimmy intended it to be.

'Your little friend here now isn't too bad either.' Clare made a face at him. 'Try to keep your head still and you wouldn't be a disgrace at all.'

'Great,' Clare said.

'Why don't you come out and play with that husband of yours sometimes? When the solicitor lady isn't around. I bet David would love a good game of a Saturday.'

'I must, but I'd be no match for him.'

'Oh, you'd give him a game, you did quite well there at the second, you were on the green in three and you only took two putts.'

'But it's a par three.'

'It's very respectable, I tell you.'

'Was it good, the golf today?' she asked him when he came home next time.

'No. I couldn't hit a ball out of my way.'

'What did you get on the second?' she asked innocently.

'Don't talk to me about the second, it's a par three, I took seven,' he wailed.

'Never mind, there are days and days, aren't there?'

He looked at her gratefully.

In women's magazines they told you to smarten up your appearance, lose weight and turn back into the girl he married. She tried wearing make-up but rubbed most of it off again, it looked heavy on her and unnatural in this part of the world. Her clothes were all right, she had a few nice jumpers and skirts and she wore smart blouses as well. She didn't need to lose weight. She was almost too thin if anything, and she was better-looking than the girl he had married. So there was no joy there. The women's magazines had never met a wife who was so tense and irritating that she had driven her husband into the arms of a country solicitor. That wasn't one the agony aunts could handle.

But still she would try. She followed every bit of an article in *Woman's Own* about how to do a perfect evening make-up.

She used the shadow and the eyeliner exactly as they directed.

She put on the taffeta skirt she had worn only once at the dance. And a nice top. She got her hair set in big loose ringlets.

Chrissie came over to the hairdresser's and stood in her dirty overall.

'I saw you coming in here, where are you going tonight?'

'Nowhere,' Clare hissed from under the dryer.

'You must be going *some*where, why else are you getting your hair done?'

'Oh go away, Chrissie,' she said.

'This is a public place, you can't order me around here.'

Clare knew that everyone would hear of the pleasant sisterly exchange between the young doctor's wife and the assistant in Dwyers' butchers.

She called in to her mother.

'Are you all right, Clare? You look as if you've been crying.'

'It's make-up, Mum.'

'Where's Liffey?'

'Nellie's minding her, I was getting my hair done.'

'Waste of money in this wind, it will be blown out before you get home.'

Jim came into the shop. Clare turned around and spoke to him, moving her lips deliberately.

'I wish you wouldn't speak to Jim like that,' her mother said. 'You make it sound as if he's a halfwit. Jim's not a halfwit, he's only idle, aren't you, Jim?' Her tone was affectionate but she got no reply. Jim hadn't seen her lips move and he hadn't realized that anyone had spoken to him.

She had slaved over a good dinner for David, he was tired and distracted, he didn't notice her hair, her eyes, the food or the way she had made everything look nice.

He said he was exhausted, they went to bed early, and David fell asleep as she was about to move towards his side of the bed.

'Caroline?'

'Oh David, don't tell me you're going to cancel the golf. I've been looking forward to it all morning.'

'So have I, no, of course I'm not cancelling it. Look I was thinking, it's such a long drive back for you after the game, why don't we have a meal before you head off?'

'Oh, that's very nice, but I don't want to put Clare to too much . . .'

'No, I thought we'd go out somewhere, you know.'

A pause.

'Yes, that would be super. Where did you think?'

'Well, I don't know why I said somewhere, there only is one place, the hotel. We can get a nice enough meal there.'

'Great, that's very nice. Give me the strength to drive back here again.'

'Good, good. I'll book us a table then. I'll ring them and reserve a table for the two of us.'

At first it was just a game of golf with Caroline, then it was golf and a couple of drinks at the club. Now it was golf, drinks and dinner. Josie was on the phone next day. Just for a chat.

'I hope the food wasn't too good last night, you'll be setting me impossible standards,' Clare laughed.

'What do you mean?'

'Well, I'm going to ask the golfers to come *here* next week, would you and Martin join us as well?'

Josie thought that would be great. She was relieved to know that Clare was in the picture about David playing golf and being seen with Caroline. Her sister Rose had come in all excited from the dining room last night to say that David Power and Caroline Nolan were holding hands under the table. But that mightn't be true. Rose had always had a soft spot for David, and Rose had been very bitter and odd since Josie had announced her engagement.

Clare asked Molly if she'd like to come to dinner next Thursday.

'It's a bit far in advance to be planning that isn't it?' Molly said. 'But that would be very nice. Do you think you could manage it?'

Angela said that under any other circumstances she would drop everything and come, but the Mother Provincial of the order was visiting the school and the nuns were having a sort of feast for her. In all the years she had worked in that school since 1945 they had never offered them a bit of food and now it was happening. 'It will be horrific, I'll take notes in a jotter and tell you later.'

'In all the years you've known *me* this is the first time I've ever offered you a bite of food, and it would be the same night,' Clare sighed.

'Is it for anything special?'

'Survival or something,' Clare said.

'Oh, you're inviting your mother-in-law?'

'And my husband's golf partner.'

'That's ambitious, what are you giving them to eat?'

'I haven't thought yet.'

'Let me give you a hint, give them something cold to start, like hard-boiled eggs with stuffing in them. Emer said that she went out to a house to dinner in Dublin and they had a whole lot of tins of sardines and lemon juice mashed up and served in a china bowl and people helped themselves and spread it on bread and it was lovely.'

'That might be fine in Dublin, but if you didn't give them soup here they'd have you taken to the county home.'

'Soup's hard to concentrate on and serve if you've got to think of the next bit.'

'Keep your fingers crossed for me, will you?'

'You'll be fine,' said Angela with no confidence in her voice.

Old Mr Kenny said that it was very nice of the young people to think of inviting him to dinner, he was very touched. And that made up her eight.

She asked Nellie to help her bring two chairs from the big house and she went through all her dishes and cutlery to make sure she had enough. She did all her preparations secretly when David wasn't there. Any time he came home she dropped the fussing. He was pleased about the dinner, that meant that he couldn't really have a great deal to hide, she thought. If he and Caroline had been up to anything more than these long relaxed conversations, the quick peck on the cheek as they said goodbye, surely he couldn't bring her into the house and act as if nothing was going on. She had phoned Caroline at work, and she too had been pleased at the idea of dinner after golf.

'What a lovely thing to suggest, Clare. Will you be able to manage?'

'Manage what?' Clare asked pleasantly, seething with rage.

'Oh, dinner and everything.'

'Gosh I hope so,' Clare said and went back to the kitchen in a fury.

She took Liffey out of the pram and spoke to her seriously. 'Listen to me, kid, this world is full of bullshit, as my friend Mary Catherine, who is your Godmother, used to say in her less refined moments. Now you and I aren't going to put up with that, we are not going to be walked on, Liffey Power. And I make you a solemn promise. If you are a good baby on Thursday, if you don't wet anyone or get sick over them or cry, I will give you a great life full of freedom and adventure, and if you want to go up in a Sputnik and your father says no, I'll fight that you can go up in a Sputnik.'

Liffey clapped her hands, pleased with all the concentration.

'So that's it, a deal. Good.'

Bones came into the kitchen.

'And you too, friend, no scratching your bum when they're here, no huge unexpected howls because you've seen a bluebottle or the lighthouse or anything. Just look like a sweet affectionate hound who loves the young mistress. Of course you could take a bite out of Miss Nolan's rear end but make it look as if she attacked you first. What will I give you? I'll tell you, I'll save you from the knacker's yard. David said you might have to be put down, I won't hear of that.'

Bones smiled at her and she went back to the cookery book.

It would have been so easy if she could have had Nellie, and Nellie would love to have helped, but the whole point of it was that she couldn't. She *had* to do it on her own. She couldn't even let Nellie know how nervous she was. Nellie's first loyalty was to her own household, she could well tell Molly that there was pandemonium out in the Lodge. That would defeat the whole thing. She had phoned Valerie for tips, and Val had said keep it simple and give them so much to drink they won't remember what they had to eat, which might have been fine for Val's people but was not much help here. Val said that she should warm the bread rolls and put cream in the soup, and to have mashed potatoes or roast potatoes because they couldn't let you down.

Chrissie said wasn't it great to be able to afford huge lumps of beef like this.

'Why didn't you ring up and we'd have sent it over to you?'

'I hoped if I came you might give me a nice cut and show me what direction to carve it in,' Clare said humbly.

'Carve it? Just cut a lump off for each person like you always do,' said Chrissie, helpful and sensitive butcher-sister who could be relied on to put your nerves at ease before an occasion.

Thursday was early closing day in the town twenty miles away. It was David's golf day, and it was the day of the dinner.

Clare thought the women's magazines would be proud of her and the way she said to David that he must bring Caroline back to the house whenever he liked, she would want to change for dinner. The others were coming about seven, so after they had a few drinks in the club . . .

'Won't we be in your way?'

'Not at all,' Clare trilled.

He kissed her goodbye on the nose and then kissed Liffey.

'Bones is creaking a lot, isn't he, I wonder is he in pain? The problem is he always seems to be smiling, you wouldn't know.'

'Oh, Bones has plenty of life in him.' She patted the dog's head. A promise is a promise and Bones wasn't going to be sent to sweet dreams while Clare was around.

Liffey deposited all her carrots and mashed potato on her best hand-smocked dress. Clare snatched it off and washed it. It might just be dry enough to put back on her again. That was the dress Molly had made such a fuss about. It was being worn in her honour. Then when she was cleaning the spoon, the beautiful silver spoon that Mr Kenny had given the baby, Bones thought it was a toy and galloped off with it.

He took it round the garden three times and then buried it in a flowerbed.

The cream was off, of all days in the year, and two of the table napkins had tears in them. In her haste rushing past the table she knocked over a jug of water so she had to put pillow cases under the corner and pray it would dry out in time.

Because Caroline would change in their bedroom Clare deliberately made it look a much more cosy and loving place than it actually was. She bunched the pillows right up close as if this was the way they normally slept, and she took out her black nighty, the one that actually looked awful on, but exotic if draped around the place. She put a bunch of flowers in the room, and a soft romantic lamp.

She had also tidied up the cupboards and drawers in case Caroline would poke around. Any shabby old shoes or things that were not meant to be seen were hidden firmly in the spare room, and she removed the bulb so that no light could be thrown on that confusion, should somebody open the door in error.

They all arrived at once.

David poured sherries and everyone said wasn't this all nice at least three times each.

Caroline looked glowing with health. Her hair looked shiny and smart. Clare had *hoped* it would have become matted and windblown. She said she'd simply *love* a quick wash, and came down in a commendably quick time wearing a long red wool skirt and white lace blouse.

'It was simply marvellous out there today,' she said. 'You really should learn, Clare.'

'Did somebody tell me you were taking lessons, Clare?' Josie asked.

Clare could have smashed her face. 'No no, but they may have seen me once with Angela up there, she's learning.'

'Oh yes.' Angela Dillon was a sore subject in Dillon's Hotel. There was great fear that Uncle Dick and the schoolteacher might well have lifted the entire golfing trade from the old hotel.

'James plays a lot in Dublin, in fact some think that he spends far too much time on the course,' Caroline said. *That* wasn't a tactful subject either. Martin's hand tightened round his glass at the mention of the perfidious James Nolan.

502

Clare decided the meal should be served.

Damn the magazines to the very blackest spot of hell.

The rolls had burned black in the oven. Black.

She sliced some of Nellie's soda bread and put it on a plate. Molly said that Nellie had one of the lightest hands with pastry and bread in the country.

'This bread is very nice too,' Mr Kenny said.

'This *is* Nellie's bread,' Clare said in despair.

The beef was tough; the mashed potatoes were dry; the sprouts were soft and the gravy was lumpy.

Clare could see a series of plates with food left and eventually had to admit that no one was having more and that knives and forks had been left together. Burning with embarrassment she cleared the table.

There was no cream for the chocolate pudding. It had been too late to go and get any more. She had cursed her mother and father for not having a phone, because they could have sent someone over with cream or even ice cream. She should have gone herself, she should have put Liffey into the back of the car and raced down, but at the time she had thought it was better to stay at her post, it seemed less flurried.

They waded through the pudding. Nobody had the cheese she had laid out so carefully with biscuits in lines.

She went to make coffee and discovered that the full coffee jar she had seen in the press was not full of coffee, it was the jar she used to keep cowrie shells in, until she found a place to display them.

She said she had to go to Liffey for a moment and crept out of the house in the dark to see could she find coffee in her mother-in-law's kitchen. It was Thursday, Nellie's evening off. She wouldn't be there. She fell over Bones and landed flat on her face. Bones barked joyfully and so loudly that Dr Power came out to see what was happening.

'My God, Molly,' he called, 'there's somebody in our kitchen!'

David was masterful. He picked up a golf club and insisted that his father stand back.

As Clare crept out of the Powers' kitchen with grazed

hands, a bruised forehead and a suspicion of a loosened tooth, Bones was baying at the moon with excitement.

'I'll kill you,' she said to the dog. 'You'll go for the chop and I won't lift a finger to help you.'

Suddenly she saw the entire party framed in the light of the Lodge waiting for her, and David advancing slowly with a golf club.

In the distance she heard the familiar sound of Liffey waking and starting a crying jag that was going to last two hours.

Angela laughed till she cried.

Clare *was* crying as she told the story.

'No I *can't* see the funny side. *Stop* all that laughing. I'm so bloody fed up. I made a *fool* of myself. I might as well have got up and danced on the table in my knickers. It was *dreadful*. They pitied me, all of them, even Josie.'

'It's your own fault,' Angela said. 'You were always the one who was great with the advice to Mary Catherine . . . tell them your father's a postman, see do they care. Why couldn't you have told them you had a coffee jar of cowrie shells?'

'Not on top of the burned rolls, the lumpy gravy, the tough meat. I bet Chrissie did it on purpose, gave me some old hindquarters of a donkey.'

'What about David?'

'He patted me down afterwards, he said first dinners are always a trial. *First!* First and last more likely. How was Mother Provincial?'

'Like a hamster, wrinkling her nose, pointed little teeth.'

'What did they talk about?'

'The decline in faith and morals. And we had egg sandwiches and tea, that was the feast.'

'I'd have loved it,' Clare said feelingly. 'Compared to what went on in my house last night it sounds like paradise.'

Gerry Doyle called in on a wet Thursday.

'I'm a bit busy, Gerry.'

'I can see that,' he said, looking at the open newspaper on the kitchen table.

'Well,' she said awkwardly.

'Well, it took some time. But it's happened.'

'What has?' Her heart was full of fear.

'David.' He stood there smiling.

Her hand went to her throat. 'What's happened to him?'

'I think he's found true love, Clare. In a caravan.'

'What?'

'Well, it's much too wet to play golf isn't it? Look at that, they'd be soaked through.' He had been sitting down uninvited, but when he had given her the news, he stood up.

'See you,' he said, and left.

David came home quite dry.

'Did you get a game or was it too wet?'

'No, we battled on, quite exhilarating you know in the wind and the rain.'

'I'm sure.'

'Horrible night for Caroline to have to drive all that way back,' he said.

'Isn't it. Should we have asked her to stay or anything do you think?'

'No, no, but I'll tell you she *is* thinking of getting a caravan here, just in case she wants to stay over. Makes a lot of sense, doesn't it?'

'Gerry Doyle is in a lot of trouble,' Clare's mother said.

'What way?'

'Well he has a big bill here for one thing, you know three months. All his groceries and cigarettes, it mounts up.'

'I'm sure it does.'

'Your father said I should ask him about it, what with my always getting on well with him.'

'And?'

'And he said he was a bit pushed. And Chrissie says he has a bill as long as your arm in Dwyers' too, and he can't

505

get credit in Costello's any more. He over-extended himself with that place, they don't get enough orders for that size of a set-up. They were fine when they had the little hut and the developing in the house. Dick says he'll have to sell up.'

'Gerry's a survivor.'

'That's what I've said always but when I asked him about his bill here and he said he was broke, I said it was all right, pay a little off it here and there to keep Tom happy . . . and he said I wasn't to be nice to him, he wasn't going out with a whimper, when he went it would be with a bang that would be heard all over the county. What can he have meant?'

'I'll take Liffey to Dublin in a week or two, show her the other Liffey, the river.'

'That's a good idea.'

'Will you go and have your dinner with your parents when I'm gone?'

'Yes, some of the time. I'll cook here a bit maybe if I feel up to it. Oh and Caroline will be in her caravan. I'll probably have a meal or two with her to settle her in.'

Gerry came again.

'I have pictures this time,' he said.

'What kind of pictures?' She was feeding Liffey and needed her full concentration.

'Can I have a cup of tea?'

'No, Gerry, you know I don't like you coming here.'

'Here, you're making an awful mess of that. I'll feed her. You put on the kettle.'

'Will you go then?'

He fed Liffey expertly, holding the spoon just long enough in her mouth for her to have to swallow what was on it.

Clare poured the tea. She had no sense of alarm. He looked vulnerable as he sat feeding Liffey and gurgling at her.

'Oh, the pictures. These ones.' He emptied an envelope

506

on the table. About a dozen black and white prints of David and Caroline making love on the cramped bed of a caravan.

She put her hand over her mouth and went to the sink. She vomited and retched.

He moved her away and turned on the tap. He cleaned the sink and gave her a glass of water.

'Drink that,' he said.

She threw it at him. It missed and shattered all over the floor. She was shaking.

Calmly he took a towel and wet it under the tap, he went up close and wiped her face, as you would wipe a child's face. She was powerless to stop him.

She poured herself another glass of water and drank it.

'What are you going to do?'

'Nothing,' she said.

'OK.' He put his hand on the door.

'Take these.' She gathered them up with a shaking hand.

'Sure,' he said.

She sat for a long time staring into space.

She told David she felt a sort of 'flu coming on, if he didn't mind she'd sleep downstairs.

He was concerned, and felt her forehead. She did seem a bit feverish.

They made up a bed for her. In the kitchen near the fire.

'It looks very cosy,' he said. 'Maybe we should move down here altogether.'

'Remember when we lived in Rathmines? It was so tiny, and the bed, the stove, the dining table were all on top of each other.'

'That's right,' he said, and sighed.

She got into bed and pulled up the sheets like an obedient child.

He kissed her forehead.

'David?'

'Yes?' He looked alarmed.

'Nothing, thanks for everything, sleep well.'

She heard him go upstairs, the lavatory flush, and eventually his shoes fall. He was in bed.

She saw the reflection of the bedroom light go off. He was asleep.

She got out of bed, wide awake. What on God's earth was she going to do?

She made a pot of coffee.

She sat up all night and only when she heard the bed creak did she get back into her own.

He tiptoed down and made a pot of tea.

He brought it to her bedside triumphantly.

'Who's a good husband?' he said.

'David's a good husband,' she said mechanically.

She looked very fluey, David thought as he went up to the big house. Funny that she hadn't a temperature – he had taken it automatically. But her eyes were bright, her forehead hot and she was white as a sheet. Or maybe it was just that he felt he could hardly look at her these days without guilt and confusion.

It was so easy to believe when he was with Caroline. Nobody would be hurt, nobody was going to make any demands, there would be no public scenes and at no time would Clare ever be humiliated. It would be discreet and it would be between them. Nobody would know. They would be the first lovers in the history of Castlebay who would get away with it.

Caroline was so relaxed about everything, she never demanded to know what he thought or what he felt. She wanted no promises, no reassurances and certainly no discussion of the future.

After a session with Clare about where they would be in ten years' time and did he really love her and would they ever have got married if it hadn't been for Liffey, it was like a warm bath to come to Caroline.

Caroline said that he must of course make love to Clare, why ever not? She wanted no stories about separate beds or lack of relations. David was taking nothing from what he and she had if he and Clare made love any more than

508

she was stealing anything from Clare by having him come to her in the caravan.

Sometimes he asked her what was going to happen. Would they have a great fight and hurt each other or would they just drift apart? She would laugh and say it was nonsensical to think of the future. It was very restful and it took all the guilt away.

Clare was still lying in her made-up kitchen bed when she heard David's car drive off on his rounds.

A minute later Gerry Doyle came in. 'Quite right too,' he said when he saw the bed.

'*Get out!*' she cried.

'Shush shush.'

'Gerry, I'm going to call Mrs Power. *Help!*'

He put his hand over her mouth gently, and his arm around her. Her thin body in the pink brushed-nylon nightdress with its long sleeves trembled. Her eyes were wild.

'What do you owe him? You saw what he's done to you. Clare?'

She wrenched herself free. And out of his grasp. On her way to the door she picked up the carving knife.

'Don't be silly.' He wasn't a bit afraid. 'Put it down, Clare, I won't touch you, put it down, you'll hurt yourself.'

She laid it down.

'I'll go now, I'll come back for you later.'

'Come back for me?'

'I think we should go away, you and I and Liffey, far away.'

'You're mad.'

'No, not at all. We leave the pictures on the table so they know why. And off we go.'

'I know you're in trouble, Gerry, I know you have money problems, could I lend you some or get you some or something?'

'We'll get plenty in time. You and I, we'll go to London maybe. I can work there, we'll have a home.'

'This is fantasy . . . you must stop.'

509

'You're not to use big words like that to me, those are for the Powers. I'll come back tonight.'

'No you mustn't, I'll tell David, I'll tell Dr Power, you can't.'

'You won't tell any of them, I know. You want to come away with me.'

'Stop, don't go, let me explain!'

'Make up your mind, one minute you're telling me to go, with a carving knife – the next you're calling me back.'

'Don't come back tonight. Don't. I won't be here. Or I'll have the Guards here and David and his father and everyone, you must understand now I do *not* want to come away with you, whatever David's done, I am going nowhere with you.'

'See you.'

He was gone.

She sat frightened, teeth chattering.

David phoned about six o'clock. His last call had left him near town, it made more sense to have a meal there than driving home through all this storm. How was her 'flu?

'David, can you *please* come home?'

'What is it?'

'In all the time we've been here I've never asked you to come home, I've never been a clinging person. Isn't that true?'

'Darling, of course it is, of course. But it's awkward now. I met Caroline, I just made arrangements to have a meal with her, as it happens.'

'You can have three hundred and sixty-five meals a year with Caroline if you just come home *tonight*.'

'I *am* coming home.'

'No, *now*. I'm frightened.'

'I'll make it an early meal,' he said. 'I'll be home then, and you can tell me what's worrying you.'

'I see,' she said, and hung up.

She left a note on the kitchen table which said, 'I feel very edgy and unwell tonight, so I've gone to the main house where there will be a lot of people to keep me company.'

That would do either for Gerry if he came, or for David.

At six-thirty she knocked on her mother-in-law's door.

'You don't have to knock, Clare,' Dr Power said. He was just about to listen to the news.

'Come on in and sit down.'

Molly was darning by the fire, they had finished their supper.

'I hope you don't mind. I've not been feeling well all day, and David's been delayed. He won't be back until about nine or ten. Do you mind if I stay here?'

They exchanged looks.

'Of course not,' Molly said.

'I think it's in bed you should be, David said you have a touch of 'flu.'

'It's not 'flu, it's just jitters, I have this awful sense of something going to happen.'

'Nonsense, it's the storm. You're even nearer the sea than we are. Don't give in to it, child. Stay with us for a bit, then I'll walk back and tuck you up. And tuck her ladyship up too.' Liffey chortled in the basket. She could only make it stretch to an hour and a half. By eight o'clock she was back in the Lodge.

Dr Power glanced at the note. 'Well, you can tear that up now, he'll find you asleep in bed when he gets back.'

He fussed and filled a hot-water bottle for her, then he went up the stairs. She was ashamed that she hadn't made the bed since last night, since David had slept in it.

Dr Power didn't make any comment.

As soon as he was gone she locked the door and put a chair against it, then she made sure the windows were fastened.

She would stay up by the fire. David could only be an hour, couldn't he? There was no way Gerry could get in.

There was a movement behind her. And there he was, in his leather jacket, smiling at her easily.

'Oh my God.'

'I was in the dining room. It's all right, it's all right.'

'You don't *understand*. You've read it all *wrong*. I'm *not* coming away with you.'

'You've always wanted me, we're the same type, Clare, I said that to you years ago. We're greedy and we want everything. Well we're going to have it. David's different, he's gentler, born into a gentle life.'

'If I did anything in my whole life that would make you think I was in love with you I swear I can't remember.'

She wasn't frightened, now, that he'd hurt her. She just couldn't bear the great fight when David came in, the producing of the pictures – and David had always thought that she liked Gerry. It was so unjust, so terribly unjust. David was the one who was unfaithful, and here was she locked into the house with Gerry Doyle.

'Will you pack your things? I have the car up the lane.'

'You are talking like a madman. There's no question of it.' Gentler, now. 'I've admired you and liked you, like everyone, but that's all.'

'Very well.'

'What?'

'You know what you are saying. I presume you mean it.'

'I do.'

He went to the door, her body was relaxing by the moment with relief.

'You'll be sorry of course. Sorry you didn't come with me tonight. You'll always be sorry. You'll wake in the bed beside your cheating husband, or in a bed downstairs, and you'll be sorry you didn't leave tonight with me.'

'No, Gerry. I won't. We'll always be able to talk you and I . . . always.'

'No,' he said.

She waited, when he was gone, hoping to hear the sound of the van starting up in the lane. There was no sound. Or the crashing of the sea and the wind drowned it if there was.

David cursed himself for having rung home. It was just that he had wanted to know how her 'flu was. *Now* look

512

what he had brought on himself. This was exactly what he knew would happen despite all Caroline's fine words. Now he was pleasing neither of them. Clare would be fretting at home over whatever was worrying her, and Caroline would be annoyed that he had to leave early, and slightly scornful. She had been like that once or twice recently. More or less taunting him, saying, *of course* he must go home to *poor Clare* if she needed him. Caroline had said more than once that there were no chains around his legs tying him to *her* apron strings. It had been very humiliating and oddly he had also felt like defending Clare. He would feel that way tonight too. The girl had 'flu, he would say, and how defensive and idiotic it would sound.

He parked his car in the little yard of the small house that Caroline rented. He had been looking forward to the evening. Perhaps he would say nothing about his promise to be home early, perhaps he could ring and say that something had happened . . .

Caroline was not in the kitchen. He had let himself in the back door. A saucepan with water was hissing on the back burner of the gas stove. He reached out automatically and pulled it away. The bottom had just begun to burn.

'Caroline,' he called. There was no answer.

That was odd. She must be at home. She still had the city habit of locking the doors when she went out.

'Caroline,' he called again. Perhaps she was in the bathroom upstairs. He didn't want her to get a fright if she came out and saw him unexpectedly. 'I'm here,' he called again.

There was a sound from upstairs.

'Are you all right,' he called, alarmed suddenly and taking the stairs two by two.

Caroline was sitting grey-faced on the bed. Both of her hands were held to her mouth.

'What is it?' Could she have been attacked? Raped even? Why didn't she speak?

'Oh my God, my God,' she said over and over.

David told himself that he was trained to deal with

513

people in shock, but it was no use, he had forgotten what to do if he had ever known. He knelt down opposite Caroline. He stroked her bent head, he unclenched her hands, he tried to get her to look into his eyes. That was the hardest bit. She wouldn't meet his glance.

'Tell me, darling Caroline, tell me.'

'I can't.'

'Did anyone hurt you, touch you?'

She shook her head.

'Please, please, I have to help you. Have you had bad news from home? Your father, mother?'

'No, nothing like that.'

'Did you see something, an accident, what is it Caroline? Tell me and I'll help you.' He went on stroking her hair and looking up as she sat on the bed, her face stricken and her eyes wild.

'David,' she said.

'Has it anything to do with me?'

'He's mad, he's mad enough for a mad home, to be locked away for ever . . .'

'Who? Who are you talking about? *Tell* me.'

'Gerry Doyle.'

'What has he done now?' David stood up in impatience.

He followed Caroline's glance to the dressing table and saw what had made her the way she was.

One by one he looked at the dozen pictures, bile rising in his throat at what had been private turning into this. 'It wasn't like that,' he said eventually. 'It was special. You know.'

That cheered her somehow, she reached out a cold hand for his.

'Why did he do this?' David looked through the pictures once more and turned them face down on the dressing table.

'Because he's mad,' Caroline said simply.

David pulled the bedroom chair up beside her and held her hands. 'Did he give them to you?' he asked gently.

'No, they were here when I came home.'

'Did he leave a note or anything?'

514

Caroline reached down and picked up a piece of paper, it had *Doyle's Photographics* on it. In small writing it said:

Delivery three sets of pictures only.
a) Miss Caroline Nolan.
b) Doctor David Power. The surgery, Castlebay.
c) Mrs Clare Power. The Lodge, Castlebay.

'My God.' David stood up. 'That's what Clare wanted. That's why she rang.'

'She's seen those?' Caroline's hand was to her mouth again.

'I don't know. She rang me, very hysterical, I mean I rang her to say I was coming here, she said she wanted me home. I said I'd be home fairly early.'

'She couldn't have, she *couldn't* have seen these?'

'No.' David was slowly going over the conversation. 'No, she couldn't have. She said I could have dinner with you three hundred and sixty-five days a year or something . . .'

'What?'

'She said I *must* come home tonight, I said I was meeting you for dinner, she said you can have dinner every other night of the year but please come back now.'

They looked at each other wildly.

'He couldn't have given them to her, she wouldn't say that if she'd seen them.'

'But why did she want me home?'

'Do you want to go back?' She sounded frightened.

'I can't leave you.'

'But suppose, just suppose he *has*.'

'He couldn't have. I'd have known by her voice.' David stood up and paced the room. 'I'll ring her, that's what I'll do.'

He telephoned the Lodge, there was no reply. They looked at each other: was that good or bad?

'She might have gone in to your mother and father,' Caroline suggested.

'No, however bad she felt she wouldn't do that.' He looked tormented.

515

'Where could he have been, just at the window of the caravan?' she glanced over at the dressing table.

'That's what he must have done. But why? I mean is it for money? His business is meant to be in a bad way, but he couldn't expect us to pay him.'

'We would, wouldn't we?' Caroline said simply.

'Yes I suppose we would. But he doesn't *ask* for money. Do you think it's because he disapproves, because he wants you and he's jealous?'

She shook her head. 'I don't think that would explain it.'

'But *why*? Why would someone do that, it's so perverted. To peer through a window . . . my God. He must be obsessed with you, it's the only explanation, he can't have you himself so he does what he can to ruin the chances of anyone else having you.'

'Oh, he's *had me* himself, many, many times. That's not likely to be the reason. He's actually lost his mind and become a lunatic.'

She had her head in both hands and didn't see the look of shock and pain on David's face. She went on talking.

'The trouble is we can't really tell the Guards or they'll want to know why, but he should be locked up, shouldn't he?' She looked up for confirmation.

'He didn't sleep with you,' David said.

'David, that's neither here nor there. You sleep with Clare, do I mind that, did I ever mind it? Once?' Her voice was getting shrill and hysterical. 'Christ, this isn't the time to do the Victorian Husband bit, everyone in the county has been with Gerry Doyle in some form or another, the point is what do we do?'

She looked young and frightened and alone.

'I know this is the most unhelpful thing in the world, but I think I should go back to Castlebay. Under the circumstances I don't think you should come with me . . .'

'No.'

'I'll ring you when I get there, I'll ring to know are you all right.'

'Sure.'

516

'I'll come to see you first thing tomorrow morning, when we're calmer, we'll decide what to do.'

'Great.'

'Is there anyone, have you any friends, anyone who could come in, or someone you could go to?' He looked around, willing himself to find her some support, hating to leave her.

'No.'

He swallowed and couldn't speak.

She turned her head towards the dressing table and the pictures that were turned upside down.

The wind and rain lashed the car, the road was strewn with bits of branches.

A steady drumming beat in David's heart. May Clare be all right, may Clare be all right. May he not have shown her the pictures, may he not have shown her the pictures . .

Clare stood at the window for a long time. She hadn't heard the car starting up. Perhaps he would come back again. But then he had been very final when he had left.

Please God he had been lying when he said he showed the pictures to David, and to Caroline. Please may David not know about them. It made everything so definite if he knew, if he had seen. She would deny she had ever seen them if David asked her. She couldn't bear to hold any discussion based on what she had seen. It didn't make her retch now, it made her sad. But she had known for months, hadn't she? All Gerry Doyle had done was to make her admit it to herself.

Please may Gerry go away from Castlebay, for ever and ever. Please, please.

Gerry closed the door gently behind him. He had never slammed a door in his life. He would like to have taken it from its hinges.

Clare had looked at him as if he were mad. As if *he* were mad! It was Clare who was mad. To have hoped that

517

she would be accepted in that family for one thing, to have looked at the evidence in black and white and *then* to decide to stay . . . That wasn't the Clare O'Brien he used to know, the Clare he had the plans for. He had been so *forgiving* towards her, so *understanding*. He had said so little when she behaved like a common *tramp* and got into trouble with the boy from the big house. No accusations had come from him. And there she stood tonight, *frightened* of him and *doubting* him.

He hit violently at some gorse that jutted out of the hedge between the Lodge and the cliff. He remembered telling a hundred girls, maybe more, about the old saying, 'When the gorse is out of bloom then the kissing's out of fashion.' They had always been surprised that gorse seemed to bloom all year round, and Gerry would laugh. He hit again and scraped his hand on the prickly branches.

How dare Clare talk to him in that frightened, teeth-chattering way? How *dare* she look up at him as if she were afraid he might strike her? She had more to fear from her big unfaithful husband than from him . . . from Gerry, who had always wanted her, *waited* for her.

He moved angrily to the cliff top and looked out at the sea.

Everything had gone now. *Everything*. Not just the business, he had seen that coming for many a month, but Clare's face tonight . . . He had not foreseen that. She was frightened of him as if he were a stranger who would do her harm, not her soul's other half. Her one true friend and love who would make a home for her and her baby, and accuse her of nothing except bad luck, as he had had.

His breath came in short bursts.

She *would not* do this to him . . . She *would not* back out now . . . Now, after *everything* . . . After all he had planned . . .

Clare! It was too much to take, too much for her to do now at this stage.

She would regret it for the rest of her life.

There would be no drive to England in the van tonight for her.

There would be no new life for her.

What did she mean by throwing back all he offered her?

She would want him in a little while, when it was too late. When he had gone. When nobody knew where he was. She would stand on the cliff and wish she had left with him tonight.

He found that he was trembling, shaking with anger. He had never known such a sensation – it was as if a great wind had taken hold of him and borne him up in the air . . .

He was shaking too much to drive. He would walk on the beach. It would clear his head.

He slipped and climbed down the path. The beach looked dark and dangerous, but the bigger waves were dying down; the tide must be going out now. It was on the turn anyway. He walked, his head wet from the salt spray and the rain; but he didn't care.

He had really blown it now.

The business was a shambles. He couldn't meet even one of the bills that were piled neatly on the desk under a paperweight for whoever would have to go through them. He hoped it wouldn't be Fiona but he couldn't think who else it might be. When the staff couldn't get in tomorrow, there would be a hue and cry but he had left no note to say that he was going to England. There would be no Guards looking for him for bounced cheques. He could always get by on credit; that's what he had always done.

There were very few lights up in Castlebay. He looked up at the outlines of the houses clustered together and the dark spire of the church. He would never look at them again from here, or at all. Once he got to London it would be a new life. It would be *exciting*. It would not be exciting to stay to see their sympathy, to work for someone else, to see Clare, lovely, *lovely* Clare put up with that *sod*. He was *glad* he had done it. He was near the rock pools. Since he was a child he had loved walking over them, balancing, teetering on the edge. It was only inches of water if you did trip over and fall in. Tonight the waves were crashing over them . . . but still, it was a temptation.

He walked around them, playing games with himself, his feet and legs wet to the knee. He cried out with hysterical excitement. It was ludicrous, but it was exciting.

The wave knocked him down and he cut his cheek on the jagged rock.

It wasn't funny any more. Here came another one. Then the drag, he felt his leg being scraped across the rocks. Desperately he reached out with his hands.

But the drag was too great.

When the third wave had reared up at him, he knew he was going to drown or be battered to death on the rock pools where he had played since he was old enough to walk.

'Clare.' He rattled the door. It was locked.

'Clare? Are you all right?' She came to the door pale but calm.

He reached out his arms for her but she stepped out of his way.

'I'm very sorry. I was frightened. It's the storm, I'm all right now. I'm sorry I called you home.' She spoke like a stranger.

'I rang, I rang twice about seven, and again at a quarter to eight.'

'I was in your parents' house.'

'Are you all right?'

'Yes I am now, I think. But I don't feel like talking. Do you want tea or food? Were you able to have your dinner?'

'No, no it doesn't matter.' He wasn't concentrating.

'Was the road bad?' Again like a person making conversation.

'Yes, branches, and in one place a tree down, you'd have to drive right up on the ditch to get past.'

'Imagine.'

'Clare.'

'You know I said I'd like to go to Dublin for a few days and you said that would be fine, because you could get looked after . . .?'

'Yes?' His voice was hollow.

'I'd like to go very soon. Tomorrow maybe.'

'You're not all that well, wait a few days.'

'I don't want to wait.'

'It's silly to take Liffey off the whole way across the country when you're not well.'

'It's sillier to stay here on my own hour after hour listening to the sea when I'm not well.'

'You don't have to be on your own here.'

'No. David, will you do me a great favour? Will you not make a scene? I've had as much drama as I can take, and I'm sure you've had a bad day too. But I want to go up to Angela and Dick tonight. Please.'

She must know.

He must have shown her the pictures. David's heart was like a stone.

'Why? What brought this on?'

'I think if I stayed here tonight it might be bad for us. We might say things that would hurt each other.'

He tried a little laugh. 'Heavens, isn't that very fanciful?'

'No,' she said. 'It's not.'

'Do you want to take Liffey with you?'

'Please.'

'I could try to explain . . .' he began.

'And so could I. But we know too well how easily people say things that are unforgivable when they're hurt or annoyed. We've done very little hurting and wounding. Don't let's risk it tonight.'

'Have you packed?' he asked.

'Yes, just things for tonight. I'll come back tomorrow when you've gone out and I'll sort out what we'll need in Dublin.'

'I'm saying yes, not because I'm weak but because I think you're very sure what you want, and I'm not, so we should go along with the one who is sure.'

He grinned at her and she almost took a step towards him.

'Thank you,' she said formally.

'Is Angela expecting you?'

521

'Yes.'

'Well.' His shoulders drooped.

'She doesn't ask, you know Angela, she doesn't ever ask.'

'I wasn't thinking of that.'

'It's better.'

'I suppose it is.'

So many times they had wished Liffey would sleep rather than struggle and chatter and try to escape. Tonight when they could have done with a bit of distraction she lay in Clare's arms breathing evenly, her long eyelashes making shadows on her cheeks.

David held his daughter tight in his arms and two tears came down his face. 'I'm sorry, Liffey,' he said.

'Why are you sorry?' Clare said gently. 'I have much more to apologize to her for. But it's only like talking to ourselves until she can understand.'

'Goodbye, Clare.'

'Goodbye, David. For a while.'

They didn't touch.

Angela had seen the car drawing up outside the cottage; she had sent Dick scurrying off to bed in case Clare wanted to talk.

Clare stood with Liffey in her arms and watched the car turning and going back down the golf-course road. She gave a little wave but David was looking straight in front of him and didn't see.

'Come in,' Angela said.

'It's very hard to explain.'

'Most things are quite incapable of being explained. I've always thought that,' said Angela.

She showed Clare her bed and made a cup of tea from a kettle which had been boiling in readiness.

'That's to take to bed on your own,' she said. Clare blinked her gratitude at the teacher who knew by magic when people wanted to talk and when there was nothing left to say.

* * *

Jim O'Brien ran back into the shop looking frightened.

'Dad, Dad, where are you, where are you?'

'Where would I be but getting out of my bed?' Tom O'Brien grumbled.

'Dad, come here will you.'

The boy looked frightened.

'Dad, come out with me . . . now, come quickly.'

Tom O'Brien pulled his coat over his pyjama top. He had his day trousers on and his shoes and socks, he had been dressing on the side of the bed when he heard the shouts.

They ran on to the top of the cliff and Jim pointed down on the beach. 'I think it's a person, Dad, it's a body.'

There was wind and spray. Tom O'Brien took off his glasses and wiped them. 'It's a shape, but it couldn't be a body, who'd be in the water in this weather?'

'It is, Dad. It *is*. I'm going down, will you get the Guards and Dr Power?'

Jim O'Brien, almost totally deaf, didn't hear his father warning him to take care. He started down the steps to the big treacherous beach at Castlebay where somebody drowned nearly every summer but where they had never seen a body washed in by a winter tide.

People seemed to know without being told. They came out of their houses and began to run down the main street. The murmur became louder, and almost without knowing they were doing it they started to check where their own families were. It was still just a figure, face down in the water. They didn't know for sure whether it was a man or a woman.

'Perhaps it's a sailor from a ship,' they said. But they knew it wasn't anyone who had gone overboard. No nice anonymous death of someone they didn't know. No informing the authorities and saying a few prayers for the deceased Unknown Sailor. This was someone from Castlebay.

They stood in silent groups on the cliff top and watched the first people getting to the water's edge; the boy who had first seen the waves leaving something frightening on the shore; other men too; people from the shops nearby and young men who were quick to run down the path. Then they saw the figures coming down the other path near the doctor's house, kneeling by the body in case, just in case, there was something in a black bag that could bring it back to life.

By the time Father O'Dwyer arrived with his soutane flapping in the wind the murmur had turned into a unified sound. The people of Castlebay were saying a decade of the rosary for the repose of the soul which had left the body that lay face down on their beach.

David had only had two hours' sleep when he heard the shouting. He thought it was still part of his dream, but it was real. He sat up in bed – Clare wasn't there. He remembered the scene last night, taking her up to Angela's house, and he remembered coming back and taking the house apart looking for any trace of the photographs. He knew Clare hadn't taken them with her – he had looked in her small bag. She had only some things for the baby and a nightdress for herself.

He had put off ringing Caroline until it was too late to ring her. Then he told himself it would be cruel to wake her when he had nothing helpful to say.

He had been dreaming that people were coming after him, waving papers or big envelopes at him, all running down Church Street calling at him in anger. In his dream he didn't know why they were so against him but he was frightened and trying to run away.

Then he realized the shouts were real. It was Bumper Byrne's voice and Mogsy's, and then his father's.

'Come quickly, there's someone on the beach, there's been a drowning.'

His heart nearly burst in fear.

He ran down the stairs in his crumpled shirt and trousers, he hadn't undressed last night.

He caught the unfortunate Mogsy Byrne who was at the doorway by his arms. 'Who is it? God damn you who *is* it?'

'I don't know . . . I don't. I don't . . .' Mogsy was stammering at the wild-eyed look of David Power who was always so calm and capable.

'*Tell* me,' David roared at him. 'Tell me or I'll break your neck.'

'He's got his face down, David,' Mogsy managed to get out. 'I left the cliff before they knew, they said to come quickly.'

He had said 'he'. It was a man, it was a man thank God, it was a man. Oh God, thank you for letting it be a man.

David's eyes had cleared. He grabbed a coat and ran to the surgery for his bag, his father was already there.

'Don't come down the steps. Please, Dad. I'll do it. Come down the other way.'

'I've been coming down those steps to take bodies out of the water since before you were born.'

'Who is it, is he dead?'

'They don't know, they think it's Gerry Doyle.'

David put out his hand to steady himself on a desk. Just beside a big brown envelope printed with the words Doyle's Photographics.

His father was already out of the surgery and heading towards the cliff. David steadied himself, put the envelope in a drawer of his own things, down at the bottom of it. And with shaking legs he followed his father to the cliff path.

They saw the group around the body and realized even at this distance that their work would not be needed. Father O'Dwyer had been sent for, he was the only one who might be any help to that body which lay spreadeagled on the beach. Even through the wind and rain and from far away David knew it was Gerry Doyle's lifeless body. He held his arm out to steady his father.

'Young fool,' Dr Power said. 'Bloody young lunatic, his whole life before him. What did he want to do that for? Bloody criminal fool to throw away the one life God gave him.'

David's heart was like stone when they turned the body over and he saw all the lacerations and tears down the side

525

of the face of Gerry Doyle. As if in deference to his father he stood back and let the older man pronounce what everyone knew, that life was extinct.

'Where's Clare, will the pair of you come in and have breakfast with us?'

'She's not here, Dad, she spent the night up at Angela Dillon's.'

'She *what*?'

'Dad, please. You asked me where she was, I told you.'

'Yes, yes you did. Well, will you come in and have a bit of breakfast? You could do with one after all that.'

'No. No thanks, I'll make a cup of tea, that's all I want.'

'And has my grandchild gone to live up with Mr and Mrs Dillon or am I not to ask about that either?'

There was a bit of a smile on his face to take the harm out of the question. But it didn't hide the worry.

'It was only last night, Dad. It'll sort itself out.'

'Clare has some kind of 'flu, she was shivery and very jumpy last night, I'm not interfering, I'm just telling you.'

'Did she say what was wrong?'

'That she was frightened, she had a cup of tea with us, I brought her back. You weren't home.'

'Yes.' Dr Power narrowed his eyes. 'Lord God, is that Gerry's van parked in the lane over there? It *is*. What on earth is it doing up here? Lord have mercy on him, poor fool. And he could be one of the nicest fellows you'd ever talk to.'

Clare slept, to her great surprise. She slept well in the strange white bed with its clean hard sheets and its hot-water bottle. Liffey slept in a cot. Clare had been surprised when Angela said there was a cot, she had forgotten that Angela kept summer visitors, and had thought it wise to invest in two cots years ago when her mother was still alive.

Liffey too had slept. Maybe it was being away from the roar and crash of the sea, or from all the anxiety.

Clare only woke because Angela had come in with a cup

of tea. To her surprise, Angela had drawn up a chair beside the bed and sat down. Surely she wasn't going to give a lecture or want a heart to heart chat at this time in the morning.

Certainly Angela's face looked drawn and strained.

Clare thanked her for the tea and waited.

'Take a big sip.'

This was different, there was bad news of some kind. She put down the cup and looked almost on reflex at Liffey as if to make sure that she was all right. 'What is it?'

'There's been an accident. Gerry Doyle was drowned. They've just carried his body up from the beach.'

Total silence. Only the sounds from Liffey's cot where she played happily with the red satin rabbit whose ears had been torn off long ago.

'Clare?'

'He's dead. Is he dead?'

'Yes, it doesn't seem possible. Gerry of all people. There was no one as full of life.'

Angela broke off as she looked at Clare's face. It was expressionless. She just sat in the white bed with her long hair tied loosely behind her pale face, staring straight ahead of her. Her hands were clasped around her knees.

It wasn't natural to react like that. Angela was alarmed.

Clare *had* been friendly with Gerry of course, very friendly maybe. Perhaps even now when Clare's marriage seemed to be going so disastrously wrong, Gerry had been on hand to give consolation. Could that be the explanation of this sense of shock and disbelief? Angela reached out her hand, hoping that if she patted Clare's arm or did something warm the girl might come out of this trance.

She was totally unprepared for Clare to throw herself into Angela's arms, sobbing and shaking. And the only words she could distinguish over and over were, 'He's really dead, thank God, thank God.'

They said it was accidental death, that had to be said, otherwise he couldn't be buried in consecrated ground.

And things were bad enough for the poor Doyles without that.

They said he must have been out for a walk and slipped, his face and side had been very lacerated so he could have been walking on the rock pools, everyone knew that Gerry Doyle loved to balance there. That's what they said but nobody believed it, not for a moment. They knew it was suicide.

It had to be suicide, his business was in ruins, it was a matter of weeks before it would have been taken from him, there was a farmer out in the country who had been making very open threats to come after Gerry on account of the farmer's daughter being pregnant and Gerry Doyle taking no interest in this state of affairs. Fiona Conway, pregnant and heartbroken, told how he had said he wouldn't be in Castlebay for much longer, but she had thought he meant he was going to England. Mary Doyle his mother said that only two days previously he had sent her £20 in an envelope with no explanation, just the words 'From Gerry'. Agnes O'Brien said that she had been saying for months that the boy was in trouble of some kind but nobody had ever listened to her. Josie Dillon said he had cashed two cheques at the hotel which had bounced but they had kept it quiet, and Gerry had thanked her and said when he went to another land and made his fortune he would think of her. She had thought he was going to emigrate, *how* could anyone have thought he would do something like this?

As quickly as they could the formalities were organized and the body was released for burial.

Gerry Doyle would be laid to rest after ten o'clock Mass on Thursday, Father O'Dwyer announced from the pulpit, and blew his nose loudly because he still couldn't take it in.

David went through his work automatically, everywhere he went they talked about the tragedy. A woman with chest pains pointed to the pictures on the walls, framed photographs of the First Communions and Confirmations.

He was a lovely boy, always a laugh, never took anything too seriously. In the next house the old man who had hardening of the arteries was more interested in what could have happened to poor young Doyle than he was about his own imminent departure to the county home which David was trying to introduce.

'He was practically born in the water that young lad, which is unusual in these parts, half of Castlebay never takes to the sea at all, but the young Doyle fellow, he swam like a fish.'

In the room of a ten-year-old girl with jaundice they talked as much of Gerry Doyle as of the patient. He told them not to be worried by the colour of her urine, it was quite natural that it would turn the colour of port wine. They nodded and said that they had heard Gerry Doyle's business was in a bad way but surely he wouldn't drown himself over a thing like that? There had to be more to it than that.

'If people drowned themselves when their businesses went wrong, wouldn't the sea be full of bodies?' asked the child's father.

David agreed absently and looked at the little girl's eyes. They were yellow and he told her that her skin would go a little bit yellow like a Chinese.

'Are the Chinese yellow?' the girl asked. 'Really yellow?'

'Come to think of it they're not, any I saw aren't yellow at all.'

'Have you *seen* a Chinese?' The girl was very excited.

'In Dublin, yes, there were Chinese students at University and there was a Chinese restaurant we went to.'

She could have talked to him for ever about it. He wondered would Liffey want to know things like that too. His heart sank again when he thought of Liffey. And Clare.

The day ended somehow and he went back to the surgery. Quickly David retrieved the envelope and brought it back to the Lodge. He saw his mother pretending not to look through the curtains at him, but he went on as if he hadn't seen.

The kitchen was tidy. He looked around hopefully for a note. Clare had been in during the day, he could see that. The dishes and cups he had left after his breakfast were washed up and put away. He noticed that she had done some shopping: a packet of tea, a pound of butter, a loaf of bread and some sliced rashers of bacon were placed on the table near the range. The bed upstairs was made and although some of her clothes were hanging in the wardrobe she must have taken others. Most of Liffey's things seemed to have gone, and one of their two suitcases had disappeared. He looked around to see if she had taken all her books. It would be good in a way if she had, that would mean she had gone through with her plan of going to Dublin for a while.

Please may she have gone to Dublin. Let her not be here for the funeral. Please.

He sat down in the kitchen, having locked the door first, and he took out the pictures. He looked at them again. Exactly the same as he had seen last night at Caroline's. Last night? Is that all it was? There was the same list in the small handwriting naming the three people to whom they were being sent. He must have given them to Clare. He must have come to this house, that's why his car was there, his big ugly van with the name of the business, parked in the lane beside their house. David's father had phoned the Guards to report it being there, they had come to collect it but it had told them nothing. But it told David everything, he must have called on Clare. That was what had frightened her so much, that was why she had wanted him to come home. But had he come in and spoken to her, shown the pictures to her personally? Or had he just pushed them through the door and said he would be back?

David opened the front of the range and one by one he put them in. There was nothing exciting about these pictures taken through a caravan window. They were not the kind of pictures that would do anything except destroy the three people they were sent to. That was what Gerry Doyle had done before he destroyed himself.

Why? David allowed his brain to start on that again. All

day he had pushed the thought out of sight while he attended to his work. But now as the flames burned up the record of his time with Caroline, time that he had convinced himself was not evil because nobody was losing and nobody was being hurt . . . he wondered again why Gerry had bothered. It couldn't have been blackmail. Caroline and David didn't have the kind of money it turned out that was needed by Doyle's Photographics, they would only have been able to pay a few pounds a week at the very most. He didn't hate David, in fact they always got on very well when they were children, and of late, well David had been a bit scathing about how easily women fell for Gerry but he would never have known that. Or if he had, he couldn't have cared enough to hound David in this way.

David had assumed that it must have been Caroline, but she had been adamant, she had said with an unattractive honesty that had revolted him that she was Gerry Doyle's for the asking, and had been – and, no doubt, would be again – so it could not have been unrequited passion that made him take the pictures.

What did that leave?

It only left Clare.

Clare.

He remembered the time he had come across them kissing on the bench over the beach, and how annoyed he had been. He remembered Clare running up from the National Library back to her hostel to see if Gerry Doyle had rung. He remembered the easy way Gerry Doyle danced with Clare in the ballroom with the glittery revolving light sparkling over them as they smiled at each other.

It was Gerry Doyle she had asked to get her post office savings book that time. Then, only weeks ago, he remembered Gerry complaining that Clare wouldn't let him come and photograph Liffey. 'She's afraid that if I take the picture, I somehow steal the child,' he had laughed. And Clare had said nothing.

The photographs were all burned. He poked around and the ashes were gone, mixed into the other ashes of the range. He closed the little gate and looked around. The clock was ticking and below the sea was crashing. Those were the only sounds. Those were the sounds that gifted bright Clare O'Brien heard all day, and all evening. That was the life he had given her.

She was too smart now for Chrissie and her mother to feel easy with her. She wasn't smart enough for her mother-in-law to make her welcome. And Gerry Doyle had loved her and wanted her to come away. He had taken the pictures to prove that there was nothing to keep her any more. He had wanted Liffey as well, she must have sensed that at the time he wanted to photograph the child.

Had he come to the house and asked her to go away?

Did he drown himself because she wouldn't go.

After all, as the father of that sick child had said this afternoon, if everyone whose business was in a bad way swam out to sea then the beach would be littered with bodies. Gerry Doyle didn't kill himself over cheques that bounced and bills that would not be paid. But if he was prepared to go to such lengths and take such photographs to incriminate her husband then he really must have wanted Clare, and wanted her enough to end his life if she wouldn't come with him.

The clock ticked on and the waves crashed on. He walked around the small house restlessly. There was no sign of Clare in this house. No pictures she had chosen on the wall. No books. There were some in the spare room but they had always looked as if they were in transit, not as if they had come to stay. On the window sill was a cookery book and inside in Clare's big bold writing were the instructions for the dinner party that had been such a disaster. That was the only evidence that this woman had lived here.

David Power put his head in his hands at the kitchen table and cried.

For *all* that had happened.

Tuesday evening. It was only twenty-four hours ago that he had come to the house sure that she would pack her things and leave in his van. Would he have killed them all? Would he have driven Liffey and Clare into the sea? Clare didn't know. He *might* have been sane, and really meant them to go to England as he said. But that in itself wasn't sane. She had been over it a thousand times, there was no way she had led him on. A few kisses years ago, a few dances holding him close. But Gerry Doyle had that and much much more from every girl he met. He couldn't have seen it as some kind of attraction or involvement. So, he knew that she wasn't very happy with David, that her life had not turned out to be the dream she once thought . . . but still.

Angela and Dick had been wonderful, but to say that, to think that was just to let the record go into a groove where it said the same thing over and over. They had always been wonderful. For as long as she could remember.

'Take the car,' Dick had said. 'I don't need it just now. If you want to go and collect anything.'

She took his car, and went back to the Lodge, she knew that both Molly and Nellie were looking out of different windows trying to see what she was up to. She didn't care. She didn't even know what she was up to herself.

Methodically she went through the house tidying it for David, she made the bed and put all the washing together in a pillowcase, none of her own things, only his. She left the place so that it wouldn't offend anyone if Molly and Nellie came in to look after poor David. She even cleaned out a particularly grubby corner of the food press she had been meaning to do for ages, and lined it with fresh paper.

She made a big rubbish bag out of one of the pillowcases, and into that she threw all the torn stockings, almost-empty marmalade jars. She sat in the unusually tidy kitchen for fifteen minutes trying to think of something to say to David in a note, and then decided there was nothing to say.

He had left her no note, after all. He had been here all night, and then they said he had been called down to the beach when Gerry had been found. Perhaps there had been no time.

With her head in her hands she sat there. Could Gerry

533

really have sent those pictures to David? Could he have left them in the van? No, the Guards had said there was nothing in the van, Angela had told her that, no photographic things even. It had been empty as if he had been clearing out.

Suppose Gerry had dropped the pictures into the surgery. Suppose Dr Power had opened them. Her heart gave a jump thinking of that nice old man seeing such indecent evidence of his son's adultery with a family friend. Then she hardened her feelings. Why should she care now? The pictures were not of Clare. She had been here minding the child and the house while all this was going on. She was not going to let herself feel sympathetic when she was the one who deserved a great great deal of sympathy.

She stood up, arranged the things she had bought for his supper where he could see them, and then loaded the car with the suitcase she had packed. She put the pillowcase of rubbish in the back, she shook more anthracite into the range, and pulled the door behind her.

'I won't stay here for ever,' Clare said to Angela.

'You haven't been here two days yet, stop being so dramatic. Aren't you company for us?'

'Not really. Not at the moment.'

Liffey asked to get up on Clare's lap and then she wanted to get down again. She waddled over to Angela with the same request.

'It's a pity Gerry didn't see Fiona's child born.'

'What?'

'Fiona's having a child any time now, you know that.'

'Oh of course, I was thinking of . . . Why do you say that?'

'He loved children. He was very good with them too. He often talked about Liffey here. Did you know that?'

'No.' Clare shivered.

Angela decided to change the subject. 'I was talking to Fiona on my way back from school, I went down Church Street. She was going in to Doyle's Photographics to sort things out . . . Clare? What is it?'

'Oh my God, my God I forgot that entirely. Can I take the car again Angela, please, five minutes.'

'Of course you can but what . . .'

Clare was out the door and into the front seat. The keys were always left in the ignition. Dick Dillon looked out the window upstairs to know who was driving his car off crashing the gears like that.

Fiona wore a grey smock with a big white collar attached to it. She hadn't any mourning clothes in maternity wear. They probably didn't make them, Clare thought.

Fiona was sorting through the brown envelopes with their codes and dates.

'I'm very sorry,' Clare said.

'I know.' Fiona went on sorting. 'It sort of helps to do this, it makes things more normal in a way.'

'Yes.'

There was a silence.

Clare had acted on such an impulse when she remembered the photographs that she hadn't paused to think how she would ask for them. Now she was here and she must speak. She couldn't let anyone discover them, nobody should open an envelope and see what she had seen on Sunday night. Nobody should be allowed to look at what she had to look at.

'Fiona?' she began hesitantly.

The perfect oval face, pale with dark circles under the big dark eyes, looked at her inquiringly.

Clare swallowed and began to speak. 'Do you know the way just when you think there's no way out of something . . . you know there's no way out and when somebody helps you. It can change your life.'

Fiona looked at her, confused.

'Surely in your life, ages ago there must have been some problem, some big worry, and maybe Gerry helped you, just said nothing, asked nothing, but gave help.'

Fiona looked at Clare, trying to read in her face whether she could have known about that first pregnancy, and how

535

Gerry had come to England to look after her. Clare felt she was walking on very thin ice.

'I suppose all of us have something like that in our lives, and if someone agrees to sort it out then it *can* be solved.'

'Yes.' Fiona was still doubtful.

'Well I know Gerry did a lot of that for people, you probably don't know how he helped a lot of people when they were in trouble, and I'd like to help him now.'

'How can you help him now?' Fiona cried.

Clare spoke quickly. 'There are some pictures, here somewhere or in a private file or somewhere, that I don't think he'd want people to see.'

'What sort of pictures?'

'Does it matter what kind of pictures if you believe me? If you believe that Gerry wouldn't have wanted them found.'

'Is it very important?'

'I think it is.'

'But why wouldn't Gerry have sorted it out before he . . . before he . . .'

'He didn't drown himself, Fiona.'

Fiona looked left and right. Nobody had said this aloud in front of her but everyone had thought it.

'But . . .'

'He couldn't have Fiona, he wasn't that kind of a person, *you* know that.'

'I didn't think he would but how else . . .?'

'Because he was upset, he must have been upset and just went climbing around the rocks. He was always doing that.' Of course it wasn't possible but it would be good for Fiona to think this, and she was beginning to believe it.

'I suppose . . .'

'And it would give a lot of people a better chance if the pictures weren't seen. I just know this, like I know I got a second chance and you probably did too . . .'

Fiona's big troubled eyes filled with tears. 'Gerry did give me a second chance years ago. I wanted to do one thing and he wanted me to do another, he was quite right as it turned out.' Almost unconsciously she stroked her stomach as if thinking of the other child Stephen, now in somebody else's family.

'Well this is what I mean.' Clare didn't want her to confess. 'If I could just . . .'

Fiona handed her a key. 'If they're anywhere they'll be in his room in that steel cabinet. By the window.'

'Thank you Fiona.'

She found them at once. There was hardly anything else there except the cheerful postcard she had sent him once from Dublin, the letter asking him to find her post office savings book and another note thanking him when he had.

It was the same brown envelope that he had showed her on the kitchen table back in her house. But there was an invoice note on it saying that there were copies being sent to Miss Caroline Nolan and David Power as well. So she was too late after all. With leaden movements she placed the contents of the drawer into her big briefcase, the letters she had written him, harmless little notes. Why had he kept them? She put it in and left the drawer open.

She leaned her head against the window.

Should she tell Fiona there was nothing, or should she say that she had found them? Which would cause less worry?

As it happened she needn't have worried, there was no decision to make. Fiona knocked on the door.

'Can I come in?'

'Yes.' Clare was still looking out the window at Church Street, at the people going about their lives in an ordinary way.

'I'm glad you came,' Fiona said.

'Why?'

'Because now I do believe for the first time that it *was* an accident. If Gerry was going to end it himself, he'd have left nothing to get him into trouble . . . or you, Clare. He worshipped you. Now I think it must have been an accident.'

'Yes, it must have been.' Clare's gaze was still on the road.

'And so he'll not have gone to hell. I couldn't bear Gerry

537

to go to hell for taking his own life, that's what I've been thinking since Monday morning.'

Clare put her arms awkwardly around Fiona and looked over her shoulder, out of the window at the view that Gerry Doyle must have seen every day as he sat in this ridiculous, over-decorated office and ran his father's steady little business into the ground.

David was looking at an X-ray with his father.

'That poor hip's worn away a lot on her, hasn't it?' Dr Paddy Power was full of sympathy for an elderly woman out on the Far Cliff Road. 'She must be in great pain with that all right.'

'She doesn't complain very much, but she's limping a lot.'

'Ah well, nothing for it, it's terrible to have to tell them it'll just get worse.'

'But you don't tell them that, do you Dad?'

'No, I tell them they're lucky it isn't malignant or anything, try to look on all the positive side of it, no point in being negative and saying it's arthritis and it just gets worse and worse . . . David? What is it?'

David had jumped up as if he were shot.

'I've just remembered something. I have to go.'

'Hey . . . come back here, leave me the notes, you've got poor Mrs Connolly's whole life story with you.'

'What? Yes. Sorry.'

'Are you all right, son?'

'I have to go out for a bit. I'll be back shortly.'

The *negatives*. Why hadn't he remembered them? They were probably in a drawer in Doyle's Photographics, unless of course the little bastard had sent them to someone else like the solicitor's firm where Caroline worked, or to Clare's parents.

He walked around clenching and unclenching his hands in the dark afternoon.

He would have to do it. He walked determinedly down Church Street.

*　　*　　*

Fiona was by herself in the shop. She looked very young and innocent. Too young for the great curve under her grey smock with its white collar.

'Oh David,' she said. 'Aren't you nice to call.'

He swallowed a bit. 'I don't have the right words to say. My father seems to know exactly what to say that helps people. I don't. Maybe when I'm older and have seen a lot of awful things I will.'

'At least you came in, that was very kind of you,' she said.

Now it was more difficult than ever.

'I'm sure a lot of people have been to say how shocked they are, how upset.'

'No. It's a bit awkward, you see.'

'Why?'

'I think a lot of them think he may have . . . that he may have meant to do it.'

It was impossible to stand talking to this beautiful serene girl who thought her little monster of a brother might have been swept away by some tide.

'Well I don't suppose we'll ever know . . .' he began.

'But I do know. I know he couldn't have meant to do it, take his own life. I *know* that.'

'No, no.' He was soothing.

'I just know.'

'Of course.'

He couldn't broach it, he couldn't say that he had really come not to express sympathy but to know if he could rummage through her dead brother's private files.

'What are you doing here? You should be at home resting,' he said in his professional voice.

Fiona looked at him gratefully. 'No, I'm better to keep busy.'

What an end to the Doyles. The bright glittery Doyles of long ago.

'That's good,' he said uselessly.

This was going to be the last time he would talk to Fiona normally. She was going through the picture orders methodically, she would come across prints or negatives, she would scream when she saw them possibly, or feel faint. She might be so revolted she would show them to someone in authority like Father O'Dwyer and ask him what she should do. She was a simple girl, simple and inexperienced, she would be so shocked by all it would mean, for Gerry as well as for him and Caroline. Could he dare?

'Fiona. I was wondering,' he began.

She raised her eyes and he saw the dark shadows underneath for the first time.

'I was wondering . . .' he began. But he couldn't do it. There weren't the words.

'Nothing,' he said, turning to go.

'Clare left her scarf here earlier, can you give it to her?'

'Clare was here?'

'Yes. About an hour ago.'

'What on earth for?' He said it without thinking.

Fiona looked at him thoughtfully. 'Nothing in particular. She just came in.'

'Of course.'

He left with a stooping walk.

Clare had come for the photographs, she hadn't come just to sympathize. If she had, Fiona would have said so.

David didn't notice anyone who spoke to him as he walked back up Church Street and turned left to go home.

Chrissie shouted something at him out of Dwyers' but he didn't hear it. He didn't notice Rose Dillon from the hotel hooting the horn of her scooter at him. Nor did he see Ben O'Brien his brother-in-law waving at him from a pick-up truck.

He turned up his collar and paused at the crossroads. Should he go up to see her now? Should he ask Angela and Dick for a few minutes to talk? What would he say? 'I believe you've got the pictures. I'm sorry.'

No, there was nothing to say. He turned and went back to the big house. He walked past it and on to the Lodge. How had he never noticed how silent the place was? And sad.

*   *   *

Clare sat in the car, motionless. She must burn them. Now. But it was much easier said than done to burn something if you hadn't a house of your own. And at the moment she didn't feel she had a house. She could hardly go to the shop: 'Oh. Hallo Mam, Dad, excuse me, I'm just going in to the range to burn a few things, I like a nice fire . . .'

And she had behaved quite madly enough with Dick Dillon and Angela already to ask them did they mind if she burned a few papers in their range.

What about Josie? Would she be able to accept Clare coming in and saying that she'd like a few moments on her own poking around at the Aga in the hotel kitchen? It was nonsensical. Her mind churned. But she would *not* leave them somewhere where they could be found. They were so awful, those pictures and their negatives, she wanted the satisfaction of seeing them burn in flames. Only that way could she begin to get them out of her mind.

There should be a public burning place, somewhere that people could go and get rid of the things that depressed them or frightened them. A public burning place in the middle of every town.

She remembered suddenly that Dr Power had made a great fuss once about there being no incinerator up at the caravan park. How were the unfortunate campers meant to keep the place hygienic he had thundered unless there were proper rubbish collections and somewhere for them to burn things? The proper rubbish collections had never been set up but the brick incinerator had. It used to burn during the summer getting rid of the worst of the campers' litter.

The caravan park. That would be a nice bit of irony, go up and burn the evidence at the scene of the crime. There wouldn't be a fire in the incinerator now, but she could make one. She had her matches in her handbag, there was a can of petrol in the back of Dick Dillon's car. The more she thought of it the more she liked the idea. She drove slowly down Church Street, past O'Brien's shop, past the bench that looked out over the cliff to the sea, and turned left down the Far Cliff Road to the caravan park.

* * *

David rang Caroline again. He had been so relieved the first time when the woman with the bad cold at the solicitor's office had said she was not there. No other explanation. She wasn't at her house either. Now he had rung her office and her house three times and had found her at neither of them. He was no longer relieved, he was worried. He hadn't wanted to talk to her, and presumably she had felt the same at the beginning. But now it was Wednesday evening – two days after the discovery of the pictures. They should talk.

'If Miss Nolan isn't in do you know when and where I could find her?' he asked the woman with the streaming cold.

'In Dublin,' the voice said.

'Has she gone on holiday?' David asked.

'No, she's gone and left. All of a sudden. Gone for good.' The sniff was full of disapproval for the flashy irresponsible ways of a young solicitor from Dublin who didn't know how things were done.

David didn't know whether he was relieved or upset. Relieved, he thought. At least in Dublin Caroline would have people to look after her, people to talk to. In the town here she had nobody. He clenched the kitchen table as he thought of it.

He seemed to spend a lot of time at this table. Sitting here while the time passed. They had thought it would be nice to have a kitchen which was also a living room, that had been the plan, but they had never really done it up or chosen any furniture for it properly. It must have been a kind of prison for Clare.

He thought of Caroline going back to Dublin, her chin raised with that determined look, driving through rain and fog in her little car. He thought of Caroline saying that Gerry Doyle couldn't have had any hopeless unrequited love for her. 'He had me.' Those were her words. Did Gerry Doyle have Caroline in the caravan park, did he share all the same things? God, God. At least David had been spared pictures of it. He only had his imagination.

* * *

It was windy and exposed up in the caravan park. It was impossible to see why so many people headed from all over Ireland and England to come here in the summer. It seemed like a different planet.

Clare knew which was Caroline's caravan. She had listened wordlessly when David had said what a good idea it was to get one, she could always spend the summertime in it fully, or in the winter it provided a place to have a change of clothes or an overnight stop when it was too late to drive back to the town. She had forced it out of her mind then. She had refused to think of it.

The same way that she had refused to think of David and Caroline making love. She had blocked it from her mind. Even on the nights that she knew with every instinct that they had she did not acknowledge it. It made things safer, like not stepping on cracks in the pavement. She had never admitted it to herself until she saw those pictures. God, but Gerry Doyle was clever. In a few more days she might well have thought he was a possible alternative to such a cheating husband. It wasn't likely but she hadn't known just how bitter and resentful she would feel. Those pictures that she had in her hand, had gone a great way towards doing what Gerry, mad insane Gerry, had wanted them to do. She must burn them. Now.

Maybe she would feel a bit better.

The wind whipped her hair as she took the can of petrol out of the boot. You couldn't light a fire on a day like this without a rag soaked in something that would leap up in flames.

The grey anonymous caravan that Caroline Nolan had rented for six months stood like a big menacing shape, not far from where Clare was standing. This was where her husband came when he was meant to be playing golf. Those pictures had been taken on a bright afternoon; Gerry must have followed them, on his light little feet. They hadn't bothered to draw the curtains. Who would look in at them? The caravan looked out to sea . . .

She was drawn to see it. Looking left and right as if anyone else would be in this wild place, she tiptoed up to it. It was stripped bare of any possessions, there were no lamps, rugs, little ornaments in it. She remembered her mother-in-law giving Caroline some cushions, two rather nice ones. They were still there, oddly. But none of the tartan rugs that had figured in the pictures, nothing at all.

Perhaps she had gone. Caroline. Perhaps when she saw the pictures she had run for it. Perhaps she was just trying to hide the evidence. She was so clever that one, you'd never know what she was up to.

She took the big envelope out and laid it down on the cold iron bars of the incinerator, she shook some petrol over a cleaning rag and watched the pictures and the negatives and the letters she had written to Gerry Doyle burn. It was a small fire. She poked and poked, they were gone, there was no way that anyone, not a fleet of detectives, could know what they were.

She breathed in the salty air. She still felt restless and jumpy, somehow she had thought that burning the pictures would help but it hadn't. It was all still here, the memory, the caravan. The knowledge of what they had done and might still do, the caravan. The loneliness, the lies he had told her. The caravan.

Almost without realizing it she was walking towards it. It was set far away from the others. She still had the petrol in her hand, the matches were in her pocket.

She paused for one long moment and acknowledged what she was doing. 'Yes,' Clare said aloud. 'Yes, I bloody will.'

The petrol soaked the bed, she put most of it there, and then more near the door. She lit the rag, threw it in and ran as fast as she could away. By the time she reached Dick Dillon's car, parked on the road outside, the flames were coming from the windows.

She drove excitedly back towards town, and stopped the car not far from her parents' shop. She could see the blaze in the winter evening . . .

She felt better than she had for a long time. She called in to her mother.

'What are you driving Dick's car for?'

'God, you were always great with the greeting Mam, I'll say that for you.'

'I've never been able to understand you Clare, never.'

'You didn't do too badly, Mam. Do you think I might have a cup of tea or is it only abuse I'm going to get?'

'Make it for yourself then. Some of us have work to do.'

'Are you cross over something in particular or what, Mam?'

'I don't know what you're up to, that's all.' Agnes had her mouth in a hard line.

'I don't really know myself, Mam, I'm meant to be going up to Dublin to see about sitting this exam again. I'm sort of on the way there – Liffey and I.'

'You're never taking that baby up to Dublin, away from her home.'

'Not for ever Mam, just to give her a taste of city life, look what it did for me.' Clare's eyes were bright, too bright.

She was still sitting on the counter sipping a mug of tea when the shouts went up that there was a fire in the caravan park.

'What's all the fuss and excitement?' Clare asked giddily.

'Lord God, child, someone might be burned to death.' Agnes was white with anxiety.

'Who'd be up there in the middle of winter?' Clare said.

'How could a caravan catch fire unless some poor unfortunate turned over a stove or an oil lamp on themselves?'

They came for David but he wasn't able to move.

'Ask Dad, take him in your car,' he stammered out to Brian Dillon who had come with the alarm.

David's limbs had stopped co-ordinating, it took him five whole minutes to pick up the phone.

The post office took what seemed like an hour to connect him to Dublin.

James Nolan answered the phone. He made a pretence that David was a long-lost traveller who had just returned to civilization. 'We never thought we'd hear your voice again.'

'Cut that out,' David said roughly.

'What?'

'Is Caroline there? Quickly.'

'Well quickly or slowly I can't tell you. Isn't she meant to live in your neck of the woods?'

'James please. I beg you.'

'Have you two had a lovers' tiff?'

'I said I beg you.'

'Very well, since you beg me so nicely, she is here but I'm not to tell you.'

'Are you sure, have you seen her, is she in your house?'

'I don't know where she is this minute but I spoke to her at breakfast and she rang me at the Law Library to arrange something for this evening. But shush, I didn't tell you.'

'No.'

'David? Are you all right?'

He had hung up.

The burning of the caravan was a mystery. It must have been youngsters playing with petrol, everything had been soaked in it. Poor Caroline Nolan.

The Guard had rung her in the big town but they couldn't find her. Still wasn't it a mercy that nobody had been hurt?

Clare drove in to the garage where her brother Ben worked. She got Dick Dillon's car filled up and also the petrol can he kept at the back. She drove back to the O'Hara house.

'You said only a minute. I was worried,' Angela said.

'Stop sounding like my mother.'

'Are you all right? You look very flushed.' Angela was conerned.

'No. I'm much better now. There was something I had to do.'

Mrs Corrigan from the other side of the road came in with the news that there had been a big fire over on the Far Cliff Road, and a caravan burned to a shell.

Angela wanted to know was anyone hurt.

'Who would be there in the middle of winter?' Clare had said, her eyes still too bright.

'People are sometimes,' Angela said cautiously.

'Well, they're up to no good then.'

Angela looked so frightened then, that Clare took pity on her.

'It's all right, Angela, it's all right, there was nobody in it. I did check.'

Clare picked up Liffey and held her tight, she was so big now it was quite a weight.

'Well Liffey, in a day or two you and I are heading off to the great unknown to seek our fortune – well, to seek Mummy's degree for one thing.'

'I'll never say. You won't, either, I hope.'

'No, of course not, but you're different, you can know everything. The good and the bad.'

'It wasn't all that *very* bad, considering,' Angela said with a smile.

'No it wasn't was it?' Clare seemed recovered now.

'Did you know that Clare's up in Angela Dillon's house?' Agnes asked Tom O'Brien that night.

'Sure hasn't she been living up there since she was ten years of age, what's strange about that?' he asked.

'No that's just it, she *is* living up there, she's been there three days.'

'Nonsense, Agnes, you must have got the wrong end of the stick. Hasn't she a perfectly good house of her own?'

'I know, but that's what I heard, so I asked her straight out.'

'And?'

'You never get a straight answer from Clare, she said she was on her way to Dublin to inquire about exams or some such nonsense.'

'Better say nothing, say nothing at all, you'll get little thanks for what you say.'

Agnes thought that for once he might be right. This could be one occasion when it might pay to take no notice.

People said that Gerry Doyle's poor mother had to take so many tablets now for her nerves that she would hardly realize what was happening at the funeral. Fiona had tried to get her a black coat and she said no, she always hated black, it reminded her of funerals. Gently Fiona had tried to persuade her that this actually was a funeral, and didn't know whether to be pleased or upset that her mother hadn't taken in the fact that Gerry was dead.

Nellie Burke's family asked her was it true that David Power and Clare were living apart. Nellie, stubborn and loyal, said she knew nothing of the sort. Her brothers' wives, who were spectacular gossips, were disappointed. They thought she would be the source of all information. So they had to make do with saying that a marriage like that could never work. They had known it from the start. She had been a silly little girl to think that a bit of education made her the equal of the doctor's son.

'Did David tell you that Caroline Nolan's packed up her job and gone back to Dublin?' Paddy Power asked Molly.
   'I don't believe you.'
   'So Mr Kenny says, remember he got her the job in the first place, very upset he is about it all. Just told them she wasn't suited to country life, worked all day and all night to get her work finished and left. Same in her house. Wrote them a cheque for the rest of the quarter and vanished.'
   'I must ring Sheila.'
   'Maybe not, Moll. Maybe not. Let it settle down a bit yet.'
   'Why do you say that?' She looked anxious.
   'We don't know half of what goes on, we might be making it worse.'
   'How could we make things worse, we're their friends, we haven't done anything to upset Caroline, to make her run off from here.'
   'No Moll, you haven't and I haven't,' he said levelly.
   She looked at him in alarm and realized he wasn't going to say any more.

'There'll be so many there they won't miss me. I'm not going,' Clare said.

They could hear the bell tolling on the cold, wet morning.

'You shouldn't hurt the living. Fiona, his mother.'

'I can't stand there and pray for the repose of his soul. It's a mockery.'

'It's what people do, it's a custom, think of it like that.'

'You don't know . . . you don't know . . .'

'Clare, stop it this minute. Of course I don't know, you didn't tell me, and you are not going to tell me now when we have to be in the church in ten minutes' time. I've arranged for us to put Liffey in Mrs Corrigan's, she'll not be going, she's got five babies in that house already.'

'No. I have to stay here and mind Liffey.'

'Clare, stop being a child. Put your coat on. Now.'

'Would you like to walk up to the church with me, son?'

'Dad, I was half thinking I wouldn't go. You know, stay here in case anyone needs one of us.'

'If they need us won't they know where to find us, where would anyone find anyone on the day the bell is ringing for a young man?'

'I know but . . .'

'There's going to be talk if you don't go.'

'That's nonsense, the church will be full, the whole of Castlebay will be there.'

'And you should be there.'

'But there are a lot of things I can't explain . . .'

'And there's no need why you *should* explain, just come up to the church with me now, come on David, it's a small thing to do, but it's a big thing if you don't do it.'

'If you think . . .'

'I do think. Come on now, the bell's ringing, your mother's gone already in the car.'

With cold hands they blessed themselves. Almost all of Castlebay went into the familiar church. The only thing

549

that was unfamiliar was the coffin up near the altar rails.
It was covered with Mass cards and there were two wreaths,
one from his mother arranged by Frank Conway, and one
from Fiona and Frank also arranged by Frank Conway.
For some odd reason other people hadn't sent flowers.
You didn't associate Gerry Doyle with flowers for the
dead.

The church always seemed colder at a funeral. In the
front row Mrs Mary Doyle knelt in the black coat that had
been borrowed for her, her eyes vacant and her hands
clasped. Beside her Fiona sat. Face paler than ever, wearing a loose black coat and a mantilla. She looked like a
Spanish widow, she had never looked really Irish at all.

David and his father arrived just at the same moment
as Angela, Dick and Clare. They exchanged the funeral
words people spoke at such times – terrible tragedy, young
man, makes you wonder at the sense of anything.

David and Clare let the others go in before them.

'Did you burn the caravan?' he asked.

'Yes. And the pictures. And the negatives.'

'It doesn't matter I suppose,' he said eventually.

'No.'

As if they were a million miles from each other they
walked into the church side by side. Angela and Dr Power
sat beside each other deliberately. David and Clare joined
them. So Castlebay was not treated to the sight of the
young doctor and his wife having a public coldness right
in the middle of a funeral. They genuflected and knelt
down, where they had been manoeuvred to be. Beside
each other.

There had never been a Mass as long as this.

When she was certain it must be the communion it was
only the offertory. When she was sure it was the last
Gospel it was only the post-communion.

Sitting, and standing, and kneeling, beside David; looking at his cold hands clasped in front of him; noticing that
he needed a haircut; seeing that his shoes were well-
polished and wondering had Nellie done that for him.

And then every time she lifted her glance seeing that coffin which they said held Gerry Doyle.

Where would she go back to? If she could go back . . .?

Before she got pregnant? No, that would mean no Liffey, and the only good thing that had come out of all this was Liffey.

After Liffey was born, had she been really terrible then? It was odd, she couldn't remember much about all that winter and spring. She must have been a poor companion. As drugged and vacant-looking as Gerry's unfortunate mother looked now.

Was that where she would start again?

David wished that she wasn't kneeling beside him, but there was nothing else they could do. She had her elbows on the back of the seat in front and her forehead resting on her clenched hands. He noticed how thin her wrist was, with the watch he had given her hanging slightly loosely on it. When he glanced at her he saw her eyes were open and distant. She wasn't praying, obviously.

There was plenty to think about. He felt a great weariness come over him. He was too tired to make her promises, to beg her to come back to the Lodge, to tell her it would all be all right. It might not be all right, and they had never lied directly to each other, they had lied by omission. He had never denied that he was with Caroline, because she had never asked him what way he was with Caroline. If it hadn't been for those pictures, they would have had a chance. Those pictures. If he could only go back to before the pictures . . .

Had she really burned them? Is that what she had been doing when she went to burn the caravan? He shivered to think of it. Suppose the wind blew the wrong way and had swept the flames towards her? But why should she have gone up to the caravan park to burn the pictures, for God's sake? Couldn't she have burned them anywhere? He turned his head and looked at her, head still leaning on one hand, her dark eyes looking ahead, her shoulders tense and full of hurt. Had he been right when he said that

551

nothing made any difference now? Was it too late?

The priest had walked around the coffin with the thurible and the sickly sweet smell of incense filled the church as Father O'Dwyer made his circle of the box that contained Gerry Doyle. Then four men, men who had been boys with Gerry and who had watched helplessly while he had taken their girlfriends away, picked up the coffin as if it were no weight at all. They walked out of the church followed by the whole congregation.

They walked, heads bent in the wind, the quarter of a mile to the graveyard which stood high on a hill. There the grave had been dug and the two gravediggers removed their caps as the funeral procession arrived.

Visitors often looked at this little graveyard and said it would be a beautiful place to come to rest. Surrounded by a stone wall, filled with the celtic crosses of years, its own little ruined church covered with ivy in the corner.

Because it was on a hill you could see the whole beach below, the white flecks of the waves coming in ceaselessly. The sand and stones being pulled out in their wake. Hardly anyone could have looked back down at the beach without remembering that this is why they were here.

The only people who didn't look were Gerry's mother and sister. Mrs Mary Doyle looked vaguely around. It was like a bad dream, everyone seemed to be looking at her she thought, but her sister held one of her arms and her daughter held the other. There was no sign of Gerry but he must be away working somewhere, he'd be here soon.

Fiona's tears were mixed with the salt wind and rain, but she felt much more at peace now, now that she realized Gerry couldn't have done it on purpose. Whatever those pictures were, Gerry would never have left anything behind him, deliberately . . . not anything that would hurt someone or ruin their life.

She listened to Father O'Dwyer, she didn't understand the Latin words, but she knew that they were necessary to set Gerry's soul at peace.

552

Angela looked at Dick. His face always looked very cross when he was upset, and he was greatly upset by all this. Last night he had whispered to her that there was a lot of violence in Castlebay, a sort of passion that was very destructive.

'It might cease now. Now that poor Gerry Doyle is dead,' Angela had said.

'No, it seems to be starting, what could have possessed that young fellow to do a thing like that. What could have been so bad that made him do it? And look at the caravan being burned out. I know that may not have anything to do with it, but it all seems very violent. All of a sudden.'

Angela said nothing. Some day she would know what it was all about.

Molly Power looked across at the O'Briens as they stood together. Agnes thin and frail always, her two sons beside her, Tom standing a bit back. That's all she had now, after rearing that huge family, two boys in England, that Chrissie married into the Byrne family. And Clare. Who knew what to make of Clare? Certainly her parents didn't; and Molly didn't. She looked over to where the girl was standing stiffly, her long hair blowing in the wind. A good dark coat, not that terrible duffle coat she used to live in at one time. She was a strange girl. No wonder David found it so hard to deal with her.

Father O'Dwyer knew how to bury the dead of his parish. He had been doing it for years. But the dead were never like this. The dead were old men and women who hadn't been able to survive a winter. Or someone who died tragically young leaving a family of small children. Occasionally the dead might be children – that was very hard, but there was something to say, about God taking innocent little souls to himself.

Paddy Power wondered what would Father O'Dwyer say to a congregation who knew what a life Gerry Doyle

553

had lived, and that he had ended up by taking that life himself.

Dr Power had reminded himself only that morning that God was merciful: and if God was, then Father O'Dwyer must be also.

The priest looked around at the cold faces all spattered by the sea spray and whipped by the wind. He would not keep them long but he must keep them long enough to do honour to the dead man. Otherwise why have the ceremony at all?

'You all knew Gerry Doyle, and as we stand here around his grave and pray that his soul is in heaven with the angels we will all remember his love of life, and how he was involved in everything that went on in Castlebay . . .

'I think it's true that since this young man personified life, and youth and energy, his sudden death will make us realize once more what a very slight hold we have on our mortal lives, how easily they can be whipped away. While we pray for Gerry this morning, let us think of the briefness of our own lives. This time next year, not all of us who stand here now may be here, and in ten years' time, many more will have gone to their Maker. But it's not only the old and those who are ready to go, it's the young who are totally unprepared to face the kingdom of heaven, and who still have so much to say to each other and to their families and their friends.

'If Gerry Doyle had been given one more day there might have been many things he would wish to have said, things to put straight, people to reassure. But the Lord doesn't let us know the time He calls us. Everyone here has a cheerful memory of Gerry. Let us keep those memories in our hearts and pray that his soul is in heaven today, and will rise again on the Last Day.'

There were the last three hail marys and the glory be to the father and then Fiona leaned forward to raise the shovel of earth, the first one to fall on the coffin that had been lowered into the ground. She looked down into the big open grave.

'Thank you Gerry,' she said unexpectedly.

554

People were almost embarrassed, nobody ever spoke at a time like this, certainly nobody expected the quiet dignified Fiona to say anything so emotional. One by one the men shovelled on earth, filling up the dark hollow space.

This was the bleakest part of a funeral. The finishing touches. People huddled closer together almost unconsciously as if they were looking for some warmth from just being in a crowd.

Clare and David moved together. Partly because they were jostled, partly because they wanted to.

It was David's turn to take the spade in his hand. He paused and looked at Clare. Her glance was steady. She didn't turn away.

David dug into the heap of clay that lay beside the grave and heard it fall on to the earth that was already on top of Gerry's coffin. He took three steps back towards Clare, she had her hand out in its little knitted glove.

He took it and they both watched the gravediggers finish off the work that the parish had begun. Two tall bony men, they had it finished in no time. The two wreaths were put on the little mound. In a year they would put up a tombstone to Gerry Doyle, Born 1935, Died 1962, and passersby would shake their heads and say he died very young.

The people began to trickle down the hill, towards Craig's Bar some of them, some to Dillon's Hotel, others to open up their businesses which had been closed to honour Gerry Doyle.

A long time ago, back in Dublin when there had been a simple sort of life, David used to take Clare's hand in its knitted glove and put it into his pocket for further warmth. He wondered did he dare do that now. Very gently he drew her hand towards him and she placed it in his pocket without him having to do anything.

They walked down the twisty road with the loose stones. Down the hill to Castlebay.

LIGHT A PENNY CANDLE

Maeve Binchy

Compassionate and delightful, this is the magnificent story of twenty turbulent years in the lives of two women. One is English, the other is Irish. Their friendship is sealed when they are children: it is warm, devoted, unshakeable and, against all odds, it survives. Their names are Aisling and Elizabeth . . .

'A really marvellous book. I couldn't put it down'   *Philippa Toomey, The Times*

'A warm, Irish, tearjerkingly readable brew'
Yorkshire Post

'This very fine novel deserves every rave review it has received'   *Publishers Weekly*

JEFFREY ARCHER'S MASTERPIECE

KANE AND ABEL

"With Kane and Abel, Jeffrey Archer ranks in the top ten storytellers in the world"

Los Angeles Times

A CORONET BOOK FROM

General — PAPERBACKS —

JEFFREY ARCHER'S LATEST BESTSELLER

FIRST AMONG EQUALS

JEFFREY ARCHER

"The latest example of the author's mastery
of the pure art of storytelling"
Daily Telegraph

A CORONET BOOK
FROM

General
— PAPERBACKS —

GREAT ENTERTAINMENT
FROM

☐   3403-37842   Light a Penny Candle $4.95
                 by Maeve Binchy

☐   3403-63703   First Among Equals $5.95
                 by Jeffery Archer

☐   3402-57334   Kane and Abel $5.95
                 by Jeffery Archer

All of these titles are available from local bookstores or newsstands in Canada, or can be ordered direct from the publisher. Just tick off the titles you want and fill in the form below. Prices and availability subject to change without notice.

GENERAL PAPERBACKS
34 Lesmill Road, Don Mills, Ontario M3B 2T6

Please send cheque or money order for books ordered, allowing the following postage: 50¢ for first book; 30¢ for each additional book ordered.

Name _____

Address _____

_____